50 Stories from Israel

An Anthology

50 Stories from Israel

An Anthology

Editor: Zisi Stavi
English Language Editor: Chaya Galai

Yedioth Ahronoth and Chemed Books

50 Stories from Israel
An Anthology

All Rights Reserved © 2007

Miskal – Yedioth Ahronoth Books and Chemed Books

P.O.B. 53494, Tel-Aviv, 61534 Israel

E-mail: info@ybook.co.il

English translation, editing, licenses and permissions by arrangement
with The Institute for the Translation of Hebrew Literature.

E-mail: litscene@ithl.org.il

Copyrights and Acknowledgements – p. 746

Editor in Chief: Dov Eichenwald

English Language Editor: Chaya Galai

Copy-editor: Miranda Kaniuk

Cover Design: Ada Rotenberg

Plates: Isralit

Cover printed by: Valigraf Ltd.

Production: Teper Ltd.

DANACODE   362-1428

ISBN   965-448-694-6

Printed in Israel 2007

Contents

The End of the Millennium

Foreword

This anthology of Israeli short stories, now presented to English-speaking readers, grew out of an anthology published in Hebrew in 1998. The same authors appear in both anthologies, though they are sometimes represented by different stories.

It is interesting to note that the short story remains a stable and popular genre among Israeli writers. A number of short-story collections, some of them very intriguing, have appeared since the Hebrew anthology was published. Young authors, now taking their first steps as writers, are not deterred by the demands of this difficult genre, which requires great effort, maximum concentration and a punishing degree of self-restraint.

It is illuminating to quote the writer Shulamith Hareven (who is, of course, represented in this anthology):

"The short story is possibly the most professional form of writing – writing as an art – because it is the most difficult to cheat with, or to employ all the tricks and make the mistakes that can be disguised in a novel. You cannot rely on psychological theories because they cannot be developed at length; you cannot use linguistic pyrotechnics or lengthy anthropological descriptions, what Clifford Geertz calls 'thick description', or whole chapters of flashback because there just isn't room. You cannot switch from style to style or – and this is the cardinal mistake – launch explanations. It is like a piano sonata as opposed to a symphony. All manner of things can be concealed in a symphony; in a piano sonata each note matters and is clearly heard. The key word in the short story is, in fact, the key word of all art: proportion. What we have is a crystal-like utterly precise structure, a work of art that must not be overloaded, in which every word is vital. If you change a word – you have changed the whole."

The anthology is in three parts:

Part One – ten stories by writers of the "1948 Generation," the generation of the War of Independence, although not all the stories were written in that period.

Part Two – twenty-nine stories by writers of the "Generation of Statehood," which constitute the core of the book.

Part Three – eleven stories published in the 1990s, to provide a picture of the contemporary Hebrew short story.

I have tried to present a broad panorama of Hebrew short-story writing since the establishment of Israel and to emphasize its multifaceted character and wide range of themes, styles and forms. I hope that its richness will be conveyed to the readers.

It goes without saying that the selection of the stories was personal and subjective and reflects my individual taste at a given period, since taste can also change with time. It is my sincere hope that my choices will appeal to the readers of the English edition.

Finally, my thanks to all who have worked hard to produce this book: the Yedioth Ahronoth publishing house, directed by Dov Eichenwald; the Institute for the Translation of Hebrew Literature, directed by Nilli Cohen, and in particular Haya Hoffman and Ayala Carmeli; Chaya Galai, the language editor of the English edition; all the translators into English; and last but not least: the writers, without whom we would not be able to enjoy these wonderful stories.

Zisi Stavi
Ramat Hasharon
Israel 2007

1948–1960

Nissim Aloni

To Be a Baker

Translated by Tirza Sandbank

When the summer vacation came round, my mother wanted me to go and stay with my uncle who was a teacher in the village. In the village the train wound its way between eucalyptus groves, and through cracks in the hard-baked earth that lined the road to the vineyard, silvery snakes would dart out their heads in surprise. One could hear the laugh of the handsome lad who had drowned in the orchard pond, and the nights were heavy with the scent of jasmine. But I had been promoted to the seventh grade, and during Passover I had already arranged with Izakino the baker that in the long vacation I would go to work in Mr. Sasson's bakery.

"In the summer vacation!" my mother had said in despair.

In the evening my father said: "I've had a letter from your uncle. He wants to know if Your Honor is willing to pay him a visit."

It was hot in the room, the window and the door were blacked out with blankets. My father was smoking a cigarette and holding a newspaper. My mother was in the kitchen with the dishes. My uncle, the teacher, sat at his desk in the village and dipped his red pen in ink to write my name, letter by letter. In his garden there was a hut, its poles entwined with grapevines, and there at noon hot moaning winds would seek me out, blowing down summer-urchins to tickle me. In the far-off Carmel hills, the trees would pounce at the shadows of elusive clouds.

"Your uncle writes that the vineyard's full of ripe grapes and they've forgotten that Your Honor burned the cat's tail."

My mother stuck her head out of the kitchen. "The devil hasn't forgotten," she said.

But I hadn't burnt the cat's tail. My uncle, the teacher, said I had though he knew I hadn't. Once, when I walked down to the edge of the village to watch a train go by, he told my father he had found me on the way to Haifa and once, when I asked him the name of some girl, he went around telling everybody in a secretive voice, the man is in love. And the time he fished me out of the pond, he said he had brought me back to life, sometimes adding that he had saved me from the jaws of death. I hadn't burnt the cat's tail, but he loved telling the story, I could never quite understand why. If he caught my astonished look while he was telling the story, he would lower his head till his shoulder touched his double chin, and wink at me disarmingly. My uncle was tall and fat, and when he talked to me the words came out cemented together like a wall of bricks, so that when he pressed me to talk, my voice simply disintegrated. When I got into bed at night, he would bring me an open book, a prodigious finger indicating the line where I was to begin reading. He also made a point of always saying goodnight, as if he were shutting a book. Why, then, should he sit down at his desk to write my name? After that story of his about the cat, they kept questioning me whether I had burnt any other tails; for it was all my fault, my mother said, that the devil had sent us seven lean years that never seemed to end.

"Has Your Honor swallowed your tongue?" my father said, suddenly.

I clicked my tongue, letting out a noise like the clatter of horses' hooves, which as usual drove my mother crazy in the kitchen.

"Can't you talk any more, brat?" she called to me. To my father she said: "Tell him he's got to go, and be done with it." She was now standing in the doorway, looking at us in turn.

My father still held the paper in both hands. "I'm writing to your uncle tomorrow," he said to me.

"Tomorrow morning I'm going to work at the bakery," I said.

One of his hands let go of the paper as he turned a perspiring face towards me. His Adam's apple bobbed up and down, his nostrils dilated, and the newspaper in his hand quivered like a cat caught by the tail and trying to jump free. I crossed my legs under the table to gain courage.

"Hark at him," said my mother, shaking her head.

My father strained his tired eyes. "To work in the bakery?"

"Yes," I said. "To be a baker."

He laid the paper down on the table and turned to face me squarely.

"To be a baker?" he said.

"To be a lunatic," said my mother.

"To be a baker," I said to the dark hollow of his throat, "to be a baker."

"You're going to your uncle's!" said my father.

"No," I said.

"No?" my mother said. "We'll see..."

Relishing every word, I muttered back: "We'll see."

For a long time my father said nothing, but sat puffing out clouds of smoke like some weary conjurer, staring at me through the veil of smoke as if he had never seen me before. His fingers kneaded the crumbs left over from the meal. I did the same. His head was very large and mysterious, and his eyes half closed. Suddenly he stood up, abruptly stubbing out his cigarette in an empty sardine tin. My mother looked at him pleadingly but he made for the back yard.

"Well, what are you going to say?" she asked, as he went past.

"What am I going to say? It's madness," he flung back, and disappeared behind the blanket.

We remained alone in the room. She shook her head and said: "In the summer vacation!" in a quiet, but sad voice.

Outside in the street, it was a summer's morning, from the sky down to the sand – a proud, light summer, like a taut white sail without a boat. Summer lay sprawled over the whole gray neighborhood, like a golden giant made of cotton-wool. I bent my head low so that it wouldn't see me, but it crouched over me, breathed on me from the dewy street corner like a glittering ocean, sticking out its million tongues and running away. I lengthened my stride to get to the bakery more quickly but it frolicked in my hair and fluttered in my nostrils. Golden summer children, taller than the houses and naked, tossed their heads out of the green crests of the palm trees and the pale strips of soft sky, and laughter drifted out of their curls, fading away before it reached my ears. I kept my head down so as not to see them and quickened my pace. My elbows jostled this clownish summer, which was not going to hold me back, not going to entice me and drown this strong desire of mine in its perfumed scents. I was running now, my forehead dripping beads of sweat.

The empty shop entrances gaped at me in wonder, cyclists railed at me, pedestrians were startled; but what could I do with this beautiful summer chasing me, trying to tempt me, while I was bent on getting to the bakery.

Suddenly everything stopped. I was standing on the pavement, just a few steps away from the bakery door and, facing me, old Sultana sat on her stool like an embalmed owl, her two blind eyes staring into the morning light.

She can see me, I said to myself.

I knew that her blind eyes could look upon the secret face of death, which stretched like pale cobwebs across the open reaches of this beautiful summer. I knew that in the morning she raised her head only to spy death out with her blind gaze. The crinkles of her face bore the traces of living death, like an open book.

She won't let me go into the bakery, I said to myself.

Suddenly I heard my name called.

Turning round I found I was standing next to Avramino Kashi's drinks stand; colored paper flags were strung out above the lemonade jars, adorning the photographs showing Avramino as a strong, famous boxer. Now he was old, except for his sparkling eyes and the white hat on his gray head.

"Where are you off to?" Avramino Kashi asked me, wagging his head quizzically. He was sipping coffee, but the cup was buried in his hands and in his yellow, drooping mustache. "Where are you off to so early in the morning?"

"To work," I said.

"To work," said Avramino, wiping his mustache with his hand. "Go, go, my son. Sooner or later, aren't we all children of one very strange God?"

I nodded assent, for Avramino always talked this way. There were very few people in the street at this hour; sitting down on his stool, Avramino stuck a cigarette into an ivory holder and put it in his mouth.

"And where are you going to work?" He closed one eye, and the other eye glared at me like a searchlight.

"In the bakery," I said. My throat was dry.

He glanced in the direction of the bakery, and, seeing old Sultana, he took off his hat and called loudly: "Good morning, Sultana my beauty!" But as he was calling, he seized my hand to pull me close and said fiercely: "What, have you lost your mind? In there, with those cursed dogs, may the good Lord forgive them? Are you making fun of an old man?"

I said: "No. I am going to work there. At the oven."

"But you're only a child," he said.

I pulled my hand away from his, saying: "During Passover I arranged with Izakino to work there." And then I added: "Izakino is waiting for me."

"Izakino," he said, shaking his head. "He's a good man, that soft bastard. A saint. How the good Lord lets him remain among us, I'll never know. But..."

Avramino Kashi again turned to the doorway of the bakery and called out in a loud voice: "Good morning, Sultana, my dear." Again old Sultana was silent. He stroked his mustache and said in a quiet hoarse voice: "Damn her!" And to me he said: "She says nothing! Doesn't answer! But yesterday, may she be eaten by lice, she tried to steal from my money plate. By heaven, I'll cut her heart out! Go, my son, go and work in the oven! If you don't keep your eyes open, she'll steal your soul!" I turned my head and saw her there, her face in the golden light and her back in the darkness of the doorway. An old tree trunk, scorched by the fire, but not consumed.

"Izakino is waiting for me," I said.

Avramino Kashi called after me. "Keep your eyes open!" But his voice and his look, the drinks stand with its colored streamers, the dewy street of the summer morning, all disappeared as I walked towards old Sultana standing in the doorway of Mr. Sasson's bakery. My sandals clicked on the pavement, but she didn't budge. I cleared my throat, and not a wrinkle moved. I heard the roar of the fire in the oven.

When my shadow touched her, she moved her head as if she wanted to brush it away. I hopped over the threshold like a grasshopper.

The room was dark with a high ceiling, and at first I couldn't see anything but the red angry mouth of the oven. Then, I made out Mr. Sasson near the oven. He was holding with both hands a shovel full of unbaked loaves. He lay in wait for the flames. Suddenly he pushed the shovel in, and immediately, as if he had stuck a spoon into an angry lion's mouth, he pulled it out again, and it was empty. I laughed, because he was very fat, like a mountain, but the movement with which he had pushed the shovel was sharp and deft, like a bird's. The folds of flesh quivered through his vest, and only his neck was motionless. With the back of his hand he wiped the sweat from his brow, pushing his cap to the back of his head.

"Mr. Sasson," I said quietly.

But he was looking at the red mouth opposite him like a wizard under a spell. My voice died in mid-air. I said to myself: When he finishes shovelling in the bread, he'll push himself in, and he'll go around the oven to see how the breads are baking. If he likes me, I thought, maybe he'll push me in too. I will cup the smell of the browned crusts in my two palms.

"Mr. Sasson!"

On the grimy wall opposite me, there was a hand made of silver paper with one finger cut off. The other fingers were spread out like those of a priest pronouncing a benediction. Above the hand hung a horseshoe covered with gold paper. Heads of garlic hung on both sides of it. Now I saw how sooty the walls were. In the corners, spiders wove cobwebs which were also sooty. There was a little table at which Mr. Sasson sat on Fridays, when he received the money for the bread from the people of the neighborhood without so much as glancing at them, and even that was sooty. But the bakers were always white. I turned my head towards the bakers' room, but no one appeared.

God, suppose Izakino's forgotten!

"Mr. Sasson, Mr. Sasson!" I shouted.

Mr. Sasson had never seemed so huge as when he came out of the red light, slowly straightening himself up. He blinked both small eyes as if I had startled him out of a dream. Suddenly, in the silence that stretched between us, there was a squeak. I turned my head towards the doorway and then I saw old Sultana standing in front of me, her chin moving up and down as if she were chewing, and the hairs of her beard quivering.

"What are you doing here, screaming like the devil, you son of a bitch!" Her clenched fists waved at me like the hands of a madman.

Her voice dug into me like the teeth of a lizard, making me blush all over. "What have you come here for? Who are you?"

"I..."

"You!"

"I want..."

"What? What do you want?"

Mr. Sasson said: "What are you yelling for, mother? He's only a child."

"Child or no child! I want him to tell me what he wants here!" Her voice was hoarse and she wheezed through her nostrils. She was standing so close to me now that I could have reached out my hand and touched the wrinkles on her face. A smell I had never smelled before wafted from her hair, her clothing, from the thin, dried-up neck, from the yellow hands. "Open your mouth, boy! What do you want here?"

Suddenly the door of the bakers' room opened and a young baker came out, covered in flour. His name was Sylvan, and his mouth always hung open. Immediately he burst out laughing and slapped his thigh, raising a cloud of white dust which at once enveloped him.

"Why it's Adirne," he said, pointing at me. "It's our friend Adirne!" And sticking his head through the doorway of the bakers' room he yelled: "Izakino, Izakino!" Turning to me again he said conspiratorially: "How's business?"

Old Sultana raised her blank eyes towards the roar of the fire where Mr. Sasson stood quietly, his hands on the empty shovel. I said to myself: Izakino's name has calmed her down. When he comes, she will get down on her knees before him.

I said to her: "I've come to work here."

She blinked her eyes. "Who asked you to?" Her voice was hoarse.

"Izakino," I said quietly.

"Izakino! Izakino!" she cried, and her anger started to bubble up again. "Who does he think he is, the boss God Almighty! Do you hear, son! You have a new boss!"

But Mr. Sasson didn't raise his eyes, nor did he say a word. He was leaning on the empty shovel with both hands, next to the red, hungry flames.

"Where are your ears, my son?" called Sultana to her silent son. "Theft, theft and trickery on the face of the whole cursed earth! My own sons are burning my heart! My own sons wish to see me dead and rotting!"

Her head stood erect in the dimness like a pointed spear and her two hands clutched the air with fingers outspread.

"Why are you yelling, mother?" asked Mr. Sasson quietly.

"Why is she yelling?" I asked Sylvan.

"She's not yelling," he said, and his mouth hung open so that it seemed as if he were laughing. "Do you have any muscles?"

"Yes," I said proudly, and I was about to stretch out my arm when the door of the bakers' room opened and Izakino came in hurriedly, carrying a wooden board laden with shiny dough, and crying: "Make way, make way!" Sylvan hurried towards him, stretched out his hand to the board, and said: "Look who's here, Izakino!"

Now he saw me: "Ah!" he said. "What are you doing here?"

My eyes filled with tears. I said to him: "The summer vacation."

"What's the matter with you, Izakino!" said Sylvan. "Didn't you decide he was going to be a baker?"

He wiped his hands on his apron and came closer. He wasn't much taller than I was. He had black hair, always neatly combed; his hair was flecked with white as was his mustache. His cheeks were always red and his bright eyes had dark rings under them. He put his hands on my shoulder and said with a smile: "I didn't forget, kid."

He turned to the others and said: "Have a good look. This is our new baker!"

Sylvan came up to me. He bent his head close to mine until it touched my nose, and then he burst into a whinnying laugh.

"Who is he?" said old Sultana.

Izakino placed his hand on my shoulder, and gesturing towards Sultana, he said to me: "Well, say something! Tell her who you are! Don't you want to be a baker?"

My heart beat wildly, but old Sultana turned her face towards the door of the bakery, her sharp, hoarse voice muttering: "To be a baker!"

As we walked towards the bakers' room, I saw the shiny head of the old woman and the thick motionless neck of her son, Mr. Sasson, and the words uttered by the sharp, hoarse voice of the old woman drummed in my ears. That day I began to paste the labels of the Sasson bakery on the bread.

In the evenings, the blue summer evenings, Mr. Sasson would sit on the balcony of his apartment above the bakery without looking out into the street. The wind played gently with his white hair, and when I passed under the balcony, I walked on tiptoe. I would stand at the corner of the street, staring at him until the darkness blotted him out. In the morning, when I came, he was standing opposite the dancing flames and he never turned his face. But his mother, old Sultana, recognized my steps, and when she heard them, the crooked line of her mouth became distorted as she cursed me. Sylvan would say:

"She's old. She's a hundred if she's a day. In Jerusalem she was attacked by Turkish bandits and they stole all her money from her."

"Why did they attack her?"

"Who knows?" Sylvan would answer, his teeth bared. "She committed terrible sins in her time. She has a touch of the devil in her eye. Didn't you see? She was once very beautiful."

"What sins did she commit, Mr. Sylvan?"

He had blue-grey eyes and he looked like a whinnying horse even when he wasn't laughing. "Isn't it strange that a man like Mr. Sasson came out of her belly?"

"He came out of her belly?" I said.

"Yes," he said, "but she'll die."

"When?" I would say.

Once he said to me: "When she was a midwife, she made a lot of money. With that money she built this oven. Haven't you heard the screams coming out of the walls at night?"

I said: "Yes, the fire screams."

But he said: "No, no, it's not the fire."

"What is it, then?" I asked.

"That's it," Sylvan would say, "the money. Do you know Salvador, Mr. Sasson's son who went to Paraguay?"

My heart beat loudly. "No," I said, and he came close to me and whispered in my ear. "In Paraguay there are a lot of Indians."

I pasted the Sasson bakery labels on the shiny loaves as if they were green Indians from Paraguay. When they were put in the oven they jumped out of the browning breadcrust as it was being baked, and danced, very thin, among the red flames, until Mr. Sasson would paste them to the loaves and take them out of there with the shovel. But sometimes the Indians would stay there and I was afraid to tell Sylvan. He stood near the giant tubs, wearing a gray, floury undershirt, pounding the sourish dough with his fists. Suddenly, as if catching a long white snake, he would take a ribbon of dough out of the tub and throw it with all his strength into Izakino's tub. Izakino would grab the dough so that it wouldn't escape, and then he too would beat it with a smile on his face, because he was talking to the dough the whole time he was beating it. Then he gently removed the dough, which under his hands had turned into a long pacified roll, and put it on the wooden board in front of him. He had a long knife with which he cut up the roll, and he quickly leaned over the pieces, patting them and smoothing their edges. As he put the pieces of dough on the scale he said to me: "Do you know what I'm doing? I'm cutting their navels. Didn't they tie up your navel?" Or he would ask me: "Nice loaves, eh? Who would have thought that from the flour and the water and the yeast and the salt such fine loaves would be born!" But I pasted labels on the loaves. Sometimes, as my fingers passed over a shiny unbaked loaf, I could hardly keep myself from sticking my finger in. I said to myself, Izakino promised to make a baker out of me. He won't forget.

One Friday afternoon, I heard the voice of old Sultana calling me. The bakery was filled with people waiting for their trays. Some of them stood next to Mr. Sasson who kept taking trays, pots and pans out of the oven. Some of them climbed up to the shelves, glancing quickly over the trays, and touching them. Some of them turned to me. My friends from the neighborhood called me by name, and as I passed by, they put out their hands to shake mine, asking me how I was. When I heard the old lady's voice I was standing on the short ladder which leaned against the shelves, looking for Shmeel's tray; Shmeel was standing below me. I looked down from my height at the old lady, but she was sitting with her back towards me, and no sound came from her. There was a lot of noise in the room, as every Friday, and I said to myself that I had just imagined it. She hadn't called me by name, she had never called me by name.

I said to Shmeel: "Go over to the old lady and ask her why she called me."

When he came back, he said: "The old lady wants you."

I took his tray down from the shelf and gave it to him.

He said: "Are you going to the field tomorrow?"

I said: "She's calling me."

Shmeel called after me: "Everybody's going," but I elbowed my way through the bustling crowd, and soon I was standing in the doorway, next to her.

"You called me, Madame Sultana?"

"Come here," she said.

"What is it?" I said to her.

"Come here, I told you."

I came nearer.

"What do you want, Madame Sultana?" I said.

She didn't turn her head. As if talking to the evening light which flooded the street, she said in a very hoarse voice: "Go and bring me a roll from one of these cursed trays."

I thought I had misunderstood. I said: "What?"

But she said: "You heard me!"

My legs started to tremble. I was afraid to look at the room. My eyes were glued to the yellow wrinkles on her face.

"They're not ours," I said quietly.

"Ours!" screamed old Sultana, suddenly turning her blind eyes towards me. "Ours!" she shrieked at me again, her mouth trembling, the hairs on her chin jumping furiously.

I said, almost in a whisper: "It's not allowed. Mr. Sasson..."

"Don't you tell me what's allowed, do you hear!"

"Yes."

"It's all mine," she said.

"Yes."

Then she lowered her voice, which was trembling, and said: "Go and bring me a roll, you cursed son of a whore!"

At night, after supper, my mother brought a large watermelon from the kitchen. My father took the knife and cut it in half.

"Watermelon," said my father. "Even kings eat watermelon." And giving me a slice, he said: "Isn't Your Honor sorry that you didn't go to your uncle's? At your uncle's you would be eating cream."

"His Honor is silent today," said my mother.

I cracked the watermelon seeds industriously. Both my parents were washed, combed and wearing freshly ironed clothes. My father had shaved his beard. A silent breeze came in through the blanket covering the kitchen window.

"There is talk about town that His Honor is going to become a baker," said my father.

"Baker, my foot!" said my mother. "He would do a lot better to go to his uncle's."

"Pretty soon," said my father, "there won't be any grapes left in the vineyard."

I said to myself, No, I won't cry here, but I couldn't forget the frozen expression on old Sultana's face. I cracked the seeds in order to annihilate her image. to smash the words which she had stuck on to me, but she kept returning like a dusty robe, and she bent over me, as if the two of us were the only people in the world,

"Stop cracking those seeds, you idiot!" called my mother.

I jumped out of my chair and ran out to the yard as if I was being chased. There, I sat down on a wide, worn step leading to the kitchen and wept. My body was heavy and sore with rough cracks, like the burnt mountains that I used to dream about when I was sick. I saw the drinks stand decorated with colored streamers and next to it Avramino Kashi, who leaned over me and took off his hat, calling in a hoarse voice: "She'll steal your soul, keep your eyes open." My uncle presented me with a huge open book, pointing with his fat finger at the line where I was to begin reading, but the words turned into old Sultana, yellow and laughing and eating rolls from trays devoured by fire.

I raised my head. Soft moonlight flooded the yard. The pieces of broken glass on the stone wall shone whitely like cats' eyes. The tall houses were silent and attentive. The leaves of the bush suddenly looked washed, and a silvery night flooded the neighborhood.

I got up, touching the leaves. I walked over to the wall of the neighboring house and stood there, drenched in the soft light. I bent down over a vegetable row in my garden, and my hand caressed a cool round tomato. I jumped into the air, as if trying to swing from the light, and the pale moon-children of summer filled the yard. They danced and twirled like pale smoke, encircling me with their cool white hands, then they disappeared beyond the fragments of glass on the stone wall, and climbed onto the houses, silent and tall like them. I climbed up the stone wall in order to catch them, and I heard my father calling:

"Where are you going?"

I came down. My father was standing in the doorway of the kitchen, smoking a cigarette.

"Come here, son," he said.

I came close to him. When I was standing next to him, he said nothing. My head was lowered and he continued smoking the cigarette.

Finally he said: "Go to sleep, son," and his voice was as soft as the light.

I passed close by him and his elbow touched my arm. I pushed aside the blanket and stood in the dark, warm kitchen. He came in after me and, in passing, he said: "Tomorrow we'll eat early. We'll go to the field together." As he came to the door of the room he turned and gazed at me and, in the darkness, I saw his smoldering cigarette. Suddenly he cleared his throat and said: "What happened?"

I said: "Nothing."

For a moment he stood silent, near the door, and then I saw the cigarette glow moving away from me.

For a long time after my father had gone, I couldn't fall asleep. I took the blanket off the window, and the moon made patterns in the glass. I wanted to look at the groves of the village and the eucalyptus trees, but old Sultana appeared before my eyes; she was sitting on the threshold of a white empty plain.

After I had worked at the Sasson bakery for a month, they raised my salary. Izakino held my palm and spread out the fingers. Then, with a solemn face and a grave, ceremonious voice, he pronounced: "In the name of the Sasson bakery, I hereby raise your salary today. Thus spoke Izakino, the baker." He fumbled in the small pocket of his trousers, and then laid half a piaster in the palm of my hand. From then on, Sylvan would say: "Lend me some money, sir. I keep the devils away." The coins which I dropped through the slot of my tin box multiplied from day to day, and the box grew heavy. When I got into bed at night, I would shake the box next to my ear. Sometimes in the middle of work at the bakery, my eyes wandered to the box and I would try to figure out how much money there was inside it. Now I didn't only paste on labels. I sifted the flour.

And every Friday I stole rolls for old Sultana. I learned to steal so that the theft would not be noticed. I learned to differentiate the rolls by their color, for old Sultana despised spinach, and was overjoyed when the rolls were filled with potatoes and cheese. She also liked the rolls filled with pumpkin. When I brought them to her, she devoured them without a moment's hesitation, as if she hadn't eaten for many days. Now when I came to the bakery in the morning, she answered my greeting, and sometimes, in the long summer evenings, she let me sit beside her in the doorway. She would sit motionless in the evening bustle which died away gradually until a silent darkness covered everything. In the darkness her wrinkles disappeared, and so did the crooked line of her mouth. Her motionless figure was like a dim stone statue.

Once she didn't get up for a long time after darkness had fallen. She is talking to the night, I thought. At night, all the sins come down from the attics and from the empty lots nearby. She is talking to her sins, her sins that join in the morning to become a secret, laughing death in the summer air.

"It's late, Madame Sultana," I said to her quietly.

She didn't answer and I thought she hadn't heard. I bent my knees to get closer to her ear, but then she said suddenly: "Isn't it a shame that you sit next to me all the time, like a stubborn camel?"

Her voice, tired and soft in the night, hit me in the face and my words faded away.

"How old are you?" she said.

"Twelve."

I saw her dark head swinging from side to side like a pendulum. "Twelve," she echoed. And then she added: "It is all one cursed dream."

A warm pleasure suddenly suffused me.

"When will you die, Madame Sultana?" I said, my voice tender, quiet and very soft.

But old Sultana got up from her stool and, taking her stick in her hand, went into the hallway and disappeared into the black darkness.

I told my friends in the neighborhood that she would soon die, for she had sinned heavily in her hundred years on this earth. She had been very beautiful, and a midwife, and she had brought terrible suffering upon the women who had given birth, because she had delivered the children in secret; they had paid her a lot of money, and given her precious stones, bracelets and gold rings. All these were hidden in the walls of the Sasson bakery, and that is why one could hear shrieks at night from the oven. That is why Izakino was the only one who molded the loaves of bread; without him the bread would have been bitter. When Sultana died, they would build a new oven, and they would put her body inside the walls, because without her the bread would fall apart. I also told about the Turkish robbers in Jerusalem, who attacked her and stole her money, and about her sons who had taken the oven away from her deceitfully and then fought over its ownership for many years. And about Mr. Sasson's only son who had become tired of his uncle's quarrels and had gone to Paraguay, to the Indians. That is why, I said, the walls are so sooty, and Mr. Sasson sits motionless on his balcony in the evening breeze. But I didn't tell anyone about the theft of the rolls.

I wanted to tell Izakino about it for a long time before he caught me stealing, that Friday. Each time that my hand was scorched from the roll in the tray, I decided to go and tell him. But in the evenings, as I sat on the threshold near old Sultana, I decided not to tell. As time went on, the awful fear that I had felt upon first waking every Friday also passed. By now, I didn't wait for her to tell me to bring her a roll. I would scan the shelves in search of a nice-looking tray, and then I would take the best of the rolls she liked, and hurry to give them to her joyfully.

One Friday towards evening, when only a few people remained in the bakery, Izakino caught me. I stretched out my hand towards one of the trays, and a hairy arm grabbed it. I turned my face and met Izakino's eyes.

"What's this?" he asked.

His eyes were dark and dim as if full of soot. I had never seen them this way. His voice was jerky, whispering, and his Adam's apple jumped.

"You?" he said.

I was silent.

"Come with me," he said.

We went to the bakers' room. There was no one there.

He grasped my two shoulders in his hands, and looking straight into my eyes, he said: "Do you want to tell me something?"

I lowered my head and bit my lip.

"You don't want to tell me anything? Me?"

I didn't raise my head.

"All right," he said. "We'll wait until they all go."

I went into the room and stood near the shelves. The naked bulb gave off a dirty yellow light in the sooty room. The smell of food and baked goods choked me. There were thick blankets spread over the door and the window, and they were covered with big green flies. When the last of the people had left, a coarse greasy silence settled on the room; the oven had also gone out.

Izakino went to the door and called towards the blanket: "Madame Sultana, would you come in please?" After some time, the blanket was pushed back, and the old woman's head emerged from behind it.

"What's happened?" she said.

"Come in," said Izakino, "and close the door after you so that the light doesn't escape."

She entered the room and he locked the door after her. When he turned, he said: "Sasson."

Mr. Sasson was sitting near the little table in the corner of the room, counting the money. He raised his tired head, and pushing his hat to the back of his head he gazed at us with his small eyes. It was as if he were seeing us for the first time.

"What is it?" he said.

Sylvan came out of the bakers' room, wiping his hands on a towel.

Then Izakino spoke in a trembling voice:

"Madame Sultana, it's you I'm talking to now. I want to ask you something, Madame Sultana. Haven't you done enough evil things in your life yet? Aren't you satisfied? Isn't there any God in your heart?"

They all froze to the spot, but old Sultana moved her head as if she were looking for the roar of the oven near which her son was standing.

"What do you want?" she asked with a snake-like hiss.

"Madame Sultana," Izakino continued, his voice trembling even more. "We brought a young boy here to the bakery, a decent boy. We wanted to make a fine baker out of him so that when we go, there would be someone to make bread for the people of this neighborhood. Madame Sultana, this is a place for learning to bake bread, not to steal!" Sylvan nodded his head as if to repeat: "not to steal."

"What happened?" asked Mr. Sasson slowly.

"Sylvan noticed it," Izakino said to him. "But I, Sasson, I didn't believe it. Who would believe it? Who would believe it if they told him that an old woman was sending a young boy to steal rolls for her from the neighbors' trays? Who?"

Sylvan said to him: "Izakino, it's not good for you to get so angry. Take it easy."

But Izakino didn't calm down, and coming towards old Sultana, he clasped his hands as if he were praying to her, and said in a tearful voice: "How could you do such a thing? It was I that told him to come. Don't you know he's like a son to me, in place of the sons that God didn't give me? How does your heart let you do it? Madame Sultana, do me a favor. Go to the boy and ask his forgiveness."

All the time he was talking her head was raised, but now suddenly she waved her fists in the air, and a hoarse voice shot like a yellow flame out of her throat. "In hell," shrieked old Sultana, and a shiver went through me. "Don't you have any shame, you – filthy dog?!" Izakino's face went as red as the fire in the oven. "Mother," said Mr. Sasson slowly, but he didn't stir.

"You spineless ninny, you come to me with fairy tales!" the old woman continued to shriek at Izakino. "Villain! Dog! The devil will eat you! The devil will devour your filthy soul!"

Sylvan came close to Izakino and said: "Izakino, leave off. Don't you see, it's not good for you."

"Aren't you ashamed?" Izakino said to her, his hands trembling.

"I should be ashamed? Listen, my dear son! Listen!" She spoke to the light bulb as if she didn't want to look at her son. "Listen with both ears! Listen to the way people malign me just because I'm an old woman whose sons stole the light of her eyes from her! Do I know him, that spoiled brat? Did he ever hear a word from me? Send him to steal... to hell!!"

A tremor shook me.

Izakino turned to me and said:

"Now answer me, why did you steal?"

I was silent.

"Wasn't it she who told you to steal for her?"

I was silent.

"Answer me, answer!"

But I couldn't answer.

He took me by the arm and pulled me outside roughly. I was dragged along behind him on the floor because my knees had given way. I felt the heavy blanket pricking my cheeks, and then I heard the door opening and banging behind us with a loud crash. After we were in the street, in the dark, he let go of my arm. I felt as if my heart had been trampled inside my chest.

"Son," said Izakino in a soft, quiet voice. "God will punish you."

Izakino died several days after that Friday. When I came to the bakery in the morning the doors were locked, but old Sultana was sitting on her stool, her head erect and her two blind eyes gazing into the morning.

I said to her: "The doors are locked," but she did not answer.

I turned away from her and I saw Avramino Kashi near the drinks stand. He was drinking coffee. I went over to him and said: "What happened?"

He said: "Didn't you hear?"

"No," I said.

"Izakino is gone. During the night."

"During the night?" I said.

He nodded his head. His white hat was dented.

"It can't be true!" I said.

"Go and ask her," he replied, nodding his head towards the bakery.

I went home. My mother hurried towards me, and asked why I had returned.

I said: "Izakino died. During the night."

She wiped her hands slowly on her apron and then sat down at the table, next to me. From the kitchen came the noise of the oil stove. I could hear the hum of the saws in the carpentry shop on the other side of the street, the noise of people walking on the sidewalk, and the roar of the bus on the main street. When I said to my mother: "It's my fault," someone in the street started whistling a familiar tune.

In the evening my father said to me: "Go to your uncle's, all right?"

"All right," I said.

Hanoch Bartov

A Familiar Face

Translated by Riva Rubin

A few days earlier, I had returned from landscapes and climates that were the opposite of this headlong pacing in the dazzle of a Tel Aviv summer. Perhaps that is why I did not remember that I had never been to Yarmous' office, which is where I was going in connection with the arbitration – postponed until my return – concerning the spiritual and financial insult suffered by my friend, the writer. It was only when I reached the corner of Ibn Gabirol and the street I was walking towards with such dizzy energy, that I realized that the number of the building – 29, 17, or 37 – had been wiped from my memory, and that I had left my diary in the car.

No problem. Resourcefully, I went over to the corner kiosk: I would find Yarmous' address alongside his name in the telephone directory. That may sound simple, but in the depths of the kiosk a thin, black-mustached youth growled something oblique, like "This isn't Information," or "This isn't a library," and paid no further attention to the pest.

The blood mounted to my head, as often happens to an Israeli just back from overseas travels. Nevertheless I bit my lip, refrained from expressing my opinion about those who make life here insufferable for the rest of us, and remained standing in front of the kiosk, considering whether to scan the street house by house, find a nearby café or pharmacy with a telephone directory, or go all the way back to the car, find the address of Advocate Yarmous and walk the length of Ibn Gabirol for the third time.

"Whose name are you looking for on this street?" I heard a loud, clear voice, but saw nobody on the sun-struck pavement.

"Was that you talking?" I hesitantly asked the mustached youth in the shaded depths of the kiosk.

"D'you see anyone else around here?"

I ignored this wisecrack, too. This is your home beside the Yarkon River, I told myself, loosely adapting a nostalgic song to soothe my mind. I added, as reinforcement from another source, that the world is but a narrow bridge, the main thing is not to be in the least annoyed and to say to the fellow, drily and laconically: Yarmous, that's the name, Yarmous, maybe, after all.

"So, 'scuse me, why didn't you say Advocate Yarmous in the first place?! For that you don't need no book! Mr. Yarmous buys tobacco here every day, newspapers, he's not just a big lawyer, and one of the best, but what a guy, Yarmous, believe me, a real *tsaddik!* If he's looking after you, your troubles are over! Look, two houses up, that one and then the next one and you're there!"

And indeed, at the entrance to number 6, a standard Tel Aviv apartment block, with locked door and intercom, a faded sign read: ADVOCATES YARMOUS AND BEN SHALOM – FIRST FLOOR. Is there really any need to go on about these rapid twists and turns, from the intoxication of the first walk in the heat of the day to the dual-faced welcome of the mustached proprietor of the kiosk? Yes, I extended a finger towards the intercom button, the whole world is but a narrow bridge and there are no crude, warm-hearted kiosk owners like ours anywhere in it, no similar intimacy – wounding, rejecting, appealing, sweet. My finger had not yet reached the button when my left elbow was lightly touched by someone who appeared out of nowhere, and a key was inserted into the lock.

I recoiled instinctively and only then saw the man, most likely one of the tenants, who inclined his head as he entered and remained thus, head at an angle, blocking the half open door with his back, his gaze unwavering. I thanked him with a nod and went in, ignoring his interrogative look. I avoided the elevator and turned to climb the stairs to the second floor. But the man, an elderly Israeli on a summer day, a knitted skullcap on cropped grey hair, short-sleeved shirt on a furrowed neck, sunken chest and flaccid stomach, remained standing in the doorway, calling out to me:

"I know you from somewhere..."

Did I mention that in the kiosk proprietor's reaction to Advocate Yarmous' name there was something that could not have been more intrinsically Israeli? That dense fabric in which our lives, stories and memories are inescapably woven together. I knew very well that I was noticing all this with particular sharpness because I had only just returned from weeks of anonymity and muteness in trans-alpine Europe, and the man with the key had laid his "I know you from somewhere" right inside my frame of mind.

Not only did the kiosk proprietor personify the double-edged aspect of this rough intimacy, but that unexpected digression also seemed to have prepared the ground for my encounter with this elderly Jew now staring at me, who had unabashedly hooked me with that "I know you from somewhere."

Of that I was sure, but my expression concealed what I was really feeling. To the man facing me it conveyed a self-effacing smile, part denial, part acknowledgement. Indeed, my face was familiar to him – secretly I knew it – except that the association imprinted on his memory had, for him, nothing to do with an afternoon in the stairwell of his apartment house. It was not out of conceit, but because it is easy to become famous in a country like ours, that I presumed I knew to which "somewhere" he was referring. I was born and raised in our little country, and when my first story was published, the local population numbered about one tenth of what it is today. Had this increase limited the chances of the average Israeli to achieve renown? If the communications revolution has shrunk the world into a "global village," in McLuhan's words, then we have become an apartment house that is all windows – everyone photographing everyone else and everyone viewing everyone else. Sufficient that a television camera in a remote corner of the studio should, for the fraction of a second, catch the back of the head of one of the audience of friends of the hero of *This is Your Life*, and a million pairs of eyes in a million apartments will view his balding gray head, the tip of an ear and a Picasso-nose, profile and full face at one and the same time, so that the next day the world and his wife can rub up against his fame and say:

"We saw you on *This is Your Life!*"

And since my face has been seen on the magic screen a few times over the years, and more often in the newspapers, I knew this was the "somewhere," this was the acquaintance. On my return from weeks of anonymity and muteness in trans-alpine Europe to our apartment building, which is all windows, it was very pleasant – I admit – for me to discover that an elderly Jew, meeting me out of any likely context, recognizes me. Something in me even prompted me to introduce myself by name and tell him where he knew me from, as it were, but I suppressed my modest smile and took the first step up.

"I know!" his passionate outburst stopped me in my tracks, "from Cracow! We know each other from Cracow!"

On the one hand, this was remote from anything I could have expected, but on the other hand it was a thousand times more amazing. I had passed through Cracow only once, about thirty years ago, one of a large group of young Israelis on the way to Auschwitz.

Was it at all possible that this Jew retained no memory of the newspapers and television, whereas one chance moment decades before – and where were we likely to have met on that one day in Cracow – was so vivid in his mind?

But before I could ask if he had indeed been in Cracow on that day in August 1962, he remembered everything:

"I'll tell you where in Cracow, we were in the same concentration camp. My name's Feldstein. Does that mean anything to you?"

What did I reply?

I certainly mumbled something, I can't recall exactly what. I hurriedly broke away from the man who remembered me from a concentration camp in Cracow and, ahead of all the others waiting to enter, I went into the office where shelves were sagging under the weight of legal tomes, and a table was entirely covered in heaps of files.

These were rapidly cleared away and I, energetically, sharply – and even with some success – spoke out in defense of my colleague's honor and pocket, but my insides were paralyzed by a vague dread. What paralyzed me was not fear, for what could be frightening about such a far-fetched mistake by an elderly Jew on a June afternoon in 1991, in Tel Aviv?

This vague dread has settled on me, and even after telling more and more of my friends where the man knew me from, and all of them responding with polite chuckles of surprise or blatant disinterest, at heart I still wonder.

What was it in my features that so stirred the memory of this Feldstein and so truly convinced him that the man standing before him was none other than he who had shared his fate, his fellow inmate in the camp, how long ago? Forty-seven, forty-eight, fifty years?

What likeness was locked in his memory all those years, and which of that person's characteristics did he find in the face of an Israeli, born in Little Tel Aviv in the 1920s? Was the person in the concentration camp a boy, as I was in those years, or was this distant figure, over sixty and with the same cast of features as I have today, perhaps a member of my lost family in Poland? And perhaps neither one nor the other, but just the hallucination of an old Jew in the heat of the day?

I will never know. But since then, whenever I hear someone say "a familiar face," that vague dread returns to haunt me.

Amos Kenan

At the Station

Translated by Chaya Galai

The station stretches as far as the eye can see. I order a cup of coffee, light a cigarette. Passengers are rushing about, suitcases in hand. The engine whistles and emits steam. A crowd of people are waving handkerchiefs. The train jerks forward. An engine hisses. The train brakes with a squeal. The passengers descend, suitcases in hand. Small convoys of luggage carts push their way through the dense crowd. The passengers move towards the exit.

I suck in cigarette smoke, and wait. Something will happen. I think I may fall in love.

My beloved approaches. I can see her in the crowd. Proud and tall. Carrying only one small suitcase. What is in that suitcase? I do not know. My heart swells.

Together we will stroll along the river bank. At twilight. The birds are twittering and the sun is setting. A big, red moon will rise over the thick forest. We sprawl in the shade on damp leaves and gaze wide-eyed at the great moon and the clear heavens. She approaches, suitcase in hand. I do not know if she will approach me or not. If she comes over, well and good. If she approaches someone else, I am that someone else.

I can't remember if it is she and if I am not someone else. The train brakes with a squeal. The passengers descend with hesitant steps and pace, suitcases in hand, towards the exit. There, outside, the big city awaits.

She is tall and beautiful. Her hair is golden, her eyes greenish-gray. On her face a shy smile.

I pick up the suitcase and we converse. Then we sit down to rest and order a coffee. I offer her a cigarette. She thanks me and takes it. I light her cigarette. She inhales deeply and blows out a stream of smoke. In the evening, I throw my clothes untidily on a chair and draw the curtains. She places her clothes untidily on a chair and covers herself with a blanket.

I embrace her with a cold hand. Her body burns in the dark. She presses to my lips a burning mouth and bites me till she draws blood. Her long nails rake my back and score red marks. I love her and she loves me. I am sad and she is sad. She gets up to the mirror, tidies her hair. I light a cigarette. We dress. The engine whistles.

Someone approaches me and asks me how things are. I answer him jokingly, I am in a jocular mood. We go off together to eat lunch.

After the meal, we order a cup of coffee, light cigarettes and wallow in memories.

Do you remember that day at the station? he asks.

Of course I remember, how could I forget. She was proud and tall, with golden hair, shapely legs. No, things like that I don't forget.

And he asks me again if I remember. I do not hear it all. The noise of the trains, the shouts of the porters, the clamor of the passengers, this constant rumble, words are lost in the air, they float and melt away. But I lend an ear, smile distractedly.

Not always, of course. One should not believe everything that is said. The first impression is always good, but afterwards, when one learns certain facts, one sees that the first impression was quite misleading. But who can tell in advance?

Not only this, of course. Something flutters within me. I see her getting off the train, in one hand a broom and in the other a basket of vegetables. There she is, sweeping the platform, back and forth, back and forth, and the vegetable basket is dragging behind her.

A very interesting woman, someone says.

A hard life, but what an aristocratic demeanor.

It's all a matter of upbringing.

Not just upbringing. A matter of character as well.

Of course. Imagine, for example, someone without a proper upbringing, but with a strong character. He can educate himself.

And, on the other hand, someone who has little in him, if you like, but shows traces of upbringing.

Or, conversely, someone who has character, but his upbringing hampers him.

And so on and so on. She had finished sweeping the platform. It shone like a new mirror. But the stream of people coming and going raises a new cloud of dust on the gleaming platform. Torn newspapers, cigarette butts, scraps and remainders. With her last vestiges of energy, she sweeps the platform one final time. Nobody will soil it now, the most recent train has left and no other train has arrived yet. With a heavy heart, she crosses the tracks, her head lowered, to the other platform. At that moment a giant, flashing engine looms up and crushes her.

We share memories.

I want to tell you a secret, he says to me, leaning his head forward. There is a crafty look in his eyes. He scatters his cigarette ash on my pants.

That calamitous day, remember? They talked about it a lot. Everyone talked. The papers made a great fuss. Well, it was me.

That's not so, it can't be.

I know it's hard to believe. But it was me. I was young, impetuous, hot-tempered and deluded. I didn't pause to think about what I was doing.

Of course, who doesn't have such experiences. I remember that day. I came to see her in the morning. Nobody was home. I told her that it was all over between us. She cried and said she had never imagined it would end like this.

Ha, ha, one can never imagine how it will end. I was impetuous and frivolous, and there you have it. Right?

I simply cannot find my suitcase. Only a moment ago I gave it to the porter, and now he has disappeared from view. I press through the dense crowd, elbowing my way along. An old woman grumbles at me.

Don't grumble, old woman. You'll be dead soon, and what will happen then?

One eye lights up, one is extinguished. One lights up, one is extinguished. Suddenly both eyes go dark. I grope my way in the dark. It seems to me that I have found the case. No, a hallucination. I fall, someone tramples on me. Someone cries out. The eyes light up. I get up. Again one eye is extinguished, one lights up. At a distance, far away, stands a motionless hunched figure.

Where to?

My heart palpitates, like a fish in a net. It quivers like a leaf buffeted by the wind. Like the tail of a comet in the cold remote darkness. Quivers.

Suddenly the quivering stops. A great peace falls, falls like night over the mountains and over the forests and the valleys. A sturdy, confident peace, with mighty chest and muscles. A proud peace.

Are you from here? she asks.

No, I say, I am from there.

Ah, and I thought you were from here. A pity.

Why a pity?

Just so.

(My heart flutters tranquilly).

Yes, I say, I am from there, beyond the far beyond.

Really?

Yes, really.

That's really funny, I was sure you were from here.

Why?

Just so. You look like someone from here.

My mother was from here.

And what about you?

I am from there. My mother went away.

And left you alone?

Yes.

Poor thing.

No, no. I manage excellently.

Truly?

Truly, truly.

That's wonderful.

Why is it wonderful?

Just so. It's wonderful to know how to manage on one's own. I don't know how.

Why?

I don't know. That's the way it is.

I... I...

Pauvre petit. Talking so much.

I'm not a pauvre petit. I just wanted...

Why want?

Why want? I bury my face in her golden hair, breathe in her fragrance, a fragrance which does not belong here. I grope my way over her flesh with a trembling hand. Her body trembles, how it trembles. Perhaps I'll have children, I will send them all to school so that they'll become respectable people. I don't want murderers in my family. One can, thank God, get along without that. She bursts into tears. I know why she is weeping. I too would like to weep. Everything around is so sad, and we are so alone, so alone. All the eyes have been extinguished and the darkness is blinding. Sometimes I grope and cannot find her. I call out in a loud voice, and from the darkness a sob answers me. A motherless kitten? A shipwrecked vessel? I weep and grovel in the dust, embracing her wet, cold body.

God has not forgiven me to this day.

The old man comes over to me fearfully and sniffs around. I signal to him to move aside – it is late. The long, long train flashes by and separates us. Intermittently – I calculate the distance between one lighted window and the next as well as the speed – intermittently I see his meager, bent figure standing helplessly, embracing the extinguished street light.

And who said that this is the way it has to be?

Right. In the fields they are harvesting with joy. A scythe gleams above the waves of golden corn. I wasn't there. I am waiting for the train to pass, perhaps I will see her again, but the train is taking a long time, a long long time. I lose patience. These days it is not worth adhering to a single objective. There are so many. Let's move on. The stars are winking and saying northward, northward. Ursa Major is nursing her cubs through the long night and the cubs are wailing in a wolf's voice on the great snowy plains.

Once I had a girl, do you remember?
  Of course I remember, how could I forget.
  She loved so much, so much...
  Maybe we could be funny, he says to me.
  Fine, let's be funny, I say to him.
  How can we be funny?
  How can we be funny? It's simple. You make me laugh, then I laugh. Then I make you laugh, and you laugh. Then we both laugh, and everyone laughs. That's funny, right?
  Right.
  So come on, make me laugh.
  Right, I'll make you laugh.
  But that's not funny.
  I know, but what can I do?
  Is it really so hard to find something funny?
  No, it's all over.
  So what can we do?
  Jump off the roof.
  That's no solution. What happens afterwards?
  Nothing.
  You see, that's no solution.
  But there's nothing new either.
  What's the difference?
  There's no difference.
  To hell with it (this is the first human note. Non-acceptance. Anger. Knowing that this is the reality, knowing that one doesn't like that fact, but not happy at this non-liking. Not saying "Thank God," saying "To hell with it.")
  Perhaps yearning?
  Perhaps dreaming?

Perhaps dreaming of yearning?

Perhaps yearning to dream.

I don't know.

I don't know.

What's clear to me is that it can't go on like this.

It's clear to me as well, but how can we go on?

I don't know.

I don't know either.

We've reached the beginning.

It isn't the beginning, it's the end.

It's the same thing.

Precisely.

Can't you see how funny it is?

No, it doesn't make me laugh.

Me neither. But I know it's funny.

Then why aren't you laughing?

I haven't the strength.

Are you tired?

A little.

Then rest. Perhaps I can give you artificial respiration.

I want a girl.

What girl?

A big, fat, yellow girl.

There are twenty-seven here like that. Which one would you like?

The fifth from the left.

Wait a minute.

I'm waiting.

Hey, you, fifth from the left. Come here? Yes, please, stand here. Look at me when I'm talking to you. What's your name?

I know three languages.

Do you have any hobbies?

I love.

So do I.

Who?

That depends.

The same for me.

You are very beautiful by the light of the pale lamp.

When I was little, I wanted to be a nurse.

And now?

Now I want to go to Monte Carlo.

Hey, and me? What about me? Have you forgotten me? I invited her first!

What does it matter who invited her first? Can't you see she loves me?

I see, but I don't care. I invited her first. She was the fifth from the left.

The sixth.

No, the fifth.

Then take the sixth.

I don't want to. I've loved her for years. There's absolute understanding between us. When I glance into her pure eyes, seventh heaven opens up. I gaze into those eyes of blue eternity and they respond with an echo that resounds down the generations with a faint roar. In her arms I am plunged into deep, deep abysses and I awake bleeding in the vale of tears. I set out to gather tears and sing songs on alien soil and a giant with one eye hurls the axe of destruction at me and I flee from him to the treetops and from there I see the remote horizon, and there, on the horizon, on a narrow strip of azure between misty borders, I read the verdict inscribed in letters, which no man can read. I close my eyes in fear and the axe hisses close to my throat. I embrace her, trembling, and we roll, clinging together, terror-stricken, from the top of the cliff to this terrible crevice down below, rolling down, screaming as we go.

Have you finished? We're going.

Will you come by later?

Sure. We'll go to the movies.

Aharon Megged

Tears

Translated by Shaun Levin

Mirtel lived in a small shed behind a hedgerow, on the outskirts of the settlement. He treated his abode with the same slovenliness with which he treated himself and his attire. There was a bed there that was never made, a lame table with a faded top that he had appropriated from the public domain, a chair, and several boxes used for odds and ends. In the corners of the dusty floor, there were always old socks, leather straps, and sometimes a work shirt or a towel caked with days-old grime. The smell of cigarette smoke never left the room.

He was a short man, but with a sturdy build. His legs were muscular and his hands were like spades. He had the hazy, somewhat baffled expression of someone who awakes in the morning from bad dreams. There was also a haziness in his watery eyes that made it difficult to see in them either joy or sadness, or even indifference. He spoke little, and when he did, his words were jumbled, his sentences chopped and scrambled, and words like "fine," "that's it," or "might as well" often substituted for the things he could not or would not say. Since he treated himself with deprecation, in his gait, his ways, and all his dealings with others, his fellow men did not feel sorry for him, nor did they bother to make fun of him. They were used to his presence as one gets used to assorted tools left lying about the kibbutz yard, nobody bothering to discard them or to put them to good use.

For most of the day he was the carter. When evening came he distributed small supplies to the members of the kibbutz, as he had done for several years. He did both tasks with meticulous care. No hint of his slovenliness was evident here. He looked after his donkey with a devotion bordering on fanaticism. He was particular about its cleanliness and its harness, and he cushioned its manger with whatever scraps he found in the chicken-coop, the stables and the rubbish heap. He never forgot to prepare its evening ration, to arrange its straw bed, and to clean the pen and inspect it; often, when it rained or the night was stormy, he would get up in the dark and rush over to the pen to see if all was well. No one dared touch the donkey without his permission for fear he might break their bones. Nothing was likely to stir up his wrath more than an injury to his beast.

The supply room, the domain over which he reigned supreme, resembled a museum more than it did a toolshed. All the items were arranged upon shelves, row upon row, cubicle by cubicle. A tag was attached to each compartment, indicating the number of units and the date as well as the item's name. The walls and the floor were spotless. Mirtel would distribute the supplies through a hatch, and forbade anyone to set foot beyond the threshold. This chamber was his holy of holies and everyone treated it as such. He kept a strict ledger in which no evidence of partiality could be found. All the same, if someone in need came knocking at his door in the evening or on the Sabbath, he never refused. He would take the keys and wordlessly walk over to the storeroom, intimating to the fellow that he should stand in front of the hatch. He would go inside and give him what he wanted.

When Heddi left the kibbutz, there was no perceptible change in Mirtel, nor could anyone tell whether he was overcome with grief or not. That summer morning he even carried her belongings from their room to the gate, and loaded them onto the truck. Some saw him bid her an ordinary goodbye, as if he would be seeing her again within a short while. And when the truck pulled away, Heddi stuck her head out the window and called back at him: "And take good care of the child, Mirtel." "Okay," he said. This scene brought a smile to the faces of those who chanced to witness it. When he walked back to his donkey-cart, one of the members addressed him with a nod, as though comforting a mourner "She left, eh?" Mirtel shrugged his shoulders and said, as if in jest: "That's how it goes, what can you do. Women, you know."

Six years earlier, when Mirtel and Heddi moved into a family room, the match caused great astonishment. Mirtel shunned the company of women, and was so shy in their presence that he would blush, stammer and say silly things when one of them turned to him with some trivial question. It was hard to picture him being intimate. Heddi was a little wild animal, a voracious she-cat in heat who knew no shame in her flirtations with men. This little creature, golden-haired and fiery-eyed, laid claim to her desires and assertively so, giving much publicity to her claims. When she worked in the clothing storeroom, she would speak of her love affairs without any modesty whatsoever, as one would talk of guzzling and boozing. She was vociferous in her love, vociferous in her hatred and vociferous in her jealousy. Yet whatever she said, she said out of innocence, and it was this trait of hers that muddled all conventional notions of morality. One could not be angry with her, just as one cannot be angry at a child's excessive sweet tooth, even if he is caught stealing candy from the pantry or smashing the dishes. It seems that our view of the sinner is determined by his own view of the deed. Heddi did not know what a sin was; hence the inclination to be forgiving towards her, even when it came to the most pious of moralists. Her stories, like her actions, never gave rise to anger or contempt. They were amusing and generated laughter that was not without sympathy, even affection. At times it seemed that she would sweep the other girls along with her, to love her "lovers," hate her enemies and burn with vengeance for her "betrayers." Funniest of all was when she gnashed her teeth and moaned about these "betrayers," or shot her verbal darts at them. Then she appeared in all her wildness, in all her animal cruelty that knew no mercy. It seemed that she was meant to scratch, pull, bite and slay. And still, it was nothing more than a good laugh.

What did Heddi see in Mirtel, whom she chose out of all her "lovers?" It soon became clear that this madness was not without method. New pleasures, like coziness, sitting side by side, and a seemingly more respected status in society, did not cancel the old ones, those of a carefree existence. For the first two or three months Heddi was as devoted to him as a maidservant, and saw to the upkeep of their new room with such vehemence it seemed their house would remain standing longer than any other. And indeed, her behavior was moderate and reasonable, and all the women commented on how she had settled down at last. Many learned a lesson from this miraculous change and said:, this is what permanence does, blessed be He who transforms His creatures. Yet once the few honeymoon months were over Heddi went back to her old ways, flying in the face of all the know-it-alls who hasten to pass judgement. Once again she would fall upon the necks of young men and chance upon the night-watchmen as they patrolled the settlement. Yet even now no sense of wrongdoing seemed to influence her conduct. She would scurry after strangers and remain faithful to her spouse, and saw no contradiction between the two. She was meticulous in her conjugal duties; not only that, she would vehemently defend Mirtel against anyone who insulted him, and fought his battles whenever she felt he was being derided. "My Mirtel," she called him at all times.

It was unclear whether Mirtel was aware of her escapades or just pretended to see nothing. In any event, he let her run riot to her heart's content. There was no indication of any breach in their domestic harmony, nor of any disruption to his peace of mind. He would do his work as usual, return to their room early in the evening, and sink into sleep. He probably never saw her coming or going. When their son, Yossi, was born, there were those who gossiped that he was from the seed of another; yet this slander certainly never reached his ears.

Their life together lasted for six years, growing neither stronger nor weaker, yet it ceased to arouse wonder and malediction until the day Heddi told Mirtel she was leaving for town. Some said she was following her lover, a fine-looking Sephardi, a driver at a taxi depot. After she left, Mirtel felt it would be improper for him to stay in a room designated for families and he moved to the shed that had once been the shoemaker's workshop.

There was no visible change in him after that, but from the day Heddi left, his love for his four-year-old son seemed to grow sevenfold.

Yossi resembled his mother in appearance, but inherited his social standing from his father. In the children's house he was insulted but did not insult and, being withdrawn, was a target for the bullies in the group. While his peers played their games, he would stand in the corner, thumb in mouth, his other hand supporting his elbow, and watch them sadly from the side. He, too, was slovenly in his attire; his trousers were always loose and soiled, the hem of his shirt trailing behind him; and always, come rain or shine, he had a runny nose. He would burst into tears at the smallest insult and seek refuge under the nurse's apron. Out in the yard he would occupy himself with solitary pastimes.

His father was his sole consolation. On seeing him cross the settlement on his donkey-cart piled high with garbage or pitchers of milk, Yossi would run to the gate in the yard, call out to him and ask to be taken along. And when Mirtel refused, Yossi would stand at the fence, his mournful look following the donkey-cart until it disappeared. When the children were let out to visit their parents it was Yossi's hour of deliverance. He would fly from the yard like a bird from its cage and run with all his might to meet his father. There was no sight more pitiful than Yossi looking for his father and being unable to find him. At night, after bedtime, Yossi's cries could still be heard in the settlement, Daddy, Daddy! He would stand on his bed and shake its iron posts like a prisoner trying to break the bars of his cell. Eventually he would lose heart and fall asleep, exhausted.

Mirtel treated his son as his equal. He spoke to him with the same matter-of-fact gravity he used when distributing supplies, and with the same confounded and stammering tongue as well. On occasion one could hear them arguing over some issue as they walked through the settlement, and Mirtel would pause, stretch out his hands, as he did in his quarrels with the work-coordinator and say: "But Yossi, you must understand that I can't... it can't be helped... that's the way it is... I'm only human after all... I can't... believe me..." And at times Yossi would defeat his father in arguments and then Mirtel could be heard saying to him: "Okay... you were right... no need to go on like that... you were right... that's that." And there was nothing in his manner to diminish in any way Yossi's admiration for his father.

In his games with his father, Yossi found compensation for all the insults he suffered in the company of his peers. He and his father would find a secluded place on a small lawn at the edge of the settlement and amuse themselves undisturbed. Mirtel would kneel on all fours and Yossi would ride on his back, waving a stick in his hands and prodding his backside to spur him on. At times they would crawl on the ground and with their hands dig ditches that became streams, lakes and oceans. But what really made Yossi's day was when Mirtel took the donkey out of its pen – the donkey he would not let anyone touch – and let him ride it before sundown. Yossi would sit atop the donkey while Mirtel held the reins and led the way. Then Yossi would be lit with majesty. He would order his father to lead him along the paths of the settlement for the children to see him in all his glory, and from the height of his seat he would look down haughtily at his friends and enjoy their envy. All the way back to the pen, the son would be silent and the father would be silent; it was Mirtel and Yossi's muted victory march through the enemy camp. They passed through the streets of the conquered town and its inhabitants bowed before them.

Not far from Mirtel's shed, near the mechanics' garage, stood the frame of an old jeep, sunk to its headlights in the sand. It was in ruins, rusted, scorched and dented, nothing more than a piece of junk; yet by some miracle the steering wheel had remained intact. Mirtel and Yossi took possession of this jeep and made it their private domain. Every Saturday they would go there, where silence prevailed and no children were to be found, seat themselves on the rusting seat and embark on their journeys.

"Where to today?" Yossi would ask.

"To Haifa," his father suggests.

"No. To Mummy," Yossi says.

"Okay, then go," Mirtel says.

And Yossi holds onto the steering wheel, turning it from side to side, screeching with his lips, honking as he sets out on his voyage. When he reaches his destination he stops and says: "Hello, Mummy, we're here."

"Okay," Mirtel says, "now to Haifa."

"Okay, now to Haifa," Yossi agrees with his father.

And in Haifa Mirtel shows him all the fine places worth visiting. The harbor, the oil factory, the oil pools, Mount Carmel, and the groves. And even though Yossi knows Mirtel's stories by heart, he listens to them as if hearing them for the first time, and even helps him along with questions.

"That's it," Mirtel ends their trip, "now we're going home." Yet the journey back is somewhat gloomy, for leaving faraway places is always a hard thing to do.

It happened one Saturday afternoon, a time when the entire settlement was asleep. Mirtel and Yossi had just returned from their journeys. Mirtel was tired and had a headache, so he left his son in the jeep and went to the shed to rest. He lay down in his clothes and shoes, and in a short while was fast asleep. He was woken suddenly by a scream – "Daddy! Daddy!"

Mirtel leapt out of bed, and from the doorway saw Yossi being dragged from the jeep by Eitan, a boy of almost eight years old, son of Peretz the dairyman.

"Stop that!" he yelled at the top of his voice.

Eitan held onto Yossi's feet and Mirtel ran to him, grabbed his hand and, pale with anger, shouted in his parched voice: "Whadda you doing to him, whadda you think you're doing?"

Eitan went blue in the face from the pain of Mirtel's large hand clamped around his arm.

"Let go..." he said, gasping for air.

"I won't let go," Mirtel still clasped his arm. "Tell me what you wanted from him."

"I said let go!" Eitan shouted.

"Shut up!" Mirtel whispered in exasperation, thrusting his finger at the boy. "I said shut up..." and suddenly he felt his blood rising to his head, flooding his skull, and his vision became dim. "I'll show you what it means to drag him by his feet," he said and slapped him across the face. "I'll show you what it means to pull him off this jeep," and slapped him again. "I'll teach you a lesson..."

The boy coiled up from the force of the blow and tried to protect his body, but Mirtel could not control his anger, and with one swipe he threw the boy to the ground. He rolled in the sand like a slaughtered chicken.

"Come," he took Yossi's hand and lifted him off the ground. Yossi sat there wailing, stunned by what he had seen. "Come," he pulled Yossi behind him, as if fleeing the scene of a murder.

He collapsed onto his bed and felt no regret. He savored the sweet taste of revenge on his palate, a taste he had never known.

It took fifteen minutes, or maybe more, before there was a loud knock on the door and Peretz stood in the doorway, holding his son by the hand.

"What did you do to him?" he said, his voice choked.

Mirtel looked at the boy and saw his bruised face and the large swelling on his forehead. He stared at him and said nothing.

"I feel sorry for you," Peretz said after a long silence, "otherwise I'd finish you off. But you won't be staying here much longer." And he left, slamming the door behind him.

In the evening, after lights-out, Mirtel went back to the shed, closed the door, and, gathering his few belongings into a pile, wrapped them up in a blanket. Then he went to the pen and put straw and barley in the donkey's trough and bedded the ground with hay. From there he went to the supply room and stuck the bunch of keys into the keyhole. He went back to his room, threw himself onto the bed and slept.

The following morning, with the gray light of dawn still outside and no one yet risen for work, Mirtel walked over to the children's house, woke his son, dressed him, and said: "Come, we're going."

"To Mummy?" Yossi asked.

"No, not to Mummy," Mirtel said and pulled him along.

"Where then?" he asked.

"Never mind. You'll see."

Yossi sensed something out of the ordinary had happened, something terrifying and ominous. And when they walked into the shed, and he saw the parcel in the corner, he burst into tears and cringed down onto the floor.

Mirtel grasped the bundle in one hand and held the other out to Yossi. "Enough crying. Enough. Come. Let's go."

Yossi wept and would not budge.

"Come," Mirtel pulled him by the hand.

But Yossi would not move.

"Come on. We're going. Everything will be fine," Mirtel tried to lift him.

But he was stuck to the floor. Mirtel did not understand how the boy could suddenly have become too heavy for him to lift. Yossi fell back each time Mirtel eased his grip.

"Don't be a baby," Mirtel tried to persuade him. "We have to go and that's that."

Yossi wept bitterly.

Mirtel did not know what to do with him. He sat down on the bed, helpless. The morning chill sent a shiver through his body. Outside it was dim, quiet and moist with dew. And the boy's tears trickled on and on, as though they would never end.

Igal Mossinsohn

Creaking Chairs

Translated by Sara Friedman

He should have told the truth. He should have told her: "Listen, my child, you know nothing. You're a delicate woman with black eyes, a soft, sensuous mouth, and your small white brow, framed by curls, is lovely – but you know nothing. 'Art is sacred!' So say you, yet you know – nothing. This life behind the scenes, under the artificial lights, the grimy makeup, the paint dripping with beads of sweat in summer, the chills that seize you when you're forced to perform on a cold rainy evening in light clothing – it's all sordid. Not sacred, not sublime – just the dull routine of people forced to make a living."

He should have told her. But in the sun-drenched kibbutz dining room, people thronging round the tables where the actors sat after the play, when a pretty girl came up to him for "a few words, just a few words," fixing her black eyes on him as if he were a fabulous creature floating among crowns and kingdoms, his very being a fantasy in human shape – how, oh how, could he possibly pull her down from heaven to the good, black earth here among the pines?

But now, when she came to his room, he would speak to her in no uncertain terms.

He stretched out on the rickety couch, clasped his hands behind his neck and stared at the ceiling. On the dusty bookcase stood a human skull, its eye sockets black. Books were heaped untidily on the single chair that stood by the couch. A full-length unframed mirror leaned against the wall in a corner. This was Gabriel Malin's room: bookcase, rickety couch, large mirror, several pairs of shoes thrust behind the curtain where his faded brown suit hung, and books, journals and bundles of newspaper heaped on the chair

If he heard two rings, he'd open the door. One ring would be for the landlord himself, and not worth the bother. In the meantime he could lie back, settle down and mull things over. In the past, after an exhausting day's work at the quarry, he'd sing along with the gang of penniless, barefoot, tousle-headed comrades: *"Yenta di roytta, Yenta di roytta, how bee-YOO-tee-ful her bandy legs"* – believing, like this young woman from the kibbutz, that art was sacred. What remained of that awe now? Scenery made of pasted newspapers, a bald pate without a trace of hair, bluish wrinkles under the eyes – nothing more. Gabriel Malin, clown! For seventeen years you've been standing on the wooden floorboards in the blinding footlights, grinning at the anonymous audience in creaking seats out there in the darkness, and going home to your little room sadder, moodier, glummer.

Say to the director: "Let me do Hamlet! Do you hear – I want to play Hamlet, King Lear, Dr. Stockman." He will think: "Have you gone mad?" "Your role, Gabriel Malin," the director would say, "your role is to bring a smile to the lips of the ticket buyers. To hop on one foot. And bump into tables. And overturn crockery. And fall in love with the eternal doll-faced, thick-limbed maidservant. You're no Hamlet, Gabriel Malin, nor Lear, nor that – what's his name? – right, Stockman. You're a clown! Your nose is flattened. Your mouth stretches to your big ears, and you walk like a clown."

"Fine," you may say, "go to hell. What's here for me? Fine, let's untie the knot: good riddance!" Why not say: "Goodbye. I'm leaving. I've had enough." "Tsk, tsk," go the tongue-clickers. "Tsk, what's all the fuss about! No need to act on every declaration so promptly. And anyway, Gabriel Malin, where will you sail off to after seventeen years? Where will you go: back to the quarry?"

They would be right, too: there was nowhere to return to. Very simple. Nowhere. And after all... when all's said and done... you don't blot out seventeen years in a single stroke. This is your home. These repulsive faces – are the faces of your friends. These cardboard crowns – they eke out your bread and butter from the audience. You won't find another place, Gabriel Malin, where your shoulder – a little slumped – would receive a warmer welcome than here, behind these curtains. To start over? Who has the strength for it!

Gabriel Malin rose from the couch and began pacing the room. He paused in front of the mirror and gave it a crooked smile. The mirror smiled back crookedly.

Well then, what would he tell her, the girl from the kibbutz? Best lock the door so no one could disturb him. He would lie on the couch, read some poetry by Poe or Baudelaire, while the skull above smirked at him: "It's all right, we're not alone in the world."

But come she will, and you must talk to her. For there, in the pine grove, you implored her to come. So be it. Make a few noncommittal remarks. Chat for a while, then send her off. After all, Gabriel Malin, here is a young person standing at a crossroads, and you have no right to turn away without indicating the path to be taken. No right at all. Very well, so be it. "Mark my words, my girl." No, best say this: "Listen, you! Get thee to the chicken coop, the cowshed, the field! Have a brood of healthy, sweet children. There's no place for the young in the theater. The theater is a cooperative, its members firmly entrenched. And by the time you get some insignificant role, you'll be weary of life. You'll have to stand around as an extra without making a sound. And after many years you'll get to say two meaningless words. And so on – until you finally despair of the whole business and go back whence you came. Whereupon other young girls will take your place, and so forth. Who will you learn from? There's no one – anyone who knows anything is too busy. There's neither point nor purpose. Go home. Go back to the field. A shame to waste all those years here. There's no place for the young in the theater. None, I tell you!"

Gabriel Malin cocked a fist at his reflection in the mirror. "You too, you lopsided mug – what, dreaming of the Danish prince?" He stuck his fingers in his mouth and stretched his lips to his ears.

Two rings.

Gabriel smoothed his wrinkled shirt, grasped his chin and rubbed it for a moment. He shot a glance at the mirror, then opened the door.

"Hello. I've come," she smiled at him. Sandals, a black skirt, a white blouse on the narrow shoulders.

"So you have. Good."

She examined the room with big, curious eyes; Gabriel could read disappointment on her alert face at the sight of his seedy room.

"A mess, isn't it?" he said, wishing to provoke her. Though, as a matter of fact, he was pleased with her candid, scrutinizing gaze that hid nothing.

"Yes, a perfect mess." Her laugh rang out, and it seemed to him that spring had suddenly burst into his room until even the holes in the skull were smiling from atop the bookcase.

Elaborately, he removed the pile of books from the chair and set them on the floor, in the corner by the mirror. "Have a seat." For some reason he was enjoying her disappointment at the sight of the general untidiness.

She sat, her thighs pressed together and the hem of the black skirt lying in folds. Gabriel Malin sank down on the couch, leaned toward her chair, and said:

"Yes, very nice of you to have come. I was thinking about that talk we had at the kibbutz. Well, then. What can I say?" he ended unexpectedly. He had meant to tell her the truth. But how could he recount the entire tale to a stranger, a young woman who considered the theater a magical world, whose sole desire was to enter it!

"I wanted to ask your advice. What should I do?" she said, her black eyes lovely: he could see them in the mirror.

"Do you think you have any talent?" He immediately sensed the tactlessness of his question, and wanted to add: "Plenty of untalented people on the stage," but thought better of it. After all, she didn't care about that.

"I don't know, that is, I suppose I do. But I must put myself to the test somewhere other than in amateur groups. If I don't try, my life will be split between reality and dreams, and I don't want that."

She spoke very softly, her voice low. Yet through her speech he sensed a strong, stubborn will: here was a person with no lack of self-esteem, though asking for help. "Many people," she went on levelly, "seek an outlet to express their feelings in color, music, drama, then ultimately discover it is beyond their power. But they must try, struggle, to give expression to the inner person. One can't give up easily. Nothing in this world comes easily, there's a price to pay. And I'm prepared to pay it."

Gabriel Malin studied her for a long moment. He didn't think she was referring to him, but rather trying to convince herself of the truth of her own words. One certainly did not abandon one's position in life lightly, in return for things of no consequence. Hence – she was struggling.

"And if one day, shall we say, after seventeen years, you should suddenly feel that you are not talented, that you're pacing the stage without a trace of emotion, without feeling the words you speak, without believing, even for a fleeting moment, in all those crowns and palaces, what then?"

She didn't understand. Shook her head, her hair flowing over her shoulder.

"If, for instance, you should feel that you have no talent, that is, after being on the stage for seventeen years?"

Now she understood. "Well, yes, of course. I would leave the theater. I'd go."

Gabriel Malin almost shouted in her face: "Go *where*?"

An oppressive silence ensued. They averted their eyes. She was of the opinion that he shouldn't have raised his voice; he, for his part, was abashed after the shouted question he had hurled in her alarmed face.

"Would you like a cognac?" he asked, trying to placate her.

"I beg your pardon, what was that?" She gazed at his lined face and bald head in the mirror.

"Will you have a cognac?"

"Yes, I'll have one. Though I don't usually. I'll probably cough," she replied, without looking at him.

He stood up and opened the bookcase doors. On the top shelf stood a bottle. He took out two small glasses and filled them. "That's for you."

"Thank you."

Gabriel Malin swallowed the cognac, his finger hooked in the skull's eye socket. He didn't know what to tell her. He had meant, once she was there, to speak out, throw cold water on her, then shut the door firmly behind her, and that would be that. Well, then? A kibbutz girl comes by and topples your entire world! But that wasn't it. It may very well be, Gabriel, that a great actress stands before you, but – the gates are locked.

He heard her cough and turned to her. "The cognac?" he asked.

"No. I thought you had dozed off."

"Where were we?" he asked, clasping his hands behind his back and leaning against the bookcase. He added hastily: "What will they say at the kibbutz if you leave?"

She replied deliberately, as if weighing her words:

"I'll be thrown out of the kibbutz. You must realize what that means to me. All my friends are there. *Everybody.* It's my home. And if I've decided to ask your advice in spite of everything, it's because I know that if I don't try, I'll always feel like half of me were missing, that I didn't realize my full potential."

"Fine... and if you fail?"

"If I fail? Yes. That would be bad, very bad. But then I would know that the burden was too much for me to bear, so I'd return to kibbutz life and take it up without any misgivings. I'd put my nose to the grindstone with the clear, calm assurance that my life was there, nowhere else. I would have peace of mind. If only we could stage our own productions! Oh, if only we had our own theatre..."

Gabriel Malin paced the room. These people with a stage of their own! Set up their own theater, would they! Oh, yes. They would find ways of solving the problem: the untalented ones – to the chicken coop, the cowshed, the stable! With all due respect, of course. Wasn't Yoske Bloch second to none in wielding a sledgehammer, yet nothing but a blockhead when it came to machinery and screws? Each to his proper place, and that was that. And as for me? I'll peel potatoes with the cooks. A theater of their own, eh!... "You must forgive me," he said abruptly. "I don't remember your name."

"How could you know it when I haven't told you?" she laughed. "My name is Tamar."

"Yes. Tamar. Fine. Good, very good." He had intended to speak from the heart yet found himself sounding dry and unfeeling. For some reason he recalled Mackenzie's play "Musical Chairs," in which people scramble for a chair; since there are more seekers than chairs, some are left standing. That's life. Here he was, Gabriel Malin, sitting tight. No one could make him budge. Not even if he *was* inept. Because he had found a chair in time, when only a few people wanted to sit down. Whereas the young ones – what would become of them, seeking an outlet for their talents? Gabriel Malin shrugged. There were enough theaters – for the hundreds of thousands in the country. But if there was a *raison d'être* for the few theaters, it was to get the pick of the crop, the outstanding actors, not those who managed to sit down first. How about: The Fund for the Untalented. Sensing Tamar's puzzled gaze on him, he broke off his musings that went round and round, only to end up where they had started.

"You know," he said, his voice husky, "you'd better go back to the kibbutz. It will be hard for you to make a living: even if you're accepted, you'll get some insignificant role. You'll have to stay in the theater all through rehearsals, with no pay. Well, then..."

"I didn't think it would be as smooth as olive oil all the way. Difficulties? Obviously. But the question is, can one study, improve? Will they give me a chance to try my hand at it?"

Gabriel Malin walked over to her, laid his hands on her narrow shoulders, felt her hair lightly brushing them. She saw faded eyes, lashless lids. The smell of cognac drifted from his mouth mixed with that of tobacco and shaving soap.

"You have a life to live," he said. "Listen, my girl, it's no life at all, don't you understand?"

She understood nothing. For a moment she thought he was reciting a part. Theatricals, she thought, should properly be confined to the stage, while in life it was preferable to speak simply and not dig unfamiliar fingers into her shoulders, not to fix lashless eyes on her own.

"Old people shuffle around onstage," he added. "*Old!* If they had trained a younger generation to learn from their experience, had encouraged them, well then... But..." Gabriel saw the lovely black eyes, slightly alarmed, and was gratified by the tremor of her body under his hand. Now she bowed her head. Gabriel could see himself when he used to pass former academy students in the street, and he too would cast his eyes down at seeing them. He heard his own voice: "A man onstage must be credible – convincing! The stage offers an illusion – but when a fifty-year-old actor plays a youth – and plays him badly – what would you call that? Still, the audience keeps coming. Thanks to whom, may I ask? Thanks to a few sublime actors. There you are. For it *is* art! It *is* sacred! No one has the power to drag Gabriel Malin off the stage, because Gabriel Malin loves the artificial lights, the costumes, the dusty floorboards, the audience, even if, possibly, he is inept. Do you hear me? I have spoken the truth. We will sit in our chairs until not only the chairs creak but our very bones rattle with gout!" He sat opposite her, his body clasped tight in his arms.

"And that's all?" she asked. Her voice betrayed her – it quavered.

"Yes, that's all. Go back home. Go! The struggle is pointless: the gates are locked. I'm very sorry, but..."

Suddenly she felt that no air penetrated here. It was an old bachelor's room and his eyes were examining her. In the far distance lay the fields, the forest on the mountain, the valley. She shut her eyes.

"I'm sorry," he repeated. He felt for her in her sadness.

"No, no. It's better to face life with eyes wide open," she said, her own eyes still closed. Now she understood that she must go back. It had been a dream; its fragments lay strewn before her. She had thought that the moment of decision had come, the choice of her path in life, and – nothing had happened: this room, and decent Gabriel Malin, desperate. "I'll go now," she said.

Gabriel Malin made no reply. They stood looking silently at the mirror giving back their oblique reflections.

"In the past," he said. "In the past I too believed. Yes... In the past. Many years have gone by since then..."

He had the feeling he was talking needlessly. For this girl, whom he barely knew, had sounded hidden chords within him. Perhaps because he was seeing himself at her age: a young man, seeking, wondering at the world.

"I must go," she said.

"Yes. Right. Of course... Forgive me. I didn't mean to go on like this, but it happens: an unplanned conversation, talking for no good reason; it all depends on one's mood. Certainly there are difficulties, but they can all be overcome. Maybe, if new blood comes in, it will invigorate us as well."

He held the door for her as she went out into the corridor.

"Well then, goodbye," she said, expressionless.

"Goodbye." He wanted to add: "See you." But didn't.

Tamar left. Gabriel Malin sat on the chair. In the mirror, facing him, also sat Gabriel Malin, and the two stared at each other and didn't like what they saw. They shut one eye and stretched their legs out, the chairs creaking under their weight.

Yes, he thought to himself, first spring enters the room in the form of an attractive girl, then autumn walks out the door. Before, you were a smiling clown, now you're a flattened nose and eyes longing for some sleep... as night wells up from the corners of the room.

Shlomo Nitzan

Down by the Dead Sea

Translated by Vivian Eden

At a certain point in time, in the thirty-ninth year of his life, Nachum Bialer lay stretched out beside the body of water lower than any other in the world. His right hand played with the stones, his left embraced a piece of driftwood which some tempest had apparently tossed up on this deserted shore. He lay sprawling there, in the broiling heat of noon, breathing slowly and deeply, feeling the sea flowing in his veins. Doing nothing at all, allowing each part of his body to breathe separately and to rest separately. The lung alone and the leg alone, the big toe and the heart. To lie thus fully content on the burning stones beneath this low sky – and to breathe in.

Slowly slowly, in this air burning like sudden grace. Like being disengaged from oneself and engulfed by the heat in a kind of somber joy, in the exhilaration of self-extinction, though no redemption was implied. He had just arrived from the north, going down, down the whole way, down hillsides which sometimes sloped gently and sometimes plunged steeply all at once to this point, the shores of the lowest water in the world. The driver could already be heard maneuvering his bus, turning it round for the journey back north. Drivers can always come down and go up at will. They do not belong, they are a race apart.

First he had arrived, and now he was filled with a passion for being here. To be engulfed and gathered in by this burning heat, and to bear it in utter stillness with neither point nor purpose, yet nonetheless with great dedication, and this too is good.

There he lay on the primal soil at the base of the world in a kind of endless time-being, facing the ripples on these waters, surrounded and imprisoned by desolate cliffs. This far, Bialer. As if you had reached the root. There is no sign of life on the soil all around, yet from this soil God created His world. The land is infinitely exposed, bare of any glimmer of green or trees, of the comfort of cool breezes, of any welcoming blossom – here, four hundred meters below the level of any civilization. To this very place God came down to judge Himself and His dread split chasms into this formless land and raised up formless cliffs which hang upon nothing.

A blow of dazzling light struck his head. Heavy heat like arid stillness wafted from the sea and swaddled him in a kind of glowing and seductive fellowship. In one direction his eyes took in, at a distance, the pole of the bus stop which was imbedded deep in the ground at the roadside, tilted to the side, like a hope grown old and shabby and hopeless, that nevertheless refuses to die. But in the other direction his eyes took in the sea, and all at once, in a flash, he saw it as if he had never seen it before in his life. Neither it nor any other sea. Without memories. Without a past. It was not memories that had begotten the sea – it was his own eyes gazing at it. And the moment he shifted his gaze to the mountain, it begat the mountain. And when his gaze rested upon the expanse stretching between the sea and the mountain – it begat that space.

He lay back down and listened to his own breathing. A stone in the field, suddenly without a past, died and lived in a single instant. His entire existence was focused at that moment on this full, leisurely breathing. All that was in him was born and died in the blink of an eye. He rested his gaze on the mountain, and the mountain was born; he looked away from the mountain, and the mountain died. His entire being was himself, and only for an instant. "I'm here," said Guli. "Go away, don't provoke me." – "I'm here here here." – "Let me be." – "But I'm here, with you." – "Let me be." – "If I came, it means you called me." – "I don't need you, let me be." – "Nevertheless, I'm here." – "Yes, I know, there's no escaping you." – "Is it my fault?" – "I don't know." – "I couldn't stand it any more, that's why." – "I've already asked you to forgive me." "Yes. It's not my love, it's my forgiveness that you wanted. Always, all the time and for everything, twenty-four hours a day for our whole lives." – "I know that, Guli." – "I'm repeating it." – "What for?" – "You called me, didn't you?" – "If only I were able not to call you." – "You wanted me to love your weaknesses." – "That's not so." – "Oh, but it is. What I wanted was to love you, not to pity you all the time." "I know, Guli." – "I wanted so much for you not to be in need of my pity, even though you had it." – "I wasn't always aware of it." – "I wasn't born a nurse, Bialer." – "But you're a strong woman, Guli." – "I'm tired of being strong." – "I have just spent a wonderful hour free of you." – "I was expected to comfort and forgive you all the time, to ignore my own needs and to defer to yours, endlessly." – "Why do you keep repeating things you've already said to me?" – "I have nothing else to say to you." – "During that wonderful hour I just spent, I came to a different understanding." – "What is it?" – "Our failure became the start of my enlightenment." – "Your failure perhaps, not mine" – "Mine was also yours, Guli, one cannot bring back the years that have gone by. Ask me why it has been the start of my enlightenment." – "Very well, I'm asking." – "Because the failure released me from all the imaginary successes and now it is as if my soul had returned to its source. I've stopped deceiving myself and you and the boy and happiness. After all, you too were something of a deception in my life, like all the other attempts. But now I'm breathing easily. Now I am something that I have never been before. I have reached a place that I struggled vainly and deceitfully not to reach. All my life, failure has been lying at my doorstep and I never acknowledged it. Everything I did, I did to cheat it. Now it has broken in and revealed itself." – "What has?" – "That which was predetermined, my companion from the womb, my redeeming angel." – "Your failure?" – "The constant trial of my life, as I now know. Now my failure has become my victory, the fountainhead of my strength. Why are you laughing?" – "You only confess as far as you forgive yourself." – "Guli, Guli." – "Or the extent to which you wish others to forgive you." – "Even now?" – "Don't you see that?"

Beyond the inn and the red tour bus and the two trucks parked languidly by the empty road, not far from the water tanks shaded by the high, crumbling cliff overhanging them, a man appeared, walking towards the sea. He walked past the bus stop of dying hope that had not yet died, and walked alone over the ground as if it were an endless sea. The sun was dazzling, blinding. The walking man left heavy footsteps in the sand and his head was uncovered. The sun was blazing hot. Treading heavily, the man reached the sea, and there he saw Bialer stretched out alone in the sun.

"They're looking for you," he said,

"There's no one here who could be looking for me."

"But they're looking for you."

"For me? My appointment isn't until five o'clock."

"So you're not from the red bus?"

"They're looking for someone from the red bus?"

"Yes."

"No, I'm not from the red bus. I came on a regular bus."

"I thought you were from the red tour bus. They're looking for someone who got lost," said the man in an utterly different tone, as if he were now speaking of things which had nothing to do with either of them, and he bent over and sat down cross-legged next to Bialer who was stretched out beside the water. Now there were two people by the water.

"Blank," the man introduced himself with easy friendliness, "that's what they call me."

"Bialer," Nachum revealed his secret, "Nachum Bialer."

"Does your name sound as peculiar to you when you say it aloud as mine does to me?"

"Why?"

"As if l were stripping myself naked."

Their voices were similar in tone, but Blank's sounded a little older as well as more sunburned, more wrinkled.

"There are mountains here," offered Blank, "many beautiful mountains in this area."

"I'm not a tourist, as I've already told you. Not from abroad and not local."

"The sulfur springs surface about two kilometers north of here, but it would be better for you to spend the night here at the inn."

"I haven't come here to bathe in the sulfur springs."

"Ah," said Blank understandingly, and at once added: "Yes." Partly to himself and partly to Bialer.

"The silence, eh?" said Blank, after a while. "There's plenty of silence here. Good, very virginal silence. Abundant and vast silence, like on the mountain peaks. At most hours of the day it is undisturbed."

"I've just arrived," Bialer said in conclusion.

"Two years ago I lay here like you and waited for my appointment with the director of the plant."

"I have an appointment with the director of the plant, at five o'clock this afternoon."

"At five in the afternoon, yes. I came down from the north looking for a job here. Two years ago, that is. I'm a chemist."

"I'm a chemist and I'd like to work here at the plant."

"If only it were possible to catch fish here at least, in this damned dead sea!" said Blank, his face serene and expressionless, like someone whose despair is silent and who is accustomed to swallowing all the petty disappointments of every day.

"My family has split up and I'd like to work down here."

"Ah," said Blank with understanding, and a tired memory flickered across his face. "The wife and children stayed up north?"

"One child."

"Of course, isn't that what I said?"

"You said children."

"That was just a general manner of speaking."

Then they were silent. In all directions, there was no living thing in sight. The sea, in its blueless tranquillity, dozed its memories and day-old sunbeams skittered playfully on the surface of the water. The sun itself was invisible, shrouded in mist, and poured its fiery wrath on the ground and on the oily, dead surface of the Sea. The mountains stood by in silence. Again and again there was this new mystery, exposed in its terrible, burning nakedness, wafting in an awesome gust and with greater force from the opposite shore – and it was greatly to Bialer's taste, so much so that he would gladly have been engulfed in it and extinguished.

"Two years ago," said Blank, looking at the sand. "Why are you laughing?"

"It's as if your voice were my own and I had changed after two years."

"Perhaps you invented me?" laughed Blank.

"Perhaps," Bialer mingled his laughter with Blank's. "Or maybe it's you who invented me."

Now they both laughed together and their laughter rang out as if it were one man's.

"How is she?" Bialer suddenly cut short his laughter and asked in a whisper.

"The wife is up north. As for me, I've been down here for the past two years. At first I used to go back up north to visit from time to time, but then I stopped doing that. Now I'm here all the time. It's just a pity you can't catch any fish here."

"You like fishing?"

"Very much. In rivers and seas and any body of water. How is she?"

"I have a feeling that quite soon I won't know either. In due time, that is."

"They think I'm very devoted to my work and they gave me a managerial position," explained Blank. "In time they may even make me a big boss."

"Your face is as dark as if you'd been born here," said Bialer.

Blank's hands examined his face.

"I suppose the sun will never be able to burn your face again."

"But I wasn't born here. I am dying here by inches."

"My face must be completely pale."

"Mine was just like yours when I first came down here."

"I know, two years ago."

"Yes."

"Two years is a long time, isn't it?"

"Sometimes long and sometimes short."

"How will things be two years from now?"

"Just like they were two years ago."

"I'll probably look just like you."

"And you'll be a manager and expect them to make you a big boss."

"I'm not so sure."

"What aren't you so sure of?"

"That I'll want to be a big boss."

"Of course you will. There won't be anything else for you to want."

At this point Bialer straightened up and the two men sat there next to one another, alone in this wide expanse spread out over the rocks and the sea. The high mountains plunged and swooped down behind them. Far off by the inn a lone automobile passed by, its motor unheard.

"A person could drown in this silence," said Bialer.

"They say that hermits used to seclude themselves in these parts."

"Yes, a few kilometers further along."

"They were also running away from all kinds of north."

"Because they wanted to be reborn in the harsh silence. That, at least, is what people say."

"But they died here very slowly, like me."

"No, not at all," explained Bialer. "They died in an altogether different way."

"That is to say, they and I each died in different ways?"

"And you, I mean, why are you here?"

"I'm not looking for anything. I live here."

"What is there to live here?" Bialer spread his arms wide.

"My defeat," Blank confided in a hushed whisper, like a father speaking the name of a beloved child. "This is an excellent place for a person to live his failure. Quietly, attentively, with moderation. Every day anew."

Bialer looked at the water and saw their two images dancing clearly in the ripples.

"It's a strange existence you've chosen," he laughed.

"I thought you understood," said Blank.

"Maybe I'll understand in two years' time."

"Like me?"

"I said: maybe."

They sat on the sand. The sky grew alternately higher and lower. Gusts of heat blew at them on all sides, from the sea and from the mountains. It was like heat from another world. It was no longer the sun, but a fiery avalanche of heat, and as it rushed down, it confounded the light. The place where they sat gradually came to resemble the bottom of the sea. It was as if they had been exiled simultaneously to the end of the world and to its very core.

"Tell me, why do you feel defeated?" asked Bialer.

"Are you asking me or are you asking yourself?"

"I'm asking."

"I could have told you about successes."

"I see."

"Many great successes."

"And they are your defeat?"

"Let's go and get something to drink."

"And each of them is like that and there's no way out, right? That is to say –"

"Why aren't we going to get something to drink?"

"That feeling, I mean... but we're evading the issue again."

"Let's go. Over at the inn they serve all kinds of drinks."

"In fact, maybe it's because of this? Maybe there's nothing we can do but evade? Everything has an explanation and every phenomenon has its own justification, but it's impossible to understand, right?"

"That's a really interesting thought."

"Like an interesting explanation and an interesting justification, right?"

"The ice will melt over there and the drinks will warm up. Every night the ice melts at the inn."

"So then you're forced to drink lukewarm drinks?"

"Yes, we have no choice. Especially when we're thirsty."

"So let's go."

They tramped heavily over the sand, the mountains ahead of them and the sun at their back. The desert was a vast land of rocks and footsteps. The fierce heat knocked the sky to the ground, and the men making their way between the sky and the earth had no air to breathe.

"And how is she, I mean?"

"Who?"

"The wife up there, in the north."

"You've asked that already."

"I still want to know."

"After two years?"

"Even after a hundred years. What difference does it make?"

"Go back up there and see."

"No," breathed Blank briefly. "Never."

The inn rose slightly out of the sand at the roadside, and instantly roofed itself and stopped growing. Right above the roof the sky started. But widthways the inn spread in all directions. First, a wide shed, then water tanks hove into view, and a little further along, large fuel tanks loomed blackly. Beyond the water tanks and the fuel tanks the land was occupied right up to the foot of the mountains – puddles of water, sprinklings of fuel oil, peelings and trash and papers and footprints, and many many trampled footprints all around. The inn was invaded on all sides – from here the mountains penetrated it, and from there – the entire sea, as far as the cliffs on the other side. In front, the water had reached the threshold, but now it was receding, leaving in its wake a strip of land which looked no different from the rest of the land all around.

Most of the visitors to the inn are transients who never return. Every bus and every car and every vehicle of any kind deposits its passengers at the inn. Parcels are opened, waiters carry platters and in the twinkling of an eye each group of travelers becomes a flock of locusts. After every such visit the shed looks like a battlefield after a battle. And that is when Weiss comes out of his hiding place, large broom in hand, and begins to trudge between the tables, slowly sweeping the cement floor, his motions very restrained. He gathers the trash and they, in their infinite variety add to it and throw down all manner of rubbish and that's how it continues all day long, but Weiss doesn't mind. He trudges and gathers, always restrained, in no hurry and not slowing down and his eyes bore under the tables, seeking what isn't to be found there. His beard springs wild and filthy from his temples straight over his cheeks, then slopes over his chin where it splits into two halves. His only shirt absorbs the sweat, which dries in the night and renews itself in the morning. His trousers are bound to his waist by a rope, like the ropes worn by the hermits who once used to live around here. His vacant eyes are indifferent towards those who pass through the inn, and towards all who pass through the world, yet at the same time hint at some concentrated and hidden flame burning within.

"That's Weiss," whispered Blank into Bialer's ear, as if offering him a secret glimpse of what might come to pass. "He's exactly what he looks like. He spends most of his time at the inn, helping out with the chores, shovelling the trash into the fire, poking around in the kitchen, lifting crates, tidying up outside, sometimes begging from the tourists."

"How did he end up here?"

"The innkeeper got him from the previous innkeeper, together with the shed, the tanks, the sea, the mountains and all the water faucets, most of them dripping."

"You talk about him as if he were a dog."

"A dog? I wouldn't say that. He's perfect in his own way."

"And the innkeeper pays him something?"

"Man, you should be grateful he doesn't kick him out. Besides, what does he need wages for? He eats leftovers from the kitchen and what the tourists leave behind on the tables. At night he wanders around outside a bit and then goes to sleep in his clothes. Over there, among the crates. Sometimes during the day too. He has no control over anyone and no one has any control over him. Look at him. Did you see? His whole appearance is the epitome of utter and total failure. Look at his eyes, at the marvellous serenity! As if far, far away some different life has been created for him, which he alone understands."

"I hear envy in your voice."

"I call him Weiss, but the others call him the Big Boss. He himself doesn't care what you call him. He responds to everyone who addresses him. Maybe he really was a big boss once, judging from the cut of his jaw and chin. The beard hides them, but even so they have a very determined look about them, ready to take the risk of making bold decisions. He was so drunk on the fact of being a big boss that one day he cracked from being such a big boss. Now he's seen me and he's coming towards us. He's a little you-know-what, but don't pay any attention. In a minute he's going to ask us if we need a manager."

"Do you by any chance need a manager, one of the best?" asked Weiss, broomstick in hand.

"Weiss, tell them to bring us something to drink. Beer? Fine. Tell them to bring us some beer."

"I'm not, but however," said Weiss.

"What isn't he?" asked Bialer.

"He said he isn't a waiter," explained Blank, "but he'll go and tell them."

Weiss went off and then came back and introduced himself, broomstick in hand: "I'm a manager by profession. Perhaps you need a manager?"

"No, Weiss, not today. Take a seat here and have a beer."

"A big manager, very good kind. And general too, that is."

"What kind of managing do you do?" asked Bialer.

"But at the moment I'm unemployed. Over there they fired me, that is to say."

"That is to say that it wasn't you who set up an appointment for me at five o'clock?" laughed Bialer.

"I never set up appointments at five o'clock!" Weiss was indignant. "Managers like me never set up appointments at five o'clock. Five o'clock? Only buses come at five o'clock."

"I see," said Bialer. "Your car has no schedule."

"I have no car."

"How can that be? Such a big manager and no car?"

"They took away my car and everything. Now I'm unemployed."

"But you're still a manager?"

"General manager. You think you can take away a person's profession? Of course I'm still a manager. Every man remains what he is, forever and ever. Even if he changes a lot. They say I'm a failure. All lies, I never failed. That is to say, not in their sense of the word. They made me fail, the people who were under my supervision."

"That's very sad, my dear Weiss."

"At first, they wanted to put me in some prison, and then into another place they called a confined rest home. You understand: me!"

"Perhaps you ran away from somewhere? Try to remember."

"The kind of manager I am never runs away from anywhere. A car takes me everywhere I need to go and a car picks me up from any place and at any time I choose. I never run away and I never even go on foot, not even to my next-door neighbor's house."

"That means that you had a company car?"

"And a chauffeur too, I was such a big manager."

"And they took them both away from you?"

"Yes. Now I'm an unemployed manager. Maybe you two need a manager, no? I'm a very good manager, first-rate. I can send you my references."

Suddenly Bialer felt as if his mouth were not in its right place and passed the palm of his hand over it to steady it. Blank's lips twitched a little from time to time in a slight grimace. But Weiss' lips and chin trembled the whole time.

When they had reached this point and heard all that, Weiss went silent all of a sudden, fixed his gaze on Bialer and examined him for a very long time.

"What is it Weiss, what do you see in him?" inquired Blank.

"My son," Weiss' lips trembled, "you've brought me my son!"

"I'm no one's son," declared Bialer.

"You're my son! You're my son!" cried Weiss triumphantly.

"Quiet," Blank said commandingly. He had suddenly become a kind of mediator between Bialer and Weiss, explaining and interpreting each man to the other. "You heard him: he is nobody's son."

"But he came from there, didn't he?"

"Yes. From up north."

"That's what I thought. They all come from the north. No one is born here. This is not a place for people to get born. From the north?"

"Yes, I told you."

"So maybe you met my son there? I have a wife up there and a son as well. I once had, that is. Many years ago. You didn't meet my son there? For a long time I thought I had no son and nobody at all, and now I know I do."

"Because he saw you," Blank explained to Bialer.

"So very much, so very much," babbled Weiss.

"He claims that you resemble his son," explained Blank.

"Are you sure not? Absolutely positively certain?"

"Leave him alone, Weiss."

"You didn't meet him? Never? I mean: never?"

"He met a lot of people there in the streets, Weiss my friend, and maybe one of them was your son."

"That means you met him?!" rejoiced Weiss.

"No, Weiss. He didn't meet him."

"But maybe some day you will? It could happen, couldn't it? So tell him he has a father. His mother most probably never told him. Tell him, so he won't think that his grandfather is his father. No, this is one thing they can't take away from me, no one can. Tell him he has a father, so he'll know."

"All right, I'll tell him."

"I'm not just a nobody!" shouted Weiss. "I'm someone who has a son! And I want my son to know that he has a father. That's very important, isn't it?"

"And the woman!" Blank suddenly burst out. "Why do you keep talking about the son? What I want to hear about is the wife!"

"My son, my son," cried Weiss gleefully. "The woman died a long time ago."

"No, no, not yet." Blank stood his ground and turned towards Bialer. "Tell us about your wife up north."

"About the boy, about the boy!"

"The wife, I beg you."

"I'm already forgetting her, gradually," said Bialer.

"Lies!" Blank hurled at him. "Don't lie! Look, I remember."

"But Weiss has forgotten."

"That's only because he's you-know-what."

"Oy," sighed Weiss. "I heard him." He sighed.

"Why did you sigh, Weiss?"

"It's so very difficult," said Weiss suddenly, and quite sanely.

"All that difficult?"

"Even more so. Terribly hard work."

"What? Living?"

"Being a human being."

"So that's why you're you-know-what?"

"I am not you-know-what!" screamed Weiss, and his beard trembled. "I'm only you-know-what in my own way."

"You know why he's you-know-what?" Blank asked Bialer. "Because he's dead. And you know why he's dead? I'll tell you. Every man is fated to have his life ruled by ambition, right? Right. So listen. Some of his ambitions died because they were fulfilled, and some of them died because he despaired of ever fulfilling them when he reached the age when a man despairs of ever fulfilling whatever ambitions he hasn't fulfilled up to that point. That is to say: for the most part."

"That's the age you're at, I suppose?" said Bialer.

"I have no ambitions!" stated Blank firmly. "Tell us about our woman up north."

"He and I," Weiss smiled at Bialer.

"What's he trying to say?" asked Bialer.

"That he and I are good friends."

"Like a single person!" chortled Weiss.

"That's right," sighed Blank, as if admitting it reluctantly.

"All of us!" declared Weiss.

"Who else?"

"You, my son!"

"Does he always talk like that, jerkily?"

"Always."

"I suppose it's his sickness and he can't help it."

"He could, but he doesn't want to."

"Why?"

"Because we're falsifying."

"Who's we?"

"You and I, that is: he. Whenever I or you or anyone else opens his mouth to say something, exactly what wants to be said deep down inside never gets said, never!"

"And that's the falsification?"

"Of course."

"And so that's why Weiss stutters like that?"

"Yes. Stuttering is closer to non-speech than to speech. A man who stutters falsifies less than a man who speaks fluently. Weiss is very sensitive to this."

"So are we all, I suppose."

"Of course. That's why he's Weiss."

"And that's why he needs you to interpret him?"

"He doesn't need anything, he doesn't care. Right, Weiss?"

Weiss was silent, and then he said: "Ask yourself."

"I'm not Weiss. It's you I'm asking."

"Are you sure?" interrupted Blank.

"Of course, him."

"He means, are you sure you are not Weiss or will never be Weiss?"

Here Weiss stuck his hand under his frayed shirt and began to moan: "Oy, oy."

"What are you moaning about?"

"Thorns are growing in my soul."

"Pluck them out."

"How can I?"

"It's your own fault you have the kind of soul that grows thorns."

"But no one can see them," Weiss consoled himself.

"They can sense them from far away."

"And I from up close," Weiss began to moan again.

"Weiss," Blank turned to him and declared solemnly, "you are the pathetic monument of my life."

"That's right," confirmed Weiss, "but don't exaggerate. Everyone and all of them together and there's nowhere to go."

"To escape?"

"Nowhere," Weiss summed up.

"No," Blank protested. "Our woman is no lie and never was a lie, never. The violin sometimes played false notes, I mean: very often. But the woman, you understand, the woman! She – I know, she's the secret umbilical cord that binds me and is never cut, even if I'm here and she's there, even if I'm alive and she's dead. And you too, Weiss, even if you're you-know-what."

"My son," wept Weiss, "is probably grown now and he never thinks about his father."

"But maybe he does think quite a lot about the father who isn't there?" said Bialer.

"In his heart there is no room for his father." Weiss pulled his lip. "Maybe they've told him I'm dead?"

"Then it doesn't matter, because fate has no time limit."

"Perhaps I truly am dead."

"Do you understand? That means: me!"

"Do you understand: I am – dead!"

"For two years I've known that we're defeated."

"I don't want to see him, but it's so good to know that he exists, my son!"

"But that doesn't change our fate. Whatever we do and however we live, there's no escape."

"What is he like?" Weiss turned to Bialer.

"That is to say, mine and hers," Blank added his voice. "I shall probably never see her, and yet we belong to one another forever and nothing matters but that."

"Sometimes I forget him but sometimes I also remember."

"Nothing! Nothing!" Blank shouted violently.

Bialer was silent. His was the third voice secretly mingling all along with the words of the other two. Wherever there is failure, he thought, there are ambitions that have failed, some dream that didn't turn out well or didn't turn out at all. The image of a life that strayed from the path.

Sometimes very, very far off the path. What ambitions did I have that brought me here? No, my dear friends, my own failure is of another sort altogether, apparently. It is the failure of my existence, the essence of my being. No doubt I would have felt it in any life I might have lived, in any success I might have had. And perhaps not? The successes would probably have hidden my true self from me, swaddled me in indulgence and illusions, and anything that is not a failure, is an illusion.

"What is she like?" demanded Blank.

"Now or two years ago?"

"Two years ago I know."

"She's different now."

"Impossible!" protested Blank.

"Different from us, I mean."

"Oh, yes, I always knew that."

"She didn't," said Bialer.

"Belongs to a different race, does she?"

"I think so."

"I think," said Weiss.

"You don't."

"I do! And so does my son!"

"That which divides is truly that which binds," said Bialer.

Here the three of them fell silent and sat together staring straight ahead, each in a different direction. During that whole time the shed had been alternately filling up and emptying. Now it was empty. The dapplings of light deepened and lay heavily on the chairs and on the tables and on the floor. The sea was shaded in the calm light, the cliffs grew dimmer and their wrinkles of age filled with shadow. It grew late. Opposite the shed a tribe of tourists gathered near their bus. Weiss picked up a rope from the floor and wound it around his finger. Bialer watched what he was doing very attentively and Blank asked him: "Do you want to hang your finger?"

"No," said Weiss emphatically. "Never."

He released the rope and tied it to the broomstick in his hand. Then he found another rope and he tied the two ropes together and to the free end he tied a crust of bread, as bait.

"Like that," he finished with great satisfaction.

Blank and Bialer looked at him and said nothing. Weiss wound the rope around the stick like a true fisherman, and turned to leave. Blank and Bialer rose to follow him. On the way out Blank signalled to the waiter and the waiter took out a notebook and wrote something down. It was obvious that Blank was as much a part of the scene here in the inn as Weiss was, even though he was not a big manager but merely a manager.

Weiss began to lope heavily across the sand, waving the fishing pole like a big pulley at the sky.

"Where to, Weiss?"

"To the sea!" proclaimed Weiss, and he did not look back but continued to hop along on his spindly legs, all the while waving the broomstick like a flag. "To fish!"

Bialer came to a halt, Blank continued on for a while, and then he too stood still, between Weiss, who stood ahead of him, and Bialer behind him.

"He's gone fishing," said Bialer, and jealousy sparked in his dimmed eyes like an alien fire. "Here, in this dead sea, fish!"

The mountains did not collapse earthwards, and the waters did not surge up. Low water touched low water and nothing was born. Somewhere there floated primeval memories of fire and brimstone, but no one bothered to gather them. Only books, as ancient as they, did. The blocks of stone were like blocks of life from all the generations that had petrified and were present and refused to die. And thus night fell on them and thus the sun will shine on them and so it will be forever.

Nathan Shaham

Speak to the Wind

Translated by Dalya Bilu

When the news of his father's illness came, Amos Nehushtan remembered Wartman. And he felt a little guilty. Before leaving for New York he had promised his father to visit his friend, but he had been busy with the Defense Ministry's procurement mission and the promise had been forgotten. Even though his father never failed to mention Wartman and inquire after his health in his letters. After a few weeks Wartman's name became a reminder of his own dereliction.

As soon as he had read the telegram he made up his mind to do his duty to his father, who made so few demands. That same day he called Wartman on the phone. The visit to Wartman, he knew, would be a chapter in the history of his father's life, which was now coming to an end.

Perhaps for this reason the visit was so difficult for him. There was no lack of excuses. His days and nights were dedicated to the work whose importance was beyond question. But even the best excuse was still an excuse. His refusal to meet Wartman stemmed from a deeper source. He didn't like writers.

His father was a Hebrew writer. And Wartman wrote in Yiddish. Ever since childhood he was used to writers and meeting them depressed him. They reminded him of what upset him about his father: vulnerability, sensitivity, and the sad humor of cripples.

He didn't know Wartman. But the fact that he was an obscure writer in an obscure language was reason enough for him not to want to see him. He imagined that he could guess his appearance and his smell: a sad little old man with the smell of carpenter's glue that came from the covers of old books clinging to him.

And there was something else which deterred him too: he guessed that the meeting with Wartman was supposed to serve as a kind of landmark. A final, clinching argument in a bitter debate which had gone on for fifty years: the historic debate between Hebrew and Yiddish. Between the Zionist movement and the Bund.

In the twenty-fifth year of Israel's existence he – an electronics engineer whose mother tongue was Hebrew, a healthy spirit in a healthy body, a New Jew, buying sophisticated components for state-of-the-art control systems – was the irrefutable, living proof that his father, and not Wartman, had chosen the right road. Tel Aviv, and not New York. Hebrew and not Yiddish.

Nobody said this. But he felt that his father expected Wartman to take one look at his strong, handsome face and admit that he was wrong. He probably wouldn't actually say anything. But his stoop would proclaim submission, the abandoning of his previous position, and the admission of defeat. The victory of the young builders. And he was supposed to look at Wartman with his father's eyes, which would not gloat, but forgive the old man for the error of his ways. A touching moment, summing up an entire historical epoch.

Something of their emotion infected him too.

Wartman lived in Manhattan, not far from downtown Greenwich Village. Amos Nehushtan took a cab. He was afraid that he wouldn't find parking. To his surprise there was no traffic in the street. It was like an abandoned city. After he got out of the cab he was obliged to return to the main street in order to phone Wartman from a public phone. The door to the building was locked and the intercom was not working.

Wartman stood at the head of the stairs on the third storey of the disintegrating building – the elevator wasn't working either – and shouted "Is it you?" in a voice tremulous with fear. Amos Nehushtan didn't know Yiddish but he could infer the meaning. He spoke Hebrew, loudly, to quieten the old man's fears. But until Wartman saw him standing in front of him he wasn't reassured. He was afraid of a trick. In the doorway he told Amos that the day before, an armed robbery had taken place in the building. Only then did he smile at him and say: "Your father's eyes, no question about it."

Wartman was astonishingly like the man he had seen in his imagination – a little old man, tired to death; a sad, shrunken piece of humanity. Only his big reddened eyes preserved a certain curiosity, which flickered on and off. Wartman knew six or seven languages perfectly, but the only one he could speak fluently was Yiddish. Even his English came out broken: every sentence included a few words in another language.

His wife didn't even know that much. She was a tall woman, ten years younger, who must have been good-looking once. She had arrived from Poland after the Second World War, and she hadn't succeeded in learning English at all. The irony of fate: ignorance of Yiddish was to her an important mark of aristocracy. In her country of origin she had spoken only Polish. She was proud of it. She stayed with them for a while, after setting out a dish of dried fruit, but the attempt to conduct a conversation in English wore her out and she retired to the next room. The sound of a sewing machine soon followed.

The conversation – peppered with words in Hebrew and Yiddish – was about literature and writers. Amos Nehushtan hardly understood half of Wartman's words, and much of what he was talking about passed him by, but he didn't mind being bored. He was resigned to playing the part of an attentive audience, to fulfil a debt of honor to his father, and he had no regrets about the wasted evening. He was glad he hadn't brought his wife with him. The meeting with Wartman would have depressed her. She hated New York. He didn't want to give her an opportunity to complain that he could have been managing a small plant in Israel instead of living in this dreadful city.

Wartman launched into a furious attack on Yiddish writers in America and the younger generation who wrote in English. He accused them of acting like "informers," "telling tales" on the Jewish community, as if they were all degenerate perverts who hated their mothers. He said that the way they wrote fed the flames of anti-Semitism. He was especially vehement in his denunciations of one well-known writer who "sold the Jews to the goyim like a kind of demonology." Amos Nehushtan, who had never read a single line of Wartman's writing, was unable to judge the extent to which the nobility of Judaism was expressed in his works, as he claimed it was.

Although he was amused most of the time, because he couldn't understand what the old man was getting so excited about, he soon began to feel a delicate undercurrent of melancholy, obscure and not entirely disagreeable, impinging on him. He thought sympathetically of the two childless old people imprisoned in their disintegrating building, and afraid of anyone who happened to climb the stairs.

He thought of their loneliness growing more absolute as the members of their generation died off, and he wondered at Wartman's strange optimism – a writer writing in a language that was disappearing from the world. He listened with growing compassion to Wartman's story about some young woman in Israel who wrote in Yiddish, the living proof that the future of Yiddish literature was "still ahead of it."

These thoughts put him in a philosophical mood, the kind of thing he had always tried to avoid, the reason he had chosen to go into the exact sciences. He believed that with the help of science he would be able to put an end "once and for all" to the oppressive burden of his inheritance. His sadness grew intense when Wartman suddenly said:

"Your father should have come to America, this is the only place where they're capable of appreciating him." He stared in surprise at the old man in the outmoded striped suit, sitting like a prisoner serving a life sentence in the faded, peeling old armchair. Then he raised his eyes to the glass cabinet full of unusable silver utensils and tasteless china animals, scanned the books and dusty old journals stacked in hopeless disarray on the bookshelves, glanced without interest at the cheap landscape in the ornate gold frame and the photographs of two old people in glass frames, and was filled with pity for his father. Presumably the old man wouldn't live to see the defeat of Wartman. The obstinate old Yiddishist dismissed all the achievements of Israel as if they were nothing. And presumably his father, too, would not value them at their full worth as long as Wartman failed to concede that he had been right. His pity for his father suddenly became too hard to bear. He wondered where he was hospitalized and whether there was anyone there who would be tolerant of his extreme fastidiousness. In his imagination, he saw his father in New York in a room like this one, surrounded by Wartmans who knew how to appreciate his true worth, each more pathetic than the other, living monuments to sharp-witted Jewish melancholy. And they were all complimenting him to his face and praising him to the skies, while he responded with an exhausted but rejuvenated spirit, and his beautiful, astonishingly youthful eyes filled with a radiant, heartbreaking joy.

Yes, something of their sensitivity infected him too.

Wartman's wife came back into the room and stood behind her husband. For a while she looked at Amos Nehushtan with glazed eyes as if remembering something, and as soon as her husband's spate of words died down she began formulating a sentence in English, whose meaning escaped him until Wartman flung at him rapidly, in Hebrew: "Don't agree to more than tea." And even though he had no intention of eating anything at Wartman's he found himself drinking tea and eating crumbly, over-sweet biscuits and listening to a new spate of malicious gossip about Jewish writers he had never heard of, a fact which caused Wartman grave displeasure. After tea he thought that the visit had ended, but he couldn't get out of accepting the invitation to dinner at a restaurant. He sensed that a refusal would hurt their feelings. Wartman said that he would be glad to go out for once with a young man, who could protect him from the "Negroes, hooligans, lunatics, junkies and anti-Semites hanging around on every street corner;" from them and from the "violent, half-crazy, drunken landlord who has no more memory than a cat, and forgets on the second of every month that he's already been paid on the first, and demands the rent for thirty days every month." Wartman said this with a peculiar kind of solemnity, like a man counting his treasures. When he said "Negroes, hooligans," he ticked the list off on his fingers.

Even though the restaurant was not far from Wartman's apartment – as he had been assured, only two blocks away – Wartman called a cab on the phone, his only means of communication with the outside world, which he also used with a peculiar solemnity, like the proud possessor of some outstanding American achievement. They left the building only when the cab stopped right opposite the door. And then Wartman jumped into it after scrutinizing the cab driver's face from a safe distance.

Wartman insisted that he was the host and that he would pay for everything, the cab and the meal, "and no unnecessary arguments, please." He gave the cabby a dollar tip, with the extravagant flourish of a man of means who need not count his pennies. To Amos Nehushtan's surprise, the cabby accepted the extravagant tip without any sign of gratitude; on the contrary, he looked at Wartman mockingly like a shrewd customer seeing through an impostor, as if he too understood that Wartman was putting on an act of success and prosperity intended to impress a sick Hebrew writer who was in hospital in Israel, and therefore unable to see for himself that Wartman was right and that America was the true fatherland of Jewish writers, not the Jewish State which did not require their clever skepticism and "morbid destructiveness."

In the restaurant, which was open to the street, Wartman revealed a surprising virtue: he knew how to keep quiet and enjoy to the full the delicious food and the girls who served it. Perhaps he also derived a certain provocative, albeit benign enjoyment from the impatience which Amos Nehushtan tried in vain to hide from his patient host while they waited interminably for the first course to appear.

Their silence was not only a matter of choice. It was a hot, humid evening and half the world seemed to have come out into the street. While the side streets were dark and empty, a stream of people flowed into the avenue like a muddy, foaming river. Conversation was a lost cause in the garden which the restaurant had carved out of the sidewalk. The noise all around them was so deafening that any attempt at dialogue was an effort. Amos Nehushtan was glad that Wartman did not force him to talk, and that he was content with his company and with getting out of the house.

The narrow streets of downtown Manhattan were incapable of

absorbing all the traffic streaming into them from the broad avenues uptown. Cars waiting interminably at the build-up opposite the traffic lights hooted at each other's tails with savage despair. Magnificent, broad-beamed limousines were stuck in the crush like tanks in the Mitla pass after the Six-Day War. They were piled up in the street like a light-and-sound spectacle documenting the death of the metropolis. Motorbikes with sawn-off exhausts, ridden by leather-jacketed youths, weaved through the cars with triumphant blasts. From time to time the muffled roar of the subway broke from the bowels of the earth, like a groan breaking the body of New York in half. Once a minute a huge passenger plane flew overhead with a loud, buzzing noise. The noise was as deafening as a buzz saw and it never stopped. In a minute it would grind the steel skyscrapers to dust. In the middle of all this commotion the hysterical wail of a police car or a fire engine would occasionally make itself heard, trying to assert its grim right of way, but succeeding only in adding its own nervous note to the general mayhem.

To Amos Nehushtan's surprise his ear isolated a human voice in the awful din. From time to time the commotion of the street was penetrated by a shrill, sudden, very brief voice, which seemed to wait for a momentary lull in the action of the giant bellows creating the deafening noise and then threaded itself deftly into the general racket, to be heard for an instant, before being covered up again in the mighty torrent and vanishing without a trace. For some time he was unable to locate the source of the sound – a hoarse shriek, heartbreaking in its despair, a brief cry exhausting the power of its owner's lungs. The screamer uttered meaningless syllables, never more than one syllable at a time, and Amos Nehushtan couldn't understand why nobody leaped up to go to his help. Perhaps he had been run over? Perhaps he had gone mad? Or perhaps he required urgent medical attention? Nothing happened in the street, which went indifferently on its way. As if nobody were screaming at the top of his lungs in the middle of the crowded street.

A city which has gone insane, he said to himself, and then he immediately dismissed the thought, partly because it was akin to his father's thinking which he wanted to avoid, and partly because a moment later he solved the puzzle of the screaming.

Its source was soon revealed as the strained throat of a man standing very close to their table, leaning on the low wall marking off the area of the restaurant. The man, tall and thin, about forty, and decently dressed, did not look in the least like someone in need of help. And his face showed no sign of insanity. On the contrary, he looked like a serious man absorbed in a job which demanded concentration. What surprised Amos Nehushtan more than anything else was that the man was screaming from notes! He held a piece of paper with large letters written on it in his hand. After a number of cries, he would lay the paper down on the wall and rub out one of the letters. In preparation for the next scream he would take a step away from the wall, fill his lungs with air, raise his eyes to the sky, and shoot out his shrieks as if he were taking aim at some invisible target. Sometimes the air confined in his lungs would choke him, since no opening appeared in the din, and he would let it out in a kind of inaudible sigh. His shoulders would suddenly slump, but he would soon fill his lungs with air again like an athlete ready to take off.

Wartman too watched the screaming man, but his expression showed that his actions were intelligible to him. The faintest of smiles hovered on his lips. Amos Nehushtan tried in vain to guess what the man was looking up at. On the other side of the street was a building which looked like a factory whose windows were boarded up, leaving only narrow air shafts under their upper arches. Occasionally he saw something like a firefly glowing at the top of the building, but he imagined that it was only a spark from an overheated engine which had flown up into the air. However, when the firefly appeared again and again, he saw that Wartman's eyes were fixed on it too. He gave his companion an inquiring look, and Wartman leaned over the table and shouted into his ear: "The woman! On the eighth floor!"

Wartman went on to explain, in a series of shouts into his ear, that the building opposite was a women's prison. The windows were boarded up to prevent the inmates enjoying the commotion of the noisy streets and their crowds. If one woman stood on another woman's shoulders, she could signal down to the street with a lighted cigarette. which was what the woman on the eighth floor did whenever the man's yells reached her ears. And then he would rub out the syllable that had served its purpose and proceed to the next one, until the firefly on the eighth floor announced that the message had reached its destination. "The power of love," shouted Wartman. "Here's Romeo, and up there is Juliet. Selkinzon, of course, would say Ram and Yael."

Amos Nehushtan had no idea who Selkinzon was, nor did he understand what there was to be so happy about. But something on Wartman's face, an expression that reminded him of the look which accompanied "Your father should have come to America, this is the only place where people are capable of appreciating him," aroused his suspicions. These were verified when Wartman roared, with a kind of smile that possessed more than an iota of triumph: "Look which side of the paper he's rubbing out from, the *mamzer!*"

What he succeeded in understanding was that the man was conveying to his wife, or his girlfriend, or his hooker, a piece of legal advice, and the cigarette verified that the message had been received. Wartman's happiness stemmed from the fact that "it's all in Yiddish! And the *goyishe* policeman stands there at his wit's end..."

A strange expression of joy was reflected in the eyes of the old writer as he shouted these things into his young companion's ear. As if the scene being played out in front of their eyes was a proof of the vitality still possessed by the language whose speakers were dwindling so rapidly.

"Men darf kannen redden," yelled Wartman and sent a warm look, full of affection and fatherly pride, at the back of the screaming man. His elation increased by leaps and bounds when the red face of the policeman on the beat suddenly loomed over their table, and gave them a shrewd, friendly wink. In a resonant bass voice, which instantly overcame all the other voices in the street, he said in an unmistakable Irish brogue: "Who does he think he's kidding, the *gonif?*" And Wartman's joy was complete.

Moshe Shamir

The Lagging Heart

Translated by Yehuda Hanegbi

Gabriel was a very amenable baby. His mother did not have much time for him especially since, not long after his birth, the family moved to a new apartment, and there was a new help in the house who was not much help, and Gabriel's older brother had to be taken to the violin teacher twice a week. Gabriel used to nurse slowly and unperturbedly, with long pulls at the nipple. He was never hungry, but on the other hand, was never quite satisfied. He didn't cry; he would just be still and hold the nipple firmly between his gums, and sometimes his mother fell asleep with him in her arms.

Childhood illnesses hardly touched him – unless there was a plot to infect him with some worse disease – and he grew up just as he was, without changing much. At the age of one he looked pretty much as at two months old, though doubled in size and weight. There are little dolls and bigger dolls and very huge dolls. Imagine an immense doll – the size of a house.

His mother never understood what attracted him to the large, darkly-polished old clothes closet. But when this piece of furniture was exchanged for a full-length wall closet, brightly painted and with many doors – the economic situation having improved when the family sold the stationery store and bought an electrical goods and musical records store – he liked the new closet as well. Actually, he may not even have liked it. He simply sat before it smiling, containing his happiness, hour after hour. His father was occasionally conscience-stricken, and would try to see whether his wife were not to blame. It would seem they weren't devoting sufficient attention to the second son. But the mother said the child could easily do with little attention. There was no need to complicate a simple matter – an easy baby, developing well. When he crawled or even walked swaying on the veranda, when he afterwards climbed on to the rails of the bannister – there was always time to grab him before he could get into trouble. One could forget him for a whole hour or two at a time, and then return to find him in the same place, holding on to a well-gnawed carrot, the same one that had been stuck in his fist in the morning. When his brother kicked him in passing while chasing a ball, he would respond late, with a plaintive little whine. Consequently his older brother, Yuda, had no respect for him.

"I have two rather unusual children," the mother would say with a smile, or at least so it was at first. The older boy was the star of the neighborhood and of the school, and the younger, who had been an unusually easy baby, became rather odd. Only at the age of three did he speak his first words. He would extend the vowel sounds, showing a preference for the long ee at the end of a word. For long stretches at a time he would sit against the wall and say eeee ee... The cats and dogs which Yuda brought home (he was so quick and agile at capturing them) did not like the little one. But when little Gabriel did catch an animal, he would not let it go until his brother came to wrest it from his grasp. This was accomplished by force, with good heavy blows to which the little one would respond only after a while with long continuous wailing, three hours of eee ee eee in some corner.

The lady from Jerusalem brought her sons to Tel Aviv to bathe in the sea. My parents rented them the best room in the house for a month, the room with the veranda looking out on the sea. Much of our boyish anger was directed at once against Mrs. Schein, the mother. Yuda became the leader of our gang – there were so many things he could do, like speaking Yiddish or telling funny stories about old men and Arabs and Englishmen. The little one, Gabriel, would stand on the veranda all day and gaze out to sea. An entire stretch of shore and sea was open to the view, while to the left lay Jaffa between sea and sky. And the sea was vast and pure. Clean white sand poured down to it from the very steps of our house. The casino stood as though with legs apart, the surging waves beneath it, like a dignified gentleman who limited himself to dipping his feet in the water. The low bath houses lay beyond it and further on there was more white sand, and waves and broad pure sea without end.

Every morning we were the first on the beach. Mrs. Schein appeared later with her two sons, a basket of food and a multi-colored parasol. She would buy some thick bananas from the Arab vendor and seat Gabriel beside her on the sand. He did not stop gazing at the sea, as though he were still on the high veranda overlooking it all. He did not run about or join the children as they leapt into the water. Still, when he was placed in the quiet little pool among the rocks on the beach, it was hard to take him out again. If he was not watched, he would sink into the water like a sack of cement. We once found him very still, sunk in the water, and we made a great outcry – but when we pulled him out and shook him, he opened his eyes and began to breathe regularly, as though nothing had happened. We subsequently tested this capacity of his and found that he could beat us all at diving. He could stay under till the count of five hundred and then raise his head quietly without opening his mouth for air.

Once Yuda buried him in the sand, to find out how long he could last without air. Beneath her gay parasol, Mrs. Schein was absorbed in gossip with another lady and the older brother piled sand on the younger, covering his legs, his back and his head which had been placed between the palms of his hands. We came out of the water and saw a huge pile of sand, which Yuda did not permit us to approach. We were sure that the little one would be smothered. I shouted to Mrs. Schein, and the silly woman began to look for Gabriel in the air and in the water. She then began to beat Yuda – all this before attempting to free the little one. We fell upon the pile of sand and uncovered the boy. His eyes and eyebrows, mouth and teeth were gritty with sand and he opened and closed his eyelids to clean them, and showed great surprise at our agitation. Then he went and dived into the water to wash himself off and stayed under for a whole five minutes. At that time he was seven years old and could neither read nor write – yet we began to feel a sort of affection for him. This was due, no doubt, to the fact that we were forced to take care of him. Everything that moved frightened him greatly and he simply could not distinguish approaching vehicles in the street. It was impossible to play ball with him: he could never catch anything.

What was it? Why was he like this? The answer was simply that he had a sluggish heart. This was discovered much later by the doctors, with the aid of all sorts of instruments and x-rays and whatnot. Meantime it was somehow decided that the boy was short-sighted, and the next time he came from Jerusalem, he had an over-large pair of spectacles perched on his nose, which only made him clumsier and more confused. For another summer after that, the Scheins rented the room with the veranda overlooking the sea and then we almost wept with laughter at the sight of Gabriel – heavy and overgrown, blinking stupidly through his ugly spectacles. He had not changed at all – he was just a little slower and heavier in his movements. Only now though, only now do we know what it was – that his heart beat slowly, that's all. But this was discovered much later. Then he sat literally for hours at a time, happy, calm and absorbed in the scene before him. A breath of smoke on the horizon became a ship, gradually progressing as though pushed by a hand on a board. And at the same time there were colors and shadows playing on the water. The green turned to bluish gray, and the wisps of white rose on the waves, then burst and returned to embracing unity. The sun moved across the heavens like a distant steam engine, moving, pulling incessantly. The waves were like muslin in the wind, rustling and crowding together into a white line always present between sand and water. The sea was alive, it was cheerful. All at one glance – a ship came out of the sea and grew big, then turned back into it and was lost; sea gulls hovered and soared and disappeared; what was dark became light, light turned into darkness, and little sailboats bobbed along and away from end to end – all in one look.

He used to watch the grass grow. In Jerusalem the father arranged a surprise, carefully planned for months beforehand by his wife – and purchased a little house and garden. The garden had grass, flowers, a cypress tree and a Jerusalem pine. Gabriel would go out to the garden in the morning and the flowers would grow slowly until noon and then they would continue to grow until evening. He would go out to the garden in the morning with half a loaf of bread in his hand and look for buds that had not yet opened, and sit down in front of them. There were seasonal flowers – zinnias, asters, dahlias – whose blossoms opened and withered in a single day. How the bud ripened and burst forth! Like wounds in the flesh, petals would appear on the virgin greenness, groping: one to the left and another to the left of the left and two to the right and another in the middle. Thus the petals emerged, brothers equal and alike. One petal was violet and its brother and brother's brother were violet. None were precocious, none tardy. All alike broadened out and expanded and stretched themselves in all directions, in a circle, arms entwined and all together. Then another, new circle of brothers sprang up among them, one circle inside the other. And within, more slowly and yet somehow following the same rhythm, the golden stamens grew, their delicate pin heads modestly bent.

One day a tortoise strayed in from the field of thorns nearby; he crawled over a rock and under a fence into the garden and wandered among the pine needles, trespassing on into the sunlight of the flower bed. A tortoise, neither too large nor too small. The right tortoise.

Yuda called the tortoise Gabriel and his mother grew angry. She did not know what to do with her two sons and how to manage them, as she herself said. In fact she became quite nervous and irritable at this time. Thoughts came to her which she tried to disperse, but they kept returning to plague her and so she started going to the movies and took her sons with her. Often in the afternoons, in the darkened cinema house, Gabriel would draw up his collar to cover his ears and screen his face with his hands. Nevertheless the garish sounds penetrated and swamped his mind – a flood of noise. Yuda pinched his soft flesh, his mother thrust his hands away from his face. Then, beyond the dim darkness he would search out the little red lights in the far corners of the hall. Yuda would notice that his brother's gaze was not directed at the screen and pinched him again: "Look, dope, look – pictures."

But Gabriel did not look. The pictures hurt his eyes like a blast of fine sand. He did not even know they were pictures. His senses could only make out a wild flurry of grey shadows. Then slowly, apprehensively, he would lift his eyes over the immobile heads around him to the far corners of the hall. There the little red lights flickered quietly, like distant boats in the sea of night. They would begin to move slowly, silently, known only to him; their little red flames flickering, sailing along the walls. Softly the waves of a sea lapped against his body and he would give himself to them entirely and sink, down, down...

Afterwards came the real joy. The cascades of noise, the storm of shadows and Yuda's pinches ceased. Everyone rose from their seats and there, where the little red boats had been all night, the sun burst through: there were four, five, six wide exits full of sun and daylight. His mother would fumble for him and drag him with a firm hand through the crowds at the exit. And there he would stand and gape at the roofs of the houses, at the clouds – now he saw pictures.

In the bus, Yuda grabbed the seat by the window. The sun came from the right, from the west, and the fine head of the older son was bathed in the soft light. Gabriel watched the golden conflagration rise, die down and reappear. Yuda looked out of the window. When they passed a row of cypress trees the light became streaked – light, shadow, light, shadow. Yuda covered his eyes in irritation: "What a darned nuisance – tick tock tick tock, sun dark sun dark..." Gabriel said: "Trrrrrr."

Gabriel took the tortoise with him when they went to the doctor. His mother had threatened to throw it into the garbage can. He was already ten at the time, but was not yet able to read or write. All he cared about was the tortoise, the garden, and the sea in the summer; and none of the doctors, not even the experts, could do anything about it. Until one day a great specialist came from Vienna and it was decided to give Gabriel a thorough examination. This time it was his father who went along. He couldn't quite manage to unfasten Gabriel's clothes. He just pulled them off and they laid the boy on the cold sofa. The fat, bald doctor leaned over him in his white smock, bringing his smells and his spectacles up close, and listened to Gabriel's heart. With every movement of the doctor's body the starched smock rustled, but on the huge white ceiling overhead, the late daylight drifted followed by shadow like a ship on a clear sea.

"He's a good boy," the doctor said at last. And he went over to sit at his big desk while the father struggled with the bundle of garments. "He's a healthy boy, just somewhat slow in his reactions. Even his pulse is lower than normal. I recommend regular examinations of the heart. Let's say every half year. Alright?" And he proceeded to write whatever it was he wrote.

Every half year. And at the end of three years Gabriel was bar-mitzva and an energetic young physician, carefully balancing a well-marked chart in one hand and a red pencil in the other, summed up the matter succinctly: "The boy is absolutely healthy. It's just that his pulse is becoming slower from year to year. We can't explain it..."

I recognized the name at once. Gabriel Schein. The father came in, and immediately my feeling of friendliness evaporated. I told myself that I pitied him and that I would save him from embarrassment by not recalling the past. I remembered him from his occasional visits to his family during those summer holidays, but he had in fact changed almost beyond recognition. He had aged and shrunk. There was something in him of the wretchedness that always frightens the fortunate and makes them fear exploitation. As soon as he began to speak I realized that I had judged correctly: he regarded his misfortunes as a bill of rights.

He began to speak before I could offer him the chair opposite me, and most of what he said was utterly superfluous. The people who came to see me were those with special requests for exemption from military service – and secretly I knew that perhaps the only sure way to obtain such an exemption was to be given a conscription officer. Mr. Schein flopped into the chair and continued to speak. His shirt collar was buttoned up under the collar of his jacket, but the usual tie was now absent. He had a frowsy, bewildered look; his speech was fragmented and for some reason he spoke in his mother tongue.

He had various medical certificates and documents attesting to his son's unfitness for the army, and while I was filling in the exemption form, name Gabriel Schein, age twenty, reason for release, etc., I inquired if there were any brothers of military age.

"No," answered his father, not anxious to pursue the subject. But my quick glance up at him from the paper may have hinted more than I had intended. He therefore tried to be more explicit. "He... he does have... he has a brother, older than he... in America."

The brief announcement that the boy was quite healthy and that it was only his pulse which was slightly abnormal, becoming slower every year, every month, and consequently every day too – this brief announcement had blotted out the father's world. After that he lived for Gabriel – nothing else had happened in the seven years since I had last heard of them. "Gabriel needs a normal heart," the father said, "and I have one."

At about the same time as they sold the new house, Yuda finished high school. He was a bright young man with a future and a girl friend of twenty. The father insisted that he go out to work and help provide for the family, but instead Mrs. Schein took the money left over from the sale of the house and from repayment of debts and absconded with her bright young son to America. They were still there, and the connection between the two parts of the family had grown increasingly distant.

"Would you care to see Gabriel, sir? He's here," the father asked lamely.

I picked up the exemption certificate and rose from my seat. I had been sitting too long and needed to move about. I thought I would accompany him to the door. There was a large, dismal line outside – it was altogether quite a dismal time, if you remember the winter of 1948. The day was gray and sullen. Old Schein's coat was wet with rain and his back was bent. At the door he did not turn to me again, yet my gaze followed him. I wanted to see his son, and I recognized him immediately.

He was standing in front of the closed window, completely absorbed in watching the drops of water on the pane. Drop after drop formed from the moisture left after the rain; and as the drops formed they began to move, sliding the length of the pane of glass, hanging delicately and gliding down to the opposite corner. There, each would break into a sparkling shower and fall to the window sill, a journey lasting... a thousand light years? A thousandth of a second? Meanwhile another and yet another drop were forming, swelling and growing heavy enough to pursue the same gliding course. They came on one after the other like dangling tears, slowly at first, then rapidly, then excitingly fast. Gabriel saw a race of quicksilver stars, the quick swing of a machine turning out diamonds, a furious contest of laughing devils. All this or simply the rain, the rain about which the children sing in kindergarten, the fresh, cheerful drops from the sky. Gabriel in front of the window pane, standing in the rain, drinking it, letting it wash over him.

Gabriel's father took his arm. Gabriel slowly turned and our eyes met. He was a big, heavy-bodied young man, whose age might be anywhere from sixteen to thirty – twenty perhaps? There was a thin covering of hair on his somewhat soft, swollen cheeks, his eyes were large and deeply set, very fine, tormented. These eyes – only now did I notice that they were a light, smoky blue – clutched me like living fingers, with an almost tactile force. He was about to recognize me.

I felt the slow, stirring, enlarging, precise working of the spirit within him. I saw the gathering of wonder, of a question, the piecing together of distant shafts of memory – one thing added to another and a picture forming like the image seen through a telescope gradually being brought into focus by an unseen hand. The whole system of opposition was also apparent to my gaze: doubts purified and sifted and finally reinforced the certainty. I actually witnessed the climbing of the positive response curve on the chart of questions and answers. In a little while he would recognize me. I could feel the moment coming closer, closer.

I was in the grip of fear and enchantment. I could not move. The next in line entered my office, sat down on the empty chair and waited. I was possibly on the verge of being recognized, but Gabriel's father suddenly tugged him and pulled him away forcibly – a sort of direct and useful sign language between them – and I returned to my room and closed the door behind me.

Gabriel's father could not always tug his son away from the boiling point of action. The workers in the social welfare office, as well as the clients, were well acquainted with a certain Samul and even feared him, permitting him to do almost anything his malicious scheming brain drove him to. Samul's brazenness grew worse from week to week. At first he contented himself with obtaining a food parcel and then getting another through his wife or one of his children. Later he began to demand a third parcel. He would come with a member of his family, get his parcel, give it to his wife or child and immediately return to the line to get another. So long as he went back to the end of the line, no one bothered to complain. But when it happened that upon arrival at the distribution window there were no more parcels, he began taking his place in the middle of the line, between two weak links such as a frightened old lady and a shy young boy. But here there were occasional protests, grumblings and exclamations. The clerks of the welfare office did not care. There was a wooden partition between them and the public; on their side was order, on the other chaos. One day Samul tried his old trick again, and after sending his parcel home with a member of his family, he thrust himself back in line in front of Mr. Schein.

The old man's calm objection, which was preceded by a light touch on Samul's shoulder, led to a vigorous response from the line-jumper. He began to curse and shout. Apparently the touch on his shoulder enraged him and became, in his mind at least, a push, a blow. "Don't you dare touch me! Take your hands off me! Who do you think you are!" Old Schein repeated that this was his place in the line. Samul laughed: "Did I say it wasn't? This is your place, this is mine and that's his – that's how it is!"

Gabriel was standing as usual behind his father, but for the moment he was forgotten. The old man now came determinedly forward and stepped into Samul's place. The people around responded at once with applause. Samul fell into momentary confusion. Gabriel tried to join his father and stepped forward to bypass Samul but the latter blocked his way by stretching out his arm. Seeing this, the father tried to move toward his son but Samul stood firmly between them, and in the ensuing tussle Samul threw the father to the floor. At the same time, Gabriel's hand touched Samul from behind. The strength of this hand upon him frightened Samul out of his wits.

A knife flashed and Gabriel's left hand began to bleed. But his right hand clutched Samul's throat. The knife fell out of Samul's fingers. The window in the partition slammed shut, numbers were dialled, there was outcry and confusion. Gabriel had by now crushed Samul to the ground, a knee on his chest and a large firm hand around his throat. Rescuers came, but too late. Gabriel did not comprehend what was happening. Samul struggled a bit, kicked feebly and was strangled to death. By the time Gabriel was finally overcome by his father and others, the matter was past undoing. A corpse lay on the floor of the social welfare office of the Jerusalem Municipality.

Your Honor. Judge – I have never been heard to the end. Very few people have ever had the patience to listen to a whole sentence from me. My father is lying in the hospital with a serious heart attack. I have to talk now, and you have to hear me out; you must hear me out, that is why you and I are here. You have to listen. These eyeglasses – I do not need them. When you sit quietly up there, Judge, and do not move, I see you well. But if you make the slightest move – it all becomes blurred. Yes, that is it – the movement, for example, which you just made. I do not know... it was too quick for me. Now I can see again... I had a brother, and when he was a big boy, just finishing high school, he once said that maybe I came from the moon. My day – is thirty of your days. The spectacles cannot help me. Nothing can help me. And every year it all moves more slowly. I am a healthy man. It is just that you are all too quick for me. When I cross the street, it is a wall of flowing fire. Your Honor, I did not strangle Samul in self-defense. I did not strangle him at all. I remember that my father put his hand on me, and after that I remember nothing. Everything moved so rapidly. I just wanted to hold on to my father, but I was unable to see anything and I wanted to see him. I did not want him to disappear, I wanted him not to be so hasty. Just for once I wanted terribly that he should go at my pace... that he be still – that he should be down and not move. I wanted just to see him properly. But everything was gray... black and white running together in a great blur. He seemed to be moving away from me, so I held on to him by force... by his neck. I just wanted to hold him so that he would not run away. And he hit me hard as well. It was my father whom I strangled.

The judge did not understand a single word in the distorted jumble of slow and clumsy sounds that came from the mouth of the accused. Gabriel was still speaking when policemen gripped him and drove him away in a closed vehicle. For three years he remained in prison under special care, until finally they despaired of him and sent him out to peddle matches in the street. Meanwhile the old man died in the hospital, even before the end of the trial, and Gabriel's best friends were now the deer and the tiger.

These lie before him in two small piles – deer on one side and tigers on the other, on a handkerchief spread on the sidewalk between his outstretched legs, in front of the gate of a yeshiva school for Jewish scholars. The animals run with him, leaping in the air, always together with him on the sidewalk where he sits leaning against the wall. And the coins come down from above in a veritable shower – one, sometimes two a day.

Tick a coin, tock a day. Light shadow light shadow. Sun darkness sun darkness. During the Passover holidays, which are the pleasantest days of the year for a visit to Jerusalem, I came upon him as I was walking about the city. I recognized him immediately by the steps of the yeshiva. I tossed a coin into the tin can between two piles of matches and remained standing there to listen and decipher his long drawn-out "Ha-pp-y N-e-w Ye-ar." Our holy days, our commotion, our suns and moons are a swift, confused gray flow, an endless repetitious murmur and movement, like the waves of the sea. Gabriel sits before it as at a window. And outside the world passes by in rhythmic alternation, like the street lamps at night – light shadow light shadow. Except that it no longer irritates. Tick day, tock night soft and gray. An express train thrusting forward past an infinity of poles, and each pole coming forward, growing, being, crying out... but who is it that cries out?

Tock his heart beats – half a year. Tock – a year, tock – another year.

T'rrrr – all of history... T'rrrrrrr.

Benjamin Tammuz

The Swimming Race

Translated by Joseph Shachter

I

One hot summer's day many years ago I was sitting in the kitchen at home, staring out of the window. The chill of the red floor tiles seeped into my bare feet. With my elbows leaning on the oilcloth-covered table, I let my eyes stray outside. The rooms were pervaded by the afternoon stillness and I felt dreamily at peace.

Suddenly, galloping hoofbeats sounded down the road and a black Arab horse-cab – the kind that plied the roads before cars took over – came into view; it was like those cabs we used to hire to drive us to the Jaffa railway station when we traveled up to Jerusalem to spend Passover with Grandmother.

The horses drew nearer and were reined in outside our house, and the Arab cabman alighted and knocked at our door. I jumped up to open it, and a musty smell filled the kitchen – a smell of horses and far-off places. The cabman's shoulders blocked out the light and prevented the sultry heat from forcing its way inside.

He handed me a letter. I glanced at it and saw it was in French, which I could not read. My mother entered and took the letter, and her face lit up. She asked the cabman in and placed a slice of cold watermelon and a fresh pita on the table before him. Leaning his whip against the wall, the Arab thanked her for her kindness, sat down at the table, and began taking large bites out of the watermelon, filling the air with the smacking of his lips. My mother told me that the letter was from the old Arab woman who lived in the orange grove. She wrote that she was well again and her pains had left her, and that she had been cured by my mother's hands, which she kissed from afar. She also wrote that now that summer had come and she had heard our holidays would soon be coming round, she hoped my mother would be able to get away from her other patients and come with her son to stay at her house in the orange grove.

The sun was about to sink into the sea as we left the house and climbed into the cab. The cabman folded back the rounded leather hood, and as we sank into the deep, soft seat I was instantly overwhelmed by a sensation of traveling to distant parts. The Arab climbed onto his high perch, whistled to his horses and flicked his whip in the air. The springs creaked, the seat sank and surged up again beneath us like an ocean swell, and a farewell whinny rose in the air. With a wrench of wheels the cab moved off, its rumble over the pitted road sounding like a joyful melody.

Before long we had left the Hassan-Beq mosque behind and were plunging through the alleyways of the Manshieh quarter. Smells of cooking assailed our nostrils: waves of hyssop, of roast mutton, of fried egg-plant and mint-spiced salad washed over us in turn. The cabman's voice filled the air, sounding warnings right and left, coaxing street-hawkers to move out of our path, bawling out the urchins who squatted in the middle of the road. The horses trotted in a lively, unbroken rhythm, their brown shiny rumps swaying from side to side. The horse on the right, without breaking his stride, pricked up his tail and dropped his dung. Turning around on his lofty seat, the cabman threw us an apologetic smile and remarked that horses were shameless ill-bred creatures and we must excuse them.

We jogged along pleasurably and restfully in our seats till the city lay behind us and the horses were drawing the cab laboriously along a track of reddish sand, lined with hedgerows of cactus and acacia. Waves of heat rose from the sand, settling beside us onto the cool seat. The sun must already have dipped into the sea, for beyond the orange groves the skies glowed crimson and a chilly dusk descended all around. Suddenly the horses stopped and made water on the sand in unison.

Again the cab lurched forward. A quiver rippled the horses' hides as their hooves struck a stretch of limestone-paved road, lined by cypresses on either side. Before us stood an archway of whitewashed stone, enclosing a large, closed wooden gate with a small wicket set in it. Near the wicket stood a girl of about my age, wearing a white frock and with a pink ribbon in her hair. As the cab drew up at the gate she bolted inside, and the cabman said: "We're there!"

You don't see such courtyards any more. And if you should happen to come to a place where there once was such a courtyard, you will only find a scene of wartime destruction: heaps of rubble and rafters, with cobwebs trying to impart an air of antiquity to what only yesterday still breathed and laughed.

But in those days the courtyard was in good repair and throbbing with life. It was square-shaped and enclosed on three sides by a two-story building, with stables and barns occupying the lower story. Black and red hens roamed about the yard, their clucking mingling with the neighing of horses. On the second floor was a pumphouse, and next to it a pool-like reservoir into which water splashed from a pipe leading from the pump. Goldfish gathered near the outlet, darting among the bubbles created by the jet of water. A wooden parapet railed in a long veranda that always lay in the shade. A colored glass door led from the veranda into a central reception room, from which numerous doors opened onto the living rooms, the kitchen and the pantries.

In the center of the room stood a long table surrounded by upholstered armchairs. In anticipation of our arrival that day, their white linen dust covers had been removed and lay folded in neat piles in a corner. Earthenware vases painted red and gold were arranged about the room; they contained large paper roses and lilies, some of them fashioned into strange unflowerlike shapes. One vase, its paint long faded, had been brought there on the wedding day of the elderly mistress of the house.

From gilt wooden frames on the walls, stared the portraits of sword-bearing men in fezzes. The old lady led my mother up to one of the pictures and said: "My husband, may he rest in peace! His father built this house. Now we live here during the summer and go back to Jaffa for the winter."

With a sigh my mother replied: "My husband's no longer alive, either. But his house and his father's house aren't here; everything remained over there, abroad, and I live in a rented apartment summer and winter."

"That's because you are newcomers, immigrants," the old lady said. "But with the help of God you'll thrive and build yourselves houses. You're hard-working people and your hands are blessed."

My mother caught the hint and threw her a grateful look, but I blurted out: "But it's not true that we're driving the Arabs out. We are out for peace, not war."

Placing her hand on my head, the old lady said: "It all depends on the individual; everyone who wants peace will live in peace."

At that moment the young girl appeared in the doorway.

"Come over here, Nahida," the old lady said, "and kiss the hand of the *hakima*[1] who cured your grandmother. And this is her son."

Nahida came hesitantly into the room and stood in front of my mother. My mother embraced her and kissed her on the cheek, and a flush suffused the girl's dark complexion. She hung her head and remained silent.

"Our Nahida is shy," the old lady said, "but her heart is kind."

Hitching up her white skirt, Nahida sat down in an armchair. The rest of us sat down, too, as though permitted to do so now that the most honored person among us was seated.

The old lady made a remark in French and my mother laughed. Again Nahida blushed and I noticed her eyeing me to see whether I understood French.

"I don't understand a word," I told her. "What are they saying?"

"My grandmother says you and I would make a fine couple."

"Rubbish!" I answered and stared at the floor.

"You can go and play," the old woman said. "We're not keeping you."

---

1. Arabic: Woman doctor

I got up and followed Nahida out onto the veranda. We went and sat down at the edge of the pool.

"Do you believe in God?" I asked her, "because I don't, not at all."

"I do, and I have a place in the grove where I go and pray. If we become friends I'll take you there and I'll show you there's a God."

"Then you fast in the month of Ramadan?" I asked. "I eat even on Yom Kippur."

"I don't fast because I'm still too young. Do you rest on the Sabbath?"

"That depends," I answered. "I rest if I've got nothing else to do. Not because there's a God, but just if I feel like it."

"But I love God," Nahida said.

"Then we certainly won't make a couple unless you stop believing."

Nahida was about to make some retort when we heard the gate open, and two men entered the yard. Nahida leapt up and rushed over to them, throwing her arms around the neck of the older man, who wore a fez and European clothes.

"Daddy, we have visitors!" she cried.

"I know," her father replied. "The *hakima* has come to see us."

I stood up and waited for them to mount the steps to the pool. The second man, who wore a *keffiyeh* and *agal* and looked about eighteen, was Nahida's uncle, her father's brother. He came up first and held out his hand to greet me. Nahida's father patted my cheek and ushered me into the house.

We had supper out on the veranda. We were served large dishes of fried potatoes, sliced egg-plant in tomato sauce with diced salted cheese, and a bowl of pomegranates and watermelons. There was a heap of hot pitas in the center of the table.

Nahida's uncle – his name was Abdul-Karim – asked me if I was in the Hagana. When I told him that was a secret, he laughed and said it was an open secret which the whole country knew about.

"Abdul-Karim is studying at the College of the Mufti," Nahida's father told us, "and he's in constant fear of your Hagana."

Abdul-Karim's face darkened and he kept silent; but the old lady, his mother, laid her hand on his arm and said: "My Abdul-Karim is a fine, loyal man. Don't you tease him."

Abdul-Karim kissed his mother's hand and said nothing. Just then, a shaggy sheepdog appeared on the veranda and wriggled under the table, butting against the tangle of legs as it looked for a spot to lie down. Finally it came to rest with its head on Nahida's feet and its tail on mine; it kept licking Nahida's feet, and its wagging tail tickled mine. The tickling made me smile and I turned to explain to Nahida why I was smiling, but when I saw she was taking my smile as a mark of friendship, I kept quiet.

When supper was over, Nahida's father said to his brother:

"Abdul-Karim my brother, go and show the children what you've brought from town."

Motioning to Nahida and myself to follow him, Abdul-Karim went into a toolshed in the orange grove and came out with a brand-new shotgun.

"We'll go hunting rabbits tomorrow," he said. "Know how to fire a gun?"

"A little," I told him. "We can have a shooting match if you like."

"We had a swimming match here in the pool last week," Nahida said, "and my uncle beat them all."

"I'll take you on at swimming too, if you like," I said.

"*Ahlan wa-sahlan!* With pleasure" Abdul-Karim agreed. "Tomorrow morning, then. Now let's get back to the house and listen to some songs. We have a gramophone."

Back in the house, Abdul-Karim put on a record, wound the handle and adjusted the soundbox. The sound of a *kamanji* and drum and cymbals issued forth, immediately followed by an Arab song, sung in a sweet plaintive voice, with delicate, floating trills. Abdul-Karim sprawled back contentedly in his armchair, his face beaming.

When the record ended he put on another, though to me it seemed as though the same song were being played over again. This went on again and again till I got bored and slipped out to another room where my mother was chatting with the old lady. But that bored me too, so I went out to the veranda and gazed at the pool and the orange grove beyond. A large moon hung just above the treetops and a chill arose from the water in the pool. Some night bird was calling nearby, but stopped whenever the gramophone fell silent. As a yawn escaped me, I thought regretfully of my pals at home who were probably roasting potatoes on a fire under the electricity pylon, having pilfered the wood from the nearby sausage factory. What had made me come here, I asked myself.

Nahida found a queer way of waking me up next morning. They had a fat, lazy cat in the house, which Nahida dropped onto my face while I was asleep. I leapt out of bed and flung the cat back into her lap. That was how we started our second day in the house in the orange grove. I was still brushing my teeth when Abdul-Karim came into the kitchen and said: "What about our swimming race?" "I'm ready," I told him.

We hurried through breakfast, got into bathing trunks and went outside. My mother, the old lady and Nahida's father had already drawn up chairs at the side of the pool to watch the race.

"Ready, steady... go!" Nahida called out, and Abdul-Karim and I dived in. Either because I was overexcited or because I wasn't used to fresh water, I sank to the bottom like a stone, and by the time I had recovered sufficiently to surface, Abdul-Karim was already halfway across. I saw my mother bending over the parapet and heard her calling out to me: "Don't be afraid! Swim fast!" I started swimming, but it was no use. By the time I reached the pipe leading from the pump-house, Abdul-Karim was already sitting on the parapet on the far side, squeezing the water out of his hair.

"You beat me in the pool," I told him, "but I'll take you on at anything else, if you want."

"At what?" he asked.

"Let's say at arithmetic."

"Why not?" he answered, and told Nahida to fetch some paper and pencils. When Nahida came back with them, I tore a sheet of paper into two halves, and on each I wrote down seven million, nine hundred and eighty-four thousand, six hundred and ninety-eight multiplied by four million, nine hundred and eighty-six thousand, seven hundred and fifty-nine.

"Let's see who figures that out first," I said.

Taking a pencil, Abdul-Karim started jotting down figures, and so did I. I was through before he was and handed my sheet to Nahida's father to check. It turned out I had made a mistake. Then Abdul-Karim handed over his paper and it turned out that he had gone wrong too.

"Then let's have a general knowledge competition," I challenged Abdul-Karim. "For instance: who discovered America?"

"Columbus," Abdul-Karim answered.

"Wrong!" I said. "It was Amerigo Vespucci, and that's why it's called America!"

"He beat you!" Nahida called to her uncle. "You see, he beat you!"

"He beat me in America," Abdul-Karim said, "but I beat him right here, in the pool."

"You wait till I'm grown up and then I'll beat you right here in the pool," I told him.

Nahida seemed about to nod her agreement, but thought better of it and looked at her uncle to see what he was going to answer to that.

"If he ever manages to beat me here in the pool," Abdul Karim said, "it will be very bad indeed. It will be bad for you too, Nahida. Bad for all of us."

We didn't get his meaning and I wanted to tell him to cut out his philosophizing; but I didn't know how to say that in Arabic, so I kept quiet.

Later we went hunting rabbits in the orange grove.

II

Many years had gone by and summer had come round once again. Tired out after the year's work, I was looking for some place where I could take a fortnight's rest. Packing a small valise, I traveled up to Jerusalem, only to find all the boarding houses full. Finally, wearied by rushing about the city, I boarded a bus bound for the Arab village of Ein Karem. As I took my seat, I started wondering what I would do there and what had made me go there of all places.

At the end of the main street stood a domed building, with a fountain gushing out from under its floor. Opposite, on a hillside that sloped up to the Russian monastery on its summit, in the shade of a clump of sycamores, some men sat on low wooden stools, sipping coffee and puffing at their *nargilas*. I walked over and sat down on one of the stools, and when the waiter came over to take my order, I asked him if he knew of a family that would be willing to put me up for a couple of weeks.

"I don't know of one," the lad answered, "but maybe the owner does."

The cafe proprietor came over to have a look at me. "A family to put you up?" he said. "What for?"

"To take a rest," I answered. "I'm tired and I'm looking for somewhere to rest."

"And how much are you willing to pay?" he asked.

"As much as I have to," I replied.

The proprietor sent the lad to the house of a certain Abu-Nimr. Before long he came back and said:

"Go up that way. Abu-Nimr is willing."

Picking up my valise, I trudged up the hillside, wondering all the time what had made me come to this place. I entered a courtyard and knocked at the door of the house indicated. A tall, bald Arab of about forty-five came out and said: "Welcome! Come right in."

I let him precede me down a long, cool passage and into a small room, almost entirely taken up by a tall, wide bed.

"If you like it, you're very welcome," Abu-Nimr said. "It's very nice," I said. "How much will it cost?"

"I don't know. My wife will tell you that," he said and left the room.

I unpacked my valise and sat down on the bed, instantly sinking into the soft bedding, which billowed up to my elbows. There was a deep stillness all around, pervaded by the familiar smells of frying oil, mint leaves, black coffee, rose water and cardamom seeds. I felt my face break into a smile as my ears strained to catch a sound that was missing in order to complete a dim, distant memory.

Suddenly I heard a tap turned on in the kitchen and the sound of gushing water made me hold my breath: water gushing from a pipe into a pool!

I got up and went out to the yard. There was no pool, not even orange trees; but there was something about the apple and plum trees, some quality of strangeness peculiar to an Arab homestead. It was obvious that the courtyard had not evolved all at once, that each generation had added something of its own. One man had planted the apple tree by the water tap, another the mulberry tree near the dog kennel, and in time the garden had sprouted up to tell its masters' life stories. I stood listening, my fantasy peopling the courtyard with Nahida and her grandmother, with Abdul-Karim, with the horsecab that would suddenly draw to a halt outside the gate and the horses that would stand and urinate.

That evening I was invited to join the family at supper, and Abu-Nimr introduced me to the people who sat round the table: his round-faced, bustling wife, who smiled into space without resting her eyes on me; his two sons, aged thirteen and fifteen, who attended high school in the city; his plump, pale-skinned daughter, married to a policeman who was away from home all week, and who came home loaded with a wicker basket containing a trussed pigeon, apples from Betar, and a dozen eggs commandeered from some villager who happened to call at the police station.

The food that was served was no more than a continuation of that faraway supper in the orange grove. At that moment I realized what I had come there for.

After supper the strains of an Arab song arose from the gramophone. Abu-Nimr asked me whether I would care to show his boys how to operate the English typewriter he had bought in the city the day before. I sat down to instruct the lads, who set about their task with tremendous awe while their parents looked on, their hearts overflowing with pride. After a while their mother brought me a glass of cocoa and urged me to take a little rest. The gramophone was still playing, and as I sipped my drink Nahida's voice came back to me and

Abdul-Karim's features formed themselves before my eyes, and out of the gloom in the passage there arose the sounds of my mother chatting with the old lady. It was then that I knew that I had been waiting all these years for just this moment, that I would relive our stay at the house in the orange grove.

Again the years went by. We were in the grip of war with the Arabs. I was serving in a company that was lined up to storm Tel Arish, an Arab stronghold in the Jaffa dunes, east of the city.

We had launched an abortive attack there several weeks before which had cost us twenty-six men. This time we felt sure of success and looked forward to the battle as a fierce retaliation.

We set out from Holon at midnight, and soon began crawling in the direction of the Tel Arish buildings. The sand dunes afforded excellent cover, and we slipped across them effortlessly and soundlessly. A west wind carried the Jaffa smells over to us, but later the wind came from behind us, from the new housing complexes going up in Holon, wafting the smell of new, white houses to us. The sand beneath us surrendered the solar warmth it had absorbed during the day, recalling the days of light we had known among the white houses, and auguring the liberty and joy that would again be ours once victory had been gained.

When the Arabs spotted us it was too late for them to do anything about it. We were already within grenade range of their position, and we stormed it from three sides. One of our first grenades burst inside their forward machine-gun nest, putting all its crew out of action. We charged inside and raked the village with the German machine-gun. The Arabs there panicked and rushed out of the houses, only to be cut down by our riflemen, who lay in ambush on our two flanks to the north and south. This left the Arabs only one escape route, westwards, and it appeared that some of them managed to slip through in that direction and escape into the cover of the nearby orange grove – the same grove where, about twenty years before, I had spent a few days with the old lady's family.

I had been expecting things to turn out like that, for that was how it had been planned. The house in the orange grove was our second objective that night. We didn't know whether there were any soldiers there, but we were quite sure that if we failed to destroy the Tel Arish position, they would easily be able to reorganize and entrench themselves in the stone building and courtyard. It seemed that they had a reserve force in the house in the orange grove, for heavy fire was opened upon us from that direction, and there were other indications that fortified positions there were ready to go into action in the event that Tel Arish should fall.

Our luck didn't hold out there, however: the battle continued till dawn and we lost six men. This only heightened our desire for revenge, and besides, we still outnumbered them. Soon the defense of the house showed signs of weakening and the fire gradually slackened off. At dawn we rushed the courtyard, got as far as the stables, laid a charge of high explosives, then withdrew. A few moments later there was a violent clap of thunder and the wing of the house next to the pool collapsed into a heap of rubble. This was immediately followed by the groans of the wounded and cries of surrender. We re-mustered in the courtyard and shouted to the Arabs to come out and surrender.

I was not surprised to see Abdul-Karim. He seemed to have expected this, too, though that was something I had never dared to imagine. I recognized him straight away. I went up to him and called his name. When I explained who I was, he gave a weary smile of recollection. "Nahida ... is she here too?" I asked him. "No," he said. "The family has left Jaffa."

Some of the boys listened to our conversation in surprise.

"D'you know him?" our officer asked me. "I know him," I said.

"Can he give us any important information?"

"Maybe," I said. "But let me settle an old score with him first."

"Want to finish him off?" the officer asked me. "No," I told him. "I just want to talk to him."

The boys burst out laughing at this. Abdul-Karim, who hadn't understood what we were saying, must have felt insulted for his hands trembled with suppressed fury. I hastened to explain to him that I wanted to talk to him alone.

"You're the victors," he said. "We do as we're told."

"As long as I haven't beaten you in the pool," I told him, "there's no telling who is the victor."

Abdul-Karim smiled. He seemed to have got my meaning. Our officer didn't seem to get it, however, for he ordered Abdul-Karim to be taken into the orange grove, where the prisoners were being rounded up. I went up to the pool and sat down on the parapet. Our reinforcements from Bat Yam and Holon began to appear and the medics set about attending to the wounded in the courtyard. I stripped and entered the water. It was warm and dirty: it must have been a long time since the pipe overhead had jetted water from the well pump.

Stretching out my arms, I swam across the pool, then back again. I closed my eyes and waited to hear my mother's voice, urging me on: "Don't be scared! Swim fast!" But instead, I heard Abdul-Karim say: "You beat me in America, but I beat you right here, in the pool." Just then I heard a shot from the orange grove. My heart missed a beat. I knew Abdul-Karim had been killed. Leaping out of the water, I pulled on my trousers and rushed into the grove. There was some commotion and the officer was yelling:

"Who the hell fired that shot?"

"My gun went off," one of the boys said.

When he saw me coming up the officer said: "We've lost that information, damn it! They've killed that Arab of yours."

"We've lost it," I said.

I went over to Abdul-Karim's body and turned it over. He looked as though he had seen me swimming in the pool a few moments ago. His was not the expression of a man who had lost.

There, in the courtyard, it was I, all of us, who were the losers.

S. Yizhar

Harlamov

Translated by Hillel Halkin

Mr. Harlamov was a big man. He was a fearless man too and when he sat himself down at the harmonium (which was a kind of piano played with a foot bellows, or a kind of accordion with legs like a piano's, an exotic instrument that served as the standard medium of instruction in Music Pedagogy and Appreciation at the Bet Hakerem Hebrew Teachers College of Jerusalem) – when he sat himself down, as big and fearless as a bear tickling a kitten, and picked out the keys with his big, fearless fingers, whose palms covered the keyboard, while pumping the bellows with his feet, the whole harmonium shook with its wheezing, creaking pedals as if about to give out in one last excruciating and unmusical gasp. Above the crash of its chords, Mr. Harlamov sang in his big, fearless voice. If he hadn't had to work the pedals he could have easily strode around the room with it instead of intermittently rearing in his seat to scan the class for anyone slacking or off-key, calling out parenthetically to the culprit without breaking the tempo of the song, You there, or That young lady in the back. Which was enough to make whoever it was cringe and join the mighty chorus.

If truth be told, the monumental sight of Mr. Harlamov thumping away at the wheezing harmonium while the class accompanied him at full volume was impressive. It was also comical, mixing giggles into the harmonies whose frequent parentheses were filled with a Hebrew that was far from untainted by Mr. Harlarnov's big, fearless Russian errors. You please to sing, he would scold. You no laugh, you. And with a scowl he went on adjusting our mighty chorus to his big, fearless notes, hunching over his harmonium and fiercely rearing up to review his troops.

There was really nothing very fierce about him. There was even an inherent good nature that might have prevailed were it not that nothing was as it should have been – neither the poor substitute for a piano, nor our voices that kept going flat, nor our young, grinning faces that showed scant respect for The Heavens Tell The Glory Of The Lord. He was constantly correcting us. C! he would shout. C Major! The more roughshod we ran over the music, the more desperately he increased the volume of the harmonium to salvage what he could of its beauty, doing his best to drown us out while bent over his instrument, a very lonely, uncompromising man.

I never had much luck with Mr. Harlamov. I didn't even notice it when, while we were singing a choral number one day, he reared up and signaled for silence so that he might spot the villain who was making a mockery of the music. For a moment nothing was heard but my unsuspecting voice, booming out the words of The Internationale. You, Mr. Harlamov whispered in a voice that made the ceiling recoil. You. Mr. Dinburg. Scram you from here! I tell Dean he give you boot. I tell you without, with no, murder music. I tell, for what I work? And maybe I tell too: if you know what is Russia and what is do to me there, you not sing that song. It wouldn't have helped if I had sworn on a stack of Bibles that it was only a harmless joke. It wouldn't even have cleared my own conscience. Why did I do it? Sometimes the only answer is because, and this because was a feeble one. Unless (but this wasn't something I could have said out loud, not even to myself) it was to make an impression on the flushed wearer of a brown sweater who was singing her heart out next to me.

Little wonder that I received a "D" in music at the end of the term and even that was an act of mercy to the young buffoon on the great man's part. Next to my "A"s in Bible, Literature, and History, it stood out like a sore thumb. (Not that my Arabic was any better; I flunked with an "F" courtesy of the esteemed and resplendent Jerusalem orientalist, Yosef Yoel Rivlin. And my English too, in the words of Mr.

Morris, a short but stern pedagogue whose heels clicked when he walked, left "a great deal to be desired." To say nothing of math, all my efforts at which satisfied neither the sphinx-like Mr. Hevroni nor the laws of algebra. I didn't do very well either when I tried pacifying Mr. Harlamov by remarking as I walked beside him, half-running to keep up with his big, fearless steps in the portico flanking the rocky lot that was slated to become an athletics field for our fabled gym teacher Mr. Yekutieli, that I, simple farm boy though I was, was so musically sophisticated that I had actually listened at my friend Habkin's house to records of Beethoven (mainly the Fifth), Mozart (the E-Minor), and Bach (the Third Brandenburg). At which point I committed the grievous faux pas of adding enthusiastically that I also liked the symphonies of Chopin. Breaking off his fearless stride, Mr. Harlamov threw me a downward, withering glance. Chopin write no symphonies! he said with disgusted finality, walking on to leave me more foolish than ever and unable to explain that I had meant Schumann, and especially the Spring Symphony, which had left me damp-eyed with *Weltschmerz*, most of all for the wearer of a brown sweater whose shy beholder found her more adorable than approachable.

The fact was that all those European names, like Schumann and Chopin, could have confused anybody, especially if he was bad at languages, and most especially if he had an idealistic father who had insisted on speaking only Hebrew at home because that was what a proud Jew should speak. But go explain all that to Mr. Harlamov. The man was as big as the steppes of Russia, where he would have had a great future had not a cruel fate reduced him to a Palestinian music teacher who did not even have a proper piano.

Who could count the times I had been corrected with a tolerant smile by Habkin, who, with his gramophone, his record collection, and his violin, had so much knowledge that, when he wasn't eking out a living as Professor Gruenfeld's secretary, he was copying scores in a calligraphic hand I never tired of watching, scrolling clefs and staffs and bars and notes, multi-angled and magical with the secret glyphs of music-making: It's not Ber Ahms. It's not Yiddish. It's Brahms, in a single syllable: Johannes Brahms.

Once, though, it was different. Once, as Mr. Harlamov was playing and singing while we sang along with him, grinning as we sometimes did, we suddenly found ourselves listening as if something were happening and we had to know what it was. All at once, without even tear or a scowl, Mr. Harlamov was transformed at the faltering old harmonium, which gasped out great chords that seemed beyond its powers of endurance. Something was definitely happening. The chords and music were no longer the same. Although Mr. Harlamov was still singing and playing while hunched over the keys like a giant snail, or an eagle feeding its fledglings between its talons, the whole class fell silent with a great, concentrated attention. He was singing differently too, as though to himself, as though he were alone and had suddenly realized something and didn't care that no one else knew, or had discovered a new truth that was now coming into focus and which only he knew, meanwhile, that it was on its way. It wasn't Tchaikovsky, in case you're wondering. It wasn't Borodin, or Scriabin, or one of your Rimski-Korsakoffs. It was different and special, not yet itself as he sang hunched like a snail in his big voice, which came through slightly muffled but clean, the way something sounds when it's true and you know it's happening and that he isn't here, and is perhaps more than you always thought, beyond all your stupid jokes when you knew nothing about it.

It was happening to us too, so that, humbled and longing for what we now knew was there and had never known before, we listened with a catch in our throats. It would be easy to spout something about the vast steppes of Russia sobbing in that harmonium, or the Cossacks, or the Tartars, or the cold winds of Siberia, or something of the sort, but it wasn't that at all. It was only a man singing and you hearing and knowing that was it, a place beyond the class and the room and the Bet Hakerem Teachers College of Jerusalem, something coming from afar, that was maybe a bit like the child Samuel when he heard the voice in the quiet of the night, the voice that said Samuel Samuel and he answered, Here I am.

Then there was silence and it was over. Nobody knew what to do next, not even Mr. Harlamov, who finally rose all at once to become as tall as the ceiling, and then let his shoulders slump and grew smaller again, his big hands dangling in the air. He wiped his big, bald skull with a handkerchief and grew even smaller, and then he turned and walked without a word to the door, and turned again when he reached it and waved a limp hand and was gone.

And still no one spoke. A few of us began getting to our feet. One by one, we stooped forlornly out of the classroom. I started down the stairs, not knowing what to say. Which way are you going? asked the girl in the brown sweater, who did not know what to say either. It was such an unanticipated question that the young man it was asked of forgot how long he had been waiting for it, and how many wonderful stories he had told himself about it, and how now that it had happened he had never imagined that it would be like this. They descended the stairs. How about you? he asked with an awkward gesture. I'll walk you. He couldn't believe that it was so simple or that he had been so bold. I live quite near here, at the bottom of Hehalutz Street, she said. The Jerusalem cold brought a flush to her cheeks, and when, in her brown sweater, she noticed that he'd noticed, she blushed until she was as red as an autumn apple in a poem. She was so scandalously red that she would have liked to run away, but she raised her collar to blush level and the two of them headed for the steps of Hama'alot Street, skipping down them as if dancing not only because they were so skippety young, but because dance is a wordless art form. Of the sort we're most in need of at this moment, she added without words, the casuarina trees dripping wet pearls on a rain-washed street that was already Hehalutz. Three or four houses further on they turned to the right and there, on the ground floor, she lived.

They stood there, the rosy girl and the young man with the wild head of hair and the too-slender back. He gives me piano lessons, she confessed. Mr. Harlamov. I didn't ask for them, but he asked me if I'd like them, and I asked if it wouldn't put him out, and he said no, he'd be glad to, I had talent and he didn't even want to be paid. Believe me, that's the kind of man he is.

They stood there a while longer without thinking of anything to say, shifting their weight from leg to leg. Then they leaned their arms against a tree, an electric charge flowing between their fingers that were not yet ready to touch, the blush gone from her face that was now simply ruddy with cold. His heart was in his throat. He couldn't think of a word. It was great, what he played, she said. Tremendous, he said. Utterly fantastic. Extraordinary. Unbelievable. The drops falling from the needles of the casuarina trees were clean and pure enough to drink.

If he were to shake a branch it would shower down on her and make him laugh at her sudden shriek. Well, she said.

Yes, he said. All right, then. She stood a while longer. I guess I'd better turn in. Good night. Good night. And still neither of them made a move to go. Well I'll see you, she said. She had chestnut hair above the warm brown of her sweater. Look how pearly the raindrops are, he said. Yes, she said. And he said, Yes, well, so long, and she came running back to him and planted a kiss on his cheek and spun around and fled down the stairs.

Incredulous, he stood there, his hand on his cheek. It was too much to take in but there it was.

Like a drunk he staggered up the wet, empty street, breaking into The Heavens Tell The Glory Of The Lord under his breath, and then beginning to hum and then to sing until he was roaring like an ox in the sleepy streets of Jerusalem whose good folk he was keeping awake. He wasn't thumbing a proletarian nose at them, he was simply letting them know the great truth newly revealed to him on Hehalutz Street, that the heavens told the glory of the Lord. He went on singing even when it began to rain so wonderfully hard that he only wanted to let it be and to turn cold and wet inside him. He only wanted to sing with the choir – *three, four!* "His handiwork is written in the sky."

1960–1990

Ruth Almog

After Arbor Day

Translated by Dalya Bilu

At the beginning of winter my father fell ill and took to his bed. He lay in bed for a long time with his bedroom door closed, and we would walk around the house on tiptoe so as not to disturb his rest.

A lot of people came to the house to inquire after my father's health, but my mother refused to let them into his room, explaining that his sick heart needed rest and quiet. Once a woman we did not know came to the house. She handed my mother a woolen scarf and said:

"You don't know me. Once I came to see the doctor with a high fever and a sore throat. He gave me medicine and also this scarf to wrap around my neck. He said that when you're sick in winter you have to keep your throat warm. Now I'm well again and I want to return it to him. I owe him money too, but I haven't got it now, and the doctor said I should pay when I can."

That was typical of my father. Sometimes my mother would lose her temper and rake him over the coals for not only treating poor patients for nothing, but even giving away medicines for which he himself had paid full price. "How do you think we'll ever make a living" – she would say – "when the only patients we get are all poor people? In any case, people only know how to appreciate what they have to pay for."

"God will help us," my father would say serenely. "God helps those who place their trust in him."

Mother told me that in the old country, too, father had been a poor man's doctor, and there too he had never taken money from patients who could not afford to pay. "I remember," she said, "how a fisherman once brought him three fish instead of money. It was on our betrothal day. His parents came to call on my family, and I cooked the fish for them. They said they had never tasted such delicious fish in their lives."

Years later, when I grew up, I went to pay a visit to the old country, and in one of the small villages, in the district where my father had worked as a doctor, I met an old woman who said to me: "So you are his daughter. Of course I remember him. Yes, of course, it's more than forty years ago, you're right, how time flies... But we still remember him, we still remember. How could we ever forget a doctor like him who never took money from the poor..."

At the beginning of that winter, when my father took ill, the rains stopped and in the afternoons, when I was doing my homework in the kitchen, my little brother went out to play in the yard. When darkness fell he would come in and play with his cars on the floor in the passage. At that hour the hall of our house would be empty of my father's patients, who were now being treated by my mother, who was also a doctor. I would go and sit there, in Mother's big armchair, and read. Sometimes, after supper, my father would read aloud to us. We would go into his room for a few moments and he would ask us about our school work and look at my brother's notebooks, which were full of all the words he already knew how to write. When I said goodnight to him, he would kiss me and stroke my hair.

At the end of the month of Tevet my father had begun to recover from his illness, and it was precisely then that the weather changed and heavy rains began to fall. It rained without stopping, day and night, and father said jokingly: "I get better, and the deluge comes."

On the fourteenth of Shvat[1] it was still raining, and my father, who was always worried about my health, said that he would not allow me to take part in the tree-planting ceremony the next day. I was dying to take part in the ceremony because I had fallen in love with our new

---

1. The day before Arbor Day, traditionally observed in Israel at the beginning of February, on the fifteenth day of the Hebrew month of Shvat.

youth leader, Raffi. All day long I begged and pleaded with my father, until in the end he gave in.

On the morning of Arbor Day it was still raining, and as I was about to leave the house my father said to me:

"Take another sweater and try not to get wet."

A fine drizzle was falling on the mountainside, and as we walked to the spot where the ceremony was to take place my shoes got full of mud. Raffi was walking next to me, and once my hand unintentionally touched his. A sweet feeling filled me for a moment.

When we reached the spot, we were met by a man from the Jewish National Fund who told us that we were going to take part in the planting of a forest in honor of the Jewish martyrs. I saw boys and girls all over the mountainside with spades in their hands, planting saplings in basins of loose soil. When I planted my own little sapling and tightened the soil around it, black earth stuck to my fingers. "Will my sapling live?" I asked myself. An inexplicable dread suddenly took hold of me. My heart went out to Raffi, who was standing next to me planting a tree. Perhaps he would say something to comfort me. I straightened my back and looked in his direction. When my eyes met his he did not smile, and I knew that he would not be able to save me.

In the evening, when I came home, I saw my father sitting in his armchair in the hall. He smiled at me. I wanted to run up to him and kiss him, but something stopped me. It was a long time since he had sat in the armchair, and now I saw that he was looking better.

On the days that followed, the rain went on falling steadily. My father wandered around the house wrapped in his brown woolen dressing gown. He would often come into the kitchen, lean over my shoulder and peep into my notebooks.

Six rainy days went by, and on the seventh day after Arbor Day the sun came out. My father sat with us at the lunch table. He sang the blessing. When we had finished eating he went out to sit on the porch. The sun was shining and a light breeze brought sweet scents from the orange groves. My mother sat next to my father and they spoke to each other.

I knew that soon my parents would be relieved of their worries about money. Soon, when my father was well again, he was going to get a job in the hospital.

I sat in the kitchen and did my homework. I soon tired and stood up. The sun had made my father's cheeks pink and his eyes were shining, and when he smiled at me I forgot all my troubles.

"Have you finished?" he asked.

"I still have to write an essay in English," I said.

"Go and do it then," he said.

I moved from the kitchen to the hall. The window onto the porch was open and I could see my father and mother, and hear them talking. Father said little, and mother too fell silent. After a while, when I was absorbed in my essay, I suddenly heard my father say in a queer-sounding voice: "I don't feel well."

As I was about to rise to my feet, overcome by panic, the door opened and I saw my father coming in, his hands clenched on his mouth, his back bent and his face very white. I saw my mother supporting him, leading him down the long passage to their room, and I went on standing rooted to the spot. Then I heard my mother's voice from the other end of the house:

"Quick, run for the doctor!"

For a moment longer I went on standing there, seeing my father's pale face before me, his eyes blank. Then I rushed into the yard, jumped onto my bicycle, and went to fetch the doctor. When he opened the door I couldn't speak.

"Hurry," I stammered, "hurry... father..." and I raced away.

Instead of going straight home, I rode to the wood at the top of the hill not far from our house. I sat down on a bench and my heart was empty. Afterwards I mounted my bike again, and as I rode past our house I saw the doctor crossing the yard on his way in, and I knew that only a short time had passed. I was afraid to go home and I rode aimlessly up and down the village streets. In the end I landed up at the wood again and sat down on the bench. How long I sat there I don't know, but by the time I came home the door of my parents' room was closed. There was not a sound to be heard. I went into the kitchen and sat down at the table.

There were a few slices of bread lying on a plate. I took a slice and started eating it. After a while the door opened and the doctor came out. I heard the front door slam behind him. A little while later I heard the front door open and a woman neighbor came in, a friend of my mother's.

"What's happened?" she asked.

I said nothing.

Then the door of my parents' room opened and my mother stood at the kitchen door. She looked at me and said: "Your father is dead," and she turned to the neighbor and said in their language: "His beautiful daughter is fatherless now." Then she turned back to me: "Come and see your father for the last time."

My father's eyes were closed. His face was blue and there was a faint smile on his lips. His face had never looked so beautiful and so kind as it did then.

When I left the room I went into the bathroom. My father's brown dressing gown was hanging on a hook on the wall. I buried my head in the gown and kissed it. Afterwards I held the empty sleeves and stroked my face with the rough, warm wool. "I won't cry," I promised myself.

The next day, a lot of people gathered in the yard of our house. Friends and relations, and my teachers and friends from school. And when the rabbi came they brought my little brother too. He walked with us behind the coffin as far as the first synagogue on the way. There he said the mourner's *kaddish* and afterwards a friend of the family took him away.

My mother did not cry, and my eyes too were dry. Once my glance encountered Raffi, my youth leader, who was walking not far from me, and for a moment the sobs welled up in my throat. I remembered the sudden dread which had seized me when we were in the hills planting the trees, and again I said to myself that he would not be able to save me.

At the cemetery they tore my mother's dress and mine too. Several people eulogized my father. The coffin was lowered into the hole and the people standing around took spades in their hands, and earth fell onto the coffin and began covering it up. I copied my mother and bent down to the ground. My fist fastened round a little clod of earth, wet and black and sticky to the touch of my palm. A clod of earth from a hard land. Perhaps there was a seed in it, and in the spring a flower would bloom on my father's grave. And perhaps then too the little sapling I had planted on the hillside in memory of the martyrs would put out its leaves too. And I – would the ice in my heart ever thaw?

Yesterday the sun shone. A mild spring breeze brought sweet scents from the orange grove. My father sat on the porch of our house and said that soon it would be spring, and that in the summer he would start work at the hospital. But now the earth was still muddy, for it had rained the whole month long: water flooded the land and the farmers rejoiced.

Aharon Appelfeld

Kitty

Translated by Tirza Sandbank

She was expected to read slowly and to memorize the sentences. She felt how the words hit the stone and returned to her, chilled. They called her name, which rustled in the starched dresses. When the dresses touched the stone they seemed to shiver. The windows glittered yellowly, illuminating the floor with little flames. Sometimes she felt the full impact of the air on the back of her neck, stifling the syllables in her mouth. But at other times the flow increased, the good words remained within her, like a warm secret which planted itself slowly, striking roots and remaining fixed.

Once a day Maria would come in. They would speak for a while. The words, for some reason, took on different proportions in the large hall, as if it was someone other than the nun who spoke then. They seemed to come from space. Maria taught her French, arithmetic, and a few passages from the New Testament, religious tenets. In her present limited state, only repetition was of any use. Maria would sit and read with her, and Kitty tried to repeat words after her with the same inflection. Sometimes it seemed as if they really communicated, but at other times, when the child tried to overcome the language difficulties, she would stammer in syllables, sounds which hardly seemed to come from her.

Afterwards they would walk in the garden. Maria would say the names of the birds and Kitty would repeat them after her.

Sometimes it would be plants. You could see the landscape, for miles around, and when you looked out, you felt the height. Steps led to this place, but the child did not know this yet, since her perceptions were still those of a first encounter. A tree, a stone, a bedraggled bush, a puddle, all these were an extension of the images taken from the hall. But outside, the universe was slacker. Outside she could take longer steps, she could stretch out her hand to touch a tree.

When she came back from her walks, the hall looked more beautiful to her. It was always towards evening. The light here was concentrated and its tones were fuller. It was a room full of flying angels, picturesque inscriptions which she didn't understand, but which suited the flight of the angels. Together they seemed to create a flowing movement. Sometimes the sound of the organ accompanied the dance.

She would return to her copybooks, reciting the conjugations, and then, in accordance with Maria's instructions, the passages from the New Testament. She had still not learned the evening prayer; in the evening they would kneel together by the bed, momentarily silent. In the meantime they found out that the Abbess was about to pay a visit. A different atmosphere now dominated the courtyard. In the rooms one could hear the creaking of furniture being moved, the sounds of scrubbing, and other sounds which seemed to indicate that some chained being lurked behind the heavy furniture, and whenever one tried to move it, it screamed. Maria tried in vain to soothe her. Kitty was affected by the uneasiness in the air, for even within these halls, isolated as they were from one another, some contact existed among people. Sometimes you could even hear the silence talking.

One morning the Abbess arrived. Her steps reminded Kitty, somehow, of other sounds. What sounds? She didn't know. The convent filled her entire life, pushing out memory, imbuing her with its solid being. At noon, she was brought before the Abbess. The hall was large, somehow different from the other halls. Waiting in the doorway for a sign, she had the opportunity to scrutinize the walls. They were in a different style. Later she found out that the treasures of the convent were stored in this hall: ancient paintings, gold crowns, silver lamps and other objects which were not suitable for everyday use. The Abbess was sitting on a chair. There was an air of practical vitality about her. She stretched out her hands, beckoning to the girl. Kitty came near and stood before her.

"Is this the girl?" asked the Abbess.

The nuns nodded.

"Has she been given any instruction?"

"The New Testament, and some French," said Maria.

"Can you already feel God in your heart?" asked the Abbess.

The nuns, in a body, turned their heads. Kitty looked at them, then turned her head back to the Abbess, and said: "God."

They spoke in French and Kitty did not understand. Mother, Father were the only words she knew. A few days before, she had recited them together with Maria. Before she was led out of the hall, the Abbess tried to ask her something, but seeing her confusion, she did not pursue the question.

The days settled down to their usual calm. No furniture was moved, no picture was taken down. Everything was wrapped in silence, in that calm that is found in deep wells. She recited the words and the conjugations, and in the afternoons Maria would come in and read with her. Memory was inaccessible. It had sunk to the darkest recesses. Thus, in her eleventh year, she made her first ardent contact with life, with a thirst and devotion which amazed Maria. Suddenly, together with the growth of her vocabulary, wonder blossomed in her: her face took on a paleness which was common to all those who have lived here for many years, even to the plants. Every month some new line, gesture, facial expression appeared; this development filled Maria's heart with rejoicing and anxiety. This human creature must have other qualities. What Maria did not reveal to Kitty, the walls would reveal to her. The air in the room, the little statue, everything surged here, flowing and expanding. "Who are you?" "We are the angels." "And who are you?" – only now was he revealed to her. It was the face of a man. The rivulets of blood flowed as far as the angel's feet, and from there to the windows. This was the first contact. He came to her from the concealed part of the picture. Neither old nor young, but suffering. The next day Kitty was sunk in deep contemplation. Curiosity died in her, and when she touched the copybook, the crude letters spoke to her. She passed her hand over them, trying to calm them. With Maria she spoke little. Her poor vocabulary made communication impossible. But Maria sensed that in spite of the progress which she had made, the child was slipping away from her. She therefore decided to improve her speech, to enable her to converse with her and thus penetrate to her inner life. For Kitty was like a dumb being, weaving a life of her own in the inmost depths of her soul. Maria noted that the concepts of the Father, the Mother and the Son were not unknown to her, and that when she uttered their names in broken syllables, a tremor of joy lit up her eyes. Her life, however, was mute and lacked expression. It found no outlet in questions, exclamations, or anger.

Once in a while, Maria would find her playing. She played with the small stones of the mosaic which had come loose in the entrance to the hall. At those moments she looked like a child, but when she raised her eyes, they held a strange look. The Abbess did not come. She left the convent to itself. The nuns worked as usual, and in the garden, the creepers, the roses and the lawn came to life. Every murmur proclaimed growth. It seemed as if even the shade encouraged it. The windows were adorned with new colors. And when Maria said: "Spring has come," her voice rang with festivity.

Maria's efforts went unrewarded. Kitty recited the verses, reading and re-reading with stubborn dedication, but her own words remained unsaid. Maria would say: "Speak." Between utterances, the silence loomed large, a solid barrier.

Summer came, and with it, the change. Suddenly, like the transition from budding to blossoming, speech came to her. It surged in her, colorful and wild, crystallizing into French words which fluttered in her like caged birds, trying to escape. They emerged only with the greatest effort, twittering syllables which took on meaning only by virtue of the voice, the fluency and the intonation. You couldn't call them words. They didn't seem to come from the center of speech: it was her whole being that spoke. The defect was now apparent. Maria had, in fact, suspected that there was something wrong with the child, but she had not mentioned it. Now the defect was prominent.

Something in the child's movements, even more than in her voice, made it obvious to Maria that lack of words was not her only obstacle. Sometimes she asked herself whether she should not take the matter up with the Abbess, as was customary in such cases. But this procedure, simple as it seemed, aroused doubts in her which made her postpone the decision. First of all, they would surely take the girl from her and put her in the care of one of the older nuns. The old ones were not very selective in their methods. They were convinced that sin stubbornly assails the young, and they sometimes rebuked them in an effort to arouse the positive forces. Maria decided to make the girl's life her own. She no longer sat nearby like a stranger, but observed her as if observing her own life. And thus, after many years of being a nun, she began to regard her life as one connected sequence, in which every detail stood out, testifying clearly to growth and development. She now could survey her own life, the life of Maria, a life which had been hidden for many years, concealed in confusion, layer upon layer of secrecy, like the walls encompassing the convent.

The days which followed brought no decisive changes. Maria felt that in her, too, something was dawning. It was a sort of pity by virtue of which she wanted to bring the girl near to her, to make her happy, to tell her about herself. How attentive Kitty's eyes sometimes seemed. A slender body, a reluctant gesture, and sadness – one could make her speak. The child spoke to herself, combining words into phrases which did not exist in the language. Only daydreams and secret desires give rise to such meaningless combinations. Sometimes a sound escaped her, as if rent from the innermost depth. Her closed being was stripped of something. Sometimes it seemed to Maria that until now her own life had been moving with evasive superficiality, barely making contact. Finally, in a moment of weakness, it had anchored and closed up, but without any essential change taking place. The years as a nun had brought no change. The vain desires of life died in her, but grace did not shine on her. Now, in her meeting with the girl, she began to feel the hollowness which filled her. Her thoughts, even the most beautiful of them, seemed to float, never becoming part of her. These feelings, which had recurred in her ever since childhood, ran through her life like a thread.

Now, with the distance of years, her youth took shape in her with remarkable concreteness. The street, the inn, the tavern. An impoverished family, the sons gone to the army, the daughters dispersed over many cities, and she, the youngest of them, finding herself in a nunnery. These were the bare facts, like the scaffolding of the building; the rest were just details, brought about by circumstance. One cannot sever oneself from one's thoughts, from the first sight seen, from oneself, from one's family, from one's sister who has taken up a dubious profession. Gradually she had realized that she was linked to them, that even in her solitude, or perhaps because of it, she was linked to them, a kind of delegate who must give account. Sometimes she thought of her father, his stubbornness, the movement of his hand; but not always. Sometimes her thoughts lay dormant and she worked industriously and devotedly with that frozen expression which one took on here. But in the hall, with the girl, her thoughts surged up in her, suddenly set free. There was a crab-apple tree in the garden and Kitty sometimes sat underneath it. The scene was like a reproduction of one of the big paintings on the wall. "Sister Maria," the girl would call, and Maria felt as if the holy infant itself was calling her. But gradually the secret came between them. The more questions Kitty asked, the larger it loomed. "And my parents?" Kitty once asked.

"We have no parents, God is our father."

She had kept this sentence in her heart for many days, and only now did she utter it. She, too, wanted to be a child of God, like the girl, with no thoughts, with no defiled past. But when she tried to dismiss her thoughts, their weight threatened to crush her.

As far as the girl was concerned, she wanted to protect her in the shade of prayer and holy studies, to have her become a nun, but not because of external pressures; to plant her in the realm of eternal silence. She began to be strict with Kitty. The war again stood at the gates of the convent. The soldiers set up a camp. Shots shattered the quiet of the night. The walks stopped. Kitty remained in the hall, her entire world restricted to the confines of its stained-glass windows.

Only once a day, in the twilight, was she permitted to look out, beyond the walls. Half-naked soldiers walked around, near the huts. Gradually this scene, different in color, merged with the scenes inside, until the contrast became blurred. She was filled with a peaceful sense of unity. Maria's presence filled her with warm intimacy. The Abbess was forgotten. Saint Matthew, Saint Nicholas, and above all the Holy Virgin became her friends, to whom she could appeal even with the smallest requests.

Then Kitty had other feelings. At first they were physical sensations, not unpleasant; then a hardening in her breasts. She realized that something was stirring inside her; it seemed to be a sign for whose revelation she must wait patiently. How lovely it was to nestle under the blanket, pulling it over her head, and to feel the body's pulse, to listen to the sweet murmurs. She wanted to tell Maria about it, but something stopped her. The sweet secret to which she had loved to listen became a heavy burden, which in dreams took on the form of a nightmare. She would sit at the back of the garden, under the apple tree, watching the ripening fruit. Indoors, they were making preparations for the visit of the Abbess. Again, the familiar squeaks were heard. Closets were moved from their usual places, pictures were removed from the walls. On the lawn a plaster bust, a lamp and a shaky table were heaped together as if to embody a new combination of the sacred and the profane. Buxom maids were brought from the villages. Carrying brooms and brushes, they looked as if they were in charge of the place. Maria, and Sister Katherine, who was older than her, took off their nuns' habits and worked side by side with the maids. Maria did not say much about the Abbess, but what she said was so full of unadulterated praise that it aroused in Kitty a feeling of uneasiness that was mingled with awe and even anxiety. Imprisoned as she was by her secret, the Abbess' forthcoming visit filled her with foreboding.

One day, during the noon break, Kitty chanced to speak with one of the maids. She was a heavily built, rather masculine-looking woman, who had apparently had a rather difficult life. Her husband had wanted to be a priest, but after becoming involved in a murder case, he had fled to Germany and enlisted in the army. She spoke fluently, in a peasant dialect, often accompanied by gesticulations in which revulsion and joy alternated swiftly as in a game full of unpredictable changes. But she did not only talk about herself. She tried, with that peasant cunning which knows how to employ flattery when necessary, to find out about the girl. A girl in a convent, thought the peasants, was a phenomenon worth noting, for she had certainly not arrived by chance.

Kitty told her that her parents had died in the war. This was the logical thing to say, for she could not tell her anything else; and besides, her new sensations seemed to point at this explanation. Sometimes she thought about it. Sometimes she saw herself as a child who had been left at the gate of a convent. But sometimes, near the sacred pictures, she would imagine that she was the child of God. At any rate, memory was of no help to her. Often Maria's reassurance filled her with satisfaction. "Not everyone is lucky enough to be God's daughter, protected under His wing," she repeated to herself. Of course, the recollection of the not-too-distant past, the visit of the Abbess and her meeting with her belied the fact that she occupied an honored position. Nevertheless, she did not lose the feeling of superiority which she kept secret in her heart.

Now, in the presence of the maid, listening to this uninhibited confession, she had a feeling of sin, but also of seductive sweetness. "Where did you come from?" – Maria's explanations seemed like a fairy tale which was real and believable, but at the same time there was now a presence which required another explanation. It was a moment of transition which only children experience, at times. It was, as it were, a realm of two truths, each with its own rights. Maria was busy with the housework and let the girl wander among the heaped rubble, left to her own reflections. She realized only vaguely, if at all, that the girl was becoming wholly absorbed in these truths.

Her meetings with the maid were marvellous; her speech was spiced with obscene words; she was large. As she dusted, Kitty felt the lightness and the nonchalance with which she walked around in the hall which had previously been dominated by silence. Usually their conversations took a rather practical turn. Peppi would speak, and when Kitty admitted that she felt a hardening in her breasts, she had the feeling that she was only acknowledging something that Peppi herself had mentioned. Peppi blurted out something in a shattered voice as if her vocal cords had burst. From then on the conversation deteriorated. Peppi described the Germans encamped in the village without trying to hide her connections with them, and she spoke about other things which Kitty probably did not understand. But she felt a sort of strange sweetness which penetrated her gradually, destroying something of her own. The next day everything was as usual. The maids were sent away and when Kitty woke up, the familiar silence was firmly in its place. The pictures hung in the hall. The smell of kerosene was everywhere. But it was not the same hall. Something had been taken away from it, from the corners, from the pictures. Her eyes looked at them, but all they saw were the drawings themselves. Maria was too busy and did not notice the change. She was taken up with preparations for the visit of the Abbess. What she did notice was a rebellious turn of the shoulder which Kitty was unable to suppress.

The next day the signs of maturity appeared. Kitty was like a vessel full of shame. She tried to avoid Maria and at night she fell onto the bed as the tears scalded her face. In her dream Peppi reappeared; in her torn dress she looked like a creature dragged out of a murky river. The next day, the dream remained with her until the late hours of the morning. As she sat over her copybooks, she said to Maria: "I am a good girl," and Maria confirmed it with a caress and a kiss on the forehead.

Later, Maria left the convent suddenly. It turned out that the Abbess had sent for her. Maria packed her belongings, and while she stood for a moment, gazing at the shining lamps, she looked unusually thin. The parting was very hasty, and as the gate creaked behind her, Kitty suddenly felt that something had been taken away from her.

Complete silence reigned as always in the noon hours. A water basin and picture frames were scattered around like creatures obliged to bear the weight of the heat, each in its own corner. The things were familiar to her, but nevertheless a certain strangeness emanated from them. She had to become reacquainted with them. Left to herself, she wandered around the building, looking for an entrance to the small rooms which were hidden from view, living their lives for many years without anyone entering them. All the doors were locked, and through the bars nothing could be seen. Finally she found Katrina sitting on the threshold. Thin, dressed in festive clothes, she seemed to be frozen in reflection. "Katrina," called Kitty in embarrassment. Katrina was Maria's cousin. Steeped together as they were in faith, they had not become intimate according to the laws of love. The enmity that they had brought with them from the outside world only deepened, daily emphasizing their past which had caused the separation. Here they had met; the hand of fate had brought them together. When the matter had become known to the Abbess, she had not been willing to separate them. She had sentenced them to remain together. Pity dawned in Kitty's heart. She came near to Katrina, trying to find a suitable expression. Katrina rose slightly. She folded her dress around her and sat withdrawn in the corner of the stoop.

"Maria's gone," said Kitty. Aside from a few words about practical matters, Katrina said nothing. She could not hide her sigh in Kitty's presence. Finally, when there was nothing left to say, she went away with the excuse that she must go to prayers. This was a hint to Kitty that she, too, should be more pious. Kitty remained fixed in her place.

She had bad dreams that night. She felt the heavy bell pressing down on her shoulders, and when the bell chimed three, it was as if the bell clapper swung inside her. She rose and prayed, trying to break out of the walls that closed in on her. Only towards morning did she discern a spark of reconciliation in the eyes of Him to whom she prayed. Peppi appeared in the morning like a good messenger from another world. With her torn dress and merry eyes she was the embodiment of total abandon. She told Kitty that the front line was advancing, that soldiers were being concentrated in the neighborhood, their number increasing from day to day. It was obvious that she enjoyed the military preparations. While talking, she threw her arms out wide, as if in an embrace.

"Maria won't return; she won't be able to. The roads are blocked.

The soldiers will break into the convent; there aren't enough sleeping quarters in the neighborhood. The Abbess is worried; that's why she called for Maria. They won't touch Katrina. Her being a nun and her anger have dried her up," – that was the way Peppi spoke. A confusion of facts and desires.

"And what about me?" asked Kitty.

"Don't you be afraid of them. Tell them you belong to me. They all know Peppi. I'll work for them in the canteen. Maybe you want to work there too? Together, Kitty? This war is going to finish us. We're going to die without having a bit of fun. We must take the gold lamp out of here. You can keep it, or me."

"No," said Kitty, taken aback.

"No," repeated Peppi, drawling the word. "No, you say. No, you say. I have something to say to you. You're a dirty Jew. They threw you into the convent, but I know. I saw. Tomorrow they'll come and take you away. Tomorrow."

"You won't escape, you won't escape" – these were not words, they were sounds escaping from a furious existence, like barks, until the gate closed them out with a bang. Kitty stood for a moment, turning her head away. Down in the valley the soldiers were encamped. They encircled the mountain without leaving a gap. Half-naked, in the radiant sunlight, they looked like moving masses of flesh. On the parade field, soldiers marched to military tunes. It was like the scene depicted in the big picture hanging in the hall. Leaning against the wall, Maria had once told her about the Crusades, which had gone on for many years until the crusaders had finally succeeded in redeeming the tomb of the Son. It was the same scene. Even the colors were similar. She was still agitated over the encounter with Peppi. "She was angry with me, or maybe she was just joking." But her heart told her otherwise. Katrina's room was locked. She did not dare to knock. She stood on the steps touching the white marble. Gradually the pattern began to emerge, at first only in meaningless details. Only later, as if aided by other sensations, it emerged and crystallized. In the evening, when Katrina came in and told her that from now on she must remain in the cellar, she accepted it calmly, as one who knows what is in store for her. Outside the dusk was fading. The sky was redder than usual. A moldy smell permeated the cellar. Jars of beets covered with white kerchiefs stood in a row on the shelves. They looked like frozen creatures in whom life was still stirring.

They're looking for me, Katrina is hiding me – there was no longer any doubt of it. Now she visualized how they would find her. The door would open, light would blaze in, first on the jars, then on her. She came nearer to the jars. The bubbling of fermentation could be heard. Gropingly, she acquainted herself with the objects around her, picture frames, broken statues, sacks of apples. She stretched out her hand and touched an apple. Its juice filled her. After a while, Katrina came down and told her that from now on she must remain here, and Kitty said she knew that it was written in the Holy Scriptures that the children of God must suffer until the light shines for them. But Katrina answered in a voice that sounded angry that she must not pride herself on this belief. "Am I a hairy Jew?" said Kitty, Peppi's voice echoing in her ears. No answer was forthcoming. Katrina was already behind the door. Her steps echoed for a while and then were silent. Now all doubts vanished. Certainty pervaded the pattern. She stroked her skin and said, "Yes, I am hairy." Now she remembered that, even in the past, Peppi used to call her "little Jewess" as she pinched her cheek. Katrina too, as she stood before the Abbess, had said something of the kind. For many hours she sat behind the bars, waiting for the light. Nothing was heard. The silence of the convent deepened. She felt the hair growing from within her, spreading around her neck and under her arms. "Yes, I am hairy," she said, as if acknowledging a fact that there was no point in denying any more.

"Who are you, jars?"

"We are jars of beets," the voice answered – "our color got lost in the dark. Can't you hear the song of fermentation?"

"Yes," said Kitty. "Tell me, am I hairy?"

"You are not hairy. You are our sister. God is hiding us."

Afterwards she curled up on a pile of hay and fell asleep. Katrina came down to her and Kitty told her that she felt well. She had many friends here. The beets were fermenting in the jars, the Wishniak gave off an aroma of sanctity. Katrina said that the soldiers were encircling the mountain. They were encamped near the walls. Maria was on the way, but could not get there. In the convent nothing had changed. Kitty stretched out her hand, touching the starched dress. A tremor went through her. Now she knew that soon she would move to another place. Katrina spoke of other worlds, and Kitty asked for details, thinking it was the thing to do.

The war was drawing to an end. A final ceremony was still needed. The convent almost begged to be broken into. Katrina said that it was not she who had hidden Kitty. At this, the soldiers burst out laughing. They no longer had any urge to kill. Now it was the game that intrigued them.

Kitty had grown taller in the cellar and when she was brought out into the light, dressed in her white nightgown, she looked even taller. The gown trailed behind her. She was led along narrow paths behind the fence. How marvellous it all seemed – like floating in space. Now all the people were gone. Angels embraced her arms and when the shot was fired, she stood for a moment, marvelling at the miracle revealed.

Yitzhak Bar-Yosef

Venus

Translated by Hillel Halkin

On his way to the cemetery Shaul turned his car onto a side road, a dirt path that led to a yard surrounded by a cinderblock wall draped with a blue-flowering vine. Large slabs of marble rested against it. From somewhere came the sound of a saw cutting stone.

He had decided not to be tight this year and to have his wife's gravestone polished and retouched, even though he was sure it would cost at least 100 shekels. And yet quickly he tried calculating what else he might do with the money. After all, what difference did it make to his wife if the letters on her tombstone could barely be read any more? Every year until now he had simply come half an hour early and dusted them off with an old toothbrush that he kept for the purpose.

A year ago he had had visitors from England, cousins whom the family in Israel put up now and then in the hope of being able to stay with them some day on a summer vacation in London. Upon being woken in the morning by the unfamiliar cries of the neighbors' roosters, they discovered that they had forgotten their toilet kit in the hotel in Hamburg where they had stayed overnight. They wanted to buy toothbrushes, but Shimon's grocery wasn't open, because having sat up all night in the hospital with his wife, who had just had a Caesarian, Shimon had decided to sleep the operation off in bed.

"Here, take this one," Shaul had said, giving them the toothbrush he used for cleaning Ruti's grave. "It's a spare. It's a little old but in fine condition."

Already a year ago at this time they had spoken of the need to retouch the 12-year-old stone. "If it's the money, Pa," said his son, who worked the night shift for an agricultural export company and earned a double salary, "leave it to me."

As luck would have it, the guests from England came down with food poisoning. They got it from eating hummus at a gas station diner on the highway to Jerusalem, but Shaul couldn't help thinking that perhaps it was because of the toothbrush. Maybe someone was angry with him, he thought. He had no idea who that someone might be, but he was sure it was a punishment, which meant that there had also been a sin.

The cousins from England had a bad time and cut short their visit. The worst attack, which came when they were on top of Masada, was very unpleasant. They had looked forward to Masada and now their trip was spoiled for them.

Shaul had gotten religion a bit in the course of the last year. It wasn't so much a matter of belief as it was of his friends from the neighborhood who had begun attending synagogue on Saturdays. "Why don't you try it?" they asked. "It's like joining a men's club." Still, he had begun to believe a little. It would make Ruti glad to see me in synagogue, he thought.

Not that Ruti was religious, either. But she had kept a kosher home because of her mother and sometimes she would say with tears in her eyes, "But how can anyone be sure there isn't a God? If the Jewish people... I mean, for so many years..." When her illness was diagnosed, she took it as proof that He existed. She was sure she was being punished.

Praying regularly on Saturdays had put Shaul in the habit of thinking about God, too. It seemed symbolic to him that his guests, who had brushed their teeth with the toothbrush he gave them, had gotten sick at Masada. Thank God it wasn't fatal, he thought. But that's the last time I clean Ruti's grave with a toothbrush.

He was thinking of this when he entered the yard of Davidov & Sons, Manufacturers of Gravestones and Kitchen Marble. It was very hot. He looked for a shady place to park his car, but the yard, which was coated with white stone dust, was bare except for a broad flame tree in the middle of it, to which a dog was tied. Though it lay there quietly enough, one of its eyes looked open.

Once, Shaul remembered, he had brought home a dog and made Ruti furious, because she disliked dogs and always had since her childhood in Jerusalem. Dogs weren't for Jews, she said. Afterwards, though, she felt sorry for it and gave it a little bowl of milk.

Shaul decided to park beneath the flame tree after all. What was he afraid of? The dog definitely looked asleep. However, the minute he stepped out of the car the animal fell on him and ripped out a piece of his pants. Only then did he notice a sign that said:

WATCH OUT FOR BITING DOG. YOU'VE BEEN WARNED!!!

He barely managed to jump into his car and back away quickly in reverse. The yard was deserted. The loud whine of a power saw came from an old structure whose roof appeared to have burned down. Beneath its blackened rafters was a new roof of asbestos sheets. Grimy white water ran in a ditch. The dog stood smugly lapping it.

Shaul thought that maybe he would just dust the gravestone with the toothbrush this year too. He had brought it with him to be safe, along with a small can of paint and a paintbrush for touching up the letters. Yet a glance at his watch informed him that he didn't have time. His son and daughter-in-law always came at ten sharp and would see him before he could finish. Once, while sleeping over at their house, he had heard his son's wife tell his son, "Is your father tight! He's been a miser all his life. And don't think he doesn't make good money at the Electric Company, either."

He got out of the car, inspected the hole in his pants, and decided not to mention it to anyone. After all, he should have noticed the sign. Why blame the dog? Its masters would just beat it, or even give it away to the pound.

He left the car at the end of the yard, by some big stacks of marble. As he was walking back, he saw a naked woman and blinked hard. Maybe I'm imagining it, he thought. He hadn't seen a naked woman since his wife's death. His sex life had stopped at the age of forty. True, half a year afterwards he had met someone at work, a clerk in the Engineering Department. Though she was three years older than he, she was a real "livewire" and he fell for her. He even dreamed of her at night. She seemed to like him, too. One night they went to the movies, after which she invited him up to her apartment. She was divorced, with two grown children, but Shaul thought it was improper when his wife hadn't been dead a year yet.

Still, at lunch, in the cafeteria, he sat with her. At first there were whispers and even laughs, but after several weeks the two of them were treated as a couple. It was understood between them that sex would have to wait "a little longer."

When Shaul told his son about it, he didn't react. The next day, though, his daughter-in-law phoned him at the office to tell him that her husband had cried all night long. "You have no idea what you'll do to him if you remarry now!" she said.

Over lunch he told his friend that perhaps they shouldn't see each other for a while. What happened? she wanted to know. He told her about the phone conversation. "I think it's best to wait out the year," he said, "and then gradually start getting him used to it. In another year we can get married. He was very attached to his mother."

"Suit yourself," said the woman. "Just remember that if someone else comes along, I don't intend to wait. I'm no spring chicken any more."

And, in fact, soon after that she met the owner of an electrical appliance store and married him right away. She left her job and went to work in the store. If Shaul bought a lamp there, or some other household item, she gave him a ten-percent discount.

As he neared the naked woman he saw that she was a statue. Several other nudes, all cast in white plaster, stood beside her; nearby were some lions and cherubs.

Someone cast a shadow on the ground. "What are you looking for, pal?" asked a young man of about thirty, whose curly hair was powdered with a film of white dust. He wore a small plastic mask over his mouth and his eyes were streaked with the same white stuff that covered the yard.

Shaul felt short of breath. He leaned for a moment on a slab of marble. Several times during the past year he had had such attacks. They felt as if a heavy rope were bound around his chest and keeping him from getting air. A mild pain crept down his neck and along his arm.

"Would you like something to drink, pal?" asked the man, motioning to Shaul to follow him. Gingerly, as if afraid of falling, Shaul stepped away from the marble and after the man. The dog cocked one eye and made a friendly sound as if to say: don't worry, that's over and done with.

They passed the entrance to the workshop. On the wall facing the road was a faded sign that said:

You can win a lot in the National Lottery!

A worker in knee-high boots was standing inside by a large saw. Jets of water cooled the machine and dripped to the floor. Shaul stepped in a white puddle and felt it soak into his socks. They entered a small shack at the other end of the yard and the man opened an old refrigerator, took out a bottle, and poured some cold water into an octagonal glass. "Here you go, pal," he said, handing it to Shaul.

A large bell outside the shack began to ring. The man picked up a telephone and shouted into it over the noise of the saw in a language Shaul couldn't understand. On the wall hung a calendar put out by a tow company. It had a picture of a naked woman whose private parts were covered by a small towtruck with a winch, from behind which several pubic hairs stuck out. She had big boobs. Shaul thought of the statue in the yard.

The man told Shaul that it would cost a hundred and twenty shekels to clean and repaint the letters on the gravestone. As long as they were doing it, though, they might as well polish the whole stone. For two hundred shekels it would look brand new and have a six-month guarantee. And if Shaul really wanted to do a job that would make him a happy man for years to come, he could have the letters recast in lead. That cost four hundred shekels, but it could be paid off in instalments. And if Shaul paid cash and didn't need a receipt, the price could be knocked down a bit.

Shaul was relieved that it need only cost a hundred and twenty shekels, or even less if he paid cash. Then, though, he thought "I'll show 'em" and ordered the most expensive job. So I'll leave them a little less when I die, so what, he thought.

The man poured him another glass of water. This time, when he opened the refrigerator, Shaul saw a large bowl of bones. The man noticed that he was looking at them. "They're for the dog," he said. After a while he added: "They're beef bones. From the butcher."

Shaul laughed embarrassedly, as if he had been caught thinking something he shouldn't have. He was pleased with his decision to order the most expensive job. "What's that nude statue?" he asked the man when he rose from his chair.

"We're expanding," said the man through his mask, which he had put back on. "We're going into Italian garden sculpture. There's lions and angels too. I'll even give you a special price, just like a regular client."

Shaul, whose largesse had put him in a good mood, asked what the nude statue cost. The man took off his mask. "Noah!" he shouted. "Noah!" The worker left his saws and sloshed toward them through the mud in his boots. He held out a hand to Shaul, who saw it was missing a finger and quickly shook it and retracted his own hand. He stole a glance at his fingers to see if they were still all there.

"Bring him a nude, Noah," said the man. "You can put it in his trunk."

"Hey, wait a minute," said Shaul. "Hold on." But Noah, his knees sticking out of his huge boots, was already on his way with an agility surprising in someone of his red-jowled, ham-handed, nine-fingered bulk. "Just a minute!" exclaimed Shaul again.

"Take it easy," said the man with the curly hair. "I already told you, I'll give you a good price."

"It's for my garden," said Shaul. "You bet," said the man, as if glad to hear that it wasn't for the gravestone.

In short order Noah was standing by Shaul's car with a naked woman on his shoulder. "Open the truck for him," said the man to Shaul. "Can't you see he's hot?"

Shaul went to open the trunk and Noah gently laid the woman

inside it, as if afraid to wake her from her sleep. He looked down at her, licking his lips and rolling his eyes. "Nice, eh?" he said. He laid a hand on her breasts and made a smacking sound.

The statue cost Shaul another four hundred and fifty shekels. "Give him a tip," said the man. Shaul took out his wallet again and handed Noah ten shekels. Noah inclined his body in thanks and sloshed away in his boots.

"You've made his day," said the man with the curly hair. "He may look like a giant, but he wouldn't hurt a fly. He's got a heart of gold, that one."

"My wife died twelve years ago," said Shaul. "Of cancer. It all happened so fast. There was almost no pain. They took her to the hospital, opened her up, and sewed her shut again. There was nothing to be done for her. It was twelve years ago," he repeated, as if anxious to avoid being misunderstood. The man put his mask back on and looked eager to get back to work. "Twelve years. I never remarried. It wouldn't have been good for my son. He was very attached to her."

"Don't you worry," said the man. "When we're through with her gravestone you'll think that she died just last week. Wait and see if it doesn't look as good as new. You'll be so satisfied that you'll keep coming back."

Shaul glanced at his watch and gave a start. It was already a quarter after ten. He got into his car and drove to the cemetery parking lot. From a distance he made out his son, his daughter-in-law, and some other members of the family standing by the front gate.

After the ceremony his son and daughter-in-law came home with him for a drink. Though he was impatient to look at the statue in the trunk, he kept saying to them, "Stay a little longer, what's the hurry?"

"There's isn't any," said his son. "Time sure does fly!"

They looked at themselves and at Ruti in the family album. "That's life," said his son's wife. "You're here today and gone tomorrow." She tried pointing in the direction you went in, but wasn't sure which way it was. First she pointed up, then down.

"You want me to make you something to eat?" she asked. "An omelet, maybe?"

"No thanks, I'm not hungry," said Shaul. He felt suddenly worried that someone might steal the statue from his car, at which he glanced through the window. It was time to mow the lawn, he thought. He would put the statue on it.

His son was sitting in his old bedroom with his head in his hands. "Come, Bubi, don't be sad," said his wife. Shaul didn't like her to call his son Bubi. His name was Baruch. True, Shaul's wife had called Shaul Uli, but that wasn't like Bubi. Bubi was like the name of a dog. What if the dog at the marble factory had peed on the statue? What if other dogs peed on it when it stood on the lawn? There must be some way to prevent it.

His son's wife took Shaul aside. "Bubi is depressed," she said. "Maybe it's because he's attached to all kinds of things in his room. You know, all that worthless old junk. Like the record player. Maybe you should give it to him." Shaul could buy himself a new one, she said. "There are these Japanese ones that come really cheap. And you can pay for them in instalments."

Shaul thought of all the things that had been transferred from his house to his son's over the years, always because of his daughter-in-law. The silver candlesticks in which Ruti had lit the Sabbath candles. The clock they had been given as a wedding present. The set of the Hebrew Encyclopedia. The exercise bicycle. The rocking chair. Baruch's wife had also wanted the large oil painting that they had bought when Baruch was a child, but that was where Shaul drew the line. He knew that the painting, whose artist had meanwhile become famous, was worth a lot of money. And anyhow, he liked it. So had Ruti. "Of course, of course," said his son's wife. "I can see you're attached to it. Keep it for yourself. When you reach a hundred and twenty..."

Another time they had awkwardly raised the subject of building a house in his backyard. They were only planning on having one child, his daughter-in-law told him, because it was unfair to raise any more than that in a crowded apartment. When Shaul said nothing she proceeded to tell him about all their friends whose parents hadn't waited to be a hundred and twenty to let their children build on their property. She even knew of cases where they had sold off a back lot and given their children the money.

"Why do you keep talking about a hundred and twenty?" Shaul once asked her.

"That's what everyone says," she replied, adding after a moment: "Of course, I'd be just as happy if you lived to be a hundred and fifty, or even two hundred." This time too she took a long look at the painting in the living room and observed how pretty it was.

Shaul looked out the window again to see if the car was still there. His son came out of the bedroom, walked briefly around the house, and settled in the kitchen, where he sat contemplating a china salt cellar hanging on the wall. On it was a picture of a little girl with wings. "Do you remember how I always asked Ma why, if the girl had wings, she didn't use them to fly away?" he asked. Shaul pretended that he did. "Yes," he said. All he wanted was for them to leave. "Maybe you'd like the salt cellar," he said. "Yes, that would be marvellous," said his son's wife. "It would be something to remember his mother by." As always when she took something, she was in a hurry to go. "Come, Bubi," she said. "Your father must be exhausted."

Shaul walked them to their car. "Come visit," said his son's wife. "The little kid misses his grandpa."

They drove away. Shaul went back inside to wait a while.

He didn't want to take the statue out of the car trunk yet. Suppose they had forgotten something and came back for it? He sat down in the easy chair in the living room, picked up the newspaper and turned on the fan.

Suddenly Noah was by his side, asking if he had seen the dog. He had some bones for him. The dog was so spoiled that lately it didn't want to look at bones. It only wanted borscht.

He was woken by the telephone. Someone wanted to know how much a water pump cost on a Subaru.

Shaul went back to his chair and tried recalling where he knew Noah from. Lately, he had noticed, he was forgetful. Especially after waking up. Suddenly he remembered the statue. He ran anxiously outside to see if his car was still there. The telephone rang again.

"Could you please tell me how much a water pump costs on a Subaru?"

He opened the trunk. The woman was lying face down with her rump in the air. Shaul had a fright. Why did he put her down like that, he wondered. Her breasts might have scratched the paint. Or been broken. He felt a sharp twinge and thought of the last time he had made love to Ruti. She was already very sick then. "Come on," she said. "Do it one more time. Who knows if you'll have another chance." Though he didn't really want to, he was carried away. He didn't touch her breasts, though. That's where her illness had started. "Was it good?" she asked afterwards.

He put a hand beneath the statue to see if its breasts were all right. The plaster was smooth and cool. Nothing was broken. He was glad to see that a blanket-like wrap around the waist hid the genitals.

A little modesty never hurt. Just then, though, he noticed that the statue had no arms. He looked in the trunk to see if they had fallen off. They weren't there. The statue's arms simply ended below the shoulders.

He phoned the marble factory. The telephone rang and rang before someone answered. It was hard to hear over the noise of the saws. "The woman has no arms!" he shouted. At the other end of the line a low drowsy voice said something he couldn't make out. He hung up. It must have been Noah, he thought. He decided to drive back and exchange the statue before anyone could say it was his fault.

The dog was no longer there when he drove into the yard, and so he parked under the tree. The office was empty. Entering the workshop, he saw Noah's broad back. He called to him several times but had to reach out and tap his shoulder to make him realize he was there.

It was too noisy to hear anything. Noah followed him out to the yard. Shaul asked him where his boss was. "Albert went to run with the dog on the beach," said Noah.

"The girl has a defect," said Shaul. Noah stared at him. Shaul noticed that he never blinked. Beside his high boots he was wearing tattered old fatigue pants and a damp red polo shirt caked with white dust. At the point where his head joined his shoulders there was almost no neck. In proportion to the head his ears were amazingly small. He had on a blue tourist's cap that said HOLY LAND. When he turned around Shaul saw that the back of it said SHALOM.

"She has no arms," said Shaul. Though he meant to sound angry, he thought: why take it out on him? He's not to blame. It's his boss who sold me the statue. And anyway, it was simpler to deal with Noah. Let him bring another statue and that would be the end of it, no more questions asked.

"She has no arms," repeated Shaul, marking with an outspread palm the place on his shoulders where the statue's arms stopped. "She's defective. Give me another one." He opened the trunk and showed Noah the statue. Noah shouldered it easily and crossed the yard to where the garden sculptures stood.

Shaul was thirsty. It suddenly struck him that the sun, which had been spanning the yard since the morning, was casting the flame tree's shade in such a way that his car was not in it. Despite the light breeze that stirred the tops of the cypresses at the far end of the yard, it was still very hot. You can win a lot in the National Lottery, said the sign. When he went over to stand in the shade of the wall, there was a strong smell of urine. There were also many large ants that came out of small holes in the ground. He thought of his father, who had had diabetes and liked to pee in the garden and watch the ants come eat the sugar from his pee. Maybe Noah also had diabetes. He was certainly fat enough. His father had been fat too. He wasn't diagnosed for years. He kept drinking and going to the bathroom. Finally, he began losing weight so fast that in two months he lost ten kilos. That's when he began getting shots. Not that it was the diabetes that killed him. It was his heart. By then he was eighty years old.

But even if you didn't die yourself, thought Shaul, people were always dying around you. The thought made him sad. From the direction of the cemetery he could hear someone shouting, "We need some men for the mourner's prayer!" They never had the ten men they needed and were always shouting for people to come running. Automatically he joined in, mouthing the words of the prayer. *Amen. May His great name be blessed for ever and ever...*

He didn't understand how he could be hearing the prayer over the noise of the saws, which never stopped working. He thought of the prayerbook that he carried to synagogue every Saturday in a transparent plastic case. He thought of God waiting impatiently for him, Shaul, to say his prayers so that He could give His attention to other things. What other things were there, Shaul wondered. He had finished creating the world long ago. Maybe He was busy creating new ones, better and more perfect than this one.

The tears rolled down his cheeks. He stood in the sun, his shoes coated white from the dust. Beads of sweat formed on his throat. He watched the cypresses sway back and forth, as if someone were playing a practical joke by shaking their trunks. He could feel himself drying up. How long can I go on crying, he thought. He thought: I should drink a lot. He thought: Ruti is dead and here I am waiting to get my money's worth. He had paid a small fortune for the gravestone and the statue of the nude woman, and she didn't even have any arms. He tried thinking what else he could have done with the money. For years he had wanted to buy a new television but had felt that it cost too much.

He wanted a new stereo too. What could be nicer than to sit on the front porch, listening to music through the open window of the living room. He wasn't sure exactly what kind of music it would be, but it would be the kind that it was nice to listen to on the porch on a summer afternoon or evening. Sometimes, listening to music on the car radio on his way to work, he would think: it would be nice to hear this at home.

He suddenly remembered how, when Ruti was in the hospital, there had been an older woman in her room who listened to music at night on a little transistor that she kept on the white locker by her bed, keeping time with her head and her fingers that drummed on the blanket. They were all in such pain that no one was bothered by it. And the hospital was always full of noises anyway, wheelchairs and wagons pushed by nurses. There were so many wagons that you might think it was a kindergarten or an amusement park rather than a cancer ward.

One night the woman didn't turn off the radio. In the morning they discovered she was dead. When her husband came for her things, he asked what music she had been listening to. No one knew, so he said he would call the radio station. He had to know what music she had died to.

There was something else Shaul had been too tight to buy: new pajamas. That's what I'll do now, he told himself. I'll buy myself some new pajamas. He was tired of the old pajamas he had slept in for the last twenty years, starting when Ruti was alive. All of a sudden it occurred to him that he might buy a whole new wardrobe. He liked the idea. I'll spend every cent I've saved, he told himself. He could smell the drawer of the little desk in the corner near the kitchen where he kept all his bank statements. He was an expert at going through bank statements. More than once he had found mistakes in them and made the bank credit him with money it had charged him for. He knew all its tricks and could prove that he was right. Of course, they could always claim that it was a computer error, but he, who worked as a bookkeeper for the Electric Company, knew that computers never erred.

Noah returned with a new statue on his shoulder. He put it in the trunk of the car and went back to his saws. Shaul went over to shut the trunk and saw that this statue was missing its arms too. He looked around him. Noah was gone. The yard was burning hot. The cypresses were motionless. The air seemed almost solid. He thought he could feel little particles of sand falling from the sky. He thought of the words, "And as the sand on the sea shore." He couldn't recall where they came from. His head was in a whirl. They were putting one over on him again.

He ran his hand over the statue. It was exactly like the first one. The same breasts, the same bare belly, the same wrap around the waist, the same amputated arms. He went to the workshop, but Noah wasn't there. It was cooler there, because of the water. Maybe Noah had gone for a drink. He went to the office, but there was no one there either. He was thirsty. At least I'll get some cold water out of them, he thought. He opened the refrigerator, as though he were in his own kitchen, and poured himself some water from a bottle. A few water bottles and the bowl of bones were all there was in the refrigerator. Maybe the bones come from the missing arms, he thought. They cut them off and feed them to the dog.

The telephone rang. That's good, Shaul thought. Now Noah will have to come answer it. But no one came. He considered answering himself but thought: what do I care, it's none of my business. The telephone kept ringing. He stepped outside to get away from it, but the bell on the outer wall of the office rang even louder. I'd better go home, he thought, though it angered him to think he was being had. If I ever hear of anyone who wants to buy a statue, he told himself, I'll warn him not to do it here. He was sure they wouldn't give him his money back and he wanted to get even.

He picked up the receiver, which was sticky and stank of cigarettes. Just then, though, the phone stopped ringing. He went back outside and into the workshop. Noah still wasn't there. Where could he have gone to, Shaul wondered. He wanted to go home but thought, if I've waited this long, I might as well wait a little longer. How can I let them rip me off like this? The statue had cost him four hundred and fifty shekels. If the arms, he calculated, were a quarter of the body, he should get at least a hundred shekels back.

He thought of his son and daughter-in-law's surprise when he told them about the gravestone. After the ceremony, the two of them had stood talking in low tones. "He's going too far, your old man," he thought he heard her say. Once, he remembered, he had read an article in the newspaper about a judge who had granted two sons an injunction against their father, forbidding him to spend his savings without their permission, since part of the money was theirs by inheritance from their dead mother. He couldn't recall whether it had happened in Israel or in America. He had better consult a lawyer, he told himself. If he didn't take some action, his son and his wife might pull the same stunt on him.

The winter before her death Ruti had wanted to buy a wood-burning stove. She had always dreamed of having one. But when they added up the figures, it turned out to be uneconomical. A square meter of wood cost eighty shekels, and they would burn at least twice that much a month, not to mention the stove and chimney, which would run them one thousand two hundred shekels to buy and install. It was cheaper to heat with electricity. I'll buy a wood-burning stove this week, Shaul thought. He thought: what else can I spend money on?

The yard was deserted. If he waited any longer, the slabs of marble might disappear too, leaving him all alone with the cinderblock wall and the blue-flowering vine. The flowers looked like they had sunstroke. They need to be watered, he thought. No flower in his garden ever looked like that. He liked to water his garden. Once he had seen an American movie about an old man who watered his garden all day. The man's son had been sympathetic. Old people liked to water their gardens.

Noah was by his side. Shaul had no idea where he had come from. He looked around as if to find the place. Noah didn't say anything. He didn't seem to want anything, either. He must be waiting for a tip, Shaul thought. On the spur of the moment he took out his wallet and handed Noah ten shekels. Noah took them and stuck them in his pocket. Shaul looked at his pants and thought that someone should tell him that money could get lost that way. His wife might even put the pants in the wash without knowing the ten shekels were there. I'll bet he doesn't have a wife, Shaul thought. I'm sure of it.

He felt a wave of sorrow. He wanted to give Noah something else, but there was nothing to give. He had already given him twenty shekels and the statue was still without arms. Suddenly he remembered that he had some chewing gum. He offered Noah a stick. Noah took it, put it in his mouth and began chewing as if he had all day. He's waiting for me to leave, thought Shaul. Maybe they don't want strangers hanging around. Who knows what they're up to. It's a shady-looking place. He thought of the bones in the refrigerator.

Noah chewed the gum noisily. Shaul had never imagined you could make so much noise chewing gum. Noah's jaws made creaking sounds, as if they were fighting a war with some strange substance. Maybe he has false teeth and shouldn't be chewing gum at all, thought Shaul. He tried looking in Noah's mouth but could see nothing wrong with his teeth amid the commotion going on there. The tongue was large and hyperactive, revolving like the beater of a dough mixer in a bakery.

He certainly seemed to be enjoying himself. But who could say what the gum might do to him? All of a sudden he gagged and coughed and it flew out of his mouth. Shaul almost bent down to pick it up, but it was already lost in the white dust covering the yard.

"There's something wrong with the statue," Shaul said. He made a motion to Noah to follow him and showed him the missing arms. Noah did not seem impressed. People whose business was graves and tombstones were probably not surprised by anything. Who knew what might be inside a shroud? It could be all kinds of amputated, mutilated, limbless bodies. Maybe the woman who modeled for the statue had been in a car accident. Maybe working as a model was the only way she could support herself without arms.

In the end, though, Noah seemed to get it, because he strode off to the corner of the yard where the sculptures stood. Shaul knew enough to follow him without being told. Noah pointed to some more female statues. They were all the same. None had arms. The lions and the cherubs had all their limbs intact. Noah kept walking with Shaul at his heels. At the far end of the yard, by some sacks of white cement, stood the molds. Noah pointed to one of a woman. Shaul saw that it had no arms either. Noah pointed to some lettering on it that said "Venus."

Shaul felt mollified. So he hadn't been cheated after all. This was how the mold came from Italy. It hadn't been nice of him to suspect Noah. How can I make it up to him, he wondered. He offered him another stick of chewing gum. Noah suddenly smiled and Shaul felt his eyes tear with happiness. It was embarrassing to cry in front of a worker in a marble factory.

He pretended to have dust in his eyes. He rubbed them with both hands and wiped them with a tissue that he took from his pocket. When he opened them, Noah was gone. He should go home at once, Shaul thought, before he made an even bigger fool of himself. He peeked into the workshop. Noah wasn't there. Shaul got into his car and drove off. The road was rutted and each time he hit a bump he heard the statue bang against the trunk. Now something will break for sure, he cursed himself, maybe even the breasts. He should never have brought the statue back with him. He could have straightened things out without it. He was certain that it was the breasts that were broken, because they were the part that stuck out. What good was a statue that had no arms or breasts?

He looked for a place to pull over and check the damage, but the traffic was too heavy. Suppose I didn't feel well, he thought, what would I do then? He had read in the papers about drivers with heart failure who ran into some tree or electric pole. One even ran over a child. I must see a doctor about my chest pains, he told himself. Though he had never smoked and had kept away in recent years from fatty meats and yellow cheese, the pains persisted. He would go see a doctor.

Ever since Ruti's death he had avoided the street where their health clinic was. He could still remember the sharp, medicinal odors each time he had gone to get her drugs. The director of the clinic, Shimshon Halevi, would step out of his office when he saw him through its glass door and engage him in loud and lengthy conversation despite the protests of those waiting in line to see him. "Well, now, how's our Ruti?" he would ask. Everything was always our this or our that with him. The impatience of the people in line slowly turned to sympathy and interest, for Shimshon knew all about Ruti's illness and talked about it at the top of his voice because he was partially deaf. The yellow hearing aid that was stuck behind his ear like a wart hardly helped him at all. He wouldn't leave Shaul alone and even walked him to the pharmacy window to make sure he was served without waiting, as if he rather than Ruti were the patient, jabbing him all the while in the chest and reminding him that he, Shimshon, had gotten Ruti the best place in the best hospital, where she was treated by the best professor. Our Ruti.

Ruti herself put up with it with a weary smile on her wan face, which had dark blotches under the eyes. Shimshon, it appeared, had been a year ahead of her in high school and had even courted her. He was no different then, a big talker. For a whole evening, on a bench in the burned copse at the end of the neighborhood, he had done nothing but tell her about his future. Even then, at the age of sixteen, he had it all figured out. And, in fact, it worked out just as he had planned. "With a few minor adjustments," snickered Ruti, who felt that her illness allowed her to be ironic toward everyone. "He was going to be an ambassador in the Foreign Office, a roving politician like one of his uncles, who was a consul in America. He was going to marry a rich woman when he was thirty. He was going to have three sons and a daughter. And it all came true, except that he married Malkaleh from our class when he was twenty one because she was pregnant and her parents wouldn't agree to an abortion, and went to work as a clerk at the health clinic – just for a few years, of course, until he found a better place – and had four daughters and no sons."

"Did he propose to you?" asked Shaul.

"You mean I never told you?" answered Ruti after a painful fit of coughing. "That's all I needed, to marry someone like him!"

Shaul took it as a compliment, though later it struck him that being chosen over Shimshon was nothing to brag about. Still, he had to admit that his own hearing was perfect. He couldn't stop thinking about Shimshon's hearing aid. And that loud, bossy voice of his. Shaul didn't like noisy people. Or demanding ones.

Now, though, he would need Shimshon's help again if he wasn't to have to wait in line for an appointment with a heart specialist. He needed a thorough checkup. It wasn't just the pain. His pulse was sometimes irregular too. And out of sheer habit Shimshon was liable to ask him "How is our Ruti?" as he had already done several times since her death before apologizing at the top of his voice and talking on and on, as if in atonement for his error, while everyone sat there listening.

In the end Shaul stopped at a gas station. He got out of his car, opened the trunk, and checked the statue. It was all right. When he was about to start out again, he noticed that he had a flat tire. In fact, it had already been low when he parked by the air pump and now it was even lower. He was grateful that it had happened in a gas station. He walked over to the tire shop next door, but it was closed, and so he walked back to the gas station attendant, who told him with a grin that the tire fixer had the mumps. He had caught it from his son. The reason it was so funny was that when a grown man got the mumps his balls blew up like balloons.

Someone who wanted to fill his tires honked at Shaul because his car was blocking the pump. When he came over to move it he saw that the car that was honking was decorated with flowers and bright ribbons. A bride and groom were sitting in the back. He headed for the diner, feeling a pressure in his chest. The driver of the wedding car was kneeling by a tire with the air hose. His shirt had come out of his pants, revealing a hairy back and the top of the slit in his behind.

Shaul leaned through the window and said, "Congratulations," but the newlyweds were busy necking. The man's hand was under the woman's dress. Shaul backed off embarrassedly, bumping into the man with the air hose. "Why don't you watch where you're going?" asked the man. "Isn't one pair of glasses enough for you, you fag, you?"

The pain in his chest was growing worse. He apologized and went to the diner, where he sat at a table by the window from which he could keep an eye on his car. He ordered a Diet Coke. Drinking something low-cal, he thought, would be good for the pain in his chest.

The waitress came with a Coke bottle in one hand and a green rag in the other to wipe the table. A small french fry fell on Shaul's pants and left a greasy stain. "It's nothing," he said. "My wife will get it out." He had already begun drinking the Coke when he realized what he had said. He wanted to call the waitress over to tell her that his wife was dead. Even when she was alive he had never talked about her that way. She was always his "best friend and life companion."

The waitress saw him looking for her and came over to ask him what he wanted. Though he didn't want anything, he asked for a slice of lemon to keep her from thinking that he was making eyes at her. He watched her hips as she went off. When she brought him the lemon he watched her bare shoulders. She was wearing a tank top that hung by two thin strings. She had a nice neck.

How can her parents allow her to work in a place like this, Shaul thought. It draws all kinds of people. He felt sorry for her. If I had a daughter her age, he told himself, I'd try to find her different work. He decided to stop by the diner regularly to check up on her. After I come a few times, she'll recognize me, he thought. He liked the thought of her coming over to take his order the minute he walked in. "I'll have the usual," he would say, and she would know exactly what that was.

He left her an especially big tip and waited to see her reaction, highly pleased with himself when she thanked him with a broad smile. He wanted to tell her that he would come again but didn't. Back at his car, he remembered that it had a flat tire. When he opened his trunk to take out the jack and spare tire, he remembered that he had wanted to check the statue. It was in fine condition. He began to crank up the car, surprised by how easy it was. But the wheel bolts were hard to free and he began to perspire. Maybe the waitress was watching him from the air-conditioned diner. It was a nice thought. He changed the tire. An attendant from the gas station came over to help him, but he was already done. The attendant stood looking at the trunk. "How much was she?" he asked, pointing at the statue. Shaul was embarrassed to say four hundred and fifty shekels. "Two hundred," he said.

The man whistled. "That's a steal," he said. "It's a real nice statue. But what'll your wife say?"

"Why should she say anything?" asked Shaul, putting the flat tire in the trunk.

"If I brought a naked lady like that home with me, my wife would show the two of us the door," said the attendant.

Shaul looked at him. He felt sorry for the man because he was fat, with a paunch that stuck out of his pants and made his greasy shirt bulge. "Not me," he said. "My wife doesn't give me any back talk."

"How about that!" said the man. "I guess you have to show them who's boss."

Shaul shut the trunk and thanked him for offering to help. The attendant went back to the gas station. Shaul checked his gas gauge and decided to top up his tank, even though it was already half full.

When he pulled up at a pump he saw that the attendant was working a different one. He wished it were this one. When his tank was filled he drove off. As soon as he did he thought of what he had said to the attendant. My God, what's happening to me, he thought. How could I have said such a thing about Ruti when she's dead?

It was a big relief to get home. He felt as if he had completed a dangerous mission and returned safely to base. The little house in the suburbs of the big city, which he and Ruti had bought a few years after they were married, had not changed over the years. Neither had the street. The cheap red concrete tiles on the roofs of the small houses had all faded to the same grimy pink and were overgrown with yellowish-green moss. Pigeons nested in the eaves. At night you could hear mice scurrying on the roof and dislodging little pebbles onto the plaster ceiling. Some of the houses were half hidden by trees that had been small or not yet planted when they moved in. Now the whole street was green. Every evening you could hear the whir of sprinklers. On Saturday mornings there was a chatter of lawn mowers.

His son's old swing still dangled from the large medlar tree that stood by the back door, which led from the kitchen to the shed. A tricycle lay among the bushes and weeds growing wild in the backyard.

The inhabitants of the street all knew each other. When someone died, everyone missed that person. Several of the houses were lived in by widows or widowers like Shaul. Sometimes people would still say, "Let's go to Shaul and Ruti's." Ruti had made a delicious jam from the guavas that grew in their yard and everyone still called it "Ruti's jam."

He left the car by the house and went inside for a drink. It was Ruti who had put him in the habit of always drinking a glass of water before working in the garden. When he tried turning the key in the latch, he discovered that the door was open. His heart skipped a beat. Lately there had been several burglaries in the neighborhood. He stepped back into the street and surveyed the house for signs of having been broken into. A hole in the wall perhaps, or a broken window pane. But everything looked the way he had left it. Slowly he approached the door and opened it. You could hear a pin drop inside. He peered into the living room. If the television is still there, he thought, that means that everything's all right. The television was there. But then he thought: who would take an old television like that anyway? He glanced at the kitchen. Nothing had been touched there either. The frightening thought crossed his mind that perhaps the burglars hadn't found anything worth taking. When that happened they took their revenge by doing things like defacing paintings or defecating on the rugs. Carefully he peered into each room, but everything seemed normal. He tried sniffing the air to see if it smelled different. It didn't. Everything was the same.

A chill ran down his spine. Was Ruti in the house? He shivered, feeling as though a fine black scarf were covering his eyes. As though he were sinking and had nothing to catch hold of. At the last second he grabbed the edge of the dining table and collapsed into a chair. His heart was pounding. His body was drenched in sweat.

A few minutes passed. The silence was deafening. He heard a cat clamber up the trunk of the avocado tree in the yard. The pleasantly crisp sound of its claws digging into the gray bark restored him to his senses. He looked out the window. The cat, which was already in the top branches, was now backing down in reverse. He smiled. Dumb cat, he thought.

Maybe I just forgot to lock the door, he told himself. The thought was so welcome that it convinced him. I'm becoming forgetful, he decided. Far from feeling anguished by it, he felt as if he were floating on a current of soft water. I should make myself reminders, he thought. Perhaps leave little notes on the refrigerator. Since Ruti died there were no more notes there telling him to buy eggs, or baking powder, or cinnamon, or two kilos of sugar. That's what I'll do, he thought. He thought: from now on I'll do what I can to make my life easier.

The telephone rang. It was his son's wife, calling to ask how he was. He knew she really wanted to talk to him about the cost of the gravestone. Had he made up his mind? she asked. A friend at work had told her a while ago that she had shopped around in connection with her parents' gravestone and that the sky was the limit. Everyone took whatever they thought they could get. After all, it wasn't a question of gold or silver, just of plain stone. They sent some Arab with a chisel or a power tool and in five minutes he was done. Why should it cost so much money? In the end her friend had found someone who did it at half price and only asked for part of the payment down. It wasn't the money that bothered them, said his son's wife. It was the principle. The men must have seen that Shaul was an intellectual type who didn't know the first thing about gravestones and charged him a ridiculous sum. Two hundred and fifty shekels was a lot of money. They themselves had to buy a new washing machine and couldn't decide between two models, because one was one hundred shekels less than the other, though the more expensive one was better and was guaranteed for ten years against rust.

"I'm sorry," said Shaul. "I've already settled on a price with them and tomorrow they're beginning work on it." He felt that he had almost said, "work on Ruti."

He debated mentioning the statue and decided against it. Let them find out on their next visit. Shaul wondered what his son would say when he saw a naked woman in the garden. Not that it mattered to him one bit. Hadn't he made up his mind to start thinking of himself? "Well, goodbye, and say hello to Baruch," he told his son's wife, hanging up with a determination that he had never known himself to possess. It wasn't easy to cut short a conversation with her. As soon as she got him on the phone she started in on him from every angle, running circles around him until she got what she wanted.

When he stepped back outside the sun had already sunk behind the large pecan tree in his neighbor's yard across the street. The birds that had hopped among its branches all day were gone. It was so quiet that you could hear the leaves swish in the breeze that came from the sea. His avocado tree, whose leaves were bigger, had also come to life and was rustling noisily, as if someone were turning the pages of a big book.

It was pleasantly cool out. Shaul was glad he wouldn't have to sweat when he dragged the statue from the car. He was glad the sky was a dark blue like the sea, with a few frilly pink clouds in it.

Shaul opened the car trunk and tried lifting the statue. Yet though he remembered how easily Noah had done it, the woman was heavy. If I'm not careful, he thought, I'll throw my back out. It had happened to him a year ago when he was mowing the lawn. He had lain in bed for two weeks, attended by his son and daughter-in-law. Anything but that again, he thought. He tried carefully lifting the statue, which was not very large but was solidly made. He glanced up the street to see if there was anyone to help him. He wished Noah were there. He actually missed him. He thought of his solidity, his boots, his helpfulness, his servility. Did he have some secret that he was keeping to himself? What a thought! Why should he have a secret? He was a simple fellow, perhaps even retarded. But that was a mean thing to think. There was nothing retarded-looking about him. Did you have to be feebleminded to keep your mouth shut and do what you were told?

It occurred to him to bring the wheelbarrow from the garden. He wheeled it up to the car and slowly began maneuvering the statue into it. Afraid the paint of the car might get scratched, he set the statue down and spread an old blanket over the edge of the trunk. Then he went back to work, feeling the effort. His heart began to beat quicker but he was determined not to stop. He glanced up the street again to see if anyone was standing there. Suddenly he felt embarrassed.

It took a few minutes to get the statue into the wheelbarrow. Shaul felt proud of himself. He steered the wheelbarrow to a place on the front lawn that was hidden from the street by a hedge of myrtle bushes. It was Ruti who had insisted on myrtle bushes, and more than once he was thankful that she had. Whenever he touched their leaves he was enveloped by a fresh fragrance. The bushes were still small when Ruti died. How she had loved them.

It was getting dark out. He was glad that no one would see him. Where should I stand the statue? he thought. He decided to put it in the middle of the lawn, right in front of the house. He would dig a small hole and stand the statue in it. He went to look for the hoe. Why did it always disappear when you wanted it? He tried remembering where he had left it. Most likely in the backyard, by the laundry line.

When he got there, though, it was dark. He had kept meaning to change the light bulb on the shed but hadn't done it. He squinted into the dim light, which was getting thicker and thicker. He tripped over the sprinkler. A sharp pain pierced his leg and something sticky ran over it. He waited a few minutes for his eyes to get used to the darkness. Now he could make out shapes. Shadows. Bushes. The laundry poles with their wires and clothespins. A few pairs of socks that he had washed by hand. He never gave his socks to the laundry with the rest of his clothes. The hoe wasn't there, though many other long-forgotten things were. The entrance to the bomb shelter looming out of the earth beneath the climbing vine that had covered it. The pile of large bricks that he had bought to build Ruti a kiln. He had always been so good to her, had always tried to give her everything she wanted. When she fell ill he had frantically tried to make her dreams come true in the time she had left. She had always wanted her own kiln. And even though she was sick, she could still make figurines and bowls. It was important for her to feel useful despite her condition. She didn't like it when he felt like making love. She couldn't cope with it.

For a second it seemed that the darkness surrounding him was not just the darkness of the night. He was afraid of what he might see if he turned around. I'm going under, he told himself. He couldn't move.

A cat brushed against his legs. He wished the furry feel of it would last longer. Cats usually die by the time they're twelve, he thought. That meant that this cat didn't remember Ruti. He was glad of it.

He bent down to pet the cat but it was already gone. He could hear it crunch over the dry mulberry leaves that were left over from last winter by the back fence. They're so fragile, he thought. The cat is so small.

He turned around. His lit-up house looked like a bright castle, full of life and gaiety. I'll look for the hoe tomorrow, he thought. When he went inside he saw that his leg was bleeding from the sprinkler. He hadn't had a cut like that or seen his own blood in a long while. He cleaned the wound and put a band-aid on it. He returned to the front lawn. The nude woman was a forlorn sight lying on her side in the rusty old wheelbarrow. He decided to stand her up without the hoe. He would firm her up with it in the morning if he had to. He slowly eased her onto the lawn and went back into the house.

He made himself supper. He was used to eating supper by himself. Breakfast and lunch he ate in the cafeteria at work. It was noisy and full of steamy, sticky smells but the prices were subsidized and most of the employees ate there.

Usually he made himself a salad, added some cheese and olives, and ate it while watching TV. Tonight, though, he didn't have the patience. He wanted to have another look at the statue. He spread some margarine on a piece of bread, took a tomato, and went out to the easy chair on the porch. He switched off the fluorescent light so as not to attract mosquitoes, and put his feet up on the little stool. It was nice out. He thought of the day. It had been different from all the other days. He felt that he had done a great deal. He felt very pleased with himself. He thought of how surprised his son's wife would be to see the statue. He remembered the look on her face when she heard what the gravestone had cost. He could read her mind. Like the time he had taken a vacation in a hotel and she was dying to ask him the price of the room.

He felt a momentary panic. In one day he had managed to spend nearly a thousand shekels. It was a menacing sum. Maybe I overdid it, he told himself. Take the gravestone. I should just have had it polished. Who needed to have the letters cast in lead? The worst that could happen is that five years from now it would need to be polished and painted again. It still wouldn't cost what I'm paying now. And then the statue. How do I even know it's a good one? He looked at the nude woman. Her back was turned to him and her breasts were pointing at the myrtles. What am I doing with a naked woman on my lawn? he thought.

He shut his eyes. When he opened them, he told himself, everything will be the way it was. But when he opened them the statue was still there. The white of its back sent a chill through him. Four hundred and fifty shekels he thought. Isn't that a bit steep?

A mosquito was buzzing around him. He tried driving it off. He felt restless. Maybe I'll try returning it in the morning, he thought. He went back to the kitchen. He washed the dishes while looking out of the window. The statue was still on the lawn, a white shape in the darkness. He went back outside. The air had a chill dampness from the orange groves at the end of the neighborhood. He ran his hand over the statue, feeling the pleasant smoothness of its female curves. He shivered. A distant, forgotten sensation passed quickly through him, like a snake in the grass. I'm going crazy, he told himself. I'm going crazy.

A plane droned far off in the sky. He watched its lights blink. He stared in surprise at the stars, as if he had never seen them before. I'd better stop going to synagogue like some senile old man, he told himself. What's happening to me? Am I afraid of dying?

He had often told himself that death was nothing to be afraid of. Ruti, despite her pain and suffering, was afraid of it. He hadn't thought of it all these years. Why should he suddenly think of it now? He looked irritably at the statue. The prudish way it turned its back on him made him angry. He reached out and turned it around, so that the woman's breasts were pointing at the house. I paid a fortune for you, he whispered. You might at least let me enjoy your breasts.

As he was watching the nightly movie on TV his heart began to act up. Keep calm, keep calm, he told himself. Perhaps I should call my son, he thought. The words "my son" seemed strange to him, like an unfamiliar vegetable in his salad instead of the usual cucumber. Maybe I'm one of those people who watch everyone around them die and live forever, he thought. I'll have to be hacked to death. The thought that he might be immortal whittled away at him like a blunt old knife. Still, the statue in the garden would outlive him. Maybe I should give instructions in my will for it to be put on my grave, he thought. He thought of the family that would buy the house when he died. They would look at the statue and say, what a dirty old man that must have been. Who knows what orgies went on in this house. He felt that he was looking at the women in the movie as he hadn't looked at women for years. Tomorrow morning I'll go downtown, he told himself. I'll be among people, among women. All of a sudden he would have liked to have a woman by his side. He thought of old Tanhum who lived down the street. His wife died when he was seventy four and a month later he married a woman he met while shopping for vegetables. Even though she turned out to be a kleptomaniac and he had to run from one store to another all day long to see what she had stolen, he refused to part with her. Even when she turned out to be a pyromaniac too and burned down the shed in his yard with a washing machine inside, he smiled tolerantly and said in Yiddish, *Hot a yid a veibele, hot a yid sakh tsoris, hot er nisht a veibele, toyg nisht fun kaporis.* That meant that while a wife was a headache, having no wife was worse.

What am I thinking about, what am I thinking about? Shaul asked himself. That's the kind of story you read about in the newspapers. He wondered what he would have to do to be written up in the newspapers himself. It would have to involve a lot of cash, or be terribly bloody or passionate. He wasn't like that. With him everything came in small change, and even that was becoming funny money. He stared enviously at the men on TV with their good-looking, well-mannered wives. He even stared hungrily at the female broadcaster on the evening news. He felt sorry when the news was over.

Before getting into bed he took a pill prescribed by the doctor for his pulse. Soon he felt himself grow calm. He lay on his back, looking up at the sky through the open shutter. Sprinklers whirred far away, beyond the orange groves. An owl screeched in the avocado tree. Here goes another night, he thought. When he had been a new recruit in the army, he remembered, his platoon had once gotten lost on a night navigation exercise. Their CO became jittery. Instead of acting cool and nonchalant, he couldn't hide his agitation. Each angry outburst of his only made the soldiers grin more. He ordered them all to sit down and look at the sky, but it was too overcast to see the North Star. Though he had a compass, he was only supposed to use it in emergencies and to report doing so on returning to the base. Naturally, that lowered the platoon's score and made it almost certain to flunk. The sky kept growing cloudier. A cold wind blew. It looked about to rain. One of the soldiers promised the CO on behalf of the whole platoon that no one would tell on him if he used the compass. That only made him angrier, but after a few minutes, when the wind got colder and the offer was repeated, he agreed. Half an hour later they were on the main road, and an hour later, back on base.

Shaul tried to remember if the CO had been found out but couldn't. It had happened such a long time ago. He pictured himself in uniform, his face young and tan, a rifle in one hand. That's when he had met Ruti, at a bus station. He tried picturing her too, her hair done up in a little bun on her neck beneath her beret. He thought of her army shirt, so rough and stiff to the touch.

He could feel himself growing drowsy. In the morning I'll take another look at the statue and decide whether to return it, he told himself. He tried picturing Noah, but all he saw was a faint transparent figure, a pile of clothing suspended in midair. The dog was laughing at him. It offered him some cold water.

When he was wakened by the sunlight in the morning he saw that he had forgotten to close the shutter and the screen the night before. It was a quarter to six. He was full of mosquito bites. He closed the screen to keep out the flies and unsuccessfully tried going back to sleep. He got out of bed, made himself some coffee, and sat down with it on the porch. The naked woman was wet with dew. Maybe I should cover her at night with a blanket or a sheet of plastic, he thought. But the coffee tasted good and his worries seemed far away. He loved the tang of it, even though the doctor had warned him that the caffeine could kill him. The birds were chirping away. A clear tarpaulin of dewdrops sparkled crisply on the grass. I'll keep the statue, he thought. I wouldn't take a thousand shekels for it.

Ehud Ben-Ezer

Madame Umm-el-Tach and Her Daughters

Translated by Chaya Amir

It happened during the Great War, at the time of the expulsions from Jaffa. Among the refugees who reached Petah Tikva was a family whose behavior so mortified the settlers that the local committee decided to banish them from the colony, an act that was – from a formal point of view – against all reason, considering that Turkish officials were among the most constant visitors to their home.

The head of the family, Reb Yankel Hirsch, a wagoner, was a Jew of small stature: dark, gaunt and trim of beard, quick in mind and body, and his strength lay in his powerful head. It was said that he could break a bottle by hitting it with his head, and this exceptional quality had stood him in good stead when he came to blows with the Arab draymen in the marketplace. He could injure them with a single whack of his head. And if one of his horses stubbornly refused to pull the wagon up the steep incline at Bab-el-Wad, Reb Yankel would get down, pound it with his fists and shout:

"Oder gey oder payger! – either get moving or you're dead!"

For many years Reb Yankel had owned a *tandah*, a wagon outfitted out with two benches, one on either side, which was usually jam-packed with passengers and bundles. He would take people from Jaffa to Jerusalem at night, stopping for an hour at Bab-el-Wad so that the passengers could rest a little, and the horses catch their breath before the big haul up. There was an inn of sorts there, whose owner – known as Shloymele Babelwader – would force each passenger to drink a small cup of bitter black coffee without sugar, and pay a kind of tax. Whoever remained seated in the wagon, refusing to get down and drink his cup of coffee, got it spilled all over his trousers and shoes by the Babelwader's servants, Arabs of course, who would then demand payment even more insistently, so that the passengers had no choice but to pay.

One night, after a particularly disagreeable squabble with the innkeeper's helpers who had insulted and humiliated one of his female passengers, Reb Yankel, his head on fire and not from wine, was vainly urging the horses up the miserable Bab-el-Wad road, which was sown with rocks and pebbles. Climbing down, he went towards the horses with his last *"Oder gey oder payger,"* and as he was about to return to his lofty seat – the passengers in the wagon behind him were groaning, crushed and crippled by the journey in the pitch dark – one of the horses kicked him, knocking him off his feet. As he fell, Reb Yankel broke his back.

From this point on the family's fortunes declined. War, locusts, famine. Reb Yankel let his beard grow. He would hobble on his crutches over to the ramshackle synagogue and back again, spending most of his waking hours in bed. His wife and daughters – either because of their wretchedness and poverty or, perhaps, their sudden sense of newfound freedom after his enfeeblement, since he could no longer use his whip on them at home or strike his wife with his head when she disobeyed him – at all events, his wife and daughters began to fend for themselves.

First the mother, a woman of prodigious proportions, whose head was always devoutly covered with a babushka and who added "God willing!" to every sentence she uttered. She herself and her specialty – fish cooked in onions and vinegar – became famous among the Turkish policemen in Jaffa, and later among the *shawishes*, the *zabets*, the *effendis* and the *beys*, in short almost everyone. And it was said of her bottom that two tugboats were needed to bring her ashore when she first arrived in Jaffa, and that one of the Arab boatmen was actually blown into the stormy sea by the great blast of wind that broke from her in her fright, and that it was only by luck that he was saved because at that very moment an absolute calm miraculously descended on the sea – and from then on she was affectionately known as Umm-el-Tach, or Mamma Boom-Boom.

The daughters, Havka the elder, thin and dark like her father, and Duba, the younger, taller and broader, pleasingly plump and fair-skinned, soon followed in their mother's footsteps, entertaining the *shawishas.* the *mudirs,* and the *effendis:* the younger one would giggle, while the elder, a frown on her dark brow, poured wine down their throats. The younger one would dance in a short robe while the older marked time on a tambourine, singing in a low husky voice. Then they would make themselves comfortable on their guests' knees, tickling their mustaches, pulling at their beards, and eventually surrendering themselves – the plump girl with a winning smile, the thin one with provocative pique. And it was hardly a year before both girls lost their innocence. Perhaps it was out of cunning that they waited at all, hoping that their value would rise, waiting for the highest bidder. Perhaps they still harbored a faint hope that one day they would turn over a new leaf, find a decent husband and put war, poverty, illness and sin behind them. But after a year had passed and nothing had changed, and the famine grew even worse, the two sisters allowed the circumcised knaves to come and take them.

Reb Yankel Hirsch, dumped like a mangled tomcat in one of the back rooms, saw it all with protesting eyes. And when he howled, coughing because of the *nargila* smoke which was choking his bleeding lungs, his room was bolted with a heavy bar. He was no longer able to hobble over to the synagogue, and kind-hearted Duba who used to carry him there on her broad shoulder was no longer in his good graces: he had discovered beyond question – hearing her muffled laughter at night – that she too was a loose woman.

One morning his wife appeared, her eyes red, her head covered and her whole body shamelessly flaccid. And when she emitted her standard "God willing!" as she did whenever she laid eyes upon him, the miserable, misshapen bag of bones let loose a stream of invective, including choice expletives from both the Torah and the Suk-el-Khan,

the marketplace where the wagons awaited their passengers next to the
Sha'aria, the Turkish government house. Enraged, he screamed at her:
"In my worst nightmares I never imagined that I married a *sharmuta*,
a whore, an Umm-el-Sharmuten – you ass peddler you... you greedy
abomination... you slut... begetter of devilish she-goats... hellfires are
burning in you... I spit on you... God willing, may you burn in hell..."

When Madame Umm-el-Tach, the wife of Reb Yankel Hirsch,
heard all this, she turned her back to him and pulled up her skirts,
revealing the whiteness of her two great bumboats, as if wishing to
express her opinion of him. The cripple was overwhelmed with fury
and tried to hurl his crutch at her, aiming at that vulnerable spot which
had just been spread open at him. By habit, he thrust his head forward
to strike his enemy – and fell, his head and his crutch smashing
against the floor at the same time. Reb Yankel died, shattered, beneath
his wife's posterior.

He was buried in the new cemetery, at the top of a sand dune in the
north of the city, and his tombstone is still there, overlooking the
graves of the nation's founders. And on it is inscribed:

> *Here lies Reb Yankel Hirsch,*
> *An honest wagoner*
> *How terrible was his fall.*
> *And when the dead shall arise,*
> *He shall drive his horses*
> *And Elijah the prophet shall stand by his side.*

After the death of the shattered Reb Yankel, the wagoner, his wife and
daughters became as riotous as they pleased. They had nights of
laughter and merriment when, at the request of Araf Bek-el-Ar'san,
Jaffa's crippled chief of police – who was from a Bedouin tribe near
Beisan – the daughters laid him on the large bed and beat his bare
buttocks with their father Reb Yankel's whip, Havka plying the whip
and Duba singing, to the tune of a Turkish military march, words she
had heard her father shout at his hungry horses: *"Stana ya kadish* – if
this horny, perspiring, club-footed corrupt stallion will wait, his ass

will bloom with grass – ha, ha, ha – furrows of blood will grow all over him in revenge on the *goyim*" – the whip whistles – "*Stana ya kadish – Ta yitla il-hashish!*"[1] – she sings as she prances around with her plump feet on the clean floor.

And Araf Bek moans and then moans again, and afterwards he washes himself in the prescribed ritual manner, asks for a *nargila* and for a dish of fish cooked in onions and vinegar by Madame Hirsch Umm-el-Tach, now wearing a red turban in place of the babushka. He pinches her bumboats and leaves the women a gift of cash, most probably from the bribes he received earlier that day from the headmen of the Jewish colonies. led by Moshe Pinchasovitch of Petah Tikva, to redeem some deserters from their colony from military duty in the Turkish army, or in place of a number of horses and wagons for *shukra*, the expropriation of vehicles for use against the British.

But they suffered nights of pain and fear when their guest was Hassan Bek Basri-el-Jabi, Jaffa's military governor, who would pace up and down the room in his riding boots and uniform, waving his elegant horsewhip at them, a whip which ended in a tuft of hair, and spewing abominations about the lewdness of the daughters of Israel and their love of fornication; and about the virility of the Ottoman Empire of which he was the embodiment. Sometimes he would strike them and treat them roughly in bed, and only the younger girl, Duba, could sometimes manage to soothe him when he was made pliant by the wine. Then, with the tears running down his beard, he would sport with her on his knee and allow her to play with the red turban wound around his head and tell her that she reminded him of his daughter. But then suddenly he would rise up again like a lion and assault her mother.

One evening a great honor was granted the two sisters and they were invited, at the suggestion of Hassan Bek, to a feast at the home of General Ahmed Jemal Pasha, the military governor of Syria and Palestine, who had led a Turkish expeditionary force against the Suez Canal in 1915. He was stopped by the guns mounted on the British battleships cruising up and down the Canal, waiting for the arrival of

---

1. Arabic: "Wait, you mule, till the grass grows."

his forces who came equipped with landing crafts, loaded on the backs of camels. He sent a *hantour*, a carriage covered by black canvas and drawn by two horses, to fetch them, and they went veiled so that they would not be recognized as Jewesses. And after the feast they awaited his summons, first the one, then the other, then one first and then again the other, spending the interludes in the general's anteroom, refreshing themselves with lemonade and baklava until his excellency exhausted himself and fell asleep. From then on, during his sojourns in the town he would send for them, particularly for the older sister, dark Havka, who was the educated one in the family and knew some French; and he would tell her of the days of the young Turks and of his comrades, Enver Pasha and Talat Pasha, and how they became the leaders of the Ottoman Empire. He would boast in front of her, but his moods were volatile: once he promised the best of everything to the hard-working Jews, especially those he saw in the agricultural colonies; at other times he would threaten to resettle them all in Anatolia, in the abandoned villages of the Armenians he had recently butchered. Then he would fall on her in a rage, uttering words in Turkish whose meaning she could not even imagine...

And how did the Jews of Jaffa react to these goings-on? Had these been ordinary times, they would probably have excommunicated them, projecting volleys of imprecations at them and forcing them to take their valuable selves back across the sea to live in comfort in the "appropriate" districts of Warsaw, in Krochmalna Street or Samotcha Street, or far off in South America, in the Jewish whorehouses of Buenos Aires, places fit for them and their kind, but – alack, alas – because of the famine and the poverty the three women were not alone in following this brazen profession: the scourge had spread and afflicted other respectable Jewish households, and not only in Jaffa but also, even more so, in the holy city of Jerusalem, woe to the eyes that behold what the ears have heard!

Furthermore, a not-insignificant number of Jews even harbored hopes that certain benefits might accrue to them from the close association of Madame Umm-el-Tach and her daughters with the *shawishes*, the *zabets*, the *beys*, the *beks* and the *kaymakams*, the commandants, the satraps, the mudirs, the mutzartarifs and the Turkish pashas, that maybe by virtue of the women's merits, the Turks would show mercy to the helpless Jewish community and, as their sister Queen Esther had done in her time, they too would be able to soften the harsh decrees. Others chose to see in them a reincarnation of Jael the wife of Heber the Kenite, and hoped that if Hassan Bek choked to death on a bone from one of the fish that Umm-el-Tach cooked and her daughters served him while he was drunk – the Jews would be saved from his cruel edicts.

But in the spring of 1917, when the order was issued to expel the Jews from Jaffa, the three women were not only helpless to change it, they were no exception to its provisions. All three were loaded into a carriage appropriated especially for them and taken, with all due respect, to Petah Tikva. There they were given – on direct orders from Yassin Bek, the Turkish governor of the colony, who took them under his wing – one of the more splendid houses, and it immediately became a Mecca for Yassin Bek himself and for the Turkish government officials who were soon constant visitors. Even the great general, Ahmed Jemal Pasha, would arrive late in the evening on horseback with his entourage, and his adjutant would remove fresh fish from the intricately woven, fringed and tasseled woolen saddlebags – fresh fish, caught that very day in Jaffa despite the fact that the Arab fishermen were prohibited by law from going out to sea because of the British battleships cruising the area, firing their cannons, besieging the city, and spying out the country.

Madame Umm-el-Tach Hirsch would stand, God willing, in one room and cook the fish in onions and vinegar, and the smell would spread through the entire colony, filled with thousands of refugees from Jaffa and Tel Aviv, while General Pasha sat in the other room, the fair Duba in her chemise on his knee, drawing her plump fingers through his square beard, the dark Havka talking to him in French of books they had both read, her eyes shooting sparks of provocation. Afterwards Duba would feed him the hot fish her mother had cooked, separating the white flesh from the bones and wiping his beard with her chemise, while Havka softly sang marches played by the Turkish military band of Jaffa in her husky voice, repressing her jealousy: *Stana ya kadish, ta yitla el-hashish*, until the general sent the two sisters from the room, and finished off his dinner on the mother herself, messing up her babushka, borne on her undulating bumboats as if she were a mare from his days as minister of the Turkish navy, trapped helplessly in the Sea of Marmara, unable to move. Four or five of his men would stand outside, holding in their laughter as they listened to the muffled titters from within, and when silence fell on the supreme command and reverberations of the great Ahmed Jemal Pasha's powerful snoring shook the walls, they would take off silently, like shadows, to the room lit only by a smoky oil lamp to enjoy General Pasha's leftovers from the fish and the Jewesses. One would take the dark fish, another the fair one, while two or three would climb on Madame Umm-God-willing to insert the mast in her surging billows.

All that summer and autumn the colony seethed. There had never been such a scandal. A number of young men, members of the Radical National Club, whose dignity had been sorely offended, decided that the women must be expelled, come what may. And to give the idea even more weight, they decided to interest the village elders in their project. They approached a few of them and explained the matter, but to no avail. All those who held power in the colony had their own excuses. There were those who suggested renting them a house on the threshing floor beyond the pale of the colony! Indeed, fear of their patrons, the Turks, hung heavily over the village elders.

The young men almost gave up hope of involving the elders, without whose agreement they dared do nothing lest the colony be punished and the inhabitants made to suffer. Finally, they paid a visit to Reb Mordechai and explained the reasons for their visit. A few years earlier there had been a great feud in the colony between the younger generation and the veterans. The young faction was led by the village doctor and Zionist activist, Dr. Jacob Bernstein-Cohen, who wanted to improve the life of the colony by rebuilding it on healthier foundations. The local committee, made up entirely of veterans, obstructed him at every turn. When he determined to renovate the schools because hygienic standards were low and the children were suffering from trachoma, and he began lecturing the teachers and a large audience of young people on hygiene, with the help of a magic lantern, the committee rose up in arms, especially the Orthodox Jews who claimed that the doctor had assembled the young people, boys and girls together, and turned off the lights to show them pornographic pictures, after which they all sang indecent songs. When he tried to organize a mobile unit of young women to provide medical aid where necessary – the committee claimed that it was a sin to expose the men to temptation by having young girls look into their eyes. It was tantamount to sexual provocation. And why should the doctor not stick to his own business, that is, medicine? Why should he stir up the colony, especially the youth? And when the struggle against him began to escalate, the committee organized a procession of women to demonstrate in front of his house, claiming that he had robbed them of their sons and daughters and was poisoning their souls with his exhibitions in darkened rooms. The young people closed ranks in defense of their beloved doctor, and a fight began, in which children took sides against their parents. The colony was split in two, with two committees, and the conflict didn't subside until even the national flag was torn, after it had been raised by the young people during a reception for the Hacham-Bashi, Reb Hayim Nahum Effendi, the chief rabbi of Ottoman Jewry, and the doctor resigned and left the colony.

And now the family of Madame Umm-el-Tach-God-willing, and the smell of her fish cooking at night in the hungry colony, reconciled former enemies. And Reb Mordechai stared piercingly at the young people as if he were testing them, searching their souls for the true reason behind their bold and dangerous plan, and after a few moments of silence he bellowed at them, as was his wont:

"Excellent! Our colony must be pure! And you shall purge the evil from your midst! Blessed are you, my sons! I am with you!" Reb Mordechai's reply surprised the young people. He no longer seemed the strict, short-tempered Jew they had known, but behaved like one of them, like a friend, with a mischievous glint in his eyes.

The next day at nine o'clock, when the young men came to Reb Mordechai's house, they found Reb Berl, Reb Wolf, and another old-timer there awaiting orders – four well-built Jews, among the founding fathers of the colony, now somewhat lean on account of the poverty brought on by the war, and all dressed in ordinary clothes and dark hats. Past feuds between the generations – the struggle for the use of Hebrew rather than Yiddish, the fight over employing Jewish rather than Arab labor, the fight to hire Jewish guards – were all forgotten and seemed no more than a vague pre-war memory. And now the small united column made its way through the shifting sands, passing by the acacia shrubs, the row of young cypresses, the corpse of a mule which had not yet been buried and the jackals had nibbled on during the night, until they reached the house of the Hirsch widow and orphans.

Reb Mordechai knocked with his cane once or twice on the floor of the terrace, Reb Berl at his side, and when the babushka-covered head and sleep-swollen, moon-shaped face of Madame Umm-el-Tach, the widow Hirsch, appeared through the window, the two bearded Jews turned their heads aside, and informed her clearly that her family must pack immediately: they were to be evicted from the colony. "God willing, where to and by whose orders?" she asked. To Kfar Saba. And they would not be given a carriage because the Turkish Army had confiscated all the horses and mules, and whoever managed to avoid the confiscation had hidden his animals deep in the orange groves, and would not bring them out for all the money in the world.

Madame Hirsch tried to raise her voice and threatened to send Havka to wake up Yassin Bek – and God only knows what he would do to them! – but then all the others came up on the terrace, including the young men, and two of them, with red turbans wrapped around their heads in the Turkish fashion, pushed open the door, walked right in and began piling up the women's belongings and stuffing them into baskets and portmanteaux, waking up the orphans and frightening them out of their warm beds as if they were chickens in a coop. Two of the young men, who once or twice had been unable to resist temptation and had come themselves to taste the remains of the fish in onions and vinegar, were unable now to look the mother and daughters in the eye, and they – naturally – were particularly imperious. Finally, a skinny old leprous mule was found, which wasn't fit for conscription into the Turkish army, for either work or transportation, and it appeared most unlikely that even the jackals would want to nibble at its carcass – and it was loaded down with the women's belongings. The widow Hirsch, her babushka covering her head, opened her white parasol, and with her free hand she held the rolled-up whip of her husband, Reb Yankel the shattered wagoner, from which she never parted. Off they went, all together, by side roads and byways to the north of the colony, in the direction of the Yarkon River, the women walking and weeping, their lips pursed, knowing full well that there, in Kfar Saba, afflicted by refugees and epidemics, no General Jemal Pasha would come to taste their fish and add his spice. At best, they would fall into the hands of some local, louse-afflicted commandant, who would undress them in one of the stables, now used as living quarters, and trample them underfoot like some wild horse.

When they reached the Yarkon River and the three women were about to cross the Sheikh Abu-Rabah Bridge, Reb Mordechai, Reb Berl, Reb Wolf and all the others left them without so much as a word, merely expectorating and huffing and puffing, old and young alike. And they had not helped them carry their belongings for even one step, treating them as if they were a band of foul lepers being banished from the holy of holies.

Madame Umm-el-Tach stood on the bridge over the Yarkon, the richness of its springs pouring out at the foot of the fortress of Antipatrus to the east. She stood bathed in the rich green foliage, listening to the croaking frogs around her and the splash of water on the wheels of the Sheikh Abu-Rabah windmills, turning their giant millstones aimlessly, squeaking and creaking, empty and hungry, for there was no grain. She stood there and she said:

"May the curses of your fathers' fathers' fathers from Sodom and your incestuous mothers' mothers' mothers from Gemorrah fall upon your heads, you kindly saints from Malabes[2] – God willing! Not many

---

2.   Arabic name for Petah Tikva.

days shall pass before you too shall have to cross the Yarkon and go off into exile with your disgusting smelly *weibers* and *kinderlach* and *peckalach*[3] – may you writhe and twist and scream as you roast in hell, Amen, God willing!"

And turning her back, which rose out of the curves of her billowing buttocks, she kicked – with the tip of her shoe – the leprous mule, bent under the weight of her baskets and portmanteaux, picked up her skirts for a moment, revealing the full span of her two massive bumboats in full sail, and snow-white except for traces of a judicious pinch here and there left by General Pasha and his entourage, and a bite or two from the native-born Petah Tikva fleas, and emitted a tremendous fart, which seemed to arrest even the movement of the millstones. And leaning with her arms on both her daughters who had supported her flaccid corpulence all the way to the Sheikh Abu-Rabah windmills walking and weeping, their lips pursed, one of them holding the white parasol, the other the rolled-up whip, Madame Umm-el-Tach sailed on to Kfar Saba in the footsteps of the mule, leaving the Petah Tikva côterie behind, stunned and ashamed, as if they had just heard the voice of God.

The widow and the two orphans spent that entire winter in Kfar Saba and their fall was as bitter as gall. The huts built by the refugees in the eucalyptus forest, planted by Monsieur Pascal of Petah Tikva, did not hold up against the fierce autumn winds and rain, and the mass of refugees had to search for shelter in the stables and sheepfolds of the small colony whose animals had long since disappeared. There was nothing to eat, and if it were not for Hawaja Shimel Erkaya, that is, Reb Shimon Rokah from Neveh Tzedek, who lived with his family in Tulkarem and would, from time to time, send the refugees in Kfar Saba a sack of sorghum and a few loaves of poor man's bread whose insides resembled a mass of gray gluten, and a jar of carob honey – the hunger would have been much greater.

At first, the commandant of Tulkarem, Ja'ud Pasha, would visit the women from time to time, but before long the two sisters fell ill in the

---

3.   Yiddish: Wives, children and belongings.

crowded stable, burning with fever and coughing their hearts out. And Slor, the pharmacist, didn't have enough quinine or other drugs to help them or any of the many people seeking some kind – any kind – of shelter from the cold and the mud and the rain of December 1917, while having to listen to the sounds of firing in the distance, and the bombs exploding in the battle for Petah Tikva which fell into the hands of the British and then back again into the hands of the Turks. And the new refugees, this time people from Petah Tikva itself, would recite the tales of Yassin Bek's cruelty, how he continued to take bribes but did nothing to stop the expulsions, and the new arrivals only increased the crowding and the hunger and the epidemics in the small colony, and the commandant of Kfar Saba became harsher towards the refugees as the front moved closer to the Yarkon River and the British recaptured Petah Tikva, threatening them with whippings and hangings should any of them try to cross the lines to the south, in the direction of the British enemy.

And many of the exiles just sat in the fields, suffering from the cold. They sat in a large circle. One shivered. Another was ill and just moaned and groaned. A third occupied himself trying to keep a dying bonfire alive with twigs in order to warm his hands, and appeared totally oblivious to the moaning and groaning of his neighbor. A fourth was wrapped from head to toe in a blanket made of sacking and resembled a lifeless object, folded on the ground. A fifth sat with a pillow on his head. The house of the pharmacist was their temporary shelter, and the exiles took turns going in for a few minutes to warm up and coming out, going in and coming out, going in and coming out.

As if to add to this recitation of the trials and tribulations of Kfar Saba, the two orphans, Havka and Duba now lie in a corner of the stable made from mud and straw kneaded together into bricks, the rafters covered by a leaking tin roof which the rain penetrates and, in spite of the terrible crowding, not a soul lies near them save their mother the widow who is taking care of them, because a rumor has spread among the refugees and has reached the ears of the dying as well... that the epidemic was brought on by the two sisters. Nor is it merely the common strain of malaria or pneumonia that is devouring them, as it devours the others, by a racking cough and fits of hot and cold shivers, writhing as they do on their ragged bed sheets or lying as if bewitched, but a rotten Turkish disease they have contracted. And whoever catches it will die in throes of agony, losing his mind before his body is completely devastated.

Madame Umm-el-Tach girded her thinning bumboats and sailed over to the headquarters of the Kfar Saba commandant to plead for the lives of her two daughters – he should please help. But what could he do. New graves were being added daily to the small cemetery in the east of the colony, and some were not even marked because no one knew the names of the deceased. Sometimes only the first name was written or the city of birth, or the fact that the deceased was a child or a man, or a woman, or the date of death. And even the names that were written down were often washed away by the rain, and when relatives came to look for the graves of their dear ones, they could find nothing.

The Turkish commandant, who had already heard of the girls' illness and whose bones quivered in memory of the first night he spent with them in the stable – rolling first on the one, then on the other, pulling at them in turn as if they were a pair of horses – dismissed Madame God-willing with a snarl, though she, a soiled babushka on her head, alternately exhorted him and entreated him in desperation. And Slor the pharmacist, who pitied the wretched family and did not believe the infamous rumors about the epidemic, who had saved some of the precious quinine for them, and even shared with them his last piece of glutenous bread – even he could not help.

The two sisters lay there embracing, hallucinating in their fever and shivering from the cold, the rolled-up whip on the ground between them. "Who shall live and who shall die," Duba intoned to her sister, their suppurating skins already tinted with death's gray hue. *"Stana ya kadish... Ta yitla el-hashish..."* "Remember how on Yom Kippur even Father's horses would fast?" Havka droned and Duba moaned. "Who in his time, and who not in his time... Who by water and who by fire," they continued intoning and droning and moaning, holding on to each other, their cracked, weak voices gradually departing from their bodies. "Who by sword and who by beast, who by hunger and who by thirst. Who by earthquake and who by plague, who by strangling and who by stoning. Who shall rest and who shall go on, who shall fall silent and who shall go mad. Who shall be calm, and who shall suffer. Who shall be rich and who shall be poor. Who shall fall and who shall be raised..."

And on the word "raised" both descended to their deaths the very same night, first the younger and then the elder.

The bereaved mother didn't utter a word, didn't emit a cry or shed a tear. She sat next to her two daughters all night, half awake half asleep, and rose in the morning, bathed their foreheads in rainwater and then put them into a sack she found in the stable, so light were their bodies wasted by hunger and shrunken by fever. She loaded the sack on her back and, her head covered, walked to the young cemetery, where she emptied her load into one of the open graves, prepared in advance since not a day passed without a funeral, covered them with earth using her bare hands as a shovel, patted the hillock round and round, found a piece of wood and wrote on it in charcoal:

> *Here lie Havka and Duba, beloved and lovely,*
> *In life and in death they were not divided.*
> *Their father Reb Yankel Hirsch*
> *Did not live to see them wed,*
> *And heaven shall be their resting place.*

From there she crossed the disease-struck, groaning colony, the feverish stables, the moribund huts and the cough-wracked sheepfolds, and once more entered the stable to look over her few belongings, taking with her, in her basket, only the most necessary items such as the rolled-up whip of her shattered husband, Reb Yankel. She opened her mud-stained parasol and, without a word to a soul, left the colony, going south-west in the direction of the Yarkon, and she followed the sun all that day and never returned to Kfar Saba.

She crossed the Turkish and the British lines and the pits left by bombs, and heard the zing of a few shots, the gallop of riders and the echoes of cannons, and towards evening she reached British-occupied Tel Aviv, and was welcomed on Herzl Street, opposite the Herzlia Gymnasium, by a troop of Australian cavalry mounted on square, broad-flanked horses – such wide girths she had never seen – and by the celebrating, carefree Tel Avivians promenading hither and to, and by the girls who would soon be as old as poor Havka and Duba, trying to flirt with the soldiers, while licking bars of Cadbury's chocolate – the likes of which she hadn't seen since the war began.

Madame Hirsch did not waste her time, and did not stay to live in cheerful Tel Aviv, licking its wounds from the expulsions and the war, and now filled with recruits from the Jewish Battalion about to be sent to Egypt for training, but immediately rented a small room in Manshia by the sea, and started cooking every evening, in onions and vinegar, the fish she purchased from the fishermen who were now allowed to fish in the open sea. The flesh came back to her massive bumboats, and she spread her sails like a seasoned old battleship. At first her room was only a meeting place for those who appreciated her food, but it wasn't long before her fame grew, and she was able to rent a whole house in Manshia by the sea and take in a few girls to help her. She had two Armenian orphans, a Turkish woman who had loved fish and men even before the war, a Greek woman from Salonika and three more girls from among the daughters of Ishmael, one of them a black Nubian. Only Jewesses weren't accepted, although quite a few pleaded with her. Her head covered in a babushka, she would speak with great respect of her late husband, Reb Jacob Hirsch, who would one day return from Egypt with her two daughters, God willing. Again and again she would exhort the Jewish girls: "What do you need it for? God willing, you'll soon find a husband, you can leave this work to the *shiksas*.[4] Has the lust of a drunken British or Australian soldier so softened your brain?"

She would sit in the large dusky inner courtyard, from which doors opened on to the smaller rooms, together with her girls, the smell of cooking fish filling their nostrils. And when a soldier left one of the girls' rooms, he would approach Madame Hirsch and receive a chit

---

4.   Yiddish: Non-Jewish girls.

from her with a number on it so that if he contracted something, the girl could be taken for a checkup. And often one of these drunks would come in, boasting and waving a handful of chits accumulated from previous visits.

At the entrance to the house, as in all similar establishments in Manshia, the British occupation authorities had stationed guards from the Jewish Battalion whose duty it was to warn the British soldiers that the place was out of bounds, but to no avail. No one dared stand in the way of a drunken Englishman or a sinewy Australian belching beer fumes. One of the guards at Madame God-willing's, Lance Corporal Shkolnik, would therefore sit contentedly, reading the Russian pamphlets he carried in his pockets, while his younger comrade sitting opposite would just as contentedly sketch the girls and the fish, their rifles lying nearby. From time to time they would try to make conversation with Madame Hirsch in Yiddish and would hear of her rich husband and two daughters, soon to return from Egypt.

And sometimes, affected by the heavy scent of perfume exuded by her chubby girls, and the smell of bodies pervading the house, and the aroma of vinegar and onions wafting from the kitchen, something would stir in her, the bereaved widow too, that familiar frisson in her bumboats, and like an old battleship about to set sail for what might perhaps be its last mission, she would choose a drunken Australian who could no longer tell the difference between a Turkish girl and an Armenian, or between a Greek and a Nubian; a broad-flanked soldier, healthy as a horse, roll him to her room and ride him all night, flogging his pink flesh with shattered Reb Yankel's whip. And with the uncircumcised goy shrieking and squealing, the mattress screeching and the bedsprings squeaking, it appeared that by the force of such momentum Madame Umm-el-Tach would soon ride her Australian all the way up to Jerusalem.

Several years passed. The soldiers returned to London, Manchester, Melbourne and Sydney. The girls grew fat as hogs. Some fell ill, some left and were replaced by others, mostly wicked and quarrelsome. Also the guests, from among the poor, were unpleasant.

Their clothes reeked not of beer, but of the acrid smell of workers' sweat, of plaster stains, of pink butchers' fingers and scale-covered fishermen's hands. They asked for fish, fried in oil or grilled. Madam Hirsch handed the place over to a Greek woman with a scarred chest, who looked more like a man and knew how to fry fish as well as men, and left for Tel Aviv. She drew her savings out of the Anglo-Palestine Bank, a tidy sum in Egyptian pounds, bought herself a shop on Nahlat Binyamin Street, and put Reb Yankel Hirsch's whip in the window for luck.

Within a few years, the shop of Mrs. Hava-Dubtche Hirsch-God-willing, whose head was always reverently covered with a babushka, became the place where Tel Aviv's young women, sporting the latest fashions from Warsaw and Lvov, purchased what they needed in the way of buttons, ribbons, lace, buckles, thread, appliqués, pins, needles, purses and later brassieres and petticoats, and exchanged fish recipes. "Hava-Dubtche, my dear, the fish I made from your recipe simply melts in the mouth." "You're telling me? I fed fish like that to Jemal Pasha! Ha ha. Ha..."

They would all laugh.

All day long Hava-Dubtche Hirsch would sit, anchored to a chair in her shop, her bumboats hardly ever stirring. One day, years after the state came into being, she got into trouble over the illegal possession of some American dollars and, not improbably, evading income tax as well. She was threatened with a heavy fine but old Hava-Dubtche was not worried. "I survived the Turks. I survived the British, I'll survive you too, God willing," she said. The tax collectors smiled. "How you going to do that, grandma? You going to call Jemal Pasha? General Allenby?" "I'm going to call somebody," she said, "but not Allenby, God willing. You'll see." And she picked up the telephone right then and there and asked to be connected to the Minister of Finance with whom she hadn't conversed in forty years, to tell him that Madame Hirsch from the Jewish Battalion in Manshia would like to speak to him. She was put through immediately, and in fluent Yiddish she exhorted him to save her from the tax collectors, and her wish was immediately granted.

With the money she saved in her last years in the Anglo-Palestine

Bank and which she still reckoned in the old currency, she bought a burial plot in Tel Aviv's oldest cemetery on Trumpeldor Street, next to that of her husband Reb Yankel, and asked me to have her tombstone engraved as follows:

Here lies Hava-Duba known as Umm-el-Tach,
The wife of Reb Yankel Hirsch
Who took people up to Jerusalem.
You who pass her grave – do not forget
The sorrow caused her by the people of Petah Tikva.

And when her body was lowered into the grave, a huge breaking of wind was heard, as if only now she had died for the last time.

Yitzhak Ben-Ner

Berger

Translated by Michael Swirsky

It is a chill, foggy early-spring dawn, the eleventh of March, nineteen hundred and forty-six, the eighth day of Adar Sheni, five thousand seven hundred and six, at o-two-hundred-forty-seven hours, when they smuggle me out of the detention cell on the second floor of Jaffa Prison, where I have been taken for interrogation; and before the sun comes up, I, the most heavily guarded prisoner in all of western Palestine – that is, the Land of Israel, or, as we call it, Free Zion – am making my way along Alkalai Bet, an unfamiliar street in the Yemenite quarter leading into Tel Aviv.

The sea breeze is very light, almost imperceptible, and the air seems to thicken and hang motionless. The odor of sewage lies stagnant in the stone streets, and the inhabitants are all asleep in the heat of their rooms behind shuttered windows. Only one old man with a few filthy wisps of beard can be seen in the narrow thoroughfare, knocking on shutters here and there to awaken the sleepers. At one of the houses he stops, like the camera of an alert photographer, his fist poised, his head cocked and his eyes upon me, one good eye, the other bad, watering with old age. Everyone knows who I am, though few have actually seen me in the flesh. If I were walking in broad daylight along Allenby Street between the sea front and the Migdalor Cinema, people would freeze in their tracks. How many of them would sell me down the river for a *grush* with a hole in it, I wonder.

My Arab robe, which looks like a straitjacket, affords little protection from the cold. Its sleeves are as full as slipcovers, and its folds keep getting caught between my naked legs. My lips are swollen and painful from the beating I got the night before, and I have lost all sensation in one arm. The frigid dawn air suddenly makes me hungry. In one of the yards, a dog eyes me, crouching between a broken-down sunflower and some pepper plants that are turning green. The pungency of the swelling pods finds its way into my mouth. I am not afraid of anyone, I say, clutching myself, a prisoner in my own arms.

Across the street, I recall, is a small restaurant frequented by early-rising Yemenite laborers. There won't be any customers yet, but the owner is probably warming things up. I have no idea of the time, maybe three o'clock, maybe four. My picture, scratched and yellowing, is plastered on the opposite wall, next to an advertisement for the Ohel Theater's production of *The Merry Wives of Windsor*. Meanwhile, the merry wives themselves are asleep in their safe warm beds, unaware of the cold empty streets just outside their walls.

It has been a long time since I last saw my own face. There was a mirror in the prison, in the entranceway next to the latrines, but they always took me there under guard, bound hand and foot. At such times, no other prisoners would be allowed in to relieve themselves, and the light would be kept low. There was only the warden's flashlight exploring the latrine, and as the Arab guard undid the buttons on my red trousers, the flashlight would illuminate all. There I stood, letting loose my arc of liquid into the darkness. There I sat, on my stool. There I lay, sleepless. Up or down, nothing escaped their watchful eye while for me, prison meant the corrosive stench of urine and lysol, sounds echoing through stone corridors, the muffled clang of metal at lockup time. And their eyes on me, constantly. One eye stared unceasingly, as though plucked from its socket, through the peephole in the heavy door of my cell. I never knew to which of my guards it belonged. Never did the eye leave the hole in the door, and when the revolving searchlight cast its beam through my barred window, the eye would gleam, pull back, and return to stare at me in the darkness.

Yet I myself have not seen my face for days, and the tattered portrait of it on the wall seems to me that of a stranger, or of someone

I once knew but whose face I have forgotten. This is not how I thought of myself during those hours I spent in rumination: the hair, now grown long, but then neatly combed on either side of the forehead; the part, flecked with white by the fading of the print; the dark piercing eyes; the heavy, bristled jaw (the dogs! never had I allowed myself to be photographed unshaven; I had always been fastidious about my appearance; no doubt they did it just to make me look repulsive); the slender nose; the fine eyebrows. It is the face of a leader, my face. That I know. Even in this poor, shredded wall poster I look like a leader. Except that in the faded photograph the mouth is slightly agape, giving me an air of mild surprise. Only now do I notice it. Could this be me? What kind of man am I, a bold leader or a wide-eyed boy? I scrutinize myself mercilessly in the chilly air: the high, smooth forehead, the combed hair, the alert eyes, the solid jaw, the cool visage of a man who knows it all – only the mouth, damn it, is open just a little, as if in surprise. A foolish boy. Maybe I don't appear to others as I always have to myself after all. Come to think of it, didn't Friedman (Ze'ev, his code name was) suddenly ask me after one of our meetings, with no connection to the grave matters at hand, if I still found time to write poetry – when I had never written poetry! Never! Now Friedman lies in a ditch between the fences, his head riddled with English bullets and his mouth slightly open as if in surprise; his face betraying, not pain, but the curiosity of a child who has taken up poetry perhaps, or dreaming. While I, on the other hand, got out of the valley of death alive.

Light reaches me from a kerosene lamp through the open door of the restaurant. What if they recognize me? Suddenly I feel as though 1 were still in the red convict's uniform, as though my rescuers had not given me a change of clothing, there in the trench between the fences, just before we were hit by machine-gun fire from the watchtowers. Then I feel the thick duck-cloth, and its strange touch brings a kind of reassurance to my fingertips; so I go in. A slender girl in a heavy sweater and drooping wool cap is hefting crude benches off the tables. A Yemenite woman, embroidered trousers under her dress, is on her knees swabbing the cement floor. From the kitchen comes a smell of kerosene and smoke, and a short, stocky man in a military jacket with a stained apron tied over it is standing at the stove. A refuge. The two women don't even look up. They are apparently used to night visitors. I sit down at one of the tables, the one where the kerosene lamp is lit, and cup my hands around the glass mantle of the lamp to warm them.

I sit that way for some time. The two women go on diligently with their work and little by little there wafts from the kitchen the aroma of hot oil and various things being dropped into it. Warmth spreads through my body. The girl has a thin black braid, and as she leans over the tables the braid dances and flaps gaily against her back, though there is no gaiety about the girl herself or the quiet of the dining room. The small gray hours of the morning are no time for lightheartedness. At this moment, I know, the CID men, the Arab trackers, the police and the army are all on my trail. My prison uniform has been given to the dogs to sniff. I know how in every police station the phones are ringing, giving orders for the hunt; how my portrait is once again being printed on sheets of poster paper, and how these will, in another hour, be plastered on the walls, as they were then. I am a very important man to them, yet here I am, sitting practically under their noses, all alone in a little restaurant in my Arab duck-cloth clothing, and I, the man everyone knows, know nothing, not even what I am going to do next.

A man comes through the door, and I hunch over the table to cover my face, the blood pounding in my swollen lips: a mere hundred and fifty days and already I have forgotten every rule of stealth. I am sitting next to the only light in the room, my face yellow in its glow. But hiding would also be out of the question. I glance furtively at the newcomer and raise my head again. It is the old man with the cataract who was knocking on the shutters. He lays his little sack on the other table and sits down, across from me, his sick eye blinking, his thin, dirty beard seemingly frozen, the features of his face quivering and his lips moving, as though he were carrying on a conversation with himself. He too seems uninterested in ordering anything. He waits. His eyes, the good one and the bad one alike, rest on me. This was how we waited then too, a whole hour, for Peter's taxi (we called him

Issachar, against his will) to take us to the RAF base in Kastina: the kind of wait that comes after great fear and before action. Our comrades had already gone out there in buses, and I, the leader, was to bring up the rear. And so there we were in the taxi, on the shoulder of the road. Very close. In full view of everything that was going on. With a great blast, the Halifax plane and the English supply depot were engulfed in flames. Then the taxi too caught on fire and I, the onlooker, found myself groping like a blind man towards the lock. Peter – I always suspected that he alone of all of them was secretly contemptuous of me; he would wrinkle his forehead irreverently, as if to make light of everything, whenever I delivered one of my thundering, majestic orations to the people and the conquerors over our radio station – Peter leaned over and struck the heat-swollen lock with his forearm. The door burst open, I rolled out into the dust and down into the bushes. From there, stunned and dizzy, I saw him break out of the flames, his clothes on fire, beating himself, a terrible sight, with no one to come to his rescue. Afterwards, the conquerors were able to identify Uri Finkel, whom we called Eitan, and Menucha, whom we called Ziona. But Peter's – Issachar's – body was burnt almost to the very bone, beyond recognition. Peter too is gone.

I have no money. I have, in fact, none of the things that connect a man with others. My belongings were all taken from me when they booked me at the prison. Now all that I have to clothe my nakedness are torn underwear, this Arab duck-cloth smock, and these heavy prison shoes without laces. In one hand I am clutching a little packet, wet with perspiration, that my friends thrust upon me on the way out; pills that I take for shortness of breath. I'm utterly penniless. Friedman or Bezalel must have had money on them – I'm sure of that – and if things had been handled properly they would certainly have stuffed a few notes into my pockets. For a long time before that, I had been used to doing without money. One of my people would always take out his wallet and gently push me aside and bargain for me with the peddlars whenever I wanted something, and I never wanted much. Those on guard duty would bring food and drink, clothing, newspapers, and cigarettes to the hideout. Women came, spent time, and left of their own accord. Now I am penniless, and hunger is gnawing at me. How will it all end?

The little Yemenite comes over to us, wiping his hands on his apron. He looks us over in the yellow light and without asking for our orders goes back into his kitchen, to return a moment later carrying two steaming, pungent tin plates of eggs in tomato sauce. He nods to me and hands me a steel soup spoon. The hot, spicy, potent concoction scalds my lips, but I am so famished that I gobble it all down before the old man has scarcely begun. Out of the corner of my eye I see him tear off a piece of warm bread, bits of burn from the oven clinging to it, and dip it into the green sauce that has been served him in a little saucer, looking at me the whole time, half clear-eyed, half watery-eyed and blurry. He does not take his eyes off me. I try to put my thoughts in order, but under his blinking gaze I cannot. In the past, I would close my eyes and fleetingly press them with my fingertips, as though silently, secretly weeping. At such times, a hush would come over the room, and everyone around the table would wait to hear what I had to say. A brief moment of complete detachment and everything would fall into place. Then I would begin speaking and explaining things one by one. Coolly, quietly, like a leader. I had never been one to speak loosely or confusedly. Always straight to the point. I could sense my eyes scanning the faces of my people, inspiring confidence in each one of them and faith in the justice of our terrible deeds. The light of the naked electric bulb. The smell of pistol grease. The picture of the slain leader, my teacher, my commander, hanging on the bare wall. The tightly closed shutters where the boy (we called him Yohai) would stand and, from time to time, peer out. And Peter, my driver and bodyguard, his forehead raised in bemusement, listening from the side, his body heavy, as he polished his big Finnish revolver with a rag. Yohai was blond and slight in build. At the meetings he was always among the enthusiasts, those for whom every loudly spoken word had an incendiary effect, touched off certain reflexes. "The British," you would say, and he would immediately add "despicable conquerors." If someone brought up Ben Gurion, Yohai would spit with contempt. At night his friends said he wept, and Peter would say derisively that he wet his bed. The girls loved him, but he paid no attention to them. What was his first name? I don't remember. I'm not sure I ever knew. During Captain Morton's raid on the room at 17 King George Street, Yohai was shot in the stomach, and after three weeks and two days of physical and mental torture, with four of the conquerors hovering over his hospital bed in their uniforms, his life came to an end. Yohai we called him. What name did his mother give him?

Thus have the good people surrounding me died, one after another – and the country is still in flames. How many are we, anyway? How long can we keep it up? Rue the day that I should be the one asking this question. The Palmach boys walk the mountain paths, hair wild and flowing, pouches strapped to their bodies, sweaters tied at their necks and wooden sticks in their hands, the girls in sandals and shorts, bursting out of their tight clothing, their hair about their shoulders. They breathe the night air of this warm land, eyes and ears trained on distant sites, while our people, still holed up in their hideouts, are ridiculed for their shorts and knee socks and branded as conspirators. Could it be that we are really just playing? That we have become so carried away with our little game that we can no longer stop but must go on killing and dying at any price? A year and two months ago, in January 1945, I was summoned to a meeting at the Jewish Agency, and people came from the other big organizations as well. How uncomfortably, how unsupportively, how disrespectfully they looked at me then – unless, of course, there was some grudging respect born of fear. And they certainly were afraid of me, for they saw in me the mysterious cruelty, the deadly isolation, the glowing penumbra of dread that surrounds a madman whose next move and next target cannot be anticipated. They listened silently to my few penetrating remarks. We are much feared, yet who have I got behind me? How many are we, all told, in the entire country? At the height of our strength there were exactly three hundred and seven of us, no more, and I alone to lead.

At the next table, the old man is sipping coffee from a bakelite cup and staring at me. The light in the doorway is brighter now, and a

Yemenite construction worker in heavy shoes and plaster-splashed overalls comes in, accompanied by a short teenage boy in sandals. They too stare at me, the stranger in their midst. They have merry eyes and a shrewd lively glance, these Yemenites. We had some in our group too. Where are they now?

There was Eli Shar'abi, whom we called Manoach[1] even when he was very much alive. He would go off to sell newspapers early every morning to support his family, and during the day he did construction work. During the season he also worked in the orange groves. But he was always ready at a moment's notice to take on an assignment, and he never failed to carry out his duties faithfully. He lost three of the fingers of his right hand in the S. raid, and still he could pick oranges faster than anyone else in the groves. In the attack on the army train he was shot in the chest and lived. During a prison break, the barbed wire tore all the skin off his back, and it festered. Torture by the English made a stammerer of him, but he never talked. Now he is awaiting death in a Jerusalem prison, an old young man, bones broken, weary, in a red uniform. He is heavily guarded. Friedman, when he was still alive, used to take a few pounds out of the organization's petty cash every week and bring it secretly to the local rabbi to take to Shar'abi's family, for they too were being watched by the conquerors to see what might turn up.

And there were others too, shrewd and alert, enthusiastic. One of them – Avner, we called him – took me once to a family celebration. A Yemenite bar mitzvah. Because of the great risk involved, I wore a ridiculous false mustache, and Dora combed my hair back. My people – there were still quite a few left at that time – circled the house unbeknown to anyone, keeping watch while I went in. Avner introduced me as his teacher, but even so, the many relatives eyed me suspiciously and were careful to keep their distance. The din of celebration seemed to diminish as I sat down among them.

In the corner of the arch-ceilinged restaurant, by the kitchen door, the Yemenite woman is sitting and mashing chickpeas in a tin pot, and

---

1. A biblical name, also meaning "late lamented" in Hebrew.

with each muffled thud of her black pestle I feel more faint at heart. I am so tired, and now I am afraid too, my face and hands ache and my thoughts are disordered. What am I doing here, alone, on a chilly morning, dressed in this heavy robe? The few people around look at me but have nothing to say. My face is drooping. Before long I won't have the strength to get up from the bench, and my thawing body will refuse to obey the orders of my increasingly dull brain. The girl is standing in the kitchen doorway wiping her hands on a rag. Now the proprietor counts some change into her hand, her wages, and she nods at each coin. From the kitchen, an aroma of coffee, strong and delicious, finds its way to my nose. My whole body craves coffee, craves the sensation of its warmth and strength permeating the tissues, but coffee which you cannot pay for is a luxury, while food, for a hungry man, is a necessity.

And so, straining and leaning heavily on the table, I get up, and all of them – the half-blind old man, the worker with his boy, the Yemenite woman, the girl, and the owner – stop what they are doing to watch me. I approach the thickset man, who peers at me, eyes shining, wiping his hands on his apron. "I have no money, sir," I say, looking straight into his eyes. He reflects for a moment, turns his head, and casts a sidelong glance at the others and at me. Does his smile mean he is afraid of me? "My goodness, it's only seventeen piasters!" he says in a near-whisper and grins. What are seventeen piasters compared to the sense of wrongdoing which suddenly grips me? But what can I do? "I have no money, sir," I repeat, the air catching in my throat, and everything seems to spin around me in this yellow light, between walls which collect heat during the day and release it at night. "You can write down my name. Berger." I am not sure he understands. "You don't have seventeen piasters?" he asks. Then, hesitating for a moment, he looks straight at me and says, "Never mind. What can you do? Let it be for a blessing." And he mutters a few more words that I do not understand, perhaps from the prayerbook. "Bring it tomorrow and straighten things out. It's nothing." And he flashes another black-toothed grin through his beard.

At this moment, a group of young building workers burst noisily into the building. They are in their late teens and carry their tools with them, prepared to earn their livelihood regardless of conqueror or conquered, of foreign rule or the struggle for freedom in this land; above and beyond all these things, they carry on with their lives. I manage to pull myself erect. The proprietor blows out the lamp, and in the dim light which they have brought in with them from the street the newcomers catch sight of my alien appearance. Their ebullient rush is brought to a halt. They stand dumbfounded and study me apprehensively. And when I look back at them, one by one they lower their gaze. What a fine new army I could make of these lads if they wouldn't avert their eyes and if my reserves of strength, of self-confidence, of clarity and ideas weren't so depleted. All I have left is my suffering.

Am I losing my grip on the table? Am I gasping for breath? My legs buckle in their weakness, and no one extends a hand to help. With all the strength I have left, I brace myself, the muscles of my face straining so hard I feel the skin is about to tear. At this, the spell cast by my strangeness seems to lift. The young men sit down at the tables and begin speaking quietly, the girl covers her hair with a thick scarf and wraps herself up in a sweater, and none of them look my way any longer. As though I had been and gone. Only the old man goes on blinking at me with his watery eye, watching me in my distress. Have they recognized me? "Go, mister, go in peace," the proprietor says, taking care to keep me at arm's length. "Only please, mister, don't tell anyone you were here, please."

"You're afraid," I say, leaning forward with my full weight, my afflicted arm sending out signals of pain now, but as if to another body, not mine. I try to look into the man's eyes, gathering all my strength for a single, penetrating glance. With great effort, I pull myself together: "Don't let your fears get the better of you, do you understand?" Could I really say such a thing, hypocrite that I am, or am I just imagining it? "Don't let them get to you! It's human nature to be afraid." He looks at me, then at someone behind me among those sitting down, all the while smoothing the apron that is tied over his army jacket. Could it be a gesture of respect for the man standing before him? I pick up where I left off. "Fear is an emotional reaction," I tell him. I always used the same words with the brightest and the dullest of my people. "No need to be scared of it or ashamed of it, do you see? It's simply a physical response that you can't do anything about. Just a matter of blood pressure and so on. You do understand, don't you?" My voice, my words, my speech, my gaze. The very things on which my power rested. Well, perhaps my strength will yet return, spreading through me like a healing balm.

Everyone listens in silence. No one nods, the way my boys always did when I spoke to them. No one moves a muscle. It is as if I were speaking from far off. Their eyes are on me. The girl hugs herself to keep warm, and quietly, coldly, looks me over. My strength is fading. I can't go on. I am even losing my grip on the table, and suddenly I sink to the cement floor, legs sprawling, ludicrous as a boy who has gotten himself into a mess and can't get out. I realize that I am no longer God's chosen one, and a great fear wells up inside me. Has He abandoned me altogether?

What is happening to me? What has happened to the conviction that I, like all self-assured people, once had that I was unique, that I was different, that I had been singled out in God's eyes and that He would never leave me? I break out in a cold, drenching sweat, and my mind is clouded by exhaustion and vague fear. Am I weeping? Not likely. My eyes are puffy but dry. The effort of the escape, the waiting beforehand, and the fear and loneliness and strangeness afterwards have sucked all my strength, and there is no hope of saving myself except in sleep. Never have I felt so deep a desire to sleep as I do now. To sleep, even on the wooden slab in the prison cell, or here on the rough, cold, concrete floor. To sleep, borne away on a cloud, receding, vanishing. Beyond all fear, the sweetness of slumber invades my every pore, poisons my limbs with a heavy, pleasant torpor and shelters me in oblivion. Come, come.

Far off, the girl appears to be conferring with the proprietor in hushed tones. Then the heavyset man comes over, looks at me, and says, still with forbearance and respect in his voice, "Mister, please to get up. Go with her. Everything will be all right. Go with her, she

says. Maybe get a little sleep, So there will be strength. No problem."
I look up at the girl but am unable to read anything in her cold, black
eyes. And so, with everyone looking on silently and no one offering a
hand, I press against the floor and the table with my fingers, lift
myself up, and shake the sleep off my body. In fear and weakness and
despair, I get to my feet. Isn't this how they always saw me: strong,
feet firmly planted, eyes narrowed in a steely gaze, collar upturned,
tommy gun in hand? Isn't this the way I always appeared to those who
feared me, who revered the mystery surrounding me?

The girl turns and walks out, and I, marveling at it all, follow heavily
in her footsteps. She does not wait for me in the empty street,
already lit by the first rays of the soft, distant winter sun. The early
chill makes me shiver in my coarse robe, the packet of pills – my
life-giving pills – still clenched in my palm. What time is it? I
cannot estimate or even guess. Five? Six? Maybe later. And how I
long to sleep. The girl neither turns her head nor waits. She walks
on, and my feet follow hers. Looking back over my shoulder, I see
the old man, the one who had been knocking on the shutters,
plodding along behind me, his head bobbing, his little sack on his
back, and his good eye flashing.
     A small, confined cityscape. Low houses, narrow streets,
curbstones not yet reached by the sunlight. Dry, hardpacked dirt paths
and heavy shadows resting in the cold spaces between one doorstep
and the next. Only the exposed windows are touched, gently, by the
sun. How good it would be if I could conduct my wars from here, I
think. I am dizzy. My body aches. My brain thirsts for sleep.
     We walk along, one behind the other, widely separated. Where are
we going? To her house? If so, why is she taking me in? Surely they
have all heard about me. And yet here, in this place, among people
who know me, she dares to take me in? After all, people talk and
people judge one another. And what is this old man to her? Why is he
always following me? Should I be afraid of him, I, who am now afraid
of everyone? Where am I going, and why, and what is giving me the
strength to continue – fear, apathy, numbness? Yet I walk on.

Here is her house. A wooden door set in crumbling stone, at the end of an alley which opens onto Allenby Street. There, halves of buses and people's heads can be seen going by in the first traffic of the morning. But these are the last stones of the Yemenite quarter, and they stand apart from the city. A green placard on the front of Allenby Cinema announces the showing of *The Invisible Man*, and her door too is green, like the entrance to an illuminated cavern. She inserts a key in the lock and steps down into the cold darkness within, not waiting to see whether I follow her or hang back. I stumble down two stone steps and hear the door slam behind me, as if of its own accord. I wait, my back to the door, for the sound of it opening and closing again, but it does not. The old man will not be joining us.

Little by little, my eyes adjust to the darkness, and I see it being replaced, almost imperceptibly, by the dim light of a small window set high in a cracked, peeling, pale-violet wall. A thick flowery blanket seals off the window and the day beyond. Haven't I been here before? How familiar it all looks. Haven't I already seen these things: the dark room, the big, messy bed, the old woman in black who gets up from her resting place on the sunken, ornate tiled floor and wordlessly puts a bawling infant into my young protectress's arms? Who is she and who is the other one, and whose baby is it? Why does my hostess lock the two of them up in this room? And perhaps I came down, not two steps but more, many more, without even realizing it.

I have been here before. I'm certain of it. The same thing happened once before. I've already seen this room with its sparse furniture. I've already felt the chill that radiates from these walls and inhaled the smell of smoke, kerosene, and hot food that emanates from that Primus stove on the trunk in the corner. And yet, perhaps not. Could I be mixing up this house with the Arab house? Not here, far from here. What is this? This is the Arab house, Habbas' house. Wasn't it here that they brought me blindfolded? But no, that was a different house, with different smells. There's no mistaking it. There was a smell of sulphur and kerosene there when we broke in, when the hand-grenade was thrown and the tommy-guns opened fire. As the smoke cleared I saw an Arab woman in a faded, embroidered dress lying on her back on the tiled floor, her eyes open yet extinguished. She had been a fortune-teller, a sorceress and a healer. She was stretched out on her back, and next to her was a chair that had been blown apart. The floor was sprinkled with blood, and there was this wall, painted violet. And when the smoke was gone we found coffee cups overturned on the table, their contents scattered. There was a crystal ball there too, a milky, opalescent beauty with a smoky white interior. I picked it up, and it was very heavy, much heavier than it seemed. At first glance it appeared to be opaque, but when I looked into it I saw past the cloudiness of milk and smoke into clear depths. And the more I gazed, the wider and deeper the vision became, until it seemed to encompass unimaginable distances. I tried to tear myself away from the ball's spell but could not – nor could I allow myself to take along with me a thing of such little obvious value. But at that moment one of my people came running through the open doorway – Al-Dahabi Habbas had apparently jumped past me and escaped just as we burst in to kill him – and, bumping me with the butt of his gun, knocked the ball out of my hands and out of my sight. The spectacular vision was smashed into a thousand thousand pieces, pieces of pieces, tiny fragments of everything the eye is capable of seeing. I still carry that sight with me, even though most of the comrades who were there are dead and only a few were imprisoned or managed to escape. This is not Habbas' house. Those things cannot have happened here. Not here.

The whole time I have been with her, the young woman hasn't said a word to me, either kindly or otherwise. The old woman leaves us with a nod, walking sideways toward the door like a crab, her eyes on me the whole time. She opens the door, goes out, and closes it behind her – and for a brief moment the ridiculous, uncouth figure of the old Yemenite man flickers there in the blinding white light. He is sitting spreadeagled on the narrow stone pavement, his back to the wall, fingering his ragged beard with infinite patience. Inside, a cold darkness returns, and my eyes, blinded for an instant by the light, once again throb with pain. A great silence falls upon us. The crumbling walls allow in no sound of the city outside. The young woman takes off her cardigan with one hand while holding the baby with the other;

and, pressed against her like a bolt of cloth, it is immediately pacified. Still holding the baby in her arms, she turns to the pot on the Primus stove to stir the scorched food. Was that motion of her head a signal to me to sit down? There is only one chair in the room, a simple, wooden affair piled high with baby clothes. Heavylimbed and weak, I sense my fear slackening in the quiet darkness. I go over to the unmade iron bed and lie down.

I am looking at her, comrades. Her back, slender and lithe in the blue wool blouse, is turned towards me as she works, when suddenly – I am so astonished that my chest contracts in pain – it occurs to me that she could be one of us; the wife, that is, of one of our people. The joy of it – and what, in fact, is there to be joyful about? – sends new blood coursing through my veins. I suppress my excitement and ask the girl if she knows... Avner. Why Avner of all people? We had so many Yemenites. Why do I mention Avner? I do not know. And she gives me no answer. "Avner," I say. "I don't remember his name, to tell you the truth. We called him Avner. Are you his wife, by any chance?" She doesn't answer, and her back seems to recoil from me a bit as she goes about her work. "There were others," I say, and with great effort, I try to dredge up names, pseudonyms, dark faces, guttural accents from the ever-so-distant past. "Why, we had Shim'on ... yes, Shim'on. And there was Oded... Really, what were their names?!... Mordechai... was his name really Mordechai? I forget. Do you know them? Here everybody knows everybody else..." I say, but she is silent. "Of course there was Manoach. That is, he's still alive, yes... Eli Shar'abi, his name was." She casts a sharp glance in my direction – or maybe I'm just imagining it – and the baby is still clinging to her. "Do you know him?" I ask, so much hoping she does. How much it would mean to me if she knew him. But she does not answer me one way or the other, only gives me this look: hard, direct, piercing. "No, you couldn't be his wife. He didn't have a wife. He was young, after all." Why do I always think of him in the past tense? He is still alive. "That is, he's so young."

Only now does she turn slowly back to the stove, and her shoulders droop. "No, Manoach wasn't married. Had no time for such things," I say, and the image of the young man's handsome face, an image growing blurrier with each passing day, floats before my eyes. "There were a lot of mouths to feed in his father's house, and he worked so hard. And besides, our... our work. You know." As if everything were clear and understood and above-board between us. "What time did I have, in the midst of all that commotion, to take an interest in my people's family lives? I'll be damned if I know." I smile to myself. "I knew them all. All of them." And suddenly a great calm comes over me. "But there was another one. Zion. Everyone called him Sa'adya. I think that was his real name." I lie back on the pillow and stretch. No need to be afraid now. Here is the old confidence, total and clear-eyed, in the very heart of danger, right under the noses of the British! "Was Zion your husband?" I ask her. "Wait a minute, yes, there was Baruch, and Avishai too. Do you know them?" I don't mind at all her not answering. I am used to speaking to silent audiences. "Those are all aliases, of course," I explain, "Not that we really need them for cover, you understand. It's just that when a person has a code name he loses his identity somehow. All those who have them become a single unit. Their individuality gets channeled, you see, into the common need, into the service of the common cause." I pause to reflect on my words and savor their aptness, just as I did in those good hard times. "Of course the public remains indebted for generations to those who fight on its behalf, and when you grasp this in all its simplicity you are able to sacrifice everything for the common good, for the good of your inferiors, without fear of disappointment."

She takes her son and the pot of food and goes to sit on the stone step under the doorway. With one hand she ladles a little food onto a plate, takes some in a spoon, and blows on it to cool it. Her baby is in her arms and she is feeding it, and when it doesn't eat, she does. Abruptly, she stops as if in puzzlement. Does she intend to offer me something to eat? "No, thanks, I'm not hungry. Thanks," I say. "I ate at..." but as I am speaking she breaks off her reverie, which evidently did not concern me at all, and goes back to what she was doing. Is she aware at all of my presence? Didn't she bring me here herself? She must be mute. But didn't she speak with her employer at the restaurant? Or she might be deaf. But then how could she have listened to all the things I said? Does she have something against me? I am suddenly seized with trepidation. I search her face for some sign of malice, but it is veiled in equanimity. What then?

"Do you...?" I begin, but do not know what to ask. At this moment I cannot find the right word. Not that I do not speak splendid Hebrew. I do. My little speeches are beautiful, well wrought, impressive. True, I know less Hebrew than French, and my Hebrew is poorer than my mother tongue – but at this moment I cannot find even in those languages the exact word with which to capture concisely what is running through my mind. "Do you...?" What, for God's sake? Poets are able to pluck elegant phrases from their imagination to express even the most bizarre and complex of thoughts. And I am at a loss for one simple word.

Outside the closed door there is the sound of a dry, hacking cough. I shudder slightly in my bed. What the hell is the time? How can I live even for a moment without a watch? In the past, someone was always around to keep me informed of the exact time. Time is those others who pass you by and who accompany you from one juncture to another. Now I am left alone, and all the others are gone. They died by the sword, were hanged, were imprisoned and tortured, escaped or left, or simply disappeared. I am all alone, myself, looking at this woman. She has something against me, I know – what, what, in heaven's name? Am I not the most wanted man in the whole country? As I watch her, she calmly uncovers a small breast, like that of a precocious young girl, and delicately positions the baby's tiny head to nurse, the faintest of smiles on her lips. Once again, I am short of breath. I feel as though I am falling apart. I take out one of my pills and swallow it. In vain.

"The struggle we are waging," I say with difficulty, "demands supreme sacrifice. And risk-taking. You understand, you are one of the risks. Or perhaps the catalyst of a risk. Don't misunderstand me, the man who took up with you took on a dangerous emotional involvement, an obligation and a responsibility. We don't forbid such things – but a member of the underground knows that these are not sensible things to do." I look at her from the bed. "Dedication cannot be divided, and one cannot consecrate oneself to more than one thing at a time. Yes, take me. What am I? I have no wife, as you undoubtedly know. I had one," I smile. Memories emerge from the fog as if it had all been a dream. "Now she's married to some Italian textile merchant. 'You hate me,' she always used to whine. 'You never come home. You're forever out on your mysterious errands.' Yes..." I laugh to myself. "Two years ago I went to Florence to collect some mail and old papers from her. Her name is Martelli now. Can you imagine? Signora Martelli! There I am at the door and out comes a fat woman with a flushed face. And how those cunning eyes of hers shone when she took her husband's hand and smiled at him. The very picture of fake contentment..."

The young woman smiles to herself and her baby, as if harboring a secret. Didn't she long for me somehow, in some way, back there in Florence, long for me to take hold of her roughly and bare her secrets, naked, as I had done when she was thin and did not blush even on the wildest nights, when her hair flew about her, and her body was hot. Yes, yes. The women were few and far between. There was Dora. Her hair was always done up and carefully pinned, and her clothes were always starched. My people brought her in to run my office and my house, though I had never really had either. And she became treasurer and secretary and confidante to me; but never did she agree to take a code name. A hard woman. We spent many hours together, alone, in the "center" at 32 Ben Yehuda Street, third floor, behind the door which bore the name "Berger." It was a rented apartment, a place for me to live and conduct business. Sometimes late at night, when we opened the heavy blackout curtains and stole out onto the balcony – the guards outside never allowed me, for my own safety, to stand there – a sea breeze would caress us, softening my grand, far-reaching thoughts and her masculine obduracy. We would gaze at the street below, dotted with lights, her hand would stroke mine suggestively, and afterwards we would go back into the room, to the yellow electric light and the darkened windows, draw the curtains, lock the door from the inside – this too against the explicit orders of my bodyguards –

move the folding bed into the corner where the lookout couldn't see it from the keyhole, and make love in the blazing light. And she would cling to me unrelentingly, to the point of pain, suddenly, in a kind of furious despair. Where is Dora now? In America, I think. Yes, a number of my people suspected her of treachery. One Saturday they saw her at the Kaete Dan Hotel with M.L. from the National Council. They wanted to put her on trial, but I objected and insisted they leave her alone. I assume they knew what had been going on between us, and there was a bad taste in my mouth when they agreed, against their will, to drop her case. Since then I've never had more than casual relations with women. After a year of abstinence, my officers hinted shyly that, if I wanted to, it might be a good idea to bring someone in for a night – "a *good* girl, to be sure" (ha!) – and I refused. I still bore a grudge against them over the woman Dora, whom they hadn't allowed even to say goodbye to me before she left the country; and I remembered my own failure. It has been a long time, a long time, since she or those who passed judgement on her have been with me.

The young woman is sitting with her blouse open, her dark-skinned infant snuggled up against her, its soft lips to her breast and its hands clutching her belly. There is a faint afterglow of sun from the window in her black eyes, and her clothes fill the room with a bluish presence. Walls of gray-violet and blue, the white of her breasts, the golden sunlight in her eyes, and the dark-pink skin of the infant. "Please, I don't want you to misunderstand our struggle. In a war like this one, there can be no concessions," I explain from my position on the iron bed. "Most people hate us, and there are only a few dozen of us left. Not more. And no one has had such losses as ours or such achievements. These conquerors must not be given a moment's rest, not one! You understand? Little by little, we've got to poison, yes, poison the water they drink. We've got to boobytrap the wheels of their cars. We've got to threaten their lives, over the radio and over the telephone. Each one of them by name. There can be no waiting, no respite. They must be tormented without letup. Kidnapping and hanging and bombing and killing and sowing fear. Constantly. Constantly. So that they never imagine for a moment that their presence in this country is accepted, so that they do not lapse into complacency. Look, that traitor Weizmann is going today to the Anglo-American Committee. Why? To sell us, to sell us all down the river. We must kill on both sides, or they'll never understand how desperately serious the matter is, even if so few are willing to sacrifice everything for its sake."

She looks up at me, and I read in her eyes what I imagine to be a quizzical disbelief. Perhaps she has not understood. Perhaps my speech has become muddled. "I know that many lives are being lost and it might all seem pointless," I explain, "but in the final analysis everything balances out. Look, even if every last one of my people is killed, there will be others to fall in behind me. There will, I tell you! Self-sacrifice is a powerful thing. Even the willingness to sacrifice has a certain power."

Saying nothing, the young woman strokes the curly wisps of hair on her baby's head, and as he rhythmically sucks her in, she begins humming a tune. All my rationales, all the persuasiveness I have left, all my charisma – everything I am blessed with lies prostrate at her short-socked feet as she sits on the stone step, here above me, yet miles away in her own remote world. Again I am left speechless. I, who am never at a loss for words, I, who set young men on fire – suddenly I am an old man, watching with tired eyes as an infant suckles at its tranquil mother's breast; and the sight is steadily fading, drifting away like smoke, smoke the color of milk.

At last, I fall asleep. Limp, dazed, I sink into the darkness, and all my aches and fears evaporate. Looking up, I see at my bedside all my heros: Eamon de Valera and Avshalom Ben David, Leib Trotsky and General Charles de Gaulle, Shabtai Zvi and Charles Parnell and Marshal Carl Gustav von Mannerheim. Am I mourning my own disintegration? Perhaps. Tenderly, these hardened men offer me their encouragement. De Valera strokes my head and wipes the sweat off my brow with a soft handkerchief. You've done enough, comrade, Trotsky says. No need to do any more. You can stay here at home now. Relax, Mannerheim tells me, so old and wise. Things will take care of themselves. It is a historical process which cannot be stopped.

You're tired, sir, says de Valera with a kind look. Fear is part of human nature. Tim O'Leary and Parnell and I used to have it too when things weren't going well. Avshalom Ben David coughs, and Shabtai Zvi smoothes my long, unruly hair, and I relax and sink back like a baby into the bedclothes.

I open my eyes and the room is full of men in uniform. Soldiers and CID men and police in their clumsy uniforms and plainclothes men in ugly, gray suits. My hands and feet are tied with coarse rope, and Captain Morton is laughing contentedly in my face. One of the others standing over me is taking notes. Sergeant O'Flynn pulls a knife from his belt and cuts me loose in a single motion. I try to get up, but I am quickly manacled hand and foot. I nearly fall back on the bed, but Morton, as if lending a hand to an old friend, grips me by the arms and helps me up - helps me back to prison, to the loneliness, to the gallows. The soldiers clutch their weapons, fingers on the trigger, nervous eyes covering every direction. Outside, brakes screech, motor cars cough with a human sound, and barricades are ready to fend off the curious.

In the corner, on the stone step, the young woman is still nursing her infant. In his mouth is the small white breast, and his hands clutch his mother's soft belly. Warmth passes from the one to the other; tenderness and delicacy flow between them. Calmly, she shifts her knees and hums her little son a quiet tune, throaty and soothing, cooing under her breath. On his way to the door, a young Scottish soldier of the conquering army, a mere boy in a baggy uniform with blue eyes and blond, close-cropped hair, casts a look of longing in her direction, and I hear him say, perhaps to one of his comrades, perhaps to himself, "There's a heavenly sight for you!"

No, I want to tell the boy, no. Far from heavenly. But I cannot find the words. The captain's firm hand is guiding me out into the blinding light of the March day of 1946. From the wall on the other side of the street, two cooks in white smile at me from a Megged Oil advertisement. The doors of a small, black Morris are opened for me, and columns of soldiers, their guns drawn and ready, line my path on either side. A boy of seventeen or eighteen leaps out of the crowd with a pained shriek, demanding that the guards set me free. But with a single blow from the butt of his pistol, Sergeant O'Flynn strikes him down. Or perhaps, as I prepare to die a dog's death, I am just imagining it. Perhaps no one has stepped forward to rescue me. The old man gets up from his position by the wall, strokes his thin beard and looks at me, his head cocked, with his good eye and his bad one. Is he waving goodbye? His hand freezes partway up, like the camera of an alert photographer. Could it be his fist that he was about to shake at me?

They push me into the car and lock the doors with a bang. A soldier sits on either side of me, the barrels of their guns in my ribs, and Captain Morton sits next to the driver. With a roar of the motor, the car pulls away. At that, the English officer turns to me and smiles, as if to say, "Welcome back, my son." And before he draws the little black curtains over the windows to shut me off from the world forever, I observe that there is not a soul in the streets; cars and buses are stopped in their tracks; and fresh, black posters display my face on all the walls. A figure to command respect. Only the mouth is slightly agape, as if in surprise. And piles and piles of corpses litter the sidewalks, as if from an epidemic of cholera. There is no movement, no sign of life. In the whole nation, in all of western Palestine – that is, Free Zion – there is no one left alive. And as we pass, the clock in Mograbi Square strikes eight, never to strike again.

Yossl Birstein

What Did I Do in those First Days in Australia

Translated by Karen Alkalay-Gut

What did I do in those first days in Australia, where I arrived as a boy of sixteen? I sewed pockets in a coat factory, and I read books to chase away boredom. Every day I went to work on the train, and in the evening I read my grandmother a poem or two I had written in Yiddish. She advised me to show them to a writer. She had heard that in Melbourne there was such a writer, called Pinhas Goldhar, but she didn't know his address. Most likely, he sat in the Kadimah Library, studying the books.

I didn't dare ask the old librarian about him, he was deaf anyway and was annoyed at me for troubling him excessively over changing books. He wasn't used to such a rapid pace. His elderly readers turned up once or twice a year to select a thick volume so as to have something to read. I wasn't choosy. When the library was open, two or three times a week, I took whatever came to hand. But I never encountered Pinhas Goldhar.

My grandmother was surprised. Either she hadn't heard right, or he wasn't a real writer – if he didn't spend his time among books. She sensed my nervousness. I turned quiet. I scratched my ears. My crotch. On the train, the bespectacled man who looked like an Italian immigrant irritated me. He took care to sit next to me and peek at the square letters. Over his glasses his heavy stare was frozen on me, observing how I turned the pages backward, from right to left. As my anger grew, I held the book partly closed. Let the Italian stretch his neck if he's so inquisitive. The books I read did not alleviate the boredom of my life. I filled notebooks with poems and didn't find Pinhas Goldhar.

"Perhaps he doesn't exist?" I said to Grandmother one evening, while we were reading by the fire, she *Ts'ena u-Re'ena* and I a similar book, because I had been infected by the old readers and had begun to choose only thick-spined books.

I wasn't surprised then when I sat down in my usual place on the train, beside the window, and saw that, in my haste, I had picked up my grandmother's book by accident. I flipped through it and lingered on the chapter "The Pure Well," which dealt with rules pertaining to men and women. This time I held the book wide open to make it easier for the Italian. Let him enjoy the dotted letters without stretching his neck.

His gaze froze on the book. Suddenly he rested his hand on it and said, in Yiddish, that he could no longer control himself. For months he had kept silent and not interfered, although the order of my reading was driving him crazy. He couldn't understand what kind of reader I was. Poetry, frivolous novels, Ghandi's philosophy, articles about trees in Argentina. He had finally calmed down when he realized that I was reading the books in alphabetical order. Yesterday he had seen me with August Babel's *Women and Socialism* and suddenly it was religious rulings about women in the *Ts'ena u-Re'ena*.

He wanted to know who I was, and then he introduced himself: Pinhas Goldhar.

Yossl Birstein

Once I Was Faced with a Dilemma

Translated by Margaret Birstein

Once I was faced with a dilemma: whether to go to a literature class or to my wedding.

This was years ago in Melbourne after my first poem had been printed in the local Yiddish paper, *Die Oistralisher Nayes*, and Yosef Giligitch, a teacher of Yiddish literature, asked me to come to his house with all my written work. After studying the thin notebook, he agreed, albeit reluctantly, to give me his honest opinion.

"So so."

I asked him to be more specific, and he covered most of his thumbnail, pointed to the exposed tip and said, "That's how much talent you have. About one millimeter of thumbnail."

"My boy," he called me, when I'd told him my age. I was about nineteen.

He handed back my notebook, and when he noted my confusion, he asked if I had ever heard of the anapest. The question embarrassed me even further, and then he softened somewhat, and volunteered to teach me the basic laws and principles of poetry. He would give me a series of lessons free of charge, but he could do it only on Saturday evenings, when most Melbournites, my girlfriend and I included, usually went to the movies. This was the only time he had free and, as he saw it, a young poet who was anxious to develop his talent ought not to think twice, and should be ready and eager to make sacrifices on the altar of poetry.

One Saturday evening, however, something different cropped up. It wasn't a case of the movies versus poetry, but our own wedding. I couldn't bring myself to confess to my teacher, Yosef Giligitch, that I, a young poet, nonconformist and rebel against convention, was about to commit such a bourgeois act. Hence, my bride-to-be and I decided not to breathe a word about it to Yosef Giligitch. That Saturday evening she would go to the synagogue and I – to my lesson.

By that time, the anapest was no longer unfamiliar to my ear, nor the amphibrach, the trochee and the iambus. While the wedding guests awaited me beside the canopy, I sat in Yosef Giligitch's house, poring over a book of poems by Leib Neidus, a Yiddish poet who sacrificed his brief life on the altar of poetry, and succeeded magnificently in marrying anapests and iambuses. What, after all, was my sacrifice compared to his? I mused, and I folded back the tablecloth, and tapped bent fingers on the wood of the table to the rhythm of his words.

I knew that in the synagogue, the wedding canopy had been unfolded and the bridegroom was awaited. My bride, her parents and grandparents, my friend, the painter Yossl Bergner, and my cousin tall Yossl. The two Yossls had promised that they would keep the gathering from dispersing by shouting, at the first sign of impatience: "Here he is! Here he is!" And I continued to tap anapests and amphibrachs on the table, in the hope that the day would come when I would bring my teacher Yosef Giligitch a new poem, and he, after reading it, would raise his thumb and show me his whole thumbnail.

Yossl Birstein

One Day, during World War Two

Translated by Margaret Birstein

One day, during World War Two, a military chaplain arrived at our army camp in the Australian outback, to celebrate the Feast of Hanukkah with us and tell us about the wars of the Maccabees. Apart from the Jewish troops, there were soldiers of other nationalities in the camp, most of them – Greeks. One of them, Papadimitrio, a giant from a village in Macedonia with the lips of a horse, had made friends with my friend Paul Wolff, a doctor of philosophy from Germany. They were tentmates and shared candies and food from the kitchen. They used to sit together in silence.

On the day of the chaplain's visit, we Jews had assembled in one section of the huge mess hut, and in the remaining area the Greeks were playing cards. The two friends, the philosopher and the villager, were sitting in a far corner. Paul Wolff was reading a book by Schopenhauer, the high priest of pessimism, and Papadimitrio, who was illiterate, was holding a closed prayerbook with a large cross imprinted on its cover, and mumbling words to a monotonous, endless melody. On his bottom lip hung the trace of a smile, as is sometimes the case with horses.

The rabbi began his sermon in Hebrew with the words: "When I kindle these candles," and immediately switched to English to recount the story of the wicked Antiochus, king of the Greeks, who persecuted the Jews of Palestine in ancient times, and how the Jews rose up against him.

The Jewish soldiers hinted that he should lower his voice, but in vain. One of the cardplayers, hearing the word "Greeks," raised his head from the cards, pricked up his ears, sniffed the air and became alert. Other cardplayers followed suit. Most of them were fishmongers, stevedores, nightclub regulars in civilian life, and they had never heard about the wars between the Jews and the Greeks. The two nations had been co-existing peacefully in the camp.

Now one of them leapt up onto the table and called on all pure-blooded men to rally to his standard on the parade ground outside. The Jews also filed out.

Papadimitrio too picked up his stick and went out to join the fray. It was a spiked stick on which he impaled the scraps of paper which littered the ground. He'd been given that job soon after being drafted, because of the way he always walked, head down and gaze on the ground.

Paul Wolff also stepped outside, but he stood apart and didn't join his compatriots. When Papadimitrio noticed this, he left his group and walked over to his friend to persuade him to join his fellow Jews.

Friendship is fine, but when there's a war, you have to fight for your own side.

Paul Wolff shook his head. He'd been through Dachau because he was a Jew, but no Hitler was going to tell him who he was. He had always shunned the crowd and he intended to make his way in the world as an individual.

Their argument was conducted in the middle of the parade ground, halfway between the two camps, with hand and head gestures, because the giant Macedonian had always contented himself with four or five syllables a day.

Someone in the Greek camp shouted out to him:

"Beat up the kike!"

Papadimitrio stood there in alarm. The stick trembled in his raised hand. Even when his head was drooping, he towered over his friend. The trace of a smile had vanished from his lower lip.

The shouts from the Greek camp continued:

"Give it to the kike!"

Papadimitrio continued to stand facing Wolff, his head bowed over his friend's, like a great merciful father grieving over his rebellious son.

Shulamit Gilboa

An Incident That's Over and Done with is Usually Boring

Translated by Chaya Galai

An incident that's over and done with is usually boring. It has a beginning and an end, sometimes there's a lesson to be learned, sometimes there's malicious gloating. In the homes of the neighbors, over slices of cheesecake or *borekas*, it's inflated to mammoth proportions. Marco oils the Czech rifles in the armory, gritting his teeth as he labors, polishing the safety-catches and the barrels; Ruthie, who is doing her army service as a teacher, hides an Uzi under her pillow at night; and people say that only Jutte, the widow, prays on cold nights that it'll happen to her as well, and then she'll serve up *lokshen* soup, a little *gefillte* fish, the smell of home on winter nights.

Whenever Marco beats Toni or slouches around sullen and dejected, everyone says, So what would he have preferred?! And when Toni's belly grows rounder, they joke and say, This time it'll be a boy. As black as night, Mazal says, winking at her husband and at the clinic nurse, who claims emphatically that they're all wrong, it's simply impossible to get pregnant while breast-feeding. The latest conception could only have happened after that regrettable incident, she repeats, and everyone hears her saying it but nobody's listening.

There's something illogical about this whole story, Roich asserts. He sends Yardena off to bring some refreshments for the committee members who are gathered in his house for their weekly meeting. And between the oatmeal cookies and the chilled seltzer, she assumes like everyone else, It could never have happened to me, ponders and decides in favor of the plastic cups instead of the glasses, including the cracked jug. But then Rabinowitz says, We ought to insist on having soldiers posted here permanently or the Border Police, and I'd like to take the opportunity of proposing that we get rid of Marco. Very true, Roich agrees, what kind of a guard is it who can't even guard his own wife, and they all start laughing and then stop, and only Yardena, who has managed to set down the jug carefully, still shakes with laughter, clutching her midriff, hunched over and aching from the muscular effort.

And I thought about the night when he walked through the hills. Stumbling on stones, scraping his knees, his calves, his fingers. How he pressed himself against the earth for fear of lights and people. Cursing the shrieks of birds, tightening his shoelaces or slithering along in boots. Black. Coarse rubber. About how he crawled on all fours when he reached the skyline and wriggled like a snake along the curve of the hillside, behind blocks of yellow stone, maybe briar bushes, maybe thorns, his eyes sore. About the daylight hours he spent in orange groves, listening to the thump of the pumps raising water to the stone conduits and from there to the mud canals snaking around heavy old trees, contemporaries of his father and planted by his hands. How he hid under the foliage of the grapefruit tree, pressing hard against the trunk, trying not to soak in the fragrance of the blossoms, camouflaging his chest and face with clods of precious red, indifferent earth. A stinking shirt. Wide black-rimmed fingernails and on the little finger the purplish-blue mark of a bruise. I thought about his hunger rumbling between his belly and his throat, about his larynx rising and falling, about the stench under his arms, the thick curls in his armpits.

Waiting minute after minute, hour after hour, perhaps day after day.

Hearing voices in a familiar language, in the smell of pita baking on the fire and an egg in olive oil. Hearing the grinding of green peppers and almost feeling the moisture spilling out of them into the sides of the mouth, and almost shouting, Give it here; something black and spongy and torn in two, steeped in margarine, smothered in onions.

And at noon, when the shadows shrink around the tree trunks, crawling cautiously, speeding towards the cold water and perhaps being startled by the random footsteps of the agricultural instructor, a *yahud* who cultivates a mustache as a disguise, and crouching down hurriedly beside the mud canal, filling up with water and coolness and thinking, Perhaps it's better to be caught earlier, before, because in any case what do I have to return to.

And perhaps not in these precise words, perhaps not in others either. Perhaps much less of a human being, more enmity in the eyes. Devious. As threatening as a sewer rat in Dickens' London. Scurrying with sharp eyes and razorlike teeth wherever his hunger takes him. Hungry for blood. For the soft noses of newborn infants. An ungovernable urge.

The third house in the northern row. A neglected yard, a small shed, a woman coming and going in these nighttime hours and some vague hope that the struggle will be easy.

Nasser, who is to be Toni's, steals forward with giant steps and hunger pounds at him, equivalent to fury.

Toni is gazing at her baby daughter. She finds it hard to believe. The curve of the lips, the flat nose, Whatever you want, my precious, she says voicelessly, smoothing the mosquito netting. Sleep, my precious, my life, and she passes a hand over her right breast. When she feels emotional, the milk flows. Yellow patches, the vestiges of previous emotions, have made inverse pear-shaped patches on the front of her robe, which is covered with the stains of applesauce and lunches.

Two in the morning. The nurse assured her that it wouldn't take more than two months. Soon you won't have to get up in the night, Mrs. Benita, if you add a little formula from the bottle, you can organize the schedule to your convenience. But Toni, six months later, hasn't made her mind up about what's convenient. The night has a special fragrance and sounds of its own, and in the bright light of day, the weeds flourish. Marco is on guard duty at night and spends most of the day sleeping. The fields have been neglected, and so have the animals. It's only his unsteady wage as substitute guard that staves off hunger and shame. Sleep, my precious, Toni hums with closed mouth, opening the shutter on the window which overlooks the back yard, with heavy clumps of fruit trees behind it, and hills.

The unaccustomed girdle is pressing on her groin. The cotton brassiere, two sizes larger than her regular brassiere, is wet and clings to her breasts. Behind the window panes the night awaits the touch of a hand, and the security lights, dispersed at regular intervals, emit a yellow corona. Things will turn out fine, Toni says as she stands at the window, her nose pressed to the glass. Olivia will grow up and help out. Things will work out fine.

The distressed bleat of the she-goat, strange at this time of night, sends shivers down her spine. Only yesterday Marco told her that Nureyev's goat had been bitten and was sick. It's hard to prevent a mad jackal from breaking in, biting and transmitting poison. Toni shivers again. The stealthy paws of rabies-stricken jackals surround her. There won't be any trouble, Marco says, but Toni senses that there is and there will be more. You smell of milk, he smiled as he went out, Look after yourselves, and Toni knows that it's precisely when things start going well that they turn bad. Groping for her coat, she shoves her feet into her rubber boots. They'll really be needing the goat's milk in a few weeks time and she has no intention of allowing it to spoil.

Outside, the cold stings her face. A light bulb outside the shed where the laying hens are kept illuminates the grass and a pile of irrigation pipes. Toni relaxes. The rusty iron handle is resting firmly on its base and the she-goat is drowsing on a bed of straw, her belly rising and falling, her udders swollen, gleaming in the narrow strip of light which seeps through the front door. Oh, those fears, Toni breathes a sigh of relief and hastens indoors. Before the birth she used to sleep so heavily that she wasn't even aware when Marco came in and lay down at her side. Seven months ago she didn't even hear the explosion that killed a family in the neighboring moshav. They came, threw the grenades and went, *Yemah shemam* – may their names be wiped out, said the border policemen who came to brief the men. All day long they sat in the orange grove and waited for dark, and nobody noticed them. Bastards. Bastards.

We would have noticed, said Aryeh, and Laniado knocked on wood, stifling a belch. But Aryeh is troubled, Toni can tell. Marco, who does guard duty in place of the more prosperous members of the moshav, knows Aryeh very well, and Toni knows how to interpret what Marco's feeling. Never mind, she says. Who knows, perhaps now we have a child, he'll change his job. Concentrate on farming. Work in the daytime.

Out of habit she found herself in the kitchen. The glasses in the sink roused her thirst. Two thirty. At six Olivia will want to nurse again, and before that she has to put out the chicken feed and let the goat into the alfalfa patch. Toni is tired. The long-handled *finjan* is heavy in her hands. Marco brought it, black and thick-bottomed, from his grandmother's house, to make real coffee for his parents when they come to visit. To give them a taste of their own home when they come to mine, he said. A heaped spoonful, a pinch of cardamom, lots of sugar. Only after she'd poured out the thick coffee, enveloped in its shameless smell, did she decide that she would have preferred milk. It's the exhaustion, that's what it is. Six months after the birth and it still feels as if she's toting heavy stones. Toni set down the *finjan* on the gas burner and sipped some water. Bubbles rose up inside her, bursting. Scattering into splinters down to the tips of her fingernails. With a sigh of relief she switched off the light, instantly concealing the front door, the table, the sink, groping her way blindly to her room, straight to the wide double bed, to the comforter which had already turned chilly. Folding her frozen feet under her thighs, she begged the God of the weary to appease Oli. Don't wake up, my precious, Daddy will guard us and please let Mummy sleep. All over the world people sleep in the middle of the night.

The sudden sound of the front door closing startled Toni. Marco? He never came in for a cup of coffee during work. Sitting bolt upright, she listened tensely to the silence, which remained undisturbed. It could have been a cat jumping up at the door, a strong gust of wind, a dream – she tugged at the blanket and called out, Mar-co? As she was thinking of lying down again, the creaking of shoes made her jump up and slide into her robe, her body atremble. God, please make it be

Marco. She was already poised to crawl under the bed, it's always better to live than to die, when she remembered the baby and ran to her, stumbling over her slippers, kicking them away, shouting Ay ay and standing with her back to the cot with something as big as a mountain and black facing her and saying to her through a long grimy mustache, *Uskut!* (Quiet!), a submachine gun in his hand.

Mama, Mama, Toni searches for comfort, with a mouth like a fish stranded on dry land, and the mountain standing beside her, his hand already over her mouth, shoves her from room to room, in search of the open or hidden presence of other people. Nobody here, nobody here, she says with an effort, with sensations in her back she never knew existed. Her feet miss the floor, bobbing on foam, responding to his shoves, straight ahead of him, covering him whenever he opens a door. Nobody here, nobody here, she tried again outside the baby's room, trying to move him on to the bathroom, to the bedroom, but being pushed in, faltering, banging against the wooden slats and waking the baby, who was startled and began to wail. My precious, she wept with her, stretching out her arms, but the man jostled her, hastily lifted the little body in one hand high over his head, staring at the mother, for a long moment weighing his moves.

Toni is frozen. Her hands are outstretched, her face distorted, clearly illuminated in the intimate circle created by the little nightlight beside the cot. The shadows of the spherical mobile suspended over the cot flicker tranquilly on the wall. In the wall-hanging, mothers are bathing their babies, and only the shadow of Olivia, clutched in one of his hands, swells to giant proportions and is broken at the corners of the room.

You keep quiet and I won't do anything. You shout and I throw her outside, he bursts out in Arabic vernacular, introducing an illusory sanity into the flat, high sobs that, she suddenly realizes, are coming from her. *Tayeb, tayeb*, she gasps, playing her part in a game whose outcome has already been settled.

Nobody here? Husband?

Nobody. Yes, there is, she thinks, befuddled. Marco, you're on guard duty outside and I'm here inside with the death in his eyes.

Your child is in his hands, and you're out there with a gun that's never been fired.

Aleppo? he asks, Tripoli? And Toni sees that he is lowering the baby and clutching her to his side, and can't hear and can't understand, just sees the marks of mud and soot on the little knitted outfit and the tiny wet face. Give me, she pleads in Arabic, She'll be quiet with me, and the words seem to emerge on their own, from a childhood in distant stone houses, from a father who smoked a *nargila* and chewed tobacco and traded in cloth. It will be all right, nobody will hear, and she moves towards him, believing in the power of words, and is hurled backwards by his strong push, and gets up hastily to pursue his wide, black receding back, as he darts through the rooms, turning the key in the front door lock twice, closing all the windows, searching the kitchen drawers and discovering the long butcher's knife and then turning back, encountering her right behind him, aiming the blade of the knife at the baby's belly and saying slowly, If you keep quiet, it will be OK. Shout and she dies, like this, no bullet, quietly.

Toni sits down on the floor, a room without walls all around her and the knife curving and straightening to the rhythm of her pounding heart. From below she sees his full stature. A big man, wide-limbed, gazing at her with curiosity, a wide gap between his front teeth.

Money, jewelry? Toni tries, stretching trembling fingers to her neck to tear off her chain, exposing, as she does so, beautiful, swollen breasts, with a heavy *hamsa* good-luck charm suspended between them. Her hands scrabble to her ears to unscrew an earring, to her fingers to pull off a ring, skipping from neck to ear to hand in the spasmodic dance of a wounded butterfly.

Not money, he says, food. And the words travel a long way before they take on meaning.

In the kitchen, her feet have a new stability. Lots of food, tons of food, Toni exults, scurrying from the refrigerator to the sink, from the gas burners to the table, piling up tomatoes, *labaneh*, *halva*, eggs, jelly, bell peppers, taking things out, dropping them, picking them up, rinsing, selecting the choicest morsels, setting out a best plate, a polished glass. She steals a glance at Olivia, pinned to the table by his left arm, and sees that her eyes are closing, and breathes a sigh of relief. The worst of all is behind her.

When she goes over to the drawer in the cabinet to take out cutlery, the stranger leaps up and closes it with a bang on her fingers, Not to touch the knives, and Toni, rinsing her fingers under the faucet to dull the pain, realizes, for the first time, that this big, dirty man is afraid of her.

All right, *habibi*, I'm not touching, just giving them to you, eat, she trills, gazing at Oli, wiping her eyes, turning into the kind of woman we'll read about some day in hardcover novels.

He eats hastily, with one hand, leaving traces of soil on the oilcloth, on the bread, on the smooth white edge of the onion. Toni flutters around him – sesame cookies from the cookie jar, *baklava* left over from Aunt Sultana, from last Shabbat, and has a sudden brainwave, accompanied by self-congratulation: perhaps even some of the whitish *ouzu* that her nephew, Shaul, brought back from the duty-free, but no.

What is your name? she tries, with her back to him, reheating the coffee in the *finjan*, prepared so recently and so long ago.

Nasser, comes the unexpected reply, hinting at something optimistic and, allowing herself to savor the homely smell, she tries again, From far away?

Here you are, catch.

Toni spins around and catches the baby as she is thrown at her, not letting herself imagine what would have happened if she hadn't sensed his intention and reacted accordingly. Squeezing the little body to her bosom, to her face, she sits down with her on a chair facing him, burying her nose, her eyes, her forehead in the baby, trying to thank him, suffused with happiness. The baby smacks her lips, squirming, burrowing, feeling the familiar warmth, stretching somnolent hands to Toni's face, sneezing and concluding by closing her eyes.

Toni is lost. Bliss, such as she has never before known, threatens to engulf her. With a saliva-dampened finger she rubs off the traces of mud, smoothes the cheek, notices the thin tendrils of grass adhering to the baby from his clothes, his hands. Her breasts ache, the flow within her drains into conflicting pain and she recalls her mother's tales about nursing mothers whose milk dried up because of terror or catastrophe. There was the story of the rabbi's wife from one of the Atlas mountain villages who was standing beside the cot of her eldest son when a horned man peeped in at her through the window, gesturing to her to come over. And she, guided by Satan or Lilith, instead of going over to her child, feeding him, covering him, banishing evil thoughts by taking the right action, hastened to the window, to close it and be rid of the man. But as she came closer, the horns disappeared and his face became rounder and he turned into the prince of the desert, and then she remembers that the window of her son's room faces a cliff and nobody could be standing there unless he possessed supernatural powers and, anxious to banish the demon, she rushed to find her prayer book, but her feet wouldn't budge and the name of her saintly husband escaped her memory, and she gazed at the stranger and said to him, What a beautiful horse you have between your legs. And the horse, which suddenly appeared out of nowhere, was black and smooth, with quivering nostrils, and the prince mounted it, smiled beneath his thick mustache, his eyes laughing, and said, Oh, my beauty, come out through the window and mount my horse with me, and she tried to curse him and drive him away and she clutched the curtain and her eyes closed – and suddenly there was nobody there and no horse either, only a crying, hungry infant, blue in the face with pain and screaming, and her milk dried up that instant.

The hiss of coffee overflowing onto the gas burner startled Toni and she rushed to pour the remainder into a little china cup decorated with flowers and serve it to Nasser. From a long way away? she repeated.

His mouth crammed full of food, his bloodshot eyes rolling, he leaps up suddenly from the table, the grenades in his belt clattering, the rifle butt banging against the table, dashes to the window and stares out at the night, listening. What can he see out there apart from the closed shed and clumps of fruit trees?

Now, thinks Toni, now. But her legs betray her. Olivia is heavy in her arms and Toni slumps heavily in her chair. And now he's coming back from the window, reassured by the stillness, unbuckling his belt, throwing Toni a measuring glance, sitting down, grasping the coffee cup. And as he gulps, he nods his head towards the neighboring village, Jabel al-Kuds, in silent answer to her question, and then gestures in all four directions as if to say, It's all mine, this moshav as well.

With her fingertips, Toni strokes Oli's forehead, where the hair is beginning to sprout. Light sweat dampens her finger. She can see a damp patch spreading through the outfit. I have to change her, she says, then stops short, alarmed, as she sees the knife suddenly pointing at her and realizes that she must have spoken in Hebrew. She's done peepee, I need to clean it, she says, reverting to Arabic, explaining slowly, taking care to use the guttural pronunciation of her mother and grandmother, sounds forgotten over the years. Turning her back, she paces slowly, clutching Olivia to her breast, towards the baby's room. The baby will catch cold.

Nasser follows her, leaving the empty cup and the still-laden table. His eyes follow her hands. Toni works slowly, dipping cotton buds in cleansing lotion. She opens Olivia's legs, lifts them, cleans the plump creases, opens the orifices and scatters more talcum powder than necessary. For a moment she forgets his presence. He isn't going to murder them, of that she's already convinced. If he'd intended to, he could have done it some time ago. And she doesn't believe he comes from Jabel al-Kuds. In the six years of living together, she would have glimpsed his face among the bus passengers or the field workers. Perhaps he was born here and fled in 1948. An infant in his mother's arms, tied to her dress. It's not a good idea to give inaccurate information about him. Afterwards. When they ask. In any case, he didn't come to murder me, her heart sang, and she folded the diaper between Oli's legs, tucking the ends under without diaper pins, the way her aunt taught her.

There's more coffee, take it, drink, before it gets cold.

With calm movements she laid the baby on her stomach, her head turned towards the wall, covered her, tightened the covers round her and turned to the door.

The knife was at face level and gestured to her to stand still.

Pick her up, he said, carry her, leading them both to the bedroom.

But I won't do anything, she wept, the restraint of the past few minutes cracking like a thin eggshell. Whatever you want, food, money, clothes, what else do you want?

How can I tell whether hunger and repletion were locked in combat inside him together with hatred and love? Perhaps it was the coffee that instilled alertness in his limbs and torpor in his brain, and perhaps it was Toni, her breasts overflowing with milk, anxious to nurse Oli, and behind her his mother, his sisters, the women he would never have.

Outside the night was still and dark and his eyes were as red as if there were no wars in the world, only a human being, a weary lump of flesh, the flow of blood. At gunpoint, he ordered her to put down the baby. Toni screamed. He swivelled round slowly and pointed to the baby. What do you prefer? Nasser has his way with Toni and her daughter lies open-eyed at her side. The knife is at arm's reach and her body is paralyzed, crushed, sprawled in the double bed with arms, legs, breasts and a vulva which fills all the emptiness in the world. Nasser breathes heavily, the stench of sweat and cow dung seeps into Toni's vagina, into her blood stream, seethes in her brain, trickles out of her eyes, fades into the rectangular shapes that the window panes cast on the wall opposite, and escapes into the yard.

When he was through, he allowed her to nurse but her milk had dried up. Stiff with terror, she lifted her drained breasts and wailed quietly. I'll boil some milk, my precious, you won't be hungry, my soul, and oblivious to her wet thighs, she went into the kitchen to boil milk, but then he jabbed the rifle into her back again and said, Food, food, and she served it. She served up the whole refrigerator. A smile sneaked through the gap between his front teeth, and when he had had enough, he gave them back their lives.

Nasser runs. None of the guards hear him. Nobody spies him. After studying the diameter of the footprints and the hollows they left in the clay soil, the trackers decided that he was more than a meter ninety tall and weighed more than ninety kilos. Marco returned home at dawn, found the two of them half fainting, one from hunger and the other from terror and shame, and alerted the Border Police.

He came, ate and went, Marco repeated to them what Toni had told him between wails and sobs. My wife talked to him in his language. Perhaps he took pity on her. What a fine figure of a man he was, how come he didn't harm her, people sniggered, She must have been good to him.

By the time they started searching for him, he must have found shelter in one of the *wadis* or in a jackal's den, or perhaps he had already crossed the border, boasting, I killed, I did things, I liberated. The curfew the Military Government imposed on the surrounding villages and a house-to-house search revealed nothing, but we knew he was there in one of the nearby villages, waiting, looking for vulnerable spots.

Lord have mercy, says Zecharia to Marco, days later, sitting beside him in the synagogue, twisting his thin beard round his finger, agreeing that food is better than a woman. You don't murder someone who gives you good food, lots of it, he says, helping Marco out. You don't beat them up either.

She fainted, Marco repeats, and the baby was crying. He's a human being too, isn't he? The main thing is that they were spared, Zecharia sums up, May the Lord have mercy on us and on all the House of Israel, and Marco nods in agreement. A small place. Small people. Cruel thoughts.

All she did was serve him food, shouts Marco, and Toni's swelling belly goads his hands to deliver hard, blunt blows, laden with hatred. Toni is shut in the house and we, staring at every male Arab, who shrivels under our gaze – perhaps it's his brother, his uncle, his son – hold avid and learned debates on which of the two versions is the gospel truth.

David Grossman

Cherries in the Icebox

Translated by Marsha Weinstein

Tonight, after we made love, Tamar cried. What is there to add? The wounded pillow, ravaged in her mouth; the foul sap oozing from her wounds; perhaps the bristling tension of my muscles, or the hiss escaping from the cracks in my body as they are hastily sealed against the particles of pain that float in the room. Or this: my lying there beside her, splayed on my back and snoring lightly, rhythmically, exuding the manliness expected of me as I lie there, stupid with pleasure and exhaustion, a naked man devoid of all desire beside a seeming-woman, beside her nine faces which are now reabsorbed into her resting features, the face that was drawn into his own cries when he clenched his teeth tight so that he would cry out the correct name of the nine, of the ninety, so that, afterwards he would sink, masking his face with contentment.

Tamar cried soundlessly. I felt the sting of sweat behind my knees and neck. I snored insistently. When we were making love, everything was as usual. Before, too. We brought the twins from Tamar's mother's, then the bedtime ritual – the gurglings over the sink, the car pool arrangements for tomorrow – and then – the tears.

I shift slightly in place. Sigh at the echo of a dreamy unease. There a woman is crying. She'll calm down in a minute. These deep sobs, they rend her body. Furrows are ploughed slowly, rustling over the marzipan surface of our bed. Tamar is crying.

Seven years of marriage. This afternoon I picked up the girls from kindergarten and brought them to Tamar's mother's. The young waitress smiled when I said we were celebrating a private holiday, and so would order the finest wine. Tamar screwed up her face grudgingly, but I gave her a lengthy stare, making her smile. We're not watching our pockets today. It's not just the money, Tamar said, and don't drink today.

The girl brought us two violet cyclamens. Her fingers were long and brittle. From the management, she said, and all the best to you. While we ate, she never ceased darting loving, moist glances at us. She's writing our story, I said, and drank from the pungent wine. Tamar followed the movements of my hands. I ask for the best wine, I said, and she brings me *havdalah* wine. Don't make a scene, Tamar said. I poured another glass.

Tamar sliced her quiche with precision. One for Daddy and one for Granny and an itty-bitty one for Annie. Tamar's hair is a bit sparse and short, her forehead white and smooth. What are you looking at me like that for? Here: the dance of the time-honored glances has already begun tracing a delicate pattern on the cheeks' parchment. What do you mean – like that? The lines of separation beginning to show. Even in her. Like *that*, like you've never seen me before. This, too, should be remarked: a faint, tired wing of destruction on the childlike chin; the earth, gently tempting, draws the corners of the mouth to it. Hey, Tami: you're cute.

It was in this vegetarian restaurant that we sat seven years ago, the afternoon of the wedding. Tamar was then twenty-three, and I twenty-six. But I love you much more today, I say to the red silhouette of my face on the wine glass. We were such children, says Tamar. I drink my winey, wavy image. Such children, she repeats.

We ate. That morning someone had hinted that next month my employment at the university might be terminated, because of the cutbacks. I didn't mention it to Tamar. Rumors like that had come and gone. I didn't want to see her nostrils flare as if in anticipation of great danger, see the determined responsibility well up in her eyes. The soup came.

What did we talk about then? I promised you I would be unfaithful within a year; I said I wouldn't pretend, not even on that day, and that

I detested the idea that anyone would think so little of me as to trust me. Really, lovely things to hear the morning of your wedding day, Tamar said, leaning her chin on her hand and glaring at me. And I'm ready, I said, gulping some soup so that steam would fog up my glasses, to renew that promise today. But I know you, she said, and I believe in you even more now. She smiled. I smiled.

Spoons touched plates. Back then I held to the absolute honesty of evil. Things need to be said, even painful ones. Especially painful ones. Terrible, Tamar said, grinning, you were a terrible child, and I don't know how I fell in love with you. It was my money, I said. Somewhere in the basin of my brain pain began to pound. And my mother's letter of recommendation. How impudent you were – a haughty, worldly, spoiled brat. Uh-uh, I raised a finger, that confidence is what captured you. No, she said sweetly, it was the fear behind it.

Seven years. The body is now smoothed. The rings of age only add beauty, ease our movements one inside the other. Saturday at your parents', Maya drank the syrup by herself. Go to bed, Tamar, I'll write a little longer. Suddenly, it's easy.

But I'm lying, she giggles, I didn't sense your fear. You were a thousand years older than me, and smart and talented and bold. Now: the loving joy kindled in her eyes; her guileless, luminous knowing that together we overpowered it, overpowered me; my diving inside; my slack, circular trawling to the cadence of pain. You used to taunt me, she giggles, because I thought Osnat was the best and most perfect of friends, because for years I let her torment me under the guise of love. You used to blanch to hear me talk about my parents – about us, too – with a tongue like an ice-pick – that's what you called it. And you revelled in feeling like a cursed man, the definitive exile and outcast. And you, and you.

The girl brought tea of fragrant herbs. We're getting married tonight, I told her with a smile. Tamar's lips pursed under the girl's slim arm. I moved slightly, catching them inside the curve of the teapot handle. I knew it, said the waitress, it's written all over your faces. Her watery eyes welled up a bit. I sipped some wine.

And those compulsive little lies of yours, Tamar said briskly, brusquely, the incessant writing of life, the cunning for its own sake. And, I said languidly, your aversion to my writing; your childish hostility toward me on the days when I have a story. Why are we bickering today, Tamar asked, her eyes suddenly extinguished. I extended a hand and drank straight from the bottle. Festive days depress me, Tamar said. I'm actually happy today, I said. A fleeting searing in my temples now joined each dull thud of pain. Someone had welded the exposed edges of the nerves together, by accident. I rhymed to myself, quickly: last hired, first fired. Why not fire the one you just hired? Also (this is pretty good!): 'The prof. is in the pudding.' By then Tamar had noticed that I was blinking nervously but didn't say a word. She touched a finger to my finger. You're having a hard time now that you're not writing, she said.

Now she cries into the pillow. A continuous, honeyed drop of sorrow drips from her, evaporating in its own warmth until it is a thin whistle, a thought, cooling and freezing like a sharp, glinting shard of glass above my carefully closed eyes. We love each other, I repeat. No outside force could spoil the movement of this relationship, because we have a kind of incessant love, I continue, etching the words on the soft inner shell of my eyelid. Now and then it creates hardship and doubt, but only so they can be resolved wisely, with a controlled flare of pain and desire; it has, I whisper to my frightened self, a complete understanding, a deep grasp of the whole process.

Afterwards we went for a walk in Yemin Moshe, down streets paved with stone. We walked hand in hand and at every third step swung an imaginary child who kicked smooth legs. But there were no children that day. I sat down on a stone bench. The orange beak of a blackbird flashed on the grass. You've changed a great deal, I said; of the two of us, you've changed more. Thanks to you, she said and sat down, placing her purse between us, her thin hair lifting as if fluttering in the wind, her eyes grayer than they were blue. The clouds caused that. Thanks to you, she said again, and in spite of you, because at first I lost myself beside you. Everything about you was dear and absolute, even your fears; only when the first years of shock had passed did I begin to fight. And you're still fighting, I said, though sometimes it's unnecessary. After all, I'm an enlightened dictator. No – with you, she jokes cunningly, one has to fight constantly. I've learned to do it without getting too tired. With a weary hand I dragged myself for anger and bitterness, but dredged up nothing.

You were so – she says with wise sorrow – so aggressive, so demanding. I had to fight for a me-I-didn't-know. And now, I said, the results I've achieved sometimes frighten me. I know, she said, but this is the only way. Adding, surprised: I really have learned. You've changed more, I said.

After that we got up, leaned into one another, and embraced. The skies grayed. Let's go to the four o'clock showing and kiss in the dark, Tamar said into my coat. Let's go to the train station and go away, I said in a pensive Russian accent. I hope my mother's coping with the girls. Today we have no girls.

On the way to the café we passed a playground. It was empty, and its shrubs and benches were furled. The slide shone like the outstretched tongue of a child, breathing and curving with metallic torpor. We sat on the rope swings, side by side. The wind whispered at our backs. The swings shifted a bit, and their damp ropes squeaked. Closing my eyes, I flooded my brain with the thick reek of a seaport. Legs kicked at the layer of gravel; muscles stretched from the gut to the tips of the toes and beyond; suddenly, the air freshened.

I remained faithful to her in an old-fashioned way. Even when the expanse of the world was for me a humid, close hothouse; even when the scented trails of glances and veiled meanings were wound around my face. I stitched my desire to her. But the heat of the body melts the iron threads, and the slivers that don't totally evaporate float in the veins, and wound. Women's-eyes' wounds. Perfume's wounds. The wounds of a lover who protects himself from the wounds of women.

And this, too: the potent agility of the imagination's sexual conscience; the longing for a sense of revulsion, which might hint at a chance of salvation; the body that rebels against you. That growls desire at you. At what is left of you. Only the bitter exile in

Tamar's placid loins. Only your love of her, her love of you, a childish pain-reliever that you skeptically swallow.

Stretching, bending the knees, leaning, Tamar passes me with blissful languor, her head arched back, her eyes closed, and I – already I sense the sinewy consistency of my muscles; already this flight sends balls of fire through me that burst in my guts and my groin and under my arms. I've been kidnapped, I'm flying, I'm the eye of the storm, I am devoured. I drag after me the slackened and the rotted. Again I weld the scattered slivers to my body. Even though I can hear Tamar's legs thud against the gravel, hear her clumsy braking; even though I can picture her wondering, still-smiling gaze. I let wildness wail in the arc of my throat, make leaden the iron weighting my body, until I become a giant pendulum slicing the air with my movements, slicing space and time in the semicircle of the swing's arc, again and again slamming against impotence to which the ropes succumb at the peak of flight as they hurl me backwards with determined softness.

Nevertheless, Tamar said at the café, we're much more alike now. Because you've managed to contaminate me a little with your dismal outlook, and I've taught you to love; you're not all sharp angles, and I'm not all soft circles.

We insisted on sitting in the café garden. Rain cubs tussled in the bellies of the clouds (I should write that down). An older waitress, short of stature and temper, was forced to clean the bird droppings off the blue plastic table. Beyond the fence the street cleared the phlegm from its throat. Tamar blew onto her palms. I asked for two hot chocolates and a snifter of brandy. That tooth hurts, I said to her. Her lips curled in anger. I didn't have the strength to explain what the pain meant: for the last few minutes I had realized, astounded, that the message my nerves had been sending me was one of – hunger. A live, reptilian hunger. As I said, someone inside me bungled the welding. Tamar averted her gaze. Tamar smiled uncomfortably.

She learned fast; she was very innocent when I first met her. That's how she was sucked into the wind tunnel where I roared. She choked on the dust of my fragmented words. That's how she was sucked into the fear that shrieks suddenly, into the froth of frightened violence. In a seemingly lost whisper, she is an opaque, corked bottle that sinks deeper into the maelstrom in my pupils.

And yet. From within her momentary helplessness springs the matador's charm: the slight sway of Tamar's slim back, and the danger projecting onto soft hammocks of amused astonishment, the sweetness of gentle mockery – is caught. A thin scarf is tossed weakly at the smoke gathering at the nostrils. You're like that, I'm like this. You see, we can be together like this, too. An evasive leap, a smile: I won't leave you, my little boy. A thick tendon pulses on a bulging neck. You make love to me as if you were at war. From on high a voice is heard, a bitter, lowing call: the bull loves the matador.

The waitress brought hot chocolate and a glass one-third full of brandy. A leather pouch was strapped to her belly by a greasy belt. We're getting married today, Tamar said suddenly, stealing a childishly crafty glance at me. Yup, that's the way it is, said the waitress, looking at us with fleeting surprise before turning to leave.

We drank. If they fire me I'll go back to writing advertising slogans and technical instructions. They'll be pleased to have me back at the offices of Peled-Arnon. The insecticide that anticipates the ants. The cigarette that smokes you. Those are both mine, and I'm wasting my time teaching literature at the university. Even the tourist office pays well for propaganda leaflets. Follow the gun and come to Israel.[1]

Anyone seeing us from a distance, Tamar said, would think we're strangers. And from up close? I scowled into the glass. Her gaze flickered. You just have to – her lips whitened – say everything, don't you, test the effect of every possible combination of words. Words are my business, I said halfheartedly. No, it's a kind of joy in destruction. I remember the things you used to tell me when I was pregnant, the evil prophecies about the inevitable hatred between parents and children. I hurt myself that way, too, I said. After all, you know there are things I must say. Angry to be telling her this yet again, I got carried away and added: Besides, you already know it's the most

---

1. The original slogan: "Follow the sun and come to Israel."

banal things that hurt me, that I can never accept them – like what you said before.

What, that you have to say everything?

No, that we're alike.

Sometimes I gnaw myself in sorrow over her. Over her being sentenced to me. The path of life for which she was intended is so clear. Of course she would have to have known me, but only as a slight burning sensation. As a lighthouse of danger. Maybe as a friend of hers and her husband's. An amusing curio you must be careful of, careful of the white-hot barbed wire cutting it in half. Someone to tell friends about, to try halfheartedly to fix up with single girlfriends, sighing fondly: He's a challenge, you'll see.

It's these clouds, Tamar said, and the empty garden and the waitress with the dyed hair, that are making us melancholy just now, tempting us to forget that, actually, on a day-to-day basis, we're pretty happy together; that we have two wonderful, healthy girls; that I'm successful in my work and you enjoy teaching and writing. That we have friends and lives that are so full and strong we can afford to talk openly like this about our relationship. No, I think we're forgetting too many things just now. It's just that you enjoy being the child you were at twenty.

I crushed the wet sugar in the bottom of the glass with the spoon. That child still has a hold on my throat; he demands attention for his pain. I spurn him because that's what I've been trained to do. But I keep him hidden away, sneak food to him. When the war's over, I'll let him be discovered.

The grains squeaked under the pressure of the metal spoon. When we met we were impossibly different from one another. Love buffeted us against one another. So we fought together to change our dreams. From this came the impenetrable wonder of the blossoming of our two girls: the code of our bodies, deciphered.

Except that all this – what is all this? – it's a fraud, a detour Tamar's learned to make. Burns she sustained passing through me before she returned to herself. From here on: her even steps; the thin, transparent slices of herself she parcels out to the world; her calm eyes. It was only in my envy of her that I understood – there was a message hidden in that corked bottle. A concealed, relentless directive: Me. Me. Me.

But now, all of a sudden, her bitter tears – the secret of Tamar in a tear – what are we two, what is left?

Really, we're happy together, I say, taking her hand in mine and kissing her on the mouth, and really, there's no need to say everything. How silly of us to expect that today of all days, on a day like this, we'd be oozing with love and optimism made to order. There, she said, you really do quite please me; perhaps I'll renew that contract with your parents after all, and lease you for another seven years. I laughed. The pain in my head suddenly abated. I laughed again. Tamar looked at me, uncomprehending, ready to smile. I laughed aloud. Perhaps I've discovered the cure, I said. She didn't understand. Come, I winked at her, let's go home. There are cherries in the icebox.

It should be noted that the house was very empty. Tiny articles of clothing were strewn in every corner. Also, blocks, scribbled-on pages, pencils, and dolls. We took off our coats. My eyes throbbed. I stood in front of the open refrigerator, furiously gobbling food. Tamar hummed to herself in one of the rooms. Suddenly I heard her voice beside me. What aggressive eating, she said, then vanished. I slammed the refrigerator door shut. Now what. I picked through the record albums. *Peter and the Wolf* and *Let's Learn to Count with the Count*, and *50 Holiday Songs for Children*. The bottom of the pile yielded prehistoric layers: Leonard Cohen and Theodorakis and Carole King. But somewhere a distant needle skipped out of its mechanical slumber and began revolving in my head in rhythmic circles, translating the grooves into sounds and sights in my memory. A rented room with the lavatory outside. A dedication in a book of poems. Hands meeting in the dark. I gave up. I still had a pickle clenched in my mouth when I placed an album on the turntable. I tried to balance the pickle between my teeth, my head angled back and my arms spread out to the sides. One, two, left, right, arms on friends' shoulders. Shlomit is building a bright green *sukkah*, that's why she's busy today. That's why I'm now a smiling, trained show-dolphin, a seal poking through a hole in the ice, the harpoon already stuck in its brain and tasting of sour pickle. And it's not just any bright green *sukkah*, left, right, caught up in the rhythm of the music, in the flashing of the sabers of pain. Shlomit is building a *sukkah* of peace, a bower of peace. My neck arches toward the ceiling and I gulp down the sourish juice. Suddenly silence, Tamar is beside the turntable, her eyes wide. The pickle glides across the room like some comic bird.

Later, after we'd brought the startled twins back home and Tamar had tried to put them to bed, I went into their room. The three of them lay side by side, and for a moment seemed to be a mirage. They were so alike, entwined. I smiled at them and went out. I rubbed my eyes roughly. That usually worked for a while, but not this time. I think I was also a bit drunk, because inside the pangs of biting hunger were slow, insistent stirrings of nausea. I stood in the hall and tried to laugh soundlessly. I contracted my stomach muscles; I pawed through my thoughts for funny things. The dance of the sour pickle, for one, or the look on Tamar's face when she was standing there. Breathing like that in the silence, my face radiant, I exhaled all the ironic poison that had collected since that morning at the university. That didn't work, either. Suddenly I knew I was ripe for a great defeat. Tamar came out of the girls' room and closed the door after her. She saw me and let out a frightened giggle. She said I looked like one of those dingy dogs that hang around gas stations. I liked the image. I pressed her to me, as if I felt better.

Afterwards, even though we were a bit dejected and careful of one another, we made love with the old passion, and Tamar's body was again my only possible home. She was tense, and when we finished she said that this time she had made love against me. Within minutes she fell asleep. *Tonight after we made love Tamar cried* – but that's only an imaginary lasso of words I was caught in that wrung startling seeds of pain from my whole body. The humming in my head became a straight, shimmering line. I knew I had to move, had to keep from being a motionless target. But I continued to lie there and wait.

Jerusalem, 1980

Shulamith Hareven

Mahogany

Translated by Hillel Halkin

The chairs were the first to go. First the kitchen chairs, then the mahogany chairs in the dining room.

Grandfather, who owned a logging firm and loved wood, spat on his right palm, then on his left, rubbed them together, reached for the ax, and chopped the chairs expertly into neat lengths; no longer our furniture, they regressed to stacks of lumber like those left for pick-up at the forest's edge. When he finished I was handed some pieces and a cleaver and carefully split kindling while sitting on the floor. The coal deliveries had stopped long ago and it was cold.

Just two weeks ago God had been in His heaven; father went each day to court; Agnieszka was in the kitchen; and there was plenty of coal in the bin. Now the Austrian porcelain in the large mahogany cupboard was reduced to smithereens, blasted in the air raid that had shaved off the three upper floors of our house and demolished the house across from us, leaving neither furniture nor people. Streaming through the odd gap, strong unfamiliar sunlight flooded the rooms along with spirals of smoke. Slivers of broken glass covered everything – the floor, the table, the beds. Their aquarium gone, the goldfish shone on the rug.

In the short breaks between air raid alerts the children played in the little park below, kicking the bodiless head of a horse like a football. When the horse had collapsed on the lawn a few days previously, the flesh had been carved from its living carcass by the neighbors and carried away in bags, at first stealthily and then in broad daylight.

One day the children came to tell me that I didn't know what I had missed: they had played that morning with a human skull. A real one, with hair. Eyes, too.

The truth was that I had heard them shrieking gleefully amid the fallen leaves but hadn't gone out to join them. I wasn't sure I would have wanted to kick around a man's head with eyes and hair. Not that I didn't understand their glee. Take *that*, you dumb grownups, take that. All summer long you wore your spiffy white suits and straw hats and danced tangos and Lambeth Walks, agog about Edward VIII, romantic isn't the word, running to Zakopane and Krynica to two-time each other with romances of your own, to take the waters, oh sure, the waters, you thought we didn't understand a thing; and when we told you how frightened we were, and how even Agnieszka said the dogs in her village were barking all night, which was a sure sign of war, and went home one day and never came back, you said don't be silly, Poland would defend us, yes, hurrah for the Polish army, to say nothing of England and France, they would rush to our aid at once. You with your porcelain dinner services with gold borders, you mahogany women with your fox stoles for the opera and your new sets of crystal to make a sister-in-law green with envy. And we listened to you and tried not to be afraid, what else could we do? Now that the whole world knows how dumb you were, and how defending yourselves, let alone us, was something you hadn't the foggiest notion of, why not give the skull a kick or two in between air raids, while the parents call out, Come home quick, the planes are coming. Why not kick free but really free of you, you'll never con us again, dearest grownups. We knew better than you. Wise, free and fast on our feet we watched you as you huddled behind your smashed windows patched with pasteboard and planks that let in a few rays of light, while you counted the bombs (God, that was close, God, that one must have weighed a hundred kilo, God, that must have been half a ton), mercilessly mimicking your groans; we who alone knew where to find a loaf of bread or in what slummy street or steamy attic laundry room where we wouldn't have dreamed of setting foot two weeks ago, milk was being distributed. As soon as we heard the all-clear, we ran to get you some. More than anything else you were pitiable.

Not Grandfather, though. On Yom Kippur he wrapped himself in his prayer shawl and prayed all day in the hallway, not a muscle twitching even when the bombs fell very close without a pause and it was hard to breathe. The whole house was full of thick, swirling dust and the smell of bombs and death, because that was the day they hit us the hardest. But the Germans did not exist for him. He had nothing but contempt for them. And when it was time for the mahogany cupboard to go the way of all wood, and Grandmother wanted to save the pieces of china and glue them together after the war, he threw them out without a glance and split the cupboard into neat boards, starting with the doors and shelves. His hands gripping the ax were the only firm things in the house. He didn't speak. Grandfather knew that nothing would survive the war. Not even the family. Only one grown-up was like us: paranoid Felicja from next door. All summer long she had stood on her balcony shouting, Idiots, how can you walk in the street, the end of the world is coming. After a while the servant girl, or her husband, or one of her two pale daughters, Bronka and Lilka, came out to drag her inside. Felicja is ill, people said, she should be hospitalized but her family is ashamed. Now she strode energetically, a tough queen ready to pounce, fetching bread, bringing milk, even getting hold of a butt-end of sausage. Now everyone knew she had been right. Her world had become clear. She spent the days in the streets, a cold bad gleam in her eyes, now and then snarling, Idiots! Later she alone managed to extricate her pale daughters, Bronka and Lilka, who never went downstairs, from the ghetto and move them to a hiding place in a village. A year afterwards, it was said, she drowned Lilka in the river for no reason. Felicja thought she was God. Or that God in those years was Felicja.

One morning it was quiet again. A sparrow hesitantly resumed its pecking and the whole neighborhood heard it. The dust was less thick too. We went outside and stood on piles of debris half as high as the house to see what was left. Some buildings had had their front walls sheared away by the bombs. It was like the raising of a curtain in a theater: floor after floor of stage sets, interiors with flowered wallpaper, a crooked lamp, an easy chair, a crib, the dangle of torn curtains, one apartment above another above another, a multi-storeyed display. Chins up, we saw that the private and the public were now one: all it had taken was a single strong puff to knock down the brick dividing line. There were no more secrets, there was no more shame; everything was set out in the open.

It was pointless to ask what had happened to the tenants of those apartments. Warsaw had no bomb shelters. Here and there a curtain on an upper floor rippled in the wind as if seeking to cover the nakedness of the cavity behind it, unaware that its job was done. Tolek, with a wolfish grin, proclaimed that there was money and jewelry up there, perhaps even something to eat; but the crumbling walls were unclimbable. From time to time something fell from the empty apartments – an armchair that had stopped fighting gravity, a heavy bathtub, a table that stood sharply tilted for days like a downhill sled before crashing loudly into the street. Sometimes a whole floor or side of a building collapsed all at once while we cheered it on and applauded, Bravo! One boy half-heartedly tried scaling a wall and scrambled down again, wiping his hands. Our dreams of plunder were abandoned.

It was quiet. The city had surrendered. In the morning there were voices of people in the street. The Germans came that afternoon. They marched in formation, in high spirits, to their brass bands bright in the sun that came out from behind the clouds just for them, singing their lovely, strange songs.

A week later I was on my way to the attic laundry for milk, my hands frozen to the bottle beneath my coat, when a German in a black uniform with a skull on the lapel and a black leather strap slanting across his chest blocked my way. Legs spread wide, each hand on a pistol butt, he yelled, "*Halt!*"

I didn't go out any more. The world turned white with fear. I sat hugging my knees on the floor, in the corner where the mahogany cupboard had stood, not wanting to move. Not wanting anyone to see me or notice me. To hear me or smell me or talk to me or pay me the slightest attention. I told no one about the man from the Gestapo. There was nothing anyone could do to protect themselves or me anyway, not that autumn, not in the years before it, not ever.

Yehudit Hendel

My Friend B's Feast

Translated by Dalya Bilu

When I came in I heard her saying from the room: And three kilos of onions, don't forget. She must have been afraid he hadn't heard. Three kilos of onions, it's important, she repeated firmly. He was already in the corridor. Don't worry, everything will be all right, he replied from the corridor.

Inside the room lay B, dying. Attached to tubes, all wounded, all bandaged on the veins and arteries of her arms and legs. In the flushed, immobile face, swollen with cortisone, only the glittering little eyes darted.

I hope he won't forget anything, she said.

He won't forget, I said.

You'll come.

Of course, I said.

Nira will cook the meal.

Naturally, I said.

I've given instructions about everything.

Naturally, I said.

When my brother Nahum's wife died, she made him swear not to get married after her burial.

She made an effort to smile, but all you could see were her trembling, sensitive nostrils.

In my case Nira will cook the meal.

She made an effort to smile again.

She's a good cook.

I didn't know what to say. I felt her eyes fixed on my face, sharp and cold, like two steel nails.

Right after that I'll die, she said.

But B, I said.

The two steel nails turned red-hot.

Right after that I'll hang on till Saturday.

Again she made an effort to smile.

I hope I'll hang on till Saturday.

Her eyes darted over me now, wild, as if she had four eyes.

I told him the exact menu. It has to be exact. It has to be just so.

I said of course it would be just so.

It has to be very delicious.

I said of course it would be very delicious.

I explained it to Alexander, she said, I explained that everything has to be just so.

He'll take care of it, I said.

Yes I hope he'll take care of it. All the time her eyes darted over me, wild. She said: The doctor's giving me two hours' leave. I can leave the hospital for two hours. I'll hang on for two hours.

Of course, I said.

He'll give me an injection first. And he'll come with me, of course. I invited him and his wife, of course.

I didn't ask her who else she'd invited. She waited.

There'll be ten, she said. Actually, eleven. And there'll be one empty place. I like one empty place.

Again she waited.

And Nira will serve the meal, of course.

I didn't know what to say. I remembered how when I was a child my mother once told me about plants that bled a red juice when they were broken. She said: I explained to her exactly how to set the table.

Now too I didn't know what to say. She said: The injection will be enough for two hours. At four I have to be back here.

I told her that she would be back here on time.

Yes, I'll be back here on time, she said.

I didn't know what to say. There was silence.

And that's it, she said.

There was silence.

After that, that's it, she said.

There was silence.

You don't know what to say, she said. There was silence. It was evident that she felt confined inside her skin. She said: After that, that's it. And next week – she tried to move her head, which was heavy, and it was evident that she felt more and more confined inside her skin.

Everything will be settled quickly, she said.

I didn't ask what.

Her eyes darted over me again, rapacious, and I could feel the hot mud in her body.

Yes, everything will be settled quickly, she said and sank her head into the pillow as if there was an abyss of air there inside the pillow.

I looked at her swollen, exhausted face. Her chin was bandaged, and I thought about the place where the animal's neck begins. I thought about the bones, the hair and the teeth. Her eyes ran over me so wild that for a moment I thought that she heard through her eyes. There was a pearl hanging on her chest. She said: I explained to her exactly how to lay the table. She breathed heavily. She said: You see, one turns into a watchdog.

Everything, like death itself, was clear and absolute. It was clear that she had taken care of everything, including what would happen afterwards. Unlike death it was clear that this too was planned. Suddenly I saw her strolling down the avenue with a white parasol. She said: I brought it from Japan but I look like a little Chinese woman. She had a sly laugh. She really did look like a little Chinese woman, strolling in the shade in the cypress avenue with a white parasol. I remembered the amusing stories of her travels, when she traveled round the world with Alexander, round the world more than once. It seemed to me that she was searching for a mirror, that she was avid to see her face in the mirror. Again I remembered the story of the mandrake plant that screamed when it was pulled up, and how my mother told me that its root was black when it was pulled up. I looked at her wounded swollen veins, and although she was all covered up I felt as if she saw through her whole body.

One can't get that thought out of one's blood, she said.

She was very quiet now, as protected as possible inside the pillow. She told me everything quietly, dryly. She told me how she intended to set the table, who would sit next to whom, and which table-napkins she had given instructions to take from the cupboard and where they were in the cupboard and under what. Which dinner service was to be used to serve the meal on and which to serve the coffee in afterwards, what to make the compote from and in what bowl, and to take out the cutlery with the long white wooden handles and not to forget mustard seeds, it was very nice to put mustard seeds in a salad. Afterwards she explained what kind of soufflé she intended making, and the quantities of courgettes, garlic and onion, and that she had asked Alexander to make sesame sweets. He is a great expert at sesame sweets. He enjoys making sesame sweets very much. That's his feast, making sesame sweets. The bandages on her arms were stained red and she looked as if she were simultaneously draining blood and words out of herself.

Enough, I said.

She didn't hear.

He's a great expert at sesame sweets, she said.

Enough, I said.

She said: And I asked him to make sugar beet soup. Everybody likes sugar beet soup. It's a pretty color, sugar beet soup.

She was speaking now neither quickly nor slowly. Her face was exhausted and only her eyes burned with the force of hostile nature.

I asked if you liked sugar beet soup, she said.

A sudden cold blew from her, as if the fever had chilled her. She wiped her mouth with a tail-end of bandage and sat up slightly. Again it seemed to me that she was searching for a mirror, that she was avid to see her face in the mirror.

I haven't got one on me, I said in alarm.

She asked what.

What? she said obstinately.

I said I liked sugar beet soup.

She looked at me and with one hand hit the iron bed, which made a sound like a musical stone. She cruelly kept silent.

It's good, especially in summer, I said.

She cruelly kept silent.

I'm talking to myself, I said.

She continued to keep cruelly silent. You thought I wanted a mirror, she said. No, I don't need a mirror.

She moved the infusion, holding her only luggage in her hand.

I'm glad you came to see me, she said. Yes, I'm certainly glad you came to see me. There was a kind of deep biological insult in her voice. She turned towards me, trying to smile.

Yes, it's good in summer, sugar beet soup, she said. Again she tried to smile. Her voice choked and quivered and she swallowed her voice and looked at me quivering from the depths of the pillow.

I feel it approaching, she said.

I didn't know what to say.

It approaches in broad daylight, she said, it will come next week.

She wept silently.

Not like a thief in the night, in broad daylight, she said.

I didn't know what to say. She wept silently. Her face was flooded, and it was hard to tell if it was wet with tears or sweat. She looked so small now in the bed among the pillows, sunk into them as if in a narrow mountain pass, waving with the infusion in her hand, making an effort to open her arms and able to move only in one direction, like a bird capable of flying only in one direction. I thought: One can't get that thought out of one's blood, that's what she said. I'm talking to myself, that's what she said. The strong women, the strong women, I thought. My clever friend B, I thought. I didn't know what to say. I asked myself how many stones made a pile.

I definitely want it to be very festive, she said.

It was very festive. We arrived at one o'clock precisely. The other guests also arrived at one o'clock precisely. The table was punctiliously laid. I counted: there were eleven places. Everything was especially gay. The napkins were colorful and flowered with little bouquets of little flowers clustered in tiny little goblets. At the door Nira received the guests. She was wearing a black dress with black lace, she had soft fair skin and the black lace emphasized her fair skin and the sympathetic melancholy of soft skin.

They'll be here soon, she said. Her face was tense and she made an effort to disguise the embarrassment in her voice. She said that there had been a problem finding something for B to wear and Alexander had driven to the hospital three times and three times she had sent him back to change the dress. One of the times she had asked for the gold sari-dress Alexander had brought her from India and then she had sent the gold sari-dress back. She said she had returned it because of the buttons which weren't properly sewn and they would open during the feast, and instead of occupying herself with the guests she would be occupied with the buttons, and Alexander said: That's better, that's better, imagine her sitting there in the gold sari-dress. And it rustles too, Nira said, and they brought her the wide floral dress.

A faint blush appeared on her cheeks as she said this. I hope she'll be pleased with what I sent, she said and added that it really was very difficult, because B was very bloated. She spoke carefully, with the same sympathetic melancholy that added charm to her voice, and she was incorrigibly sympathetic too when we heard the sound of the car approaching and when we heard it entering the yard and Alexander thundering: There, we made it, you see.

It must have seemed a little strange when we all formed up in a row. There was silence. She got out slowly and approached slowly. The doctor supported her on one side and Alexander on the other, and she walked silently down the long green garden path with her eyes making a big circle that instantly swallowed up all of us standing in a row. She smiled.

We're lucky it's a nice day, she said. She was wearing her jewelry and her eyes stood out in her face like big brightly colored glass beads.

Wonderful, thundered Alexander, you see. There was a dead cigar butt in his mouth and his breathing was loud and excited. He was a big man with long legs and big steps and he always had magnificent wooden boxes full of big cigars.

I told you it would be a lovely day, he beamed.

She didn't look at him and only swallowed us all up as if we were some kind of shapeless stain. Then she took a small step forward. And she took another step forward.

Truly, what luck, a lovely day, she confirmed.

You see, thundered Alexander.

She took another small step forward. Her head was heavy and she stepped carefully onto the lawn with one foot and then stepped carefully with the other foot as if there were landmines under the lawn. Her bowed head betrayed the thin depleted hair and the ominous bald spots. She raised it, stretched, and hit her body with both hands. There was a metallic sound and I saw her standing in the gold sari-dress that Alexander had brought her from India with the power of a short queen who had lost her kingdom but not her authority. And she set off on her race, the sick old mare.

You mowed the lawn in my honor, she said.

In my childhood, in Nesher, I once saw a huge rock torn from the mountain. First it crumbled slowly, for days, maybe for a year, maybe for generations. When it fell it wasn't rock any more. It only looked like one. In reality it was crumbs of soil.

But in my childhood in Nesher it hung huge in the air on the mountain and I thought that it was holding the mountain up. One day, at noon, in summer, when the sun on the mountain blazed and the rock was all gold like my friend B in the gold sari-dress she wasn't wearing, suddenly the rock tore. But in my childhood in Nesher it was still hanging there for years in the air holding up the mountain, and at noon I would look for it on top of the mountain whirling and crumbling in the air all summer, and it seems to me the summer after that too. Afterwards came the winter and I asked myself how long it took for a mass of rock hanging on the mountain to fall off the mountain, and I asked myself what material it was that held grain to grain and sometimes I remembered that when it fell I was afraid that the sun had fallen. Every day I looked at the quarry then.

The table, the table, said my friend B. This was after she had already crossed the lawn, still stepping on it with small careful steps as if there were landmines under the lawn. By then she had already extricated herself from the support of the doctor and the support of her husband, leaving the two embarrassed men behind her and us behind her as she proceeded alone along the narrow path, advancing with tremendous effort forward into the house, her house. Her hands were limp, exposed, and again she beat them like two wings against the two sides of her body as she approached the door and stood for a moment on the threshold, and then entered with a sudden decision with the strong movement of a person setting out in stormy weather. It was hot. Her face was flushed. But it gave off a chill which was hard to bear.

Wonderful, she said.

She said this three times, in the same tone, but each time the temperature changed and the chill grew more unbearable, as if with each statement something was happening in her body. After that her eyes narrowed and she looked only at the table. Now she stood alone, apart form everyone else. She drew herself up a little, exhausted, and her eyes darted low, narrowed on the table. Everything was green. Everything was a lie. And she stood there, as if in the gold sari-dress apart from everyone else, and there was no way either good or bad. And only everything was green, everything was a lie. And apart from everyone else she began to walk towards the table as in ancient times those sentenced to die walked towards the hills.

Wait, raged Alexander.

Wonderful, she said.

She turned towards us, her confused audience.

Really, they've made it look wonderful, no? she said triumphantly.

Her sick eaten body was already stretched as far as an eaten body could go and she stretched it further and further and further, her eyes on every single one of us still standing there in that miserable row. And everything was green. Everything was a lie. And all that existed was only the chasm between one look and the next and one moment and the next and the passion and power which she now possessed.

She smiled.

She had a blue shadow under her eyes, and the smile took its time passing from one eye to the other.

Really, they've made it look wonderful, no? she said, drugged and poisoned, with the eyes of a she-wolf.

She knew the price of the performance.

Really, they've made it look wonderful, no? she said triumphantly.

She spoke slowly and it took time for her to get from word "a" to word "b," from place "a" to place "b," and the only thing she didn't have was time.

She knew that too.

The table really did look wonderful. It was covered with a red cloth with airy stripes woven in, so that the color of the wood of the table showed through. There were eleven places round the table, eleven little straw baskets for bread, and eleven slender-stemmed glasses with white garlands engraved around their rims, eleven tumblers of Hebron glass in purple, green and blue and a khaki color for cold drinks. In the center stood a huge glass jug with a silver handle, silver tongs, a heap of little square cubes of ice and flat round slices of lemon floating in the water, and another eleven tumblers of low Hebron glass with a few low flowers stuck loosely in each of them to look like bunches of wild flowers dotted about. And then there was the dinner service, not the splendid one used for formal occasions but the pseudo-simple, pseudo-crude one used by the family, a clay service in a clay color with a narrow brown stripe encircling the plates like a slender ring. And of course there was the cutlery with the long white wood handles. The table was ready for the feast. On every clay plate stood a small clay plate with an artichoke on it, and scattered about the table stood saucers of lemon and dill sauce for dipping. The wine bottles stood on a little table next to the main table, in front of the window, and there were plenty of salt-cellars, pepper pots and rolled-up napkins.

She was still standing at the door, flushed, examining the intricate colorful setting which really was magnificent. Suddenly she took a small step forward, then she approached the table and stood there for a moment in agitation, and then she said that you didn't put red table-napkins on a red tablecloth and she had specifically asked for the antique-rose damask set. Alexander apologized and came back with the antique-rose damask set. She said: You put table-napkins in rings, don't you know that you put table-napkins in rings, what, didn't Nira remember? I specifically asked for it, she said. Alexander brought a pile of narrow wooden rings and inserted each napkin into a ring and she circled the table with little steps and examined the cards and the names on the plates. It'll do, she said, and after that Alexander's voice rose thunderously and he called the guests in from the garden to the feast. B sat in her usual place, opposite the window. Opposite her sat Alexander, with his back to the window. Nira sat next to him as the guest of honor at the meal. They began with chilled wine. Alexander asked everyone what wine. There was vermouth, a dry white wine and a rosé. B said: I want some too. Alexander fumed that it wasn't allowed. The doctor said nothing.

It is allowed, she insisted.

I knew it, he whispered angrily.

Full, she said exultantly.

Her eyes were bulging and she tried to make her voice sound gay.

Full, full, she said exultantly. She raised the glass carefully and set it down carefully.

In vain I try to remember what was said. I can't, but I remember exactly what we ate and even what every dish looked like, the color, the quantities and the combinations, the gleam of the cutlery and the gleam of the glasses, and from which side they began serving, in what order, and what. There was nothing out of the way during the meal, everyone kept to the unwritten contract and nobody knew, or remembered or saw. B sat next to me, speaking now neither too quickly nor slowly, but laughing very slowly, with a kind of hidden violence, and it was clear that the same program would continue running till the end of the meal, and in this wretched lost battle all the data were positive, there was all the time in the world moving in endless directions. She let this be understood with every look, throwing out short packed sentences, gulping water, jealously guarding the next wave of words. Her hands were wounded, and she made an effort to hide them, trying to eat bunched up and move her fingers as little as possible. She tore off the artichoke leaves and dipped them in the lemon and dill sauce; seated at the head of the table, at the most convenient vantage point, she didn't miss a move made by anyone. They said what a pleasant breeze. There really was a pleasant breeze. They said what a delicious sauce. The sauce really was delicious. After that they served the soup and she said to Alexander that she would dish up, and to put the tureen next to her. To my surprise it wasn't sugar beet soup. It was consommé. She smiled, inclining her head slightly in my direction, and it seemed to me that we both understood the code. The tremendous difficulty was the words. Today I'm not so sure about it any more, returning to the handsome dining room with the big wide windows, the bright locks of light and my friend B sitting there wearing her jewels and sweating beneath them. She shifted them from place to place on her neck, and today when I read a little book about birds I remembered her, my friend B, sitting burning, with drooping shoulders and swollen hands, like a bird feeding on its own blood.

Consommé, excellent, she said.

She laughed.

There's nothing like hot soup on a hot day. She laughed again: Alexander, the ladle, please. We'll begin at the end, Nira's first.

She said this slowly, quietly, and smiled a little smile, as if the fact that they had changed the soup made her feel especially cheerful. Then she sank the ladle into the middle, making a little whirlpool in the center, in the middle of the tureen, holding onto it hard as if she were holding a heavy wooden stick in her hand. Her eyes bulged, glassy, two balls of celluloid which did not move, fixed on the ladle, their gleam getting duller from minute to minute; and you could feel how from minute to minute, together with the cancer, the hatred of strangers bloomed in her body.

It's important to mix it well, to get the "heart of the soup" into every plate, she said, and we'll begin at the end, Nira's first. She smiled a little smile again. Her forehead was bathed in sweat and she wiped her forehead.

Suddenly it's grown hotter, she said with the same little smile, looking round the table from one to the next, and suddenly she began to count aloud.

Don't worry, there'll be second helpings, she said and drew the tureen towards her, trying to increase the gaiety in her voice.

Over-enthusiasm is weakness, writes Tolstoy in *War and Peace*, but my friend B, for all her cleverness, trapped in a narrow strip of life for this one hour at noon, forgot; feeling, for this one hour at noon, her old power, and trying, for this one hour at noon, to remove some misunderstanding as she ladled the consommé with her forehead bathed in sweat; she wiped it away making the same movement over and over again but it kept on coming back. Her face was alternately red and white and she dished the soup out slowly, plate after plate, stirring it with the ladle after every plate to make sure that everyone got the "heart of the soup." And everyone around the table held out his hand with the empty plate and then drew back his hand with the full plate and smiled and said: Thank you, you're wonderful. And she said: Marvellous, and everyone around the table knew that it was murder, the disease had murdered her body.

They ate and talked and ate and talked again. Someone said he had bought a movable air-conditioner and that a movable air-conditioner was a wonderful thing, and someone said that he hated movable things, he liked things fixed to the wall. After that they talked about how Haifa had become a dirty town. Someone remarked that it had never been clean, it only had the reputation of being a clean town, and after that as usual they asked why we were still living in Hadar instead of moving up to the Carmel, there was nothing left in Hadar but lawyers and prostitutes, and she said with a laugh that she knew Zvi would say that of the two he preferred the prostitutes, and she agreed with him, but precisely at that moment a wind sprang up and he asked something about the poplar.

It will have to be pulled up, said Alexander.

Someone asked why.

Alexander said that it would raise the house.

Someone asked how a poplar could raise a house.

Alexander explained that it had long roots and it could raise a house.

A house? the doctor asked.

Alexander explained that its roots were so long they destroyed the foundations under the ground. The house remains whole but it has no foundations, it has nothing to stand on, it falls down whole, do you understand?

Strange, said the doctor.

Why? said B. She was apparently in pain. She smiled: And it never stops shedding its leaves. It always seems it's going to be left naked.

The doctor sipped his soup.

Yes, he said, growth.

B turned towards him, leaned over to the middle of the table and took the salt-cellar.

It has to be strong, it acts as a wind-break, she said.

A wind-break? said the doctor.

She went on playing with the salt-cellar.

It has scars on its leaves. When the wind goes through it whistles.

It wasn't clear what the connection was, and she repeated: It has scars on its leaves. Haven't you noticed that it whistles? There was passion in her voice. She said: I'm very fond of the whistling.

You're tiring yourself for nothing, said Alexander.

She put the salt-cellar down immediately and pushed it to the center of the table.

Yes, I'm tiring myself for nothing, she said, and she picked up the salt-cellar again and put it down again on the red tablecloth. Then she paused in order to gain control of her voice.

Her face blazed.

The tamarisk tree has leaves with salt nodules.

Her face blazed even more.

Didn't you know that the tamarisk has leaves with salt nodules, didn't you know? It's doomed to die in the desert, she said. She asked if anyone had heard of the Dead Sea apple, the apple of Sodom. Haven't you heard of the apple of Sodom? The apple of Sodom, she repeated and Hell, haven't you heard of Hell? There are lots of synonyms for Hell, didn't you know? And the apple of Sodom, nobody's heard of it, nobody knows?

She laughed again. She had strong teeth when she laughed.

Once people believed there was an animal that breathed for ever. Alexander, what's the name of the animal? They cut off its head, you know, and it goes on breathing after they've cut off its head.

We're in the middle of eating, Alexander thundered.

Oh, I forgot, we're in the middle of eating, I apologize.

Her face was full of blood. I forgot, we're in the middle of eating, I certainly do apologize. She held onto her hands which were trembling hard, as if an electric shock had passed through her body. And a table like this too, with one's husband and one's best, one's dearest friends.

She looked around her, unable to control her hands. Really, best and dearest, I really do apologize.

You're going too far, Alexander thundered.

Yes, I'm going too far, I'm definitely going too far, she said. She said this now in a dry, matter-of-fact tone, and she still couldn't control her hands. And the table-napkins, Alexander they're the antique-rose damask table-napkins, you know. It's my memory, you know, I've simply forgotten the animal's name.

Instead of eyes under her forehead, her two celluloid balls bulged – blank, glassy, a foreign body in her face. Again she tried to make her voice sound cheerful.

You can serve the salads now, she announced, tugging at the wide flowery dress which revealed ravaged shoulders, all bones, her arms hanging from them as if they came from some other place. I read this week, I don't remember where, that ever since 1945 the world has lost its stability, she said.

Since '45? Alexander inquired.

Yes, since '45, she said.

Why since '45 precisely? asked Alexander.

It's a fact, the world really has lost its stability. But nobody knows yet what the attributes of the new, unstable material are, she said.

The two celluloid balls suddenly raced round feverishly.

And it can be anybody, she said. She spoke as if her voice had been wounded. Material engineering, it's a complicated business, she said.

Suddenly she raised her back, tilted her body backwards and pressed hard against the back of the chair, raising her head too as she looked hopelessly in front of her for a moment, wringing her hands. You can't live outside your home, that's what it is, I think that's what it is, she said suddenly and straightened up violently as if she wanted to increase the volume of air around her. She was breathing fast, and I thought that pain, like fire, duplicated itself in the process of burning. She kept on wringing her hands. It's a cannibalistic thing, she once said to me. Living inside a sack, she once said to me. And all the time the leaves are rustling, she said.

She was still sitting erect like a dog.

The poplar has a concert voice, she said.

Around the table there was a sudden stir.

I've already said that I have great difficulty in remembering what was said during the meal, and yesterday I called someone to ask. She didn't remember either, nor did her husband. They only remembered that nothing special happened until someone mentioned Beilinson Hospital, and B said: No, I'm not going to Beilinson. Alexander said that no one wanted her to go to Beilinson and she went on looking at her plate. Alexander said that she wouldn't even go into a street called Beilinson. Her face was full of blood now too. She bent over and began sipping the soup with small sips and said into the soup that nobody was going to name a street after her. Alexander shouted, but she didn't raise her face from the soup and said that that was what she wanted, not to have a street named after her. You'll be able to walk freely in all the streets, she said. Alexander hastily removed the napkin from his knees. He stood up, but she went on eating her soup. Like mountaineers, advancing by stages, she said into her soup. Then I didn't yet know the story and I only understood later that people, like history, repeat themselves. It was told me years later, on the telephone from Haifa to Tel Aviv. The lines were busy and I couldn't hear very clearly. The doctor joked that it wasn't so easy to get a street named after you. B didn't hear. She ordered the meat and salads to be brought, but before that for Alexander to tell the story about the cobra.

They all knew the story about the cobra but they all liked the story about the cobra too, and he lit a cigar, drew a breath and loudly and lustily recounted what he had already loudly and lustily recounted dozens of times before, how he had brought this cobra back with him from the UN conference to the Tel Aviv zoo on the plane in a suitcase, and how over the ocean the cobra had escaped from the suitcase. It was night time. The passengers were sleeping. And when he opened the suitcase, it was empty. And he drew a breath and went on telling how he had closed the suitcase, already knowing that the cobra was taking a walk over the ocean between the seats on the plane, and in all the seats people were sound asleep, and he drew a breath again and stretched his long strong legs, settling back in his chair, and she looked at him, her eyes concentrating more and more on one point of his face as she tapped her plate with the tip of her fork like background music accompanying his loud voice. You could see her eyes grow smaller and smaller, narrowing on a smaller and smaller point in his face, moving along some strange, slanting, oblique line and after that this same oblique line moved around the table, passing glassily from plates to faces and faces to plates and together with it moved a faint little smile, but it was impossible to tell to which side.

You can serve the meat, she said.

The oblique line now moved on to Nira.

On the big wooden platter; and averted her face with the movement of a person crossing to the opposite pavement. I hope the color has been preserved, she said, cooking ruins the colors. She breathed hard. Have you noticed, most vegetables go red when they're cooked, have you noticed? She breathed hard again. The vegetable peel, it's all in the vegetable peel, she said, looking for words, but the words didn't meet, like objects that don't belong to each other. You never know how materials will behave, she said. She laughed a little. I like this dinner service, this clay one, she concluded.

Nira scattered the salads over the table (I've already said that there were mustard seeds). Then she served the soufflé and the quiche and a variety of baked goods, and added ice cubes to the beautiful jug for cold water. There was red cabbage cooked in wine, a dish of tiny onions in wine (a delicacy of which B was particularly fond), sweet and sour sugar beet, and green beans with almonds. After that a magnificent platter arrived with a magnificent crown of rice decorated with mushrooms and almonds and raisins and thin slices of crystallized fruit. In the end came the meat, a huge joint lying on a thick board of pale wood and surrounded by pieces of chicken cooked in orange juice and wine. Alexander began to carve the meat and he asked us all what we wanted, and B said that Alexander was a master meat-carver and all the time she followed his movements and looked at him. The inner meat, the inner meat, please, she said, and all the time she looked at him, and all of us knew that she was the one who took care of everything for him including the woman who would take her place. She was the one who had brought her into the house, taught her the dishes he liked and how he liked his shirt-collars ironed. And she had learnt quickly. She had soft graceful steps and she passed round the table with the salad bowls and dished up with soft graceful steps, and after that she brought potatoes in aluminium foil with cream sauce and put them in the center of the table, and as she walked she bent over and the doctor asked if there was garlic in it. B said: Yes, there's garlic in it and so what if there's garlic in it? Today I'm eating garlic too, today I'm omnipotent, and she asked Nira to bring the peach melba and the apricot whip and the iced soufflé. And Nira went into the kitchen a few times with soft graceful steps and piled the peach melba, and the iced lemon soufflé and the apricot whip in an exquisite black dish on the table, and all the time B looked at the table and where she put everything down on the table, and then someone suggested drinking a toast to her and everyone stood up and drank a toast to her and she stood up and drank too. Her face was still flaming and you could feel the heat of her breath burning her.

We can begin the meat, she said.

She exhorted them not to forget the gravy and said that Alexander always forgot the gravy. Afterwards she said that the gravy was out of this world and suggested that after the meal we should all tell a story and Alexander would be first. He asked which one.

The one about the cobra.

There was silence.

The one about the cobra, everyone likes the story about the cobra, she said.

There was silence.

Why not? said the doctor.

She laughed a nervous laugh.

I forgot, you already told it, she said.

I can tell it twice, why not? Alexander thundered.

Certainly, you can tell it twice, she said. Her voice sounded hoarse, like a sad croak, and she looked at him now, very concentrated, in the way a person might look at a point in a flashlight.

Never mind, she said.

The arteries in her neck suddenly filled with blood and she bent down and held the nape of her neck as if her neck was broken.

The meal, as usual, took longer than expected and I saw the doctor stealing a glance at his watch. She must have seen it too, because she turned to me and raised her hand, making a sign with her hand. No, the two hours aren't over yet, she said, and went on staring distantly at her hand as if it were the hand of some other body, and to this day her voice runs after me through the years: No, the two hours aren't over yet. And packed into this brief statement, like gunpowder, lay the entire foreseeable future. Her breathing was rapid, her eyelids pink, and she was already playing her role with only partial success, failing to fill in the gaps. After we finished eating she announced that for coffee and the sesame sweets we would move to the living room, and that Alexander had, indeed, made sesame sweets. He adored making sesame sweets. Here too everything was ready and waiting. There were eleven seats, a lot of little tables and a lot of bunches of flowers. The window was open, high and wide, and it was possible to see the sea from end to end, limitlessly. B sank into an armchair slowly, laboriously, supporting one hand with the other. Then she relaxed her wrist, this too slowly and laboriously, as if it was the hardest thing in the world to relax her wrist. Suddenly she looked exhausted. Instead of the flush there were little brown spots on her face, like flakes of rust, and every time I remember that picture I think that there are machines that can withstand field conditions but not transport conditions. And moving into the living room, ah no, with that my friend B could not cope, and how she got there making her head move and her hands move advancing as if she were swimming by means of a strong backward motion. And I said to myself something about the heavy soul in the light shell; I caught myself thinking: A deciduous tree, the poplar tree. I remembered the leaves with the salt nodules and how she said: The inner meat, the inner meat, please, and he said: But what do you want, and she said: My strength, I want my strength, and he said: What side should I begin on, and she said: The green-blue light the blue-green ray, the laser is a weapon that blinds. Everyone remembers windows, doors, she said, everyone knows only a few details, the body is a particularly deep grave, she said, brushing crumbs off the antique-rose damask napkin, and I wish you all a pleasant day, she said, and to this day I cannot remember the second incident and only that a wind began to blow, the huge poplar trembled and a whistling sound came from the poplar and the table rose and the tablecloth rose, the doors and the glasses and the chairs and the bottles and the antiques rose, and my friend B remained sitting there next to an empty table in an empty room of a house being raised by a poplar tree.

Suddenly she said: Wait a minute, first Alexander has to bring the sesame. He hasn't brought the sesame yet. We forgot the sesame.

She laughed. As I said before, she had strong teeth when she laughed.

Everything's fading out like in the movies, she said.

I didn't know what to answer and I smiled and she looked at me and to this day I can't forget the way she looked at me. Then she turned her head ninety degrees and looked at me again. Her face was strange now as if it were cut in half and like you sometimes see in the movies as if she had two faces, one superimposed on the other, and she no longer wanted to remove the second layer before the first. These faces were now facing me fully, two faces one on the other in two silhouettes with thick contours. It seemed to me that she was still trying to hide the fear but not the poisoned life, and that it was impossible to stand it for another minute and I saw her suddenly bending the upper half of her body forward so hard that it seemed to me the fear was cutting her in half like a butcher's knife. But she didn't say a word. One contour was distorted and underneath it a contour with strong teeth laughed. Again it seemed to me that it was impossible to stand it for another minute but she stood. We all sat and she stood. She even straightened up, stretched her neck and looked round for a minute at everyone sitting there with a soft look, a look like shot silk.

I'd like to hear a violin, she said.

We can put on a record, said Alexander.

No, a live violin, she said.

There was silence. Her glance strayed round the seated square with a circular movement, one by one, with the face that recalled her face, its intelligence, and with the two contours that ran over it wildly with the tremendous desire to live. We were still sitting and she stood, looking at the tables and the cupboards and the antiques (I remembered how conscientiously she used to dust them) and all the fixed and the movable objects and the dozens of different signposts of time scattered here as if they were things forgotten somewhere by mistake.

Yes, a live violin, to see the fingers on the strings, she said.

Her look suddenly grew vague.

I'd like to hear a live violin, she repeated staring in front of her frozenly. Even her eyelids didn't move and it was clear that everything was behind her, everything was over, existing in some distant time, old and buried, and only that tremendous desire to live was streaming through her arteries like a powerful shot of morphine.

She selected words as if they were precision instruments.

I stood up before the coffee because I wanted to say something.

Her face turned a silver shade.

My plan was –

Enough, roared Alexander.

She looked at him with a desperate squint, shifted from one foot to the other and, swaying slightly, pressed both hands tightly to her body as if she were wearing a straitjacket.

My plan was –

I don't agree, roared Alexander.

She shifted from one foot to the other again, and the red blotches returned to her face and one eye suddenly grew black and swollen with a bruise under the eye. She looked as if she had been given a punch in the eye.

My plan was – she began again, but the words came out of her mouth strangely as if they were going in the opposite direction, from the mouth to the heart, and had disintegrated on the way.

She began again: My plan was –

In the story, as in life itself, there's a moment when it seems unreal to die in the middle of summer, forever. It's tremendously hard to bear the continuing dryness in the mouth, the burning in the feet, but it's unreal to think that suddenly thoughts stop and a human being turns into a corpse. But perhaps B was not concerned with all this. She was poisoned with morphine, her time was running out and she still wanted to say something. Again she shifted from one foot to the other, her one eye grew increasingly black increasingly swollen and her skin and her face were now completely opaque and their color made you think of a material resembling coral.

She looked very exhausted but nobody dared stand up and the doctor didn't tell her to sit down either, and she stood there, with her one black eye, shifting from foot to foot, the other eye glittering large and open, devouring the trees and the windows and the rays of light in the windows, unbelievably bright, transparent, endless, penetrating the surface of the skin without leaving a scar.

Nobody dared get up and the doctor didn't tell her to sit down either, and she went on standing and looking and seeing and looking, not moving, unblinking. It was hot. The poplar whistled. She made a strange movement with her head, the eye with the black bruise fixed on the poplar, the other eye on some other place low down on the trunk, as if she were trying to separate the shape from the background or the treetop from the ground. It seemed as if she were looking not at the objects but at the margins of the objects and everything looked really huge, really tiny, really split-second. Again she strayed over the faces of the seated people with staring eyes. Time passed. More time passed. And I saw her strolling to and fro on the long veranda opposite the poplar tree in the way you sometimes clearly see people you once knew in places where they have never been at all.

Have you ever looked at a plant after it has been chopped down or after a fire, and what happens to the bitter hairy poisonous fruit? Have you ever looked at the hard round seed and what happens to the hard round seed? The fruit of the birch tree, for example, is ground up. Ground up it's used for rat poison or for spraying fish. Have you ever seen a bare tree blossoming? The tree shines, naked, pink, even the trunk is visible in the distance, so pink and shining it is in its beautiful blossoming. Some people say it's the tree on which Judas was hanged after he betrayed Christ. Others say it was used to crucify Christ. Since no material is ever lost in the world perhaps a bit of it is still hanging on a tree somewhere and has become part of the naked trunk or the beautiful blossoming.

She turned to Alexander again, squinting desperately, and you could feel the wild cat bursting from her body.

My plan was –

Instead of contracting into a ball of pain, her body expanded and she opened her fingers, still able to fly, but they were heavy, swollen, made more of lead than blood, and she dropped them and remained standing for a long time without moving.

My plan was – for each and every one of the people sitting here – who are all very dear to me – she took a breath – to say one sentence to me – she took a breath – and also –

She took a breath.

My plan was – to tell each and every one of the people sitting here – who are all very dear to me – she took a breath – what role they have played in my life – she took a breath – but it's impossible – it's impossible.

She took a breath.

It's impossible, I can't do it.

She took a breath.

In any case, I have to go, time's up, she said.

Her face was wet and she wiped it with her hand, like a little girl.

And in any case I'm burning, I'm on fire, she said and wiped her face with her hand, like a little girl.

When she was standing at the door she stopped suddenly, and turned round.

I'm sorry we didn't drink the coffee, she said, you'll have to drink it without me. Nira will serve the sesame and the cake.

In the middle, when she entered the living room, there was another incident that I forgot to tell and skipped over. It was before she collapsed into the armchair. She asked Zvi to sing her a song. He asked what song.

Never mind, whatever you want, she said and, unable to keep standing, fell into the armchair. He knelt at her feet and began to sing:

> *Seven mice and a mouse*
> *Are eight I suppose*
> *So I take my chapeau*
> *And say goodnight.*

She didn't move. Her hands trembled on her knees. They were cold and damp and stuck to her knees like clamps. She hummed:

> *Seven mice and a mouse*
> *Are eight I suppose*
> *So I take my chapeau*
> *And I say goodnight*
> *I take my chapeau*
> *And off I go*
> *Where can you go so late at night*
> *All on your own.*

A week later, on Saturday, we were there in the garden and there were a lot of other people there too, who had come to condole Alexander. He came up to us and stood with us for a moment next to the poplar tree.

I don't want you to hear it from strangers, he said, Nira's living here.

We didn't know what to say.

I thought you realized, he said. A strange smile crossed his face.

– That's why she had the feast.

We didn't know what to say. Zvi mumbled something. Then he said he would go and get us something to drink and I said: All right, I'll wait here, and I stood and looked at the beautiful garden and the beautiful woman moving round serving fruit and lemonade and iced coffee. Among the other antiques and jars and capitals there was a sarcophagus which I forgot to mention, made of wonderful white stone, standing open in the garden, and my friend B would sometimes sit on its rim as if it were a bench. I couldn't resist the temptation and I sat down on it too as if it were a bench, and looked at the beautiful woman moving round there in the garden and she suddenly seemed to me like a small detail of no significance to the whole story, moving round the garden with little steps as if she had been moving round here all along. I've already said that she had a soft walk and a soft neck, and I saw him standing in the kitchen passing his hand over her soft neck and I said to Zvi, let's go home. He said: Yes, let's go home. The poplar made a loud concert sound and on the bench sat my friend B. On the other side of the bench. Her black eye had disappeared and her eyes were china blue, a warm blue, sparkling on the rim of the sarcophagus, and inside it her head swayed like a giant marionette beating the stone of the sarcophagus. I was very tired. I said to Zvi, let's go home. He said: Yes, let's go home.

When we left, he asked if I remembered what she had said.

I asked what.

Yoel Hoffmann

Kätzchen

Translated by Eddie Levenston and David Kriss

Kätzchen[1] drew a picture of a woman without any legs. He pulled one of her hairs upwards and curled it around the edge of the page. Then he looked at the woman and thought that her face was a little frightening, but she did not frighten him at all. Still, she might frighten someone who had not drawn her.

Uncle Arthur squeezed the bird's head at the tip of his cane and the skin on his knuckles turned white. "*Komm!*"[2] he said, and stood up. Once Kätzchen had seen a cypress swaying in the wind. But that was before his mother had gone up to the sky. He thrust the woman into his trouser pocket and followed Uncle Arthur.

Once they were out of the bank, Uncle Arthur leaned his cane against the window of a bookshop. On the other side of the glass was a stone castle with gray clouds floating about its turrets. Kätzchen thought the bird could see the tower, and for a moment a sort of happiness for the bird passed through him.

Uncle Arthur placed his hand on Kätzchen's head and Kätzchen thought, "Now Uncle Arthur will say *'Verfluchte Welt'*."[3] Uncle Arthur said "*Verfluchte Welt,*" and added, "now Kätzchen's going to have an ice cream."

Uncle Arthur was normally of the opinion that chocolate or vanilla

---

1. Kitten, a term of endearment. (All translations are from German unless otherwise noted.)
2. "Come!"
3. Cursed world!

were the only two colors which might decently be eaten, but that day he seemed tired of propriety and bought Kätzchen a green ice cream studded with different types of nuts.

Kätzchen first passed his tongue over the ice cream until the twin peaks which rose from the cone had rounded into one. He wore down the mound until the nuts stood out and then he caught them between his teeth. His tongue was cold and his teeth ached with frost. When the mound had been flattened, the walls of the cone were exposed and Kätzchen nibbled around them. All the while, Uncle Arthur's eyes were fixed on the sea. Kätzchen looked up from the ice cream and asked, "*Wohin?*"[4] Uncle Arthur withdrew his gaze from the sea and said, "Now we go to another house. Perhaps to Tante Oppenheim."

Aunt Oppenheim was the sister of Kätzchen's mother and had never married. In Vienna, Aunt Oppenheim had sung in the opera house but in Palestine she sat in the coffee house on the sea shore and ate cream cakes. Once, she had held Kätzchen between her legs, pressed his head to her belly and said, "Kätzchen will not be a swine, nor a *Schakal*[5] like all the others." Since then, a sort of distant memory lingered in Kätzchen's nostrils and whenever he thought of his life he would see himself walking along a path flanked on either side by swine and jackals. At the end of the path perfume wafted from a silk curtain. Sometimes, when he was unable to sleep, he would place himself on this path and walk along it until he reached the end and was swallowed up in the silk.

Kätzchen was about two and a half years old when he first heard that his father was *krank*.[6] His mother placed a bowl of fruit on the table and walked out of the house. Kätzchen's father sat silent in the armchair, and when Kätzchen offered him an apple, a tear appeared in the corner of his eye. Kätzchen opened the doors of the sideboard and arranged the silverware, on the carpet. Then he surrounded his father's

---

4. "Where to?"
5. Jackal.
6. Sick (here, mentally sick).

slippers with the silverware and the father's feet inside the slippers did not move. After that, Kätzchen made a habit of asking whether this or that person were *krank*. By the time he found out other people were *nicht krank*[7] his father was already in "the institution."

After Kätzchen's father left there was Herr Druck. He kissed Kätzchen's mother on both cheeks and asked Kätzchen, "Vot you learn today?" Kätzchen's father, who was *krank*, leaned back against the armchair while Herr Druck leaned forward, with only half his bottom on the armchair. Kätzchen distinguished between those who were *nicht krank* and those who were *krank*. The bodies of the *nicht krank* were tense while the bodies of the *krank* were limp. The *nicht krank*'s shoes were black and their socks were pulled up tight, while the *krank*'s feet shone in shades of silver. Herr Druck would come and go and Aunt Oppenheim said to Kätzchen's mother, "Beware, Margarethe. That man is a *schakal*." Kätzchen's mother looked at Kätzchen and said, "The boy needs somebody." Years later, Kätzchen read in a book that "there are some animals that resemble dogs, but they are no more than distant relations," and was reminded of Herr Druck.

Aunt Oppenheim opened the door and smiled at Kätzchen. Kätzchen wanted to twitch his nostrils and take in the odor of perfume given off by his aunt. Then he decided to wait a little longer until he had walked past her and entered her room.

"*Schon wieder hat man uns herausgeschmissen!*"[8] said Uncle Arthur, and Aunt Oppenheim said, "Kätzchen will sleep with me." Then Uncle Arthur and Aunt Oppenheim sipped tea from china cups and Kätzchen was given raspberry juice in a glass.

Kätzchen compared the color of the raspberry in his glass with the color of the tea in their cups and thought to himself that the color of the tea was only the color of raspberry which had faded. Then he thought that, like their tea, Uncle Arthur and Aunt Oppenheim were

7. Not sick
8. "They threw us out again!"

children whose color had faded. It had grown dark meanwhile, and Aunt Oppenheim lit a yellow lamp. Shadows danced on the ceiling and Kätzchen thought up a story at the end of which all the devils died.

When Kätzchen opened his eyes, he saw a ray of light which stretched from the curtain to the wall opposite. He put his hand into the light and his skin glowed. "Now Kätzchen will eat porridge," said Aunt Oppenheim, and when she leaned over him her face was white. Kätzchen considered whether he should ask what happened to her face or where Uncle Arthur had gone. "With a lot of sugar," he said.

Suddenly he saw himself in the wardrobe mirror. His body was wrapped in a pink lace nightgown. Kätzchen brought his face closer to the face in the mirror until his nose touched the nose in the mirror. Then he stuck out his tongue until it touched the tongue in the mirror. "There are two Kätzchens," he thought. Then he said to himself maybe there were two Aunt Oppenheims as well. In a little while he would sit on the white bench in Aunt Oppenheim's kitchen and eat sweet porridge, and the other Kätzchen would sit in the other Aunt Oppenheim's kitchen and eat sweet porridge too. When Kätzchen looked away from the mirror his reflection disappeared. Kätzchen consoled himself with the thought that the wardrobe mirror was not the real mirror. The mirror in the wardrobe was framed on all sides and images entered it and left it, while the real mirror covered the whole world and there was nothing which it did not double.

"Arthur is already old. Maybe Kätzchen will live now with Tante Oppenheim. Also Margarethe in the sky wants Kätzchen to live with Tante Oppenheim," said Aunt Oppenheim. This confused Kätzchen's thoughts for some time, since he no longer knew where to place the mirror which doubled the world. If he placed it in mid-air it would separate the world below from the world in the sky and hide his mother from him. Kätzchen decided that the mirror reflected on both its sides and doubled both the worlds – the world below and the world above. But then the fear began to gnaw at him that his double in the mirror would take over his mother in the sky while he himself would only be left with her reflection. Eventually, Kätzchen decided that the mirror was crystal clear and that even its reflections were real things.

"At night I will sleep here and in the day I will be with Uncle Arthur," said Kätzchen, and he thought to himself that it would be better to eat breakfast with Aunt Oppenheim because her sweet porridge was tastier than Uncle Arthur's bread and margarine. Aunt Oppenheim gave a quiet smile and said, "Uncle Arthur is *krank* like your father. One day people will find out." Kätzchen felt a sudden yearning for his uncle and said, "Now I want to go to Uncle Arthur."

Meanwhile, Aunt Oppenheim drew black lines above her eyes and smeared two pink patches on her cheeks. Then she pursed her lips until they formed a ring, and painted them red. Kätzchen thought to himself that women's faces were white at night and colored in the daytime, while men's faces, which were white during the day, were colored at night. Kätzchen decided he would look at Uncle Arthur's face at night and see what color it was. "Doesn't Kätzchen love Tante Oppenheim?" Aunt Oppenheim asked the mirror above her dressing table. Kätzchen looked at the mirror and waited to see how it would answer. But when he saw that Aunt Oppenheim's eye in the mirror was looking at him, he returned her glance and said, "He does." The eye stared at him and asked, "Kätzchen loves Uncle Arthur more?" Kätzchen blushed and did not know what to answer. He suddenly remembered when he had been little and had walked next to Uncle Arthur in the rain, and Uncle Arthur had taken off his coat and wrapped Kätzchen up in it and carried him close to his chest, and the coat smelled of Uncle Arthur, and Kätzchen had almost fainted with the pleasure of it. Kätzchen looked into the mirror and saw that Aunt Oppenheim's eye was no longer there, and concluded that the time for an answer had passed.

While Kätzchen's father was still at home, Uncle Arthur would come every day when the clock on the wall struck five. Uncle Arthur sat on the chair next to the table, his face towards Kätzchen's father. Margarethe touched the shoulder of Kätzchen's father in the armchair and said, *"Ernst, dein Bruder ist da."*[9] Ernst, who looked at his brother out of the corner of his eye, shook his head from right to left and said nothing. A hidden sense told Kätzchen that the movement of his father's head was not intended to deny Uncle Arthur but was a way of saying in *krank* language, "Ah, my long-limbed brother, have you come once again to see the face of your brother whose spirit has been turned inside out?" Uncle Arthur sipped the chicory which Margarethe placed before him and spoke to Ernst. He sipped and spoke and Ernst said nothing. The things Uncle Arthur said to Ernst always began with *schon wieder:*[10] *"Schon wieder* autumn has come." *"Schon wieder* I need a walking stick because of the rheumatism." *"Schon wieder* the landlord told me to move out of the room." In course of time, Kätzchen understood that the difference between his father Ernst and his Uncle Arthur lay in their power to resist this *"schon wieder."* His father had been beaten by *"schon wieder,"* while Uncle Arthur stood up against it like an old stone wall.

After Ernst was sent to the institution Uncle Arthur would come only once or twice a week. He would suddenly appear at the door, sometimes in the morning and sometimes in the evening, and seat himself in the same chair. Only now the armchair which faced him was empty. Kätzchen, who knew that Uncle Arthur was staring at emptiness, would come and stand beside him. Uncle Arthur would sip the chicory Margarethe had put before him and place his hand on Kätzchen's head. Then he would remove his hand, take another sip, and replace it on Kätzchen's head. At that moment it seemed to Kätzchen that Uncle Arthur's resistance to *"schon wieder"* had slipped somewhat.

When Aunt Oppenheim had finished painting her face she put on a dress strewn with various flowers and said, "Now Kätzchen is coming with Tante Oppenheim to the coffee house." Kätzchen inhaled her perfume and Uncle Arthur was forgotten. Outside, the scent of her perfume mingled with the sea salt. Aunt Oppenheim's hand encircled

---

9.   "Ernst, your brother is here."
10.   Again.

Kätzchen's like a warm blanket and Kätzchen was afraid to move it lest Aunt Oppenheim loosen her grip and allow the air to enter between her flesh and his. In her other hand, Aunt Oppenheim held a green handbag. Once she had told Kätzchen that this bag was made from a crocodile and he was seized with wonder. The crocodile in Kätzchen's picture-book had a gaping mouth filled with sharp teeth. Kätzchen often imagined Aunt Oppenheim astride the crocodile, forcing it into submission and turning it into a handbag. When Aunt Oppenheim was in the kitchen, Kätzchen approached her dressing table and passed his hand over the handbag. "If the crocodile who has turned into a handbag should turn himself back into a crocodile," thought Kätzchen, "he will devour me in the twinkling of an eye." But the handbag did not turn into a crocodile and Kätzchen commended himself on his bravery.

On her way to the coffee house Aunt Oppenheim nodded to a shopkeeper and to another man. Then a man in a suit placed himself in her path and Aunt Oppenheim let go of Kätzchen's hand and extended her hand to the man's mouth. The man bowed his head and kissed her hand. Kätzchen thought to himself that Uncle Arthur greeted people in only one way while Aunt Oppenheim had two ways of greeting them. If they wore faded shirts she nodded to them, but if they wore suits she stretched out her hand to be kissed.

In the coffeehouse red tablecloths fluttered in the wind. Aunt Oppenheim sat herself down by the balcony wall and Kätzchen sat next to her. Kätzchen saw black ants going in and out of the wall. A man dressed in white clothes bowed and said, "*Guten Morgen*, Frau Oppenheim."[11] Kätzchen thought to himself that the ants in the wall also had a coffeehouse. A white ant was placing two cream cakes on an ant-table and the Aunt-ant was sipping coffee and the Kätzchen-ant was drinking cocoa from an ant-glass. Aunt Oppenheim wiped the corners of her mouth with a paper serviette and asked, "What is Kätzchen thinking?" Kätzchen said, "*Ameisen*."[12] Aunt Oppenheim

---

11. "Good morning, Mrs. Oppenheim."
12. Ants.

stared at Kätzchen in amazement and said, "Arthur is wrong. Kätzchen must go to school."

Kätzchen remembered that Uncle Arthur dressed him in a white shirt, took his hand and led him to a school with gray walls and taps in the yard. A woman who smelled of toothpaste sat Kätzchen down at a little wooden table. Kätzchen saw that something had been scratched into the table and read, "SARAH IS MAD." Then the woman put a book in front of Kätzchen and told him to copy:

> *Higgledy, piggledy, my black hen*
> *She lays eggs for gentlemen*
> *Gentlemen come every day*

When Kätzchen came back from school Uncle Arthur looked at what he had written and said, *"Unsinn!"*[13] During the break the children would throw a ball to one another and shout, "Here! Here!" or, "To me! To me!" Kätzchen stood under a fig tree and waited for a girl with two black pigtails to laugh and show her teeth. A few days later, Kätzchen was ordered to copy something else from the same book:

> *To see what my black hen doth lay*
> *Sometimes nine and sometimes ten*
> *Higgledy, piggledy, my black hen.*

When Uncle Arthur saw what Kätzchen had written he said *"Unsinn!"* again and banged the table with his fist. Uncle Arthur did not send Kätzchen to school anymore and the whole affair left Kätzchen only with a faint feeling of regret that he had never seen the mad Sarah whose name was on the table.

Meanwhile, the coffeehouse had filled up with people and Aunt Oppenheim stretched out her hand to be kissed three or four times. Kätzchen saw a big ship sailing in the sea and looked at it until it disappeared. A boy, a little older than Kätzchen, stood below the coffeehouse with a bundle of newspapers under one arm. He waved one

---

13. "Nonsense!"

newspaper in the air and shouted, "Baat... elson... Koree... Anfront!" Kätzchen thought to himself that people give names to the days of the year and call each day by a different name. And in order that everyone should know the names of the days, they write them in big black letters on the newspaper and everybody buys them to find out what that day is called. Kätzchen leaned over the edge of the balcony, looked at the newspaper in the boy's hand and read: "BATTLES ON KOREAN FRONT." Kätzchen asked Aunt Oppenheim, "*Was ist* front?"[14] Aunt Oppenheim laughed and loosened the top button of her dress. Kätzchen peeped inside and Aunt Oppenheim said, "But for this Kätzchen is too little."

Afterwards, a dog ambled up and sat itself down in front of Kätzchen. Kätzchen stroked the dog's head and the dog wagged its tail. Kätzchen gathered the cake crumbs from his plate and offered them to the dog, and the dog stretched out a warm tongue and licked Kätzchen's palm.

Kätzchen did not see Uncle Arthur at all that day. In the evening, Aunt Oppenheim undressed him, put him into the bath and washed his whole body. While she was dressing him in the pink nightgown, she told him about a man who used to drive up in a horse-drawn carriage and bring her bouquets of flowers. Kätzchen asked if they were big horses, and Aunt Oppenheim said that in this story what was important was not the size of the horse, but the size of the *Liebe*[15] between herself and that man. Kätzchen said that when he was big, he too would drive up in a horse-drawn carriage and bring Aunt Oppenheim bouquets of flowers. Aunt Oppenheim kissed Kätzchen on his forehead and told him that every child has his own special angel who always guards him from harm. Then she taught him a prayer for the angel to come and lead him to the Land of Nod. At night, Kätzchen dreamed of a big ship sailing across the open sea. Then the ship turned into Aunt Oppenheim who skimmed across the waves with her dress rolled down to her waist and a garland of flowers on her head.

---

14. "What does 'front' mean?"
15. Love.

In the morning, Uncle Arthur arrived with Max the Hungarian. Max's mustache, which was thick underneath his nostrils, grew progressively thinner until it petered out into wispy strands on both sides of his chin. When Kätzchen saw Uncle Arthur he ran to him and Uncle Arthur lifted him up and pressed him to his chest. Max clicked his heels, took Aunt Oppenheim's hand, bowed his head slightly, and kissed it. From his place against Uncle Arthur's chest, Kätzchen could see that Aunt Oppenheim's eyes had softened. Max returned Aunt Oppenheim's hand, looked at Kätzchen and said, *"Gozemeber."*[16]

Then Uncle Arthur, Aunt Oppenheim and Max sat around the table and drank chicory, and Kätzchen sat under the table and looked at their shoes. Blue veins extended downwards from Aunt Oppenheim's knees and the flesh of her feet, which were too big for her shoes, bulged out in swollen hillocks. Uncle Arthur's knees were pressed together and his legs were pulled backwards. The tips of his gray shoes peeped out from under the chair and only his cane was placed, like a sort of extra limb, under the middle of the table. One big, black shoe had also situated itself here. Max's other shoe hung in the air between Aunt Oppenheim's legs. Kätzchen thought to himself that each man puts on his shoes and is on his way. But then he changed his mind and decided that each shoe inserts its foot – and the man at the end of the foot – and is on its way.

Meanwhile the skies outside had darkened and it was raining. Uncle Arthur said that *schon wieder* it was winter and Aunt Oppenheim asked what was going to happen with the boy. Uncle Arthur said that he, and Max agreed with him, was of the opinion that schools in Palestine caused more harm than good and that he and Max would teach him themselves. Aunt Oppenheim asked Max if he was still with that *schwarze Frau*[17] and Max said, *"Jawohl."*[18] There was silence at table-top level and Kätzchen was sorry he couldn't see Aunt Oppenheim's face from where he was sitting under the table. Then Aunt Oppenheim said that the boy was thinking about ants and all he

16. "Rascal!"
17. Black woman.
18. "Yes."

wanted to do was look down women's fronts. Uncle Arthur said the boy was *begabt*,[19] and Max said that grown-ups don't understand what children are thinking about at all.

The rain rapped against the window panes and Aunt Oppenheim lit the stove. Kätzchen crawled out from under the table and sat himself down on Uncle Arthur's knees. He picked up Uncle Arthur's cane, tapped it on the carpet around Uncle Arthur's foot, and thought to himself that old people walk with their legs and support themselves with a stick, while he, Kätzchen, was not even touching the ground and the stick alone was supporting him. Then Aunt Oppenheim sang what she had once sung in the opera in Vienna and Max sang a song in Hungarian. When he had finished, Max explained to Aunt Oppenheim the meaning of the song: he is sad, and drinks until he can no longer remember his name, but nevertheless women still love him.

Kätzchen looked at the picture which hung next to Aunt Oppenheim's grandfather clock. In the picture, there was a palace and around the palace there were – fir trees, and a horse-drawn carriage, and the horse's head was turned towards the palace. The horse's foot hung suspended in mid-air and Kätzchen waited for the horse to put it down. Then Kätzchen brought his face up close to the picture and saw that the palace and the trees and the horse had all been embroidered, and remembered that he once saw how Aunt Oppenheim had embroidered a peacock. The peacock was standing on both feet and had already spread its tail, but its face was half in the picture and half in Aunt Oppenheim's spools of cotton. Because of this memory, Kätzchen thought about Margarethe, his dead mother. She was sitting on the sofa, young and beautiful. In the armchair opposite sat his father, Ernst, while Margarethe embroidered him, Kätzchen, ever so slowly. At first she embroidered his shoes, then his legs, and his body, and his hands, and his neck. When the thread hung from his neck Margarethe stopped, holding the needle between her thumb and her forefinger, with her three other fingers spread in the air like a bird's

---

19. Talented.

wing. "We will make ourselves a beautiful child," she said to Ernst, and Ernst nodded his head. Then she embroidered Kätzchen's face, and when she had finished the hair on his head, she cut the thread. "What shall we call the child?" asked Margarethe, and Ernst nodded his head once again. "So be it," said Margarethe, "we shall call him Kätzchen," and she embroidered the name "Kätzchen" above the child's head.

Meanwhile, Max the Hungarian had stood up, spread out his arms, and was singing *"Meine Liebe Ist Wie Eine Rose."*[20] Kätzchen saw that tears were streaming from Aunt Oppenheim's eyes and he remembered the man who drove up in a horse-drawn carriage to bring her bouquets of flowers. That carriage in the picture, thought Kätzchen, must be this man's, and the palace is Aunt Oppenheim's. She sits in the room in the palace and looks out through the window. Tomorrow Aunt Oppenheim will take a spool of thread out of her sewing box and embroider the foot of the horse again. And the horse will put its foot down. Then she will embroider the feet of the horse as they rise and fall until the horse reaches the gates of the palace. And when the horse reaches the gates of the palace she will embroider the man descending from the carriage and offering her flowers.

As they walked away from Aunt Oppenheim's house, Uncle Arthur held one of Kätzchen's hands and Max the Hungarian held the other. The rain had stopped and gray clouds sailed towards Kätzchen, Uncle Arthur and Max the Hungarian and passed over their heads. "If Uncle Arthur and Max the Hungarian had chosen to take me to where the clouds are sailing," thought Kätzchen, "the wind would carry them up and they would float in the sky." As they walked down the steps to the sea, Max said, *"Eins, zwei, drei – hop!"*[21] and Uncle Arthur and Max lifted Kätzchen up, carried him through the air for a distance, and put him back down on his feet. When Kätzchen was in the air he saw the sea, and when Uncle Arthur and Max put him down, the sea

---

20. "My Love is like a Rose.
21. "One, two, three – jump!"

284 ◆ Yoel Hoffmann

disappeared. It seemed to Kätzchen that it was the sea, and not he that rose and appeared, sank and disappeared.

When they arrived at the bottom of the steps, the sea stood still and spread out before them. Uncle Arthur dropped Kätzchen's hand, placed both his hands on the bird's head, and leaned his body on the cane. Kätzchen saw that the tip of Uncle Arthur's cane was sinking into the sand and the fear stole up on him that the sand would suck Uncle Arthur under, into the earth, and he, Kätzchen, would be left alone on its surface. But Uncle Arthur pulled his cane out of the sand, and held Kätzchen's hand again.

Kätzchen lifted his eyes and noticed that they were standing near a hut smeared with tar paper. Out of the window of the hut peered a head with gold-rimmed spectacles on its nose and a white beard hanging from its chin. The head moved from one shoulder to the other, and said, "Oy vey! Oy vey!" Max the Hungarian looked at the head and said, "*Guten Tag,* Herr Schneider."[22] The head moved once more from one shoulder to the other and said, "Oy vey, oy vey, and vot is so good about such a day?" Max the Hungarian laughed and said, "Herr Lumpenschneider,[23] this is Kätzchen. Now Kätzchen is also *Lumpenproletar.* Then he grabbed Kätzchen and lifted him onto his head. From his seat on Max's head, Kätzchen saw that the head in the window was attached to a body – and that the body was sitting in front of a sewing machine. "A good boy, a good boy," said the tailor. Max said, "Not just a boy. This is a *Prinz.*[24] And now Prinz Kätzchen is coming to the palace of King Max." Kätzchen remembered that Max's eyes were blue-green and thought that Max was King of the Sea, who sits on the beach and looks at the sea all day long. When his eyes are blue, the sea is blue – and when his eyes are green, the sea is green.

Max turned away from the tailor and entered an alleyway which ran between the huts. Now the wind blew against their backs and the clouds came up behind them and drifted into the distance. Kätzchen

---

22. "Good day, Mr. Tailor."
23. Mister Tattered-Tailor
24. Prince

turned round and saw that Uncle Arthur was leaning forwards, as though the bird on his cane had spread its wings and was pulling his long body upwards.

Max lifted Kätzchen down from his head. Then he brought his two fists in front of his mouth like a bugle and called out, "Avigail, Avigail, open up the palace. Emperor Franz Joseph, the King of Hungary and the Little Prince are here!"

At the door of the hut appeared a woman with dark skin and black hair. She stared at Kätzchen, pointed a brown finger in his direction and said, "Ooooo-aa! Ooooo-aa! This must be Arthur's nephew. Welcome to my humble abode. Avigail will call you Pussycat!" Kätzchen looked into Avigail's black eyes and thought to himself that she was a sort of *Hexe*[25] who used spells and turned children into animals.

Avigail sat Kätzchen down at a table and placed a bowl before him which gave off white steam. Kätzchen thought to himself that there was a magic potion in the bowl and when he drank it, he would turn into a cat. But the bowl also smelled of meat and pepper and Kätzchen swallowed the potion down to the last drop.

The sun stood in the window of the hut like a red wheel. "When the wheel of the sun sinks down into the sea," thought Kätzchen to himself, "I will be no more." His eyelids were heavy and through his eyelashes he could make out Avigail's figure, close by and far away, far away and close by. When she picked him up in her arms he closed his eyes and remembered the angel Aunt Oppenheim had told him about. "This angel," thought Kätzchen, "is smooth-skinned, and smells of wild grass, and will always guard me from harm."

At night, Kätzchen heard voices and opened his eyes. Rain beat down on the roof of the hut. Uncle Arthur stood at the window looking out to sea. From the bed at the other end of the hut rose Max's voice, "Jesus Christus! Jesus Christus! Jesus Christus!" he cried. And Avigail's voice answered him, "Ooooo-aa! Ooooo-aa! Ooooo-aa!" Kätzchen strained his eyes and saw that the bodies of Max the

---

25. Witch.

Hungarian and Avigail were going up and down, up and down. Uncle Arthur walked over to Kätzchen, covered him with a blanket up to his chin and said, "*Schlaff mein Kind, schlaff!*"[26] Water streamed down the window panes. Then Max and Avigail fell silent and Kätzchen lay for a long time listening to the voice of the rain and imagining that he was turning into a cat.

In the morning Uncle Arthur was standing by the window facing the sea. Kätzchen remembered what he had seen in the night and looked at the bed at the other end of the hut. In the bed lay only Max, his mouth gaping wide. At that moment, Avigail appeared in the doorway with some herbs in her hand. "Does Pussycat like *na'ana*?"[27] she asked. Kätzchen who did not know what *na'ana* was, nodded his head and said, "*Ja.*" Avigail placed some earth-colored tea before him, suspended her fingers in the steam which rose from it, and let the herbs drop. The herbs sank down to the bottom of the cup like a sort of forest on the seabed. "Drink, Pussycat, drink," said Avigail, and watched Kätzchen with black eyes. As he sipped at the drink, Kätzchen lowered his eyes to see whether cat's fur had already begun to grow on his hands. Then Avigail placed before him a sort of round bread sprinkled with small seeds. As the bread was hard, Kätzchen dipped it into the cup and saw that the end of the bread was peeking through the herbage like a fish head. Kätzchen chewed the bread and thought to himself, "Pussycat eats fish." But when he looked at Avigail again, she was braiding her hair and her lips were smiling. "Arrturr," said Avigail. The sound of Uncle Arthur's name rolled around her mouth like a train on iron tracks. "I'm going out with the boy to the beach." Uncle Arthur did not turn away from the window.

Black crows jumped on the sand. The sea was green but the sky was cloudless and light blue. Avigail slipped off her shoes, held them in one hand and held out her other hand to Kätzchen. Kätzchen saw that Avigail's feet were brown, and remembered Aunt Oppenheim's foot, which was white with the little toe bent inwards, and covered by a sort of

---

26. "Sleep, my child, sleep."
27. Arabic: mint leaves.

thick crust. Avigail's toes were all straight, and along the sole of her foot ran a kind of line which divided the brown skin above from the white skin below. Kätzchen felt the urge to touch Avigail's feet, and without wanting to, and without knowing why, suddenly said, "Jesus Christus."

Max said, "Now I tell from the beginning. *Mah ze hayim?*"[28] Kätzchen was reminded of Chaim Heiventreiger who used to throw four stones up in the air. As the stones were on their way up, Chaim Heiventreiger would pick up another stone which he had placed on the ground, turn his hand palm up, and catch the stones he had thrown up as they came down. After Chaim Heiventreiger's parents moved to Jaffa, Kätzchen never saw him again.

"You think," continued Max, "that life is gas, and then amoeba, and then fish, and then fish which come out of the water with legs, and then monkey and then man. Life is not gas, not amoeba, not fish, not fish with legs, not monkey. Kätzchen hear the music of Liszt and understand life. Max with woman – Max understand. Life is secret, life is secret," said Max twice, and fell silent. Kätzchen remembered what he had seen the night before and thought to himself that the stones which Chaim Heiventreiger threw went up only once, while Max and Avigail go up because they come down and come down because they go up. The same thought persisted in his mind until it took on the form of a picture. Black crows jump on the beach. Avigail, swathed in a white robe, floats barefoot across the sand. And on the water walks a fish with four legs and the face of Chaim Hieventreiger. He throws four stones into the air, catches them in his hand and calls after Avigail: "Wanna try? Wanna try?"

Then Max walked over to a box in the corner of the hut, placed a sort of handle inside it, turned it seven times and said: "Arthur *soldat*[29] of Franz Joseph. Max *soldat* of Franz Liszt. Kätzchen know what is *Zigeuner?*[30] *Zigeuner* steal chickens and make beautifulest music.

---

28. Hebrew: "What is life?"
29. Soldier.
30. Gypsy.

This, teacher in school not know. He know only liberation of Jews. Music is liberation of man."

From the box came the sounds of a melody which rose higher and higher. Then it fell down, down, and then up and down, up and down. The sounds sent Kätzchen spinning round and round. They entered his ears, his mouth, his nostrils, and sent a shudder through his chest and stomach. At first, Kätzchen saw a man with a drooping mustache drawing a violin bow across the back of a large rooster. Then the man disappeared and the rooster flew slowly up into the darkness. Thousands of birds circled the sky. The birds' wings were on fire and the sound of their voices reached from one end of the world to the other.

Then the music came to an end and Kätzchen saw tears running down the cheeks of Max the Hungarian. Kätzchen thought to himself that Max was crying over the birds that burned. He looked at Uncle Arthur and saw that his eyes were clear. Kätzchen climbed onto Uncle Arthur's lap and clung to his chest. Uncle Arthur stroked Kätzchen's head and said, "*Genug*,[31] Max."

In the afternoon, the tailor with gold-rimmed spectacles on his nose came and sat at the table. Avigail placed a bowl of soup in front of him and the tailor bent forward and put his beard in the steam. Then he raised the bowl to his lips, took a sip of soup and said, "*Nu nu!*"[32] Max looked at him, his eyes aflame, and said, "*Nu nu ist garnichts.*"[33] The tailor looked at Max and said, "*Gurnischt is gurnischt.*"[34] Max said, "*Nu nu is gurnischt.*"[35] The tailor said, "What have you got against me today?" Max made no reply. The tailor turned to Uncle Arthur and said, "*Nu?*" Uncle Arthur rested his chin on his hand and said, "*Nu nu ist etwas.*"[36] The tailor smiled with satisfaction. Max fixed his eyes on Uncle Arthur and said, "*Was ist nu nu?*"[37] Uncle Arthur tugged at the

---

31. Enough.
32. "Well, well," a world-weary sigh common among Eastern European Jews.
33. German: "Nu nu is nothing."
34. Yiddish: "Nothing is nothing."
35. Yiddish: "Nu nu is nothing."
36. Yiddish: "Nu nu is something."
37. "What is nu nu?"

end of his chin and said, "*Nu nu ist alles.*"[38] Max said, "*Alles ist garnichts.*"[39] The tailor said, "*Gurnischt is gurnischt.*"[40] Max said, "*Nu nu is gurnischt.*" The tailor said, "*Nu nu.*" Kätzchen remembered that his mother, Margarethe, used to look at his father and say, "*Ja ja,*" and was filled with affection for the tailor.

At night Kätzchen had a dream. A wild-haired woman set the forest on fire and Max ran after her shouting, "I am King of the World! I am King of the World!" High above floated a large grandfather clock whose face was the face of the tailor. The hands of the clock were gold-rimmed spectacles and the pendulum beneath it was a white beard. And at the edge of the picture was Uncle Arthur leaning on his cane and saying, "This is mad Sarah."

When Kätzchen woke the next morning the sky was gray and the sea was stormy. Max sat at the table, his face somber, and Avigail stood in the corner of the hut with her face to the kerosene cooking stove and her back to Kätzchen. Uncle Arthur saw that Kätzchen's eyes were open and sat down next to him on the edge of the bed. Kätzchen asked Uncle Arthur, "*Sind alle Frauen verruckt?*"[41] Uncle Arthur smiled and said, "*Nein.*" Then he told Kätzchen in German that Margarethe, his mother, had been a beautiful woman in her youth. "Margarethe chose Ernst," he said, "because he was the more stubborn. But Ernst was afraid to lose her and went out of his mind. Women are not mad, but neither are they sane. Only men go in and out of their minds because of the women."

Kätzchen remembered that he had once heard his father speak. Suddenly, Ernst had lifted up his head and said, "*Warum?*"[42] in a deep voice. Margarethe rested her hands on Ernst's shoulders and said, "*Alles ist in Ordnung, Ernst, alles ist in Ordnung.*"[43]

---

38. "Nu nu is everything."
39. "Everything is nothing."
40. Yiddish: "Nothing is nothing."
41. "Are all women mad?"
42. "Why?"
43. "Everything is in order, Ernst, everything is in order."

Then Uncle Arthur told Kätzchen that if it hadn't been for Zionism he would have married Gertrud, who was not as beautiful as Margarethe, but always knew the right thing to do. But because of Zionism he traveled to Palestine and Gertrud remained in Vienna. But even if he had stayed in Vienna, Gertrud might not have married him since Gertrud believed in three Gods while he (like all the Jews) believed only in one.

All the while, Avigail had been quietly humming to herself by the kerosene stove. When Uncle Arthur fell silent Kätzchen could hear Avigail's song curl like cotton wool clouds and spin itself out in a wail, "*Ya howwa ya howwa.*" Avigail suddenly looked at Kätzchen and said, "*Howwa* is the wind." Kätzchen saw that Avigail's cheeks had reddened as though on fire. "*Ana wa'inta fi ilhowwa min zar'ina sowwa ya howwa, ya howwa, ya howwa, ya howwa,*"[44] sang Avigail. "This is a song of two children in the desert," she said to Kätzchen, and then she looked at Max, and Kätzchen understood from her eyes that the child Avigail had loved in the desert was not Max.

Kätzchen looked at Max's face and saw that he had no eye in his forehead. Once Margarethe had told Kätzchen about the Cyclops. "He who sees with two eyes," she said, "closes one eye when the sights he sees are painful. If he is also pained by the sights he sees with the eye that remains open – he closes both eyes. But the Cyclops never closes his one and only eye." On hearing this, Kätzchen closed one eye and saw that there was not a great deal of difference between the sights he saw with one eye and the sights he saw with two. Then he closed the eye that remained open and thought to himself, "Now I will never see anything ever again." But then, when his eyes were closed, an eye in his forehead opened. The sight he saw with this eye was not clear, but it held a kind of transparency missing from the sights he saw with his other two eyes. When Kätzchen looked in the mirror he could not find the eye in his forehead, but when he closed his eyes again he knew for sure that the eye was there. After that day, Kätzchen knew that he was a Cyclops and would look at people to see if they had an eye in their foreheads.

---

44. "I and thee in the wind from our childhood together."

Once Herr Druck, who used to come to Margarethe, said, "Call me Zelig. All right?" Kätzchen felt the eye in his forehead opening. He closed his eyes and saw that Herr Druck did not see him, Kätzchen, at all, and was speaking to Margarethe alone. But the Margarethe Herr Druck was speaking to was not Margarethe his mother, who was thin and chewed her fingernails, but a full-bodied Margarethe whose fingers were painted red. Kätzchen opened his eyes and said, "Zelig." Herr Druck said, "That's good. That's good." Kätzchen looked at Margarethe, his mother, and saw that she too was a Cyclops but what the eye in her forehead saw pained her, and she closed this eye and opened her other two eyes. Kätzchen understood that Ernst, his father, was also a Cyclops. But Ernst was no more than a Cyclops and could only see through the eye in his forehead. If Herr Druck had been swallowed up inside my father, thought Kätzchen to himself, Ernst too would have been able to see like other people, and they would not have sent him to the institution. Kätzchen felt pity for Herr Druck who ran to and fro between Margarethe and himself and did not know that they were Cyclopes. Later, when Herr Druck had dwindled and faded away, Kätzchen was sorry. He was not sorry because of Herr Druck, but because of the eyes which Herr Druck had and his father did not have. Once Kätzchen said "Zelig" a hundred times and hoped in his heart that the word had the power to reach the institution.

Meanwhile, Avigail had placed herb tea on the table and bread sprinkled with seeds. Max sipped the tea but did not reach for the bread and his face was as somber as before. Outside the sea raged. Suddenly, Uncle Arthur said, "Kant." Max raised his head and said, "*Keren Kayemet.*"[45] Uncle Arthur looked at Max and said, "Heine." Max looked at Uncle Arthur and said, "*Kofer ha-Yishuv.*"[46] Uncle Arthur said, "Franz Joseph." Max said, "Franz Liszt." Uncle Arthur said, "Arlozorov."[47] Max said, "Sheinkin."[48] Uncle Arthur said,

---

45. Hebrew: Jewish National Fund
46. Tax paid by Jewish residents of pre-state Israel
47. Chaim Arlozorov – pre-state Jewish labor leader
48. Menachem Sheinkin – Zionist leader.

"*Schinken*,"[49] and they both laughed. Avigail laughed too. Kätzchen saw that everyone was laughing, and laughed as well.

"*Wo ist Kätzchen?*"[50] Aunt Oppenheim's silhouette stood in the doorway of the hut like two umbrellas joined together. "Two days," said Aunt Oppenheim, "I am worrying about Kätzchen." "*Komm herein*,"[51] Uncle Arthur said, but Aunt Oppenheim stared at Max and Avigail and did not budge. Sun entered the cabin round Aunt Oppenheim's head and between her legs. Kätzchen went up to her and pressed his head against her stomach. Aunt Oppenheim's stomach was soft and her dress smelled of perfume. Uncle Arthur got up from his chair, took his cane and went outside. Aunt Oppenheim took hold of Kätzchen's hand and followed Uncle Arthur. Kätzchen saw that for every step which Uncle Arthur took, Aunt Oppenheim took two, and thought to himself that people walk the way their hearts beat. Uncle Arthur, whose heart beat slowly, walked slowly and took long steps, while Aunt Oppenheim, whose heart beat quickly, took short steps.

At the end of the alleyway the head of the tailor peered out of the window. "*A giten tug*,"[52] said the tailor's head and added: "*Ist die gnadige Frau ihre Schwester?*"[53] Uncle Arthur heard the tailor speak German and looked at him in amazement. The tailor removed his head from the window, appeared at the doorway of the hut and presented his entire body to Aunt Oppenheim. "*Ich war in Wien*,"[54] said the tailor. Aunt Oppenheim's eyes softened and she nodded her head. The tailor said, "*Meine Frau ist gestorben.*"[55] Aunt Oppenheim looked into the tailor's face and smiled.

The tailor extended both hands towards the interior of the hut and said, "*Kommen sie herein af a gleisl tee.*"[56] Aunt Oppenheim's eyes,

---

49. Ham.
50. "Where is Kätzchen?"
51. "Come in."
52. Yiddish: "Good day."
53. "Is the good lady your sister?"
54. "I was in Vienna."
55. "My wife passed away."
56. "Please come in for a glass of tea." (This sentence begins in German and ends in Yiddish).

which had softened now hardened again. She looked away from the tailor and said, *"Es tut mir leid."*[57]

Kätzchen pondered what Aunt Oppenheim had said. At first he thought Aunt Oppenheim's sorrow came about because the tailor's wife had died. Then he thought Aunt Oppenheim's sorrow was not because of the tailor's dead wife but because she didn't want his cup of tea. As he was thinking these thoughts a picture emerged in his mind. The tailor sits next to a sewing machine in front of the window. His wife who died approaches him with a cup of tea in her hand. The tailor sips the tea which his dead wife puts in front of him and the lenses of his spectacles steam over. His fingers extricate a slice of lemon from the tea. He sucks the lemon between his lips and says, *"Nu nu."* This picture made Kätzchen feel a sorrow of his own for the tailor and Aunt Oppenheim's sorrow was forgotten.

Uncle Arthur and Aunt Oppenheim held Kätzchen's hands and walked down the steps to the sea. Kätzchen remembered how Uncle Arthur and Max the Hungarian had led him down the same steps and lifted him up in the air and how it seemed that the sea, and not he rose and fell. "Now," thought Kätzchen, "the sea doesn't rise and doesn't fall, it stands still." As soon as Uncle Arthur and Aunt Oppenheim came to the beach they let go of Kätzchen's hands and turned to each other. Uncle Arthur said that Kätzchen should be *"bei mir"*[58] while Aunt Oppenheim disagreed and said that Kätzchen should be *"bei mir."*

Kätzchen saw a shell. Once his mother Margarethe told him that shells contained the sound of the sea, and even if the shell was far away from the sea, in the mountains, or the desert, the sound of the waves is always in it. Kätzchen lifted the shell to his ear. The sound of the sea came out of the shell and seemed to Kätzchen to be saying *"bei mir, bei mir."* Kätzchen looked at the sea and saw a ray of light descending from the sky and painting a slice of the sea gold. Once Uncle Arthur had pointed far out to sea and said, *"Dort ist Zypern."*[59]

---

57. "I am sorry." (Literally – it causes me sorrow.)
58. "With me."
59. "There is Cyprus."

Kätzchen thought to himself that Zypern was a land of gold and that the people who lived in the sky went down that ray of light and came to Zypern.

"Onkel Arthur and Tante Oppenheim want Kätzchen to go to a good place," said Aunt Oppenheim. "Now," thought Kätzchen, "I'll sail in a ship to Zypern and there I'll meet Margarethe." A wave of joy rose from his stomach and spread through his chest. "To Zypern? To Zypern?" asked Kätzchen, and Aunt Oppenheim said, "To kibbutz."

When Kätzchen and Uncle Arthur came back from the sea, the tailor's head was back in the window. "Women," said the head, "are the work of the devil." But Uncle Arthur held tight to Kätzchen's hand and said nothing.

That evening, Uncle Arthur packed Kätzchen's clothes into a suitcase. Avigail placed Kätzchen's socks on her knees, threaded a darning needle and quietly hummed, "*Ya howwa, ya howwa.*" Max sat at the table with an angry face. "Arthur," said Max. Uncle Arthur raised his head from the suitcase and looked at Max. "*Warum kibbutz?*"[60] asked Max. Uncle Arthur returned his gaze to the suitcase and was silent. Then Uncle Arthur took Kätzchen's shoes and polished them with brown polish. "Arthur," said Max, "you cannot repair a big evil with a little good." But Uncle Arthur did not raise his head. Kätzchen was suddenly filled with longing. He looked at Uncle Arthur, who was stooped over his shoes, and understood that this longing was for Uncle Arthur, and was filled with amazement that he could long for Uncle Arthur even though he was right next to him.

That night Kätzchen had a dream. But by the morning, when Uncle Arthur woke him up, he had forgotten it. Avigail smiled at Kätzchen, placed an apple in his hand and said, "Goodbye Pussycat." Uncle Arthur picked up the suitcase and said, "*Komm, mein Kind.*"[61]

The moon still lit the sky. The tailor's window was shut but Kätzchen could see light through the blinds, and the tailor's shadow moved along the opposite wall. "A man's shadow," thought Kätzchen,

---

60. "Why kibbutz?"
61. "Come, my child."

"lives inside his body at night, and in the daytime the shadow comes out of the body and walks behind him. A shadow is also a kind of man, and a man's name is also his shadow's name. The tailor has a shadow and its name is Schneider, Uncle Arthur has a shadow and its name is Uncle Arthur, and Kätzchen also has a shadow and its name is Kätzchen."

By the time they reached the bus stop the moon had gone away and it was daylight. A woman was sitting at one end of the bus, and a man with a swollen neck at the other. Kätzchen looked at the man's neck and thought to himself that the man's shadow also had a swollen neck.

After the bus had left the city streets, Kätzchen looked at Uncle Arthur and saw that his head was bent forward but his eyes saw nothing. Uncle Arthur's cane leaned against the window and the bird's head faced the fields.

As Uncle Arthur and Kätzchen entered the gate of the kibbutz, Uncle Arthur turned to a man dressed in blue clothes and asked where he could find Herr Grossman. The man pointed to a house and said, "In the office." Uncle Arthur held Kätzchen's hand and set off towards the house the man had pointed to.

Suddenly, Kätzchen saw a cow. Kätzchen looked into the cow's eyes and the cow looked into Kätzchen's eyes. Since Kätzchen had come to a halt, Uncle Arthur rested his cane against the fence of the cattle-pen, and stood still. Then Uncle Arthur picked up his cane again, took Kätzchen's hand and said, "*Komm, mein Kind.*" As they were leaving Kätzchen looked back and saw that the cow had also turned its head and was looking at him.

Herr Grossman was not in the house but a woman there told Uncle Arthur that Herr Grossman was not a *Herr*[62] at all, and there wasn't a single *Herr* on the kibbutz, since everyone who came to the kibbutz left the *Herr* outside. Kätzchen wondered where the *Herr* had been stuck to this Grossman and how he'd removed it when he arrived at the kibbutz. Then the woman looked at Kätzchen and asked, "And what's your name?" Kätzchen said, "Kätzchen." The woman said,

---

62. Kibbutz members call one another *haver* (comrade) instead of *Herr* (Mr).

"That's a suitable name for Germany. Here we'll have to call you by a name that's suitable for a kibbutz." Kätzchen remembered Avigail and wanted to tell the woman his name was Pussycat but from her face he understood that Pussycat was not a suitable name for a kibbutz either.

Meanwhile, Herr Grossman had arrived and said, "This is the boy?" Then he looked at Kätzchen and said, "And what's your name?" Kätzchen was silent. Herr Grossman asked Uncle Arthur, "Doesn't he speak Hebrew?" "He does," said Uncle Arthur, "but his name is not right for a kibbutz." Herr Grossman asked, "And what is his name?" Uncle Arthur said, "Kätzchen." Herr Grossman said, "You're right, that's not a proper name for a kibbutz. Let's go to the school."

Herr Grossman walked out of the house and Uncle Arthur and Kätzchen followed him. Outside, a man in blue rode past Kätzchen on a bike. The wind blew. When they passed the cow-pen the cow was standing there looking at Kätzchen. Kätzchen looked into the cow's eyes and said, "*Ich bin* Kätzchen!"[63]

At the door of the school Uncle Arthur patted Kätzchen's head and said, "*Mein Kind.*" Then he turned his back and walked towards the gate of the kibbutz, and it seemed to Kätzchen as though Uncle Arthur's cane was groping its way along the path like a blind man's stick.

Herr Grossman placed his hand on Kätzchen's back and led him into a room. "The new boy," said Herr Grossman. Children with untidy hair and a man holding a sort of carving knife immediately stared at Kätzchen. The man put down the carving knife and said, "Good. And what's your name?" Herr Grossman said, "I'll talk to you about that later." The man looked curiously at Kätzchen and said, "Sit down." Kätzchen sat down. The man picked up the carving knife again and, with his other hand, took a green leaf from the table. Then he looked Kätzchen in the face and said, "Since city-dwellers have distanced themselves from nature, nature has distanced herself from them. Have you ever heard of photosynthesis?" Kätzchen thought the man was talking to him in German and said, "*Nein.*" The children

---

63. "I'm Kätzchen."

laughed. The man said, "Don't you speak Hebrew?" "No. Yes," said Kätzchen. The children laughed again. The man looked angrily at Kätzchen and said, "The leaf absorbs sunlight and turns it into chlorophyll." Then he cut the leaf with his carving knife, turned back to Kätzchen and said, "Have you ever seen a leaf through a magnifying glass?" Behind Kätzchen's back one of the children called out, "*Nein*," and they all laughed for the third time. The man smiled and said, "Children, we must give the new member a warm welcome." Then all the children looked at the leaf through a magnifying glass, but Kätzchen, whose eyes were filled with tears, saw nothing.

When the children went out into the yard they clustered around Kätzchen. One pointed at Kätzchen's shirt, which was buttoned up to his collar, and asked why he wasn't wearing a tie. Another said that Kätzchen's coat was funny. Kätzchen turned his head and walked away. By the side of a road, near a tree, he saw a ladder. He lifted his eyes to see what was at the top, and saw a woman in blue. The woman had a saw in her hand and was cutting down the branches. "The work of the people in this place," thought Kätzchen, "is cutting. Some of them carry carving knives and cut leaves, and some of them carry saws and cut branches." Kätzchen remembered that when Herr Grossman came to the kibbutz they cut off his *Herr*. "Soon, when the people here turn to me," thought Kätzchen to himself, "they will cut my name off." And as Kätzchen thought of his name, he remembered the cow. He walked along the paths of the kibbutz to the cattle-pen to see the cow, but the cow was not there. Kätzchen raised his eyes and saw green fields lying beyond the kibbutz. He left the kibbutz and walked into the fields to look for the cow.

When his mother died, Aunt Oppenheim told Kätzchen that Margarethe had gone up to the sky and this statement seemed right to him. Once Kätzchen saw Uncle Arthur reading a book. Kätzchen stood behind him and looked at the picture in the book. In a field, inside a pit, stood a man with an ugly face holding a skull in his hand. Kätzchen asked Uncle Arthur, "*Was ist das?*"[64] and Uncle Arthur said,

---

64. "What is that?"

"*Der Tote von gestern und der Tote von morgen*,"[65] and this statement of Uncle Arthur's seemed right as well. "The dead," thought Kätzchen, "go out into the fields, fall slowly on their faces and the earth covers them. Then slowly they break through the earth and go up to the sky."

Now grass soaked Kätzchen's trousers and mud covered the shoes which Uncle Arthur had polished. Clouds covered the sky. In the middle of the field stood a man surrounded by sheep. The man looked at Kätzchen, but Kätzchen, who was looking for the cow, continued on his way.

At the edge of the field Kätzchen saw a ditch with a stream running along the bottom. When Kätzchen climbed down into the ditch a big crab was startled and ran into the water. Before the crab disappeared, Kätzchen saw on its back two eyes looking at him. Then Kätzchen wandered along the side of the stream until he saw a tree trunk half in and half out of the water. Kätzchen climbed onto the tree trunk and walked, step by step, across the stream. When he was half way across, the tree trembled and Kätzchen's body trembled with it. But then Kätzchen heard the lowing of a cow. His body straightened up and he crossed over to the other side of the stream. As Kätzchen climbed up out of the ditch the shadow of a mountain was spread across the fields. "In a little while," thought Kätzchen, "I'll find the cow. Then I'll fall on my face and the earth of the field will cover me." "*Mutti*"[66] said Kätzchen. But when the sound of his voice reached his ears, it seemed as though the word had not come out of his mouth. "*Mutti*," said Kätzchen again, but it was as though his lips were not his own. "*Howw...*" blew the wind; "*waa...*" blew the wind. Kätzchen listened to the sound of the wind and remembered Avigail's song. *Howwa* is the sound of the wind and *howwa* is the name of the wind, thought Kätzchen. When the wind blows you hear its name and when you hear its name it blows. "Wi-ind," said Kätzchen. "Wi-ind," and this word too sounded to Kätzchen like the sound of the wind.

And as things and the names of things became one, the fear in

---
65. "The dead of yesterday and the dead of tomorrow."
66. "Mommy."

Kätzchen's heart disappeared. "*Mutti*," he said for the third time, and this time the voice was his own and the lips were his own. "Have you lost your way, my son?" Kätzchen heard Margarethe say. "*Ja*," answered Kätzchen, "I have lost my way." But there was no doubt in Kätzchen's mind that he would soon find his way, and follow it until he reached the cow. And the cow would look into Kätzchen's eyes and say: "There, you have found your way, *mein Kind*, and you need never stray so far again."

"*Min hadda?*"[67] said a voice from out of the darkness, and metal clicked against metal. A black shadow approached Kätzchen. "*Min inti?*"[68] said the shadow. Kätzchen saw that the shadow had the face of an old man with a large mustache on both sides of his nose and white hair covering his chin. When the old man saw Kätzchen's face he hung the rifle over his shoulder and said, "*Min neyn jit?*"[69] But Kätzchen looked at the old man's face and said nothing. The old man also looked at Kätzchen's face and remained silent. The old man and Kätzchen looked at each other for a long time.

Then the old man turned his back on Kätzchen and walked away. His figure was swallowed up in the field but the barrel of his gun stuck up and moved across the clouds. "That gun," thought Kätzchen to himself, "is Uncle Arthur's cane with the bird at the top, and the bird is turning its head and looking at me." Kätzchen picked up his feet and ran after the bird. "Onkel Arthur," cried Kätzchen, "Onkel Arthur?" The bird appeared and disappeared between the clouds. Kätzchen's shoes tangled in the weeds and his legs hurt. "To the sky," thought Kätzchen, "to the sky. Birds fly to the sky. Margarethe is in the sky. Uncle Arthur is in the sky." Suddenly Kätzchen's body seemed as light as a bird and he was floating above the earth. "At last," thought Kätzchen, and closed his eyes.

When Kätzchen opened his eyes, he saw the old man standing over him. A black robe covered his body and on his head he wore a cloth

---

67. Arabic: "Who's that?"
68. Arabic: "Who are you?"
69. Arabic: "Where are you from?"

kerchief tied with black rope. Kätzchen looked around and saw a tent made out of black sheets. In the corner of the tent embers were glowing and on the embers stood a kettle. When the old man saw Kätzchen looking at him, he offered him some thin round bread and said, "*Kol.*"[70] Kätzchen took the bread from the old man's hand and chewed at it. Then he raised his head and saw that he was lying on a mattress scattered with cushions. The old man hunched down with his legs tucked under him and his haunches brushing the floor. He laid his hands on his knees and looked at Kätzchen.

Kätzchen ate. From time to time the twigs on the fire crackled, and black shadows leaped across the flaps of the tent. The old man rose from his place and handed Kätzchen tea that smelled of flowers.

Suddenly, it seemed to Kätzchen that he had once been in this place, and had once eaten what he was eating, and the old man had once sat like that and looked at him. "Never," thought Kätzchen, "will I have to leave this place again." His eyes felt heavy and through half-shut lids he saw the old man standing over him with a woolen blanket in his hands. "*Nam,*"[71] said the old man and pressed lightly on Kätzchen's shoulder. Kätzchen lay back on the mattress and folded his legs into his stomach. The old man spread the blanket over Kätzchen's body and tucked the sides into the mattress. Before Kätzchen closed his eyes he saw the old man take the kettle and pour himself some bitter-smelling coffee into a tiny china cup.

"*Komm,*"[72] said Uncle Arthur and shook Kätzchen's shoulder. Kätzchen opened his eyes and saw the face of the old man. "The old man," thought Kätzchen, "is a kind of Uncle Arthur. Sometimes he talks in Uncle Arthur's language and sometimes in another language."

The old man placed a glass of milk in front of Kätzchen. Kätzchen drank the milk and it was very sweet. The tent smelled of morning dew and other, more pungent smells which Kätzchen had never

---

70. Arabic: "Eat!"
71. Arabic: "Sleep!"
72. "Come, get up!"

smelled before. *"Nimshi,"*[73] said the old man. *"Nimshi,"* thought Kätzchen, "is a word with a beautiful sound. When I meet Uncle Arthur again I'll teach him this word."

The old man walked out of the tent and Kätzchen followed. Outside Kätzchen saw a donkey. Kätzchen looked the donkey in the face and the donkey looked like the eyes of the cow that Kätzchen had gone to look for in the fields. Black goats stood in a stockade made of dry branches and looked at Kätzchen. *"Ziegen,"*[74] said Kätzchen to the old man. The old man gripped Kätzchen's waist and sat him on the back of the donkey. Then he took up the rope tied around the donkey's neck and led the donkey into the fields. Kätzchen turned round and saw that the goats were still looking at him. When the old man reached the edge of the field he led the donkey for some while along a path which ran between two fields. The old man climbed up a hill and the donkey climbed after him. When the donkey reached the top of the hill the old man gripped Kätzchen's waist and lifted him down to the ground. At the foot of the hill Kätzchen saw little red-roofed houses. The old man pointed to the houses and said, *"Yahud."*[75] Then, he removed from his neck a little horn which hung from a thread, and placed it around Kätzchen's neck. *"Ma ee-saleme,"*[76] said the old man. He turned his back on Kätzchen and began to climb down the hill. Suddenly he looked back and saw that Kätzchen was looking at him. The old man returned to Kätzchen and said, *"Shu ismak?"*[77] Kätzchen said, "Kätzchen." The old man said, *"Ana ismi Ahmad."*[78] Then the old man left with the donkey and Kätzchen was left alone on the hill.

Suddenly it seemed to Kätzchen that the old man was not a real old man and the donkey was not a real donkey, but they were more like the sights he saw at night; pictures transparent as air on the finest of all cloth. Once, the picture of a dragon appeared in Kätzchen's mind.

---

73. Arabic: "Let's go."
74. "Goats."
75. Arabic: "Jews."
76. Arabic: "Farewell."
77. Arabic: "What's your name?"
78. Arabic: "My name is Ahmad."

If he had been able to, Kätzchen would have preferred to imagine a different picture, but even if the dragon had left the picture and stood in front of him, Kätzchen would not have been afraid. The dragon would open its mouth and spit fire, but Kätzchen would stand his ground and look the dragon in the face until the dragon understood that it was not a real dragon.

"The things I can touch," thought Kätzchen to himself, "are real," and he touched the horn on his neck. But the horn, and his hands touching it, moved away from Kätzchen and he couldn't find in himself other hands with which to feel his hands. "All this is a dream," thought Kätzchen, and he found this to be a very strange thought. Storks flew across the sky. Kätzchen tried to picture in his mind the storks he could see, but the storks he imagined were not the storks he had seen, and once more Kätzchen did not know whether storks had flown across the sky or whether this was only a picture in a dream. And because this strange thought refused to leave him, Kätzchen decided to think about it until it disappeared. "I think all this is a dream, but it isn't," said Kätzchen to himself. "This thought," thought Kätzchen, "is my thought, and it's strong enough to get rid of the previous one." But as he was thinking this thought, it too moved away from him, and once again he didn't know if it was his own thought or not. "The more my thoughts roll around," thought Kätzchen, "the more I lose myself." And because he was looking for himself, he remembered he had once asked his mother Margarethe where Kätzchen was before she was born. "You are my child," said Margarethe. "When I was a little girl I went for a walk in a field of cabbages. The field was full of cabbages and in each cabbage lay a baby. All the babies were asleep and only one baby was awake. 'Do you want to be my baby?' I asked, and the baby said, 'Yes.' When I grew up I married Ernst, and we had a baby. I looked at its face and saw it was the baby I chose in the cabbage field."

Suddenly, Kätzchen longed to go back to the cabbage field. "I will lie inside the cabbage," he thought, "until Margarethe finds me. And when she finds me she will stay with me forever and never go up to the sky again." "The cabbage field," thought Kätzchen, "is near those

houses with the red roofs. I'll go there and look for the cabbage field."
But as he climbed down the hill he began to worry. "When I was a
baby," he thought, "my body was small and it could fit inside a
cabbage. Now my body is big and my legs will poke out and
Margarethe will not want such a child. Now I'll have to look for the
biggest cabbage in the world."

While Kätzchen's thoughts were revolving around the cabbage he
saw a little man with curly side-locks hanging from his temples.[79] The
man stood and looked at him. "This man," thought Kätzchen to
himself, "is a sort of dwarf. The houses here are small, and the people
who live in them have small bodies, and they could climb in and out
of cabbages with ease." The man turned his head towards his house
and called out, "A child of the Ashkenaz! A child of the Ashkenaz!"[80]
Immediately, a little woman walked out of the house. The man and the
woman approached Kätzchen and said one after the other in a strange
accent:

"Where have you come from, child?"

"Who is your father?"

"Where do you live?"

"How old are you, child?"

Their words rang in Kätzchen's ears like some kind of music
without questions or answers, played only for him to hear.

"Come and eat something, child," said the little woman and took
hold of Kätzchen's hand. When Kätzchen walked into the house he
saw a horse and rider on the wall. For a moment it seemed to
Kätzchen that the man on the horse was the old man he had met in
the field. But the land on the wall was different, all sand dunes, and
in the sky hung a crescent moon. Kätzchen remembered the picture
in Aunt Oppenheim's room. "The rider of this horse," thought
Kätzchen, "is the lover of the woman who lives here, and he is
searching for her in the desert. And when he finds her he will get
down from his horse and offer her flowers." The woman saw that

---

79. A Yemenite Jew. The Yemenite Jewish community immigrated to Israel en
masse in 1948.
80. Ashkenazi Jews are of European origin.

304 ◆ Yoel Hoffmann

Kätzchen was looking at the tapestry on the wall. She pointed to the horse and said in the same strange accent, "We came from there on eagles' wings."[81] A picture took shape in Kätzchen's mind. The man on the horse is galloping to his beloved through a cloud of sand. But as he draws near and can already see her face, a huge eagle descends from the sky, snatches the woman in its beak and carries her up and far, far away. Kätzchen wanted to ask the woman if the man in the picture was still riding his horse through the desert and searching for her but the woman placed a bowl of spicy-smelling food in front of him and said, "Eat, child."

Suddenly Kätzchen saw that on the floor, in the corner, an old man was sitting with a pipe in his mouth. A tube extended from the pipe and entered a bottle, and in the bottle there was water. Kätzchen, who had never seen such a strange pipe, put down his spoon and looked the old man in the face. The old man looked back at Kätzchen and said, "Where have you come from, child?" Kätzchen pondered the old man's question for a little while and said, "Cabbage." The old man fell silent and sucked at his pipe. Then he removed the end of the pipe from his mouth and asked, "Cabbage... kibbutz?" "*Nein*," said Kätzchen, "Cabbage... field." The eyes of the old man widened. "A field of cabbage." The old man shook his head from right to left and from left to right and said, "Poor child. An orphan."

Meanwhile the man and the woman had left and Kätzchen found himself alone with the old man. The old man saw that Kätzchen had finished his food and was sitting and looking at him, and he said, "Come here, child." Kätzchen went and sat down beside him. The old man thrust his hand under a nearby pillow, pulled out a book and said, "Do you know what this is, child?" Kätzchen looked at the book and said, "*Buch*."[82] The old man said, "In the tongue of the Ashkenaz it might be *Buch*, but in the holy tongue it is called *Teyro*."[83] Since he

---

81. The Yemenite Jews believed that the air-lift which brought them to Israel was a fulfillment of the biblical prophecy that God would return his people to Zion "on eagles' wings."

82. "Book."

83. *Torah* – Bible in Yemenite Hebrew pronunciation.

wanted to please the old man, Kätzchen repeated the word and said, *"Teyro."* The old man said, "And this is the Law which Moses set before the Children of Israel." Kätzchen repeated, "And this is the Law which Moses set before the Children of Israel."[84] The old man's face beamed. He wound the tube around the neck of the bottle and placed a sort of shawl with black stripes running across it round Kätzchen's neck. Once Kätzchen saw a man with such a shawl around his neck and asked Uncle Arthur what it was. "It's not the kind of thing," Uncle Arthur said, "that people put on for decoration. These people put the shawl around their necks for their *Gottesdienst.*"[85] Kätzchen thought such people were very lucky to have an enchanted shawl. They could spread the shawl in front of them and see God through it. But when he asked Uncle Arthur what the people saw through the shawl, Uncle Arthur said that they saw nothing, but God, who sees both them and their shawls, laughs. "There is no harm," thought Kätzchen to himself, "if God laughs, as long as I don't upset the old man."

The old man opened the book and read from it: "In the beginning God created the heavens and the earth." Kätzchen listened. and asked, "Created?" "Created. Made," said the old man. "The heavens and the earth?" said Kätzchen. "The heavens and the earth," said the old man. Kätzchen said, "And the air?" "And the air," said the old man. Kätzchen said, "And the stars?" "And the stars," said the old man. Kätzchen thought about what the old man had said, and asked, "Where is God?" The old man took the end of the pipe from the neck of the bottle and placed it inside his mouth. For a long while he sucked at his pipe and said nothing. Bubbles rose to the surface of the water. Finally, the old man took the pipe out of his mouth, looked at Kätzchen and said, "He has neither form nor body." A picture took shape in Kätzchen's mind. God makes the earth and leaves it. He makes the sky and removes Himself to the air above the sky. He makes the stars and removes Himself beyond them. And after he has made the sky and the earth and the air and the stars,

---

84. Deuteronomy 4:44.
85. Religions devotions.

there is no room left for Him in the universe, and He gets smaller and smaller until He disappears beyond the last star and nobody can see Him anymore. Once Margarethe had also been in the world, but after she gave birth to Kätzchen her body shrank and removed itself from the world, and now, when he calls out Margarethe's name, his voice gets lost among the stars. "God," thought Kätzchen, "gave birth to the world and died. And now the world asks for God in vain. A child sees his mother for only a short time, when he is a baby, and then, for the rest of his life, he asks for his mother who has no form and the mother who has no form asks for her child." Kätzchen saw that Margarethe's sorrow was no less than his own and he pictured Margarethe's short time, when she was little and lay in her cradle, and her mother, who had not yet lost her form, was still beside her.

"Mother of God," said Kätzchen. The old man lifted his arms into the air, a book in the one, and the end of the pipe in the other, and cried, "Be astonished O ye heavens!"[86] Then he averted his face from Kätzchen, closed his eyes, and only his lips moved. Suddenly Kätzchen saw in the face of the old man that he too had once been a baby, and was filled with wonder. The old man opened his eyes, replaced the end of the pipe on the neck of the bottle and said, "Child, He is the first and hath no beginning." Kätzchen remembered that he had once opened his eyes at night, in the dark, and could not see a thing and did not know where he was, and his hands groped through the air and found nothing, and at that moment he was alone in the world, and did not remember what had been and did not know what would be.

"The earth was without form and void," read the old man from the book, "and darkness was upon the face of the deep; and the spirit of God moved across the face of the waters. And God said: 'Let there be light.' And there was light." The wheel of the sun stood in the window and clouds sailed across. Outside a dog barked and the old man went back to blowing bubbles through the water. When Kätzchen looked at his face, he understood that his own sorrow, and the sorrow of the old

---

86. Jeremiah 2:12.

man, and God's sorrow, were all one sorrow, and a great happiness filled his heart.

"Is this the boy?" asked the policeman who stood at the door.

"This is the child," said the woman whose lover searches for her in the desert. "Come along, son," said the policeman. The old man rose from his place in the corner, lifted up his hands and cried, "The child is an orphan. He shall live with us." But the policeman placed his hand on Kätzchen's shoulder and led him outside. "Why did you run away from the kibbutz?" asked Herr Grossman's head which peered out of a car window. "He knows that my name is Kätzchen," thought Kätzchen. The policeman bent his knees until his head reached the same level as Kätzchen's and asked, "Why did you leave the kibbutz?" "I was looking for the cow," said Kätzchen. "You like cows?" asked the policeman, and Kätzchen saw in his face that he had once been a child and his mother had pressed him to her breast and he laughed, and she said, "Again?" and he laughed, and said, "Again."

At the gate of the kibbutz Herr Grossman got out of the car and said to Kätzchen, "Come along, let's go." A picture formed in Kätzchen's mind. Herr Grossman returns to the kibbutz and says the name "Kätzchen." A man in blue waves a knife and says, "What did he say? What did he say?" A woman descends from a ladder, her saw cutting through the air, and says, "He said it! He said it!" Kätzchen looked into the policeman's face and said, "The cow is not in the kibbutz." The policeman laughed and said, "Maybe she went to the fields to look for a boy." Herr Grossman said, "He's been placed in our care." The policeman said, "We'll see," and they drove away.

On the way, the policeman pulled the steering wheel right and left and left and right and sang, "Ti-na Ti-na, come to Palesti-na." Kätzchen thought of Tina, sailing across the sea past the strip of gold which was Zypern, with the prow of her ship turned towards Palestina. Birds rose from the fields. "And who do *you* love?" asked the policeman. "It's because he's thinking of Tina that he thinks of other people's loves," thought Kätzchen, and he said, "Avigail." But when he tried to think about Avigail she faded into the distance and he could not remember where she was or what she looked like.

When they reached the police station the policeman said, "Sit down," and went away. "All I ever do," thought Kätzchen to himself, "is come and go, and come and go." But as he was mulling this over he was uncertain again whether it was he who came and went, or other people came and went while he stayed in the same place.

Next to Kätzchen sat a woman. Perfume rose from her body. "Between your legs," said the woman, "lives a little dwarf and he does what he likes." This amazed Kätzchen and he asked, "What does he do?" The woman said, "At night, he wakes up, stands up straight, and goes off to look for another house." "And does he find it?" asked Kätzchen. The woman smoothed her fingers between her legs, rubbed her shoulder against Kätzchen's shoulder and said, in a voice whose melody unfurled like a roll of silk, "Come to me my prince. Come to me my dove. What you lack you can always get from me." Kätzchen looked into the woman's face and saw that her lips were red, and her hair was gold and she had gold rings on her fingers, and thought to himself that the dwarf could hear this melody and was pricking up his ears, longing for her, and going out to look for her. "When you grow up your dwarf will come to me as well," said the woman, and Kätzchen was filled with joy. Then the policeman walked in and said, "Come on," and Kätzchen followed him.

In a room with green walls, policemen were sitting and eating. Through a hatch in the wall Kätzchen saw a huge pot and a fat cook with a white hat on his head. When the cook saw Kätzchen he looked up at the ceiling and barked like a dog. Then he stuck his head into the hatch and asked, "Do you want a cat as well?" "*Ja*," said Kätzchen, and the cook meowed like a cat. Kätzchen meowed and remembered

the song Aunt Oppenheim used to sing him until he fell asleep –
"Ein Hund Kahm In Die Küche:"

> *A dog came to the kitchen*
> *And stole the cook's fresh stew.*
> *The cook picked up the carving knife*
> *And cut the dog in two.*
> *All the other dogs came round*
> *And wondered what to do.*
> *They wrote these words above the grave*
> *For everyone to view:*
> *A dog came to the kitchen*
> *And stole the cook's fresh stew.*
> *The cook picked up the carving knife*
> *And cut the dog in two.*
> *All the other dogs came round*
> *And wondered what to do.*
> *They wrote these words above the grave*
> *For everyone to view:*
> *A dog came to the kitchen*
> *And stole the cook's fresh stew.*

"This story has no end," thought Kätzchen, and decided to go back to the beginning. But when he went back to the beginning it seemed to him that even the first dog who came to the kitchen was not a real dog, but was only the story of the dog which the other dogs had written on the gravestone. "This story doesn't have a beginning either," thought Kätzchen, and was filled with wonder.

"Eat!" said the policeman. Kätzchen dipped his spoon into the bowl and took a sip of the soup. When the taste of the soup entered his mouth, doubt left his mind. "The soup I am eating is the soup I took from the cook," thought Kätzchen, and understood that the story begins with the taste of the stew.

That night Kätzchen slept in the policeman's house. There was another man there, whose name was Naim, and the two of them rolled a dice across a wooden board divided into lots of triangles. The policeman sang "Tina, Tina, come to Palestina" and from time to time asked Kätzchen if he fancied some tea. When Naim's eyes met Kätzchen's eyes, Naim said, "So how are you doing?" and Kätzchen said, "Fine."

In the morning, the policeman hit an egg until its shell broke open, and then poured it into a frying pan. When the edges of the egg turned brown, the policeman tilted the frying pan and the egg slid into a plate. He placed the plate before Kätzchen and said, "Eat!" Then the policeman brought Kätzchen to a man at the police station and went away. Kätzchen looked at the man's face and saw that he was thinking hard. "Right," said the man, "let's play a little game. I'll say a word, and you immediately say what comes into your head. 'Old'." For a moment it seemed to Kätzchen that the man was calling him "old" and he was surprised. But when he thought about it he understood that the word had only been said so that he could hear it and immediately say what came into his head. Kätzchen remembered Uncle Arthur's cane and said, "Bird." The man wrote down what Kätzchen had said and said, "Family." Kätzchen said "Cow" and the man said "Milk." Kätzchen said "Arab" and the man said "War." Kätzchen said "Kibbutz" and the man said "Mother." Kätzchen said "Zypern" and the man said "Sea." Kätzchen said "Avigail" and the man said "Bible." Kätzchen said "Pipe" and the man said "Father." Kätzchen said "Herr Druck" and the man said "Who's that?" Kätzchen turned over the question in his mind and finally said, "*Schakal.*" "The man looked at his notes for a long time. Then he raised his head and said, "So, you think people are like animals?" "Not all of them," said Kätzchen and the man frowned. "Now draw something," he said. Kätzchen picked up a pencil and drew a dragon. "Right," said the man, "and who is the man you drew?" "That's a strange question," thought Kätzchen. Had the man asked, "What did you draw?" he would have answered, "A dragon." And had he asked, "Is this a man?" he would have answered, "It's a dragon." But since he wanted the man to be satisfied, Kätzchen drew Herr Druck with a hat on his head next to the dragon. The man looked at Herr Druck and asked, "So who is that?" Kätzchen said, "Herr Druck." "Herr Druck... Who is he?" asked the man, and Kätzchen said, "*Schakal.*" The man frowned for the second time and said, "Now tell me what you dream about." Kätzchen remembered and said, "Mad Sarah." The man's face lit up and he wrote something down. Then he said, "And who is this Sarah?" and Kätzchen said he didn't know. The man frowned for the third time. "So," he said, "now go outside and play." But Kätzchen remembered that the hall outside was empty and he did not know who he could play with. "Another game," said Kätzchen. The man eased himself back in his chair and said, "Good. We'll play with words again." "Now," said Kätzchen, "I am first. Photosynthesis." The man looked at Kätzchen and his eyes widened. His lips moved but no words came out. "He only knows how to play," thought Kätzchen to himself, "when he goes first."

The policeman came back. He placed his hand on Kätzchen's shoulder and said, "Your uncle is no longer with us." "If Uncle Arthur is no longer with us," thought Kätzchen to himself, "he must be with someone else." "And your aunt," continued the policeman, "has returned to Vienna." "Now," thought Kätzchen, "Aunt Oppenheim will meet her lover and he will offer her flowers." Then the policeman turned to the man and said, "His father is alive but he..." and the policeman leaned over the man and whispered something into his ear. The man said, "The boy is also..." and whispered something into the policeman's ear. Kätzchen looked at the policeman and said, "I'll be with Ernst." The man said, "No. He has to go to..." and whispered something into the policeman's ear. The policeman looked at the man, then looked at Kätzchen and said, "We'll see." Outside, the policeman raised his eyes to the sky and sighed. Then he bent his knees until his head was at the same level as Kätzchen's and said, "Your father is ill. Do you know?" and Kätzchen said, "*Ja.*" The policeman sighed again and said, "That man doesn't want you to go to your father." Kätzchen told the policeman that the man makes up games but doesn't know how to play them. The policeman laughed and said, "You know what, I'll take you to your father."

On the way, Kätzchen told the policeman a woman in the police station told him that the dwarf between his legs would come to her one day. The policeman laughed and said, "That was Shifra. Your dwarf would do better to go to Avigail." Kätzchen was filled with affection for the policeman and thought to himself, "I hope Tina comes to Palestina." Then the policeman led Kätzchen to a man selling ice cream and the man handed Kätzchen a green ice cream studded with nuts. And when Kätzchen passed his tongue over the ice cream he remembered the ice cream Uncle Arthur had bought him once, and understood that Uncle Arthur was dead.

"Ah," said a man dressed in a white coat, "Ernst is the man you're looking for. He's quiet. You can see him." When the man left to look for Ernst, a woman sidled up to the policeman and said, "The clothes on your body are very nice." The policeman laughed and said, "The clothes on your body are very nice too." The woman said, "You're thinking about something else." The policeman asked, "What am I thinking about?" The woman said, "What I'm thinking about." The policeman looked at Kätzchen's face and said, "You see? There's no difference between the people here and the people outside." Suddenly Kätzchen felt afraid that the Ernst who was here would not be his father. Meanwhile, the man in the white coat had returned with another man and said, "This is Ernst." Ernst pointed at the policeman and said in German, "He is not my son." "No," said the man in the white coat and pointed at Kätzchen. "This is your son. The policeman just came with him." Ernst snatched a quick glance at Kätzchen's face and immediately turned back to the policeman. "Now," he said, "I have to talk with my son about my will." The man in white hesitated for a moment and then said, "All right. Go with him to your room." Ernst turned his back and walked away, and Kätzchen walked behind him.

In the room, Ernst stood by the window and looked outside and Kätzchen knew from his back that he was his father. "*Verstehst du mich?*"[87] said Ernst, and Kätzchen, who did not know what he had to understand, said "*Ja.*" Ernst spoke with his back to Kätzchen. "You must choose. Small and important or big and worthless?" At that moment Kätzchen knew with absolute clarity that if he made the wrong choice he would lose his father again. The sound of a bell rose from the street and a man shouted, "*Kerosene! Kerosene!*" "Big and worthless," said Kätzchen.

"*Gutt!*" said Ernst and opened the window. "Outside!" First he held Kätzchen by the waist and lowered him through the window until Kätzchen's feet touched the ground. Then he too climbed out through the window. When they stood outside, Ernst said, "One and one are one," and the two of them left.

When they reached the fields on the outskirts of the town Ernst looked over Kätzchen's head and said in German, "Now we will rise to the heavens in a chariot of fire." Then he placed himself in the middle of the road and spread out his arms. A lorry the size of a mountain screeched to a halt and almost touched Ernst's body. Out of the window glared a head with a black beard and shouted, "Are you mad?" Ernst lifted his eyes to the man and said, "Elijah." The man opened his mouth and his eyes widened. "You know who I am?" he asked, and Ernst said, "Yes." Ernst climbed up and seated himself next to the man with the beard and Kätzchen climbed up after him. The man closed the door and they drove off. The noise was deafening. "Who are you?" shouted the man, but Ernst closed his eyes and said nothing. The man looked at Kätzchen and shouted, "Where does he know me from?" and Kätzchen, who did not know what to say, said, "Maybe from Jerusalem." "From Jerusalem?" shouted the man, and Kätzchen shouted, "Yes." The man fell silent, immersed in thought. Then he looked at Kätzchen again and shouted, "The British Army?" and Kätzchen, who did not know what the question meant, shouted, "Yes..." "Ah," shouted the man, "I know." When the fields came to an end they went through hills, and when they came out of the hills another town stretched before them. The lorry stopped in the middle

---

87. "Do you understand me?"

of the town and the man with the beard slapped Ernst across the shoulder and said, "Wake up mate. Here we are." Ernst also said, "Here we are." Then he opened his eyes and climbed down to the pavement without looking at the man. "What's the matter with him?" said the man to Kätzchen, and Kätzchen said, "He's thinking." "Oh well," said the man, and gave Kätzchen his hand. "If you ever need anything you can always rely on Elijah Zisskind. Those were good times in the British Army." Ernst had already disappeared around the corner of the street and Kätzchen ran after him, shouting, "*Vater, Vater.*" Ernst did not stop, but slowed his pace. After they had walked together some way through the streets of the town, Kätzchen asked, "*Vater, wohin gehst du?*"[88] Ernst stopped. He looked at Kätzchen and said, "Never ask a question like that again." "*Warum?*" asked Kätzchen. "Because time," said Ernst, "is not a line, and place is not a space." And although Kätzchen did not know what his father was saying, he understood that from now on both of them would look only through the eye in their foreheads.

Meanwhile the day had grown dark. Kätzchen saw Ernst's shadow on the pavement and said, "*Schatten.*"[89] Ernst stretched out his hands in front of him, distorting his fingers into talons, and said, "*Ratten.*"[90] Kätzchen looked at Ernst's hands and said, "Jesus Christus." Ernst laughed and said, "*Ich.*"[91] Kätzchen laughed too and said, "*Auch ich.*"[92] Smells of cooking wafted out of the houses. Suddenly Kätzchen longed to know whether his father remembered he had once sat in the armchair with slippers on his feet and Kätzchen had scattered the silverware around him. "*Ja,*" said Ernst, and Kätzchen was not at all surprised that his father had answered the question before he heard it. But then Ernst saw something that frightened him, and said, "*Nein,*" and Kätzchen understood that his

---

88. "Father, where are you going?"
89. "Shadow."
90. "Rats."
91. "Me." Also in Hebrew – "A man."
92. "Me too."

father remembered the sights but hadn't the strength to look at them.

Since Kätzchen was thinking of memories, he remembered Frau Kurtz's photograph album. It was because of Joachim that the paths of Frau Kurtz and Aunt Oppenheim crossed for a time in Vienna. And when they both found their way to Palestine they made it a rule to see each other, one week at Aunt Oppenheim's house and the following week at Frau Kurtz's house.

When Frau Kurtz saw Kätzchen with Aunt Oppenheim, she always said, "Look, look, we have a special guest today," and Kätzchen knew that Frau Kurtz would then say, "And it just so happens that I have sweet biscuits." Frau Kurtz would take down a tin box, on which brown cows grazed in a field of flowers, and extract from it two sugar-coated biscuits. Frau Kurtz put the biscuits onto a plate and the plate in front of Kätzchen. Kätzchen was convinced that the two biscuits were for the two times that Frau Kurtz had said, "Look," and hoped that one day Frau Kurtz would break her habit and say, "Look, look, look," and place three biscuits before him. Aunt Oppenheim and Frau Kurtz sipped coffee with cream from china cups and Kätzchen drank cocoa. Then Frau Kurtz picked up the photograph album and opened it to where Joachim lay. First, they looked at the photograph of Joachim as he was when he still had both his legs. Then they looked at Joachim as he was when he had only one of his own legs, and the other, which was made of wood, was stuck to his body, and said, "*Der arme Kerl.*"[93] And when Kätzchen asked if they had chopped down a tree to make Joachim's wooden leg, Frau Kurtz said that was not the point. The point was that Joachim had given his leg to Germany, and Germany gave him beautiful decorations to pin to his chest. A picture formed in Kätzchen's mind. Joachim enters a shop and looks at the decorations displayed there. He points his finger and says, "That one and that one." The German takes down the decorations which Joachim pointed out and places them in front of him. Joachim lifts his leg and places it on the counter next to the decorations. The German picks

---

93. "The poor fellow."

up a saw and cuts off Joachim's leg. Joachim pins the decorations to his chest and hops out of the shop on one leg.

In Frau Kurtz's photograph album there were other people as well. Some stood alone and some in groups, and at the end of the album, where it was written "Palestina," the people had taken off their elegant clothes and stood in short trousers. Behind their backs were mountains strewn with boulders and between the boulders grew thorn bushes. Frau Kurtz placed a finger over the face of one man and said, "*Der ist schon tot.*"[94] But when she removed her finger and his face reappeared, the dead man smiled, and did not leave his place.

"Before my eyes," said Ernst suddenly, "there is glass and a bird pecking at it all the time." Kätzchen looked at his father's face and saw that his eyes did not see what was in front of him. "Before my eyes," said Ernst again, "there is glass and a bird pecking at it all the time." A picture took shape in Kätzchen's mind. The bird approaches the glass, its eyes getting bigger and bigger. Then he heard the sound of the beak pecking at the glass. The sight and the sound emerged in German and Kätzchen was filled with wonder that even a picture needed a language to draw itself. If Ernst had spoken Hebrew, thought Kätzchen, he would have looked through the glass without seeing it and the bird would have flown elsewhere. "*Vater,*" said Kätzchen, "*Warum sprichst du nicht Ivrit?*"[95] "Hebrew?" said Ernst, and the very word sounded like German in his mouth. "*Ja,*" said Kätzchen, "Hebrew." Ernst was silent for a long while, and then he said in a strange incantation, "*Be-reyshis boro elohim es ha-shamayim ve-es ho-oretz.*"[96] Suddenly, Kätzchen was filled with fear that his father would leave him and said, "Before my eyes, too, there is glass and a bird pecking at it." "The same glass," said Ernst, and Kätzchen understood that his father was not mad. "And the bird?" asked Kätzchen. "And the bird," said Ernst. A distant memory came back to Kätzchen's mind. Margarethe is asleep in her bed, her face to the wall.

---

94. "That one's dead already."
95. "Father, why don't you speak Hebrew?"
96. Hebrew: "In the beginning God created the heavens and the earth."

His father lifts him out of the cradle and brings him ever so slowly towards his face. And through the lenses of Ernst's glasses Kätzchen sees the eyes of his father coming closer and closer.

Ernst went through the door of an inn and Kätzchen followed him in. Once they were inside, Kätzchen saw that the innkeeper's head was big, and his body carried his head as though it had done it a favor by transporting it a short distance, and now that it had been delivered as promised, the head refused to get off and wobbled on the thin neck. *"Ein Bett,"*[97] said Ernst, and Kätzchen knew his father could see what he saw, and was not asking for a bed for himself but for the innkeeper to rest his head. *"Far zwei?"*[98] asked the innkeeper. Ernst looked at the innkeeper's head and said, *"Farzweifelt."*[99] The innkeeper took a bunch of keys and opened the door for them. In the room stood a large wooden bed, with legs carved into the shape of lions' feet. Ernst looked at the legs of the bed and said, *"Ein Lowe."*[100] The innkeeper's head nodded violently. *"Sehr angenehm. Friedman,"*[101] he said, and walked off. Ernst knelt down and touched the lion's feet. *"Schau,"* he said, *"ein Lowe."*[102] *"Vater,"* said Kätzchen, *"hast du Geld bei dir?"*[103] But Ernst only smiled to himself and said again, *"Ein Lowenbett."*[104] Suddenly, his father took on the shape of a lion in Kätzchen's mind. "Soon," thought Kätzchen, "the lion will get onto his couch and fall into a lion's sleep." And instead of being filled with wonder that his father had turned into a lion, Kätzchen turned himself into a lion cub. For a long while the lions paced around the room. Manes covered their necks and the movement of their feet was slow and serene. From time to time the big lion growled and the little lion answered with a

---

97. "A bed."
98. "For two?"
99. "Full of sorrow."
100. "A lion."
101. "Pleased to meet you. (My name is) Friedman."
102. "Look, a lion."
103. "Have you any money on you?"
104. "A lionbed."

growl. Afterwards, the two lions climbed into bed and stared at the ceiling of the room with yellow eyes divided by a black streak.

In the morning, Ernst looked into the mirror and said, "*Gott, wie hasslich dieser Kopf ist.*"[105] Ernst looked at his face as though he had never seen it before in his life and was relieved that the face looking back at him was not his. Once, Kätzchen looked at Uncle Arthur looking at his face in the mirror, and saw a sadness in Uncle Arthur's eyes that the face trailed around with him all his life. But Frau Kurtz looked in the mirror as though it never crossed her mind that the face looking back at her was not her own. On the piano in her house stood the head of Beethoven, and Frau Kurtz looked at this face too without amazement, as though it was the only face he had. Once Frau Kurtz had taken Kätzchen with her to the market and by the way she was walking Kätzchen saw that she was sure what happened to her was bound to happen, and that what didn't happen was bound not to happen. This aroused a kind of anger in Kätzchen and he distorted his face like a madman. The people who happened to pass them looked at Kätzchen in surprise, and Frau Kurtz, who noticed the looks on their faces, looked down at Kätzchen. But Kätzchen quickly put on a different face, as though he too was sure everything was as it should be, and Frau Kurtz, who could not understand what had suddenly gone wrong, was overcome with embarrassment. In the market, Frau Kurtz bought a chicken. When she returned home she chopped off the chicken's head. Then she poured out its entrails and cut off its wings. And when the chicken was left without a head, and without entrails, and without wings, Frau Kurtz cut off its legs. Kätzchen wasn't at all sorry about what happened to the chicken, but Frau Kurtz's eye took on a look of satisfaction, as though she was sure the deeds she was doing were her own deeds, and it was only proper they be done just as she was doing them. At the table, Kätzchen tasted the dish and praised Frau Kurtz on the taste of "the dead bird," but Frau Kurtz was not dismayed and merely commented that in German, one says "*Huhn.*"[106]

---

105. "God, how ugly this face is."
106. Chicken.

The innkeeper's head was in the kitchen. "A fried egg?" he asked, and Ernst extended his arm, pointed at his head, and said in German: "This head is holy." Kätzchen said, "Yes," and the innkeeper put two fried eggs in front of them. Ernst looked down at the fried egg and said, "What does this eye see?" and Kätzchen said, "*Iss, Vater.*"[107] Ernst put the fried egg into his mouth and swallowed it in one go. Then he turned to an invisible audience and said, "Never laugh at a big head." It seemed then to Kätzchen that his father was a kind of prophet who knows what was, and knows what will be, but Kätzchen did not know if his father knew what is. "Herr Lowe," said the innkeeper in a strange sort of German, "will you be staying tonight as well?" "Herr Friedman," said Ernst, "when a man comes into the world, he stays until he leaves." Kätzchen heard this and was filled with joy that his father remembered the innkeeper's name, but Ernst, as though he saw what Kätzchen had thought, said, "God did not make a man without a name. He made Friedman." "May God bless you and everything you do," said the innkeeper. Ernst thrust his hand into his trouser pocket, pulled out a leather wallet, and placed it before Kätzchen. Kätzchen drew two notes from the wallet and placed them in the innkeeper's hand. The innkeeper put the two notes into his pocket and said, "When my wife, may she rest in peace, was still alive, everything was better." "Him too," said Ernst, and pointed to Kätzchen. "His wife is dead." The innkeeper's eyes widened and he looked at Kätzchen. Then he moved his eyes back to Ernst and saw what he saw.

When they walked out of the inn, rain was falling on the town. Kätzchen looked at the rain and said, "It's raining." Ernst, too, looked at the rain and asked, "What's raining?" At first it seemed to Kätzchen there was no sense to this question but when he turned it over in his mind he understood that it had only come out of what he himself had said. When Kätzchen was small it had rained, and Uncle Arthur had taken off his coat and wrapped Kätzchen in it so that the rain would not wet him, and the coat was filled with the smell of Uncle Arthur. "*Vater,*" said Kätzchen, "*Onkel Arthur ist gestorben.*"[108] Ernst turned

---

107. "Eat, father!"
108. "Uncle Arthur is dead."

his head towards Kätzchen and looked at his mouth. "If Ernst understood that his brother is dead," Kätzchen thought to himself, "he would look into my eyes." Then Ernst looked away and walked on, and from the sight of his back Kätzchen understood that he was pacing out "*Arthur ist gestorben*," an *Arthur* pace, an *ist* pace, and a *gestorben* pace, and again *Arthur* and *ist* and *gestorben* and again and again. Water dripped from Ernst's ears. Suddenly, Kätzchen longed to tell his father that Uncle Arthur always said, "*mein Kind*," but since he knew Ernst was thinking that Arthur died because his father was born, he said nothing. Kätzchen had once seen a picture of his grandfather. The photograph was yellow and out of the brown suit peeped a round watch. "Your grandfather," said Uncle Arthur, "the father of Ernst and myself, rode a horse in the army of Franz Josef." A beard sprouted from both sides of his chin, and under his nose was a thick mustache whose ends twirled upwards. But by then, the grandfather who looked out of the photograph was already *gestorben*, and when Kätzchen asked, Uncle Arthur told him that the horse his grandfather rode was also *gestorben*. The grandfather's eyes looked through Kätzchen to some other place, and Kätzchen, who saw what he saw, decided that when he was big, he would find a picture of the horse and place it in front of the picture of his grandfather.

Suddenly, Ernst said, "*Margarethe liebte den Arthur*,"[109] and Kätzchen remembered that Uncle Arthur told him Margarethe had chosen Ernst because he was the more stubborn, but Ernst, who was afraid to lose her, had lost his mind. Then Ernst turned his head towards Kätzchen and looked at him as though he had never seen him. "*Und wo ist Margarethe?*"[110] he asked, and Kätzchen said, "*Im Himmel*."[111]

When Margarethe was already dead, snow covered the town and Uncle Arthur took Kätzchen out to see the snow, and when Kätzchen stepped in the snow he remembered the sweetness of porridge he had

---

109. "Margarethe loved Arthur."
110. "And where is Margarethe?"
111. "In heaven."

eaten when he was a baby. On that day it seemed to Kätzchen that if the whole world turned white Margarethe would come back to him. But some of the branches on the trees remained gray, and by evening the snow was already mixed with mud. *"Und wo bin ich?"*[112] asked Ernst, and Kätzchen, who did not know how to answer his father, was silent. A woman dressed in black walked out of a gate in the wall. Kätzchen understood that Margarethe was already a long way from Ernst, and that his father saw what he saw and his heart was broken. And since he wished to make Ernst forget his sorrow, he told him that one day the dwarf between his legs would come to a woman he had met at the police station.

Meanwhile, Kätzchen and his father had entered the alleyways of the market. "Now," thought Kätzchen, "I will raise my hand and everything will freeze." Kätzchen raised his hand but nothing changed. A vendor weighed tomatoes and a woman felt pears. Kätzchen remembered Aunt Oppenheim's foot that was white, with the little toe bent upwards, and covered with a thick crust. *"Vater,"* he said, *"Der Fuss von Tante Oppenheim."*[113] *"Ja,"* said Ernst, *"eine traurige Geschichte."*[114] From his father's words Kätzchen understood that raising his hand had been an act of foolishness, and he raised his hand again to make everything stay as it was. Kätzchen's hand made the woman put tomatoes in a basket and the vendor stretch out his arm to pick up an apple. *"Und alles ist eine Geige,"*[115] said Ernst suddenly. *"Alles ist eine Geige,"*[116] repeated Kätzchen after Ernst. *"Und alles ist eine Geige,"* said Ernst for the second time. "What my father says," thought Kätzchen, "is not exactly the same as I said." And in order to remove the doubt, Kätzchen again said, *"Alles ist eine Geige."* *"Und alles ist eine Geige,"* said Ernst for the third time. Kätzchen looked around and saw that *"Alles ist eine Geige"* was sheer nonsense, while

---

112. "And where am I?"
113. "Aunt Oppenheim's foot."
114. "A sad affair."
115. "And everything is a violin."
116. "Everything is a violin."

"Und alles ist eine Geige" was the naked truth. "My father hears smells," thought Kätzchen to himself, and he too said, *"Und alles ist eine Geige."*

Kätzchen and his father had by now left the town and were walking through the fields. Where the fields ended stood a mountain, its peak wrapped in clouds like a white bandage. Suddenly, Kätzchen understood that what was had already been, and what was to be would not be. *"Vater,"* said Kätzchen, *"ein Berg."*[117] Ernst lifted his eyes to the mountain and said softly, *"Ja."* Kätzchen saw there were brown spots on the back of Ernst's hand and touched them. Ernst took Kätzchen's hand and brought it to his stomach. At that moment Kätzchen knew that the difference between himself and his father was getting smaller and smaller, and that all that would remain of it would be the size of their bodies. Birds passed over their heads. Ernst looked at the birds until they disappeared behind the mountain. Then he looked at Kätzchen. And when Kätzchen looked into Ernst's eyes his soul turned over. "My father's eyes can see!" thought Kätzchen. He knew that a great disaster was at hand but his heart quivered with happiness. *"Weist du wer ich bin?"*[118] Kätzchen asked his father. *"Ja,"* said Ernst, "Kätzchen."

---

117. "A mountain."
118. "Do you know who I am?"

Amalia Kahana-Carmon

I'm Not Paralyzed, You're Not Mute

Translated by Jeffrey M. Green

After I was gripped by the paralysis which the doctors despaired of curing, I was sent here.

The idea was Alex's. Because Alex said that anyway I'm of no use anymore and perhaps the country air would put me back on my feet. Not in those words, but that was the general idea. As for me, I remained indifferent, it was all the same to me.

Now, transferred by the farmer Basset from my wheelchair to the chaise longue near the window, in the room that is going to be my room, and the farm-hand is bringing in my trunk, I looked around with eyes still unfocused.

Young Basset's hair had gone grey, and he was no longer young. Years ago, his hair like fire, he chased after his horse, shouting "Where's that cursed devil running to," and his mother shouting to him "And where did Dicky run."

The farm-hand, carrying the heavy trunk as if effortlessly, moving it into the corner, now as then is wearing a shabby RAF tunic, and the bottoms of his trousers, which lack belt-loops and are held by a black leather belt, are crammed into his Wellington boots. With an unlit cigarette butt in his mouth and a hungry look in his eyes, of an animal, he used to cross the yard carrying buckets of milk. However, when I passed by the place a few years ago, he was the one I saw again. Leaning on the gate, gazing. Lantern-jawed, his eyes bloodshot, his neck wrapped. No longer a look of hunger in his eyes. Nothing. No, he didn't remember me, he answered, he didn't recognize me, he said taking out a cigarette he had rolled himself, lighting it carefully.

This time I didn't bother. Of all the places in the world, to return to this one was Alex's idea. And so, to reintroduce myself, to try to remind them of things, I wasn't going to take the trouble. From my seat on the blue velvet chaise longue with thin red lines, and its single, high, side-rest, I looked outside unseeing, through the large window at my side. And through the small round recessed window, approximately above the dining-table, with branches pressing against it from outside. A candlestick, with remnants of orange wax, thick and dusty, was put there as an ornament, standing on a terra-cotta saucer. My gaze travelled over the whitewashed wall-stones, protruding like rough swellings. And over the windowsills, that are like old boards in public baths, uneven in width, which have dried out. And the dark supporting beam cutting through the ceiling overhead. Nice. So be it.

The farmhouse which had been extended was a guesthouse now. Closed down for the off-season. But a small separate wing has been opened up for me, as much as possible, and it was a room that in my time had been the spacious kitchen and the pantry.

The farmer Basset, in long strides, lighting the lamp on the dresser and drawing the curtains that resembled yellow bed sheets, for it was late afternoon, grey and soggy, pointed at the farm-hand:

"Garrick. He'll help me. We're here to provide you with the basic needs of life."

"Only you two are here?"

Neither answered. For a moment, like a shock, a distant shock from the bowels of the earth, suddenly I could see: they were alike. But in what way. Like doubles?

"I hope I won't be too much trouble," I mumbled, therefore, in Garrick's direction, as though introducing myself in my turn, forcing a faint polite smile.

Garrick merely stood and looked. And did not answer. Then turned and left.

"Garrick doesn't speak," Basset explained to me.

"Since when?" I asked, as if startled again. Over there, in the far away distances.

"And now we'll make you a fire," replied Basset, poking in the grate. On straightening up, turning to crumple large pieces of newspaper and throwing them into the grate, as if offhand, but by instinct throwing low, from the side, like bowling – did he really smile a little; well, he definitely didn't smile when he turned round to me, and said: "You'll find out. None of us speaks much."

"Why?" I asked, looking at the large window. It was all the same to me.

I'm in exile, I reflected. So what, it's a long time that I'm in exile.

But I recalled his father. The straight old man, with leather patches on the elbows of his sleeves. Was he really old, or was I that young. How he once brought a bunch of sweet peas to Mrs. Mortram on her deathbed, how he sat rubbing his eyebrows. And how, rising, trying to show sympathy, he said, "I'll send a man to trim your hedge: it's about time," and hurried out.

Basset was kneeling now in front of the broad hearth. The hook for hanging the big pot was still embedded in it. Scraps of newspaper, shreds of plywood – he arranged them with his hands, finished and straightened up. And with a sure movement which suddenly brought him to mind more than anything, he put out his foot, placing it on the white stone step before the iron rail, and waved the leather scuttle, tall and narrow like a rigid, tapered tube, back and forth, throwing down, as though from a funnel, a quantity of rolling coals. But now it's as though he had become a forest wildlife, I mused. They are like forest wildlife! – for a moment, was it for the third time? As though I were caught by the silence and seriousness of falling night.

"Once I knew how to light a fire in a fireplace," I said and turned my head away from him. It was all the same to me.

Basset, who had stooped down in the meantime to light the papers on every side, quickly putting out the match, didn't answer. He only stood again, inspecting the fire, as he wiped his hands against each other.

"What about tea?" he suddenly asked. "I'll bring what's needed."

"I ate in the train."

"Excellent," he said and left. I remained by myself. I crossed my arms, and only looked around me, my mind going blank. I didn't know how long I was sitting that way. I forgot I was there.

A knock at the door. Garrick. Silently he took out the dresses, the coats, the underwear, the handkerchiefs. Removing things and hanging them up, removing things and laying them in drawers.

"The tartan traveling-rug, please," I asked.

He cast a glance at it, lying on the bed now. He took it. Leaving it folded in two, he spread it on my knees, and like a nurse tucked it snug under me and went away.

Finally on my own.

Great tears started rolling down my face. It was fatigue, fatigue from the trip, showing signs of itself at last, I said to myself, trying in vain to wipe them. Closing, pressing my eyelids in vain. Despairing, I just sat and looked through them at the rough walls. At the lines in the knots of the wood. Floating over the surfaces of the unfashionable furniture. And that's how I fell asleep, leaning against the only, rather splendid armrest.

A knock at the door was heard. Basset stood in the doorway. In his coat, with its collar raised. A powerful torch in his hand. A brimmed hat, shabby but still a bit rakish, on his head. I didn't even raise my head, which was leaning on the armrest. I just looked at him. And at the night, of air and chill, beyond him. With a weak glow, distant, like that of a city's light thrown up to the heaven, on sections of the horizon.

He closed the door behind him.

"I'm bringing dinner," he said.

"What time is it?"

"Late. We didn't want to wake you."

He lit all the lights. Passing with his long, fleet strides. The big room is small for him.

I sighed and arranged myself, therefore, comfortably in my seat. He laid the dishes on the table professionally, observing all the formalities. Throwing the ironed napkin down in the end. He transferred me to the wheelchair.

"My watch stopped. And the electric clock, over there in the drawer, isn't connected yet," I apologized.

He opened the drawer, took out the clock.

"While you're at it. The other electric appliances. Perhaps you could have a look at them. Maybe they aren't suitable. For the local current. They're foreign."

The clock, the transistor adapter, the calculator adapter, the hair dryer, the ladies' electric shaver. In the same drawer as the stockings, the tights, and the underwear. He took them and spread them out on the bed. They looked very odd here. Bringing them close to his eyes and then far away, he tried to read the numbers stamped on them.

"One moment. I too have problems with my eyes. I carry a magnifying glass with me. Where's my handbag?"

He took no notice. Taking my pen from the roll-top secretaire, tiny as a toy, and he began, still standing, to copy the numbers onto the back of his hand.

"One moment," I quickly wiped my mouth on the napkin. "Tear off a sheet of paper. From the pad of writing paper."

"Papers get lost, don't they?" he answered over there, as he kept on copying, straining his eyes. The edge at the opening of his diamond patterned pullover was frayed here and there. His forehead ridged with furrows.

"Since school, before exams, I haven't seen, I forgot it was possible, to write down things on your hand, on your knee," I mumbled with my mouth full, while he, apparently, went out. Alone again.

I finished my meal. I pushed the crockery and things away from me. I remained seated. With a hand supporting my head. Once, outside, I half-heard Basset's scorched voice. Most likely busy at some job, talking, in his way, not from the man's depths. Answering out loud. To a woman's voice, probably coming from across the wall of the private lane. Like noises of the night. "Yes. That's the problem. In the winter. But," he said, "we are actually thinking of buying the

Bird In Hand. Now, that he's about to retire. Maybe that's the solution for winter. Some kind of a solution," and I understood they were talking about me, about my arrival. A small village.

Afterwards the woman's voice answered, not from her depths, with a parting ring: "And what he will do now that he's retiring is still a mystery to us all, isn't it."

Basset didn't answer. A small village. But with houses very isolated. I remained seated. My arm, with my elbow on the table, supported my head. It was all the same to me.

Garrick came. He made the bed. He tidied up. It was like being in hospital, I accepted it. But one must admit, an out-of-the-ordinary kind of hospital, I said to myself. Garrick cleared the crockery and cutlery from the table, as though he were disposing of litter. He went away. While for a moment, they were opened again there, recalling themselves, the freshness of the night, the air and chill outside. And the door closed on them once more.

I rolled myself over, to the door, to the lamp standing beside the chaise longue, to the lamp on the dresser, putting out the lights. Only the light of the blue reading lamp on the night table remained. Then I rolled the wheelchair over to the bed, pulled the night-gown from under the pillow. But I gave up. I changed my mind. I threw it aside. Just stayed sitting in the chair. Oh, my God, I think I'm lost here, I said to myself.

A knock at the door.

"Who's there?"

Basset, with his torch. As was his way, he stood for a moment in the doorway, in the black. And he entered, the shoulders of his coat and its lapels sprinkled with droplets. He wiped his feet vigorously.

"Where are they?" he asked briskly, putting down the torch, the coat, on the coarse box-chair by the door.

"Who?"

"Your things," and clicking loudly with his tongue, with three fingers, the middle one raised, he made as if to stick a plug into a socket.

"My electrical appliances? Garrick put them back. In the drawer."

Basset strode over and lit the lamp standing on the dresser. He laid down there, within the circle of the light, on the white crochet strip, a screwdriver and pliers. He bent over and took the appliances out of the drawer. Leaning his shoulder against the wall, his legs crossed, he began to change the plugs, talking as though to them: "I found out. I managed to get them for you," he raised his glance, looking at me without expression, and he lowered it again. "By adding these," he took them out of his pocket and lay them on the dresser, "the plugs, the numbers, now they'll fit."

"Why are you standing?" I murmured absentmindedly. I think I'm lost here, I think I'm lost here, I repeated to myself.

"Me? I always stand. Here," he went and tried them one by one in the lamp socket by the chaise longue, "You see?"

Then he came, next to the night-table near me, setting aside, without fuss, the small table; and going down on all fours and crawling to reach the socket behind the bed, he unplugged the reading lamp, to add the double socket there. He put it in, plugged it in. Rising to his knees in front of me, he set the clock by his watch. And he got up: "See?" He held it out to me like a barber holding a mirror.

"I think I'm lost here," I spoke out loud, "I think I'm lost here. If you don't mind me saying it, please. I think I'm lost here."

Standing, he let drop the hand that was grasping the clock, continuing to grasp it, and he observed me.

"The basic needs of life, the man said," I wrung my hands, "I suppose you meant a roof overhead. Food. Clothing."

"Right," he agreed, examining me.

"But what I'll be missing here is what comes after them on the list," I placed the lower part of my face in my two hands.

Basset stood the clock on the night-table, with his head turned towards me above the lamp. For the first time I could see his eyes fully; very light beneath the eyebrows that were still somewhat golden. Looking at me, penetrating. I was alarmed.

"No. No. I don't know what comes after them on your list. On my list, it's people. Company. I shall die here!"

Since when is company on my list, I wondered to myself.

"That's not accurate," I lowered my head, "the truth is this. I, I already died. A long time ago. But why be buried in this tomb as well?"

"You should calm down, I think," he said. And I saw, he too, in his way, was lost. Perhaps at a loss. He moved away, took up and put the screwdriver and pliers in his pockets. He put out the light on the dresser.

"Wait, wait a moment, Gerald. No, don't go. Sit down please," I pointed to the armchair.

He didn't respond. Recoiling, he immediately stood in military at ease:

"My name? That's my name. How did you know?"

"I've been here before," I whispered, looking straight forward, my eyebrows raised in surprise. "Once. Many years ago. I stayed here, lived here. You had horses then," I said, as though stepping, for a moment entering a dream again. "And cows. With calves. I used to buy from you. Baskets of eggs. That were waiting for me. Right here, on the back steps," I pointed to the bath cubicle. "And here, in the corner, among the brooms and brushes, your rifle used to hang," I said, as though discovering it for myself too, with growing surprise, with my head moving from side to side. "Yes. I lived here." And with a choked voice, I turned my head to my shoulder as far as I could. "Once. Years ago. Many. When I was still among the living, that is."

I in the wheelchair, he came, sat on the edge of the bed, turned me around in the chair to face him: "You're a strange girl," he took my hand, pulled it to him, held it on his knee.

I moved a finger, as though trying to erase them, over the numbers in pen, scrawled on the back of the hand that was covering mine. "Now it looks," I bit my lip, "like a tattoo on your hand." I took it, brought it close, pressed it against my cheek: "I don't think I'm that strange," I cried, "just lost. Simply lost."

"You won't be lost. You'll see. And now we'll put you to bed," he pulled, brought the night-gown near, helped me undress, dress, transferred me to my bed. "My weight is fifty-five kilos," I said, my lips approximately above his hair. "Oho," he teased me. He covered me up to my chin, and bending forward, he tucked the blanket on both my sides: "Better?"

The light of the leaping flames alternately reddened and darkened his face, his hands, his chest, as he rummaged in the fire, and with one foot forward over there waved, poured with the same motion, back and forth, a cascade of coals. He dug around again, looking at the fire:

"They said at the time that you came from London?" he said as though talking to the fire, "that you're professors? Is that it?"

"Yes. My husband. And I had a baby girl."

"Yes. You were pretty. Pretty. I remember. The vicar said you were interesting."

"The vicar? He said?"

"What difference does it make now. Now go to sleep."

"Gerald."

"Yes."

"My name is Tamar."

"Yes. All right. Now go to sleep."

"Yes. All right."

"You know what, at that time you seemed just like a child-bride to me. That's what you seemed to me. But now go to sleep."

"Yes."

"And do you remember? Once I offered you a ride?" He was about to take his coat off the chair near the door. Instead, he turned the low chair around and leaned on it, his arms before him, arching his back. "I opened the door of the car and I said: 'Come in. With this ice on the road you'll break a leg.' Was that you? Were you very shy with strangers? Did you blush a lot? 'What sign were you born under?' you asked. And I said: 'Scorpio.' Wasn't that you? Maybe another girl. Another girl-woman. It doesn't matter. Now go to sleep."

"Gerald?"

"Yes."

"Twenty-one years have gone by since then. Exactly twenty-one."

"Yes. Life is short."

"Short, the man says. Short? It doesn't seem so to me. No, to me it certainly doesn't seem so." I turned myself over in bed with my elbows, and with my face in the curve of my arm on the pillow, what's happening to me today, I, who haven't cried for many years, started crying again, with a quivering back, unable to stop, the sobs coming like sneezes.

Gerald came. He repositioned me, placing me on my back again, straightening and putting my arm by my side the right way: "It's short, I tell you. Like this." With his hand somewhat raised he swiftly snapped his third finger against his thumb, "and that's why – listen – that's why," his lips wandered over my face, covering my face, while he was taking off his jacket, turning off the lamp, pulling up the blanket and getting in with me without losing time. I made room for him. "No, don't run away," he spoke into the pillow, arranging himself. "So much a woman. And so worried, tense, you came here. It isn't good. It isn't good," he said still into the pillow. Pushing the blanket, tossing it with his feet, his trousers and the rest, to the floor, did he throw back my useless legs around his shoulders? His arms? He burrowed into me, rose, pressed and squashed; all taking place beneath my navel, all happening so fast, I didn't know exactly what was going on. While from my navel up I was alone.

He fell onto me. I made room for him again, I pulled him to me. But he refused, got up, covered me, dressed and went to his shoes and coat at the chair by the entrance.

I transferred myself therefore to a sitting position, the pillow at my back, leaning against the headboard, and from the drawer in the night-table I took my comb and mirror.

Gerald came back. He stood above me, waiting, his hand in the area of his belt, looking with soft mockery at the slope of the ceiling. Already, on his own, he decisively took the mirror, the comb, put them in the drawer that had remained open, closed it with his fist. He sat casually on the edge of the bed, only the red light of the fire partially illuminating him, setting off the big shoulder, the corroded skin of his face, his moustache, his hair. The threads, still reddish, sparkling in it. The strong cut of his chin and cheeks, that slightly buries, with the forehead, the eye. That proud head, who would believe it was in me. Above the blanket he tapped my thigh now:

"Child-bride. Now go to sleep."

"Gerald. I want to tell you something," I held my palm out to him.

But, streching towards me, he closed my hand and put it back in my lap, leaving it with me. He plucked briefly at the bit of hair that always escapes sideways over my left ear-lobe. And he got up: "Not now. Now, by order, you go to sleep."

"But I want to say something."

Gerald turned away, stepped over to the chair, picked up his square lantern there, fussed with it, lit it, turned it out, and kindled a beam of light on the floor:

"So much a woman. So, silly things, very well. Say them. Perceptive things, not now," he smiled, already turning towards the exit, only his head turned to me.

"You're in a hurry."

"Yes. Good night," he lit me for a moment as though with a searchlight: "You're sweet, very. You give. Good night. Now you'll sleep." He went out, and with him the short dazzling light.

I remained sitting in the dark. My eyes on the flames in the fireplace. On the black shapes in them.

No, Gerald, no – I mused, slipping down again from a sitting position to lying down. I'm not a child-bride. And I have the right to speak. But I'm alone. And what am I to do, therefore? What am I to do – I didn't know, and the soft inside within me weeping inside of me, getting harder.

I'm not paralyzed, you're not mute, that's what I wanted to say. But that's where I was wrong. My mistake. And I wanted to say that I wasn't the one you once offered a lift to. Your mistake. It doesn't matter. Perhaps for a moment you came towards me. Perhaps for a moment, with me, in your own way, you, some source was opened up in you again. Which, like water joining up with water is joining up with itself, for a moment it abolished, swept by and passed as through spider-webs through those thin cloth curtains, and like a substance of the quality of a soap bubble, through the non-existent protection of the windowpanes. To join up with the freshness of the night, the air and the chill.

As though I found you again, I wanted to say. But only as though. As though I had come home. Always just as though. It doesn't matter. For a moment you came towards me. For a moment some source was opened up in you again. For a moment perhaps we caught up with each other. The paralytics, the mutes, maybe they shouldn't ask for more.

I brought the wheelchair closer to me. Taking a long while, for the first time, I did the trick, shifted myself somehow into the wheelchair. I rolled over to the big window and pulled a curtain back a little. Darkness. Almost absolute. With silhouettes of unknown masses, near and distant. Far off, a man with a lantern passed through the courtyard. He stopped. I saw the lantern leave the trees, approach and grow closer. And already the steps in the mud. And a wheelbarrow of galvanized iron, next to the wet wall of a store-room, against which a galvanized iron ladder leaned. A large dustbin in muffled black sparkled. And puddles.

He walked to the window. Stooping slightly, he leaned a hand on the frame. He lifted the lantern and lit his face and mine: Garrick. In a fur cap with ear-flaps. I didn't move. And he turned, walking away.

What are they now. Like when the waning moon is already the thinnest thread of light. Superimposed. Upon the fullness of the disk in black. Fitting in. In the silence and seriousness of night taking over. Setting on the ends of the earth which are still in last light. A memory: once, at home, I read in the newspaper. A short report about a German shepherd dog. Which joined a pack of wolves. Thus he was discovered one day by hunters. In northern Syria? In Lebanon? – I tried to remember and couldn't manage to.

Strangers they will walk in the big city now. Suspicious, reserved, he was on the telephone. No, that's not it. They don't talk, I mused. Because they are stronger in their silence. It is by their silence that they are dangerous. It is by their silence that they command. Secret, acting alone, homing in on the goal. The perfect sense of proportion says when to attack, when to move on. And they never tell. They never boast. Their self-respect, the authority, intact, I mused. I thought about Gerald. Like about an animal you cannot tame. Despite the ravages: only the thin, delicate skin, smooth as a baby's forehead, tells what the open air, the upheavals of the climate, and the years, did to the exposed skin. Like the way geological configurations indicate the unceasing working away of the elements, I mused. And perhaps I dreamed it all – I wondered to myself.

I turned around into the room. As I rolled by the fireplace, I stopped. There were no more flames: the bright canyons, among the reddened mountains of splendor, glowed and rustled, like halls and corridors in a ready inferno. I tried to pick up the leather scuttle, in which not much was left. I picked it up. I tried to wave it, back and forth, to pour in coal, the way he did. And already the whispering columns of smoke. Hurrying to the chimney, seeking, trying, and trying again, to flare up suddenly in bright, leaping cock's crests. Like twisted handkerchiefs thrown in the air, floating burning. Afterwards joining together.

The small amount of power that began to collect in me now. Don't I derive it, open to it, through you, from your strength, I thought. And I broke down unexpectedly: Oh, Gerald, Gerald. Oh, a bewitched day. A bewitched place. Oh, my God. What could I have known about these when I was here, standing unsuspecting on the bank. A child-bride. And your father, you know, once gave me. A gift. When I donated to the bazaar some sort of large tongs. They were new. For making American waffles. That I had received as a present. And couldn't get the knack of them. They were relegated to the toys box. I don't know why your father was so impressed with them. And gave me as a gift a little decorated bowl of bulbs. Crocuses. That he took down from a row of identical bowls like that, arranged on the broad shelf that was fixed, right over there, on the pantry wall. I appreciated it a lot. I was a girl who was interested. In the names of plants. Oh, Gerald. I want to be with you. Why. Everywhere. Why. At all hours. Why. I want to put the best there. Everything. And to start growing. Not a child-bride. Differently. Like you. May I. Enter. The other club of the afflicted. Alex, as usual, was right – speaking and not knowing what he's saying – the country air will put me back on my feet. Or is it a form of suicide.

Alex? – I won't go back to Alex, I knew suddenly. And my heart stopped beating. I entered a state of silent shock. Gerald? No. Not at all. Now I almost forgot Gerald. He was dissolved now, turned into the ghost of the man. Not because of Gerald. Because of me – I was astonished without understanding. Not because of me. Because of the spark of life, I said to myself with a kind of unfathomable relief and liberation, heady, like intoxication. Or maybe this is a form of suicide, I wondered, with the same freedom, the same joy.

Yoram Kaniuk

The Beautiful Life of Clara Shiato

Translated by Ruvik Danieli

She always remembered the hidden fear. When Clara Shiato was twelve years of age, she stood by the window and hung curtains. Before the clowns passed by, on their way to the circus, she saw Shmuel Abuman with his brother. He raised his eyes and saw Clara, and then a strange fear filled her, and her eyes, those bright eyes, grew dark and she felt as if the blood had drained from her face. She quickly hid behind the curtain but heard Shmuel Abuman ask his brother who this beauty was, and smile. She didn't see the smile but she heard the word smiling in his throat and she felt a knot deep inside her. She knew that her legs had become cold and remembered that she had been told the dead have cold legs, and so she felt her heart to see if she was still alive. Shmuel Abuman's brother said: Her brother is a weight-lifter, and Clara hastened to disappear, as if wanting to be swallowed by the orange curtains and never be seen again.

Before the arrival of the uncles from Saloniki who brought the presents and the laced dress, she heard Shmuel Abuman sing the *Haftarah* in the Great Synagogue. She sat in the women's section and didn't look in his direction. The women said that no boy had sung thus in Izmir since Abutbul the Great, the grandson of Rabbi Tam. She knew that without having to be told. But she felt the need to defend herself against something that suddenly filled her with a too strong desire, and said to herself softly: he has a funny voice, he sings without feeling, he is beautiful and he sings like a too beautiful child. She didn't hear the whole *Haftarah* because the window was full of birds that flew to faraway countries and the skies were clouded, and Clara cried into her embroidered handkerchief until her mother jabbed her with her elbow and whispered in her ear, but she didn't understand what her mother was saying.

Shmuel Abuman was betrothed to the daughter of an angry man who was a butcher in the market-place, who cut his meat with vicious strokes, and after marrying her he moved to another town. Clara grew up in a yard full of children, and loved fat foods, sweet cakes, hot spices and mint tea. The house was full of whispers and different rumors flew about, and Clara waited to be told what to do. Once she dreamed that Shmuel Abuman came to her, and handed her a wreath of flowers, but she awoke with such suddeness that she couldn't remember if she had taken the flowers or not. And so, between rumors, a husband was brought to her. His name was Sasson and she gazed straight into his eyes and knew that he was beautiful and that he loved her at first sight. He trembled as he talked to her. She remembered Shmuel Abuman and sang a portion of his *Haftarah* to herself and recalled that his eyes were green-gold, and their expression was one of despairing sadness. Fear entwined her, coiling with a strange joy, and she wanted to cry and laugh at the same time.

Her husband, Sasson, took her to a small town in Greece, by the sea. She loved the sea that stroked the sand and said to herself: God, let me live my whole life by the sea. I want to die as the setting sun sinks into the horizon and the red sky kisses the water's ripples. Sasson carted things in a wagon hitched to a horse and she bore five children. Something inside her expected them to have green-gold eyes but their eyes were Sasson's dark eyes, except for the fifth whose eyes were green-gold. She learned to love Sasson with a pure and silent devotion. He was a soft and pleasant man and whispered sweet words to her, and at night he cried as he made children in her.

He had a fish's slippery body, dark eyes, and hands as soft as a candle flame. She called him Mr. Sasson and he sang her sad songs in a language she didn't understand, songs about the mountains and forests of Anatolia where he was born and from which he had fled after the great fire destroyed his home. Once he told her of how the house had burnt and his parents had roasted in the flames. Drunken people had been there, who had wanted to see him in the flames too, wanting to see a small boy turn into a torch, but an old man had saved his life. His mother was dust and they buried her without his seeing her again. And on nights when no candles were lit he would look for burning candles to snuff out. And on nights when the full moon shone and he looked for blazes to extinguish, none could be found. They lived by the sea and the trees were few and far apart. He longed for the high mountains of Anatolia and he cried as he dreamt of the places where streams ran into big rivers and hard-faced, mounted men brandished swords, and Clara would hear him crying in his sleep and knew what dreams he dreamt.

Her dreams were so bitter that her face, as she slept, was as soft and smooth as a baby's face. Mr. Sasson searched for Clara with his wise hands, and knew how to pity and protect her, and loved her as one loves good wine, and drank her slowly as if his whole life were ahead of him, and she let him flow within her, and bore him two dead children and three living, and said to herself: I really do love Mr. Sasson and he is a beautiful, soft man. Sometimes when she dreamt of a man with green-gold eyes she would wake trembling all over and drink spiced mint tea and watch her husband's dreams of terror and that way she could smother the bitter fear that burned inside her. She learnt of Satan and Asmodeus from wise *Hakham* Amram and knew they had green-gold eyes.

When Clara's mother died, her father called her to come to him in Ismir. She bade farewell to Mr. Sasson and her children and went to her father. He was old and sight had left his eyes. He lay in bed and longed to join his wife, Marioma. In the night he asked Clara to lie by his side. She warmed his dying body with her own for three days and three nights, and he called her Marioma and yearningly stroked her face. His longing for her mother frightened her, for though she knew she loved her husband, she didn't miss him. She thought that she had never yearned for anyone, but deep in her heart she knew that her longing for those green-gold eyes that pierced her body in her sleep was without bounds.

As she caressed her father's eyes she no longer knew whose eyes she was stroking. And when he died in her arms, she locked his dead eyes shut, closed his gaping mouth with a kiss and couldn't resist the impulse to lay her hand on his legs. His limbs were cold and Clara knew she had actually died when she stood by the window and was twelve years old.

After the funeral her husband took her back to their town. He stood by her during the funeral and held her hand. She didn't cry. She didn't miss her father after his death. A young man with hate-filled eyes passed by them on their way back and threw a dead bird onto Clara's lap. She stroked the bird not knowing it was dead. Only later she said: God help us. The young man circled their house many days. It was said that Clara was the fairest among the town's women and he wished to buy her. Clara only smiled because she didn't know that married women could be bought. She had an open face and eyes that smiled of themselves. The young man was attracted to those receiving eyes and wanted to slide into them. When she asked him what work he did he answered that he fed sardines from cans and she laughed.

Her three sons grew and she taught them all she knew, knowing how little she knew. Mr. Sasson said he knew a few things about wild mountains and forests, but he couldn't teach his sons anything except decent behavior and the love of God. Such was the blossoming in the house by the sea, accompanied by a sad awareness of some resignation. The children mocked the young man who circled the house awaiting the right moment to love the fairest of women. Mr. Sasson fell ill frequently and lay feverish. Later the Germans came and at night they fired from nooks and crannies. Clara didn't understand why they were being banished from the sea. She loved the smell of the water and the muffled roar of the whispering waves. Mr. Sasson loaded their trunks on the cart and talked with the young man who said he was willing to hide them. Mr. Sasson kissed the young man's hand. When Clara saw Mr. Sasson kiss his hand, distant fears filled her and she remembered Shmuel Abuman. The young man led them to a small house by a stream whose waters reached the sea. There was a small windmill and people there grew poppies. At night, by the light of the lamp, Clara saw that the young man's eyes weren't the color of the dead bird's eyes. They were green-gold. She spread her hands with the same dull, silent pleading of wounded dogs run down by a cart. She froze into his arms, while her husband slept in the loft of the barn. He was older than he looked at first, and had a gentleness tempered with cruelty that reminded her of the smile she never saw. She cried when she was in his arms and her body surrendered into his, and she understood why Mr. Sasson cried when he made children in her. She played with the young man's curls and rested his head on her breasts, and groaned with such feeling that he laughed joyfully.

She knew she was committing a great sin but a demon laughed in her heart. She was terribly frightened of this pure and pungent joy she felt she didn't deserve, but now she did what she had perhaps always wanted to do: she kissed a demon. The demon inside her touched a demon, and the bliss was sharp, like pain touching pain. He told her his name was Borkas and that there was love in the world. She told him she didn't understand why she was kissing him and he decorated her body with flowers he had picked by the stream and he said: Your beauty is so frightening, Clara, and your skin is the color of water.

The young man left on the third night and her husband came to her bed. Mr. Sasson spat blood and she wondered where she drew the courage to rest her unwashed body next to her beautiful husband's body. Outside there were policemen. Through the window above the bed she saw the policemen behead Borkas as a warning to all who hid Jews. The severed head no longer answered her that there was love in the world. Clara searched for Borkas' eyes and found her husband's eyes by her side and his mouth spitting blood.

The policemen loaded the children onto the wagon and shouted at her to hurry. She dragged the bags and Mr. Sasson came after her, bent and stooped. They mounted the wagon and traveled in a convoy.

At one place she met her aunt Rosa. She was giving out black coffee and her eyes burnt with a dry hate, fitting the rags she wore. Clara whispered something in her ear and Aunt Rosa said: Your brother is a weight-lifter, and the gentile who has died will be killed again by hands of steel. But the weight-lifter had already been burnt in Auschwitz and there was no one who could kill Borkas again.

They traveled from place to place and Clara shut her eyes and thought of how beautiful the young man by the sea had been. A German officer caught Clara's breasts in his hands and said: These Hebrews, they have giant smooth stones instead of breasts. And then they stripped the women. The beautiful women cried and the old women trembled and tried to cover their nudity with their hands. Not all of them died. Those that were raped were killed immediately. Clara's anger erupted when she saw the German kill her aunt. The black coffee in her aunt's hands, like black tongues crisscrossing her body, horrified Clara, and she fell on the German, scratching him with her fingernails.

The German received her blows impassively, and then she understood what Doctor Hirsch, who had put himself at the head of the convoy, had meant when he had told her in Greek that the German looked like a Greek sculptured by a blacksmith. She noticed with dread that as her anger at the German grew, so too grew her pleasure from the touch of his elegant white hands, and she couldn't help but think, even at that moment, of what she'd always known deep in her heart, that the devil had chosen her body to live in.

When the partisans came, the German's blood was still on her nails. She didn't remember how long they stayed in the forest but Mr. Sasson's strength returned and he became a changed man. The partisans, who at first mocked and ridiculed him, began listening to his advice and Clara's heart beat with pride. Mr. Sasson led them over hidden paths and could predict when the rains would come and when the cold would be unbearable. He found food for them in hidden places, and sweet grains in dark forest clearings, and once he came to her at night and didn't cry. She stroked his head, his hair, stroked him and saw the great pride in this man, the pride that had been quenched by the sea and had come to life in the mountains.

The children disappeared and were later found near the white monastery. Her two eldest sons were happy to see her and asked her what had happened to Mr. Borkas. Her youngest son came to her wearing a monk's white cloak and a rosary, and his face, always pale and beautiful, was more pale and beautiful than ever, and she saw once more that the devil's eyes were green-gold. Her son spoke to her about Jesus who died to save us all and she shut her ears to his words. The partisans drank the wine that the monks brought and laughed, and Clara screamed when Mr. Sasson hit his son. She wasn't screaming at her husband but at the whole world, and suddenly it seemed that her entire life had been sliced with a knife. She saw her son's grieving eyes and they were like rimmed steel. Clara wore a necklace made of a stream pebble tied to a string, and walked stooped, as if she carried the burden of the sky on her shoulders. At night the sad stars shone in the sky and a somber halo, like the cold sorrow of the mountains, lay over the trees and the last of the forest bears roared from afar.

Two years passed and they arrived in the town of Fiume. Her youngest son stayed behind at the monastery with his white cloak and rosary. In the town the houses were blue, as if the sky had fallen into the clean, narrow streets. She wandered through the streets and joined a funeral procession. Women in black mourned, a wooden Madonna painted red and gold shed tears, and the women wailed. A curly-headed lad gave her an orange. She knew who he was for she recognized the color of his eyes. He told her that God loves dead Jews and she said, this funeral is not of Jews. He told her that he came from Tel Aviv and she knew that Mr. Sasson was waiting for a ship to take them to Tel Aviv even though she didn't know where that city was. She had heard of the golden wall and of Zion but she didn't know these places really existed. The young man said he was searching for his uncle and she asked if his uncle had green-gold eyes, but he couldn't tell her as he had never seen him, and then she asked if his uncle's name was Shmuel Abuman and he answered, yes, and how would you know that, and she burst out laughing. The terror his looks had aroused in her gave way to laughter that flowed through her constantly. She didn't know how she had known, as she didn't know if Shmuel Abuman and Mr. Borkas were one and the same or not. The years in the mountains and the forests had blurred, in her mind, the relations between things that would appear to be clear.

Mr. Sasson dragged sacks onto the ship and ate his fill of oranges. The young man led Clara to the boat. Her sons waited for her on the ship's ramp with a camera they had stolen from a dead German in the street. She wanted to throw the camera into the sea but her sons laughed and kept it. All the passengers boarded the ship and the *Pan York* set sail for the Land of Israel. They lay in the ship's belly, deprived of both air and light, crowded like sardines, and Clara remembered how Mr. Borkas told her once that he fed sardines from cans, and she smiled to herself. Mr. Sasson fell sick, vomiting constantly and even spitting blood. He didn't go up on deck with everyone else three times a day to breathe fresh air and eat the canned meat that two curly-headed lads and two girls doled out to them from cartons. The sea was stormy and Clara loved its fearful splendor. She met Shmuel Abuman on the deck, Shmuel Abuman whose hair had grayed and whose skin was wrinkled. She trembled at the sight of him and tears flooded her eyes. Shmuel Abuman said: I remember you well, your name is Clara. And she said: Your words smiled of themselves, and you sang the *Haftarah* more beautifully than Abutbul. He said: So much water has flowed, and looked at her yearningly and stretched out his arms and immediately returned them to their place. And she spread her hands as if beseeching for his soul more than for her own, but she knew that she was pleading for the soul of another man who had once worn the semblance of Shmuel Abuman. He said: My wife lies sick below and her fingernails are sharp from envy, and then Clara said something, she said: Maybe we have lost everything? And he said: But we still live, Clara, and all the others are dead, and she said: Maybe it would have been better if we had died, and told him, reluctantly, about her son, who had stayed in the forest wearing a monk's cloak. She didn't tell him how strongly her son the monk resembled him.

She didn't see Shmuel Abuman again but she was conscious of his name in the cold nights. Everyone sang when they reached Haifa in early morning and the Carmel range appeared from afar, and Clara prayed to Zion and longed to see the wall of gold. They were taken to a city of tents and she stood in line and was given a kerosene stove, some mattresses, blankets, rice, flour and onions. Mr. Sasson lay ill and Clara suddenly desired to see her youngest son. The hate that burned in his eyes was compassion in hers and in her heart she called him Shmuel Borkas. When Mr. Sasson recovered he went to work as a construction worker. Clara found work in an institution for the aged and scrubbed the floors. It was before huts were built for them and electric poles put up in the *ma'abara*. There was no meat and they ate eggplant and fish. Then there came a hard winter and it rained for six days on end. The tent filled with water and they prayed to God. They moved to the hut suffering from severe influenza after lying for several days in the leaking tent.

Later they moved to a ruined house near Jaffa in a place called Jabeliyeh. The houses were almost demolished; Arabs had once lived there. Some Poles opened a bakery across the street and the smell of fresh bread filled her with fierce desire. People said she was the most beautiful woman in the neighborhood. The young men returning from the war appraised her and Mr. Sasson was taken to the hospital in Sarafand.

Every evening Clara went to visit Mr. Sasson and brought him food she had cooked for him. He stroked her face and said: I wish I were dead. She said: Don't say that, Mr. Sasson, here we are free in our own land, there's Ben Gurion and a state and all Israel are brethren. And suddenly, without realizing how, she knew things she had never known. She learned Hebrew slowly, but everyone spoke Ladino except for the Poles and the Rumanians who opened a restaurant that served black market steaks on wooden platters. Clara washed dishes and scrubbed floors. She learned to cook Rumanian food but she knew that Shmuel Abuman would prefer the food she cooked for Mr. Sasson. She didn't know where Shmuel Abuman lived, and once she dreamt his wife came to her and scratched her with sharp fingernails and she didn't know if she'd scratched a German with elegant hands or a woman who suddenly didn't have a face at all. In the Rumanian restaurant she met Mr. Halphon who wanted her to be his wife. She said: What do you mean, I'm married to Mr. Sasson, and Halphon said: And if he dies what will you do? How funny he talks, she thought, but how terribly. There were tears in his eyes as he ate, and she couldn't understand why she didn't love people who wanted her to pity them. But she learned something she had never known, she almost learned to pity herself, and she said: Mr. Halphon wants to marry me and the children have no clothes for winter, I mop the floors and my legs hurt. But she derided herself for this thought when Mr. Halphon showed her photographs he had brought from there and she saw a deep furrow in the ground and people standing naked in the snow and Croatian soldiers with rifles to kill them, and a priest incanting a final blessing. She didn't know if the priest was her son but then she thought, why not? So she went to the woman who had driven the devil from Mr. Sasson's lungs when he had returned from the hospital still spitting blood, and asked her to take her son from her.

She lay on the bed, and the woman and the turbanned man who crumbled holy bread into a glass of water with cloves of garlic in it cast her son out from inside her. His leaving was a fierce pain but she restrained herself and didn't cry. She remembered his birth and how sweet and beautiful he had been then. But her womb was now clean of him and his memory left her for a long time. Mr. Sasson was unable to work anymore and her eldest son, Meyuhas, was on probation. Meyuhas smiled and whispered to her that he was called Trigger of Death. His smile looked strange to her, as if it didn't come from within him but had been stuck onto his face to protect him from something frightening. After he was jailed for the first time, she left the Rumanian who sold camel steaks and pushed her into dark corners, and went to work for the Ronen family on Ben Yehuda Street.

The Ronen family had a large apartment with many books and pictures and three children who looked to her like ice-cream cones. Mrs. Ronen told her she was more primitive than the Arab women who had worked for her in Jerusalem before the war, and asked her to bring her smoked fish from the black market. She brought Mrs. Ronen smoked fish for lunch and was given murky soup. She polished the floor until it was fit for the dainty feet of the children who looked like ice-cream cones. Meyuhas wrote her from prison and she couldn't read his letter. And then Shmuel Abuman came to live in Jabeliyeh. He was given a ruined house larger than hers and he rebuilt it with his own hands. His wife stayed indoors and Clara never saw her face. But the windows were so dirty that Clara couldn't resist and came at night with a washcloth and a pot of water and soap and polished the windows and didn't know if the eyes that watched her from inside were her own or somebody else's, as she couldn't make out their color in the dark. Men accosted her in the streets and she said: You want girls to love and I am old, and laughed in her heart. Shmuel Abuman became a municipal worker and distributed tea. He told her that he was called Shmuel the Great and she laughed; this was at the Tripolitanian grocer's, while she was buying matches. Shmuel Abuman told her that he knew what she'd done to the windows and he thanked her for it, and she covered her face with her hands and went home. Sasson was taken to the hospital again and no longer returned. She thought: I really do love Mr. Sasson, he was soft and beautiful and made me two live children and two dead ones and one neither alive nor dead, but she thought of Mr. Sasson in shrouds. At night she sewed herself a dress from black velvet she had found in the flea-market. Mrs. Ronen was angry and said she didn't like cleaning women who came to work wearing glittering party dresses like floozies. A day later she said that the children couldn't sleep because of nightmares and dismissed her.

She said: You told them about death. Clara didn't know what the Hebrew word for nightmares meant but she said, I think of Mr. Sasson in shrouds because he is approaching his Maker and I mourn the light of my youth. Mrs. Ronen said: I am sure you slash with a sword and your eyes are fountains of tears, and laughed as she walked to Café Roval where she sat with her friends and talked about the new clothes being sold in the fashion stores sprouting in the city like mushrooms after many days of rain. Clara stepped off the bus and stopped at the Tripolitanian's and he too didn't know what the Hebrew word for nightmares meant, but a woman who was dipping her hands in a cask of salt fish said that it meant bad dreams. Sad and weary, Clara went home. The house was quiet and birds wailed on the roof. She saw a black scorpion beside the doorway and crushed it with her foot. The house felt empty: Meyuhas was in jail and her second son, Abram, was roaming the streets. She went to Yehuda Halevy Street and asked the letter-writer in black sunglasses to write a letter for her. He inserted a page in his huge typewriter and wrote:

> *Subject: My dismissal from work.*
> *Dear Mrs. Ronen...*

Clara stopped him and said that she would tell him what to write. The man was offended. He crumpled the paper in a hand covered with black cloth and lit a cigarette. He said: I've been writing letters twenty-three years and I know how to write letters. But Clara, who knew nothing, said: Maybe you know how to write but I'll tell you what to write. And he looked up and saw the tough beautiful woman, threw away the cigarette, inserted a page into the typewriter and waited for her words, and then wrote:

> *Mrs. Ronen,*
> *I'm a hard woman. Maybe not a good mother because Meyuhas is in jail and that's a bad sign. All that is true. That wasn't a party dress but tears for the light of my youth. Why tell me your children have nightmares!!! That they can't sleep! I know they do sleep. They sleep in the softest beds in the world. They have nice things and nice things make sweet dreams. They have a record player, you live in a nice street with trees and shutters. It isn't nice to talk to me like that. You're not dismissing me, I'm quitting because of myself and because of Mr. Sasson.*
> *Goodbye, Clara*

She paid and the man said: I wrote all the mistakes you said and don't tell anyone who wrote this letter, and Clara looked at him with a smile that suddenly shone from her and said: What are words and what are letters, what's important is the heart, and you have a good heart. The man lit another cigarette and said: You know, Mrs. Clara, the heart, that's what gets lost here. I was in Baghdad and Jews were Jews to one another, and here it's like Gentiles, everyone at the other's throat, and who's this Mrs. Ronen who lives on Ben Yehuda Street and whose son goes to whores? And Clara said: She doesn't have a grown-up son, she has three small children, and then she thought: Maybe, maybe, and Clara laughed and thought of Mr. Ronen and of her son Meyuhas in jail. Then she went home, and the evening descended, embracing the trees in amazing silence. She hummed an old song that the fishermen had sung in the faraway village where she had borne her children, the live ones and the dead ones and the one neither alive nor dead, and the laughter didn't leave her face even after she'd bought a stamp and put the letter in the red mailbox.

Meyuhas was in jail again when Abram began roaming in the street of the bitter people. He was courting Ziona and wanted to marry her. It was said that the people in the street were bitter, and had blue numbers on their arms. When Mr. Sasson died she escorted him to his grave and didn't cry. She thought: He has joined his maker and I don't miss him. Meyuhas, who was brought to the funeral by a policeman, escaped during the service, and the policeman shouted at Clara and said: You helped him, and she said: No, no, but he stared at her with hate in his eyes and didn't see that her bright eyes were stroking Mr. Sasson's thin body for the last time. On her way home she thought a few thoughts. The first was why Meyuhas had decided to escape during his father's funeral, and Clara said to herself: Maybe he didn't want to grieve his father, and pitied him. Her second thought was why hadn't Ziona, Abram's fiancée, come to the funeral. And then she thought: Everything blends into one thing. The gaiety she'd latched onto was consolation of a sort, and she said to herself: See, Meyuhas has done something, maybe he wanted his father to be proud of him, and she thought that if she could, she too would run away. But she knew that all her life she'd been running away and getting nowhere and then she thought maybe she'd never run away and something inside her always remained rooted in some place, and to run away is not to arrive, it's not like standing still. At home she sat and thought of Borkas. The mourners had long since gone and she asked herself: Did Mr. Sasson know about Borkas? That night she went to the cemetery. Over Mr. Sasson's fresh grave there was a small, painted sign with his name on it, but she couldn't read. It was night and the wind rustled through the branches of the trees. She said: Mr. Sasson, light of my youth, did you know about Borkas? And Mr. Sasson said: I knew, but I also knew how pure your love was. She said: There was a demon inside me and still is, and Sasson said: Your demon was what made you beautiful. And she said that it wasn't fair to be beautiful because of a demon and not because of the Angel Gabriel. Mr. Sasson said: Gabriel has a white beard and looks like a rabbi. But the demons are beautiful and they have the faces of angels and God is what is the opposite. She thought that these strange thoughts didn't suit a woman who couldn't read or write, and returned home and sat among the flowers that had wilted in their vases and dreamt a terrible dream. In the dream three men came to her and each said: I am the father of a son you killed with your own hands. The three men were her aged father, Shmuel Abuman, and Borkas, who came headless and whose hands held her throat until she thought she would choke and she awoke screaming.

Shmuel Abuman came to her house and saw vases with wilted flowers. The air was stale and she wore black and watched the rain in the window. Shmuel held her hand and she stepped outside and picked an anemone and gave it to him. Winter was raging and many anemones grew among the ruins. It was said they were the blood of the Arabs who'd lived here once.

Abram learned to drive and became a ticket collector for the Dan bus company. Clara felt like an uninvited guest at his wedding. They moved to Givatayim and Clara went to work for Yolanda who looked like the wooden Madonna that had wept in Fiume. Meyuhas was released from jail and brought girls home. He said they were sick and needed rest. At night a doctor came and did things to them and in the mornings they lay like the dead, brightly painted, with false hair, and smoked cigarettes. Meyuhas put in a bath so his girls would be able to wash and Clara began to shower in cold water every morning and looked cold and refreshed. Trigger of Death said the girls were his friends but she knew they worked in the backyards for him. He bought her a radio and a refrigerator and a set of silk sheets. But she hated the painted stares of the girls in Meyuhas' bed, with cigarettes in mouths which smiled derisively as if she had lived for nothing, as if she was made of air.

She loved Yolanda with the careful love of a bereaved mother. She wanted to give birth to Yolanda and bequeath her the castles she didn't own. Yolanda spoke English and a funny Hebrew and had a toothpaste voice, but she was the most delicate and mysterious thing Clara had met in her life. Clara knew in her heart that Yolanda was a queen and so she could bequeath her the castles she didn't own. Yolanda found out that Clara liked sardines and cream and bought her sardines and cream. They sat in the kitchen like two sisters and talked about life, in general and in particular. Aya went to kindergarten and Yolanda helped Clara clean Yolanda's home. When Yolanda stood in the kitchen with the insecticide spray and cried, the shoemaker came in his stocking-cap and wanted to kill Clara with a hammer. Yolanda cried with the spray in her hand because she couldn't kill the roaches that had suddenly crawled out of all the cracks and even from the sink. She cried because she couldn't kill them with the spray. She knew them all, because she'd seen them coming out of the cracks and the sink and Yolanda couldn't kill living things she knew personally. The shoemaker with the stocking-cap sat in the street below and mended shoes, and burst into the apartment because the door was open.

The door was open because Yolanda never locked it. Clara thought that if she should ever give Yolanda the castles she wanted to bequeath to her, they would probably be stolen from her. And then she thought: Maybe my son Meyuhas would come and steal them and she felt a great pride mixed with an endless sorrow. Clara shouted at the shoemaker: Get away, you fool, and he burst into tears and told Yolanda that he didn't have anything against Clara, who was beautiful, only against Trigger of Death. Trigger of Death had taken his daughter to Clara's and had an abortion done on her, she was a whore in the street, she'd come home with a disease and stolen his savings to give to Meyuhas. My daughter spits on her father, he said. and beautiful Clara doesn't know what's going on in her own home. Clara said: He isn't my son! He isn't my son! She went to the bathroom, lay down in the tub and cut her wrists. In the ambulance she told the policemen she wouldn't bring charges against anyone and didn't remember anyone trying to kill her with a hammer. The policemen said the shoemaker had told them he had come to kill her and she said it was probably a joke and they said he wasn't joking at all. She told them about Meyuhas and his girls, about the doctor who came and performed abortions. The police watched the house and arrested a girl and a doctor. Meyuhas escaped and came back the next day, beat Clara who was bandaged after her release from the hospital, and took the radio and the refrigerator.

Yolanda gave Clara new clothes, an old refrigerator and a radio and Clara killed all the roaches when Yolanda went to the kindergarten to bring Aya home. On the day she returned to work she heard that Meyuhas had murdered the doctor from Neve Sha'anan. He got life imprisonment and she went to visit him. He said that he forgave her for informing on him but he asked her to bring him hashish. Clara borrowed money from Yolanda and bought hashish from a Yemenite in a neon-lit street and brought it to her son in her mouth. She kissed him between the bars and passed him the hashish from mouth to mouth. He wanted more and more and it became hard for her to find the money. She wanted to buy a new dress and repair the shutters for the winter but Meyuhas would spread his pleading arms and say: Mother, it's all I have here, and her heart melted.

That winter it rained a lot. One day it even snowed in Jaffa and everything was frozen and wet. Clara remembered a snowman she'd seen in the mountains, at the time of their flight, and suddenly sensed how all the years had piled up on her, and inside her, and maybe she was old, she didn't even know her birthday. She wanted to rest but she didn't know where. Ziona, Abram's wife, said that her house was too small. Angelina, Abram's daughter, fell in love with a terrible man who had a red Mustang and Ziona said that it was all because Clara's eldest son killed people and her youngest sold Jews to the Germans and only Abram had been saved from her touch. Angelina laughed at her father, who wanted to beat up the man with the red Mustang, and then Abram suffered his first heart attack and people said: What troubles that whore of a daughter brings him.

After three winters beautiful Angelina stopped laughing. Now her face was bitter like everyone else's, she started wearing glittering clothes and looked like the girls Meyuhas had brought to Clara's in the days before he killed the doctor from Neve Sha'anan. Angelina became hard and sad, but was beautiful like all the Shiato women. She looked so like Clara, that Clara could sit looking at her for hours, remembering how she herself had walked beside the sea and played with her children when they were still babies and people said: Beautiful Clara's playing in the sand. Angelina's face became like a white inscrutable sore. People in the street said: It can't be, as if beauty such as hers was unforgivable. And they wanted to kill her because she was so beautiful. On the night when her terrible man came home drunk and beat her, Angelina took a thousand lira from his jacket and brought them to Clara. Together they went to the neon-lit street to buy hashish. And Clara came every week and kissed Meyuhas with hashish in her mouth and felt as if she were kissing bars.

Great laughter erupted in the prison when Clara was caught with hashish in her mouth. The policemen laughed, the warders laughed and the prisoners laughed. Clara said nothing and sat silent. Yolanda brought her journalist husband to the trial and he told the judge the story of Clara Shiato's life. Clara refused to speak and only smiled blankly, and the judge said: Blessed are the sons of farmers for theirs is the simple wisdom of life. And he said: What a pity that people become apathetic and stop fighting. Maybe, he said, maybe only Meyuhas is in the right. The judge was a sad and serious man and said things that perhaps he shouldn't have said. He said that only those who are born angry can really escape the strangling noose, but too much anger can be dangerous, just like apathy. Clara sat up, stopped smiling, and said they'd inherited the anger from the demon always nesting inside her but the judge said that he was lamenting the apathy, the fact that people say: We're lost and it's all over before it can even begin. Yolanda's husband signed a bond and Clara swore not to bring Meyuhas any more hashish. Meyuhas told her she needn't come at all.

Before Angelina vanished, she came to Clara. Her face was slashed with a razor and her hair was tangled. She said she was pregnant and Clara gave her the little money that remained. Angelina went to Galilee and Abram suffered his second heart attack. It was said that the Angelina caused it. Ziona demanded that Abram go to the synagogue and renounce Clara as his mother. He went to the synagogue and swore that Clara wasn't his mother and Ziona bought him a keyring with a little angel made of almost pure gold. Angelina came with her slashed face and said: Maybe you aren't his mother but you're my grandmother, and she went to work on the street. When she brought Clara money and stood outside, in the wind, her beautiful face lit with a strange glow. Clara threw the money out the window and Angelina waited outside, her belly swollen, and picked up the money. She returned it to her glittering purse and cried. Her man was waiting for her with the red Mustang, and the pallor of her face against the Mustang was like a wound that hurt Clara to see. As if someone had drawn a window into the astonishment of her life. Yolanda bought Clara warm clothes for the winter, for her body ached from the damp and the mold. The years passed between words. There were days of sun that not everyone saw. New apartment buildings were built around the ruins of Jabeliyeh. Shmuel Abuman said he was distributing tea in a new city hall with elevators. The years slid down Clara's body into the ground and waited for her. Clara had once seen Shmuel Abuman cry. She couldn't place the picture. She didn't know if he was crying now or long ago. And if long ago, when? As if she'd been detached from the wandering of days and had turned into something fixed in some unseen landscape. Shmuel said: Clara, Clara. And then she felt, even outside the framework of time, how old she'd become. And once she put on the earrings Angelina had brought and stood in front of the mirror and laughed and saw a demon laughing in the mirror.

At night Clara felt she was going to die. She said to herself: I'm dying and only the thought remains, and didn't know which thought. The body flies, she said, and the thought lies in bed. And she sensed something sweet inside her, and angels stroked her eyes and she knew that wherever she went and however she was defeated, she'd arrive at places she'd already been to and from which she was drawing away. Clara went outside, into the dark night that hung between the new apartment buildings and the ruins, and did what Jewish women never do. She stood by the castor tree and made the sign of the cross, and for the first time in many years she thought of her son in the monk's robes. She felt as if a great train was roaring inside her, bringing her death or maybe sweet intoxication. And she said: God of my dear son, I love him with all the love of the demon inside me, let me see his face before I die... I know he's been cast out of me and my womb is cleansed of him, but I so want to see him once more before it all ends, before what was always between the words begins. And then she saw that the castor tree was witnessing her shame. She hit the tree and spoke bitter words to it and the tree wasn't moved. The next day she went to *Hakham* Joseph and told him what she'd done. He advised her to go to the Wailing Wall and pray with true intent. She left for Jerusalem a few days after Angelina, who had not come to see her for a long time, brought her daughter and said: I called her Clara, after you, Grandmother, and Clara wept and hugged the girl and knew that her end was drawing near.

She feared that she'd only get to see her son the monk in the world-to-come, but was also afraid that the world-to-come was divided into different wards, for Christians and for Jews, and maybe she'd be forced to see him through bars. Abram she hadn't seen for a few years. Sometimes she went to Abram's street and stood opposite their house, beside the flower shop, and saw Abram in the window, sick. The light was on, and there was her son's face in the window, staring. She saw how hopelessly sick he was and wanted to go and embrace him but the house was locked to her and Abram had sworn in the synagogue that she wasn't his mother.

She traveled to the Wailing Wall and met a Greek family who remembered her as Clara who lived in the small house by the sea. They were alarmed to hear Mr. Sasson was dead, as if someone's death foretells things that are too clear. Clara prayed beside the Wall but didn't feel that the large stones had heard her. She searched for God among the stones and saw he wasn't there. There were tourists and children there, and women wailing. It was after the war, everyone came to the Wall. She'd long known the Wall wasn't made of gold but she hadn't known that instead of tears she'd find such heavy stones. She knew that God was something sad, like a butterfly with heavy legs, who doesn't like being stone or wood. But she believed that *Hakham* Joseph knew things she didn't know. And in the bus on the way to Jaffa she laughed inside. She thought: Maybe all these people know how to read and write and maybe they know things they shouldn't know but she knew one terrible thing they didn't know. She knew the stuff from which life was woven, the stuff from which life was embroidered.

At night, when she felt that death was approaching, she'd go outside. She wore the black dress she'd made for Mr. Sasson's funeral and strolled among the ruins of Jabeliyeh where the red anemones, and even the poppies, had ceased to flower. As if not only her own blood had stopped flowing but the blood of the Arabs too, in this forsaken spot between the new apartment buildings and the giant city being built around them. She didn't walk by the castor tree for the castor tree had seen her make the sign of the cross. She went walking because she thought that if she should die in her house, she would rot without anybody knowing. Abram died of a heart attack the day he heard that Angelina had given birth again and no one knew who the father was. And Ziona came to the rundown house for the first time in her life, took the feathers out of the pillows and scattered them round the house, and said: This is where my daughter whores. That night Clara thought she was dead. It was a quiet night and dogs barked from afar. Beyond the ruins, between the skeletons of new houses under construction, were the dark crosses of the English cemetery surrounded by a sandstone wall. The moon was full and something pure and wonderful hung in the air. She was surprised when among the crosses she saw her son who burned inside her like a disease, walking as if alive. He wore a white cassock and his face was pale in the moonlight. When he spoke she sealed her ears even though she knew that it was her prayer to his God that had brought him to her, to the place where she'd crossed herself for him, where the castor tree had seen her shame. She didn't hear what he said to her but she brought him home and suddenly death flew from her, and her body was light and danced into her house. She helped him wash in the bathtub Meyuhas had brought for his girls, sat him down beside her and spoke to him as if he were a little child. She sang him old songs she hadn't sung for many years and he sat bent over with heavy tears in his eyes. When he spoke she sealed her ears but she cooked food for him and kissed his green-gold eyes. After visiting his brother in prison, he went on to Jerusalem. It was said that he lived in a monastery. Sometimes he wrote her but she didn't open his letters and didn't ask anybody to read them to her.

When Shmuel Abuman's wife fell ill, Clara began to come to his home. She cared for the sick woman and Shmuuel Abuman's wife thought she was a nurse from the Dejani hospital. The woman was deaf and blind and her body disintegrated in appalling exhaustion. She wilted, and soon nothing remained of her save a shadow between the sheet and the blanket. Clara fed her and she spit out the food. She placed her on the chamber-pot and washed her but little remained of the body save sharp fingernails and a wilting shadow. Clara sang her songs in Ladino but the woman was too deaf to hear. When she died she was holding Clara's hand. Her hand was clenched with a strength she hadn't had for a long time, as if it was locked in the rigor of death.

Shmuel Abuman stood behind her and stroked Clara's silver hair, and maybe that was why she laughed. She didn't laugh at the dead woman of whom nothing remained save a shadow; her laughter came in place of a shout that had been hiding inside her for a long time, a laugh not at all gay. She heard her own laughter and was frightened. She detached her hand from the dead woman's and fled outside. In the chords of her laughter Clara heard the distant echo of the *Haftarah* Shmuel Abuman had sung more beautifully than the grandson of Rabbi Tam. Later she vomited and lay ill a few weeks. The doctor gave her cloves of garlic and cast spells and Yolanda gave her a hundred lira to go to Jerusalem. She saw her son beside the Wailing Wall. His clothes were different and his face was shrivelled and transparent as if something terrible was occurring inside and through it she could see his heart fluttering, like the mechanical doll Clara had once seen in the window of a store on Allenby Street with its small motor exposed. When she saw the agonized dread on her son's face, she wanted to do what a mother never does, to take him to Meyuhas' streets, to give him a woman for six days and six nights, but she was afraid that a mother couldn't give such a present to a son with the eyes of a demon and the face of a martyr. They dined together and he bought her a black scarf of silken lace. He said that in Jerusalem he'd heard God's voice and because of that he'd repented. He told her his cross was hidden under his bed because he didn't regret what he'd done in those days, he said, in the mountains. God had shut his eyes to those who didn't wear crosses, now God had returned to his people. Clara didn't understand how the great, terrible and merciful God could leave and return, but she hugged her son in great apprehension and told him: You were always my favorite, and now you've returned into me. Years ago I was afraid of your eyes that pierced my body and I asked that you be cast out of me and I didn't cry even though you hurt terribly. Now you've come back and within me an orphaned womb laughs.

When she returned to Jaffa the solitude was unbearable. Shmuel Abuman came to her on the third evening and brought her flowers. They talked in Ladino about the things they had known separately yet so together. They ate and liked the same fatty foods, the same sweet cakes and mint tea and suddenly the house didn't seem so empty. Shmuel told Clara that his brother had died and left him a house in Tiberias by the sea. He said: I've retired and I have soft silk sheets, furniture, I have a General Electric refrigerator eleven cubic meters, I have a radio that can pick up Turkey. I am lonely, I have no one to eat with and talk Ladino with, I bought a fishing rod with an automatic reel. Why don't you come be my wife?

She said nothing and gazed at him with quiet eyes like two storms extinguished on a distant star. As if her whole life, all the long days she had lived, the dead children she'd borne, dead Mr. Sasson, Borkas, Meyuhas behind bars, the repentant monk by the Wall, strangling hands, and Angelina with the slashed face – all these had only been for this one moment. Therefore she could say nothing. After sitting silent for a long while, feeling her heart fluttering and her legs cold like the dead, she said: I'll ask Mr. Sasson. Come tomorrow.

That evening she went to Mr. Sasson. She said: Mr. Sasson, light of my youth, Shmuel Abuman has come and wants to make me his wife. Meyuhas is in jail, Abram is dead, Ziona is full of hate, Angelina comes and goes, there is no one to cook for, the house is empty save for sadness, the sheets I bought you lie clean on the shelf with the shop's sadness in them, your coverlets are orphaned in the closet, what should I do, Mr. Sasson? And Mr. Sasson told her: Love of my eyes, I ought never to have been your husband. You were born to be by the sea and I was born for mountains and forests. I know that Shmuel Abuman should be your husband and sleep in the sheets and rub against the white coverlets, and she said: No, no, but he said: I know you loved me, but the demon in you loved him.

Her son with the green-gold eyes came from Jerusalem especially to put up the bridal canopy and everyone said how much he resembled Shmuel Abuman. Shmuel couldn't break the glass and succeeded only on the third attempt, and everyone wished them well. Yolanda and her husband the journalist looked conspicuously different, and everyone asked: Who is this man, for they'd seen him on television. There was a big dinner and they played and sang songs from faraway places.

Meyuhas was brought by a policeman and didn't try to escape. In a year he'd be released for good behavior. Ziona wrote that Abram was turning over in his grave from shame, but no one read Clara the letter. The rundown house remained empty, waiting for Angelina, and Clara went to Tiberias with Shmuel Abuman, to the sea. Clara wanted to die by the sea, maybe inside it. Shmuel said: Here is my home and here is yours and now they are one. Clara cooked Shmuel Abuman food he liked, they talked Ladino about things that had happened, and they liked touching each other. Sometimes Shmuel would catch a fish. In a few years the two would die together, as if they were created to be born together. People say: What a beautiful couple. Clara is radiant and her skin is smooth and its color is the shade of the water. In summer Angelina came with the two grandchildren. The water didn't ask who their father was, nor was it important. They bathed in the sea and swam and laughed. Shmuel threw pebbles that started ripples. It was a moonlit night and lights glowed beyond the Golan mountains. It was warm and young people from distant countries sang songs by the sea, around campfires. The smoke mingled with the moonlight and the radiated light from the mountains and everything merged into something awesome in its longing not to change. Shmuel Abuman went into the warm water in his clothes, and Clara undressed and swam naked. Later she laid her hand on her mouth and wailed like a mourner but in some fierce wild joy, and Shmuel Abuman saw what a wonderful and frightening demon lived inside the woman he had married, and was as excited as a child. He swallowed water and she swam and sang. Later they sat in the room opposite the little window with the blue vase and drank mint tea, and Shmuel asked: Clara, what are you thinking about, and she said: About life, and he said: What, and she said: Oh, how sweet life was, how beautiful it was, this life of mine.

Yehoshua Kenaz

The Three-Legged Chicken

Translated by Dalya Bilu

One day at the end of summer they laid the old man they called grandfather on the floor in the big room, lit candles at his head and closed the double doors on him and on the people standing around him. The last rays of sun filtered through the colored panes of glass at the tops of the windows and the veranda door to say their last farewells, staining the walls, the floor and the body with violet, green and orange lights and making the flames of the candles look very thin and pale in comparison.

When his mother emerged from the big room she stood opposite the boy and bent over him, bringing her face level with his so that she could say what she had to say to him in a very soft voice. She smiled for a moment, a strange smile that he had never seen on her face before, and he did not know if it was anxiety or malice glittering in her eyes when she said to him: our grandfather is dead, our grandfather is dead – but it was obvious to him that she knew she was hurting him for nothing, and that this was what she wanted, and in this matter there would be no concessions.

He asked when his father was coming, because he knew that at a time like this his father was bound to come and restore order and security, but there was no reply. The old man they called grandfather, who used to come every evening when the boy got into bed, to urge and beg him again and again to say: "*Shema Israel*," if only for his sake, did not come to his room that night, just as he had not come on any of the previous evenings of his brief and final illness. And knowing this, he wanted to say *"Shema Israel"* to make him happy, to repeat the words after the old man as he wished him to do and to give him love in return for his love.

All night long it seemed as if people were walking about on tiptoe in the rooms and passages of the house in the dark, seeking, secretly laboring at all kinds of tasks whose meaning there was no way of knowing. For hours the boy wracked his memory for the words of the prayer which had suddenly vanished, as if the old man had taken them with him on his journey. For hours he could not fall asleep, and no one came to the doorway to peep into his room and see how he was. All night long he waited for his father to arrive home from work and to hear his voice and know that he had someone to take care of him. Until late at night the quiet bustle continued, and when the searching and silent prowling between the rooms ended there were only the brief, businesslike whispers of people parting from each other for a while until they met again to set out on a journey together.

And when silence fell the boy heard the voice of the woodworm again, friend of the sleepless, burrowing in the depths of the old wardrobes, laboring and pausing in her labors and beginning her nibbling again, momentarily taking fright and listening to the sound of his breathing in order to ascertain that it was rhythmic and he was indeed asleep: and if not – the woodworm would stop and make an effort not to disturb him and wait until he fell asleep; but no sooner had she conquered her drive for a moment than it would reassert itself and overwhelm her with its strength. And the boy would outwit her and restrain his breath. And the worm would wonder if he had really fallen asleep and she could go ahead without anything to stop her, and she would send out tentative signals, groping in the dark. Very hesitantly she would venture an experimental nibble, nibbling and stepping, afraid of exaggerating, trying to discover how much she could dare at once without bringing down wrath and catastrophe on her head. She was so full of a sense of the significance of the deed she was destined to do, and so full of the prudence demanded by the importance of the task and the need to perform it stealthily, obsequiously, and ingenuously. And nevertheless, as soon as she plucked up courage, or simply succumbed to her drive and went back to work, she would be overcome by an urgent, panic-stricken need to cram as much as she could into one short moment, in order to make up for the time lost in the pause of the past and counteract the paralysis that would take hold of her a moment later, when her senses were alerted to the danger again. With blind enthusiasm she would plunge into her labors, the other possibility receding as she did so, and until the fear came back again she would accomplish whatever she could. And when she stopped, it was obvious that she was in the grip of terror and great remorse, and that she was playing a cunning game of deceit and make-believe: clinging tightly to her place, shrinking into herself as far as she could, and pretending to be bodiless and spaceless, a concentrated point of alertness to spy out the silence. And whenever she stopped work for longer than usual, breaking the accustomed rhythm, the boy would cover his face silently with the sheet and roll his whole body into it, very slowly, so that not the slightest sound would reach her, and he would lie motionless, barely breathing and imagining that he, too, was all closed in and wrapped up in himself, and since his eyes were closed his bed turned into one of the deepest, most hidden veins of the wood, shrouded in eternal darkness, warm and protective, and thus he and she would listen to each other in the silence, and she would always be the first to give in to the illusion of safety, send out a tentative, experimental signal, a tiny sound to test the reaction; and since nothing happened to arouse her suspicions that a trap was being set for her in the silence, and since her appetite had been whetted and her passion had blinded her to all sense of caution and danger, she would fall to work again. And sometimes she would go on for longer than usual in her enthusiasm and oblivion, and the boy would wonder how far this eagerness of hers would deafen her to the danger signals from outside. After a long moment during which she did not stop, he would cough loudly and she would fall silent immediately, and her silence would go on and on, as if it were taking her a long time to recover from her terror.

At that moment the boy remembered the big room and the old man they called grandfather, who had been left there by himself. He opened his eyes and suddenly the sounds of the night broke into his room from outside: the sound of crickets rising from the furthest reaches of the house and the yard, and the chorus of frogs gathered by the cowshed and in the garden, and the howling of the jackals in the citrus groves – all these silenced the soundless game between his breathing and the whispering of the woodworm, and with them the ample light of the moon came flooding into the room. And since he was accustomed to this pattern of sounds and its regular sequence, he did not even raise his head from the pillow to see what was happening around him. The shadow of the oil lamp standing at the end of the passage stretched like a long dark triangle from the threshold of his room to a corner of the house which was invisible from where he was lying. And he wanted to get up and see what was in the big room at this hour of night, but his body refused to respond to his will, as if it had been turned to stone.

From all the corners of the room, the dark and loathsome thing advanced on him. He opened his mouth to scream, but his lips and voice were paralyzed, and only the muscles of his throat strained to call for help or break the evil spell of the moment, but in vain. He felt that he was not dreaming, but this was how he always felt when the thing came at him out of the dark, and only in the morning, when he recalled it to his memory, would he wonder if he had been dreaming or if he had really been awake when he saw it. And only the vestiges of the scream that he had wanted to utter but couldn't remained like a painful sensation in his throat.

In the morning he would get up and look for the trickle of powder that had fallen from the wardrobe, the worm's nightly work and a concrete proof that those moments were real, and he would crumble the powder between his fingers until it disintegrated and was absorbed into his skin, and much as he wanted to derive some secret knowledge from it and its touch, all his efforts were in vain.

The quilt and mattress renovator sat on an empty crate next to one of the citrus groves and took a hard-boiled egg, about a quarter of a loaf

of black bread and a few olives and tomatoes out of the little
haversack slung over his shoulder and got ready to eat his breakfast.
The instrument he used to tease the cotton wool, which resembled a
big harp with one string, stood leaning against the fence and at its
foot a bundle of tools tied up in a coarse cloth of a blue-gray color.
There was not a soul to be seen and the only sound was the murmur
of the water in the irrigation canals coming from the citrus groves. It
was already quite late in the morning. The quilt and mattress
renovator took the egg and aimed it at the middle of his forehead.
Although there was no audience to witness his tricks, he could not
suppress the buffoonery which in the course of plying his trade had
become second nature to him. He held the egg opposite his forehead,
squinted at it with both eyes, moved it away again, with his eyes
squinting at it all the time as if in alarmed anticipation of the blow
which was about to descend at any minute, and which indeed
materialized immediately as the man smashed the egg on his forehead
and burst out laughing. He held the egg with its shattered shell in his
left hand and started removing the bits of white shell very slowly and
meticulously. When he had finished he inspected it carefully to see if
there were any bits left. His face was serious now, but his eyes hinted
to the empty sun-washed spaces in front of him that there was one
more joke in store for them: again he squinted at his nose and all at
once he dropped the whole peeled egg into his wide open mouth,
where it vanished without a trace. He looked about him as if to test
the reaction of his nonexistent audience and then slapped his cheeks
with both hands, as if to hit the egg from one side of his mouth to the
other, like a tennis ball. After this his shoulders heaved convulsively,
as if he had swallowed the whole egg. Then he spat it out into the
palm of his hand, took a few olives from the handkerchief spread out
in front of him, stuck his teeth into the quarter loaf of black bread and
started chewing with his mouth open, while at the same time
humming a cheerful tune and swaying his head from side to side in
time with the tune.

Two men appeared at the end of the road, one of them carrying a
suitcase and the other a kind of square box covered with a sack, and

began advancing towards the quilt and mattress renovator. When they reached the place where he was sitting they stopped and exchanged a few words with him. Then they consulted with each other, put the suitcase and the sack-covered box down on the ground, sat down next to the man, and began to roll themselves cigarettes. They rolled one for him too. The three of them smoked peacefully in almost total silence.

The two men lay back on the ground, rested their heads on their hands and closed their eyes. The quilt and mattress renovator kept darting glances at the sack-covered box and an ugly smile appeared on his face, as if he had remembered an obscene joke. Then he looked at the two sleeping men and his face suddenly fell. He stared at the fields and citrus groves and his eyes scanned the dirt road beside which he was sitting, which twisted and turned and receded into the distance until it disappeared around a corner next to the horizon. He remembered to cast a glance from time to time at his one-stringed harp and his bundle of tools, but he would immediately turn his head away and start staring into space again, and there was a great sadness in his eyes. He too would have liked to lie back like them and take a nap, but since he had promised them to look after their things until they had recovered their strength he did not stir from his place, nor did he dare to hum his songs for fear of disturbing their sleep.

When the two men rose after a little while he asked them to take him with them, and they laughed at him. They pointed at his tools and he promised that he would sell them and give the proceeds to the men, or even abandon them where they lay and follow the men with no more ado. He took their hands and begged them, saying that he would do anything for them if only they would let him join them. They laughed. They straightened their clothes. One of them picked up the suitcase and the other the box covered with the sack, and the quilt and mattress renovator called out to them. They set out. He leapt up and ran after them.

They did not turn their heads and he walked along behind them. Until the man with the suitcase picked up a stone and threatened to throw it at him; but still he was not deterred. And seeing that the man was still following them and that he was already far away from the citrus grove and the fence where he had left his tools lying, they stopped and turned to face him. The man with the suitcase picked up a stone again and this time he threw it with all his strength at the quilt and mattress renovator and hit his leg. He jumped into the air as if he had been bitten by a snake and then stood rooted to the spot again. They continued on their way without turning their heads again, and he yelled curses and entreaties and abuse after them. Until they disappeared from view and he returned unwillingly to the place where he had left his tools. He sat down on the crate and began humming his songs and staring into space again.

In the morning they sent a cart to the ice factory to fetch ice and the boy did not know what they wanted the ice for. His uncle, his mother's brother, stood in the back yard facing the cowshed, and he looked at him for a long time without saying a word. The sound of the Arab playing his fiddle drifted out of the dark doorway together with the smell of the cows and their fodder. No one had told the Arab to stop playing his fiddle. His uncle called the boy to him softly, gave him a few coins and told him to go to the little market to buy the newspapers. They wanted to see how the funeral notices had been printed. And the boy really wanted to stay and wait for his father to come, and to see when the cart came and what they would do with the ice and if they would leave any of it unguarded. But the people who up to that day had belonged to him were now busy with their own affairs. And also the old man they called grandfather who, during the boy's illness, had prowled restlessly around his bed, sighing bitterly and bringing him glasses of lukewarm water sweetened with sugar to sweeten the pill of his sickness a little, and saying indulgent things to him in a broken voice with his peculiar accent, and stroking his forehead with a heavy, hesitant hand – he too had joined the conspiracy and lay motionless on the floor in the big room with candles burning at his head, waiting for the blocks of ice they had sent the cart to bring for him for a purpose the boy could not fathom.

His father was working then in one of the army camps near Haifa and came only for Saturdays. On Friday evenings the boy would go and stand in the street long before the time his mother told him to, waiting to see the figure of his father appearing in the distance and coming toward him from the top of the road, to examine his face and his body and touch his clothes that had come from far away and get to know him anew all over again and wait for him to throw him into the air and hug him. His father had not yet come but he knew that he would come, even though it wasn't Friday evening.

He put the money in his trouser pocket and went to put on his sandals.

That morning they brought Bruria home for the summer vacation from school, which was far away from the town. Her mother and father got up early in the morning so that they would have time to bring her back and take her home before too many people saw her. When the bus arrived Bruria refused to get off until her parents promised to buy her new shoes. She was wearing lace-up boots and her parents tried to persuade her that these boots were healthier for her feet and prevented them from getting tired. But Bruria stamped her feet and said that she would not budge from her place in the bus until they promised to buy her the most modern high-heeled shoes, in Tel Aviv, nowhere but Tel Aviv would do. All the way from the bus station to their house next to the little market they kept her quiet with arguments and promises: Who ever buys new shoes just like that on an ordinary day in the middle of the year? On Passover Eve we'll buy you new shoes. And anyway the ones you've got on are still new, they look as if they've just come from the shop. When's Passover Eve? asked Bruria. It'll be here soon. In a little while. After these holidays? asked Bruria. Yes, said her father. After the winter? Yes, said her father. Bruria reflected for a moment and her father said: But only if you're good and do what you're told and listen to your mother and don't talk to people.

Passover Eve, said Bruria, Passover Eve, Passover Eve. After the summer and after the winter. In a little while. Soon. And in Tel Aviv, in the most modern shop? And thus she gave in to them and went home with them, dreaming about her new shoes. But as soon as they got there she forgot all about their promises and sat down on the sofa and scowled angrily at her big boots. What's gotten into your head about your shoes? Did somebody at school say something about them? asked her mother. But Bruria did not reply, only stamped her feet in hatred and humiliation and then fell furiously upon her boots, quickly undoing the laces and taking them off and hurling them into a corner of the room. Afterward she took her socks off too and sat barefoot. Her father said to her: If you don't behave yourself we'll take you back to school and we won't buy you new shoes on Passover Eve or ever in all your life.

When the boy went into the street there was still no sign of the cart returning from the ice factory. He saw Molcho sitting next to the notice board and whispering something to himself, as if he were hatching some evil. Molcho was hostile to the boy because of some forgotten quarrel, or perhaps there had never been a quarrel at all and the boy had simply walked past his house on the street of the Sephardim and Molcho had tried to hit him. And when he saw him coming Molcho stood up and started shaking the dust from his trousers. He gave the boy a hard look and his lips were parted in a challenging smile. The boy started walking without looking at him. But he imagined he could hear Molcho's bare feet padding behind him like some wild cat, and he knew that the moment he heard them quicken he would run away as fast as he could. But as long as he kept on padding softly behind him he wouldn't anger him by sudden flight. He concentrated all his senses on listening and on the effort to check the flight begging to break out in his feet and keep them on the alert so as not to miss the moment when it would become necessary to bound forward and run. For a moment it seemed to him that he no longer heard the bare feet padding behind him but he was afraid to turn his head and look. Until he gathered up his courage and looked and saw Molcho standing a few steps behind him, beckoning him to approach. But the boy did not budge. Come on, I won't hit you, said Molcho. The boy approached. Your grandfather's dead, said Molcho. It's not true, said the boy. Who said so? I'll hit you if you lie, said Molcho.

And the boy said nothing. They've brought Bruria home for the holidays, said Molcho. I saw her. He looked for a moment at the windows of the house, and since there was nothing to see he turned his back on the boy and walked away. The boy let him go, and when he was about to turn into the little market to buy the newspapers he heard her voice calling him from the window: Little boy, little boy, come here for a minute.

He went into the yard and stood facing the window. He saw her face, the face of a pretty child, pale, dark-eyed, and her hair which was already full of gray streaks. Don't be frightened, little boy. You can come into the house, my mother and father have gone out and I'm alone, said Bruria. But he stayed where he was and went on looking at her face. In the window frame she looked like a figure in a portrait, from the waist up. She leaned with her elbows on the sill, one hand dangling and tapping the wall and the other patting her hair into place. On Passover Eve they're going to buy me new shoes, in Tel Aviv, the most modern shoes there are! With high heels. She fell silent for a moment and closed her eyes. There was a triumphant smile on her pale, pretty face. At night I'll dance with all the boys! I'll be the belle of the ball! And I'll dance with the boys all night long!

Opposite the big faucet next to the cowshed, in the back yard of my house, a long time before all the times I have ever known, I experienced something like an awakening from a dream into a new dream. I always spent a lot of time sitting opposite the big tap and playing with it, because the handle of the tap had been removed to stop it from dripping, and also perhaps to prevent me from opening it and playing with the water as I loved to do. But I kept plugging away and never gave up trying to open it with stones and bits of wire, nails, and even my teeth.

Until I resigned myself at last and passed my fingers over the thick, cold pipe, seeking something to take hold of, some secret catch which would make everything work like magic. The cowshed with the two steps at its door and the dim light inside it always looked blurred, and the Arab sat inside it playing his fiddle.

And as I sat stroking the stem of the tap a great and mysterious spirit passed over me, over me and the world around me: before my eyes, the wall of the cowshed and the two steps took on their final, definitive form, and the strains of the Arab's fiddle emerging from the doorway sounded as if they were coming from the bowels of the earth. The earth steaming with a pleasant warmth and the dusty sky and the wooden fence and the trough, the little back shed next to the urinal and the smell of the cows, the sourness of the sacks of fodder and the flock of birds suddenly startled into flight from the roof of the cowshed, shooting like an arrow of little black dashes to the tops of the trees and from there to the limits of the horizon – the more fixed and formed and self-sufficient they became the further they receded from me, shrouded in strangeness and perhaps even hostility. At the same time – from unknown depths inside me – there rose a voice, and the voice said: I, I, I, I. And although the voice came from inside me it wasn't my voice. The voice was quiet, solemn, redeeming and very dangerous; it stiffened my hand on the chilly metal of the big tap which had become rounder and more slippery, trying to shake my fingers off and put an end to all my games. And the voice filled me with dread and a joy whose cause I could not tell, but I felt that it was greater than I was. Out of the twilight silence the voice spoke to me and I looked around me, tried to rise to my feet but could not, like at night in my bed when the dark, loathsome thing came at me from all the corners of the room. The vividness of the shapes awakening to a life of their own before my eyes and the painful and liberating current flowing through me, strong and silent, coming from an unknown source and spreading through all my limbs, brought the scent of the greatest of all possible adventures before me. And the voice rising from the depths of my being pushed onto my lips the words, which slipped out as silently as if it were not I saying them but a stranger sitting inside me, calling without stopping in great astonishment: I, I, I, I.

A heavy load descended on my shoulders and squatted there, like an uninvited guest with the right to stay forever.

My hand fell from the snub-nosed tap and the Arab went on playing his fiddle inside the cowshed. The sound of the Arab's fiddle with its thin notes dragging out endlessly like the voice of some strange beast, heartbreaking in its sobbing, moaning its longings for other places, told me that from now on every step I took, everything I did and everything I touched would be a secret known only to me and never to be revealed to anyone else in the world. For my hands had touched the last wall of all – behind which there was nothing.

A hidden hand dragged Bruria away from the window and her cries rose from inside the house: Handsome boys and girls in party dresses are dancing together all night long, and I'm going to dance with them too!

And then the boy heard the sound of blows and Bruria screaming. Her old father came out onto the porch and approached the boy: What are you doing here, he asked, with your grandfather dead?!

She called me, said the boy.

Go home, said her father.

And he stood on the porch waiting for the boy to go. The sound of Bruria's shrieks rose from the house and her mother drew the blind and shut the window where Bruria had been standing before, as if she were in a picture.

When he went into the street the boy saw the little market in front of him and a crowd of people outside Yardeni's café. He approached the people and they told him that the three-legged chicken was on display inside the café. Two men, they said, had obtained the chicken on loan from its owners, who had brought it from abroad, and there was nothing like it anywhere in the world. The two of them were passing through the town on their way and they had agreed to stop for a few hours to put the monster on display. The next day they would leave for a tour of the surrounding towns and then they would take their show overseas. The sound of laughter rose from Yardeni's little café, which was packed with people. Strange, obscene cries were heard from the interior. The entrance fee, explained the people standing outside, was divided equally between the owner of the chicken, the two men traveling around with it, and Yardeni, who had made his café available for the show. The faces of the people emerging from the café after the five minutes covered by the entrance fee were exhausted with laughter and astonishment. The boy drew nearer the doorway, pushing his way through the crowd of curiosity-seekers and people waiting in line to pay the entrance fee. Suddenly he felt a hand on his shoulder and Molcho's face was very close to his, steaming with heat and smelling of sweat.

You want me to look after you? I'll look after you forever, just as if you were my brother.

And Molcho did not cease clutching his shoulder.

A chicken, with three legs, said Molcho. It talks and dances and pulls faces.

The boy put his hands in his pockets and felt the coins; he knew that he would not buy the newspapers which he had been sent to fetch, and that he would never again see the face of the old man lying on the floor of the big room, and the cart they had sent to the ice factory, and a great anxiety swept through him and drew his heart toward unknown things. He stretched out his hand to Molcho's shoulder and clasped it in great fear.

You can come and swing on the swing in our yard whenever you like, with my brother. He gave him the coins he had taken out of his pocket.

I'll look after you for always, said Molcho, even more than my brother.

The monster stood inside its little cage made of flimsy wooden slats, which had been placed on top of a high box. There was a handful of grain in the corner of the cage but she did not touch it. She kept rolling her eyes around and swiveling her head from side to side so as not to miss anything that was going on around her. And she would hop on her two healthy legs and jump backwards, as if she was trying to escape from the danger surrounding her on all sides, and her extra leg, her sick leg, stuck out behind her, defiant and provocative. Yardeni stood next to the cage guarding it against the blows of the people who were trying to tease the chicken and elicit grotesque and surprising reactions from her. A certain cart driver, a very heavy man who always wore a sweaty cap on his head, kept cupping his hands round his mouth like a trumpet and imitating a cock's crow in order to awaken her longings for a male, and every movement she made would then be interpreted as a response to this simulated mating call, seductive and very obscene, giving rise to loud guffaws of laughter. The two men who had brought the chicken sat at a table next to the door and took the entrance fees. And every now and then Yardeni glanced in their direction to make sure that they weren't putting any of the money into their pockets before giving him his share.

The drunkard sat at his usual table in the corner untouched by all the commotion. He was in a quiet, very thoughtful mood. And only when a very loud burst of laughter rose from the crowd around the cage, in reaction to one of the spectators' comments or one of the monster's movements, the drunk would raise his eyes, shake his head dismissively, and whisper: Vanity of vanities, vanity of vanities.

There was a bad smell in the crowded café, and the boy did not connect it with the congestion and the sweat but with the presence of the chicken, and especially her third leg, infected with some disease from foreign parts. Molcho stood next to him opposite the cage and stared at the spectacle, fascinated and perhaps a little frightened too. The boy knew that his father would not have come to stand among these people and stare at a chicken with three legs, and he missed him very much. And although no one had ever condemned such spectacles to him, he knew that they were wrong. The anxiety that had been in him before he entered the café and had drawn him to the spectacle and the company of these people and the friendship of Molcho now brought ominous pictures before his eyes. Every now and then the corners of Molcho's lips twitched in a smile, as if he were seeing things in a dream. And the boy pretended to be very amused and tried to look closely at the chicken, who was hopping from side to side of her little cage, as if she were fighting some hidden enemy, and he was ashamed of his ignorance of the secret which would have enabled him too to enjoy and admire the spectacle. He waited impatiently for the time he had paid for to be up so that he could leave. During those moments he felt such a sense of desolation that he thought it would never leave him.

The sound of a quarrel broke out at the entrance to the café, where the quilt and mattress renovator could be seen trying to force his way in past the two men sitting by the money box, who were pushing him back and hitting him. Yardeni looked anxiously at the door, wondering whether to leave his post by the cage and to go investigate the reasons for the fight and restore order, or to let it alone and guard the chicken.

The quilt and mattress renovator shouted something from the doorway to the people inside the café, and the people asked one another: What's he shouting there, what does he want? With carpenter's glue, he says, they stuck the leg on with carpenter's glue.

The alarmed Yardeni was driven to take a few steps forward again in order to have a few words with the two men, but before he could reach the doorway he had to return to his post by the cage to guard it and restore order in the café where the outcry was growing louder by the minute; and there was no knowing if the outcry was due to excitement and high spirits or to indignation at the fraud, or whether the people's frenzy was simply seeking a pretext for erupting after it had been inflamed by the sight of the freakish, contemptible chicken; in any case, the heavy cart driver with the sweaty cap brushed Yardeni out of his way, lifted the cage into the air with both his hands, hit the flimsy wooden slats with his fist and shattered it with a couple of blows. He removed the chicken, brushed aside her tail, and inspected her third leg. All the people crowded round and the chicken flapped her wings and squawked in pain as the cart driver attempted to tear the third leg out of her flesh. Again and again he tried to part the leg from the flesh of her body, pulling harder and harder as Yardeni entreated him: Have pity on dumb animals!

And suddenly they all saw the leg lying on the palm of the cart driver's hand and drops of blood falling from the chicken's white feathers. The people in the café burst into angry cries and laughter and they all rushed to the doorway to see the two men in all their guilt. But their places next to the table were empty, and the money box was gone too.

The cart driver dropped the chicken and threw the third leg in disgust at Yardeni, who recoiled in horror. Although drops of blood were still falling from underneath her tail, the chicken ran frantically about the cafe looking for the door, but she could not find it for the people filled the room and hid the light from her.

And when she bumped into the legs of the people who recoiled from her in disgust, because they had not forgotten her third leg, she flapped her wings and tried to fly away as if she were a bird. Only the drunk, who was in a very quiet and thoughtful mood all this time, smiled at the panic-stricken chicken, held up an admonitory finger, and repeated: Vanity of vanities, vanity of vanities.

They stuck it on with glue, with glue, said Yardeni and clapped his hands despairingly, remembering the two men who had escaped with the money and left him with the chicken and the uproar in his café. The crowd began to leave. When they were outside Molcho said to the boy: You want to come and swing now or some other time? Some other time, said the boy. What a chicken, sighed Molcho, remembering with emotion the impact of the experience. They stuck it on with glue, with glue. It's a shame my brother didn't see it. And once again he stretched out his hand to clasp the boy's shoulder as a gesture of friendship. But the boy evaded him. Molcho went on his way without another word, and the boy knew that next time he encountered him Molcho would try to hit him again, as he always did, but he no longer cared.

When the boy reached home he stood outside the gate for a minute looking at the windows. Then he climbed the steps and the front door was locked. No one answered his knocking. He walked around the house and everything was shut up tight. He went into the back yard and saw the Arab sitting on the steps of the cowshed, without his fiddle, his head on his hands and his eyes staring vacantly.

In the afternoon Bruria's parents left the house and walked with her to the bus station. Bruria was quiet all the way, but when she saw the bus she shrank back and promised that she would be good. But her parents paid no attention to her promises. She wept silently and her mother too wiped a tear from her eye. But her father said: Let this be a lesson to you for next time, let this be a lesson to you.

I don't want the shoes anymore, said Bruria, I'm sorry. They got on the bus and Bruria covered her face with her hands and cried without stopping. Her mother, who sat beside her, embraced her and put her head on her shoulder, and her father, who sat in front of them, pretended not to know them.

The boy circled the house again, to see if anyone had come back in the meantime, but the doors and windows were all shut, and there was no one to be seen. He returned to the back yard and sat down opposite the big tap. He held the stem and wondered if the same thing that had happened before would happen again, but everything stayed the same and the afternoon hours stretched out endlessly.

In one of the deserted fields behind the citrus groves, outside the town, the quilt and mattress renovator lay on the ground with his eyes open, staring at the sky. A column of ants crawled over his arm and climbed up to his neck and down to the ground again, as if he too was part of the earth, a hump on its back.

It was a dreary summer afternoon and everything was empty and too quiet. The Arab rose lazily to his feet and went into the cowshed and started raking the manure into the gutters and from the gutters outside. The raking sounded like a scratching in the heart of the darkness. A slow drag of the rake, then a short silence, then a drag of the rake, then silence again. The boy looked around him and waited for the thing to happen again, and he was seized with rage at the indifferent touch of the big tap, and affronted at being left alone. He said softly: I, I, I, I – and the magic did not work.

And suddenly his body was lifted sky-high in a familiar, well-beloved movement, and immediately he felt his father's face, with its prickly stubble against his cheek. And the boy could find nothing to say to his father for shame filled him with a kind of fog. But he was afraid that his eyes would fill with tears and betray him if he did not open his mouth and say something, and so he whispered into his ear: Our grandfather is dead, our grandfather is dead. And his father hugged him and said nothing in reply, but carried him to the house and put him down next to the door and took him by the hand. Together they entered the house and his father led him into the big room and there was a secret smile on his face. They went into the big room and the boy looked around him and saw that nothing had changed and the room was the same as always. As if no one had ever lain there on the floor, and there had never been candles or anything. And the colors of the windowpanes as always cast purple, green and orange stains on the walls and tiles. And the boy did not understand what was before his eyes or the contradictions rising in his memory. He looked questioningly at his father, and then again at the room, and afterward he smiled at his father as if to ask: Did it really happen? And his father smiled back at him as if to say: Indeed it did.

Yeshayahu Koren

Barazani

Translated by Dalya Bilu

It was the third time we were going into Lebanon, and I wanted to go to the collection point with Barazani. I arrived at his metal shop and pushed open the door. A clot of dust blocked my nose. A sharp whisper cut the air: the notice hanging on the door had torn. The shop was quiet, but muffled voices came from the far end of the room.

I sat down on an inverted crate and waited. I didn't like going into the back, into the storeroom, alone. Barazani had only taken me in there once. There were various coins arranged on the shelves of an old glass-fronted cupboard. From the Bar-Kochba period, from some town in Germany or Italy where they had once used Jewish money, from Persia, Iraq, from the British Mandate, and coins dating from the first years of the state.

Next to me there was a low table. It was covered with a sheet of cracked glass, underneath which were notes, newspaper cuttings, and dusty pictures of soccer players. On top of the glass used and new football pool forms lay scattered, some of which had various calculations scribbled over them in pencil. On the corner of the table stood a pile of old records with a half-full cup of coffee on top of it. There was no steam rising from the coffee. Yonah Barazani, as usual, had forgotten to finish it. Torn, oily rags and dirty, sweat-soaked clothes were strewn over the floor. I was thirsty. But Barazani emerged from the storeroom and said: "Let's go. The car's outside."

"What do we need the car for?" I said. "Everyone's waiting in the municipal park, it's less than a five-minute walk from here."

"I've decided to take the Volvo," said Barazani. "Like in the good old days."

"You're crazy," I put my suitcase down on the floor. "Lebanon's not the good old days, when you could drive to maneuvers, or even to the front line, in your car. No one'll let you in."

"Bullshit. Last time I found a way."

"Look here, Barazani," I said quietly, "I'm telling you you can't do it, and don't forget I'm your platoon sergeant."

"Don't give me that crap. If we only did what we were told, where would we be today?"

"I'm not joking. We've got enough problems as it is."

"Everything's ready. I went to the stores yesterday. All our stuff's already in the boot. Come on, gimme your case and stop acting like a kid."

Barazani was the oldest soldier in the company. About forty-nine years old. A mustache, black hair, white hair. His face was brown, strong, and lined. He picked up my suitcase, turned towards the door and said: "Who the hell's gone and torn my notice now?"

It was a notice advertising the Betar Jerusalem soccer team's matches for the next few weeks. He tried to mend the tear, then he pointed at the notice and said: "I can do without the game two weeks from now. It's a weak team and there won't be any problems, even if it's an away game. But this coming Saturday – make a note of it! I'm getting leave. We're playing Hapoel Kfar Saba and we've got to get back the points we lost in the last round."

I knew that he was actually ordering me to give him leave. Barazani was a fanatical Betar fan, he contributed money to the club, brought rattles from his shop to the games, came home hoarse and voiceless after every match. The only thing he didn't believe in, he told me once, was "that business of letting doves loose. Doves don't mix with football."

"Why not?" I asked. There was a heap of old programs and blueprints, rusty screws and pipes next to the door.

"Because they don't. I get into arguments about it in the club too." He pushed the pile of rubbish out of the way with his foot, and a torn, open magazine hit my suitcase.

"You'll get leave," I said. "But now let's go to the park and get on the bus like normal human beings."

He locked the shop door, descended the stone steps to the sidewalk, opened the trunk of the car and shoved my case inside. Our weapons, which were lying there, he transferred to the back seat of the car. "Without prior conditions," he said. A police siren wailed in the main street. There was a smell of oil mixed with onions, garlic, and spices coming from the felafel stand. Yonah paused for a moment at the stand, looked at me and said: "Let's flip a coin. If you win – we won't take the car. We'll go by bus."

I knew him and his coins. He was an expert at flipping two-mil coins from the Mandate period. He knew exactly how to swoop his hand, catch the coin, and win. I took out a cigarette, lit a match, and said: "If you say so!"

He rummaged in his right pocket and asked: "Tree or Palestine?"

"Pali," I said.

He went on rummaging in his pockets, and finally produced a greenish, copper-colored coin. He spun it round in front of my eyes. His lips were pursed. He snapped his thumb and flipped the coin into the air. The coin flew up, turned over, almost hit a branch of the tree in whose shade we were standing, and began spinning down. I saw his lips tighten. His gleaming blue eyes following the progress of the coin. His back was hunched, his hand stretched out, taut. About half a meter before it reached him, Barazani swept his hand out in an arc like a reaper, waited, and clenched his hand around the coin. There was a silence. His face was tense and guarded. He straightened up. He opened his fist. Seven leaves peeped through the greenish mold covering the surface of the coin.

"Okay," said Barazani, "We're taking the car." It was tree.

A cold wind blew through the alley. We got into the Volvo. He put on the heater, the car turned into the main street and approached the collection point. "What's up?" I asked.

"Go and see if they've all shown up." The way he was always trying to run my life for me was annoying, but I couldn't be mad at him.

Two of the buses had already left. The last one was still waiting for late-comers.

"I guess everyone's here," said the company Sergeant Major. "We'll pick up a few men on the way, and in Nakura. What about you guys?"

"We'll get there in the Volvo," said Barazani.

"You'll have to leave it at Rosh Hanikra."

Barazani said nothing.

The Sergeant Major mounted the steps of the bus, counted the men again, and said: "Apart from Shlomi everyone's here."

"Shlomi'll be late," I said.

"How d'you know?"

"As usual. Problems with his girlfriend." But even before I reached the end of the sentence I saw him. He was running down the street, his pack bouncing on his back. Occasionally he stopped, looked behind him, and began running again. A brown boot, hanging by one lace, dangled from the pack.

At the bottom of the front window, over the dashboard, was an old family photograph. Barazani with fewer lines on his face. Black hair. His wife, plump, long frizzy hair, her lips thick and dark with lipstick, her face smooth and fair. Three children. The oldest, a boy of thirteen, straight blond hair falling over blue eyes. His daughter, in a red plaid dress, was hugging her little brother who was plump with a round face and curly brown hair.

Barazani looked at the picture, and the car skidded to the side of the road. The wheels bounced on a row of stones, and when they steadied on the road again, Barazani took out a cassette and inserted it in the cassette player. It was a cassette of dance music from one of the army programs. He looked at the picture again. The glass misted over and I turned on the windshield wipers for a moment. Barazani turned them off and indicated his older son in the picture. "Seventeen and a half already," he said. "In six months' time he'll be going into the army, goddammit. It's him who records these cassettes for me. And look at Shlomi. Out of the army for a year already. And don't tell me he doesn't look like a kid to you still with that hair in his eyes, always turning up in the same old pair of pants?"

"Come off it," I said to him. "Shlomi's been out a year already and he hasn't even found a job yet. Trouble with his girlfriend all the time."

"And we haven't got troubles? That's exactly the reason I like him." Barazani laughed loudly. "So what if he roots for Hapoel Kfar Saba, who took the cup away from us in '75. I'll still get him for that." He took a cigarette out of the packet tucked into the pocket of his khaki shirt.

"He doesn't remember a thing about it. He was still a kid then."

"That's just why he remembers. No kid would ever forget a game like that."

I pressed the cigarette lighter on the dashboard, took it out and checked it, and when the delicate coils turned red, I raised it to the cigarette in his mouth. Barazani inhaled deeply and coughed, and I put the lighter back in its place. "Pick up your foot," he suddenly yelled. Ash fell from the cigarette onto his trousers. Smoke blurred his face and stung my eyes. "Can't you see you're treading on my program?" It was a purple photocopy, and I picked it up and threw it onto the back seat. It fell onto weeklies, old sports magazines, an empty plastic carrier bag from a department store and an open wooden box. Inside the box, among the screws, pliers and screwdrivers, were a few beer cans, some empty and some full. Barazani leant over and picked up one of them and offered it to me. "Have a beer," he said.

We arrived at the Rosh Hanikra border post and got out to get something hot to drink at one of the stands. Trucks and command cars, tanks and M-113s were crowded into the parking lot on top of the cliff overlooking the sea. Soldiers milled around and disappeared into the narrow lanes between the many vehicles: private cars, jeeps, officers' Landrovers, and big Mercedes with green Lebanese numberplates. An MP was passing down the lanes and checking entry permits. We came back from the kiosk. The MP stopped, and when Barazani walked past him he said: "Where's your permit?"

"Hang on a minute," said Barazani. He opened the car door, rummaged around in the glove compartment, and then, after making sure that the MP wasn't looking, pulled his call-up papers out of his shirt pocket, straightened up, and held them out to him.

"That's your call-up papers. That's not what I meant. Where's your permit?" The MP leant against the car. His eyes were webbed with sleep.

"What? You mean that's not it? Our company commander told us to meet them on the Kasmiyyeh Bridge. I gotta get moving. This is the tenth time I've gone through here."

"But that's not a permit. Anyway, you know private cars aren't allowed in." The MP scratched the ginger beard fringing his face. His shirt was old and there was a pale patch on the sleeve.

"Every day you change the goddamn rules here," said Barazani. Cars were honking behind us. "This ain't the first time I've gone through here."

"Move aside," said the MP.

"How the hell am I supposed to move here?" said Barazani. Cars and buses full of soldiers were blocking our way in all directions.

"Move aside," said the MP again. He signaled to the driver of the jeep behind us.

"I want to talk to the checkpoint commander," said Barazani. The cigarette in his mouth was getting shorter, the ash was getting longer and it almost touched his lips. Barazani took another drag. The ash reddened and fell onto his trousers and his old shoes.

"It won't help you," said the ginger MP. "At the checkpoint they check again, and they won't let you through."

"Let me try," said Barazani.

"So they can say you made a fool of me?" said the MP.

In spite of the cold wind that was blowing, I thought I could see beads of sweat glittering between the lines on Barazani's forehead. He took the packet of cigarettes out of his pocket, but it was empty. He threw it away, suddenly smiled, laughed, and said: "Okay. You have to do your job. So clear the way for me at least, so's I can get out of here." He came up to me and said softly: "It won't work. We'll have to go back."

"Let's wait for our buses," I said.

"By the time those buses get here we'll go crazy. If they want us to screw them, it's their own lookout."

He went back to the kiosk for a minute to buy cigarettes, and I rummaged idly in the glove compartment. A scrap of a newspaper article, carelessly torn off the page, was stuck onto the inside of the compartment door: "A few days after the war, among the crowds of Israelis flooding Hebron was a well-known Jerusalem antique dealer. Next to the Tomb of the Patriarchs he got into a cab and asked the driver to take him to an antique shop. The cab drove through the alleys, and after a while it seemed to the Jerusalem dealer that they had left Hebron behind them and were already in the heart of the Judean desert. He panicked and asked the cab driver: Where are we going? The Hebronite looked at the elegant Jerusalem antique dealer and said: I didn't think an ordinary antique shop would interest you. I wanted to take you to the place where they make them."

Clouds accompanied the foam of the waves advancing in the sea, opposite the cliffs of Rosh Hanikra. But what with the heating and the parka and the smell of smoke filling the car I was hot. I was sweating. There was no point in getting out of the car and waiting for the buses. They always drove slowly and stopped at kiosks at all the junctions. There weren't all that many alternatives. Barazani had won after all.

He got into the car, lit another cigarette, and switched on the tape again. There was stubble on his cheeks. Lonely late-night tunes filled the car. We returned to the Northern Road intersection. And, even before we passed the fields and left them behind us, I suddenly felt homesick for those green fields, for the straight avenues of trees in the orchards, for the round, concrete reservoir sticking up on top of the hill. Near Hanita we turned off the road and drove back towards the border. The fence there was completely broken down. An occasional solitary car passed us on the road, with a train of dust accompanying it and then dying down, falling and covering the low bushes. I looked again at the photograph of Barazani's family stuck in front of us, and it too seemed to be covered with dust. In the distance, on the crest of a hill, was an Arab village whose name I didn't know. In the abandoned school to the right of the road children were driving an old car. They zigzagged jerkily between the trees and a broken basketball pole. The songs were slow. Barazani hummed something. The jolting motion put me to sleep. I dozed off.

"*La Comparsita!*" I woke up to a yell which filled the car. My feet were sweating, I stretched, yawned, and looked at Barazani. He turned his head towards me, blinked his eyes and laughed. His cheekbones stuck out, his lips were clamped shut. Again he looked at the picture in front of him and cleaned the dust off it with his finger. The cassette stopped playing. The windows were closed. The heater gave off an exhausting heat, and I too lit a cigarette.

"I like old tunes," said Barazani.

"And I don't even know them," I said. I didn't yet know then that *La Comparsita* was an old tango, from the early forties, or maybe before.

A reconnaissance jeep came speeding towards us. In the wake of the column of dust it raised came an old military ambulance. A safari command car, with helmeted soldiers sitting back to back, drove behind the ambulance. There were black and gray clouds in the sky, and a north wind beat against the windshield in dry waves.

"An ambulance means there's still hope," said Barazani.

"Where do you get that from?"

"They took Yoel away by helicopter."

"Yes," I said, "and it was too late. But there isn't always a helicopter available."

A few drops of rain fell. Heavy drops. They fell on the dust that covered the hood. Barazani mumbled something, his eyes fixed on the road, and it sounded to me as if he was yelling again: "*La Comparsita.*"

We crossed a low bridge. Barren cherry trees grew thickly on either side. Barazani bent down and pulled the M16 out from under the seat. The car swerved off the road and he stopped for a minute. A bird crashed into the front of the hood and went on flying.

Barazani put the M16 down next to him and opened the window. The bird flew over our heads and he said: "Put your Uzi on your knees."

I didn't answer, and he said: "It's no joke. Put it on your knees."

In the distance I saw the green domes of the mosques of Nabatiyeh. The Uzi was lying on the back seat, among the newspapers, the photocopies and the parcels. I turned round and pulled it towards me. When I turned my head back, the picture of Barazani's family loomed up in front of me again, with the straight blond hair of the oldest son.

"He really does look like Shlomi," I said suddenly. A dark oil stain spread over my trousers, above the knee, because of the Uzi. Barazani too looked at the picture and grinned.

A terrible stench assailed us. We were in Ansar. We passed the checkpoint on the outskirts of the village. We drove round the prison camp. But the wind kept on blowing the smell of the sewage running through the camp into our faces.

A half-track drove past us. We shut the Volvo windows and Barazani said: "Maybe we can drop in on Nabatiyeh and do a bit of shopping."

"We should stay put and start getting organized," I said.

"You've got time till they arrive. Just getting out of the bottleneck in Nakura takes hours. Look at my shoes. I have to pick up a couple of pairs here."

The camp commander, a gray-haired guy with a thin, gray mustache was walking round between the huts, and when he saw us he said: "Hi, Barazani. I see you brought the Volvo again. One day you'll get it in the neck. Hide it in the back. Behind the detention tent.

"Where's our billet?" asked Barazani.

"Over there, at the end of the camp. In the precast blocks."

"Blocks, shmocks. Is there anything hot to drink?" said Barazani. We drove there. Barazani walked around between the precast huts and in the end he stopped next to the one before the last. "We'll take this one. It's at the end and not at the end. And we can park the car between these two shmocks." He got into the car, parked it, and opened the trunk.

The buses arrived.

Shlomi got out first and ran towards Barazani's car. As soon as he reached me, he said: "I have to get leave on Saturday." He was panting. His eyes were red. His hair was wild and covered with a thin veil of dust. The M16 was hanging carelessly from his shoulder. He was holding a newspaper in his hand.

"Hold your horses," I said. "We're not organized yet, we haven't moved into our rooms, we haven't done anything. And you're already talking about leave."

"I'll do whatever you say. But I've got to get leave on Saturday," said Shlomi. His face was shrunken and his hair ravaged by the wind.

"What's wrong?" I asked. But he was silent. When we were in Lebanon the first time, too, he had asked for leave. Then he had a story about problems with his girlfriend, and it was true. She was in France at the time, and it really was a problem.

"Is she back?"

"Long ago. And I have to get leave. Believe me."

"I heard you," I said. "But you're not the only one. We'll take you into account."

He wanted to go back to the bus, to get his pack, but everyone got off at once, pushing and shoving, and he stood to one side, next to the pile of gear they were beginning to unload from the top of the bus. The wind ruffled his newspaper. He tried to fold the pages but they creased and one of them tore. Packs were thrown down anyhow on the ground. Someone asked in a yell if they couldn't put them down properly so they wouldn't get dirty in the mud, but nobody paid any attention to him. Only Shlomi went up to him, took a cigarette from him, succeeded in lighting it with the third match, and removed it from his mouth. He held the cigarette with his two fingers as if it was the first cigarette he had ever smoked in his life.

Barazani got organized in the room. He found an old ammunition box and stood it next to his bed. Then he took a tattered notebook out of his pocket and began making various calculations about the coming Saturday's football games.

"Filling in the football pools?" I asked.

"It's got nothing to do with the pools," he said. "The pools is a different system altogether."

Afterwards we cleaned our weapons and in the evening we went on our first patrol. When we drove through Nabatiyeh, Barazani said again that he wanted to buy shoes.

"You're out of line," I said.

"What's wrong?"

"How can you go out on patrol in civilian shoes? You should have worn boots."

"Boots don't fit my feet," he said. The shoes he was wearing were scuffed and shabby, and the uppers were coming apart from the soles. Tiny thorns were sticking to his socks and the hems of his pants.

The next morning we sent details to man the checkpoints and the rest of the men were allowed to sleep till noon. Barazani woke up early and drove to Nabatiyeh to buy shoes for the children and himself, and slippers for his wife. In the distance, on the roofs of the houses, I saw black flags and big pictures of some Imam of theirs who had disappeared in Libya, and I remembered the way they had whipped themselves in the streets the year before.

"It's some holy day of theirs," I said to Barazani. "You shouldn't have gone there."

"Look," he said. "As long as they're selling, I'm buying. The shoes are comfortable and they're cheap too." Shlomi also got out of the Volvo. He was carrying a blouse embroidered in red, green, and white.

"He needs leave on Saturday too," said Barazani.

"He told me. But there's no end to it. Anyway, this time I think they're going to do it by company. Is anything wrong?"

"You mean you don't know?" said Barazani. Shlomi went into the room, and Barazani and I stood next to the Volvo.

"What can already be wrong with her?"

"Let's not talk about it."

A command car carrying prisoners with wispy beards drove past on the red, muddy dirt road in front of the camp. Planes flew overhead. A little rain fell, but the wind kept blowing, and the stink from the sewage canal of the prison camp reached us in waves.

In the night the Sergeant Major arrived and asked us to evacuate the room. They wanted to set up the company commander's office in it. Barazani refused, but suddenly he started laughing and blurted out: "Tree or Palestine?" "Pali," said the Sergeant Major and sat down on the yellow ammunition box next to Barzani's bed. Barazani took a coin out of his pocket, flipped it high in the air, crouched down, reached out his hand, and when the coin approached his chest I saw his tense face and I knew that the Sergeant Major had lost. Barazani caught the coin, opened his fist and said: "Tree! You've had it!"

The Sergeant Major stood up and leant against the door frame, his lips twisted, and Barazani said: "Never mind. You lost, but we'll do you a favor and get out anyway. The CO's the CO whichever way you look at it." The Sergeant Major was silent, and a soldier arrived at a run and said: "The deputy CO said it's okay. They've found a better place."

In the evening Shlomi went off to phone, and his unintelligible shouts reached the big Indian tent which served as a mess hall and bordered the operations tent. I was playing cards. Barazani was drinking coffee and working out his calculations about the soccer matches on Saturday. He wrote things down on the margins of a newspaper and glanced occasionally at his tattered notebook. Afterwards he stood up and walked around with the coffee cup in his hand. Then he returned to the table and said: "There's nothing for it, they need my voice there on Saturday. I have to get leave."

A command car drove past on the road. There was the sound of an explosion in the distance. Nobody moved. Only the soldier on guard at the entrance to the camp lowered his gun from his shoulder. The big oil stain on my pants was caked with dust.

On Thursday, by the time the patrol force set out, and the two checkpoint details took over from the previous shifts at the camp intersection and the exit from Nabatiyeh, it was already 10 p.m. The generator hummed. No one had gone to sleep yet.

We sat in the Indian tent. The Sergeant Major, the cook and the CO's driver were playing cards, and the Sergeant Major asked me if I wanted to take a hand. "In a minute," I said. Two young soldiers were sitting next to a dangling naked bulb, drinking beer, reading parts of yesterday's newspaper, and arguing. "The place for history lessons is the university, not here," a tall soldier said to them. His hands were stuck in an oil-stained parka. He stood at the entrance to the tent, looking at the black orange grove covering the opposite hill. Then he turned round, took a letter out of his pocket and gave it to Barazani.

Barazani was sitting on a long wooden bench. He already had a bunch of letters and football pool forms he had been asked to deliver in Israel in his hands. Only three people had been given leave, and Barazani, in view of his veteran status in the unit, had been granted a special pass as an exception. He had promised to bring back special stands for the checkpoint machine guns from his shop, so that they wouldn't just sit there on the ground but would be ready for firing. The old-timers remembered that in the Six-Day War, during the alert before the war broke out, Barazani had organized similar stands for the company machine guns on the command cars. "Convenient for sitting, observing, and for reacting efficiently," said the CO, justifying the pass to himself. "All for some lousy soccer game," I said to myself, and saw the tattered notebook sticking out of Barazani's pocket.

Shlomi sat down opposite me. He didn't touch the coffee in front of him, and he tried to persuade me that he had to go on leave. I said that I didn't have anything against him going, but it had already been decided that he wasn't going. "Think about the guys who've got families," I said.

"They've got families," he said quietly. "Right."

I didn't know what to say to him. "Speak to Barazani," I said.

"Barazani's not part of the quota," shouted the Sergeant Major, raising his cards to his eyes, "he's an exception."

"So what," I said. "You can substitute one exception for another."

"Impossible. That would mean four men going on leave."

"Barazani's not a human being as far as you're concerned?"

"The CO wants you," the company clerk arrived and said to the Sergeant Major.

"What's up?"

"We have to bring the inventory up to date."

"So bring it up to date, dammit. Can't you do anything without me?" But he shuffled the cards in his hands together, slammed them down on the table and left the tent.

Barazani shoved the letters and football forms into the pocket of his parka, stood up and went over to Shlomi, and said to him: "You want to go instead of me?"

"No," said Shlomi. "I don't want anyone to give up their leave for me."

"It was decided that only three men are going," I said. "You can go next week." I kept quiet for a minute and then added: "Go call her and get it over with."

"I call her all the time," said Shlomi, "I can't talk to her on the phone."

"It was decided that only three men are going," the tall soldier repeated, "and that's why only four are going."

"You'll go next week," I repeated to Shlomi.

He kept quiet and then blurted out: "Next week's too late."

"Goddammit," I said, "You've only just been discharged. Have you forgotten already what being in the army means?"

"I haven't forgotten. In the army I'd have gone AWOL. Here on reserves with all these old men I wouldn't feel right."

"I'll talk to the Sergeant Major again," I said.

I went over to the operations tent. The Sergeant Major was busy fixing the inventory and bringing it up to date. I could never understand what was so difficult about adding up the number of soldiers in the unit and getting one clear result. The clerk copied the lists, the Sergeant Major corrected them, erased, added on, changed the order, and then the clerk copied them out again. By platoons, by units, by the alphabet, by rank. And whenever he was asked how many men there were in the company, as of now, the Sergeant Major would reply: "About 79, 1 still have to check."

"Get off my back," he said when I mentioned Shlomi.

"He's a kid."

"So let him have his candy first," I said, "and then he can wait until his turn comes round again."

"From your platoon Barazani's going. It's your headache. I don't give a shit who goes. Just let me know so's I can bring the inventory up to date."

I went back to the mess tent. Barazani was roaming round between the tables. The wind blew through the tent flaps and covered his suitcase with pale dust. Shlomi stood next to the pole supporting the tent corner and his head rubbed against the canvas. The two soldiers who were reading the newspaper were still arguing: "We should never have moved in here in the first place."

"What difference does it make? Now we're in up to our necks. Even if we withdraw."

"What's that supposed to mean?"

"It's not supposed to mean anything. But that's the way it is."

I didn't want to talk to Barazani, but when I sat down he came up to me.

"What're we going to do about Shlomi?" I said.

"Let him go. What difference does it make? Who cares?"

"I can't. It's not just ongoing operations. There's an alert on too. They say we're gonna stick it to them good and proper tomorrow night."

"As long as we don't stick it in too far. Afterwards we'll have a hard time getting it out again."

"They say it'll be the last push."

"Every day they say something different."

"I dunno, but it looks like they need everyone. To stop up all the gaps."

Barazani said nothing. He had a folded, creased sports magazine in his hand. He tore a little strip of paper from the margins. "Nothing'll come of it," he said. "Don't you know them by now? They've always got some reason." He bent over his suitcase and tucked the magazine under the handle.

A cloud of dust rose from the corner of the tent. Shlomi approached me and said in an undertone: "Did he say something to you?"

"Enough!" I yelled. "You can't go. Only if somebody else lets you go instead of him. Forget it."

There was a noise of M-113 engines outside. The patrol was back. "The checkpoints'll have to be relieved soon," I thought. A strong wind beat at the tent flaps. It was cold and dry. The Sergeant Major returned and resumed his place at the card table. The tall soldier yelled into the telephone. Shlomi stood at the entrance to the tent, huddled into his parka.

"To hell with it," said Barazani suddenly. "It's him or me, right?"

"It doesn't have to be," I said.

"So let's flip a coin." He stood up, suddenly laughed, and said: "Let them manage without me." Then he turned to Shlomi standing at the entrance to the tent. "Keep smiling, Shlomi," he said in English, "and don't take everything to heart. So what side do you want: tree or Palestine?"

"Pali."

"Damn," said Barazani. He rummaged in his trouser pockets and in the end came up with his old coin. A two-mil coin from the British Mandate.

Everyone was watching and gradually they got up and drew closer. Even the card players laid their cards face down on the table and got up to join the circle. I knew what the outcome would be, but I kept quiet. The Sergeant Major touched Shlomi's shoulder and said: "Why should he flip the coin? You do it." But Shlomi pushed his hands into his parka pockets and he didn't say a word.

Barazani's eyes darted round anxiously. He looked from side to side, wiped the spit from the corner of his mouth, and moved the coin around inside his fist.

"He's cheating," called someone. But Barazani had already flipped the coin high into the air with his thumb. I knew what was going to happen, and probably the old-timers who knew Barazani did too. I saw his tense face when he crouched, his hand on a split-second alert next to his knees.

Shlomi stood outside the circle. The coin fell, and when it was parallel with Barazani's chest, but before it could touch him, he reached out and snatched it. His head thrust forward, his eyes darting round his audience. He turned around, and when he saw Shlomi he opened his fist in a flash, and said: "Pali, goddammit, you've got leave."

There was a noise in the tent. In the distance a few bursts of fire were heard. Flames spread over one of the hills. Shlomi laughed, grinned, and ran to the phone. "Hello, hello," he yelled, and I heard him say, or maybe sing: "I just called to say I love you, I just called to say how much I care." But when he put the receiver down he went back to the tent pole and fine clouds of dust rose from his footsteps. Barazani went up to him and gave him the bunch of letters and football forms that were in his pocket. Shlomi smoked a cigarette. Somebody else was whistling the tune now.

On Friday, at 4 a.m., they drove off.

Barazani got onto the half-track setting out on morning patrol. He was wearing the new shoes he had bought in Nabatiyeh. The other pairs he had left on the shelf in the room, lined up according to size.

He was standing behind the company machine gun, broad, sturdy, unshaven, his eyes burning in the wind, with the old balaclava he dragged with him from reserve duty to reserve duty covering his head and forehead. It was cold, and the men were all huddled in the faded parkas that were handed down from intake to intake and were full of oil stains.

They drove out of the gate of the camp, and before returning to the room I went back into the mess tent. My lips were dry from the wind, and I needed something hot to drink. There was a jug of tea standing on one of the tables, and I took a few sips. Next to the tent pole I saw Shlomi's pack. There was a gray sweater tied to the buckles. Inside the folded sweater was a packet with the letters and football forms peeping out of it. I looked around, but the tent was empty.

I went back to the room. I couldn't close the shutter. The wind beat against it and the hinges creaked. I didn't fall asleep and at about 6 a.m. I went outside. A soldier came running out of the operations tent. I went inside and heard over the radio that a grenade had been thrown at a half-track, shots were fired and there were casualties.

The Sergeant Major called the doctor. The ops officer ordered a helicopter to evacuate the wounded. We drove to the scene. Barazani lay on the hood of the half-track without moving. The doctor said there was no pulse and that he had been killed on the spot.

The medic took care of him. He straightened his legs and laid his arms along the sides of his body. He opened Barazani's clenched fist.

A coin rolled out of it onto the hood and fell on the destroyed road surface. I bent down, picked up the coin, tossed it from hand to hand, and when they let off a smoke grenade to show the helicopter where to land, the smoke spread over us all and rose broad and spiralling into the sky. I blinked my eyes which were full of tears, and looked at the rusty two-mil coin from the Mandate period, and at the word written on it in English, Hebrew and Arabic. Both sides of the coin were the same: Palestine.

The helicopter descended noisily. Grains of sand, mud, leaves, scraps of paper, dust and dirty plastic bags flew into the air. "But there has to be another coin," I shouted at the medic who had emptied the pockets of Barazani's torn and charred uniform. He was standing next to me, looking at the approaching helicopter, his eyes blinking and watering in the wind. "Here," he said in a hoarse, weak voice, and held out the other coin.

It was the other side of the coin. On both sides of the greenish rusty copper was a slender, upright olive branch, with seven leaves spreading from its sides.

Israel, 1985

Yitzhak Laor

Rachely's Father
Who Was an Actor

Translated by Sheila Jellen

Rachely's father was an actor. He called her Rucheleh and made her work with him. They went from town to town presenting skits and ballads in Hebrew and Yiddish. Rachely would go around the audience after the performance and ask people to put money into a hat or a headscarf. Afterwards she would go with him to the restaurant for some soup. Rachely's father was a Holocaust survivor, of course. He never spoke about it explicitly to us, but we knew enough to ignore the screams we heard from their house and to forgive Rachely for her strange behavior in all sorts of matters, because of the fact that her father was a Holocaust survivor. There were two other, quieter survivors in the neighborhood, but they admired Rachely's father because he was from Auschwitz, and Auschwitz was a different story. That's what they said. My family were real Israelis, old-timers, and all I knew about the Holocaust was the Eichmann trial, which I remember very well, especially the way the writer Katzetnik fainted in the middle of his testimony.

I went out with Rachely for a long time. That is to say, we were an item, she was my girlfriend. But I was only the second person to sleep with her. When Rachely was my girlfriend, she was still a virgin.

Once I went along with Rachely and her father to one of their shows. It was in a town, part of which had once been an Arab village, and there were no Yiddish speakers in the café where they were performing, but Rachely's father insisted on singing a Yiddish song, and Rachely had to translate it. People gave money, I think, only because of Rachely's beauty – she was already seventeen. Afterwards, we went to a café that had a sign with the name of the owner, and the name proved he was a Yiddish speaker. Rachely's father swore in Yiddish. She was very nice to him, but very tired too. I knew how much she hated him. You see, she once cried on my shoulder about what a monster of a father she had and why did she have to take all that. Rachely's father ordered cake and coffee for all of us and asked me when I was going into the army. I told him they had postponed my conscription because of medical problems. You're sick? A little, I said, very ashamed. But he didn't care, because he wasn't an old-timer. Polacks talk about their ailments very openly. Then Rachely said: Let's go home. The young man sitting near us was irritating her. He was wearing a striped suit and had a big brown suitcase. Her father laughed and said that was how he himself had looked when he first came to Israel, and it's no big deal that he's staring, maybe he wants to marry you or maybe he wants to figure out how to speak this hard language.

That evening I went with Rachely to see a movie in our neighborhood, which never gets any decent movies. It was sentimental, full of wars and goodbyes and sickening music. I was grossed out. Rachely cried and I stroked her back and shoulders as she shuddered. I thought she liked it so I kept going and really got into it. But afterwards, outside, she told me sharply never to touch her that way again. She couldn't take my softness; I was at the height of cramming for my matriculation exams, and the truth was that my hands were too soft. But I was sure they would toughen up after basic training. Sometimes I forgot that I wasn't going to be a combat soldier and I imagined myself as a hardened trooper. Tough but moral, I swore to myself.

In Rachely and her father's show, he was a prisoner who's always looking out of his window. He sees his beautiful daughter and sings her a song about a distant land. Not you, what I'm praying for, he sang, yes you, but something further, more beautiful. When he sang in

Yiddish, he used coarse words, Rachely told me, and cried and screamed. When he spoke Hebrew, he was more in control. Sometimes he'd fling himself down at the end of the show, and Rachely would ask the audience to give money for her sick father who had been in Auschwitz. She was never embarrassed about using that tactic. Once, when I brought it up, she looked at me with scorn. Maybe that was when she decided not to let me be the first.

When we were small, Rachely's father knew how to recruit us all to work in his yard. My mother always said that I didn't mind helping other people, though at home I wouldn't help at all. But it wasn't like that. They were poor and they were a team, Rachely and her father, and we all knew the score. Once Rachely's father even explained to us why he couldn't stand his wife, Rachely's mom. Another time he told us the truth about sex, and even though we knew all about it his explanations felt different than those we heard from the older boys, who talked dirty. He explained it all in the most minute detail, and every once in a while he'd give this weird laugh. Rachely acted, at those moments, as if she were a queen and her father was minister of the royal court.

That summer I was drafted. Again I forgot that I wasn't going to be a combat soldier, and again I cried in secret when I had to face that fact. My mother ached for me and told me that I could make a valuable contribution anyway. My dad said that if I had really wanted to I could have pulled one over on the doctors, but apparently I hadn't really wanted to; in any case, now was the time for me to put my best foot forward to serve my country. I decided not to tell Rachely. Basic training was long and hot. I was selected for a secret military course I couldn't tell Rachely about, especially since I wanted her to think I was a combat soldier.

I got one letter from her during my whole time in basic training, and it was one long indictment of her insane father, who screamed all night and acted the buffoon all day and did all those outrageous things I knew about from all the hellish years she lived next door. When basic training was over, I went to visit her. I had a crew cut and my face and hands were sunburnt. She said that I looked like a real soldier, and she smiled at me. Her new boyfriend was on his way over, she said. My heart shrank. All those kisses and touching, on the chest and between the legs, had seemed to me like a commitment, maybe even a mutual one, and here she was telling me about her new boyfriend. I pretended to be indifferent and good-natured. I even used some slang I'd picked up in training. Then her boyfriend came in. He was a kibbutznik. I knew deep down that he was stupid and had no real culture, but I had no real proof. The whole thing just threw me for a loop.

Only people whose families were old-timers were in the socialist youth movement, and only those of them whose parents had been in the Israeli Workers Party. I personally couldn't stand the whole business, with all the field trips, the truck reeking of canned food and sandwiches, and the so-called serious discussions about the military government and S. Yizhar, and the couples. Rachely didn't think much of the movement. When she saw me standing there with the gang from the movement, she wouldn't come over, even if it was on our street or in the center of town. But then along comes some youth counselor from the kibbutz while I'm at basic training, and gets all friendly with her. He was very nice to me, he asked me about basic training and he seemed to get the fact that I wasn't in a combat unit. I told Rachely that I'd come back some other time, and she smiled and said that I should knock at the door first. What was that supposed to mean?

When Rachely first arrived in our neighborhood from some faraway immigrant transit camp, we were still very young and we would drive them crazy. That is, when we saw her father, who screamed in his sleep, we would call after him: "Billy goat, billy goat, mk, mk, mk," and all sorts of other inane chants from Max and Moritz. Rachely would cry and try to throw stones at us, and her father would laugh, he'd bust his gut laughing, and then she'd turn her rage on him and pound him with all her might. And he would keep laughing. For a long time she wouldn't let us into her house, and if we went in, two or three of us from the block, she'd kick her father out. Now Rachely is all grown up. She doesn't yell at her father anymore and his whole story just seems tragic to her. Her mom never goes out; there's a big mystery there.

I went back to the base where the secret course was going to take place. On the way, I dropped a letter into Rachely's mailbox in which I poured out all my bitterness at her betrayal. I loved her. She was beautiful. Most of the kids never even noticed her or her beauty, because she wasn't one of us.

There was someone weird in a striped suit with a suitcase standing by her house. The whole way to the base I tried to remember who he was, and only when I got there did I remember that we saw him at that Ashkenazi café in the town where we'd performed. I requested special leave to investigate the matter, which of course I didn't get. In the middle of the week we were given a furlough. I didn't go to see Rachely, even though I really wanted to see her. First, she might have been off performing. Second, she was probably busy with her kibbutznik. Third, I didn't want her to know I was a noncombat jobnik. But after it got dark I allowed myself to go out. My mom called after me to ask if I was going over to Rachely's, and I let loose a barrage at her as if it was her fault things weren't going my way. Near Rachely's house I saw him. He was tall, and the light coming from the kitchen cast his shadow toward the empty synagogue, which was very close. I wanted to scream, but I didn't want Rachely to know I was home, and it wasn't a good idea to ruin my spy mission in the middle either. When I was little, I dreamed of rescuing her from the hands of evil men, and now here was an evil man, thin and with a wide-brimmed hat on his head. Suddenly he saw me, he looked at me, his shoulders shook and he took off through the synagogue courtyard into the parallel street. I went back home, called a few friends from my class, guys, some of whom hadn't yet been drafted, and was glad that none of them was home. I think I wasn't the only jobnik. Other people certainly were lying too.

The windows in the classroom at the base were covered with black curtains, and white fluorescent light flooded the room, tiring our eyes. We weren't allowed to write anything down, and the building itself was surrounded by barbed wire. I could have been very proud about the whole production, but I wasn't allowed to tell anyone about it. Besides, out of twenty-five recruits, twenty were girls, and they preferred combat soldiers too. Anyway, I was in love with Rachely. I fantasized about the kibbutznik dying in a car crash or a reprisal raid. I hoped that he would see, just once, the ceremonies Rachely's father conducted at night and that he would regret having gotten mixed up with that whole insane crew and I would be the only one left who could tolerate it.

Rachely wrote me a frightened letter about the strange peeping Tom who had started hovering outside her window. From her letter I understood that she had progressed quite a bit in her sexual exploits with the kibbutznik. At least in comparison with what she had allowed me. The kibbutznik was very nice to her, but he was there to lead a youth group and get married, not to solve her problems, especially since he had his own. She said that her father's rituals were starting to get longer and that her mother didn't have a life anymore outside these rituals. I answered with a long letter, in which I also complained that she hadn't responded to my previous letter. In the meantime I decided to start something with Dina, who was sort of fat and not at all pretty, so I figured it would be easier to start something with her and learn all those things I missed because Rachely hadn't let me get anywhere. One class, while they were running a training film, I put my hand on her knee and she didn't stop me. I couldn't stop thinking about the peeping Tom and I was very tense.

I went to Rachely's house the first night I was back in the city. She'd gone out with the kibbutznik, her father said. He looked sick. I knew I had interrupted his ritual, but I couldn't tear myself away. All the dolls were sitting around the table, and Rachely's father went back to his place at the head of the table as if I weren't there; her mother served the usual courses and he read from the Passover Haggadah. Neither of them looked at me. I trembled with fear. I knew about the rituals. I could hear them through the wall. But I had never seen his eyes with that sick flash and the spittle and the woman in her old-fashioned outfit. The whole dead family was there, and he spoke to them in Yiddish and sang almost angrily. I fled. The next evening I called Dina and asked her to come over, and when she arrived we went to the shed behind the house. I unhooked her bra and she asked if it wasn't dangerous, so I joked that my military profile was too low for me to try anything dangerous, and she said that she accepted me just the way I was and it didn't matter to her. I got her good and hot because I didn't want her to suddenly remember to stop me before I got inside. I was about to come and I was thinking about all sorts of other things so I shouldn't come, especially about the advice the Moroccans give you in basic training. I was praying she wasn't a virgin because they said that girls get attached to their first and I was planning to dump her as soon as the kibbutznik took off. Besides, I wanted to learn a lot about how to be soft and hard in exactly the right balance. Actually she wasn't a virgin, but she swore it was like her first time, because she had done it before with this older guy who was very bad to her and I was good. She hoped she wasn't pregnant, and next time I would have to be careful. I kept myself from shouting with joy that I had slept with a girl. I wanted to tell my mother, because she's the only person who gives a damn about me, but I knew she wouldn't be too thrilled with the casting, the staging, or the script. Dina talked, and I counted midnight butterflies. That's just an expression. What I mean is that I waited for time to pass in order not to hurt her feelings. She said that I wasn't talking because I was just like the rest of them, but I said no, I was just so happy that I wanted to be quiet, and she kissed my eyes and said that kisses like that you only give to people you love. I knew that those were kisses that would work on any girl from now on. Finally I walked her home. Rachely was standing with the kibbutznik on the sidewalk in front of her house. She was crying. We went over. I was a little embarrassed to have Dina hanging on my arm. She was so fat and Rachely was so beautiful, so heartbreakingly beautiful. Rachely said that the peeping Tom had just been there and she didn't want to go back home and she didn't know where to go. I told her to go in to my mother and that when I got back I would go after that creature, but it didn't work: (a) I couldn't quite come out and say all that because Dina and the kibbutznik were right there; (b) I was embarrassed; and (c) I was afraid that my mother would blurt out some bullshit about me being a jobnik or something like that.

Rachely's mother shrieked. Our blood froze, even though it happened all the time. Dina didn't understand what was going on. The kibbutznik, who seemed to know what was up, said something to Dina about the Holocaust. We left. I had never said anything to Dina about Rachely, it was better that way. I hoped they would still be outside when I got back, but by then the buses had stopped running and I had to walk half way across town on foot, swearing the whole way. But actually, I had good reason to feel satisfied: the combat soldiers from my class would die to go all the way with the first girl they made a pass at in the army. So I wasn't too caught up with the whole Rachely thing.

The next day Dina smiled at me in class and we started making a regular thing of sleeping together every night behind the girls' tent, by the old firing range. I was very careful to pull out in time. Dina loved me. The more she loved me, the more I tried to hide the whole thing from people around us. Because of Dina, who called so much, I didn't get to see Rachely when I was on leave or vacation. The course would soon be over, I thought, and we would each be attached to a different unit. On one of my leaves, at a hitchhiking station, I ran into Rachely's kibbutznik, who was on reserve duty. The way he opened his heart to me made my head spin. He told me everything, and I didn't know what to say, I just prayed that some car would stop and pick up one or the other of us. He told me that he'd had a girlfriend for many years but she was a Christian and he didn't want to marry her because love is love but what about the Jewish people, and that he didn't love Rachely but he had grown attached to her and it was a shame that it was all over between them because of that new immigrant. After all, he was her first. He'd opened her up and he would have liked to remain the only one. He had been a naval commando when he was in the regular army, and now he was an officer in the armored corps. The theater of war is just theater and you can't stay in the theater your whole life, can you? he concluded. After that or before that he told me about this exercise they had in the commandos, where you're taken prisoner and the other soldiers have to beat you up, for practice. The interesting part of this exercise, according to the kibbutznik, was how people would really get into the spirit of the beating, even when the guy being hit was their best friend. They'd really give it to him, until the blood poured off him, and the minute the exercise ended and the show was over, the hate disappeared. He asked me if I knew what he was getting at, and I rushed off to Rachely to see if I could rescue her from the new immigrant or from this raving kibbutznik.

The immigrant was the peeping Tom with the ridiculous outfit. He had taken Rachely with him and they were living in a hotel on the other side of the city. The kibbutznik hadn't slept with her at all. That's what she said in a letter she'd left with her father for me. He was impotent and those callused hands were deceptive, she wrote. I was very happy. In the final analysis his hard hands were worthless, while my soft hands had disturbed Dina's peace night after night, during the course and on our furloughs. Rachely had taken off with the immigrant, who was ridiculous even compared to other new immigrants with their gold teeth. She spoke Yiddish with him. She'd sleep with him, no problem about it. When I found the hotel, late that night, I asked the sleepy front-desk clerk if there was a beautiful girl named Rachely there with a tall Polack with a gold tooth in the front of his mouth. I told the clerk that our father was sick, that I was her brother and had to bring her home. Her father really did look pretty sick. He told me he didn't care that she had gone off to a hotel to sleep with that man. He'd seen a lot in his life and he didn't care one way or the other. But it was terrible that a man terrifies her and follows her around like the angel of death, and suddenly she loves him. How can you turn fear into love? That was something he couldn't go along with. And who was going to perform with him now, and who would help Mother, who was so weak she had no energy left? From working so hard, he added, after a pregnant pause. Then he asked if I had slept with Rachely, and I was stunned. I looked at the letter I was holding and wondered if he had read it. I don't read Hebrew, he said.

At the hotel they didn't let me go up and I waited outside all night.

In the morning the new immigrant came down and smiled at me. Rachely, when she came down, was not at all surprised to see me. As usual, everything about where we stood was quite clear to her. He went to the market, I think. Rachely said that he was selling all kinds of clothes in various places and that's what he was doing with that suitcase. We went down to the beach. She'd wanted to kill herself, she said, but he saved her. She was going to bring him home. Her father would love him. He's one of us. He grew up without parents and how he got here was a whole other story.

I gave up on Rachely. A lot of time passed. On Fridays I went to parties with my old class. Some of them had their driver's license and they showed up in their parents' cars. I tried to forget Dina too. Sometimes I called her, and even though she was mad, we would find some corner where we could catch up on what had happened in the time since we'd last met, while we were busy deciphering secret codes in our different army units.

One night – it was when I was going home from the base every night, and I wasn't even that embarrassed about it, that is, I was used to it – Rachely knocked on my bedroom window, the way she used to when we'd help her and her father work in the yard at night. I went outside, like I did back then, in my pajamas and I took her into the shed and turned on the light. When I held her hand I got very excited. I had dreamed about this for so long, and suddenly, in the middle of the night, Rachely comes to me, just like when we were kids, and I lead her through the yard. She was pale and her wrists were bandaged. She had tried to kill herself. Her immigrant had gotten her pregnant. But that's not it, she said. That's not the problem, because she was going to get an abortion and had already been to the social worker who was assigned to their family and they'd get permission for her. Now she burst into a storm of tears. It was totally the opposite of the terrible dryness with which she said: he got me pregnant, but what was worse – she started practically shrieking – he's my brother, do you understand? He's my brother. I didn't know what to do with this story. I had fantasized often enough about rescuing Rachely from various disasters, but I didn't understand how all of a sudden he could be her brother. She started hitting me the way she used to hit her father when he laughed at our curses. It worried me. I moved, taking the opportunity to close the shed door. I was terrified that my mother would wake up and hear. She calmed down for a minute and explained that they hadn't gotten along so well. He was Polish, do you understand? And I'm not Polish and I don't know what I am. And his stories about the Holocaust drove me crazy. He lost his parents there, and he had a picture of his parents and brothers. I can't explain any more, do you understand? I was an only child, but I'd always been repelled by the idea of sleeping even with my cousin. It really was awful. I asked her if she had told him. No, she hadn't. And her father? Not yet. What was she going to do? She burst into tears again and swore she would kill herself. We fell asleep on the floor of the shed. Obviously I didn't try any funny stuff. That is, she slept and I shivered and coughed.

I took my annual leave. Rachely came to our house. I explained to my mother that she had to check into the hospital for some procedure, and my mother wondered whether it had anything to do with me. I didn't mind if she got the wrong idea, actually Rachely looked like a pale, sickly angel on the gurney in the hospital. Woozy from the anesthetic, she tossed and turned on the green gurney, and I got a little poetic. I arrived in uniform and everyone treated me like a man who had gotten a woman pregnant. When we left, I took a taxi and she cried. This time she cried quietly, whispering something about the ugliness that was still clinging to her. Her tears were big and hot. My mother had made up a bed for her, and my father, who was asking all kinds of crude questions like he does, caught hell from my mother, and I was very proud of her for working everything out so well. That evening the doorbell rang. It was the actor, Rachely's father.

He knew, of course, that she was at our place. He sat down beside her and didn't ask anything. Then she said that she had something important to tell him, and did he have his heart medicine on him, and could I close the door. I could stay if I wanted to, she said, but I decided to leave. When he came out, a long time later, he was hunched deep into himself. I asked her what she had told him. She hadn't explained everything. But he didn't want him as a son. I heard him calling to me from outside. I went to him and he hugged me. He told me to go over to their house and tell the young man to leave them alone. And not to say another word about the whole family thing. He went back into Rachely's room, without knocking. He didn't wait to watch me knock on the door of their house. I had always wondered about his lack of interest in houses and families and privacy, the way he told us all sorts of things about his wife, Rachely's mother. Tell him to go. You understand me, right? We don't have a choice, do we? After all, you're the smartest boy in the neighborhood and Rachely admires you very much. I never knew that, that she admired me. I ran. I stopped in front of the house, feeling heavy and slow. I wanted to cry or swear. I wanted to tell Rachely that I was no combat soldier. Then I asked him to leave them alone and go make a life for himself somewhere else. And not be always looking for his relatives because that wasn't what was important in life. Rachely's father was angry about the pregnancy, I lied. He had been sitting next to Rachely's crazy mother, showing her pictures of his family from the Holocaust while she giggled. Then, after I told him what I told him, he went to pack his things, which he had just finished unpacking. And after he had left, the crazy lady set up all the dolls again around the table and waited for Rachely's father to come home.

Israel, 1976

Shulamit Lapid

Thread

Translated by Ora Cummings

A wall stood to his right, dim and misty, and to his left stood a wall, dim and misty, and from the place where he lay, slowly drifting into slumber, a dense, steamy cloud rose up to fill the abyss. He felt a fine hair moving across his upper lip each time he breathed out through his nose, and this fine hair caused him to stay awake, and although he was being drawn into sleep and could feel himself sinking into its depths, he knew he wouldn't be able to pitch into it until he was rid of this capillary floating above his upper lip. He raised his hand to brush away the hair. His hand felt very heavy, as if cast in lead; he had to make an effort to lift it and he knew that this effort would probably wake him from the sweet lethargy enfolding him. He brought his hand to his mouth, found the hair, grasped it between thumb and forefinger and carefully removed it from his lips. But the hair was longer than he'd supposed and continued to float above his lips. He tightened his grip, afraid of letting go, and pulled some more, but to his dismay, the more he pulled, the longer the hair became. His movements grew more forceful and less careful. He wasn't sleeping, and wanted to get rid of the hair. The hair wasn't as fine as he'd thought. This was a strong hair and it was lodged somewhere in the obscure depths of his throat. He pulled on it, trying to reach its root, and began winding it around his finger. He was entirely awake by now. He coiled the thread around his finger, swiftly twisting and coiling, feeling the spool thicken around his bound finger. He then peeled the spool from his finger and laid it in his palm, still holding on to the hair with his thumb and forefinger: what had begun as merely a bother had turned into anxiety. From where within him was all this hair coming, and when would he reach its root? He could feel a dull pain in the depths of his chest and began worrying that the hair had become entwined with the tendons around one of his internal organs. If he wasn't careful he might tear off a piece of intestine or lung. Maybe the hair had been stuck in a piece of bread he'd gobbled down, or shed onto his pillow and inhaled into his lungs while he was sleeping.

The hair he was holding between his fingers had, by now, become thicker than it had been when he'd first touched it. He could feel, without seeing it, that it had turned into a weft-thread, one of those twisted flaxen threads that he used in his shop to tie up bundles of cloth. The thread felt familiar. He held on to it and wondered what he should do. Obviously the hair had got itself entangled with this thread which was buried in his stomach or intestine, and it was now pulling on the thread. Many a time, he'd bitten off a piece of thread with his teeth when he was in a hurry and there were no scissors or knife to hand. He would swallow any fibers left in his mouth; he could hardly spit them out when he was standing in front of his customers.

His throat ached. He relaxed his jaws a little and lay still, staring into the darkness. He wanted to tug at the thread, but it was stronger than the hair and if it was really braided into one of his inner organs or wound around it, he might dislodge that organ or bring it out through his mouth. He wondered if those fibers he'd swallowed in the store could have interwoven inside his stomach, to become a whole thread.

Something tickled his memory and he caught it, and held on until he remembered something that had happened three years before, when he'd been on a visit to London.

One Sunday, some relatives of his had invited him to visit Petticoat Lane Market, and at lunchtime they'd gone to Bloom's. They were in high spirits from their pleasant walk and because of the good will they'd shown their relative, and now they ordered for him all those delicacies they remembered from their parents' home. Chopped liver and borscht and stuffed goose neck and steamed red cabbage with raisins and cinnamon and, of course, salt beef and pickled cucumbers – Bloom's salt beef and pickled cucumbers.

His legs ached from the walk, his eyes were misted and blurred from all the sights he'd seen and he was thirsty and hungry. Cooking smells filled the large restaurant, which was crammed with eager, red-cheeked families who'd come here as on a pilgrimage to an ancestral tomb.

He put a morsel of food into his mouth and suddenly felt a piece of thread, which the cook had used for tying up the stuffed goose neck and had obviously forgotten to remove before sending the dish from kitchen to table. He poked his fingers into his mouth and pulled at the thread and spat it out with a loud uncorking sound, together with the piece of food he'd swallowed. What a fright he'd had, and what a relief when he saw on his plate the piece of stuffing in its skin and the thread tying them together! He quickly covered up the little pile with his starched napkin, sipped from his cool wine, cleared his throat, apologized, and again cleared his throat with tears pouring down his cheeks. Only after he regained his breath and composure was he filled with shame in front of his relatives. They insisted that he eat something else, stuffed fish perhaps, or meat dumplings with bread crumbs – no one does them quite like Bloom. He agreed at last and ordered some stewed prunes, if only for the sake of peace, and studied the skins and stones with suspicion, imagining all the dangers these were laying in the path of an innocent tourist from the Holy Land. He knew his relatives were revolted by him. But then, wouldn't he himself be revolted by someone who noisily burped up his food? He knew that every time his name was mentioned in their home, they were reminded of his table manners, their faces twisted in disgust, and he continued to send them cards for the Jewish New Year and to wish them happy holiday at Passover in self-exoneration and atonement for the unpleasantness he'd caused them at the end of that agreeable walk.

But this was not that same thread. That one was finer. It was the kind of thread that dressmakers and tailors use for tacking clothes. The thread he was now gripping between his fingers was coarser. White twisted flax – he knew it was white – used for tying up light bundles.

Again he opened his mouth, pulled on the thread and began winding it around his finger until, once more, he felt those same cramps beneath his ribs. He hadn't the faintest idea about anatomy. He was a healthy man, and apart from the usual seasonal cold, or occasional bout of diarrhea, he was not over-concerned with the workings of his body. And that was why he didn't know now what it was that he was pulling out of the hidden caverns of his body.

He was frightened. He decided to stop pulling on the thread and lifted himself up in bed. He did not turn on his bedside light, scared of what would confront him if he did, seeing in his imagination the mucus-covered pile of hair and threads. With his free hand, he took a pair of scissors out of the drawer, pushed them into his mouth as close as he could to his throat and snipped the thread, being very careful not to injure his tonsils or tongue. With three or four deep gulps, he swallowed the remaining thread until it sank and disappeared down his gullet. Only now, as he rested it on the blanket, did he feel how painful his arm was.

He took regular breaths and forced himself to imagine black velvet unwinding itself from a cardboard tube, being spread out under a black sky full of stars twinkling on the black velvet, as in a lake. But no matter how hard he tried to sink into the black velvet, he was unable to make himself forget the unpleasant experience. He remembered how, two weeks ago, Rina, his shop assistant, had brought him a packet of linseeds – good for the blood and for regular bowels, so she'd said. He wondered now if the seeds had not germinated in his stomach, wily things that they were, and grown into this thread. Every few months she would bring him something to improve his health, although he'd tell her over and over again that there was nothing wrong with his health, thank God, and he didn't need any help either from nature or from doctors. From the day he'd hired her to work in his shop, she'd had her eye on him, showing exaggerated concern for his physical and mental well-being. Now only a pathological examination would disclose the truth – but not to him – as to whether the linseeds were the source of the thread. In his imagination, he could see Rina walking after his coffin, wiping away her tears and murmuring: "He was a healthy man, never missed a day's work in his life..." Men like him were sought after by women, hard workers, responsible men, slogging away day after day, year after year, stable and serious, the kind who are not likely to become addicted to drink or cigarettes, or other women.

It hadn't been a good thing to cut off the thread and swallow it. He could see now that he'd never be rid of the thread until he'd pulled it out with its roots and seed. Still, what was done, was done.

He decided to think pleasant thoughts, but remembered his twin brother, who'd drowned at sea off Netanya when a boat they'd hired capsized. A girl he'd been engaged to had later made the accusation that his devotion to his mourning was stronger than his love for her.

I am gliding in the sky, he said to himself, I can see fields of grass with red and yellow patches down below me, those patches are poppies and dandelions. But his thoughts kept returning to his brother, and Rina, and the thread, neither to swallow it down nor to vomit it up. And so, in this muddle of hungry sea and fields of flowers, he finally managed to fall asleep.

If he dreamt any dreams, he remembered nothing of them as dawn broke. After he'd showered and shaved, and patted scent on his cheeks, he opened the shutters and sniffed in the fresh morning air. The sky was a clear blue. He spread his bedding on the railing of the balcony, put the scissors back in their drawer, tossed the ball of hair out of the window, picked up his briefcase and went to the shop.

Savyon Liebrecht

Hayuta's Engagement Party

Translated by Marganit Weinberger-Rotman

Fifteen days before Hayuta's engagement party, which was arranged hastily because of the youngsters' unexpected announcement, nobody had thought yet about the disgrace that Grandpa Mendel might heap on their heads. Everybody was busy with guest lists, musicians, food, drinks, dishes to borrow, neighbors willing to lend chairs and tables, and the presents the prospective bride had expressed a wish for in case someone asked what to buy. Bella, Hayuta's mother, was appalled at the sight of the house: the stains on the green couch were so conspicuous; the drapes were frayed at the edges; the wallpaper in the dining room showed a faded line where the three chairs used to stand. Thus a list of upmarket upholstery stores was added to the existing lists, as well as the names of wallpaper experts.

In the middle of all this commotion, Bella suddenly remembered that she had not yet decided on the dress she was going to wear for the occasion. After rummaging through her wardrobe, and trying on dresses in shops for two days, she came to the conclusion that the success of her dress depended on the style of dress Ran's mother – her daughter's future mother-in-law – was going to wear. She had already heard that the mother was a tall, pretty, well-connected woman. If she herself chose a frilly and elegant dress, Bella reasoned nervously, while her future in-law came in a tailored suit – it might make her look provincial while the other mother looked like a sophisticated woman of the world. On the other hand, if she chose a suit, while her in-law selected an elegant dress, then she would look stodgy – and

Ran's mother would look glamorous. The choice of color was also a complicated matter. If she wore red and the mother-in-law wore black, then she would look vulgar and the other one, refined. If she wore black and the other wore red – why she would look dreary and the other would look vivacious. And the size of the buttons, the length of the hem and the width of the belt were also problematic questions. The more she thought about these matters, the more hopeless they seemed.

Dealing with furniture, clothes, food and invitations saved Bella from having to think about the cause of all this commotion: Hayuta, almost twenty-three years old, about to finish college this autumn, had managed, with perfect timing, and before the first wrinkles appeared at the corners of her eyes, to find herself a clever, and energetic husband who was – so people said – from an educated and well-off family. Perhaps the full meaning of this engagement would only sink in later, after the party, when the guests had left, the band had packed up its instruments, and the hallway had been swept.

After several days of hectic activity, things were falling into place; the chairs and tables had been collected from the neighbours and a way had been found to set them up in the backyard: most of them would flank the garden wall, while the side rows would stretch diagonally like two open arms welcoming a child; the middle of the yard would remain empty. A representative of a catering company came and displayed an array of colored photographs featuring different methods of presenting the food.

Following lengthy deliberations, it was decided to order the utensils, the meats and the salads from him and to leave the baking of the cakes to the lady of the house, as that was her forte – this after an understanding had been reached regarding the terms of payment. Inside the house, too, work proceeded apace, despite the gloomy predictions. For a special fee, the workmen diligently applied themselves to the task. Even though she had not been completely happy with the choice of wallpaper, and claimed that the haste with which it had been selected resulted in a pattern which did not go well with the style of the chairs, it looked quite nice when she saw it on the wall. The question of the dress was also resolved; since her daughter refused to cooperate in spying on her future mother-in-law, Bella hit on an ingenious solution and chose a dress that was both elegant and charming – a blue suit-like silk dress with raised white piping and a little, pointed white collar.

Only then did she find the time to think about her father, Mendel. By a strange coincidence Hayuta, too, was thinking about him during her final exam in Jewish history. After lunch the two of them were ready to discuss him.

"If he ruins my party, I'll never forgive him, never!" Hayuta said, her mouth full of radish.

"You're right," her mother agreed.

"This isn't just another Seder or holiday meal," Hayuta explained as if facing opposition. "The whole family knows him by now, they know his history, and they forgive him. But Ran's parents don't know him, and his sister and some of their closest friends will be here too. I don't want them to get the impression that there are strange people in my family. I'm telling you right now that if he does it in front of everybody, I'm just going to drop dead!"

"God forbid," exclaimed Bella, truly distressed. "So what's one to do?"

"We'll have to find some solution." Hayuta searched with her fork among the slices of cucumber, looking for radish rings.

"But we can't very well not invite him," said Bella in the tone of someone arguing with herself. "After all, such an occasion – his first grandchild is getting engaged. This is something very special for him, the dream he's always talking about – a large family. I don't see how we can not invite him. We'll never forgive ourselves afterwards. Don't forget, he's already eighty-two. How many more parties like this will he be able to attend? What are we to do? Can we possibly not tell him?"

"We could send him on a trip," said Hayuta pragmatically, having just had a brainstorm. Bella looked at her daughter and shuddered: here she is, already getting rid of him like an unwanted object, with that typical nonchalance that this new generation has. Hayuta had already forgotten how he raised and coddled her, ready to give up his food for her. And all these years, when she herself was busy at the plant with her husband, Grandfather – no longer a young man – used to take his granddaughter to ballet lessons and art classes, and wait for her patiently outside, rain or shine.

"Perhaps we could talk to him, explain that this time he has to control himself," Bella tried. "After all, he's not senile or anything; on the contrary, he's quite alert."

"Talking's not going to help, and you know it," Hayuta stopped her. "Would you be able to stand the suspense all evening? Just wait and see when he's going to start?"

"I'll convince him, you'll see. I'll explain it to him clearly. I have an idea: we'll seat him next to Shifra. She'll keep an eye on him and shut him up the moment he opens his mouth. Shifra won't let him talk, you can count on her. I think that's a good solution, what do you say?"

"I say I'm going to find out what trips the municipality is organizing for senior citizens. I saw an ad in the paper once. It's better this way, for him and for us."

Monsters, thought Bella in disgust as her daughter went to answer the phone. We are raising monsters. At first they look like babies, then like children, but behind the innocent facade – hearts of stone! I've heard of children throwing their old folks into the streets, waiting for them to die. Just like that – shamelessly to evict Grandfather from your engagement party!

After Hayuta had gone, Bella calmed down and had to admit to herself: there's no doubt about it, he would cause a disaster at the party. At the sight of all the food, he just wouldn't be able to help himself. On such occasions, words just gushed from his mouth, beyond his control. In the last few years, the situation had worsened considerably. It seemed that in his mind distant memories overcame those of yesterday, as often happens with old people. Up to about six years ago, he was really in good shape. Until then he didn't talk about what had happened to him during the war. When he returned from the concentration camp to the house of the Polish peasant to whom he had entrusted his two children for four years, his little daughter Bella only barely recognized him. His face was emaciated, his cheekbones and nose prominent, and his hair was cropped short. At the sight of him the peasant woman crossed herself and said: "Mister Goldberg, all night I dreamed that you were coming. Your children weren't sick even once! I took care of them as if they were my own!" He bent down and gathered the children in his thin arms; the rancid smell of his body hit them when he said: "We'll forget everything, everything. We'll look for Mother and then we'll go to America."

However, they did not find their mother and they did not go to America. Years later he married another woman in Israel, and she raised the children as if they were her own. Only when they got sick, she would urge them to get well quickly. Up until six years ago he never said a word about what had happened to him in the war. Once, in his room, she found a memorial book produced by survivors from a small Polish town, and between the pages were newspaper clippings announcing memorial services. His children never asked him what had happened to him during all those years when they were scrambling and shuffling in pig dung on the peasant woman's farm. As if all of them had vowed to force those memories into oblivion. When his wife died, years after his grandchildren were born, he refused to live by himself, and refused to move in with his children. He arranged a room for himself in an old folks' home. He would spend the Sabbath and holidays with his family, coming and going by bus, never letting them drive him. He would talk with wit and animation about the economic situation, Russia and America, topical events he read about in the papers. But the war – as if part of him were dormant all these years – he never mentioned.

The change in him, Bella calculated, occurred six years ago. The tables laden with meat, fish, chopped liver, glazed carrots, stewed prunes, triggered something inside him, like a coded message. A secret door to the memories of the war, and what had been shrouded in blissful oblivion for decades, suddenly burst open. It all started on the eve of Rosh Hashanah. Around the table laden with food, everyone raised their glasses, and Mordechai, Bella's brother, turned to their father and said: "Dad, now say a blessing for a good year."

The old man turned a little pale, he already sensed something buckling inside. He raised his glass to the expectant eyes and said in Yiddish: "May we have a happy new year. A year of peace and family bliss and many happy feasts. I want to tell you something, and I'm glad we are all gathered here together and the children are listening. During the war – for four years I didn't eat any meat. We all looked like skeletons, you could see every single bone in our bodies. When rumors started to spread that the Americans were coming, the Germans became nervous and we had even less to eat. When we saw a German starting to run, Shloyme Bermanski and I pulled a sausage from his belt. I smelled it once and started to throw up, but Shloyme started eating like a pig. He ate the whole sausage, and half an hour later his eyes bulged and he fell down dead, even before the soldiers arrived." Around the table everybody looked at him, aghast. Bella and her brother exchanged astounded looks. Yehiel, who had come from Netanya with his wife and children, fidgeted uneasily. Shifra, his daughter-in-law, looked around her in disgust, as if an ill omen had been introduced into their midst. The old man, however, oblivious to the silence around him, raised his glass and added: "Let's have a happy new year. And let the children grow – that's the main thing. *Lechayyim!*"

The people echoed *Lechayyim* faintly and raised their glasses to their lips. The embarrassment lingered in the air for a while, as often happens when a shock dispels, but as the evening progressed towards the prune dessert, the tension subsided gradually. When the host told a story about a newlywed who, on his honeymoon, went to borrow a newspaper from a neighbor and returned only at dawn – everyone laughed loudly. By the time dessert was served, the memory of Grandpa Mendel's embarrassing moment had dimmed. Yehiel and his wife started singing in Polish about a girl with a long braid who goes to wash her hair in the river and is watched by a boy behind a blackberry bush who does not dare to declare his love. Perhaps it was the dessert or the mention of the blackberry song, or perhaps something else altogether, but Grandpa Mendel rose to his feet again, lifted his right arm, as he had done earlier when he was holding the wine goblet in his hand, and said: "In the camp, every day two or three people would die in our barracks. We used to drag them to a corner. Those that died during the night were already cold. Those that died in the morning weren't quite so cold. But those who died in the evening had started to smell by morning." Shifra rose to her feet and stood rebelliously in front of him, and then, defiantly, left the table and went into the next room. The old man followed her with his eyes and resumed his speech. "Once I found a potato in the pocket of one of them. We used to look in their pockets; we would take sweaters or socks off them. What use were socks to them now? I have no idea how he got that potato. He didn't work in the kitchen. I asked around, but nobody knew. And I couldn't figure it out. Where did he get that potato?"

His son Mordechai tried to shush him. The initial astonishment was over and now he could find words more easily. "Dad, this is a holiday. We want to celebrate and eat and not remember such things. On holidays one should be reminded of happy things."

"But where did he get that potato, I'm asking you. Maybe you read something, maybe you have an idea?"

"No, I don't. Look, Bella is bringing in the cake. Look at that cake! This is a sign that we won't be short of cakes all year!" He bent towards Hayuta, who was then in her senior year of high school and said to her jocosely: "Isn't that a sign that we shan't lack cakes all year?" But the cloud was already hovering over them, even the children sensed it.

The years that followed hardened their hearts gradually. It became a habit: over the laid tables on Sabbath and holiday eves and birthdays, Grandpa Mendel would tell them about people who dropped dead in the streets of the ghetto and about other passers-by who trampled them or robbed them of their shoes or kicked them aside and covered them with newspapers; he told them about those who died of starvation, with bloated bellies and sunken eyes; about the man who put an end to his misery by throwing himself on the electric fence and, in a second, became a piece of charcoal; about the man who came to the camp and saw his younger brother hanging on the gate; about the man who sorted the victims' clothes and found his wife's dress with pearls embroidered on the front, the dress he had bought her when their son was born, and which you couldn't mistake because the hem had torn and was repaired with red thread, and when the German saw him linger over the dress in his hand, he suspected him of trying to steal the pearls and lashed at his neck with a whip; and he told them about the boy who carried the bodies to the crematoria and found his mother among the dead. They let him talk, blocking his stories from the path to their hearts. Whenever he rose to his feet and lifted his right arm with the wine glass in his hand, they knew that the moment had arrived. The children would go out to play, the hostess would start clearing the table, so as not to waste time. The others would start whispering or drifting into thought, letting the next few moments pass, like a raging hurricane which would soon blow away, like an airplane that zooms overhead and takes its roar with it.

While other members of the family were resigned to these descriptions of hunger, death and putrefaction as part of holiday celebrations, his daughter-in-law Shifra rose up against them. "He is ruining my evening," she would complain, knowing full well that her words reached his ears. "We've suffered enough, and we've heard enough. Don't we have Memorial Day and Holocaust Day and memorial assemblies and what have you? They never let you forget for a minute. So why do I need to be reminded of it at every meal? I don't understand how you can go on eating so heartily when he goes on and on about festering wounds, blood and vomit – but that's your own business. As for me, the moment he opens his mouth, the holiday is over." And she would slam the table with her fist. Bella, on the other hand, was especially attentive to her father. When preparing a meal in her house, she would listen from the kitchen; when they visited others, she would listen from her seat at the table. Suddenly a window opened for her, a key to the riddle that had haunted her all those years: had he erased from his memory everything that had happened to him in the four years she and her brother spent in the pigsty of the Polish peasant? For a few moments she found herself walking the village roads, smelling the sty as if it were a reality and not a distant memory. She felt the wet snouts of the piglets in the palm of her hand, their skin hardened with mud. Had her father forgotten the death and the fear and the hunger? How could he lock them in his heart and never mention them for forty years? And now, how had his locked memories awakened in him, in the presence of all the abundance and songs and the harmonious atmosphere of lighted rooms on holidays? It's a psychological mystery, Bella concluded, and perhaps it can only be resolved at the level at which man is totally denuded – he will take it with him to his grave.

But this time, she admitted to herself, it's a difficult situation. How could they not invite Grandpa to the engagement party of his beloved granddaughter, who was named after his wife, Haya? On the other hand, how could they jeopardize the whole party, perhaps even Hayuta's own future, and cause the family to irrevocably lose face in front of all their guests. And in front of the new in-laws?

Towards evening she hit on another idea and was about to suggest it to her daughter, but Hayuta anticipated her by saying, matter-of-factly: "I talked to Ran. He says we have to invite him."

"Did you explain the problem?"

"Yes. He says it won't be civil not to invite him."

"And what if – "

"I've already spoken to him."

"To Ran?"

"No, to Grandpa."

"You spoke with Grandpa? When?"

"This afternoon."

"And?"

"I explained to him how important it is for me that everything goes smoothly."

"And?"

"He promised he wouldn't say anything except 'Lechayyim' and 'All the best.'"

Bella sighed with relief and leaned back in her chair. "I really think this is the best solution. We would have felt awful if we had sent him away on a day like this. Is that what he said? Nothing except *'Lechayyim'* and 'All the best.' Well, you've got to hand it to your Grandpa, he's certainly got a sense of humor."

"And you've got to hand it to his granddaughter, she knows danger when she sees it. I'm going to stick to him like glue all evening – to be on the safe side."

"Everything will be fine." Bella smiled and touched her chest with a fist. "My heart tells me so."

The night of the party the air was exceptionally pleasant. It was no longer the end of summer, though fall had not yet started – those in-between days of beauty and clarity. Bella, who had finally begun to grasp how momentous the occasion was, was circling like a sleepwalker among the elegant guests, all strolling about with wine glasses in their hands, in the soft little halos of light that the round garden lanterns were shedding on the lawn. The rapid flashes of cameras added a touch of importance to the atmosphere. She scrutinized her in-law from the corner of her eye, pleased to notice that she was indeed rather tall, but also excessively skinny; the front of her dress, which had layers of folds to camouflage the flat, boyish chest, apparently failed to fulfil its function. The rest, too, turned out to have been a false alarm; her pink dress was too pale, and its sash was tied in such a complicated knot that it required constant tying and undoing.

Walking around the garden as in a dream, Bella experienced an almost palpable happiness. Everything seemed to be perfect: the immaculately set table, the bowls that kept refilling as if by magic, looking as if the table had just been laid; the small band playing pleasantly, loudly enough to be heard, yet softly enough so as not to drown the conversation. Hayuta followed her grandfather with her eyes, like a trained hunter. Even when she turned her back to him, responding to well-wishers, she still sensed his movements.

The old man looked radiant and festive, responding to those who greeted him and patting children's heads. Once in a while, when she thought he was talking too much, she made her way to him, as if by chance, brushing by his back, listening. At one point she sensed danger and stiffened. He was facing the set table, looking at the guests loading their plates with food. She recognized the look, the raised hand, which always heralded the lofty words. He opened his mouth to talk, but was pierced by her harsh look. Across the long row on the table, he suddenly smiled at her mischievously, as if caught red-handed, and called: "*Lechayyim*, Haya'leh, *Lechayyim!*" And then added, as if reminded: "And all the best!" And he laughed like a child who has managed to fool an adult.

Hayuta joined in his laugh, relaxing for the first time since the first guest had arrived. She raised a hand holding an imaginary wine glass to him and called: "*Lechayyim*, Grandpa, and all the best!" The photographer, from his vantage point by the door, caught them in his lens, standing face to face saluting and toasting each other across the table. He darted his flashes at them and smiled, contented, seeing the finished product in his mind's eye.

From then on, Hayuta felt at ease as she mingled with the guests, catching a glimpse of her grandfather in the crowd from time to time. For a little while the photographer took her and Ran away from the guests and seated them on the sloping garage roof that was covered with sprawling ivy. He shot them facing each other, in each other's arms, until Hayuta remonstrated: "Enough with this kitsch. This is so banal!" And she waved her hand at the camera in protest, and pulled Ran by the arm.

From the roof she suddenly saw her grandfather. He was staring at the people crowding around the table. The meat platters had been removed and replaced by plates of cakes. People were helping themselves to slices of cake, and from where she was standing, Hayuta could discern the excitement on her grandfather's face vis-a-vis the new extravagance, the new commotion around the table. His eyes shone with a familiar light, and his arm, though no longer holding a glass, rose by itself. His other hand thumped on the table, drawing the guests' attention. People were looking at him from all corners of the garden; several came closer, waiting respectfully for him to talk. He waited a minute for the conversations to subside, like an expert orator, and then began. Silence fell on the garden, as before an important announcement.

"Grandpa, no!" Hayuta yelled from afar, from her shaded corner, and he raised his face to her, straining his eyes to see her beyond the peoples' heads, near the darkening ivy.

Suddenly he ducked and disappeared from view. Hayuta could see the sudden commotion in the crowd, people pushing and gathering at the empty place he had just occupied. She tore herself from Ran's arms and rushed there, tearing through the barrier of people around him, but by the time she got there the table had already collapsed, the strawberry, cheese and chocolate tortes, and the tall, layered cake were lying ruined on the grass, and her grandfather was rolling among them, his face and his suit spattered like an actor in an old comedy, who had just been hit by a cream pie.

In the bedroom, they could hear Mordechai's voice trying to stave off the guests who came to inquire about the old man. He sent them back to the table, which had been hastily restored and to the band, which had resumed its playing. "He got very excited, now he's resting. No, please, don't disturb him. I'll tell him. He needs his rest now. He'll be okay. Please go on dancing." His voice, and the music and the murmurs of the people came from a great distance.

Inside the room it was very quiet. Hayuta, with the wreath of roses still resting on her curls and her face very pale, took out a paper tissue from a pop-up box that spewed out thin rectangles of paper one after the other and handed it to her mother. Bella dabbed her wet face and wiped the jam and the chocolate chips that had smeared the front of her dress and her white collar when he was carried inside and she held his head close. Then she took another tissue and very gently, as if she could still inflict pain, wiped the anguished face which knew no final release, and the handsome mustache, and the closed eyes, and the lips that were tightly pursed under a layer of sweet frosting, firmly treasuring the words that would now never bring salvation, nor conciliation, nor even a momentary relief.

Reuven Miran

Tzipori

Translated by Dalya Bilu

Yaakov Eizner stood alone in the square. The sun was over his head and there was no one around. The neighborhood houses were white. All the shutters were closed. The streets were empty. I wanted to kill him. I took my slingshot down from my shoulder and cocked it carefully. The back of Yaakov Eizner's neck darkened inside the gunsight. Gray clouds suddenly closed in on the sun. The sides of the sight closed in on the nape of Yaakov Eizner's neck. He stood alone in the square. It was summer, but suddenly gray clouds closed in on the sun and a warm rain started falling. Yaakov Eizner moved, and I stood still under the heavy drops of warm rain which had started coming down so unexpectedly. He ran home.

"Coward," I whispered. "I'll kill you."

The warm rain came down harder. The drops were big and heavy. The clouds shifted restlessly from place to place. There was a high wind in the sky. On the ground it was hot and stifling in spite of everything.

"Rain," cried Michael.

"Maxie, Maxielein, come home," a woman's voice called from behind one of the closed shutters. She was talking German. She always spoke to her husband and children so loudly that her voice broke through the shutters and traveled around the neighborhood.

"She's calling her fatso again," said Tzipori.

A round figure emerged from a distant stairwell and ran towards the woman's voice, which abruptly fell silent.

"Stinking Germans," hissed Yoram.

426

"Hitler," said Sammy the Iraqi, "and now all of a sudden it's raining in the middle of summer." His eyes were reflective.

"It's because there's a storm in Europe," said Michael.

"Aha," said Sammy.

And only I was silent. I was thinking about Yaakov Eizner. I wanted to kill him.

The next morning Tzipori's father knocked at our door. My big brother opened the door a crack and said that our mother and father had gone to work. But Tzipori's father wasn't looking for our mother and father. He was looking for me. I was wearing my summer pajamas, but Tzipori's father didn't care. He came into the room with a heavy and determined tread. With one hand he dragged Tzipori who was as red as a pimento, the kind that were always hanging up to dry on Michael's grandfather's balcony. In the other hand he held a big brown packet, which he waved in front of me and asked: "Do you know what this is?"

"Me?" I said.

"Yes, you, you," cried Tzipori's father angrily. "Don't you be smart with me."

Tzipori looked at me sadly. My big brother, as usual, kept aloof.

"Yes," I said, swallowing hard, "I know what it is. So what if I know what it is?" Suddenly I knew that I had nothing to lose. I would kill Yaakov Eizner in any case. But I had made a mistake when I entrusted the packet of dynamite to Tzipori. He looked to me now like a stupid little chicken.

"Where did you take it from?" demanded Tzipori's father.

I was in no hurry to reply. Suddenly I realized there was no need to hurry. In any case Tzipori's father hadn't gone to work, and I asked myself if it was all in my honor. I looked at Tzipori and I pitied him. He looked at the whitewashed wall as if he had never seen a whitewashed wall before. His little brown eyes stared straight ahead. It seemed to me that he was trying to bore a hole in the wall and disappear inside.

"It's a strong wall, Tzipori. There isn't a crack in it and you'll never get out that way," I said loudly, but to myself.

428 ◆ Reuven Miran

"Answer my questions," yelled his father. His face was flushed and beads of sweat began dripping from his nose.

I looked at my big brother. He was tall and thin, an outstanding student in the tenth grade. And he was silent.

"We didn't take it, Mr. Tzipori. And your son had nothing to do with it anyway." I thought, in my innocence, that Tzipori would be insulted. But he heaved a sigh of relief. For the first time he took his eyes from the wall and looked at me.

Tzipori's father advanced on me. I was wearing my yellow summer pajamas that were at least two sizes too big. It wouldn't be easy to escape in them. I inched toward the door. My big brother kept aloof and said nothing.

"It's from the ruined positions on the hill," I suddenly blurted out. Tzipori's father stopped.

"From the positions on the hill?" he repeated with disbelief. "And the detonators? Are the detonators from there too?"

"No," I replied unwillingly. "There aren't any more. We found them in the woods."

Tzipori listened curiously. My fear was replaced by a violent desire to laugh.

"Tell me," said Tzipori's father (as if I hadn't told him up to now), "why did you give it all to Yerucham?"

I laughed.

"Yerucham?" I asked, "who's Yerucham?"

For the first time a slight smile appeared briefly on my brother's long face. But he went on standing aside, saying nothing, and the smile too disappeared.

"Ah," I said as if it had just occurred to me, "you mean Tzipori. I asked him to look after it for me."

"You little fools," sighed Yerucham's father (I started getting a kick out of the name). "There could have been a fatal accident."

It wasn't quite clear to me what he meant by "fatal," but I didn't say anything.

"But Yerucham didn't look after it," I said quietly, without taking my eyes off Tzipori. His eyes escaped to the wall again. Tzipori's father said nothing. He took a few measured paces around the room. He seemed to have calmed down. My big brother asked: "Won't you have something to drink, Mr. Tzipori?" – and these were the first words I had heard from him in quite a while. But Tzipori senior didn't even bother to reply. He stroked Tzipori junior's head and asked me in as gentle a tone as possible: "What for? What did you want all that stuff for?" I couldn't tell him that I wanted to kill Yaakov Eizner and nothing else came into my head. I looked into Tzipori senior's gray eyes and saw how much he resembled his son.

"*Nu*," he said in the same gentle voice, "the main thing is that nothing happened."

And with these words he departed, dragging Tzipori junior behind.

"It really is dangerous," said my big brother, my big brother who had never laughed in his life.

"Yes," I said, "I know." I didn't look at him. My big brother.

That night I had a dream. I was in the big eucalyptus grove. It was daytime, perhaps late afternoon or early evening. But all at once it was night. I was strolling alone among the trees. If I meet Yaakov Eizner now, I thought, I'll kill him on the spot. I was sure that I would. I knew that I had to kill him. And as soon as I was quite ready, he appeared. He stood there in the middle of the path and smiled. In one hand he was holding a big brown paper packet. Yaakov Eizner. How long I had been waiting for him. He approached and without a word he held out the packet. I recognized it immediately. It was the packet of dynamite and the detonators that I given Tzipori and he had handed over to his father.

Yaakov Eizner said nothing. He held out his hand and offered me the packet.

"Take it," he whispered.

I took the heavy packet from him.

"You want to blow me up, don't you?" whispered Yaakov Eizner.

"I don't like you," I said.

He shrugged his shoulders. The darkness separated us, although we were standing very close together.

"Good," he whispered. And as I had once seen someone do in a movie, he glided towards the ground and fell flat on it.

"Scatter it over me," he whispered.

I scattered the dynamite over him, especially in the region of his head and chest. The strong sharp smell filled the close darkness and out of the darkness Yaakov Eizner offered me a detonator attached to a fuse.

"Have you got any matches?" he asked in a whisper.

And suddenly I understood everything. He was giving me orders and I was obeying them.

"No," I said, "I haven't got any matches."

"Here," whispered Yaakov Eizner in what was almost a scream, "here, take them." He offered me a box of matches. I didn't take it.

"You won't get away with it," I said. "You won't get away with it, Yaakov Eizner. I'll kill you."

He started writhing on the ground at my feet.

"Light it," he begged.

But I left the detonator, fuse, and box of matches in his hand.

"Goodbye," I said, "goodbye, Yaakov Eizner."

"Come back," he cried, "don't leave me like this."

"I'll come back some other time," I said and went away.

And then I woke up. I knew that it was a dream. Yaakov Eizner was a new immigrant, and he didn't know Hebrew. So how could he have spoken to me?

After that I stopped speaking to Tzipori. At home no one said anything to me about the packet. But my big brother, who was in high school and read a lot of books, didn't forget. Every now and then he looked at me with eyes that seemed full of suffering, and this look gave me a very unpleasant feeling. Since I wasn't on speaking terms with Tzipori junior, I excused myself from greeting Tzipori senior too. In the evenings I would slip away to the hill, crawling about and looking for things in the ruined army positions. Our agriculture teacher had told us that this hill had always been an important strategic place. Even under the Turks, he said, bloody battles had been fought on the hill, until the last autumn of the year when the British had gained the upper hand and driven their enemies from the whole of the Sharon. Our agriculture teacher was as well up on all the wars that had been fought in our country as if he had taken part in them himself.

He told us about the War of Independence, too, but when I crawled into the ruined positions which were full of pieces of broken, faded green ammunition boxes and rotting tatters of army capes, I only remembered the red sky of the last autumn from which the agriculture teacher never returned. Everyone was sure that the war would break out in Qalqilyah, where the murderers came from by night. Some even spoke of the need to chop down all the orange groves next to the border, in order to help the Border Police in their patrols and manhunts. And one day we heard the principal of our school shouting during recess that he had never heard such rubbish in his life. "An eye for an eye!" yelled the principal furiously. "We have to destroy them in their homes!" In his excitement he spilt his tea and added a new stain to his trousers.

The orange groves were not chopped down and war didn't break out against our neighbor Qalqilyah. The white village clustering on the bare mountain slopes to the east was not destroyed. The only one who knew this beforehand was our agriculture teacher. "There's no need to destroy anyone," he said, "let alone an entire village." He said that the war would break out in the south, and I remember how they laughed at him. "Look at all the soldiers dug in on the hill," they said to him. "You think they've brought them here just for Esterika the whore?" The agriculture teacher didn't even bother to reply. And I knew that he was cleverer than the rest put together.

One night, in the middle of autumn, we were sitting on the balcony of our apartment, drinking raspberry juice with sparkling water. It was still hot, although the High Holidays had already come and gone. Suddenly I heard muffled noises and then the eastern sky was lit up and turned as red as blood. We sat on the balcony with our faces frozen like photographs in an album. My father looked at us and then at my mother. My big brother retreated into himself and muttered something incomprehensible. I looked at the half empty glasses. The sparkling water was clear. The red raspberry juice had sunk to the bottom of the glasses.

The whole neighborhood was gathered in the street. They were counting the shells falling in the east and smiling. I thought about our agriculture teacher. Had he made a mistake? I felt a burning in my throat. In the street they were roaring with joy.

"Sixty-five!" someone cried. "Sixty-six, whaaam!"

"They're only shooting at the police station," shouted Michael's big brother. "You can see everything from the water tower!" He raced down the sandy street on his bike and the narrow beam of light from the lamp jumped over the houses. I wanted to go out after him but my father told me to go to bed. I didn't go. Had the agriculture teacher made a mistake? I forgot about Yaakov Eizner. All I could think about was the agriculture teacher. Had he made a mistake? And what had all the soldiers really been doing on the hill? Amusing themselves with red-lipped Esterika? Yaakov Eizner had stammered that soldiers always amused themselves with girls. He knew. His parents had told him and he himself remembered. They were in the big war, far away from all our little wars.

"After Yaakov learns Hebrew we'll ask him to tell us about the big war he was in," the agriculture teacher had said one day.

Now Yaakov Eizner stood in the street counting the shells in a loud voice and another language. The sight of the crowd below drew me like a magnet, but my father said if the neighbors wanted to stand as if they were watching a football match or basketball game, that was their business. I stood still on the balcony and hated them. With every exploding shell my heart shuddered. I saw the agriculture teacher's face and the faces of other people I knew and did not know, and I wanted it to be over.

The next morning we went to school as usual. I waited for Tzipori and Yoram. They laughed, as they did every morning when the woman cried from behind the closed shutters: "Hurry Maxielein, *schnell!*" We didn't like Maxie the fatso, and Yoram never forgot to add: "Dirty German!" On the way we were joined by Sammy. Michael was sick. I didn't see Yaakov Eizner until we were already sitting at our desks. His eyes were sunken and circled with black rings. He spoke to his neighbor in a hoarse whisper. Straight after the bell the teacher Bilha came into the class and we fell silent. Her eyes were red. She said: "Good morning," and her voice shook. She couldn't go on. She was crying. The tears poured down her cheeks, and she didn't stop them.

"What happened, Teacher?" asked Pnina, who was on the class committee and the first to recover.

Bilha sank into her chair and cried onto the table until it was all wet with her tears.

"Your agriculture teacher," she stammered, the words coming out all broken and strangled. "Your agriculture teacher was killed in the fighting last night."

Thc floor started shifting underneath me, and so did the walls and ceiling. Everything spun around and around. Only Joseph the janitor's arm was steady, strong and sure as it carried me outside. In the infirmary I lay next to Bilha. She was lying flat on her back with her eyes closed and a damp white towel folded on her forehead. I raised myself and sat on the edge of the bed. We were alone in the room. Then I stole out on tiptoe and ran home.

The next day I stayed at home. I lay in bed leafing through my only agriculture notebook again and again.

There wasn't much in it. He didn't make us write down everything he said. "Write it down in your hearts and minds," he would say, although none of us, I think, understood how it was possible to write down agriculture in our hearts and minds. My notebook was nothing to be proud of. I didn't know how to draw or write fancy letters. With every page I turned, new tears flooded my eyes. My beloved agriculture teacher had made a mistake.

After the tears were over I felt calmer and I knew what I had to do.

After Tzipori's father had confiscated the bag of dynamite which I had collected with so much effort, I looked for another way to kill Yaakov Eizner. In the evening I would steal out to the hill and prowl among the dugouts. The soldiers were gone and all that was left were some empty cans and a lot of olive pits and cigarette stubs. Two weeks after my agriculture teacher was killed in the attack on the Qalqilyah police station, the real war broke out, and it was exactly as he had told us it would be. Although I remembered very well that he had known about it even before he died, I told him all about it, and also about everything else that was happening in the country as I wandered about the deserted hill. Sometimes I asked his advice, but only on insignificant matters. I didn't tell him that I was going to kill Yaakov Eizner. I knew he would never have agreed to that.

The only way left was to kill him with my gun. So I took my slingshot to the hill, stood one crate on top of another, and drew a little circle with chalk on the top. Inside the dugouts I found some lead shrapnel fragments and I shot them into the little circle. I went on shooting until the sun set. Then I took a long look at the parched bare hills in the east. They were bathed in a very clear, bright light. I could make out every bush, every rock, every dry creek. The agriculture teacher had gone there and never came back.

One morning, at the beginning of the vacation, I was awakened by the noise of a big truck engine. My big brother had gone to study French in Herzlia. An old truck was parked in the street under the balcony and two movers were dragging furniture out of the apartment opposite. Yaakov Eizner's apartment. His parents were supervising the movers while Yaakov himself was scrambling about on the truck arranging things one on top of the other. I looked at my watch. It was half past nine. Tzipori suddenly crossed the road. He dragged his feet slowly through the sand, warming up in the morning sun. I hadn't spoken to him since he had given his father the dynamite. But now he called out to me: "They're moving! They're going to America!" I said nothing, but Yaakov Eizner paused for a moment and raised his curly black head to me. I think our eyes met. I went into the room and took my gun from the closet. When I returned to the windowsill there were bright stars shining in my eyes, and among them I saw the face of my beloved agriculture teacher. I selected a particularly smooth lead pellet and cocked my slingshot. The taut rubber bands reddened in the sunlight. On the ground below, the movers had almost finished loading the truck and Yaakov Eizner's parents had vanished into the driver's cabin. Yaakov Eizner stood on his parents' dining room table, tightening the leather straps that held it to the wooden ladders, which went down the sides of the truck. I aimed my slingshot at his head. The black nape of his neck filled the sight. I heard him counting the shells exploding in the eastern sky. The red sky covered the whole neighborhood. I saw my agriculture teacher's lips whispering: "There's no need to destroy anyone, let alone an entire village." The floor slipped from under my feet. I squeezed the trigger and felt myself ascending into the sky.

By the time I recovered, at the beginning of the second half of the vacation, my big brother was already registered for an English-language course. I myself went on wandering among the deserted dugouts on the hill. The warm summer rain had stopped falling. Every morning I climbed the hill. I broke the slingshot and scattered the pieces in the trenches. The grass covered everything.

A number of picture postcards arrived from Yaakov Eizner. His parents sent them to the people who lived downstairs. They showed high buildings, big parks, and long lines of motor cars. Michael showed them to me, but I wasn't interested.

At lunchtime I would come back from the hill. I spoke to nobody and nobody spoke to me. From time to time my mother commented that I had apparently not fully recovered from my illness, and she was probably right. I would go into the bathroom and lock the door. There was a big mirror there and I would stand in front of it with my head lowered but my eyes raised. I would look straight into my own eyes and my gaze would pass between my father's shaving gear and my mother's cosmetic vials and come back to me.

"You're in America now," I would whisper, "but nothing, nothing is over."

There was a hard look in my eyes and sometimes it even frightened me.

After the long vacation I moved up to the seventh grade.

Yitzhak Orpaz

Talitha Kumi

Translated by Dalya Bilu

In September everyone's looking for an apartment. Especially in Jerusalem. Especially students. This is the busy season for Yochanan Dvir, apartment renovator and owner of a few of them himself. Two small apartments which he renovated in Nahlaoth he rented out immediately for 400 dollars each. He was on the point of renting out the third, a one-room apartment in Abulafia Street, for 300 dollars, but before he could sign the contract Haimke Levine called him from Tel Aviv and said: "Listen. Maybe you've got something for my daughter. She's been accepted at the Bezalel art school and she needs a one-room apartment."

Yochanan said "Yes." Without hesitation.

Haimke Levine had helped Yochanan when he was in big trouble. He had fallen in love. Suddenly he understood the meaning of the words "for love is fierce as death." And the girl – a high-school student. He stopped working and ran around like a lunatic. One day he began taking an interest in the Shalom Tower, walking around and counting the floors. Haimke went with him, ate with him, refused to leave him alone. And all the time he told him horror stories about this one and that one and how they all, thank God, survived in the end. And were getting along nicely too. Once he even jumped into the Gordon swimming pool for him. He shouted "I'm sick of it!" and jumped in at the deep end. He didn't know how to swim. Yochanan naturally jumped in after him and pulled him out. Afterwards it turned out that Haimke was once the junior swimming champion or something. He simply never left him alone. This was four years before. Yochanan got over it, and in the end he even got married (and divorced again). They didn't see much of each other. But Yochanan kept a warm spot in his heart for Haimke. And when he called and asked a favor for his daughter, Yochanan immediately saw before his eyes Haimke's floury face, his soft laugh, and the exposed gums at the front of his mouth. He wouldn't hear of an implant or a prosthesis. He claimed that he couldn't afford it, that the child support he paid for his two daughters ate up everything he earned teaching mathematics at a crammer's. As far as this was concerned Yochanan didn't believe him. In Yochanan's opinion, Haimke knew that the exposed gums were part of his elderly charm. In any case, Yochanan was delighted to have the opportunity to repay him. He had never seen Haimke's daughters.

"Her name's Dana," said Haimke Levine. "You'll recognize her immediately. Innocent-looking with big eyes."

They arranged for Yochanan to meet Dana the next day at seven o'clock in the evening next to Talitha Kumi,[1] to show her the apartment and give her the key.

"How much?" asked Haimke.
"Don't insult me. We'll talk about money later."

His watch was fast. Sometimes ten minutes and sometimes twenty. This didn't bother him. He liked feeling that he was running ahead of time. He took his shoulder bag, but instead of wearing his regular jeans which he used for work too, he put on a striped shirt and wide cotton trousers. He checked his beard after shaving too, smelled his armpits after showering, and combed his short, strong hair, and suddenly it occurred to him – and he wasn't even surprised – that he was getting ready for a blind date.

---

1. Talitha Kumi: "Arise, little maid," words spoken by Jesus (Mark 5:41) on resuscitating a young girl. When the school by this name – a school for Arab Christian girls established by German missionaries in the 19th century – was demolished to make way for a shopping complex in downtown Jerusalem, some of the features of the historic building, including an arch with a clock, were preserved and reconstructed as a little edifice on the plaza in front of the Mashbir Latzarhan department store.

But he didn't change the contents of his shoulder-bag. The usual pliers and screwdriver, he never left the house without them. Any repair or renovation, big or small, you began with them.

And there was also a thick notebook with a hard black cover in the shoulder bag, on whose first page, under the word "Diary," the opening date was written in green ink, and after that nothing. And there was also a thin book published by the Open University in a soft cobalt blue cover, the color of his Subaru car, on the subject of quantum theory. The fate of the universe had been worrying him lately.

Equipped with all the above, he made for Talitha Kumi. The clock on the facade of Talitha Kumi said six-thirty. He compared it with his wristwatch, which said six-forty. He trusted the Talitha Kumi clock, which left him enough time to duplicate a key for Haimke Levine's daughter, who appeared in his imagination as a pale, fragile girl who spoke in a whisper and whose big soft eyes shyly caressed his face.

At about the time Yochanan was putting the finishing touches to his mental portrait of the girl he was going to meet next to Talitha Kumi, the man finished duplicating the key. Yochanan was pleased by this synchronization, it seemed to him like a vestige of some longed-for harmonious world which had once existed, but was now lost. It also held out promise for a successful meeting. He looked for a key-ring and found a gilt medallion with a picture of Madonna. He supposed that she would want Madonna. He himself detested Madonna. The duplication of the key cost him four shekels, the key-ring eight. This seemed exorbitant to him, and he almost bought one in the shape of a Dutch clog for four shekels, but at the last moment, for the sake of Haimke Levine, he decided to buy the medallion with Madonna nevertheless.

A wonderful feeling of generosity flooded him. He didn't exactly know what to do with it. He dropped a whole shekel into the violin case of a street musician, and called up one of his two tenants, a new immigrant from Russia, and asked him what he could do to help him. The new immigrant said: "Everything. Everything. *Nye harasho.*" Yochanan promised to come and see what he could do. Maybe that very evening. He knew, of course, that the faucets had to be fixed, but his experience as a landlord told him that if he didn't do it, the tenant would. The tenant, however, who misunderstood the landlord's good intentions, said something in Russian which sounded to Yochanan like a curse.

Yochanan thought that this was unfair. But he made up his mind not to let it spoil the rendezvous. He returned to the Talitha Kumi plaza. On his arm he carried a black anorak. As a native Tel Avivian he mistrusted the Jerusalem weather: suddenly in the middle of summer, especially here, you would be hit by a freezing wind. Even without a wind, it was September now, and September evenings in Jerusalem meant sweaters and anoraks.

Talitha Kumi is the place where everybody meets everybody, especially at this hour. The light took on a kind of bluish hue – he was always astounded by this color of light in Jerusalem, in the last ten minutes before darkness gathered. Perhaps they would be in time to meet inside the blue. Now he saw her as a Japanese silk doll. Deathly pallor worked well on his hormones. He was glad that he had been given the opportunity to discover this side of himself. Not only would he give her the gilded key-ring studded with glittering stones, he would show her the apartment and ask her what it lacked, and after she told him shyly what it lacked, he would say to her, casually: "It's on the house."

He liked these thoughts. He wanted to cry. His ex-wife's words still rang in his ears ("You only think of yourself"), and in view of all this abundance he was about to shower on his friend's daughter, he was overwhelmed by a swelling surge of self-love. After a long time of dulling his mind with house renovations and apartment rentals, together with abstract concern for the fate of the universe – he suddenly felt good, and he was almost happy.

The watch on his wrist said ten past seven. Another ten minutes at least, he said to himself. Maybe fifteen. He looked forward to a delightful hour, and in the meantime, in a kind of eagerness hitherto almost unknown to him to do something for others, he went up to a particularly vociferous group clamoring near the edge of the plaza, and suggested that they state their case quietly. One of them, holding a placard with the clenched fist of the Kach movement, bent down and roared into his face: "Are you for or against?"

Yochanan thought that the man was joking, but he was afraid to laugh. At a distance of a few steps from there a young man in a teeshirt and shorts was standing and muttering: "No more war, no more bloodshed."[2] Yochanan wanted to tell them that now, when the world was about to collapse anyway, there was no point in worrying about trifles. Most of all he wanted to shout: *"I'm happy! I'm happy!"*

But the lout with the placard, puzzled by the mumbling of the weirdo – who at this moment opened his arms as if to embrace the world – lowered his heavy head with a roar:

"Are you for or against?"

The question was definitely unfair. Yochanan saw the dagger flash under the flapping shirt of the armed giant with the cobalt face who was threatening the world.

He thought of inviting him to discuss the problem over a cup of coffee in Café Atara, but in view of the urgency of the matter, he immediately declared:

"I'm for or against."

The clenched fist of his interrogator remained suspended in the air, enabling Yochanan to withdraw in a more or less orderly manner.

As he retreated, walking backwards, Yochanan admitted to himself that the Cobalt Man's question had a certain justice, if not in its style then in its content. He had never completely made up his mind whether he was for or against anything. It seemed to him a little beside the point. For example, if he happened to bump into a high-school student with a murmuring voice and caressing eyes, he wouldn't ask himself if he was for or against, he would simply die for her.

Dana, for instance.

At this moment he realized that he was imagining the kind-hearted Haimke's daughter as a kind of double of the high-school student for whose sake he had almost thrown himself off the Shalom Tower. This moved him, and he couldn't come up with any good reason to fight

---

2.   In English in the original.

against this wild flight of his imagination. Somewhere deep in his heart he was always ready to forget his apartments and the child support which had turned him unwillingly into a landlord with apartments to rent, and the never-ending worry about the imminent destruction of the world, which appeared to him in the form of a cobalt-colored booklet shooting out of his bag and exploding into a million scraps of colored paper – a real celebration! – and to begin the adventure of his death from the beginning.

A few useful details about the life history of Yochanan Dvir:

Motherless from the age of six, a bookworm to the age of sixteen, fatherless from the age of sixteen, apprenticed to a renovations contractor from the age of sixteen, non-registered student in the departments of Jewish Mysticism and Business Administration at Tel Aviv University, a six-month course in Japanese flower arrangement, two years as a pilgrim at a temple in Nepal, whence he returns bearded, smiling, and silent, to work from the age of twenty-four at odd jobs, and between one job and the next to lie on his back and smile at the ceiling. Sometimes he announces, alone or among casual acquaintance, over a glass of beer, in response to urgent events: "It's impossible to know anything." In this manner ten years go by. At the age of thirty-four he is pushed into marriage by two of his acquaintances, themselves married, who are unable to bear his provocative bachelorhood. From the age of thirty-nine, divorced with a child. At this age, one day after his divorce, he bought a thick notebook with a hard cover and wrote under the word "DIARY," printed in large letters: *"Begun on the 15th of September 198 – Yochanan Dvir."* The date was important, since it was his birthday. But Yochanan did not believe in horoscopes and the signs of the zodiac, and accordingly he did not see the date as having any significance beyond the date itself. Ever since then he had carried the notebook around with him wherever he went, in a special compartment in his shoulder-bag. Apart from the opening date he didn't write a single word in the notebook. After his divorce, his wanderings, the death of his parents, and his first love, he was sure that he would have something to write in the diary. But when he sat down to write in it, everything seemed to him trivial, meaningless, and incomprehensible, and the notebook remained empty. Nevertheless he never stopped believing that one day he would find something to write in his diary. When he fell in love with the beautiful high-school student, who spoke to him – her private tutor in mathematics – in a soft voice and with a caressing look, he decided that this was the thing he had been waiting for, and everything assumed a tremendous significance. Her name was Dana. In his dreams she smoked his pipe (he had never smoked a pipe) which had a gigantic stem. He immediately understood that the sights of Nepal were intruding here and signalling to him: This is your bride. This is your betrothed. He almost began to write in the diary, but then the girl made it clear to him that she had a boyfriend, and that if he continued to harass her she would call the police, and he began to contemplate suicide. Yochanan was sure that there had been a misunderstanding here, that she was meant for him, and that it was only because of some fault or hitch in a dark corner among the stars – of which he could know nothing because of the immanent uncertainty stemming from quantum theory – that it had not come off, and the little high-school student had exchanged him in her blind naïveté for some stupid athletic boy who still had pimples on his face.

According to the same logic, Yochanan argued in his own favor, as he lay on his back for days at a time looking at the ceiling, it was possible that some other, opposite fault, a kind of anti-fault, in some other corner of the universe, would cancel them both out, and the girl would return to him as naturally as the sun returns to its course in the morning, and his life would be saved.

Equipped with these thoughts and a full measure of self-pity, he stood for hours in front of the Shalom Tower and counted the floors from top to bottom, without any intention of committing suicide, but full of gratitude to Haimke Levine who took his tears and threats seriously. From the age of thirty-nine he worked as a renovations contractor, both because of the need to pay child support for his son, whom he hardly ever saw, and because of the opportunities offered him by the Jerusalem building market, which began to boom with the mass immigration from Russia; but mainly because of an inner consciousness that Jerusalem was a place in which everything was still possible. He soon found himself with apartments to rent. He had an accounts book, also in a hard cover, in which he wrote down his income and expenditure at the end of the day, but he did not take this notebook with him in his shoulder-bag. He thought: if what he had heard a scientist saying on the radio was true, that it was enough for a butterfly in Kamchatka to flutter its wings in order to create a cyclone in the constellation of Sirius, then mixing up the two notebooks could be really dangerous.

Yochanan shook his arms as if they were crawling with vermin, but for safety's sake he also sent a conciliatory wave in the direction of the lout, who had not yet recovered from his stupefaction.

The twilight blue dissolved into the cold neon lights of the evening, and Yochanan asked himself if he had done everything possible to be worthy of the frissons of delight awaiting him at the appointed hour. In the meantime he scratched his back between his shoulder-blades, where a kind of scabies had taken up permanent residence during one of his journeys. A cold wind descended on the plaza and went away again, and the crowds of people, of all races and ages, who momentarily raised their heads as if to see where the cold wind was coming from, immediately returned to their searches or their wares, jewelry and balloons, knitwear, missionary leaflets and prayer-books for the High Holidays; the violinist to his violin, the messiahs to their demented mutterings, and the quarrelers to their quarrels, and a rabble of faces and garments moved to and fro like sleepwalkers around the stone arch bearing the name of a young girl who had come back to life – and they all looked as if they were searching for their blind date.

Yochanan put on his black anorak, which up to now he had been carrying over his arm, examined the way it lay over his white shirt with the brown stripes, and leaving the sleeves unbuttoned for an effect of careless grace, he looked at the Talitha Kumi clock and was shocked.

The clock still said half past six.

The anticipated frissons of delight gave way to confusion. On principle he was against confusion. And so he resolutely exchanged the confusion for paternal concern. What had happened to the girl? His dear friend Haimke had entrusted her to his care, and now where was the girl? Irrelevantly he remembered that he hadn't had any supper. He bought a hotdog for three shekels, demanded mustard, crammed half of it into his mouth with one bite, and immediately spat it out into the municipal litter bin, into which he also disgustedly threw what was left in his hand. There. In spite of his hunger, he had given up the hotdog. This seemed to him a worthy sacrifice. His watch said seven forty. How was he to tell if his watch was fast or slow? Suddenly he no longer trusted his watch. He wanted to swear, but he couldn't find the right word, and so he ripped it furiously off his wrist, but he couldn't bring himself to throw it away and he put it in his pocket instead. He asked someone who looked serious: "What's the time?" "I'm not from here," said the man. Another man asked Yochanan if the No. 4 bus went to Kiryat Yovel. Yochanan, who believed in the supreme importance of maintaining your presence of mind under stress, explained patiently that he could go to Kiryat Yovel with No. 18, 20, or 27, and that the nearest bus stop was in Jaffa Street. But the man interrupted him with a dismissive gesture and said: "All I asked was if No. 4 goes to Kiryat Yovel."

Suddenly he had the distinct feeling that all the people here, waiting on the steps of the monument and milling around it, had been waiting and milling around since yesterday, since the day before yesterday, and maybe forever. And they had all missed their appointments because of this bloody Talitha Kumi clock, which had probably stopped two thousand years ago at least. In the grip of this defeatist thought, he turned to a pale young girl, who was sitting and writing from left to right on a letter pad, and asked her, after apologizing in two languages, what the time was. She said: "Eight o'clock." In Hebrew.

Her voice was soft, something delicate and painful tightened her lips. For a moment he hoped that she was Dana. In the terrible pressure he felt in his guts, he was ready to compromise, and so he asked her if she was by any chance Dana Levine. She whistled a few words between her almost-closed lips, among which he identified one English word he knew: "Asshole."

A mumbling, bearded messiah-freak who was standing with his back to the big display windows of the Mashbir Letzarhan went on mechanically repeating, in a nasal American accent: "The last train, gentlemen. It's not too late." Only now, perhaps under the influence of the words of the mad, self-anointed messiah, Yochanan grasped his new position: that he was late. By a simple calculation, while he was duplicating the key, phoning his tenant and messing around with the morons from Kach, Dana had been looking for him. He was at least half an hour late. Dana had waited for him for half an hour and left. He dismissed out of hand the possibility that she had not recognized him – in such cases your eyes met with the force of an electric shock. By a simple calculation, the cold wind had descended on the plaza at exactly half past seven, and that was supposed to be the minute at which it would happen. I'm thinking like a madman, thought Yochanan. He immediately formed a two-pronged plan. One: call Haimke – Dana had undoubtely phoned him to tell him what had happened. And if the first move failed, then the second came into operation: he would go to the apartment in Abulafia Street, within spitting distance, and there – he could see the picture in front of his eyes – she walks past the entrance, lingers for a moment, and her big eyes caress the iron door, and she rings the bell, and listens, and when nobody answers she leans against the doorpost and waits.

He inserted ten tokens, anticipating a long conversation with his Tel Aviv friend. There was no reply. He proceeded immediately to the second move. But half-way there, as he crossed Mesilat Yesharim Street, he remembered that he hadn't retrieved the telephone tokens. He decided not to make an issue out of it and to continue on his way. But in the narrow alley, Avi, a skinny youth with a stealthy step, known in the neighborhood as something between a thief and a junkie, barred his way. Avi's mother was sitting on the steps of the Hagoral synagogue, holding a chicken in her lap and stroking it. She always sat on the same step with a chicken in her lap. In the neighborhood they said that she saw everything, but she had one eye stuck permanently shut. Her son, Avi, stood barring the way with his legs wide apart, and took a deep drag from his cigarette. The alley was narrow, barely one and a half meters' wide, and it was impossible to pass without pushing up against him.

"I've got somebody for you."

His voice was menacing.

"Thank you. I've already got someone," said Yochanan.

"A girl, right?"

"How do you know."

His heart was full of foreboding.

"There was some female here," said Avi. "Don't worry. I'll give you a girl you can rely on, just right for you. Two hundred, maybe two hundred and fifty – what the hell's the matter with you!"

Yochanan charged forward, almost knocking him over. He ran, but immediately slowed down. He rang the bell and knocked on the door of his house, as if Dana were inside. But Dana wasn't even outside.

He went up to his apartment. For a moment he wondered why Dana wasn't there. Then he wondered at his wonder. In the meantime he promised himself that even if she wasn't there, she would come back, of that there could be no doubt. After all, she belonged here.

The thought that Dana belonged here and that she would therefore simply return here, was so pleasing to him that he awarded himself a laugh in front of the mirror, rubbed his teeth with his finger and smelled it, and in order to give full expression to the feeling of relief, he stretched his arms out to the empty room and yawned a deep yawn. And then he was seized by a terrible panic.

Maybe something had happened to her!

Yochanan Dvir found himself at this hour, inside his house, in a state of total uncertainty as to where to go and what to do, but with the clear knowledge that he had to do something, come what may. This being the case, he took his accounts book and began to write down his expenditures for the day: duplication of key – 3 shekels; keyring for Dana Levine – 8 shekels; hotdog, telephone calls –

A police car, or maybe an ambulance, drove past with a wail, right under his window. The situation seemed urgent, even threatening, but on no account could he clarify to himself where things had gone wrong. The Talitha Kumi clock appeared before him, confident and eternal, its hands on six-thirty. He tried to phone Haimke and found the line dead. It must have been that junkie Avi who had cut the line. The neighborhood boss. Skinny as a dried fig, and lording it over everybody like a rooster. He had to phone the police, but the phone was dead.

Yochanan resolutely dismissed the idea that everyone had conspired against him. The effort he invested in this refusal made him sweat, especially in his armpits. He smelled his armpits. The smell wasn't so bad, but nevertheless he sprayed himself with a deodorant. He liked deodorants that smelled of tobacco. He liked his body. He still saw himself going to keep his appointment with Dana. He drew encouragement from his short, hard haircut, and decided to act with presence of mind.

And immediately, as if he had gone beserk, he began to run. In his catastrophe-haunted heart he immediately connected the nervous wailing of the police cars and ambulances arriving from the direction of the Talitha Kumi plaza with the inevitable death of Dana, hope of his life. As he ran he tried to connect his permanent anxiety about the collapse of the universe with the death of Dana, but they wouldn't connect. The little pimp with his eternal cigarette barred his way, this time facing the opposite direction. Yochanan decided that with the wailing of the sirens in the background and Dana hovering between life and death it wouldn't be so terrible if he knocked the little bastard out of his way. He did it. "I don't believe it," he said to himself in surprise. "I don't believe that I did it." Judging by the squawking of the chicken, Yochanan guessed that the little pimp had rolled onto his mother.

But Yochanan's heart was already elsewhere. His Dana lay dying

on the Mashbir plaza, at the feet of the Talitha Kumi archway, covered
with a blanket, and they were already pulling a stretcher out of one of
the ambulances. He heard shouts: "Kill them, they work for Jews and
come at you with knives!" He crossed knots of people, shouts, wailing
sirens. He sensed huge powers in himself. Policemen grabbed him and
he eluded them, and fell on the body. He tore the blanket off the body
and lay down on it full length and shouted "*Kumi*, get up, Dana my
soul, get up, Dana my heart –"

That was as far as he got. The policemen grabbed hold of him and
dragged him behind the arch of Talitha Kumi and seated him on the
concrete step.

Someone brought water.

Yochanan rejected the water. The sweat was pouring off him. A
policeman wiped the blood off his face.

"Take it easy," said the policeman. "Is this yours?"

Yochanan nodded and the policeman hung the shoulder bag on his
shoulder.

"Are you related to her?"

"She's my brother's daughter."

"What's your brother's name?"

"Haim Levine."

His answers were lucid. He didn't look anywhere. He knew that all
in all he was the hero of a tragedy and the victim of a great love, and
decided to act accordingly.

"What's your name?"

"Yochanan Dvir."

"How do you know that she's your brother's daughter?"

"That's an idiotic question," said Yochanan.

The policeman put the side of his hand in position for a dry chop.
But another policeman intervened:

"Leave him alone. Can't you see? The guy's in shock."

"What's her name?"

"Dana. Dana Levine."

The second policeman, the one who had spoken before, rummaged
in a small denim knapsack and pulled out a document that looked like

a passport. He paged through the passport and showed Yochanan the photo.

"Do you know this woman?"

"No," said Yochanan.

"Her name's Sandra Lee, Arkansas, USA. Is that your brother's daughter?" asked the policeman.

"No. But..." said Yochanan, "it's not too late."

He stretched out his finger and pointed it at the level of their eyes. The second policeman exchanged a glance with the interrogating policeman.

"You can go," said the interrogating policeman.

Yochanan felt slighted at not having been taken in for more serious questioning. What could you expect from policemen who saw the world through the nickel of their police badges? There had been a big mistake here, of that there was no doubt. A colossal mistake in his opinion, but completely comprehensible. If they had given him a chance he would have opened their eyes to see that there was something more, something else, more than the human eye could see, and that it was not an everyday matter. Yochanan's mind, which had in a certain sense been clouded, but in another sense been granted clarity, immediately connected everything with the great imminent collapse, when the bodies racing toward nothingness, toward the gathering darkness, would open up to each other like lovers at the hour of their last farewell. What's the wonder that my Dana, Dana my soul, came back to life.

Pityingly he now looked at the two ignorant policeman, who didn't understand what they saw. One thing was absolutely clear: as long as he waited for his Dana, as long as he waited for his Dana, his Dana was alive.

These are good thoughts, said Yochanan to himself. He went up to the battery of public telephones to call Haimke, but remembered that he had no tokens left, and turned round to go home. His whole body hurt, but the sacrifice was worth it. Even if he never saw Dana as long as he lived, he had done his bit. At the same time, however, he wasn't sure if the cosmic forces which had assisted hirn to bring Dana back to life would be enough to protect him from the swift knife of the little pimp, who was presumably lying in wait for him in the alley. Accordingly he made a detour round the neighborhood via Agrippas Street and approached his house from the rear, stealthily, and immediately phoned Haimke.

He was sure that Haimke knew everything. The hand which had previously cut the line had now repaired it. Haimke was on the line.

"Listen, Yochanan. It's a good thing you phoned. Danka's found something else. A friend of hers has rented a two-room apartment and she's going to share it with her. Not far from you, by the way, in Bezalel Street."

"But..." said Yochanan in bewilderment. "She. You know. That's to say..."

"Yes. Of course. She came to tell you. You sound... is anything wrong?"

"No."

"Then bye for now. Drop in some time."

Yochanan leant on the table. He was very tired. And now he also felt a pressure at the base of his head, where it joined his neck. This he imagined was where the plug connecting all the positive cosmic forces was situated. He felt exhausted. He wasn't sure that he would be able to play his role in maintaining the system. He needed concrete proof. Accordingly he phoned his Russian tenant and the moment he heard the word "faucets" he went for him and told him not to expect any refunds or repairs from him: "Listen here" – he yelled at him –"you fix those faucets yourself. I'm telling you. Everyone has to do his bit, and that's that."

What he said sounded to him barbaric. But completely justified. It was high time they learnt Hebrew.

He went into the bathroom and tested the hot water. There was hot water. He left the faucet open. He liked seeing the steam rising from the hot water. As he pulled off his anorak and kicked off his sandals, he reviewed his day with detached interest, like a person examining someone else's clothes. He vaguely remembered the clock set into the stone arch of Talitha Kumi. The clock said half past six. Why half past six, for God's sake?

"Here's something to open the diary with," he said to himself.

In the meantime he got into the bath.

"It can wait till tomorrow," he said to himself.

Amos Oz

Nomad and Viper

Translated by Nicholas de Lange
and Philip Simpson

I

The famine brought them.

They fled north from the horrors of famine, together with their
dusty flocks. From September to April the desert had not known a
moment's relief from drought. The loess was pounded to dust. Famine
had spread through the nomads' encampments and wrought havoc
among their flocks.

The military authorities gave the situation their urgent attention.
Despite certain hesitations, they decided to open the roads leading
north to the Bedouins. A whole population – men, women, and
children – could not simply be abandoned to the horrors of starvation.

Dark, sinuous, and wiry, the desert tribesmen trickled along the dirt
paths, and with them came their emaciated flocks. They meandered
along gullies hidden from town dwellers' eyes. A persistent stream
pressed northward, circling the scattered settlements, staring wide-eyed
at the sights of the settled land. The dark flocks spread into the fields of
golden stubble, tearing and chewing with strong, vengeful teeth. The
nomads' bearing was stealthy and subdued; they shrank from watchful
eyes. They took pains to avoid encounters. Tried to conceal their
presence.

If you passed them on a noisy tractor and set billows of dust loose
on them, they would courteously gather their scattered flocks and give

you a wide passage, wider by far than was necessary. They stared at you from a distance, frozen like statues. The scorching atmosphere blurred their appearance and gave a uniform look to their features: a shepherd with his staff, a woman with her babes, an old man with his eyes sunk deep in their sockets. Some were half-blind, or perhaps feigned half-blindness from some vague alms-gathering motive. Inscrutable to the likes of you.

How unlike our well-tended sheep were their miserable specimens: knots of small, skinny beasts huddling into a dark, seething mass, silent and subdued, humble as their dumb keepers.

The camels alone spurn meekness. From atop tall necks they fix you with tired eyes brimming with scornful sorrow. The wisdom of age seems to lurk in their eyes, and a nameless tremor runs often through their skin.

Sometimes you manage to catch them unawares. Crossing a field on foot, you may suddenly happen on an indolent flock standing motionless, noon-struck, their feet apparently rooted in the parched soil. Among them lies the shepherd, fast asleep, dark as a block of basalt. You approach and cover him with a harsh shadow. You are startled to find his eyes wide open. He bares most of his teeth in a placatory smile. Some of them are gleaming, others decayed. His smell hits you. You grimace. Your grimace hits him like a punch in the face. Daintily he picks himself up, trunk erect, shoulders hunched. You fix him with a cold blue eye. He broadens his smile and utters a guttural syllable. His garb is a compromise: a short, patched European jacket over a white desert robe. He cocks his head to one side. An appeased gleam crosses his face. If you do not upbraid him, he suddenly extends his left hand and asks for a cigarette in rapid Hebrew. His voice has a silken quality, like that of a shy woman. If your mood is generous, you put a cigarette to your lips and toss another into his wrinkled palm. To your surprise, he snatches a gilt lighter from the recesses of his robe and offers a furtive flame. The smile never leaves his lips. His smile lasts too long, is unconvincing. A flash of sunlight darts off the thick gold ring adorning his finger and pierces your squinting eyes.

Eventually you turn your back on the nomad and continue on your way. After a hundred, two hundred paces, you may turn your head and see him standing just as he was, his gaze stabbing your back. You could swear that he is still smiling, that he will go on smiling for a long while to come.

And then, their singing in the night. A long-drawn-out, dolorous wail drifts on the night air from sunset until the early hours. The voices penetrate to the gardens and pathways of the kibbutz and charge our nights with an uneasy heaviness. No sooner have you settled down to sleep than a distant drumbeat sets the rhythm of your slumber like the pounding of an obdurate heart. Hot are the nights, and vapor-laden. Stray clouds caress the moon like a train of gentle camels, camels without any bells.

The nomads' tents are made up of dark drapes. Stray women drift around at night, barefoot and noiseless. Lean, vicious nomad hounds dart out of the camp to challenge the moon all night long. Their barking drives our kibbutz dogs insane. Our finest dog went mad one night, broke into the henhouse, and massacred the young chicks. It was not out of savagery that the watchmen shot him. There was no alternative. Any reasonable man would justify their action.

II

You might imagine that the nomad incursion enriched our heat-prostrated nights with a dimension of poetry. This may have been the case for some of our unattached girls. But we cannot refrain from mentioning a whole string of prosaic, indeed unesthetic disturbances, such as foot-and-mouth disease, crop damage, and an epidemic of petty thefts.

The foot-and-mouth disease came out of the desert, carried by their livestock, which had never been subjected to any proper medical inspection. Although we took various early precautions, the virus infected our sheep and cattle, severely reducing the milk yield and killing off a number of animals.

As for the damage to the crops, we had to admit that we had never managed to catch one of the nomads in the act. All we ever found were the tracks of men and animals among the rows of vegetables, in the hayfields, and deep inside the carefully fenced orchards. And wrecked irrigation pipes, plot markers, farming implements left out in the fields, and other objects.

We are not the kind to take such things lying down. We are no believers in forbearance or vegetarianism. This is especially true of our younger men. Among the veteran founders there are a few adherents of Tolstoyan ideas and such like. Decency constrains me from dwelling in detail on certain isolated and exceptional acts of reprisal conducted by some of the youngsters whose patience had expired, such as cattle rustling, stoning a nomad boy, or beating one of the shepherds senseless. In defense of the perpetrators of the last-mentioned act of retaliation I must state clearly that the shepherd in question had an infuriatingly sly face. He was blind in one eye, broken-nosed, drooling; and his mouth – on this the men responsible were unanimous – was set with long, curved fangs like a fox's. A man with such an appearance was capable of anything. And the Bedouins would certainly not forget this lesson.

The pilfering was the most worrisome aspect of all. They laid hands on the unripe fruit in our orchards, pocketed the faucets, whittled away piles of empty sacks in the fields, stole into the henhouses, and even made away with the modest valuables from our little houses.

The very darkness was their accomplice. Elusive as the wind, they passed through the settlement, evading both the guards we had posted and the extra guards we had added. Sometimes you would set out on a tractor or a battered jeep toward midnight to turn off the irrigation faucets in an outlying field and your headlights would trap fleeting shadows, a man or a night beast. An irritable guard decided one night to open fire, and in the dark he managed to kill a stray jackal.

Needless to say, the kibbutz secretariat did not remain silent. Several times Etkin, the secretary, called in the police, but their tracking dogs betrayed or failed them. Having led their handlers a few paces outside the kibbutz fence, they raised their black noses, uttered a savage howl, and stared foolishly ahead.

Spot raids on the tattered tents revealed nothing. It was as if the very earth had decided to cover up the plunder and brazenly outstare the victims. Eventually the elder of the tribe was brought to the kibbutz office, flanked by a pair of inscrutable nomads. The short-tempered policemen pushed them forward with repeated cries of "*Yallah, yallah.*"

We, the members of the secretariat, received the elder and his men politely and respectfully. We invited them to sit down on the bench, smiled at them, and offered them steaming coffee prepared by Geula at Etkin's special request. The old man responded with elaborate courtesies, favoring us with a smile which he kept up from the beginning of the interview till its conclusion. He phrased his remarks in careful, formal Hebrew.

It was true that some of the youngsters of his tribe had laid hands on our property. Why should he deny it? Boys would be boys, and the world was getting steadily worse. He had the honor of begging our pardon and restoring the stolen property. Stolen property fastens its teeth in the flesh of the thief, as the proverb says. That was the way of it. What could one do about the hotheadedness of youth? He deeply regretted the trouble and distress we had been caused.

So saying, he put his hand into the folds of his robe and drew out a few screws, some gleaming, some rusty, a pair of pruning hooks, a stray knife-blade, a pocket flashlight, a broken hammer, and three grubby bank notes, as a recompense for our loss and worry.

Etkin spread his hands in embarrassment. For reasons best known to himself, he chose to ignore our guest's Hebrew and to reply in broken Arabic, the residue of his studies during the time of the riots and the siege. He opened his remarks with a frank and clear statement about the brotherhood of nations – the cornerstone of our ideology – and about the quality of neighborliness of which the peoples of the East had long been justly proud, and never more so than in these days of bloodshed and groundless hatred.

To Etkin's credit, let it be said that he did not shrink in the slightest from reciting a full and detailed list of the acts of theft, damage, and sabotage that our guest – as the result of oversight, no doubt – had refrained from mentioning in his apology. If all the stolen property were returned and the vandalism stopped once and for all, we would be wholeheartedly willing to open a new page in the relations of our two neighboring communities. Our children would doubtless enjoy and profit from an educational courtesy visit to the Bedouin encampment, the kind of visit that broadens horizons. And it went without saying that the tribe's children would pay a return visit to our kibbutz home, in the interest of deepening mutual understanding.

The old man neither relaxed nor broadened his smile, but kept it sternly at its former level as he remarked with an abundance of polite phrases, that the gentlemen of the kibbutz would be able to prove no further thefts beyond those he had already admitted and for which he had sought our forgiveness.

He concluded with elaborate benedictions, wished us health and long life, posterity and plenty, then took his leave and departed, accompanied by his two barefooted companions wrapped in their dark robes. They were soon swallowed up by the wadi that lay outside the kibbutz fence.

Since the police had proved ineffectual – and had indeed abandoned the investigation – some of our young men suggested making an excursion one night to teach the savages a lesson in a language they would really understand.

Etkin rejected their suggestion with disgust and with reasonable arguments. The young men, in turn, applied to Etkin a number of epithets that decency obliges me to pass over in silence. Strangely enough, Etkin ignored their insults and reluctantly agreed to put their suggestion before the kibbutz secretariat. Perhaps he was afraid that they might take matters into their own hands.

Toward evening, Etkin went around from room to room and invited the committee to an urgent meeting at eight thirty. When he came to Geula, he told her about the young men's ideas and the undemocratic pressure to which he was being subjected, and asked her to bring along to the meeting a pot of black coffee and a lot of good will.

Geula responded with an acid smile. Her eyes were bleary because Etkin had awakened her from a troubled sleep. As she changed her clothes, the night fell, damp and hot and close.

III

Damp and close and hot the night fell on the kibbutz, tangled in the dust-laden cypresses, oppressed the lawns and ornamental shrubs. Sprinklers scattered water onto the thirsty lawn, but it was swallowed up at once: perhaps it evaporated even before it touched the grass. An irritable phone rang vainly in the locked office. The walls of the houses gave out a damp vapor. From the kitchen chimney a stiff column of smoke rose like an arrow into the heart of the sky, because there was no breeze. From the greasy sinks came a shout. A dish had been broken and somebody was bleeding. A fat house-cat had killed a lizard or a snake and dragged its prey onto the baking concrete path to toy with it lazily in the dense evening sunlight. An ancient tractor started to rumble in one of the sheds, choked, belched a stench of oil, roared, spluttered, and finally managed to set out to deliver an evening meal to the second shift, who were toiling in an outlying field. Near the Persian lilac Geula saw a bottle dirty with the remains of a greasy liquid. She kicked at it repeatedly, but instead of shattering, the bottle rolled heavily among the rosebushes. She picked up a big stone. She tried to hit the bottle. She longed to smash it. The stone missed. The girl began to whistle a vague tune.

Geula was a short, energetic girl of twenty-nine or so. Although she had not yet found a husband, none of us would deny her good qualities, such as the dedication she lavished on local social and cultural activities. Her face was pale and thin. No one could rival her in brewing strong coffee – coffee to raise the dead, we called it. A pair of bitter lines were etched at the corners of her mouth.

On summer evenings, when the rest of us lounged in a group on a rug spread on one of the lawns and launched jokes and bursts of cheerful song heavenward, accompanied by clouds of cigarette smoke, Geula would shut herself up in her room and not join us until she had prepared the pot of scalding, strong coffee. She it was, too, who always took pains to ensure that there was no shortage of biscuits.

What had passed between Geula and me is not relevant here, and I shall make do with a hint or two. Long ago we used to stroll together to the orchards in the evening and talk. It was all a long time ago, and it is a long time since it ended. We would exchange unconventional political ideas or argue about the latest books. Geula was a stern and sometimes merciless critic: I was covered in confusion. She did not like my stories, because of the extreme polarity of situations, scenery, and characters, with no intermediate shades between black and white. I would utter an apology or a denial, but Geula always had ready proofs and she was a very methodical thinker. Sometimes I would dare to rest a conciliatory hand on her neck, and wait for her to calm down. But she never relaxed completely. If once or twice she leaned against me, she always blamed her broken sandal or her aching head. And so we drifted apart. To this day she still cuts my stories out of the periodicals, and arranges them in a cardboard box kept in a special drawer devoted to them alone.

I always buy her a new book of poems for her birthday. I creep into her room when she is out and leave the book on her table, without any inscription or dedication. Sometimes we happen to sit together in the dining hall. I avoid her glance, so as not to have to face her mocking sadness. On hot days, when faces are covered in sweat, the acne on her cheeks reddens and she seems to have no hope. When the cool of autumn comes, I sometimes find her pretty and attractive from a distance. On such days Geula likes to walk to the orchards in the early evening. She goes alone and comes back alone. Some of the youngsters come and ask me what she is looking for there, and they have a malicious snicker on their faces. I tell them that I don't know. And I really don't.

IV

Viciously Geula picked up another stone to hurl at the bottle. This time she did not miss, but she still failed to hear the shattering sound she craved. The stone grazed the bottle, which tinkled faintly and disappeared under one of the bushes. A third stone, bigger and heavier than the other two, was launched from ridiculously close range: the girl trampled on the loose soil of the flower bed and stood right over the bottle. This time there was a harsh, dry explosion, which brought no relief. Must get out.

Damp and close and hot the night fell, its heat pricking the skin like broken glass. Geula retraced her steps, passed the balcony of her room, tossed her sandals inside, and walked down barefoot onto the dirt path.

The clods of earth tickled the soles of her feet. There was a rough friction, and her nerve endings quivered with flickers of vague excitement. Beyond the rocky hill the shadows were waiting for her: the orchard in the last of the light. With determined hands she widened the gap in the fence and slipped through. At that moment a slight evening breeze began to stir. It was a warmish summer breeze with no definite direction. An old sun rolled westward, trying to be sucked up by the dusty horizon. A last tractor climbed back to the depot, panting along the dirt road from the outlying plots. No doubt it was the tractor that had taken the second-shift workers their supper. It seemed shrouded in smoke or summer haze.

Geula bent down and picked some pebbles out of the dust. Absently she began to throw them back again, one by one. There were lines of poetry on her lips, some by the young poets she was fond of, others her own. By the irrigation pipe she paused, bent down, and drank as though kissing the faucet. But the faucet was rusty, the pipe was still hot, and the water was tepid and foul. Nevertheless she bent her head and let the water pour over her face and neck and into her shirt. A sharp taste of rust and wet dust filled her throat. She closed her eyes and stood in silence. No relief. Perhaps a cup of coffee. But only after the orchard. Must go now.

V

The orchards were heavily laden and fragrant. The branches intertwined, converging above the rows of trunks to form a shadowy dome. Underfoot the irrigated soil retained a hidden dampness. Shadows upon shadows at the foot of those gnarled trunks. Geula picked a plum, sniffed and crushed it. Sticky juice dripped from it. The sight made her feel dizzy. And the smell. She crushed a second plum. She picked another and rubbed it on her cheek till she was spattered with juice. Then, on her knees, she picked up a dry stick and scratched shapes in the dust. Aimless lines and curves. Sharp angles. Domes. A distant bleating invaded the orchard. Dimly she became aware of a sound of bells. She was far away. The nomad stopped behind Geula's back, as silent as a phantom. He dug at the dust with his big toe, and his shadow fell in front of him. But the girl was blinded by a flood of sounds. She saw and heard nothing. For a long time she continued to kneel on the ground and draw shapes in the dust with her twig. The nomad waited patiently in total silence. From time to time he closed his good eye and stared ahead of him with the other, the blind one. Finally he reached out and bestowed a long caress on the air. His obedient shadow moved in the dust. Geula stared, leapt to her feet, and leaned against the nearest tree, letting out a low sound. The nomad let his shoulders drop and put on a faint smile. Geula raised her arm and stabbed the air with her twig. The nomad continued to smile. His gaze dropped to her bare feet. His voice was hushed, and the Hebrew he spoke exuded a rare gentleness:

"What time is it?"

Geula inhaled to her lungs' full capacity. Her features grew sharp, her glance cold. Clearly and dryly she replied:

"It is half past six. Precisely."

The Arab broadened his smile and bowed slightly, as if to acknowledge a great kindness.

"Thank you very much, miss." His bare toe had dug deep into the damp soil, and the clods of earth crawled at his feet as if there were a startled mole burrowing underneath them.

Geula fastened the top button of her blouse. There were large perspiration stains on her shirt, drawing attention to her armpits. She could smell the sweat on her body, and her nostrils widened. The nomad closed his blind eye and looked up. His good eye blinked. His skin was very dark; it was alive and warm. Creases were etched in his cheeks. He was unlike any man Geula had ever known, and his smell and color and breathing were also strange. His nose was long and narrow, and a shadow of a mustache showed beneath it. His cheeks seemed to be sunk into his mouth cavity. His lips were thin and fine, much finer than her own. But the chin was strong, almost expressing contempt or rebellion.

The man was repulsively handsome, Geula decided to herself. Unconsciously she responded with a mocking half-smile to the nomad's persistent grin. The Bedouin drew two crumpled cigarettes from a hidden pocket in his belt, laid them on his dark, outstretched palm, and held them out to her as though proffering crumbs to a sparrow. Geula dropped her smile, nodded twice, and accepted one. She ran the cigarette through her fingers, slowly, dreamily, ironing out the creases, straightening it, and only then did she put it to her lips. Quick as lightning, before she realized the purpose of the man's sudden movement, a tiny flame was dancing in front of her. Geula shielded the lighter with her hand even though there was no breeze in the orchard, sucked in the flame, closed her eyes. The nomad lit his own cigarette and bowed politely.

"Thank you very much," he said in his velvety voice.

"Thanks," Geula replied. "Thank you."

"You from the kibbutz?"

Geula nodded.

"Goo-d." An elongated syllable escaped from between his gleaming teeth. "That's goo-d."

The girl eyed his desert robe.

"Aren't you hot in that thing?"

The man gave an embarrassed, guilty smile, as if he had been caught red-handed. He took a slight step backward.

"Heaven forbid, it's not hot. Really not. Why? There's air, there's water..." And he fell silent.

The treetops were already growing darker. A first jackal sniffed the oncoming night and let out a tired howl. The orchard filled with a scurry of small, busy feet. All of a sudden Geula became aware of the throngs of black goats intruding in search of their master. They swirled silently in and out of the fruit trees. Geula pursed her lips and let out a short whistle of surprise.

"What are you doing here, anyway? Stealing?"

The nomad cowered as though a stone had been thrown at him. His hand beat a hollow tattoo on his chest.

"No, not stealing, Heaven forbid, really not." He added a lengthy oath in his own language and resumed his silent smile. His blind eye winked nervously. Meanwhile an emaciated goat darted forward and rubbed against his leg. He kicked it away and continued to swear with passion:

"Not steal, truly, by Allah not steal. Forbidden to steal."

"Forbidden in the Bible," Geula replied with a dry, cruel smile. "Forbidden to steal, forbidden to kill, forbidden to covet, and forbidden to commit adultery. The righteous are above suspicion."

The Arab cowered before the onslaught of words and looked down at the ground. Shamefaced. Guilty. His foot continued to kick restlessly at the loose earth. He was trying to ingratiate himself. His blind eye narrowed. Geula was momentarily alarmed: surely it was a wink. The smile left his lips. He spoke in a soft, drawn-out whisper, as though uttering a prayer.

"Beautiful girl, truly very beautiful girl. Me, I got no girl yet. Me still young. No girl yet. Yaaa," he concluded with a guttural yell directed at an impudent goat that had rested its forelegs against a tree trunk and was munching hungrily at the foliage. The animal cast a pensive, skeptical glance at its master, shook its beard, and solemnly resumed its munching.

Without warning, and with amazing agility, the shepherd leapt through the air and seized the beast by the hindquarters, lifted it above his head, let out a terrifying, savage screech, and flung it ruthlessly to the ground. Then he spat and turned to the girl.

"Beast," he apologized. "Beast. What to do. No brains. No manners."

The girl let go of the tree trunk against which she had been resting and leaned toward the nomad. A sweet shudder ran down her back. Her voice was still firm and cool.

"Another cigarette?" she asked. "Have you got another cigarette?"

The Bedouin replied with a look of anguish, almost of despair. He apologized. He explained at length that he had no more cigarettes, not even one, not even a little one. No more. All gone. What a pity. He would gladly, very gladly, have given her one. None left. All gone.

The beaten goat was getting shakily to its feet. Treading circumspectly, it returned to the tree trunk, disingenuously observing its master out of the corner of its eye. The shepherd watched it without moving. The goat reached up, rested its front hoofs on the tree, and calmly continued munching. The Arab picked up a heavy stone and swung his arm wildly. Geula seized his arm and restrained him.

"Leave it. Why. Let it be. It doesn't understand. It's only a beast. No brains, no manners."

The nomad obeyed. In total submission he let the stone drop. Then Geula let go of his arm. Once again the man drew the lighter out of his belt. With thin, pensive fingers he toyed with it. He accidentally lit a small flame, and hastily blew at it. The flame widened slightly, slanted, and died. Nearby a jackal broke into a loud, piercing wail. The rest of the goats, meanwhile, had followed the example of the first and were absorbed in rapid, almost angry munching.

A vague wail came from the nomad encampment away to the south, the dim drum beating time to its languorous call. The dusky men were sitting around their campfires, sending skyward their single-noted song. The night took up the strain and answered with dismal cricket-chirp. Last glimmers of light were dying away in the far west. The orchard stood in darkness. Sounds gathered all around, the wind's whispering, the goats' sniffing, the rustle of ravished leaves. Geula pursed her lips and whistled an old tune. The nomad listened to her with rapt attention, his head cocked to one side in surprise, his mouth hanging slightly open. She glanced at her watch. The hands winked back at her with a malign, phosphorescent glint, but said nothing. Night.

The Arab turned his back on Geula, dropped to his knees, touched his forehead on the ground, and began mumbling fervently.

"You've got no girl yet," Geula broke into his prayer. "You're still too young." Her voice was loud and strange. Her hands were on her hips, her breathing still even. The man stopped praying, turned his dark face toward her, and muttered a phrase in Arabic. He was still crouched on all fours, but his pose suggested a certain suppressed joy.

"You're still young," Geula repeated, "very young. Perhaps twenty. Perhaps thirty. Young. No girl for you. Too young."

The man replied with a very long and solemn remark in his own language. She laughed nervously, her hands embracing her hips.

"What's the matter with you?" she inquired, laughing still. "Why are you talking to me in Arabic all of a sudden? What do you think I am? What do you want here, anyway?"

Again the nomad replied in his own language. Now a note of terror filled his voice. With soft, silent steps he recoiled and withdrew as though from a dying creature. She was breathing heavily now, panting, trembling. A single wild syllable escaped from the shepherd's mouth: a sign between him and his goats. The goats responded and thronged around him, their feet pattering on the carpet of dead leaves like cloth ripping. The crickets fell silent. The goats huddled in the dark, a terrified, quivering mass, and disappeared into the darkness, the shepherd vanishing in their midst.

Afterward, alone and trembling, she watched an airplane passing in the dark sky above the treetops, rumbling dully, its lights blinking alternately with a rhythm as precise as that of the drums: red, green, red, green, red. The night covered over the traces. There was a smell of bonfires on the air and a smell of dust borne on the breeze. Only a slight breeze among the fruit trees. Then panic struck her and her blood froze. Her mouth opened to scream but she did not scream, she started to run and she ran barefoot with all her strength for home and stumbled and rose and ran as though pursued, but only the sawing of the crickets chased after her.

VI

She returned to her room and made coffee for all the members of the secretariat, because she remembered her promise to Etkin. Outside the cool of evening had set in, but inside her room the walls were hot and her body was also on fire. Her clothes stuck to her body because she had been running, and her armpits disgusted her. The spots on her face were glowing. She stood and counted the number of times the coffee boiled – seven successive boilings, as she had learned to do it from her brother Ehud before he was killed in a reprisal raid in the desert. With pursed lips she counted as the black liquid rose and subsided, rose and subsided, bubbling fiercely as it reached its climax.

That's enough, now. Take clean clothes for the evening. Go to the showers.

What can that Etkin understand about savages. A great socialist. What does he know about Bedouins. A nomad sniffs out weakness from a distance. Give him a kind word, or a smile, and he pounces on you like a wild beast and tries to rape you. It was just as well I ran away from him.

In the showers the drain was clogged and the bench was greasy. Geula put her clean clothes on the stone ledge. I'm not shivering because the water's cold. I'm shivering with disgust. Those black fingers, and how he went straight for my throat. And his teeth. And the goats. Small and skinny like a child, but so strong. It was only by biting and kicking that I managed to escape. Soap my belly and everything, soap it again and again. Yes, let the boys go right away tonight to their camp and smash their black bones because of what they did to me. Now I must get outside.

VII

She left the shower and started back toward her room, to pick up the coffee and take it to the secretariat. But on the way she heard crickets and laughter, and she remembered him bent down on all fours, and she was alarmed and stood still in the dark. Suddenly she vomited among the flowering shrubs. And she began to cry. Then her knees gave way. She sat down to rest on the dark earth. She stopped crying. But, her teeth continued to chatter, from the cold or from pity. Suddenly she was not in a hurry any more, even the coffee no longer seemed important, and she thought to herself: There's still time. There's still time.

Those planes sweeping the sky tonight were probably on a night-bombing exercise. Repeatedly they roared among the stars, keeping up a constant flashing, red, green, red, green, red. In counterpoint came the singing of the nomads and their drums, a persistent heartbeat in the distance: One, one, two, One, one, two. And silence.

، VIII

From eight-thirty until nearly nine o'clock we waited for Geula. At five to nine Etkin said that he could not imagine what had happened; he could not recall her ever having missed a meeting or been late before; at all events, we must now begin the meeting and turn to the business on the agenda.

He began with a summary of the facts. He gave details of the damage that had apparently been caused by the Bedouins, although there was no formal proof, and enumerated the steps that had been taken on the committee's initiative. The appeal to good will. Calling in the police. Strengthening the guard around the settlement. Tracking dogs. The meeting with the elder of the tribe. He had to admit, Etkin said, that we had now reached an impasse. Nevertheless, he believed that we had to maintain a sense of balance and not give way to extremism, because hatred always gave rise to further hatred. It was essential to break the vicious circle of hostility. He therefore opposed with all the moral force at his disposal the approach – and particularly the intentions – of certain of the younger members. He wished to remind us, by way of conclusion, that the conflict between herdsmen and tillers of the soil was as old as human civilization, as seemed to be evidenced by the story of Cain, who rose up against Abel, his brother. It was fitting, in view of the social gospel we had adopted, that we should put an end to this ancient feud, too, just as we had put an end to other ugly phenomena. It was up to us, and everything depended on our moral strength.

The room was full of tension, even unpleasantness. Rami twice interrupted Etkin and on one occasion went so far as to use the ugly word "rubbish." Etkin took offense, accused the younger members of planning terrorist activities, and said in conclusion: "We're not going to have that sort of thing here."

Geula had not arrived, and that was why there was no one to cool down the temper of the meeting. And no coffee. A heated exchange broke out between me and Rami. Although in age I belonged with the younger men, I did not agree with their proposals. Like Etkin, I was absolutely opposed to answering the nomads with violence – for two reasons, and when I was given permission to speak I mentioned them both. In the first place, nothing really serious had happened so far. A little stealing perhaps, but even that was not certain: every faucet or pair of pliers that a tractor driver left in a field or lost in the garage or took home with him was immediately blamed on the Bedouins. Secondly, there had been no rape or murder. Hereupon Rami broke in excitedly and asked what I was waiting for. Was I perhaps waiting for some small incident of rape that Geula could write poems about and I could make into a short story? I flushed and cast around in my mind for a telling retort.

But Etkin, upset by our rudeness, immediately deprived us both of the right to speak and began to explain his position all over again. He asked us how it would look if the papers reported that a kibbutz had sent out a lynch mob to settle scores with its Arab neighbors. As Etkin uttered the phrase "lynch mob," Rami made a gesture to his young friends that is commonly used by basketball players. At this signal they rose in a body and walked out in disgust, leaving Etkin to lecture to his heart's content to three elderly women and a long-retired member of Parliament.

After a moment's hesitation I rose and followed them. True, I did not share their views, but I, too, had been deprived of the right to speak in an arbitrary and insulting manner.

IX

If only Geula had come to the meeting and brought her famous coffee with her, it is possible that tempers might have been soothed. Perhaps, too, her understanding might have achieved some sort of compromise between the conflicting points of view. But the coffee was standing, cold by now, on the table in her room. And Geula herself was lying among the bushes behind the Memorial Hall, watching the lights of the planes and listening to the sounds of the night. How she longed to make her peace and to forgive. Not to hate him and wish him dead. Perhaps to get up and go to him, to find him among the wadis and forgive him and never come back. Even to sing to him. The sharp slivers piercing her skin and drawing blood were the fragments of the bottle she had smashed here with a big stone at the beginning of the evening. And the living thing slithering among the slivers of glass among the clods of earth was a snake, perhaps a venomous snake, perhaps a viper. It stuck out a forked tongue, and its triangular head was cold and erect. Its eyes were dark glass. It could never close them, because it had no eyelids. A thorn in her flesh, perhaps a sliver of glass. She was very tired. And the pain was vague, almost pleasant. A distant ringing in her ears. To sleep now. Wearily, through the thickening film, she watched the gang of youngsters crossing the lawn on their way to the fields and the wadi to even the score with the nomads. We were carrying short, thick sticks. Excitement was dilating our pupils. And the blood was drumming in our temples.

Far away in the darkened orchards stood somber, dustladen cypresses, swaying to and fro with a gentle, religious fervor. She felt tired, and that was why she did not come to see us off. But her fingers caressed the dust, and her face was very calm and almost beautiful.

Dorit Peleg

Ariel

Translated by Chaya Galai

Ariel is an angel. Ariel is an angel who sits at God's right, and even though he doesn't know he's an angel, I know it and I keep telling him though I know I shouldn't. Ariel, you're an angel, did you know, I say. Quit all that nonsense, Ariel scolds me and shakes his halo off his forehead. Ariel has a golden halo that God gave him when he chose him to be an angel, which was just before he was born. There were blue clouds floating in the sky and God said: Ariel, you shall be my angel and guard my creatures through the thick smoke of joints and the dirty coffee cups and Supertramp's howls of longing, and as a sign I am putting my seal on you in the shape of this golden halo, which will adorn your head and blur your vision always so that it is never too clear, because that is not in the nature of angels. You're giving me a headache, you and your visions, Ariel grumbles, anyone might think you're tripping and you're the only one here who doesn't even smoke. Ariel doesn't like it when I talk about him, especially not when I mention the fact that he's an angel, and yet you can see it so clearly. Even Nissan doesn't try to argue when I say it and laughs at me through the smoke, his eyes expanded and his pupils all gone. Why, a real angel, I swear you've got it right, someone with this kind of stuff could even be a seraph. What d'you know – did you hear that? Seraph, what stuff, stuff it, sheriff... and he roars with laughter, trapped inside his own joke and quite forgetting the beginning, which was the only important part: Ariel the angel.

When Ariel was born the gates of heaven opened wide within a

470

great stillness, and a myriad bright stars drifted down to the ground in celebration of Ariel's birthday. All the senior angels hovered in the gateway and stretched out their necks to see Ariel floating down to earth. But they didn't come out to escort him on his way because it's forbidden for grown angels to step outside the gates of heaven from the moment they grow up, which is a moment decided on by God and they're not free to change it or to keep it from him. At that moment they must stop flitting among the raspberry bushes that grow wild in my yard and they're no longer allowed to hide among the daisies in the field on the way to school. They have to go up there instantly and report to God, and after they've told Him what they've witnessed on earth they must join the guard of honor and the cloud cleaners and the rip patchers, and the heavenly gates close behind them for all eternity and they're not allowed to leave ever again. But Ariel will never become a grown angel and he will never fly up there to be shut in behind the gates with their lattice of bars and two eternal cherubs puffing above them, their cheeks swollen out forever and ever without a moment's respite. Not Ariel. He'll never be hemmed in by the winged shoulders of the archangels because he can't change and I won't allow it. Ariel too has fledgeling wings under his armpits, soft down like the fluff of newly hatched chicks, and I love to stroke them, to smoothe them up and down when he lets me, which isn't always. Just sometimes. But Ariel's down will never turn into great wings with a wide span and smooth, hard feathers. No, Ariel's down will always remain soft and fluffy and so translucent it's hard to decide when you touch them if they're really there. Because Ariel is the kind of angel who never grows up, which is the rarest kind, and you can see it clearly from the fact that he has a small body neither thin nor rounded, just simply Ariel's body, and hands whose nails are sometimes, in fact most times, grimy with charcoal and the pencils he draws with, and his mother says that Ariel draws like an angel. Which just goes to show that she doesn't know what she's talking about, because how can an angel draw like an angel.

But I don't like it when he smokes because then he gets lost in the kingdom of heaven and I can't reach him. And sometimes when he's floating in a cloud of cigarettes and Colombian stuff it seems to me that he's a fallen angel. An angel who has stood guard and seen everything and now there's nothing left for him to do except float around in the sweet smoke that smells like nothing else in the world and behind it you can always see the transparent glint of the needle. And I hate the needle, hate it hate it because when Ariel holds the needle with his fingers that are neither thin nor large, just Ariel's fingers, the needle is no longer transparent but instead becomes milky and thick and Ariel presses it into him into his arm which only I am allowed to press up against, and then he disappears with a bang. With a mighty roar and it's not Ariel at all because with Ariel everything's so quiet you hardly notice, except that with Ariel everything is so distinct in its quietness. And then Ariel dances and shouts and sings and that's strange because most people when they use the needle they become silent and look as if they've been nailed to the picture of Janis Joplin on the wall with her hair twisted into snakes like Medusa and sometimes they wake up in panic and cling to me or whoever and sob out that they're frightened, but not Ariel, never. Ariel dances and shouts and sings and never clings to me after the needle and that's the only time I don't even want him to, because it's not Ariel at all and in his eyes there are burning witches. And they know who I am.

But Ariel doesn't allow the needle to press against him very often. And usually it just lies there in the bottom drawer of his writing desk under the unfinished charcoal sketches his mother never takes out to show her girlfriends at bridge mornings because they're not pretty enough. And usually he remembers me when I'm standing beside him and lets me look over his shoulder while he whistles to himself and sketches, whistles and draws lines in charcoal which aren't thick and aren't thin and suddenly there's Rahamim from the grocery store, or there's his mother with whipped cream from the cherry tart she always serves smeared on her upper lip, though I've never seen her smeared with even a drop of cream, or there's horses galloping up to heaven. I like the horses best as they lift off their front hooves plunging and their leg muscles taut as though in a minute the gates will open up for them and they'll gallop in. But he never draws the gates themselves though he knows them well, being in and out of them every day, and he gets angry if I ask. It's time you got all this out of your system, he says, it's been going on for too long and you're overdoing it. So I try not to talk about the gates or the drapes of silk and old lace nor about the organ music, especially if I want Ariel to play the guitar. And sometimes he agrees when I ask him to and sometimes he doesn't, but when I pick up the guitar and start pulling at the strings and short harsh sounds come out wailing for Ariel to play, he snatches it away from me because I'm hurting it and he starts stroking it to calm it down. And he plucks at the strings softly, each one with its own special touch, and he coaxes the sounds out quietly without pain, each sound slipping out and then falling like sugar drops on a cake. And I sit at his feet and catch the sounds in my cupped hands as they drop and I stir them and they make a sound jingle jangle when they strike against each other like little glass sticks.

But sometimes, at very rare moments, I too am allowed into the kingdom of heaven and that's sometimes at night. When Ariel and I snuggle together under the covers and I look deep, deep into his eyes until I fall in because then Ariel allows me everything. And then I see the horde of angels big and small fluttering among the puffed-up clouds or the shrunken ones they're supposed to puff by beating at them with a broom, and I see the ministering angels pumping shreds of persimmon out of the sinks with red rubber plungers and Ariel rolls about laughing and between bouts of laughter he gasps: Why, you funny thing, it isn't the same thing at all. But I don't care because when Ariel laughs he's completely with me and nowhere else.

But sometimes at those moments I don't see in his eyes the hosts of angels and the long wooden tables with the executive chairs and the remains of the wild boar who wasn't at all in pain when they killed it, I don't see a thing except for the gray mist that seeps out of Ariel's eyes and wraps itself around me and swallows me up. And I hold on very tight to Ariel's neck so he won't lose me while we're flying up there because I'm not an angel and I can't fly by myself and it's only thanks to him that I'm there at all. I hold on very tight and my eyes drown in his and I'm not at all afraid as we soar higher and higher and the gates of heaven open before us. And everything fills with radiance.

But for quite a few days now Ariel has been pacing up and down his room and his legs follow one another in all kinds of directions, and he scarcely talks to me. And even when I pick up the guitar and the sounds burst out and wound him he won't play, he just takes the guitar without looking at me and puts it up on top of the closet where I can't reach it. And his eyes are blank, like the frosted glass in the door of the bathroom where his mother took the needle she found by mistake when she was looking for his old report cards from grade school to show to her friends, took it and smashed it on the floor and trod on it and cried and cried. To think that my son... And her eyes were red and swollen. And yesterday she came into the room and said to Ariel without looking at him Ariel we've decided that you need treatment. And we're sending you to the best place in the country but what's money when you're our son and what have we done to put you in such a state and she started crying again. And then she said and I don't know what's going on with you and she pointed to me you're a weird one you don't talk at all I wouldn't be surprised if it were you who got him onto this and she started crying again and wouldn't stop. And Ariel raised his head and made her look him straight in the eye and said get off her back, she's not on anything. And you have no rights over her to torture her. And she said are you trying to say that we torture you and she started crying again and then I saw that she was in fact made out of a giant drop of liquid held in by a thin pinkish skin and that if you made a tiny puncture in her with a pin she'd start leaking and leaking until she was empty and shriveled and nothing was left of her except for a tiny wrinkled lump of pink skin. But I wasn't mad at her.

All the same I wasn't worried because Ariel is an angel and you can't do anything to angels because a voice would instantly come down from heaven and burn everything up by lightning and I've seen lightning how it strikes sharp and blinding and sudden and trees go up in flames. So nobody would be stupid enough to want to harm an angel once they've seen something like that. Even if they're bad enough to want to. But I forgot one thing. I forgot that there are demons and fiends whose job is to harm angels and I should have feared them and taken measures against them but I didn't. And yesterday they came and they took Ariel who screamed and kicked and clung to the closet and even to me and I was surprised because he hadn't pressed the needle in so why was he screaming. But their faces were like the white masks that Ariel showed me at the Japanese Museum, white and cruel with red slashes at the mouth and their eyes were as blank as the slits in the mask that the eyes hide behind. And they took no notice of Ariel's screaming and kicking even though I told them, I explained to them that Ariel didn't want to go otherwise he wouldn't have been screaming because Ariel never cries out except when he's pressing in the needle, and I even grabbed their sleeve when I saw that they didn't understand what I was telling them and when I tugged at their sleeve Ariel's mother grabbed the collar of my white shirt and pulled it so hard she almost tore it off and she yelled get out of here you disgusting child you're a symptom. And when Ariel comes back he won't want to look at you ever again. And then Ariel stopped shouting and looked at her, at her eyes that were leaking black and said very quietly don't you touch her. And she let go of me and I fell because she'd been holding me so tight. And the demons that were looking at Ariel's mother and me weren't holding Ariel so tight, and he came over to me and picked me up from the floor and wiped my eyes because by then I was crying too and he said don't cry, because I'll come to you every night and look after you. And I asked will you fly to me? and he blinked and said yes, I'll fly, you funny thing and went off by himself with the demons. He walked very straight and tall. And then I went too because I didn't want to remain in the house all by myself with Ariel's mother but I wasn't crying any more because I knew that Ariel would come to me and there was nothing to worry about.

And he really does come to my room every night even though in my bed it's much less comfortable because it's narrow and quite small, not wide with lumps and hollows and games like Ariel's, but that doesn't matter because in any case as soon as he comes we hold each other tight and I look deep into Ariel's eyes and we soar up, high up above the parade ground and the white buildings of the institution and the demons stand down below with their red mouths open in the white masks of their faces and we hang high above them and laugh, and then we stop laughing and just fly and the gray mist deepens in Ariel's eyes around me and the houses and the streets and the trees disappear into it and I hear a guitar playing the only melody Ariel taught me, and I know that right now the gates of heaven are opening.

Yotam Reuveny

Dream Time

Translated by Chaya Galai

At night I fall asleep late, sometimes after four in the morning. Till then I tell myself fantastic stories of which I remember nothing by the early afternoon which is when I wake up, either because the telephone has rung or because someone in the house is making a noise, or simply because the body has had its fill of sleep; I remember nothing, then, apart from this – that I have succeeded, perhaps for a very brief time which will end terribly and miserably (since for the time being I am not paying my old debts, and interest is interest, and I am in danger of being sued) in being Scheherezade and Dunyazad and King Shahriyar. How I longed, several years ago, to enjoy a single night in which I could spin myself fantastic tales and remember nothing about them in the morning, apart from the fact that I had been allowed, however late in the day, to live as I chose. But at the time I was the prisoner of that Communist upbringing imposed on me for eight years of my childhood, an upbringing which does not acknowledge needs such as this need of mine – namely, to tell myself stories and be Scheherezade and Dunyazad and Shahriyar – but only the external, what one might call social needs; to work and work and then work again. And there it is, for years I worked and made a great deal of money and it was all squandered in the course of my travels on wine and strange love, which brings a blush to my cheek now. How that love sullied my memory, and gradually the crisis came. Gradually there came this flight inward, through wine, to the secret lair of these tales which will never be recorded in writing and which affect me like strong sleeping pills, like sedatives whose chemical ingredients seep into the blood and flow to the fingers and the eyes and return to the heart and set out on another journey, through the blood, until restless sleep comes, followed by dread, peopled with figures and events which I cannot recall when I awake. And then, to protect myself, I try to postpone as long as possible the admission that I am conscious, my acceptance of wakefulness. I hide under the blankets, stop up my ears against noise, ignore the telephone when I am alone at home, and try to restore to myself something of childhood, something of the nocturnal tales I weave. If only the encounter with what lies beyond the blankets, outside in the other room, with all the objects there, and the need to admit that I cannot go on like this and that I must revert to being productive, in a newspaper office or a factory or as a book editor, if only that encounter could be postponed, and meanwhile these gloomy superfluous days would pass; but now deprived of that strange love for whose sake I committed so many mistakes, if I could only be granted those nocturnal moments in which – like a monk imagining that he has been granted a moment of grace and sensing the presence of God in his cell – I can be what I wish: Scheherezade and Dunyazad and King Shahariar. If only I could postpone the encounter with whatever is not part of the secret world of the nighttime tales. Ah, only the rich can compose the right tales, now that distress and disease are no longer of interest, now that death is no more than a television commodity, like the highly complicated and unhappy loves of the characters in British drama series. Rich romantic heroes, created in order to compensate the unfortunate for their misfortune, for their humiliation and mean status, their sorrows and calculations of income and their numerous, neverending payments.

Is it really possible to flee to a little workshop in Jerusalem? No. No, it is not. And regret hardens and overwhelms the mind and takes over the heart. And the stories too become practical or admonitory or else are told in order to compensate the writer for insults of the kind a policeman inflicted on me when he threatened to arrest me for forty-eight hours because I returned home at four in the morning and had no papers on me, and he carried out his threat and I was arrested for forty-eight hours.

I. The great enemy. But there, at the Abu Kabir detention center, among the filthy blankets, the detainees suspected of murder and rape and other crimes against morality – there, submitting to the madness of a meticulously planned routine, there, bearded as I was, dressed in grimy clothes, I was permitted, without interruption, to be Scheherezade and Dunyazad and King Shahariar, and until I was released, I told myself dozens of stories which, naturally, I cannot now recall. And now, now that I have ceased to tread the wine path to that strange multifaceted love, which seemed to me in the end like some painless, unnecessary, brief surgical operation, once again there is nothing with which to occupy the selves of the night until quiet reigns in the streets of the big cities, till not a sound from outside disturbs the man lying in the dark, smoking in the dark, imperceptibly touching himself, by now without faith, without hope and without will, weaving complex plots about people I might have encountered had I not been forced by circumstances to meet the people I met, most of them perhaps not the people who were needed, but people who passed me by fleetingly before I had time to detain them, to see their faces, like that naked man I saw once in a dream. He lay in a pool of water, its sides made of glass, and I came and wanted to see his face. I wanted to see his smile, but he was silent, and only the clear water remained, and I was forced to admit that this same man, who should perhaps have told me something, have indicated a direction, or some consolation perhaps yet to come, vanished as the nights vanish, and the days as well, without purpose and sadly, in this silence, which fills me even as I stand in a noisy street, ride the bus, lie in bed, on mornings of productivity, of army service, of politics, asking, pleading to distance myself from all this turmoil and to gain some illusory or real freedom, the freedom to be Scheherezade and Dunyazad and King Shahariar.

As against these nights, there were nights of anxiety in which every sound from the hallway infected me with dread as if people were coming to end my life so that I could no longer dream, no longer disrupt routine, nights spent in rented rooms or hotels with that same vast, indifferent urban solitude which was the only thing I found, the only thing, at the end of my hallucinatory journey to the great cities, a journey which began on distant nights in another country, when the child I was then could not fall asleep, did not want to fall asleep, and dreamed about all the good things and the glory awaiting him in the great cities. Nights of dread of a boy, an adolescent, a twenty-year-old, nights in which I could not tell whether my dread stemmed from the meaning of the acts I had committed or from the acts themselves, those nights seemed then the most terrible, the most barren; and the acts of license and abandonment of all prohibitions in search of that lost freedom which, so I believed, could be found outside myself, seem now so innocent, so unlicentious, so befitting the vitally necessary attempts that I and my young companions made at that time to somehow put an end to the unease, the dread and the shame entailed in the need to admit that we would never be what we had dreamed of being; at most we would hold positions, and several of us would marry and have children and a few would die in wars and road accidents or as a result of acts of excess, excess meaning rebellion, as did in fact happen. And I, who sought to be a witness to their deeds in order to record my testimony in writing – the sole skill which was never in doubt, but now I doubt that too – gave up the idea of higher studies and took up various trades. In the naïve conviction that in this fashion I would be a child of my time and of my place and thus my testimony would have some validity, while the others forged ahead and built, and I watched all this in wonder. Aghast at the minuscule value of the deeds I witnessed. Their minuscule value made me doubt the need for a witness. Which happened. People met and perhaps fell in love. They married, then came children, then came doubt. Then came falsehood. Small misdemeanors. Greed and sex. The flight from routine became a routine of flight. What actually remained was routine alone, that same routine that shatters all hope, crushes all belief and no longer evokes fear – as it did in the nights in the rented apartment on Chen Boulevard or in another apartment in Ramat Gan – but merely disgust and the desire to lie in bed at night and invent fantastic tales and become Scheherezade and Dunyazad and King Shahariar. And then there were other nights of cruising, between the nights of dread and the nights of renunciation, cruising which became more frequent because of the conviction that the night could not remain empty, that one could not admit so soon that it was over, that it was now time to return home and go to bed to sleep alone, to be alone at a time when nothing could have been more abhorrent, more intolerable than that nocturnal solitude. And on some of those nights of dread I sought succor in records and the radio. The distant, tranquil voices of the announcers, unreal voices, artificial and uniform, merely sharpened my fear of failure which inescapably had to be admitted, to the glee of all those who had anticipated failure, awaited the moment, at the end of the nights of dread, at the end of that terrifying glide through the rooms, at the end of the attempts to lie down, to switch off the light, to climb out of bed again and glide through the room, gripped by anxiety, of which I could say very little then and which it is now impossible to describe; at the end of all those, therefore, I shall announce that I am joining the ranks of those who gave up from the outset. Such an announcement could mark my return to that distant self, the self of my first few weeks in Israel when children despised me for not knowing Hebrew, for trying to join in their battles without possessing a weapon, a supplicant at the gate begging for a pitchfork, a shovel or a stick so as not to be exposed on the battlefield. But then, memory could not contain all the selves it now contains who could be asked for help, almost at any moment. Then, there was only the emptiness of the lonely, not only the anxiety of one rejected (which surfaced again in those Tel Aviv nights, stronger than ever before, based on additional selves, on earlier nights of anxiety) and left out of the games and parties of a group of high-school students in Ashdod in the mid-Sixties, but the dread of utter rejection, in accordance with some inexplicable and terrible scheme, in whose execution I was powerless to intervene: first the death of my mother, then detachment from all that had gone before, from all that I was and could have been in the place where I was born, and now rejection by a handful of high-school students who are the new country. But I was unable to take a stand against them and so I shut myself in at home and read and read because of my pathetic desire to know Hebrew even better than the native-born. But now, when I dare to write about it, the selves of those nights of dread return. Physical anxiety, deep in my gut, in the trembling of fingers, in the weakness of limbs. But the additional selves which have come into being would be capable of prevailing over the dread-ridden selves (if a battle were to be waged), armed with the amazing nonchalance of the child who dreamed of big cities, the child who comes to me and frees me of anxiety about my present debts (problems at the grocery store, a debt to the bank), so that I no longer yearn to escape from dread to strange love through the portals of wine. Anxiety of another kind: all my life I have been accustomed to living in solitude. When I worked, when I was productive – who would have thought that a day when I could touch (gingerly, fearfully, yearningly) the things about which I wrote, would seem to me more productive and important than all those days and nights, the five years that I worked at a well-known newspaper – when I worked, then, I could afford an apartment, whereas now I cannot afford one; and I fear that one of the members of this household, where I am now a guest, may come in suddenly and discover me, while I am writing about the nakedest truth of all; and then I will go out, I know I will, without completing the writing of these words, to roam listlessly through the now wintry streets of this great city. But this faith in the significance of a day on which I succeed in touching, succeed in recording in writing that which, if it does not touch on the essence, is at least the prelude to reaching the essence, the crux which is indefinable but can perhaps be sensed because a few pages, a certain paragraph, do indeed touch the essence – even this conviction, therefore, cannot entirely obliterate what happened at night, within the dream. Together with my love of the dream, with the feeling that I was succeeding in becoming Scheherezade and Dunyazad and King Shahariar, together with that sensation and alongside it, there was another need, the need to revert to the Communist-educated selves: to get up in the morning and go to the employment office, to register as one of the forty-seven thousand unemployed who, apparently, loiter on the esplanade and wait for work or love. And another thing: to organize my personal effects, to make sure that I can rent an apartment in the near future. In the night it was clear to me that I was going to get up early and do as I had planned: employment office, tidy my belongings, laundry, apartment – but in the early morning, when I was supposed to get up and put the plan into action, I suddenly felt the desire to linger between the sheets and it prevailed over the other desire (I was like someone who hates traveling so much that the day he has to set out on a necessary journey he is glad that it is raining and he can cancel the trip, even though he has bought his plane tickets and is dressed to go). And there is the faint nausea I am suffering as a result of too much coffee and cigarettes. And the cold. I can see how the self I was two hours ago, when I woke up, is receding – the self that remembers the night when I was Scheherezade and Dunyazad and King Shahariar. He is leaving, walking through walls, not touching the trees, like the invisible knight in one of the stories I used to read at night, in a distant city, and then I would put down the book, switch off the light and fantasize about great cities.

And, on those distant nights more than twenty-two years ago, in a strange city whose buildings I no longer remember, when I could hear my mother breathing in the next room, then, already then, I preferred fantasy and great cities to the most exciting adventure stories. And I preferred them in particular after my mother's death in the village, because after that my father returned to the village of my birth; he returned beaten and loveless, and I heard him weeping at night and calling my mother's name and repeating: *Ce mult te-am iubit.*

Now I can hear his voice, louder than the ticking of the clock and the hum of the electric heater blowing warm air at my feet. I did not think then that dread would visit me in great cities, that I would be alone in great cities, so alone that I would even prefer to lie in bed in the dark and seek a child's fantasies, set them up against all odds, never leave the house and eat irregularly, just so that there would be no need to confront the total discrepancy between what was actually to be found in great cities and what I had hoped to find there, in those cities I traveled to so eagerly with money saved with considerable effort. And I came back from there more beaten than my father, because there was no love like my love for the big cities, the cities from which I returned weary, forced to prefer fantasy, the stories about people who could come, those nights when I am Scheherezade and Dunyazad and King Shahiriar. Oh, no need to lament. It is pointless. Now it is evident that nothing, nothing at all of what I wanted then, when I lay in the dark and dreamed of great cities, could have happened the way it did in fantasy – neither love nor other fascinating events with which my imagination peopled the streets of cities, which were alien then and are alien even now, when there is no consolation apart from television and some illusion of good in encounters with people to whom time should have connected me, but didn't, either for me or for them. Several of them – it is, after all, possible – try, at night, to cling to the fantasies of the children they once were, so as not to be entirely alone, a body suspended in darkness; so as to create some foothold, some connection between the love they anticipated then, and the woman who is already sleeping, she too, perhaps, submerged in a similar search for connection (through childhood fantasies) with the man – clerk, engineer, teacher, carpenter – whose breath is exhaled on her sheets. As for love, I have nothing to say (for the time being) about myself apart from those comments about strange, multifaceted love, which brought no salvation and was at most a continuum of unpleasant occurrences. But fantasy, that force which summons up people, places and events, of which nothing is recalled when the fantasy is over, when I, the fantasizer, disappear – mostly because of some unanticipated external disturbance – returns to us like some force which rouses us from sleep, like some force which lulls us to sleep. We float blissfully in its fields, but we feel guilty for having permitted ourselves to be seduced in so practical an era, in an era when specialization is the rule and the craze, when people value only external achievements. A man – I, for example – who dares to choose fantasy, the possibility of being

Scheherezade and Dunyazad and King Shahariar, is doomed to solitude in addition to the necessary, self-evident solitude which is despised and murdered through never-ending activity, through endless talk, through television programs and aimless telephone conversations. But at night, after days of resolving to seek work and renouncing the resolve, I succeed, like an invisible knight, in walking through the walls of the castle and the heavy iron gates, reaching the place where no importance is given to humiliating and superfluous deeds (such as editing books and editing in general, and matters concerning love that I have already mentioned), to money and the race after money, to fear and advantage and to industry that is being operated, as I speak, by a metalworker from Kiryat Shalom whom I met under special circumstances; and there, far removed from it all, beyond the fortified borders of the blanket which not even the most modern fighter planes can penetrate, there I grovel in my sin and immerse myself in my crime.

David Schütz

Angels

Translated by Chaya Galai

When the shot sounded, the woman was detailing for the Arab laborer his chores for the following day, pointing as she did so at the thickening clouds on the horizon which were slowly blocking out the last light. In the west, they were piling up in heavy, clumsy lumps. A cold gust of wind battered at her shoulders. She tightened the pale knitted shawl around her and saw that the Arab was shivering from the cold and breathing on his hands.

"There's no need to irrigate tomorrow," she said, "in any case it's going to rain, but the cowshed must be cleaned out and the poultry run as well." The Arab nodded. He had a long, red nose like a mole's, a hairy face and big prominent ears. Even for an Arab he's unusually ugly, the woman thought when she first saw him, even among them you don't find such hairy people. Something about him reminded her of a goat, particularly when he laughed suddenly and soundlessly, baring his yellow teeth, and his eyes, like two black olives surrounded by murky oil, were half-closed in a malicious smile. Apart from the fact that he was in the habit of pissing in the courtyard indiscriminately whenever he was in the grip of some great happiness or terror, pissing on every wall or tree, at the same time wearing a fixed ingratiating smile (a dog-like deceitful expression, as her husband said succinctly), she succeeded in getting what she wanted out of him and was reasonably satisfied with his work.

The woman stretched out a hand to the rain which had started falling, her eyes on the sky, and the Arab watched her, confirming with a movement of his head that it was in fact raining, and then the shot exploded.

"Who's that?" the woman exclaimed, surprised at the panic in her own voice, and saw the Arab shrink as if trying to move closer to her to gain her protection. "Who's shooting?" she exclaimed again, and tightening the shawl over her shoulders, she moved at a hesitant gait towards the buildings in the yard. The Arab stood alone for another moment, his protruding ears absorbing the patter of the raindrops falling on his exposed skull, his fingers clutching his old buttonless shirt to his chest; then, without changing his position and sockless in his worn shoes, he began to run with strange skips after his employer, hopping like a grasshopper over the gathering puddles.

"Oh, it's you," the woman shouted and her sigh of relief resounded in the rainswept courtyard. "I didn't know who it was," she went on apologetically. Her husband was standing there, leaning on his army rifle. His large head was outlined sharply against the clouds. He didn't turn towards her, ignoring her shout, her fears. "What happened?" she asked again, walking towards him across the dreary muddy field. The last light had almost completely faded. Here and there a dark mound of dung could be seen in the field. He didn't answer. With a wave of the hand, he indicated that she should move away and, his eyes fixed on one spot, he lifted the rifle to shoulder height and fired into the thick bushes at the end of the courtyard. Beyond them, she knew, was solid white rock.

She shivered, unheeding. It seemed to her that she heard a groan after the shot, but she wasn't sure. Now that she was close to him, she could see saw how terrified he was. His heavy shoulders trembled under his sweater. His face was pale, inflamed with an evil, greenish light. "What happened?" she asked again, trying to control her voice and to make out the precise expression on his face in the dim light.

"Don't know," he replied. He spoke with an effort, very slowly. "Something white was flashing over there," he pointed with the rifle to the darkening bushes in the corner of the courtyard, "something white was moving up and down, up and down..."

"And then," she whispered, clinging to the wet sweater despite his silent protest, and grasping his head with her strong hands, "what happened then?"

"Don't know," the man went on. "I heard birds and I saw something white, shining. I fired. It didn't stop. And again something landed, something white like a very big bird..." He fell silent. She could distinctly hear his teeth chattering.

"We have to go over there," the woman said quietly, realizing suddenly that the Arab was behind her, urinating noisily into a puddle. Without turning her head, she ordered him to go back to his hut and not to come out till tomorrow, because in any case it was raining.

Like a dark mass, their heads close together but not touching, holding their breath, the woman and her husband stood, pricking up their ears and waiting for the Arab to finish what he was doing and leave them to themselves. The man stirred first, left her in the dark and returned with a flashlight and an axe in his hand. "It was here," he whispered, casting a pale beam of light on the dripping black bushes. She advanced slowly, clearing a path through the bushes, following the broad back. She knew clearly that she mustn't abandon him now, when his teeth were chattering and he was pacing ahead of her with his raised axe; she must follow him now, even if the water was soaking through her thin shawl to the skin.

"Perhaps it's nothing," she tried to say, and then she heard the noise. It was a mighty flapping of wings, as if a giant bird had been trapped in a net. The dancing beam of light encountered something pale. Warily, they moved forward to the rock and saw two figures lying there. One of them was motionless, rain dripping on his exposed still face, the second was writhing, trying with all his strength to raise himself with the aid of his wings. His white body was stained with mud and blood.

"He's been wounded," said the woman.

"A good shot," confirmed the back standing in front of her, focusing the beam of light on the squirming figure. Then he turned to her, thrust the flashlight into her hand and positioned it firmly, approached the injured figure and with one chop of the axe slashed the delicate wings off his back and threw them aside.

"That way he can't escape," he blurted thickly into the trembling flashlight, but she heard nothing except the ugly smash of the axe as it jammed into the living flesh. Only now did she see that the two figures were completely naked. She marveled to herself that she hadn't noticed till now. They seemed soft to her. Their fair curls fell to their shoulders, their lips were as red and juicy as those of children and their bodies, surrounded by an aura of light, were tender and white and plump. One of them had closed eyes, and seemed to be sleeping or engrossed in prayer. His friend with the cropped wings did not shift his gaze from her. Without understanding how she had been told, she removed her shawl and wrapped it round the prone figure, trying to alleviate his pain. He was very close to her. His clear gaze caressed her face. To her astonishment she could detect no pain in him, only a kind of insolent, mute challenge which confused her. Intoxicating odors assailed her nostrils and she smiled weakly at the thought that both the dead figure and the injured one had been drunk when they infiltrated the yard. A hand gripped hers. "Let's go," said her husband close to her ear.

As they passed the Arab's hut, the woman halted, touched the rough beams and said: "He can see us." Her husband did not reply. But when they were inside the house – he threw the bloodstained axe into a corner, switched off the flashlight and put down the rifle cautiously – he said that the time had come to get rid of him, in any case he was a lazy bum who did nothing but piss, and the rainy season had arrived.

"I'm sure he saw it all," she replied irrelevantly. "So what," her husband insisted. "So nothing," she replied angrily, ashamed at having to apologize because that goat had seen them chopping off the wings.

"He shouldn't have been allowed to come close," she persisted. She knew only too well that the Arab had seen the beautiful fingers stretched over the chest and the fleshy, fragrant lips over which she had suddenly drawn her fingernails.

"He didn't see a thing, nothing at all," her husband assured her. "You sent him away, didn't you."

"Yes," she agreed. "I sent him but I'm convinced that he was loitering about. That's his nature, to loiter around."

"There's something in what you say," her husband confirmed. He pulled the wet sweater off his skin. The woman was standing at the window. Without looking at him, she knew that he was standing, dark and well-muscled, in the center of the room, unbuttoning a white shirt in order to put it on. She caught his sour smell. She could easily identify the outline of the hut outside, the single window inside which, she knew, olive-shaped eyes set in murky oil burned and watched her.

"You're attributing importance to a load of rubbish," her husband cut short the unpleasant conversation. "I can get rid of that miserable mute anytime I like, chuck him out." And he went into the bathroom and rinsed the terrible axe in water. She heard him shouting to her from there, his voice prevailing over the rush of the water; then he turned off the faucet, wiped his hands thoroughly and went over to the telephone. She heard him talking to several people, telling them about the events and realized, through a thick curtain of exhaustion, that all hell had broken loose. She was unable to tear herself away from the window, and until her husband dragged her away and sat her down on a chair – just before the room filled with anxious armed men – she didn't budge from there.

The next day no trace remained of the storm. Wisps of white cloud floated across the sky, and the woman who was still lying in her bed, indulging herself and watching them through the open window, wondered a little at the fears that had overwhelmed her the previous day. The night had indeed been unbelievably stormy. She started up suddenly and saw, to her dread, that the room was entirely white. The dazzling light cruelly exposed the old closet, the figure curled up at her side, the nightgown and her fingernails. Everything was white to the point of madness, shining and dazzling like a blaze of flickering lightning. It was as if a bolt of lightning were poised directly over her house, tightly binding heaven to earth. Fearfully, she heard her husband's rhythmic snores fading away in the silence. The rain seemed to have ceased, she thought, and then the earth was shaken by a clap of thunder. It was so close that her heart seemed to shatter with dread. A white glare continued to filter through her tightly-shut eyelids. Beside her the tranquil snores continued.

She tiptoed over to the window on her bare feet. He was there in his hut. He had been there with her and seen the white ladders stretching down from up there, the white fire raging with restrained fury. "I'm tired," she said to herself, the way she had done when she was a small child, terrified of storms. "I'm tired, very tired." The cold seeped into her bare feet. "I'd better go to sleep," and she curled up beside her husband, huddled up and warming her frozen feet, trying slowly to wake him, to attract his attention, to talk to him. And still his chest rose and fell to the steady rhythm of his snores, and it seemed to her that he was trying to speak to her in a single clear and simple sentence which she had never succeeded in understanding.

Now, the morning after the storm, her limbs were weary, even the lids of her eyes which had gazed up at the clouds. All the same she got up, glad at the replete quietude which had descended on her and, scratching her head and yawning, she went into the kitchen. There were signs that he had left hurriedly some time ago. The dregs of coffee were cold, the morning paper lay on the floor, its pages crushed.

Outside the sun reigned with full force in a clear sky and the Arab was there, skinny, abashed and awaiting orders. She commanded him to stay where he was, to wait for her, and as if she had recalled something of vital importance which for some reason had slipped her mind, she turned and walked rapidly towards the bushes at the edge of the field, slipping easily into last night's gloomy undergrowth. She halted close to the gleaming white rock. There was nothing there. Neither the dead figure lying on his back with a blackened bullet hole close to his heart, nor the sweet wounded figure writhing in the mud, neither the lopped-off wings nor even the blood-stained feathers. The woman knelt down, groping carefully with her fingers for the marks of the violent struggle which had taken place here last night. Suddenly she heard the familiar sound of the Arab pissing nearby. She stood up in a fury, grumbling that she was going to be forced to send him away after all if he couldn't learn, once and for all, to control his bodily functions. And then she saw him. He tottered towards her in his ridiculous shoes, his mouth gaping in a kind of voiceless shout, clutching something white in his hand which flapped in the wind like a great kerchief, like gleaming white wings. As he held the shawl out to her, he stood, as was his habit, at a proper distance, his broad smile exposing his rotten teeth. And unblushingly, she hid her face in the soft enfolding wool, wildly inhaling what was left of its magical sweet fragrance. Then she wrapped the shawl around her carefully; she wanted to say something to the Arab, but instead she dropped her hand, turned and went back into the house.

Dan Benaya Seri

Mother Pickles Cucumbers

Translated by Eddie Levenston

I

She went back to the well. This time it seemed she was not frightened of the snakes. Nor of Tamar's dumb, scaly eyes. She walked barefoot, holding in her small hands the clay pot, spilling over below her knees. Weary. She thought the dirt path would never end. The boiling sun pounded on her head, dazzled her eyes, and the ash-gray rocks high on the hills threatened to overcome her. Even the cracked earth, the yellow bushes dying all summer, joined in pursuing her with grim anger. Why are the stones crying again, she thought, listening once more to the sounds. Father had told her, but she didn't understand. Wandering solitary between the rocks, his huge figure gradually disappeared, grappling with the rocks like a wrestler. When, hurting his hands on wild thorns, he suddenly shouted, she knew he was drunk again. Sometimes, when she was climbing with him to the hilltops, he would crouch down in the dirt, slowly crumble lumps of parched earth and mumble in a tired whisper: "Once these were mountains." And still she did not understand.

The air was already humming with flies, driven crazy by the oppressive khamsin. The torn earth crept by sluggishly, gasping like a viper. At a bend in the path, beyond the rock, lay the carcass of a wild pigeon. The torn flesh was decomposing in the sea of insects that fed upon it. "Be careful!" her mother was always appalled by such a horrid sight, "they eat people too." She stood and looked into the tiny eyes of the little creatures. Once again tears welled in her eyes. She thought about Mother's ugly wrinkles, her heavy legs, Father's silence. Always alone. A heavy man. Harsh. A primitive animal among the mountain crevices. He believed the power of hatred was enough to pulverize them. Wildly he would charge the openings with his fists, striking them again and again to the heart, like a madman, with his huge body till he bled. Till the redeeming explosion. Only then would he stop, gather the split rocks in his hands and clutch them to his heart. That is how stones cry, she thought at the time.

Why didn't he kill Tamar as well, she grieved. She yearned so much for him to do away with her and her long body. Slender. Sinuous and tense. Scraggy bones like vermin. Only her teeth are concealed. Simmering the poison within them. She and he will dig the pit together. They won't have to make much effort. A shallow trench will suffice. Like that for the pigeon carcass.

Sometimes he would take her as far as the edge of the sea. There they weltered among myriad small smooth pebbles. For hours he would finger them in amazement, lost in thought. Trying to decipher. "They are only fish," he would repeat to quell his fears, his face wet with tears, fixed on a horizon of breaking waves, grieving for Grandfather who was dead. She tried to console him, taking the pebbles from his hand. To look, just once more, into his sad eyes. Perhaps he would embrace her now. And Father wept. Grandfather. Grandfather.

Mother would be waiting for them in the hut. "Go and wash!" she would shout, tearing the dress off her back and throwing it with the rest of her rags into the laundry box. "And you too. Where have you been?" staring at him with defeated eyes, taking in with a wicked glare the hidden stains in his trousers. Father said nothing. Dragging his chair behind him, he went through the doorway of the hut. She pursued him there. "The girl is crazy," throwing at his feet the pebbles she had removed from the pocket of the dress. The way she always drips poison in his ear. "Hills. Rocks. Where did you get this lunacy?

Where? Where?" Father doesn't move. He keeps quiet. Perhaps such suffering is his way of tormenting her. What is he thinking? Grandfather is dead. Grandmother too. What is left? The air around him is turning gray. He rises from his chair like a cloud of dust and goes off towards the last houses in the village.

He'll come back at night. And Mother will be waiting for him. As always. With a desolate look. Sitting forlorn beside her wooden distaff, and spinning yarn from coarse goat's wool. Her face is plowed with a forest of wrinkles, her feet enclosed in cotton socks. Every day the same. Like some hopeless disease. Sometimes she is filled with hope, and puts on an apron. And always alone.

Women seldom visit her. They come for a moment and leave in amazement, as though they had lost their way. Mother is the same. She never visits them. She loathes them all. Only the goat skins. Desperate and sullen, she makes them into winter cloaks. And in the village they laugh. Who is to wear them. It's a short winter. Without a single puddle of rain. Maybe sometimes a little wind and even that, like scraps of torn paper, is in a hurry to disappear behind the parched ridges. But Mother remains rebellious, let them laugh, the scum. Furiously she bites the tough hides. Her eyes fill like udders. Investing all her rage in the accursed needle, thrusting through the reeking wool. Perhaps in her tempestuous soul she is still dreaming of the white snow she left behind in the beautiful tiled town, and the little children scampering about like grasshoppers, flying around in bare goatskin coats. Her eyes have darkened now and her face become sour. Now she will turn on her. "Why are you quiet all the time?" Thus she tyrannizes her always. And she, her hands twitching, tries in desperation to touch her. Drags the heavy bucket to the outside latrine. Perhaps that will ease her day's labor. "Mother," beseeching her to absorb her gaze, but in vain. "The two of you will be the death of me." She drives her away. And as always, at that ominous hour of the setting sun, she heightens the flame on the oil stove and boils herself some tea. Pours it into the copper cup and poisons herself from a large jar of sugar. Perhaps it will keep the wrinkles at bay.

At night, hidden under the thin woolen blanket, she could hear her latest beratings. She blamed Father for the ugly wrinkles that disfigured her face. For her swollen legs. For the insane way he fled to the houses of other drunkards, wallowing like a donkey in a bug-ridden barrel. Leaving her here, alone, amid the stench of goat's wool, with a mad, almost mute child.

And she cursed the villagers to his face, she spared none of them. A pampered woman, they whispered behind her back, but she asked no favors. "What is there for me in this wilderness?" she rebuked Father, as though just now remembering how he had brought her to the village for the first time. At that time he had already begun to keep silent. Keeping back in the shadows. If he had listened to her then, they might now be living in a stone house, in town. With a flowering hedge. A lemon tree. And there, on the edge of the sky, a roof of red tiles. Fine people, like those in a holiday procession. No carts, no donkeys, and no filthy, stinking cow dung. Father remains quiet, he doesn't lose his temper, even when she throws at him the copper cup that Grandfather in his madness left to her. Silently he picks it up from the floor and examines the engraving.

Once again the tea is brewing in the kitchen and Father is tossing and turning in bed, swaddling his throat and holding his breath so that she, a small half-crazy girl, should hear nothing, how his gall rises and is spewed on the bed. She had always thought the tears of adults have a sour smell, like a crumpled linen bed covering.

Sometimes Mother could not restrain herself. She would pack her few clothes into her small suitcase and flee to her relatives in town. For a day, sometimes extended to a week, swearing she would return to such a wasteland only in her coffin. Father never went looking for her. She could see from his sad eyes that he knew Mother would eventually come back. Stooping, submissive. Failing eyesight, hair turning gray, a silent lifeless individual keeping people at a distance.

Inside the hut she tried to beg compassion for Mother, perhaps she had merely gone to town to bring some lemons. She washed the dishes in the sink, polished the two windows and before Father had time to extract himself from Grandfather's chair, she was already hurrying to remove the dirt from the concrete floor. Father tried to console her: "Enough crying," wiping the sweat from her brow with his fingers. But not raising his face to hers. She knew, his eyes then were red and his trousers covered with the stains that drove her out of her mind. She stood with him and the two of them gazed at the dirt track where vehicles drove up towards the village. When darkness fell he would take hold of her hand, "Come," dragging her behind him. That was how they always ran off to the rocks. It was hard for her to understand how they had once been mountains. One day she asked him who had killed Grandfather and Father was shocked. He held her hand, as though suddenly reduced to tears at the sight of Scorpion's Rock. "Grandfather did not die," he cautioned her. "Grandfather was a great mountain." Whenever he felt afraid of death he would create the world anew. "Look over there," he pointed, his hand thrusting at the darkness, "over there in the sea."

At midday the old bus would arrive. And Mother would get off with her tattered suitcase. For a moment she would look at the vegetable garden, stare at Father praying silently to be ignored, then stride into the hut, turn up the oil stove and as usual go back to killing herself with a hillock of sugar.

At night Father would disappear again with the drunkards. She thought a lot then about the mountains and the sea. She knew he was lying. There are no mountains in the sea. There are only fish living in the sea. And Grandfather was crazy and Tamar is not dead.

II

She wanted it so much. Every day she yearned for the death of Tamar. Prayed to see her melt in the sun. Dissolve between the hungry teeth of maggots. Skinny Tamar. There were days when she looked upon her slender body with contempt. Just skin and bones, she chuckled to herself with undisguised pleasure. If young men hold her, she'll injure them. She didn't understand why she would injure them. Father said so, and she felt happy, even though on that evening of khamsin it had seemed terrible to her. Father was sitting in his heavy wooden chair, his broad back leaning against the wall of the hut, slurping noisily at the hot mushroom soup Mother had brought him. She had been crouching in the dust with Tamar, beyond the wooden floor, the two of them using a lizard's tail to scatter a column of scared ants that had emerged from a crevice in the anthill. Tamar did not hesitate. She trapped the fleeing ants and squashed them into a sticky paste. Suddenly the chair moved. Father's face was red. He flung down the soup bowl, pulled off his shirt and sat there with his hairy chest.

"Now play Horses," he startled them, using his shirt to wipe the sweat off his face.

Tamar was the first to rise; she smiled at him, amusement on her face.

"Are you afraid?" his gaze was challenging.

"No," she grinned.

"Over there then," he pointed to the cold embers of the fire.

And looked at Tamar again. At her lithe body. Skittishly she gathered the ends of her dress around her hips, almost naked, exposing her slim legs. For a moment Father rose from his chair but instantly sank down again.

"Now," he said.

"But she's afraid," Tamar giggled, pointing at her with a look of scorn.

"No," she had shouted.

And she stayed crouched on her knees, her gaping eyes fixed on Tamar's bare feet.

"Get up," Father scolded her.

And she sprang forward.

But Tamar easily leapt over her, and with a shriek of joy pushed her face into the ground.

"I told you," she laughed at Father, "she has no strength."

Angrily she stood up again. She tried to grab Tamar's ugly legs. To dig her teeth into the repugnant flesh. She could feel the humiliating strength flowing through the scraggy bones. The friction, almost burning, of torn metal. She breathed heavily. Wheezed. Spat saliva from her mouth. Jumped again on Tamar's back and stumbled as before. Rose and fell once more. Her strength was fading. Her mouth gaped wide as she gasped for breath. She inhaled as though from a foul vial of poison. And Father was silent. What does he think of her. A little girl. Almost useless. Immersed like her mother in a filthy pen of goats' wool and like her hanging up stinking tails on the washing line. Get up. Get up. His staring eyes have strayed from her, contemptuously, fixed again on Tamar's fin-like bones, on her hateful sticklike legs. The salty dust was still clinging to her mouth as only now she strove in vain to evade the blows of that awful knee jammed deep between her legs. "Aah," she groaned. With the last of her strength she spat the muck from her mouth. She rolled over onto her back, spluttering in despair, squirming away from the trampling leg. But by then Tamar's hands had grabbed her. Pinching her like a scorpion, Tamar had hold of her, dragging her helplessly towards the ashes of the fire. Father was wiping his mouth again with his shirt. "Enough," she heard herself sob. Tears softened her cheeks. She was exhausted. She stopped struggling. She allowed Tamar to drag her like a corpse towards the sooty fire trench.

And then Father's chair was pushed back and bumped on the floor of the hut.

"You haven't won yet," he jumped down, grabbed Tamar and swung her off. Tamar smiled like a little girl, then suddenly dug her knee in his paunch and pulled him hard. Father stumbled. For a moment he swayed like a wounded eagle, his arms outspread, and then before he collapsed he tensed his body and sprawled on top of her with a thunderous roar. Suddenly they were both quiet.

"Have I hurt you?" he remained bent over her.

"No," she gave him a different look.

"Really," his face was red with mushroom soup.

Through a crack in the window curtain Mother's silent face appeared. Father climbed off her and rose to his feet.

"Just skin and bones," he smiled and brushed off his dusty trousers, "you'll injure all the lads."

Mother let go of the curtain and let it drop.

III

When she reached the well, she stopped, put down the pot and leaned against the trunk of the old olive tree. The *khamsin* mist that had dogged her footsteps seemed to be slowly dispersing. But the sand beneath her feet was looser. Perhaps it was the dark vipers that had come back to burrow among the stones, longer and thinner, she seemed to see their eyes. Narrow and smiling. And Father was stooping, trying to stroke their heads, as though stroking invisible braids between his fingers. She inspected the broken olive branch. Lifted it off her and gazed at the tiny missing leaves. She remembered, this was where Father had stood, his large face wordless. Stunned, he pulled off his trousers and looked at Tamar. She did not flinch. Nor did she move when he enfolded her. Only her bare feet moved and her mouth, which trembled suddenly, as if silently digesting some awkward prey stuck in her gullet. For a moment his hand explored her back, his nails clawing, and then they both stumbled and wallowed soundlessly in the sand.

An east wind had begun to blow from the gaps in the hills, dragging the first dust clouds with it. She knew, in their wake would come the herd, tired and panting. They would fall upon the drinking trough, crumbling the stony ground in their thirst. And the shepherd, with startled eyes, would stare at her. Breathing rapidly. She let the branch fall through her fingers and peered at the bottom of the pot. She had so much wanted to bring Tamar with her today. To tempt her. To see her, just one more time, rolling in the rough sand in front of her. She had been sure she would refuse, but still insisted.

"We won't stay long," she lied, "just a little while."

"I mustn't."

"We can even bathe in the trough, the sun is not burning hot today."

"But can't you see," she squirmed on the mat, "I'm sick."

"What's the matter with you?"

"Something," she smirked.

"The herd is coming today."

"I can't stand the smell."

Her moist eyes gazed up at her. Her slim neck twisted like a worm. Her ribs writhing against the fibers of the mat like the rubbing of scales on sand.

"And the bulls," she said aloud, "and the new shepherd."

"Stop it."

"Why?"

"Your mother may blame me."

"What for!"

"For everything," she suddenly chuckled, "like now, when I'm delaying you."

"Aah!" she burst out in despair, and ran out.

IV

Mother had never openly blamed any of the inhabitants of the village. Certainly not Tamar. Even when she noticed the derisive looks of the young men and the humiliating attempts of the old women to offer consolation, she held back and concealed her real feelings from them. When Father first brought her to the village, she was already three months pregnant. Stunned, almost petrified. Father was a young lad, Mother four years older. He didn't know how to reveal his secret to Grandfather and went with her first to the doctor. In the evening he went in fear to Grandfather and asked if he could borrow a little money for clothes. Grandfather was not a religious man. Just a simple almost crazy man of the earth who believed that people died like mountains. He would not let Father make a fool of him. Father began to cry. He talked about the grove of fig trees beside the dirt road and Mother's short dress that had got caught in the foliage. She asked him to pick her some figs and he didn't know why she suddenly lay down to rest. Afterwards she cried and said she had forgotten the fruit in the grove.

Grandfather had no pity for him. That same night they harnessed the two horses to the cart and drove off together to Mother's family in town. They came back the next morning, unharnessed the tired horses in the stable and with tears in his eyes Father kissed Grandfather on his forehead.

There were very few witnesses at the wedding. Mother did not dress for the occasion and Father wore only the minimum essential *Shabbat* clothing. When they returned to the village Grandfather gave them a small hut and told Mother she was not to go to work with Father. At that time he already wanted to die.

No one could release Grandfather from his delusion. He believed that the child about to be born would cause him to die. Would inherit his soul. Always the same dreams. There were no spare souls. Just enough to go round. No one is born until another has passed away. The soul of a horse. A hawk. A man. Just enough to go round. The days before the birth drained his spirit. He prepared himself for the journey. For long weary hours he would gaze at the chain of hills and fashion his coffin from them. A full beard covered his face. His cheeks were prominent. Only there – he pointed to the great burial niche between the jaws of the cliffs. At night he kept opening the window. The hills flowed down towards him, dark and soft. For a moment he seemed to have leveled them to a plain. Only then would Grandfather wipe his eyes and go back to bed. In the morning his body was stricken with mosquito stings.

He had no pity for Father. What was it about those trees? He kept shrugging his shoulders in amazement. And Father held his tongue. Fig trees, Grandfather yelled again. How can it be. How can it be. This desert has never produced a single fig tree. The whole region is full of the stench of cattle. And Father cried, Don't die. Holding Grandfather's hand and kissing it in despair.

But in vain. In the evenings, before sunset, he would drag Grandmother from her old chair and take her to the window. Shouting "Bury me there!" and gesturing with menace towards the needles of rock wrapped in darkness. Grandmother laughed. By that time she was already deaf in both ears. She would look at the grove of olive trees on the slope of the hills and nod her head. Yes, she remembered, in that grove of trees in her eighth month she had given birth to Father.

Grandfather didn't die. One night Mother left the hut and

miscarried her child next to one of the cliffs. When the rumor reached the village, people believed that now Father would have his way and send her back to her parents. But Grandfather, crazy as ever, bade Father take her in this time as well.

No one had compassion for Mother any longer. She was given all forms of field-work. In the morning she would follow Father out of the house, carrying the plowshare on her back, and do his bidding. The carrot plot. The squash. The double row of tomatoes. In row after row she loosened the soil. And hoed yet another double row. Her hands became as tough as a tortoiseshell. Blisters hardened into calluses. In the corners of her eyes the first wrinkles formed. Something in her withered gaze harbored a secret. Perhaps she had conceived. But Father was oblivious. She had not yet turned over the soil in the watermelon patch.

For five years Mother did not give birth. Who was accountable? Perhaps it was the pests that ruined the pumpkins. Secretly, Grandfather lay in wait. Why does she not conceive? Even the two full dresses that Grandmother sewed for her from Grandfather's riding coat did not cure her. Her stomach began to contract. Suspended from her hips as from two loose pegs. Her eyes failed to see into the distance. She looked through the window pane, as though startled by the bleating of a stray goat. Father plodded after the plow, tearing the earth apart in fury. His strength increased, concentrated in his fists. He opened his hands and scattered the seeds in the womb of the furrows. And in her heart Mother prayed for the rains suddenly to return.

Grandfather knew no rest in his hut. His spirit failed in this barren wilderness. He could endure the doubt no longer. From the time that Mother miscarried the fetus, bad thoughts had begun to sap his vigor. He believed it was now his fate to live in place of the baby. Till the end of the generation. Weary of soul and with fading eyes. His delusions diminished his strength. He had already ordered Grandmother to feed her medicinal herbs. To fill her stomach with pea soup. And at night, a cup of boiling onion juice with plenty of sugar. In the morning he would open the door of the hut and stare hopelessly at the clouds above the hills. His gait was feeble, like a man who has striven with the Angel and not prevailed. He found it difficult to till the soil. The field of melons dried up. The almond trees withered. Stones emerged from the belly of the ground and stifled the delicate palm shoots. And in summer the *khamsin* returned.

Mother's family were summoned from town. What had been found wrong with her? They brought a wise old man who cited relevant texts from the Bible. Sarah was barren, Hannah was barren. Rachel too had difficulty with childbirth. "Look," they found new hope in the ugly pimples that disfigured her face. "Maybe she'll vomit tomorrow," they hinted at the possibility. Grandfather refused to listen to them. He sent them away in shame. He had never known such disgrace. He grabbed hold of Mother and dragged her into the hut. "Tell me, why are you like this? Why? Why?" And Mother remained silent. What could she say? Everything Grandmother put on the plate in front of her, she ate.

There was plenty of gossip in the village. People took malicious pleasure in her misfortune. It was whispered that Father had been seen wasting his vigor in the stable. Women murmured among themselves. Their bodies were not at fault. Mother sealed her ears. She did not have the strength to silence them. Even the roof beams of the hut conveyed her shame. She fled their malice, to the very end of the village. Grandfather also suffered. He knew now that his fate was sealed. No mountain for him. He would end as dust. All summer he would rest on the pine needles and in winter, when the light rain fell, he would be swept away with the mud and swallowed up in the sea.

Suddenly, in the sixth year, Grandfather was restored to life. At first, it seems, no one noticed. It may have been the heavy *khamsins* that loomed over the woven roofs and sprinkled black raindrops against the walls. That morning Grandfather rose and, contrary to his usual habit, took off his night clothes and bathed in the tub of chilly water. When he was dry, he took his clean clothes out of the old wooden closet and put them on. His pale face glowed with fire, his beard bristled, and through the hairy thicket of his eyebrows his eyes were different, alert. He went down into the cellar and came up brandishing a bottle of old wine. "Go and fetch her," he told Grandmother. He placed two glasses on the table and when Mother came in, he put one in her hand. "It's good," he refilled her glass from the bottle. Mother sipped with assurance. It was sweet raisin wine. She raised her eyes and then she saw what was in Grandfather's. "More," she stretched out her glass towards him. But Grandfather held back. He took the old kerchief off her head and let her long black hair fall on her rounded shoulders. "Why don't you comb your hair," he trembled. Only then did he harness the horses to the cart and bundle her into it.

All the way there he was silent. Speechless, he harried the horses. Would not let them rest. Mother curled up in the corner, at ease. She had always drunk such wine with pleasure at home. Four full glasses one Passover. And at night, furtively, the forgotten fifth glass, next to the old man's chair. "Faster, faster," she urged Grandfather to whip the horses. They were slack. Something cold and dark from her past history floated to the surface of her forehead.

Towards evening the horses left the road and went down a deserted path to the sea.

When they returned to the village, it was already growing dark. Mother's full-throated laugh filled the whole lane. She was the first to jump out of the cart and burst into Grandmother's hut. The bottle was still standing there. She grabbed it firmly and drank. Grandmother, in her way, said nothing. "How are all the family?" Mumbling in the stillness from her straw chair. And Mother was exultant. Clutching in her hand the tiny seashells she had gathered on the shore and kissing her forehead. "We didn't go there."

A few weeks later Mother suddenly felt better and one morning she began to vomit. Father left nothing to chance. He went to town and came back with a doctor. "She has been like that for five days," was Grandfather's greeting at the entrance to the hut. The doctor drove everybody out and shut the door behind him. When he came out he stood and shook Father's hand with joy. Grandfather could not contain himself. He seized the doctor by the arms and carried him out to the waiting vehicle.

Mother gave birth to her, as Grandmother expected, in the eighth month. A healthy baby with spots on her shoulders. "Father was born like that," Grandfather said, fumbling her proudly. Ugly old Grandfather, when she was born he no longer had faith in his huge body. He went and trimmed his beard, like one of the young men. The festive meal lasted two days. All the villagers came running. Mother's family also turned up in strength. "I told you so," the wise old man reminded Grandfather.

Father sat next to Mother at the table and drank just a little of the plentiful wine piled in front of him in flasks. He didn't talk to Mother and she didn't answer him. They addressed their silence to Grandfather, who went around dancing attendance on his guests and plying them with the strong liquor that Mother's family had brought with them from town. His body was heavy and he was panting, like a clumsy grizzly bear. A kind-hearted animal with the moist eyes of a drunkard. "What a man! A fine man!" he shouted repeatedly at Father's table and returned to fill his throat with the burning liquor. He was always crazy. Overflowing with strength like the sweat of horses. He believed that people beget rocks and die in their place like mountains. And Grandmother was deaf, and Mother ill, and Grandfather tall as a shadow, scattering grain to the wind, and then he went to the stable and saw the silent horses. He bought Mother a fine headscarf and pointed shoes to dazzle the eyes of the women in the village. He made her swear she would not go down to the sea again. He was afraid of the dreams of seashells and thought that the evil fish begot only dwarfs.

Close to midnight the arak got the better of him, his arms slumped and he fell to the ground like a tub. Only then did Father rise from his place and show the guests the door. Mother quietly stood up after him and turned off the lights. They left him there, sweaty and snoring on the floor.

V

Mother's family were in no hurry to leave for town. They stayed a month in the village, idling in the sun. They climbed the walls of the sheep pens, swarming like sleepy animals. From time to time they would wake from their slumber. "Why are you sad?" they rebuked Mother, and fell asleep again. The khamsin heat beat down on their bodies, and though it failed to burn them, it tanned and baked them. Their eyes grew dim. Their speech slackened. At noon, when they climbed down from their imaginary hammocks and gathered round the table, it was as though they had melted like lead.

In the evening, when Grandfather came in from the fields, they quickly admitted him to their company. Whispering, they repaid his hospitality. With great secrets. Item by item they revealed the mysteries of their craft. "The fundamental principle is the cask. The wood must be oak. Sealed with wax." He learned to make wine from dried grapes. "What's more," they warned him with covert threats, "you must never reveal this secret to any man." Grandfather was captivated by their charm. That same week he went with the father of the family to the vineyard of a Muslim in the heart of the mountains. He paid the full price for the small yield of a virgin field of vines and told the stunned farmer to stretch cloth bags over the ripe bunches and leave them hidden from the sun. They would become raisins.

By the second year his affairs were thriving. His reputation spread far and wide. People flocked to him from the ends of the town. But Grandfather was inflexible: "Only for respectable families." He rose at dawn, loaded the clay jars on the cart and went on his way. When he came back his clothes had changed. Ornamented with copper buttons. His youthful trimmed beard flourished again, thickening like a lion's mane. On his head a white straw hat. With a double brim. He was patient with his mutinous horses. He taught them good manners. Don't squint at the women, flicking them affectionately with his whip, displaying as he did so the glory of his huge paunch, swathed in a deerskin belt. "This is how the rich dress," he would shout in Grandmother's deaf ears. But she remained the same. "How are the family?" On with the old bonnet. Her ostler's stick. And then Grandmother was laughing, transformed in the new dress that Grandfather had bought her in town, fingering the lovely seashells that Mother had brought her before she conceived.

He quickly dispensed with his old cart, exchanging it for another. He hung amusing bells round the necks of the animals and on cold days he covered their backs with colored bridles. His clients were insatiable. "More, more," they pestered him politely. And Grandfather made fun of them, "Only if you pay me in gold coins."

The villagers kept their distance from his enterprise. He was giving the place a bad name. All their lives they had been simple folk. Shut in behind soft curtains. Suddenly their space had been invaded. The wall breached. Why? Why? At first they sent him a delegation. Their request was courteous. "All our lives we have managed with donkeys," they explained calmly, "and now look," they pointed outside the window with concern, "the whole road is full of cars." Grandfather listened tranquilly. His guests lacked for nothing. Figs. Dates. Sweetmeats on a glass dish. Coffee in porcelain cups. "The world is changing," he excused himself for his source of income. But the villagers were not appeased. "What's wrong with donkeys?" they repeated their charge. And thus evening fell.

It was the heavy stones that first aroused Grandfather's suspicion. They used them to seal the entrance to the cave where he kept his jars cold. He moved them away with his cart and loaded the flasks. The next day the same thing happened. He removed them and they put them back. Likewise with the stable. The nights were full of intrigue. It didn't take him long to find carrion in the fields. Someone had killed them deliberately. From the walls of the cellar the eyes of the first rats peered out. The horses moved slowly. Some unknown disease irritated their hide. The animal doctor had no difficulty in concluding: "They have been maltreated."

In the village store they made a fool of Mother. "They don't want to sell to me," she said, skulking in the kitchen. Grandfather consoled her in greedy fashion. "Never mind, shop in town. Like the rich people do." Glass jars. Cardboard boxes. Tins imported from abroad. The whole town was crazy. Sweltering in silk trousers. "Here, take more money." Furtively, he stuffed more gold coins into her hand, "make the bastards' eyes pop with jealousy." Grandmother willingly agreed with him. She moved through the doorway of the hut, driving off the mosquitoes with her feathered stick. Perhaps she believed that they had made her deaf.

That night the three horses were found dead.

All day Grandfather remained shut in the stable. He thought he could bring them back to life. Towards evening he took his pickaxe, climbed up into the hills and dug three pits. Only then did he go down into the cellar and bring up his old plow. He exchanged the old rusty blades for new ones and began wildly to turn over the soil of the vegetable field as far as the edge of the stony ground. In fury he removed stones, dug irrigation trenches with a hoe and planted slender vine seedlings. "Here there will be a new vineyard," he swore.

The villagers gathered their strength. That same month they converged on the hut and threatened to overturn it. Grandfather was not deterred. On the contrary, he went out to them empty-handed. For a moment they appeared to be regretting their initiative. Hesitantly, they began to withdraw. But then the younger men approached. Holding wooden poles. They seized Grandfather and thrust him aside. Suddenly the cry went up: "Destroy!" and a stone from somewhere struck the window and shattered the glass. That was the sign. Grandmother, as though cured of her deafness, flew through the doorway on mosquito wings and charged the attackers. But the villagers, more daring than ever, quickly threw her off and broke down the door. And there they found Mother. Standing silently in front of them, holding a kitchen knife. Her eyes melted their onslaught. They recoiled slightly. But the women blocked their way. Scornfully, they swept round them and fell upon Mother. They took the knife out of her hand and ripped the neck of her dress. Her bare flesh blinded the eyes of the young men. With renewed strength they burst their way in. "Whore!" they screeched in despair. And then came Grandfather's madness. Roaring, he leapt into the tool store, brandished the huge pickaxe with which he had buried the horses and single-handed put the rioters to flight.

All this time, no one had noticed Father's disappearance. He reappeared at night and went out with Grandfather to look for Mother in the hills. They walked in silence, examining every cranny. Only at first light did they find her, crying by the cliffs. Then, for the first time since he had brought her from town, Father raised his hand against her. "Crazy woman!" It was a miracle the jackals had not found her first.

VI

From that day on Grandmother never recovered her health. They believed it was the severe *khamsin* that made her ill. The doctor who came to visit supported them in this belief. "The important thing is to drink a lot," he soothed them. But Grandfather, who had noticed the serenity on her face, refused to believe. "She wants to die," he sobbed.

He abandoned all his affairs and began to look after her by himself. He would not allow anyone else to come near her. Even when Mother came in, carrying a bowl of soup, he was unpleasant to her. He told her to leave it by the door. Something of his strength seemed to be undermined by Grandmother's quiet breathing. She did nothing. Nevertheless, he continued to sob: "Don't die." Now the sounds from outdoors made him fearful. He dreaded how the mountains moved by night. He could hear their footsteps approaching. The air beyond the window, filled with the howls of foxes, also betrayed his schemes. The old nest of crows on the roof of the ruined house also added to his fears. He closed and bolted the door of the hut and boarded up the window. No one would take her away from him, he held her two hands strongly. And then the viper crawled under her bed. He crushed its head with a hoe, but no longer trusted his own strength. He knew his enemies had won. Weeping, he climbed into her bed and clasped her to his heart. "Don't go," he adjured her. Slowly, Grandmother's eyes lost their fullness. Now she was also blind. She did not want to pain him. She died while he was standing in the kitchen, cooling her soup.

When the old women came to purify her body, Grandfather would not open the door. He locked himself in and would not respond even to the entreaties of the rabbi who came from town for the funeral eulogy. At noon, when everyone had given up hope, Father appeared with the pickaxe, broke down the bolts of the door and took Grandmother from his arms.

In the evening, when they came down from the hill, he told a different story. "She died during the night," he assured the mourners.

VII

The first pests were discovered in the vineyard. Grandfather no longer went out to exterminate them. Sick plants withered in the silence of dry autumn leaves, and the smell of decay spreading from the belly of the earth hastened the death of the other vines. The supporting props fell apart, the wire fences collapsed. The disgrace was clear to all. And one day Father went out and plowed up the whole vineyard.

Grandfather's sickness did not seem to break down Father's taciturnity. Days went by as before. He left for the fields in the morning and came back at the end of the day. He would sip his soup and stand in the doorway of the hut. Sometimes he would climb up to the other hut. "What did he eat?" he would casually inquire and Mother would hesitate. "Just tea." He would look at the bed and go away. "Even the doctors had nothing else to say," he commented.

A delegation of village elders came to visit. They sat for a while in a half circle, then rose to go, saying nothing. Their serene expression could not conceal their joy. His fate was sealed. He would alarm them no longer with dreams of wine.

Mother still washed his clothes, cleansed his body and plowed a path through his hair with the iron comb. Occasionally a miracle would occur. Once again he looked like a farmer. He would hoist his iron pickaxe on his shoulder and set out along the snake path. There his enemies gathered. When he returned he was mocked. Silently carrying the dry pelt of a rat. He reverted to his bad old ways, shouting aloud, howling like a wounded animal at the mention of Grandmother's name. He believed that now that she had become a great mountain among the high peaks, she was cured of her deafness.

Through weary nights he would rock her empty chair, talking to her endlessly. "Do you remember?" with a drunken smile, laying the old sea shells in her imaginary lap.

People tried discreetly to intervene. Perhaps he could be sent away, somewhere else. No, it was not that he was a nuisance, God forbid, but all the same, he couldn't just be left alone, abandoned. After all that had happened. A man rich in possessions. He may have been impoverished, collapsed like a pauper. But land is still land, favoring those who do not rise above themselves. And Grandmother, as everyone knew, had been ill a long while. That was the way things were. Dust to dust, everything returns to its place. What one hand takes, the other restores. All the same, it cannot be denied, he had transgressed. Offended the villagers. But now he had been cleansed of his sin. He had been forgiven, with a full heart. And Father was grave, sitting despondently on the wooden steps, gazing silently at the hut higher up. "No one is going to send him away," he warned them.

Sometimes he seemed to awake from a black rage. "He wants to drink," Father would say threateningly. And Mother would hurry, carrying the boiling kettle up to his hut. She dragged the girl along with her too. She gave her all the degrading jobs to do. Taught her how to wash and dress him. He was thin and enfeebled, lying there in his filthy clothes, his legs suppurating. "First his head," pulling the bowl towards her and wetting his goatlike hair, rubbing it with a towel and then pulling at his trousers, "Use your strength."

Time for soup. It was hard for them to feed him. His jaws were clenched tight. They opened them a crack with a kitchen knife, forced the food down his throat. "Eat, eat," Mother implored him desperately. In vain. His bowels turned over noisily and he slobbered onto her dress. "Ahh, that man is driving me crazy," she fled screaming from the hut.

In the end she left the girl alone with him. "You try," grimacing, she flung the towel over the bowl. She approached him slowly. Grandfather was blind by now. He saw only snakes. Full of the venom of wadis. Belts. Ropes. Foul woolen blankets. He scrunched them all with his hard boots. Like Mother, she knelt down and tied them back on his feet. "Grandfather, grandfather." Through the dark hours. Soup again. Softened crumbs of bread. "Just once more, Grandfather," she coaxed and wheedled. Wonder of wonders, his eyes slowly grew moist, he opened his mouth and chewed from her hand.

In his madness he learnt to grope for her fingers, her neck, her thin cheeks. "Who are you?" in a terrible mumble. "A young girl," she answered. Grandfather cackled. He closed his hairy eyes, fumbling gently for the tassels of her clothes. "Grandmother was the same," clear-sighted, shaking himself free of his depression. His hands with peeling skin resting on his body like the sagging chrysalis of a larva. That was how he held Grandmother's hands before she died. "You know what happened there," sobbing at the grief of the mountains in desolation, remembering that they had begotten only one child in their lives. Father. And Grandmother dreamed in her new palace. Her hands were still full of sea shells. She died, sailing in a fishing boat.

Stories came unbidden, in a jumble. His crumbling brain cast them out of secret hiding places. He took her hand and laid it on his chest. All his stories. He spoke in a whimper. Moaning insistently. Mother's face was pale, her skin breathing like a curtain. Father was foolish. He loved to lie down in the sun with the donkeys and come home full of fleas. He had never wanted to marry Mother. He was always asking after the donkeys. He never knew he would meet her in the fig grove. And Mother was as foolish as he. She thought figs only had a smell. Grandfather said so, his face screwed up in thought, charring the roots of his hair. She was older than Father and he was only a child. He thought the women in town came out of pictures. "Both of them were crazy," declared Grandfather with feeling, drawing himself up to his giant height and beating in terror on his emptied chest. The baby died at birth and Mother was unconsolable. Like a snail she crawled up into the hills There she suckled a jackal's cub. Perhaps she already wanted to die. Always to die. Like dry leaves. Like the tears of a barren tree. What could grow out of her? Crazy. Just a fistful of young shoots. Once she went into the sea and never came out. "I pulled her out of the sea, swollen like a barrel, with a child nearly full-grown in her belly. That's how you were born, tiny like a snail." And Grandfather cried, Grandmother's imaginary fingers stroking his face, the fading sun in the west shining through the window, its rays as mad as he.

At night the shouting returned.

Mother's strength waned. Grandfather's shouts were wearing her down. "He has to be brought down from there," she implored, digging her nails in the ugly wrinkles on her face, "maybe put in an institution. In town perhaps. Or even here," pointing at their room in despair, "only not up there." Father remained silent. "Let him stay there," he decreed. At that time his face was grimy as ash. Sitting on the wooden step, drinking with loathing from the soup bowl. Something in his soul was gaining strength. He glared at Mother, venting his anger on her. "Tell the truth," and Mother is dwarfed. She swears by her life. "You know," he thunders darkly. Her entreaties bring no salvation. He confines her to the net like a dangerous animal. "What did you do? What did you do?" Mother's sobs are endless. "The child is crying," again she begs for mercy. But Father's eyes are ugly, sharp as fangs. She looks vainly at the pair of them, her eyes like frightened rabbits. Perhaps it was at this moment, as he stood there furious, that she understood for the first time why Grandfather killed all the snakes. "Father," she sobbed. But his voice showed no recognition. The air in her lungs was blocked. "What did you do there? What did you do?" And Mother was mute, dragged across the floor by her two feet, her back bleeding. Screaming as though through a suffocating pillow of down. "I wanted to drown." For an instant Father is also silent. The two of them listen to the insane howling coming down to them from the hut. But in a trice his strength increases, he swings Mother high in the air and flings her on the bed like a piece of rubbish. "Lies. All lies." And Mother strains her throat: "I swear." The bed shudders again. "Both of you!" Then silence. Father's feet disappear into the mountains. The sea is still far away. Even on quiet nights its roar cannot be heard. Perhaps it was Father who stood there alone on the shore and prevailed. He gulped down all its waters. And only that same monster towered there, and Mother did not cry out for help.

Suddenly the shouts ceased. Mother hurried out of the hut, looking up in fear. Father stood there petrified, holding on to the open door.

His face was frozen, faded, as though he had sloughed off his skin. She came up to him slowly and placed her hand on his: "I swear, I wanted only to die." His eyes did not budge from the doorway. "Come in," he said. Grandfather lay stretched out dead among Grandmother's wooden spoons, his boots tied to his feet. His face was composed, one hand reaching forward. "He wanted to go," Father followed her. Mother took the towel, moistened it and washed Grandfather's face. "So old," she sobbed, and wrapped him in a sheet. Then she looked at Father. "Now you can kill me too."

At midday the villagers assembled and dug his grave next to Grandmother's.

VIII

"Grandfather was a great mountain," Father made her swear to believe it, "he died at night." He began looking for his tracks now among all the rocks. The horizon mapped the path of his wanderings. A man like Grandfather is never interred. He seeps down through the earth and makes the volcanos grow. "Here, take a look." Amazed, he held the small stones between his fingers. "Once they were mountains." So it was with Grandfather. Father stifled his tears. He learnt to raise his eyes like an eagle and scan the range of hills that stretched beyond the desert. "One day we shall go there," he wiped his face with his hand.

Mother remained, Father seemed to have forgotten, and now that Grandfather had died it was as though the last taste of the village was lost to her. She groveled before him as before and wept. Maybe now that they were fatherless they could buy themselves a small house in town. One room would suffice. "This village is killing me." She did not blame the villagers for her disaster. She merely wanted to explain. But Father was tired and her voice was feeble. They had become like two trees growing inextricably together. Quiet words at night. Falling leaves. And always in stillness. As though language was wasted. She cooked and he sipped. What else did they need? Even if the soup had no flavor, he did not complain. He left it on the wooden step and tried to raise his eyes above the wilderness of stars.

In the evenings, like someone who detested life, he began to range beyond the village houses. Mother asked no questions. Mutely she gave thanks as each day ended. Her wooden distaff revolved slowly between her dry fingers. She held the goats' wool, plucking viciously at the fibers. Wrinkles again furrowed her cheeks like cart tracks. She no longer lamented. Thus her face would remain forever, incised by tunnels, or was it the look in her devastated eyes, seeing only into the distance? The house was forgotten. The street. And one small tile, red as the divided plumage of a bird, lying on the roof. Her face was downcast. The dream had flown. She no longer rubbed her hands with cream. When would she be dead and gone?

Beyond the snake path towered Father's silence. What was behind it? He had grown stronger. And his actions. The plow. The field of vegetables. The crash of his old pickaxe. And again the silence. The persistent stare at the heart of the desert. Driving tunnels through the wild earth. What are his eyes plotting? And then, one evening, for the first time since Grandfather's death, he opened the door to the cellar and brought up the cold bottles. Removed a cork and drank. Removed another and drank again. From high above, two hawks swoop down. Glide as though over the top of a chimney.

Dark men have come to join him in the cellar. Rolling on the ground with him. Bottle after bottle. Stillness again. "Come," deceitfully Mother clasps her to her bosom, covering her with the thin blanket, "you don't have to know." At dark they all go away, and Mother listens to their footsteps till they reach the last houses of the village. Women's voices can also be heard there.

When he comes back he throws his trousers on the floor and flops on the bed. He smells disgusting, foul. Singeing the wings of mosquitoes in flight. Mother is at her spindle, restraining herself, staring at his trousers in rage. She is never going to wash them again. He can wear them in sin. In her innocence she believed that evil deeds brought on death. Her legs were swollen. The ligaments ossified. Hampering her gait like scarred lizards. She moved awkwardly. Drank cup after cup, the kettle boiling. Perhaps in her heart she is listening to the whimper of the water, still yearning to drown. New signs spread menacingly across her cheeks. Her skin was withering. "This is the end," she stood silently in front of the wardrobe mirror. And then, when she could no longer endure her anguish, she came to the girl's bed, hugged her little shoulders and told her weeping that Father had never had black spots on his shoulders.

IX

In the distance she could make out the sand clouds rising above the herd as they grazed. In clumps. Black, moving lazily. The sun was blazing in the sky above. Yellow, a *khamsin*. Two wild doves cut across the sun's rays and were swallowed up in the bowels of the dust. She knew the herd would loiter here until the heat faded. She clutched the clay pot fearfully to her stomach and watched the animals.

The first to burst forward were the dogs. Then the cows moved slowly. Exhausted. Some of them sank hopelessly onto the sandy thorn bushes, others mooed plaintively as they gored the stones of the trough. The cowherd prodded them from behind, his scorched hands pulling at the tired carthorses and keeping them away from the herd. He jammed heavy stones against the wheels, only then free to water the animals from the well.

The ancient trough was awash with water. Cows and young calves milled about angrily, plotting desperately to smash the blazing stone platform. Again and again the cowherd would haul up the bucket and cool their discontent. His face was haggard, etched with muddy sweat. Behind him the horses pawed the sand, their nostrils exhaling strange fire that threatened to burn up the parched wild bushes the herd was trampling as it moved around. Suddenly a wild groan was heard from inside the wagon. The cowherd turned his head anxiously.

"What's that," she emerged from her hiding place behind the tree trunk.

"Be careful," he called out to her. Slowly the animals slaked their thirst. Their fleshy bodies relaxed. Some wandered off among the bushes and the others sank silently to the ground and dozed. The fierce heat damaged their skin. Their tails hung listlessly. Only their eyes revealed a trace of rancor, the frothy discharge like the last foam on the grapes she had seen in Grandfather's casks of wine. The horses remained standing in their places, their bodies black with sweat. From time to time they twitched their manes, gazing malevolently at the sealed entrance to the wagon. The cowherd paid no attention to them. He pulled up another bucket from the well and turned towards the wagon.

"Is it a bull?" she asked from afar.

He nodded dryly. His muddy face was animated. He poured the water through the close-set wooden side beams and looked inside with concern.

"Is it sick?" she came nearer.

"No," he threw down the bucket.

Suddenly she felt his gaze on her body. Slow-moving, stringy eyes exploring her as though nibbling in disgust at some poisonous plant.

"Who are you?"

"From the village," she replied quickly, "down there," pointing to the small wooden huts scattered along the downward slope of the stone path.

"And the pot," he examined its clumsy form with surprise.

"I was going to draw some water," she said hesitatingly, apprehension in her voice.

"Are there no pipes?" he asked her suspiciously.

"They're polluted. Mother wanted clean water, for pickling cucumbers."

His torn shirt was sticking to his chest. His hard bones were covered in thick hair.

He strode resolutely towards her and rudely snatched the pot from her hand.

"It's heavy," he sniggered.

"Yes," she shivered. "It was always Father who came to draw water."

"And now."

"Mother doesn't ask him any more."

"Why not?" he gave her back the pot.

"Once he went to the well and broke the pot."

She thought he was making fun of her. The mud on his face had faded, leaving his coarse skin pitted.

"And since then Mother has sworn..." she fell silent.

Screams of pain echoed across the sky. Two wild doves swooped out of the yellow clouds. A group of birds of prey came flashing after them. She watched as the patch of bright sky between the birds dwindled. For an instant they were unified in a confused brawl, then the air parted and crumbled into a thin sprinkling of plucked feathers.

"They are dead," she said.

He looked at her, almost with contempt.

The wooden wagon began to shudder wildly. The heavy stones that jammed the wheels seemed to be gradually splitting. Suddenly the herd also began to grow restless. The look of Grandfather's last wine was once again alight in the eyes of the cows, sensing almost with horror the danger latent in the horses. The cows that had been lying now rose and moved together in one huge block. A sour smell of salt and raging flesh came wafting from their midst. Dazed, she retreated, dropping the pot against the trunk of an olive tree. Smiling in spite of herself, she felt a strange softness seeping into her belly, flooding her with a dreamlike peace. The groan of the bull awoke her from her daze.

"What's the matter with him?" she shouted.

He looked at her almost disdainfully.

"He's crazy."

The herd advanced, their feet plowing towards the sides of the wagon. The cowherd watched them moving threateningly. He leapt towards them, and calling the dogs to his aid, fell upon the animals, smiting them heavily on the back, shouting and dragging them by their thick necks towards the stones of the trough. His hands were full of frothy saliva. His shirt had been torn off his shoulder. Scorched, brown flesh blinded his eyes. The deep grooves on his face were drenched again with sweat. She saw him rise again and spring forward. Slowly the herd began to retreat. Several cows that had been beaten moved away beyond the sparse thicket of bushes. Suddenly the leading cow, black and weary, dodged aside and charged towards him. The cowherd evaded the animal's angry snout and lunging, jumped onto its back. With his scorched arms he tried to hang on to its back, but to no avail. The cow was stronger. It raised its huge head and nudged him in the chest. Then the dogs joined in. They dug their teeth in the cow's belly and tore the flesh.

"They're killing it," she screamed.

The cow kicked out at them with its back legs, exposing its heavy udders threateningly but they gnawed at everything, biting its tail, its ribs, throwing themselves at it from all sides, as though feeding on a carcass. Finally the cow was defeated, tossing its head in flight, swallowed up among the last cows behind the bushes.

The cowherd remained alone, puffing and blowing. Tensing at the dark hostility of the beasts' despair. For the first time she noticed the hesitation of surrender in his close-set eyes, the fear with which he gazed helplessly at the heavy wooden beam that sealed the door of the wagon. Unwittingly, she felt sorry for him. Such a young lad. He was holding another bucket of water and cooling down the roof of the wagon. The bull shuddered, banged its body against the side walls and bellowed with rage. The cowherd recoiled, staring alarmed at the stony glare in the eyes of the pent-up animal. All this time the horses had been standing in silence, scraping, almost savagely, deep trenches with their hooves. The cowherd approached and swilled their backs too with water. They did not move. For an instant a covert tremor flared their nostrils. They buried their muzzles again in the ground. What were they plotting? She suddenly found herself walking towards him. Her bare feet were burning in the sand.

"You're sweating," with a trembling hand she took her kerchief from her pocket.

She held her breath. His eyes were grinning again as he squinted at her exposed thighs. A strange fear twisted her back. Suddenly she felt a longing for her mother's soup, for her mute countenance, her broken teeth desperately fraying the sheep's wool. Pulling at her dress, she smoothed it prettily round her legs.

"Keep away," he exclaimed in a hoarse voice.

His speech was aggressive, humiliating. Offended, she stepped back a few paces, sliding away from him. As though for the first time, she felt drugged by the smoke of the oppressive *khamsin*. What would have happened if the cow had got the better of him in its rage. If it had trampled on him with metallic hooves. The dogs would have been no help. Like a pack of rats they would have fled yelping to the distant desert caves. The wagon was creaking. The cows would have swept over the sides of the vehicle like a breaking wave, shattering the side beams. The startled bull would be caught in their bellowing, its belly swollen. They would have dragged him with them as far as the stone cliffs, emptying his boiling blood into them. At night they would have killed him. An empty hulk. Drained. Flung away like a torn sack. And there, at the edge of the dry trough, the cowherd would remain. His body ravaged, silent, the flesh destroyed by the sun, maggots squirming among his cavities. By the time the other cowherds appeared, his stench would be rising to high heaven. They would gather up his corpse, and throw it, with its terrible swarming sea of creatures, beyond the pile of stones.

In the evening she will go back there with Father. There, on the forsaken hills, he will continue to give the stones frightening names, transforming terror into a children's story. Mountains are always sad men with cliffs for beards. They never die. They merely change their size. Even when she pretended to be stupid, he believed she understood his drunken storytelling. Yet she loved the pungent odor of strong liquor that wafted from his throat, the desperate caresses as he stroked and disentangled her braids. Red, imploring eyes that created nothing but mountains. "You will die by night," he soothed her, "a great mountain like Grandfather." She tried to hold him, to keep him from stumbling. Three bottles, sometimes more. And those harsh, almost scorching gasps. Together they will reach the cairn of stones. His face grim. Why are the cowherds laying waste his beautiful desert? He will stand in silence with her by the cairn, staring sadly at the bones of the shepherd with their moldering flesh. Mumbling, how could it be? Such a small rock. A crumb of a stone. He still found it hard to make sense of. A lad. Hardly more than a boy. He may never have known a woman. Come, dragging her after him, let's go back to the village.

As they approach the paths to the huts he will turn again toward the well, his eyes still moist from fumes of wine. Did you see, dead like an animal. His face weeping. Stumbling over every stone. With her two small hands she will support his huge bulk. And Father weeps. Such a young man. Almost the ribs of a mountain. And yet, just a small stone. Gravel. Like Mother's final dust. And Mother, listening in the kitchen, hears, and holds her peace. Biting the goatskin mantles with her missing teeth. Praying in her harsh silences for the winter that will not come. Apart from the snow that will give her cheeks a flush of color. She could not watch her suffering. "I'm going to draw some water," she told her. And there, beyond the window curtain, Father was wrestling with a broken heart. Perhaps we ought not to have run away – Father grieved over his disgrace – but buried him there. Covered the wretch with sand. Poor Father. When he embraced her, sobbing at her from eyes sick with sour wine, she believed that Mother had acted stupidly in not leaving the village when the baby died.

X

The cowherd was cautiously feeling his saliva-damp hands. He seemed to her still afraid. Covertly, with weary eyes, he watched the suspicious movements of the herd. And the horses worried him. Their long-suffering silence was full of menace. The bucket he had placed in front of them was still full to overflowing. They had not touched a drop. Hesitantly he removed his shirt and used it to wipe his sweaty face.

"You're hurt," she cried when she saw his hairy stomach.

"I told you," he said, driving her away again.

His voice was unbearably harsh. He did not conceal the contempt he felt. The disdain with which finally he looked at her. A little girl, not much more than a silly baby, with her father's pot of liquor. Anxious to make excuses, to explain things, to tell him about Mother's latest folly – pickling cucumbers in strange glass jars that her relatives brought from town. With dill and vine leaves and cucumbers yellowing like the dead fish that Grandfather gathered from the sea. Laboriously lining the small wooden shelves and covering them with sacks of flour. And Father losing his temper. Why in jars? Why not like all the other sensible women in the village? What's wrong with deep jugs? Or wine casks? And anyway, who is going to eat all that stinking stuff.

At night he'll come home, tottering as always, falling over his feet. He'll crawl over to her small bed on the other side of the partition and fearfully embrace her narrow shoulders. "My little girl," he'll groan, "my little girl." She won't know what's happening in the dark, only the salty wetness that wounds her skin. A shudder, and another shudder, and another, with despairing pleas: "my little girl... my little girl..." and then his insane moans, the horrible dribble, the stench, the ensuing silence as with the body of Grandfather at the end before he died.

Mother is shouting from the kitchen. The goat skins have broken her spindle again. Who is going to mend it this time? Her family are far away in town. They haven't come visiting much since the day Grandfather died. Who can she charge with carrying the heavy instrument? Her eyes close as she ponders, filtering the rest of her life through them. Perhaps she is dreaming again of being buried in a stone house in town. Pots of geraniums decorate the windows. A moist autumn breeze cools the furrows on her face. In the dirt patch in front of the hut, the white jasmine is in blossom. She can stretch out her hand and touch the sky. And once again, her eyes gape. She has remembered. There are still two empty jars left on the table. She will stuff them too with decaying cucumbers, leave them in the entrance of the hut for Father to look upon in defeat. Stupid old Grandfather, he didn't have to fish her out of the sea.

XI

The heavy wagon continued to grind the large stones jammed against its wheels. The crazed bull had no mercy. Again and again it launched its body against the bars, bellowing frantically as if it had been disemboweled. The horses made no response to its distress. Wickedly silent, they went on pawing at the sand, stubbornly ignoring the bucket of water which was emitting drowsy vapor. Father had once told her how they used to drug the bulls before mating them with the cows. "They used to dip them in a tub of spirit," he said. She listened quietly. His eyes were tense, filled with fibers of light. And Mother never stopped moving her out of earshot, even though it was hopeless, away from Father's drunken ramblings. "He'll turn you too into a dishrag," she warned her. All the same, she went with him to the cowshed.

Suddenly the herd was noisy, and she was deafened by a shrill scream.

"Run away. He'll kill you."

The wounded cow charged again from the bushes, galloping madly, and gored the wagon door. The body of the bull was shifted from its resting-place on the floor, and as though it had been flung up towards the ceiling, came thumping down. The enraged cow would not leave it alone. She charged the wagon again and her two front legs caught on the roof.

"He'll kill her," she shouted, as she caught sight of the bull's two horns protruding through the cracks in the beams.

"Get away from there, girl!"

He moved in a crawl behind the silent flanks of the horses. Slyly, little by little, he allowed the thick lasso to slip between his tough fingers. He tensed his body like a fox, covertly advancing, his arm projecting like a camel's hump, and then, when the cow came back, this time pushing in between the bull's horns, he leapt from his hiding-place and with a quick lunge looped the lasso round the cow's neck.

"Aahhh," he summoned the dogs to his aid.

The savage animals deferred to their master. They came yelping forward and hung on to the cow's udders. This time her awesome bellowing was not enough to drive them off. They kept on harrying her like wasps, lapping the blood that dripped from her flesh as though they were suckling. At her back the cowherd dug his heels in the sand and dragged the cow by the lasso. She was no longer bellowing. Wounded and defeated, she let them drag her like a carcass. There, beside the tree of knowledge, the cowherd bound her to the trunk. Her body slumped listlessly. Her eyes were bloodshot and a murky fluid, as though after protracted weeping, suffused her nostrils.

She stood and gazed helplessly at the cow. The humbled body sprawled in the sand. It lay there quiet, sweating, as though pinned to the ground by wooden spears, moist and dripping, staring upwards, eye torn and awash with blood. Tiny olive leaves stuck to its damp hide, like flies on the lethal strip of honey that Mother hung in the kitchen. She wondered in amazement how Father could have brought Tamar here that day. He had poured so much wine down his throat that morning. Perhaps he wanted to drown. Or through the rocky eyes that destroyed his head he saw a leopard prowling around the cowsheds and was plotting to kill it. Then, when he threw his trousers quivering over the branches of the tree, she believed he wanted to kill Tamar on the sand. Even her screams were different then, as though Father was pressing on her throat with a huge rubber bar. From her hiding-place behind the stone cairn, she had hoped the strange madness that suffused his eyes would be the downfall of her enemy. He seized her, twitching, and sank with her to the ground. Now he would grope with his fingers for the stone. See, there, beside the trunk, she shut her eyes so as not to see the encounter between the rock and the skull. And then came the shout. Fainter than she had hoped, a kind of groan, but it was enough. She and Father would dig a small trench together and cover her with a little sand. Like carrion. Dainty bones that injure young men. There would be no need to leave her in the sun. She would molder like the snails in the shade.

She remained hidden a long while before she dared to open her eyes beyond the stone wall. Father looked ridiculous, down on his knees, confusedly pulling his trousers away from the branches of the tree. Tamar was not dead. Annoyingly agile, she rose to her feet, peering at her thighs derisively. "So much hair," she laughed and twitched it with her fingers. Father was still struggling with his trousers, ripping away the broken branch that had got twisted between the buttons.

On her return home, she told Mother nothing.

Mother interrogated her: "Did you find Father."

"No."

"Where did you look."

"Everywhere."

"Including next to the well."

"He wasn't there."

"Take this. I'll go and look." She threw the midday fish towards her. "Just clean it for now."

After a time she came back, put her apron on and took out the meat grinder, cut up the fish into slices and put them through the machine.

"That man will be the death of both of us," she moaned.

When he came back, Mother tried to pacify him with mushroom soup.

"I'm not hungry," he exclaimed.

"There's fish too."

He threw his clothes on the chair and sprawled on the bed.

"Where did you eat."

"In the fields."

"I was there," she said.

He said nothing.

In silence she took the dish back to the kitchen. She examined his ruined clothes. What had he done to them? Slowly she lifted up his trousers. "So many leaves," her eyes blinking as she threw the remains of the branch on the floor. She fixed her eyes on her too. A silent stare. Thinking no doubt of the many places to which she had sent her to look for them. But she had sworn she had looked there too, how could she possibly have found them. They must have been hiding from her on the sand. Mother was mumbling again, pretending to be ripping the goatskin mantles with her broken teeth. Now her voice was free of restraint, floating in the air like a stray dove's feather in a region of hawks. Perhaps, downtrodden, in her mind's eye she was back again with her distant relatives in town. For some time now the only news of them was Job's tidings. Her old uncle had died. And then another uncle. And quite suddenly her young brother-in-law. The widows, brokenhearted, unable to endure the suffering, were soon gathered to their fathers. Mother, here in the village, was more alone than ever. And Father was drunk. And the child again speechless.

In the evening Mother rubs her face with fish oil. Perhaps at long last it will heal her skin. In the morning her face is disappointing. And her feet are swollen again. The cursed desert has no pity on her, inexorably shortening her days. There are no roads, no vehicles. Only bug-infested walls. Goatskin mantles moldering in the cupboard and what is left of the jars. Sometimes, with a firm show of resolution she packs her old suitcase and fills the villagers with hope. "This time surely she will stay there," they congratulate Father. But Father is not fooled. He knows her time of departure and her time of return. Always in shame and disgrace. More sullen than ever. "My uncle died," she mumbles. Perhaps in this way she seeks the same fate.

The women of the village clap their hands as though in grief. "She's back early again." Their disappointed expression shows compassion for Father. What was his sin? An innocent lad who once went astray in a grove of figs. And for that he has to uproot the whole orchard. Father remains silent, plods along the rows of vegetables, striking them with his hoe. His face is dreamy. What does he wish for in his heart? Perhaps for Mother to die at daybreak. Vanish like the morning dew. But no. Mother will not do the bidding of the village. She will die in darkness. Standing firm on her own two legs. All night the Angel of Death will wrestle with her, striving to overthrow her. In the morning the brow of heaven will still be covered with his sweat. Father will stand distraught by her room. The blanket in shreds. The room furniture overturned. And Mother, her two arms wounded, lying supine on the floor. Her face smooth. Gazing serenely at the ceiling. And Father weeping. How his eyes have faded over the years. A great mountain. A giant. For the first time he will fall at her feet and whimper like a dog. The whole desert.

XII

Tamar's laughter still remains there beside the tree trunk. Rolling and squirming under the boiling innards of the anguished cow. Her breath rises like smoke, collecting among the branches like stray wisps of mist in the days before winter. Perhaps her death will begin like that. She will die on a very cloudy day. Like the beginning of the rains. And Father will not know. He will open the door of the hut to look for her and all the empty air will be swept away.

XIII

Again the cowherd drove the herd ahead. His face was tense, seamed. The dogs, more excited than before, continued maliciously to chase the alarmed cows towards the rocks. On the cliff slopes the noonday sun was kindling the desert scrub. The smoke from the fires hovered motionless, drawn quietly upwards, as though sucked through vast transparent chimneys. "You see those snakes?" Father used to say excitedly, gazing with startled eyes at the flames of the khamsin, "they are plotting to kill God." Father's drunken fairytales. Perhaps in his heart he thought death had no dominion without God. He would reign alone throughout the desert. A spirit that knew no bounds. Father. Father. She remembered, Mother had spent all night removing the olive leaves from his trousers. And Father lay sprawled speechless on the bed, digging his head into the wall, sucking at the last of Grandfather's bottles. So lost. Powerless. A child dreaming of a basket of figs. A tiny heap of sand. Not a mountain. Not a stone. If a flake were to fall from the ceiling on to his head, it would crumble to dust. With a dry rag Mother would cheerfully flick it towards the windowsill. Father. Father. Totally lost, she walked towards the wagon. Again she took hold of the bar of the padlock. The hewn trunk of a tree. Its bark hurt her fingers. She felt the blood pulsing between the horns of the feverish bull. The sky continued without cease to withdraw, escaping the poisonous fangs that threatened to reach it. Father. Father.

Suddenly the wagon shook. The wooden bar fell from her hand. The door was wrenched from its place and the massive bull galloped off towards the sand. It hovered for a moment on its back legs and then, as though clutching an unseen ladder, took possession of the wounded cow and drew her in. Only then did the horses wake from their silence. They rose on their hind legs, whinnying in triumph.

The cowherd rushed towards her, striking her viciously in the face. The furrows had suddenly vanished from his face. His teeth were bared. And sticky. She was too small to take everything in. Again and again he beat her without mercy. "Mad!" She opened her mouth to scream, but remained silent, swallowing the air from his teeth, as though from some last slice. Columns of poison touched her flesh. His shirt tore between her nails, strangely baring his tanned skin. His teeth did not let go, digging in to her neck, stifling her spirit. She struggled to push his body off her. The sand was scorching her back. Mother's wrinkles cried aloud to save her, hopelessly imploring. It was as though the sea had sneaked into her hut, and swallowed her together with him, like a useless husk. And then the flesh burst out of him, choking her strength to the ground.

Eventually he relaxed. Silently he pulled up his trousers and calmly fastened them. He summoned the dogs and set them on the tired bull, driving it into the wagon. Only then did he look at her again. "Such a child," he said.

In the afternoon he left with the herd.

XIV

After a while, she stopped crying. She stood up and brushed her dress clean of sand. Lying on the ground were the shards of the pot that the bull had shattered when it broke out. She picked them up, still thinking about Tamar. Why had she laughed? Now she must be snuggling on the mat in her hut and chuckling to herself. Chewing a piece of sugar cane between her teeth and laughing again. Her face content. She is wrapped in the dress that Father brought her secretly from town. She'll go to her. When she comes in, Tamar will squirm on the floor again. Giggling, she'll try to make a face like a woman in despair. And she, for a long time, will hold her peace, delving into her eyes as though pouring poison into them. And it will be taken in, be absorbed into her blood. Her thin body will collapse. Desperately, she will tear at her new dress with her nails, unstitching it like a caterpillar sloughing its skin. Water, she will grunt, saliva frothing at her mouth, water, water. One last twitch of a muscle in her dry lips. And the rest of her bones will stiffen into the fibers of the mat. Water, water. But she will continue to gaze at her serenely, throwing the fragments of the pot on her cold body and smiling. Can't you see, the pot is broken.

XV

When she came home she found Mother outside, hanging the washing on the line. She slipped into the shed where the latrines were, praying that Father would be back before she had to confront her. She almost believed it, until she heard her wooden clogs approaching.

"Is that you there?"

"Yes."

"Why are you late?"

Hopefully she kept quiet.

"Are you sick?"

She was tempted to lie.

"No," she froze.

"And the pot?"

She bit her lips.

"What?"

"It broke."

She knew Mother's face had paled. Now she would shout. She would slam the door on her. But no. Only a tired whisper.

"Just like your father."

The clogs withdrew slowly into the distance. Her body slumped to the ground. From somewhere she heard weeping. Her wounded fingers climbed up and dug into her throat, as though only now she had strangled a poisonous snake.

Mother will pickle no more cucumbers this summer.

Yaakov Shabtai

Departure

Translated by Dalya Bilu

Little by little my grandmother died. Like a strip of brown land, receding from the eyes of the travelers on a ship until it merges into the horizon and disappears into it, so she faded away. And during all that time we continued to keep kosher and separate the milk from the meat.

At the beginning came the fits of weakness which were accompanied by pallor and shortness of breath, and the valerian drops whose sharp smell clung to her and to her clothes and hung in the air of her room. She would put on her reading glasses and drip the brown drops with a trembling hand into a pale green wine glass, counting them in a low, tense voice, as if whispering an incantation to drive away the evil spirits.

Afterwards came the coughing. At first it was a slight, insignificant cough, as if a crumb had lodged in her throat. But from day to day the cough grew deeper, more stubborn and troublesome until in the end it conquered her entirely, with only an occasional and unexpected respite. She would shuffle round the house in her brown slippers, broad as a goose's feet. and cough and cough. She coughed at her prayers too, and also at night, in her sleep. The kindly, red-cheeked Dr Gottlieb would come, smile at her, pat her shoulder affectionately, and the medicines on her bedside table multiplied. And still she pursued her daily round without bitterness, punctiliously and serenely.

Because she slept so lightly, she would wake up even before the ringing of the alarm clock, which she would set every night and place on her bedside table. Slowly and wearily she would raise her grey head from the thick pillow, lift the vast down quilt, and rise from the depths of the mattress in her limp, white nightgown. All of them – the pillow, quilt and mattress – had been brought from Poland in carts and trains and on board ship and had gone on serving her here as they had served her there, at the end of that distant century. With a careful movement of her hand she would take the clock, wind it, and return it to its regular place on the shelf in the kitchen. Her son Aaron had given it to her many years ago. It was a tin clock with thin little legs, a ridiculous bell-hat and long hands with ornamental tips, like the tufted letters of an old Bible. It was always slow and sometimes it stopped, and Grandmother would shake it like a bottle of medicine to bring it back to life. In addition to telling the time, it was fitted with a gadget that was supposed to switch off the light in her room on Friday nights. But if it failed to do so, she would throw me a rapid glance, and I would do it instead, quickly and as if without her complicity in the act.

The Sabbath prohibitions were of no consequence in my eyes, as they were of none in the eyes of my parents. Nevertheless, I was taken aback by her behavior and I would wait curiously, with some anxiety and more than a little animosity, to see what God would do. It was clear to me that he did not exist, but at the same time I was still somewhat in awe of him, in the guise of my step-grandfather, my German grandfather, who had died in the meantime, who was brown and irascible, who when he was alive had sat in the dim light of the entrance hall on his Pharaonic throne, mumbling his prayers, or gulping watery, yellowish soup from an enormous silver spoon, keeping an eye on everything that went on in the house, and aware of the slightest transgression committed in each and every corner of its rooms.

After taking out the chamber pot and washing and praying and tidying her room, she would go out and come home flushed and panting with her shopping, which was barely enough for a bird to live on. Then she would sit down at the kitchen table to do her accounts. Meticulously she would set down large figures on the margins of a newspaper, from time to time wetting the point of the indelible pencil with the tip of her tongue. This was invariably a miniscule stub of a pencil, which was kept in the drawer with the *parve* cutlery used for dishes that were neither milk nor meat, and which was so small that she could barely get a grip on it with her thick, carpenter's fingers. Concentrating intently, she would add up the sums, whispering the numbers to herself in Yiddish as if she were praying, check the result, exclaim at the exorbitant prices, and copy the total into her black notebook. Life had taught her to calculate carefully, to darn old stockings, to peel potatoes with the thinnest parings possible, and to try not to be dependent on other people's favors.

In the early evening she would say her prayers from the brown prayer book, whose pages were the same color as her face. Afterwards she would sit in the heavy armchair and read *Ze'enah u-Re'enah*, a popular pious work of biblical commentary and homiletics in Yiddish, considered particularly suitable for women, or some other book. But sometimes she would still knit things for her grandchildren, patch worn garments, exchange views on politics, give cautious advice, or settle some dispute that had flared up in the house. She did this by means of snatched, whispered conversations which she would conduct, apparently casually, with the different parties in the bathroom, the little storeroom, or the corners of the rooms. In the same way she fought for my brother when he was going out with a divorced woman, causing a great commotion in the house where divorcees were regarded as distant relatives of whores. Grandmother saw nothing wrong with it. In her own way she was a free woman in her world.

In the evenings she would entertain guests, read the Labor Party newspaper *Davar*, or brown copies of the Yiddish weekly the *Amerikaner*, or else she would write letters to her son and faceless sister, Idel, in America.

All her life, until the appearance of the ballpoint pen, she wrote with an old-fashioned wooden pen, dipping the long thin nib in an ink-pot and blotting the ink with blotting paper. The pen lay in the table drawer next to the ink-pot, the writing pad, the airmail cards, the reading glasses, the calendar, the long hairpins, the mirror, the brown comb and the red chocolate box in which she kept her Sabbath wig.

She lived in great economy and intimacy with her belongings, reserving for each its proper place and time and use like objects in the performance of a rite.

From day to day she faded. Like a chick inside an egg, death grew inside her, while she herself shrank. A permanent flush bloomed palely on her sagging cheeks, whose flesh was the color of clay, and suddenly her coughing stopped. Now she passed through the rooms without a sound, the nostrils of her broad nose like the two halves of an empty walnut, and her clever eyes, which had sunk deep into their sockets, grew very wide and strained, with a strange, baffled stare. And still she went on salting the meat, cooking her meals in little enamel saucepans, doing her accounts, dragging herself to the rabbi with her questions, lighting Sabbath candles, quoting old proverbs, spitting to the right and the left against the evil eye, trapping roaches in bits of newspaper and hurrying, gritting her teeth in disgust, to throw them into the lavatory and pull the chain. Sometimes she would still even sing little songs in Yiddish and Polish in a dry, hollow voice, smiling a weary smile as she sang. It seemed that in spite of everything, she was glad to be alive.

Her friends kept on coming. The wealthy Mrs Abeles, her heavy face shadowed by elegant hats which were smothered in flowers or embellished with feathers and net veils, who filled the house with her loud, rough voice, hoarse as a cigar smoker's. Old Leibshu Knipp with his tanned face, who wore a bowler hat, guffawed coarsely from time to time, and noisily slurped glasses of black, boiling tea, breaking the sugar cubes between his strong teeth. On every visit without fail he would repeat the tale of the two widows, one of whom he wished to marry, only he could not make up his mind between the one who owned the kiosk and the one who owned the orange grove.

Grandmother refused to give her opinion in this matter, just as she preferred to say nothing in response to the stories of Shmuel Zilberbaum, who would turn up at intervals like a fresh spring breeze, wearing an old striped suit with a spotless handkerchief in the breast pocket, a large ring on his finger, and milk-white shoes with holes punched in them on his feet. He would sit on the edge of his chair, drum on the table with a white finger, and hold forth to her on his business affairs and his chances of making a fortune from stocks and shares and land speculations and currency deals. Grandmother's reaction was reserved. She rejected such feats of financial wizardry, which bordered, she felt, on fraud. And she didn't believe in them either, just as she didn't believe in lotteries or miracles and suspected anything that smacked of the supernatural. Among those who came to see her were also the synagogue treasurer, the gardener, the grocer, the *landsleit* from the old country, neighbors and members of the family. But the one who came most of all was Mrs Chernibroda.

She was a busybody of a woman, skinny as a thorn and sprightly as a grasshopper, dressed in frocks of thin black silk. They would sit side by side, Grandmother with her broad face, and Mrs Chernibroda with her sparrow's face, and conduct long, peaceful conversations.

Now Grandmother no longer went out, not even to the synagogue. But the calendar of significant days and the deeds appropriate to them – holy days, birthdays, anniversaries of the deaths of brothers and parents and grandparents – continued to be observed.

And on Fridays, after setting the table in her room with the two glass candlesticks, which were decorated with colored crystals, and after covering the plaited challah loaf with its pink silk cloth, she would get dressed in her Sabbath dress and sit down to put on her wig. She did this with silent concentration and a ceremonious air, repeatedly examining her face in the mirror. When she had finished, she would wind the clock, put it in its place, and bless the candles. And then it was Sabbath.

Afterwards they took her to the hospital, and she was already very small. From there she was transferred to the sanatorium. One day my mother came home carrying a bundle of clothes, brown slippers, a few copies of the *Amerikaner*, a pen, two airmail cards, a calendar, a prayer book, reading glasses, hairpins and a picture of the family.

When we came home from the cemetery we sat in the kitchen and my mother served tea. A number of friends and relations came and sat with us. There was a feeling of weariness and emptiness, but also of relief. It seemed as if we had all come back from the docks, after seeing off a departing member of the family. It was all over. The radio spoke, someone read the evening paper, my mother set the tea on the table, and people spoke quietly to each other. From time to time they mentioned Grandmother, but as if she were someone who had set off on a long voyage from which she would return. After all, she had left all her belongings here.

No rites of mourning took place and the days passed without being counted off from the day of her death. "Grandmother's room" remained open and we went in and out of it as when she was alive. All the furniture, clothes, and other things remained where they were. And so did the meat-salting board, the old china jug in which, and only in which, she made the Sabbath raisin wine, and the tin clock which stood perpetually at twenty to eleven, since nobody had bothered to wind it after she was taken to the hospital.

One day Mrs Chernibroda appeared and took away Grandmother's clothes and bedclothes to distribute to the needy. Two floral silk dresses, a coat, a thick woollen scarf and the crocheted bag in which she used to carry her reading glasses and her prayer book to the synagogue, Mother gave to the Yemenite maid who had been in the habit of leaving part of her wages with Grandmother in order to save something from her drunken husband. Her purse and towels she gave to a poor old man. He used to call on Grandmother at regular intervals and she used to give him milk, soup, rusks, tea and fruit. Now he announced that he would pray for the elevation of her soul. The candlesticks and the pink silk challah cover were taken by Mrs Abeles. A few months later the pillow and quilt, the bed and armchair and brown wardrobe were sold for a song. The account books, together with the old receipts, the certificates attesting to donations made to yeshivas and orphanages, the prayer book, the knitting needles, the balls of wool, the scraps of cloth and needles and thread in the old tin tea-caddy with the picture of the sailing ship on its lid, were piled up untidily on the table standing in the middle of the room.

This was a heavy, dark brown, oval table with carved legs and an expression of stern antiquity. Worn carvings of tendrils and flowerets also embellished the two austere wooden chairs which stood beside it like two loyal bodyguards, the dark eroded remnants of a defeated army. There was something strange and foreign about them that belonged to another century, to the remote country towns whose peculiar names fell so naturally from Grandmother's lips, together with the names of vanished relatives and kinsmen, of rabbis, emperors and lords. There she had been a child and there she had married her first, beloved husband, and her second husband too. There she had lifted heavy bolts of cloth, measured with a tape-measure, felt with her fingers, traveled days and nights in carts and steaming trains, bargained humiliatingly at fairs to save a few zlotys, given birth to children, concealed bread baked from potato skins under her clothes when pogroms broke out against the Jews and wars raged about her unsuspecting head. There she saw squires and communists and preachers and the German soldiers of Kaiser Wilhelm, who treated her politely and gallantly, and even gave a big doll to her daughter, my mother.

Mr Singer came to take the table and chairs, he smoked a cigarette, stroked the table with a callused hand and said with satisfaction: "Very nice. Very nice."

He meant the wood.

Two workmen carried it all downstairs, and my mother took the opportunity to get rid of all the worthless objects. In the room, which grew very big and full of light, all that was left was the bedside table, upon which reposed the prayer book and the red chocolate box, and the big portrait of Grandmother hanging on the wall in a dull gold frame, which was already peeling here and there.

In the portrait she appears seated in her dark Sabbath dress, one hand resting serenely on the arm of the chair and the other on her knee, the Sabbath wig on her head and a serious, formal expression on her face. Thus she sat now and looked down from the heights of the wall on her empty, light-filled room.

That year we did not hold a Passover *Seder*. This involved some doubts and a certain feeling of uneasiness, but the nuisance of making the house kosher and all the other preparations tipped the scale against it. We ate a big meal, and everyone went about his business. The special Passover dishes – all kinds of bowls and jugs and pots of clay and copper and iron, vast plates and cups of white china rimmed with blue and gold, old silver forks and knives and spoons, ladles, salting boards and pastry boards, blue kettles and black pans – all these remained stored away in the storage space above the ceiling, packed in sacks and big wicker chests, pirates' chests locked with black locks. But at the end of summer, when some modest renovations were made in the apartment, my father went up to the storage space and brought down the dishes. Most of them were sold, but a few were added to the everyday household stock. Among them were some pots and jars, the Prophet Elijah's goblet, and the basin for ritual handwashing, which was now used for soaking small items of laundry.

At the same time Grandmother's room was whitewashed and furnished with light, pale furniture. Only her portrait remained hanging on the wall as before. On the opposite wall my brother hung photographs of horse races and car races, which he cut out of magazines.

In the meantime, the milk and meat dishes were mixed up. The change took place as if of its own accord, and without anyone being able to stop it. In the period immediately following her death we were careful to observe all the dietary laws, just as we had done when she was alive, but gradually our meals became mixed, and we even began eating forbidden foods. At the same time, however, we were careful to eat meat from the meat dishes and milk from the milk dishes, but not for long. Convenience overcame the old customs, which no longer seemed to have any point. And besides, most of the old metal utensils were found in the course of time to be clumsy and impractical, while the china kept breaking. I myself dropped the splendid dish meant to hold herring. On its lid reposed a plump, amazingly lifelike herring, which never failed to arouse my admiration. It was Grandfather who had brought Grandmother this dish from Leipzig, which he had once visited on a business trip. In place of all these dishes now came utensils of glass and stainless steel and plastic, which had never been either milk or meat. They were light, handsome and elegant as bridegrooms. Among them one could still come across the occasional old fork, big as a pitchfork, or a tremendous soup spoon, the curve of its bowl reminiscent of the belly of a plump fish cast upon dry land. They put me in mind of rejected poor relations, and gave me an uneasy feeling, as if we had tricked Grandmother in her absence.

The first anniversary of her death passed unmarked. It passed like any other day of the week and like all the anniversaries of the deaths of vanished grandmothers and grandfathers and uncles whose names we bore and who, ever since Grandmother's death, had been torn from the calendar too and wiped out completely. And the same thing happened to Mrs Abeles and Leibshu Krupp and the synagogue treasurer and a number of the *Landsleit*, who stopped coming to our house and were forgotten. And the same thing happened to the unfortunate Aunt Idel. As soon as Grandmother stopped writing letters to her in Buffalo, her fate was sealed and she vanished into thin air without anyone taking any notice. But my mother remembered the day and so did Mrs Chernibroda. She called on us early in the evening, sat in the kitchen, drank tea and conversed calmly with my mother. The tin clock was still standing on the shelf, its hands pointing, as usual, to twenty to eleven of the day or night of some unknown date. As they spoke, my mother remembered the Sabbath wig, which she had hidden at the bottom of the wardrobe.

Mrs Chernibroda took the wig, together with the red chocolate box. My mother wished her "Till a hundred and twenty," and she smiled, thanked her, and left.

And one day, a few years later, I was rummaging in the bookcase when my eye suddenly fell on a thick, brown book. I took it out and saw that it was the old prayer book. I turned the rough pages and felt the special smell, the smell of old books, which reminded me of the smell of my grandmother sitting on the stool in the kitchen, the brown woolen shawl around her shoulders and the faintest of smiles on her face. When I was about to close the prayer book I saw that there was something written in ink on the white page preceding the title page. And this is what was written there in Grandmother's handwriting:

Yaarzeit fun Tate z"l –16 tug in Tummuz
Yaarzeit fun die Mamme z"l - 10 tog in Ellul
Yaarzeit fun Aaron z"l - 4 yom in Hanukka[1]

I strained my memory to remember the date of her death, but all I could remember was that it was a cold, cloudy day.

---

1.   Father z"l died 16 Tammuz
      Mother z"l died 10 Ellul
      Aaron z"l died 4th day Hanukka
      (z"l from Hebrew *zikhrono livrakha* – of blessed memory)

David Shahar

The Fortune Teller

Translated by Yehuda Hanegbi

As will become readily apparent, it's not the fortune teller that I want to talk about here, but my uncle Kalman. The fortune teller was no more than a kind of railway junction that redirected the train of my uncle Kalman's life onto tracks which led nowhere – or nowhere, at least, that anyone could see. I have compared the fortune teller to a junction because, like a railway junction, he didn't know what he was doing. As a matter of fact, the fortune teller did nothing: it was his absence that led to what happened. If he had stayed where he was supposed to be – that is, chained to his wife's bedside or unchained – then whatever it was that did happen wouldn't have happened.

Twenty-five years ago, when I was a boy of nine, the fortune teller lived in our house. It seems strange, and even a little frightening, that I already have clear memories of things that took place so long ago – a quarter of a century ago! But to get back to our story: over the window of his room, facing the street, hung a sign on which the words "Fortune Teller" were inscribed in the old-fashioned style of Torah scribes, letters with soft rounded corners and sharp pointed tips like thorns. Also painted on the sign was the head of a man with a black tarboosh and a glazed look in his eyes, as if he were gazing into the depths of the future; and all around the face were little drawings interspersed with flying letters. Over the years most of the drawings had faded away, but the letters could still be deciphered. In winter the sign would creak in the wind and bang against the ancient stones of the wall, and drops of rain would flow like tears from the glazed eyes into the mossy cracks in the wall.

The fortune teller lived with his wife for two years in the little room in the corner of our yard, and at the end of the second year, about a week after Kalman was released from prison and came to live with us, we woke up one morning to find that both of them, the fortune teller and his wife, had disappeared, simply run off with seven months' rent still due to us. During the two years that he spent in our house there wasn't a single soul in the whole neighborhood who didn't come to have his fortune told at least two or three times. In this respect, the fortune teller resembled old Dr. Lewinstein, who was intimately acquainted with the pains and the heartaches of everyone in the neighborhood: like him, the fortune teller had four or five ready-made formulas for every occasion, and like him he had two or three steady customers who had need of him every two or three days. One of these was Rahamim, the old stonecutter. Rahamim himself could not remember how old he was, and when anyone asked him he would say: "Old enough, Praise the Lord, much older than seventy..." and his tongue would dart in and out, trembling all the time, like a snail peeking out of its shell this way and that to have a look at the wide world. He used to consult both Dr. Lewinstein and the fortune teller regularly on the question of his virility. And then there was the old Bukharan crone, so fat she was incapable of rising from a sitting position without assistance, who used to sit at the door of her basement all day long, muttering to herself in the language of Bukharan Jews and sucking at the mouthpiece of her *nargila*. She too used to come to the fortune teller at regular intervals to ask him when the letter was due to arrive. The secret of the letter was known only to the two of them. And I remember the fortune teller's wife too, and her two brothers, both of whom rose in the world to become taxi drivers on Ben Yehuda Street, and eventually even managed to acquire a taxi of their own. As for the fortune teller himself, I never laid eyes on him.

"Hanna's tied her husband to the bed again," said my uncle Kalman to my mother, and he laughed. I loved my uncle Kalman more than anyone in the world. He was a good, happy man and he used to sing all kinds of songs – Yiddish songs from the days when he was a yeshiva student, and German songs from the days when he was a student at the Lemel School, and French songs from his schooldays at the Alliance Israélite and the records of Maurice Chevalier, and even Turkish songs which had somehow remained in his memory from the depths of his early childhood. But I couldn't understand why he laughed when he said that Hanna had tied her husband to the bed again. Hanna's husband was the fortune teller. And whenever the two of them quarreled, she would tie him to the bed. To my mind there was something obscure and vaguely threatening about the whole situation. How could a woman struggle with a man, overcome him, and even tie him to her bed! Why, it was impossible – or else the fortune teller must be a very small man, a sort of midget. Obviously, a fortune teller couldn't be an ordinary person. He was a midget then, sitting on a pillow in the middle of his wife's big bed, sipping Turkish coffee from a tiny cup and telling his clients their fortunes in a hoarse, piping voice.

"How can Hanna tie him to her bed?" I asked Kalman. "After all, she isn't so very strong!" "Strong enough for the purpose, it seems," said Kalman, "and he's evidently quite content to let her have her way."

What he said made no sense to me at all, but I didn't argue with him. In those distant days I hadn't yet developed the urge to argue with everyone, and certainly not with my uncle Kalman. I always agreed with everything he said, drinking his words in thirstily even when I had no idea what they meant. It was only years later, when I was already a student of philosophy, that I was drawn into an argument with my uncle Kalman once, when he was expounding the main tenets of his system of thought to me. And the "philosophical" discussion I had with him then has since become one of my most painful memories. I shall never forgive myself for it. As befitting one of my philosophy professor's most "brilliant students," I was self-satisfied, conceited, and intolerant, and had in full measure the special kind of arrogance that characterized all diligent disciples who have grasped the main tenets of their master's teaching and learned from him how to turn everything into a game of words which they use to triumph over any thinking, feeling human being trying to express himself verbally. So I crushed my uncle Kalman simply by reducing everything he said to words, and then asking for the precise definition of every single one of them. But the main thing I shall never forgive myself for is that in the depths of my heart I was angry with him. Yes, angry with him – just as I was angry with anyone who dared express an opinion on "professional" philosophical matters without having taken the trouble to study the latest discoveries in the field of logic and semantics. That particular stage in my life, however, has nothing to do with my uncle Kalman.

What was Kalman doing in our house twenty-five years ago when the fortune teller was still living in the room in our yard? As a matter of fact, he wasn't doing anything at all. True, when the urge took him he used to help my mother with the housework – emptying the garbage pail in the morning, going on urgent errands to the grocer or greengrocer or butcher, washing the dishes, and even mopping the floors. Once his industry reached such heights that he got up early in the morning, polished all our shoes and placed them in a straight line on the bench outside for us to see when we woke. These attacks of energy, however, were neither lasting nor frequent. In this, as in other matters, Kalman was a little peculiar. If he really felt like it, no work was too hard for him – he was ready to turn the closets upside down and scrub their backsides. But when he was in the grip of idleness, nothing in the world could make him budge from his place on the couch. He would lie there, sprawled across it, his head resting on a pillow propped against the wall, his feet, with shoes on, crossed on the only upholstered chair in the house, one hand holding a cigarette and the other an ashtray, his eyes fixed on the ceiling with a calm, distant gaze. When he reached the higher degrees of idleness he didn't even take the trouble to find an ashtray and would drop cigarette ash all over his shirt and trousers, on the floor and in the water jar. No wonder that by the end of the week he spent in our house before moving into the fortune teller's room, he had managed to burn holes in all my father's shirts. The miracle was that he didn't set his bed on fire, for he fell asleep with a burning cigarette in his mouth on more than one occasion. He used to fall asleep stretched out on his back, his hollow cheeks sunken as if he were sucking them in his sleep and his prominent nose, more prominent than ever, emitting an ill-humored snore. It was my father's shirts he burned holes in, because when he came to our house he had only the shirt on his back and that was thrown into the garbage soon after his arrival, where it was followed by his trousers, his underwear, and even the battered little suitcase whose contents have remained unknown to this day because my mother threw it away without even bothering to open it. In those days the people of our neighborhood were in no hurry to throw old clothes away, and if Kalman's garments were treated in this summary manner it was only because there was absolutely no alternative. On that day he looked like a fierce, plucked bird. A bird set free, whose heart was still beating wildly within him. Altogether, there was something sharply birdlike about him, and when he put on my father's clothes, which were much too big for him, this impression became even more pronounced. All his life, in fact, Kalman wore trousers which were too big for him, since the trousers in the shops were all too wide for his narrow hips and he never had the means or the inclination to have any made to measure. It was because of these baggy trousers, I think, that he acquired the hopping, sidling gait that was characteristic of him.

On the day of his arrival, even before crossing the threshold, he said to my mother: "Give me some of Eli's old clothes and throw mine straight into the garbage can. Do you have any carbolic soap?" Eli, of course, was my father, and my mother understood at once that her brother Kalman was full of lice and bugs. Before he was caught and put in jail, Kalman had been hiding for weeks in the cellar of Levi, the mad Georgian porter who never spoke anything but Yiddish although he was a Sephardi Jew. And he had come to our house straight after spending twenty-one days in jail. Everything had conspired against him at once – all his creditors had descended upon him and taken him to court just when the judge had ordered him to pay five pounds a month for his wife's support.

He sought refuge in Levi's cellar, hiding first from the court clerk who was trying to deliver the summons, then from the law enforcement officer who was trying to serve him with the first and then the final warning notice, and lastly from Trachtenberg, the policeman who had been ordered to arrest him. Trachtenberg the policeman lived in the same house as Levi the porter and about once a week he would go down to the cellar to talk to Kalman about women and politics. Before taking his leave he would complain about his harsh fate and mention the great dangers that lay in wait for him should the English police officer ever get to know, Heaven forbid, that the sentenced criminal Kalman was hiding in this very house. He, Trachtenberg, would be fired and put into prison as well. Whenever this imminent peril was mentioned, Kalman would thrust his hand into his trouser pocket, take out some coins, and slip them to the policeman. Once, when he could no longer find a single copper in his pocket, he borrowed ten piasters from Levi the porter. After a few weeks Kalman got sick of the whole situation and gave himself up to the police. Then he sat for twenty-one days in prison, appearing twice before the Arab judge, to whom he spoke of matters of the spirit. The judge enjoyed these conversations so much that he found mitigating circumstances for all Kalman's transgressions of the law and ordered him to pay off his debts at the rate of only twenty-five piasters a month; he even reduced the sum he had to pay to his wife from five to three pounds a month.

The whole matter of Kalman's wife requires some explanation or, perhaps it would be better to say, justification. The truth is that I don't really remember his wife at all. Not because I never saw her, but simply because she made no impression on me. In fact, if I had parted from her and then bumped into her again by chance half an hour later, I doubt if I would have recognized her. All I remember is that she was considerably taller than Kalman, that her voice was rather deep, and that she was always talking about "support." She wasn't a bad woman, and if it had only been a question of "support," she probably wouldn't have taken Kalman to court at all, but would have tried to supply whatever was lacking herself. After all, what did a woman need in those days? I think that most of the women in our neighborhood didn't even know that electric refrigerators existed. Pots that had to be kept cool were wrapped in wet cloths and left standing on the window sill in basins of water, and all the housewives were quite content with this arrangement, including Kalman's wife. She would probably never have become involved in shameful, distressing legal proceedings if it hadn't been for the energetic interference of her family. She had a secret fear of my uncle Kalman. He frightened her with his opinions, his talk, his sudden bursts of activity and prolonged bouts of idleness, and his behavior in general. In time, she even grew afraid of his singing, his laughter, and the look in his eyes. For some years she contrived to hide her fears from her family and neighbors, and she would even defend her husband, whom they regarded as a loafer of the worst sort, from their attacks. He liked sitting with the drunken British soldiers and policemen who frequented the cafés in the vicinity of the Edison Cinema. When she was asked what her husband did for a living, she used to say he was an "agent," and once, when she was pressed to be more specific, she said he was a "dry goods agent." For some reason, this branch of commerce had a particular importance in her eyes, and during the five years of their life together, she did her utmost to make Kalman open a dry goods store. Her father was even willing to rent a store and fill it with the requisite goods, but the person chiefly concerned, namely my uncle Kalman, flatly refused to rise to such heights. He was quite content with his own way of making a living, which consisted of writing letters for people and filling out documents for them in the languages he had acquired at the Lemel School and the Alliance Israélite. His wife – and here I realize that not only have I forgotten what she looked like, I can't even remember her name – claimed that she would have been prepared to make ends meet, even on this meager income, if only it had been steady. He, however, preferred to read useless books or lounge in cafés. Finally, things came to such a pass that she felt it was better for him to be sitting in a café than to be lying on his back in the yard chatting with the neighborhood children. His café sessions could at least be explained by the fact that he was "negotiating... you know... business deals." She never dared admit her fears and anxieties even to herself, until one day her mother arrived at the house to "have it out with her," "say it like it is," and save her from her husband before it was too late. As luck would have it, her mother turned up precisely on the ill-fated and disastrous day that had seemed to start out so well with Kalman in a particularly good mood and intent, or so it appeared, on effecting a reconciliation between them. After a long period of estrangement, he had approached her and embraced her in a manner that moved her to the point of tears. He said that it was impossible to continue in this way and that something had to be done. Her heart began to beat wildly in anticipation of the fulfillment of her dream of a dry goods store and the end of shame and the beginning of prosperity and respectability. But slowly something in his words began to jar and trouble her, reawakening all her anxieties. Suddenly she realized that he was speaking of his own suffering, saying that he was "rotting away," that he had "no one to talk to about really important things," and that he lacked "proper conditions for study and reflection." She was struck dumb, unable to utter a word. That very evening she agreed with her mother that the time had come to "take action."

My mother had no carbolic soap, but she did have laundry soap in plenty. She lit the two big oil stoves and heated up water for Kalman to bathe in. At that time there was no running water in the whole of the neighborhood and we used to draw our water from the cistern in the courtyard. In the corner of the yard, next to the fortune teller's room, stood a little wooden hut which was used both as a bathroom and a laundry, the big washtub doing double duty as a bathtub when the occasion arose. Kalman scrubbed himself in the washtub, singing Maurice Chevalier's "Beneath the Roofs of Paris" at the top of his voice. Then he emerged wrapped in my mother's dressing gown, and asked if there were any sardines in the house. We had *gefilte* fish and meat and other products of my mother's cooking, but Kalman wanted sardines and I had to run to the store and buy some for him. After squeezing a whole lemon over them, Kalman ate the sardines straight from the can, standing in the kitchen, and washed the lot down with a glass of cocoa. During his twenty-one days in jail, he told me, this was the meal he had longed for. When he had finished eating, he fell onto the couch in his usual position, flat on his back with his head resting on a pillow against the wall and his feet crossed on the only upholstered chair in the house, and immediately fell asleep. He slept for ten consecutive hours.

About a week after Kalman was released from prison and came to live in our house, the fortune teller vanished from his room together with his wife and our last hope of ever obtaining the seven months' rent they owed us. A long time later we heard that he had settled down in the Arab quarter of Tiberias where, it was rumored, his affairs prospered. When the fortune teller disappeared, Kalman moved into his room.

I have already mentioned that Kalman had the look of a bird about him, with his wizened, beaky face and darting, beady eyes. He was about forty-five years old when he was released from jail and set up house in the fortune teller's room. Something had happened to him there in prison, and I am not referring to the more or less respectable way of life which he adopted on his release – the Arab judge, as will be recalled, had ordered him to pay back his debts at the rate of twenty-five piasters a month and pay support for his wife at the rate of three pounds a month. Thus he had to earn at least six pounds a month in order to pay all his debts and provide for himself as well, which he did by translating letters for the orphanage nearby, spending no more than three hours a day at it. As I say, I am not referring to his way of life which was more or less normal and respectable, nor even to the fact that he played gladly with the neighborhood children and sang songs for them; he had always been a friendly, good-humored man. Something had happened to him there in prison, something very different from anything we can imagine. For instance, he would often lie flat on the ground for hours on end, watching a line of ants winding their way from a crack in the paving stones to some mysterious destination of their own and back again; and he would be so entranced by what he saw that I could sit down on his back and he wouldn't even realize I was there. All living creatures fascinated him; not necessarily lions and tigers and exotic beasts in the zoo, but the cats and dogs in the street, the sparrows on the roof, the little lizards that crawl into your hand. And not only creatures but also plants, and even the simplest most ordinary things. On the day he went down to live in the fortune teller's room – you had to go down seven steps to reach it, but it wasn't called a basement because its windows were high enough to overlook the street – he gave my mother a real fright. When she came in to see how he was getting on she found him sitting crosslegged on the floor, staring at a stone – an ordinary, unpolished stone. And when she asked him whether he wouldn't like to stay with us a little longer until his room could he properly whitewashed, he made no response at all because be neither saw nor heard her. Mother was afraid that he was ill or that he'd fainted, and it was only after she had shaken him and shouted: "Kalman, Kalman, what's the matter with you?" into his ear that he came out of his trance and answered her in a surprised tone of voice: "But I told you, there's no need to have the room whitewashed."

Years later, when I was already a student of philosophy, he said to me (in the course of the conversation to which I have already referred) that in his opinion a person could "grasp the essence of things by rapt contemplation, by the annihilation of the self," and that it didn't matter what the object of contemplation was, even a piece of stone. "Once you grasp the essence you no longer see anything as separate or whole, beautiful or ugly, good or bad." And later in the course of that same discussion he also said: "The suffering of a child is the punishment which God inflicts on Himself when he awakens from the intoxication of His love of Himself in individuals and time."

And all this began in the prison cell. One night, when he was sitting on his mattress, he became aware of a drop of water suspended from a stone support in the wall. It took on the typical pear shape, full and extended to the utmost, of a drop of water just before it falls. Only it didn't fall, it remained hanging there. The drop seemed very near and very far away. It was the center of all things, and all things were related to it and far removed from it. The cell expanded immeasurably, and everything was engulfed in an infinite calm, and

Kalman became part of this living calm. From that moment on, he felt that he could no longer understand the anxiety, the worry, the anger, the irritation, the fuss, and the bother of the people around him, in the prison and outside it.

Once he had installed himself in the fortune teller's room, Kalman became a fortune teller himself. On the first day he opened his eyes in that room, the old Bukharan woman rolled in, puffing and panting and muttering to herself, to discuss the matter of the letter. She was not at all put out to find that the fortune teller had changed his form and countenance and denied that he was himself. On the contrary, she was glad of an excuse to go over the whole history of the letter again from beginning to end without omitting a single detail. Kalman listened to her patiently and told himself that he must remember to remove the sign over the window facing the street. On second thoughts, however, he decided that it wouldn't make any difference if he did, and that in any case it wasn't worth the trouble. To this day, I believe, the sign is still there, creaking in the wind.

To the Bukharan woman he said: "The letter will arrive in seven days and seven nights and seven hours and seven minutes and seven seconds."

"Blessings on your head," she said, and the blessing immediately materialized, not on his head exactly but in his hand, in the form of a loud moist kiss followed by a five-piaster coin.

"It's not necessary, really it isn't," he said, referring to both aspects of the blessing, the one of sentiment and the one of substance, but she firmly refused to take the coin back. Seeing that she seemed offended, Kalman reconsidered and decided that in the long run, in the ultimate reckoning of what was good for her own soul, he should take her money. When she had gone he decided to sit down and write the letter at once so that she would get it in time, but on second thoughts he realized that he would be doing her more harm than good if he put an end to her hopes by fulfilling them, so he did nothing.

She had barely departed when the other one came – Rahamim the old stonecutter. Rahamim was a suspicious old Jew. As soon as he glanced in at the doorway and saw the figure of my uncle Kalman, he raised his eyebrows and pursed his mouth in a petulant question mark, but he made no move to retreat.

"Please come in," Kalman called. "Come in, sir, please." The stonecutter did not wait for any further invitation. "I am the servant of a servant," explained Kalman, "the apprentice of an apprentice of him who sees the end in the beginning, reads the history of the generations before it is written, and remembers the future because it is past."

These words, clear as the sun, pure as the moon, and fragrant as myrrh and frankincense, immediately set the mind of the stonecutter at ease and completely dispelled his suspicions. At once, without any preliminaries, speaking as man to man, he launched forth on the long, hard problem of his virility, and since his lips trembled as he spoke and his tongue protruded like a soft snail poking its head out of its shell, the problem grew longer and harder to follow with his every word.

"I see," concluded Kalman, "that the happy turn of events is near. It will happen as it must and will stand firm in its glory when Miriam cometh."

The stonecutter extracted a ten-piaster coin from the folds of his striped sash, slapped it down on the table, and said: "Your Honor will understand, as usual – the rest on account."

"How much on account?"

"Fifteen piasters, no more. That's what we always pay, the cash and fifteen on account."

"And the others, the Bukharan?"

"I always get a discount," the stonecutter explained. "I haven't had a job now for over twenty years."

"Why, that old woman cheated me," Kalman thought to himself and began to laugh aloud until tears came to his eyes. The stonecutter stared at him in concern, bade him farewell, and hurried away.

Well, said Kalman to himself, this seems easy and enjoyable work; he liked listening and not being listened to, seeing and not being seen, getting others to talk and putting their minds at rest. Strange how it was only his own wife's mind that he was unable to put at rest. Or perhaps it wasn't so strange after all, for in order to put her mind at rest he would have had to change into another person, and that was patently beyond his powers. The mistake lay in his ever having married her in the first place. But then he had only married her in order to put her mind at rest. Well it certainly seemed easier to tell other people their fortunes... Suddenly he felt that he was losing his own peace of mind, that he was becoming involved, that he was lying. He tried to concentrate on the water jug on the table, but the great calm did not descend to envelop him again. He rushed out to the corner of the street and slipped the fifteen piasters he had received from his clients into the blind Yemenite beggar's box. Then he wandered about the alleyways of the neighborhood until sundown, repeating to himself, without knowing why: "The dark night of the soul, the dark night of the soul." He sensed something horrible threatening him, something not connected with anything in his immediate surroundings. The fifteen piasters he had taken for telling fortunes had opened a thin crack for the dark night to seep into his soul.

As the sun began to set he returned to his room, sat down, and waited. From the first moment he knew, from the moment her shadow in the doorway blocked out the rays of the setting sun. She was beautiful and dignified even in her distress. Very restrained and delicate, almost apologetic at troubling others – even if it was only a fortune teller whose business it was to be troubled – with her pain and suffering. The very fact that she had come to a fortune teller could have only one meaning, so clear that further explanations were superfluous – it was the end. There was no hope. Her eleven-year-old son Gili had cancer of the glands. She had come to him furtively in the dusk, embarrassed and ashamed of herself for coming, and her eyes were imploring, tearless, and stretched wide open.

"You are Mrs Greenfeld," he said to her, "Dr Greenfeld's wife."

Her husband was a lecturer in biochemistry. Once when Kalman had been waiting in the courtroom to have his detention period extended he had seen Dr Greenfeld and his wife appearing as plaintiffs in a case involving an accident in which a truck driver had lost control of his vehicle, hit a child, and finally smashed into their little black Morris.

Her eyes gleamed with hope, as if she were on the verge of the revelation of a miracle.

"I know your name because I happened to be present at your court case. There's nothing to wonder at."

"My husband must never know that I've come to you," she said apologetically.

"Yes, of course. He doesn't believe in fortune tellers and miracles and suchlike superstitions," he replied. "Neither do I. I'm not a fortune teller. It's a mistake. A lie. Once a fortune teller did live here, but he's gone now. I'll take down the sign tomorrow."

She sat still on the stool, shrinking as if she had just received a blow and was waiting, resigned, for the next. Kalman looked at her. The darkness in the room deepened. Since he was facing the door, she looked to him like a silhouette with only the glass buttons on her blouse glistening in the dark.

"If so, I must go," she murmured at last, but she remained seated.

"I'd better light the lamp," he said.

He lit the kerosene lamp, and the little flame leaped and flickered until the whole wick caught, and then it steadied itself into a tongue of light. One of the glass buttons on her blouse reflected the radiance faintly, sending little rays of light in all directions with every breath she took. Suddenly the button became fixed, a motionless center like the drop of water in the prison cell, and everything ebbed away from him in a smooth rapid movement, calm and full of life.

"If you don't mind," he said, "I'll come with you to the hospital." He felt that he ought to see the child with his own eyes.

Again she stirred expectantly. They walked quickly and silently, side by side, through the streets. The full moon had already risen and the shadows of the houses were sharp and clear like a woodcut. Three weeks had passed since the doctors had concluded that it was "the end, only a matter of days." But the body refused to die. The boy lay wrapped up on his bed, behind a screen separating him from the other two patients in the room whose condition was not so desperate. He was small and shriveled, like a little skeleton, and only his swollen neck and belly protruded. Every once in a while he would quiver in a spasm of pain. His mother sat on the chair by the bed and looked at him with wide-open eyes. The night nurse peeped into the room. "The doctor said that tomorrow they'll give him another blood transfusion," she said to the mother. She was evidently trying to cheer her up. So long as they were giving blood transfusions there was still hope.

Kalman went out of the ward on tiptoe. He knew that he ought to say something encouraging to the mother. She needed the lying encouragement of the fortune teller more than the fat old woman or the feeble old man, more than any other human being, but he could not bring himself to say a single consoling word to her. He wandered about the streets for hours on end, with no notion of the passing of time, until he became aware of the fact that he was walking in circles around the prison. He returned home after midnight and fell onto his bed like a stone. When he awoke in the morning he knew at once that he had to hurry to save a life in danger. He jumped out of bed and hurried to the blood bank to donate blood for the child Gili Greenfeld. "We must do everything necessary, everything known, everything possible," he said to himself as his blood dripped into the fat-bellied bottle, and all the time he knew that at best the blood transfusion would do no more than prolong the child's agony for another few hours or days.

A child's pain. What greatness, what glory, what power, and what goodness was there in the world, in all the worlds, in all the vast space of lightyears, in all the galaxies, in all creation, in God Himself, if He allowed a single child to suffer such awful pain? These terrible torments, why were they created, for what purpose did they exist?

"You can have a cup of coffee and then get a meal in the hospital kitchen," the nurse said as she undid the rubber tube on his arm.

"Thank you, I'll just have the coffee," he said. He swallowed the cup of coffee in one gulp and rushed out as if he were in a great hurry. But in fact he had nothing to do, nothing at all. There was nothing to do. That night he returned to the hospital and the porter let him in as soon as he mentioned the child's name – the special privilege of the families of the dying, thought Kalman, they can get into the hospital outside visiting hours. In the courtyard, on a bench beneath a tall pine tree, the boy's mother sat weeping quietly while his father walked up and down giving vent every now and then to a muffled groan. Kalman went straight to the mortuary, drew back the sheet and looked at the child's face for a long time. He looked as if he were sleeping soundly. All the lines of pain had faded from his face. His body, that had now once again become part of the whole of existence, had nothing whatever to do with the anxiety, fear, sorrow, suffering, and pain of living in individuals and time. On the other side of the little barred window, the branch of an olive tree glowed in the light of the street lamp, and Gili's soul did not need to go anywhere. It existed.

Kalman left the mortuary with a strange feeling of release, and as he went out of the hospital he felt a great hunger. He went into Abulafia's restaurant, ordered a plate of hummus, and then a double portion of shishlik and kebab and pickles, which he swallowed down with the assistance of a glass of cognac, and finished his meal with a cup of Turkish coffee. When he rose from the table he was slightly dizzy and his knees felt weak. "So giving blood does weaken you after all," he said to himself aloud. "They take three hundred grams of blood, I believe, from your body..."

As soon as he reached home, he fell onto his bed in his usual position, his head resting on a pillow against the wall and his feet crossed on a stool. On the wall opposite him was a large black nail upon which the fortune teller had once hung a big calendar illustrated with the signs of the zodiac. Kalman's eyes now fastened themselves on this nail. Instantly, as though struck by a beam of pure light, he became aware of the great calm of life in its essence and its nothingness, and he knew that it was greater than the God who had created life in individuals and in time. In the beginning God created the universe as a mirror to give Him back His own reflection so that He could preen Himself, and as soon as He wanted to see His own image in a mirror, He fell to the level of the pettiest of tyrants trying to get his picture in the newspapers. And the way is open for me to be greater than He, great as the great calm of life in its essence and its nothingness, which is greater than the God who created life in individuals and in time. The calm which has no separate parts or differences, and no past and no future, because it is the eternal glory of the present moment.

The blackness of the nail expanded until it enveloped him entirely and he fell into a deep sleep.

A.B. Yehoshua

Flood Tide

Translated by Miriam Arad

A storm has been raging over the Southern Islands for the past fortnight, and day by day it grows more violent. In an instant everything will go misty and a mass of clouds will come to rest on the plain like piles of dirty cotton wool. A burst of hard clear hail will sweep the wasteland and batter the gray prison house. Is it any wonder that tonight, in the dead of night, with the storm at its wildest, the Chief Warder should suddenly order the sentry to my cubicle to wake me from my wide-eyed sleep and summon me to the office, to receive startling midnight instructions?

The words of the messenger are still echoing around the dark walls I when, and I alone, crawl naked from under the rough blankets, and all the other actors in my dream perish among the wrinkles of the sheet. Shivering with cold I don the stained service overall, and while my hands race down the long, long row of buttons my face is turned to listen to the mounting gales. I am newly come to this jail and still a novice in the service. Hence I am awake to everything about me and eager to excel in my work. If it wasn't for the dreams unsettling me at night I would consider myself an exemplary jailer. It is but a month since I graduated from the stiff course for jailers; there I was taught to shoot a submachine gun and never miss, to jump over high hurdles, wrestle in hand-to-hand combat, and understand the tersely worded Regulations Manual. Was it my taciturnity that made them think I could restrain my passions too, and made them send me to serve at this small jail on its remote island? True, the men confined here are real criminals, murderers reprieved from the gallows and sentenced to life imprisonment; but they are few, and they are very old.

I fumble for my shoes in the dark. I do not light a candle for I am sparing of property belonging to the King. Does there exist a regulation that permits jailers to let their thoughts wander while on duty? I do not know. As long as I haven't studied every last dot in the Regulations Manual and made certain either way, I can grant myself the benefit of the doubt. But I know that, though I am silent, my face betrays me, at least to this Chief Warder for whom I am bound now, proud and thrilled, correctly dressed though it is the middle of the night. I cross the eternal twilight of the cell-lined corridor, dimly lit over its whole length and into the deepest corner of the prisoners' cells ranged along both sides, ascend the three steps to the office and present myself, saluting as laid down in the rules.

He is sitting behind his desk, alert and watchful whatever the hour. A middle-aged officer, short, his hair graying, his face dry and strikingly severe; a member of the old school, which I venerate. The curtains are drawn over the barred windows, and the huge red emblems of the kingdom are displayed on them in all their glory. His two long-legged dogs squat on the carpet and look at me with mournful dignity. Only the hail lashing against the windows disturbs the grave imposing silence that graces our prison. My commanding officer turns his eyes full on my face, and his eyes burn, bold with lust, in utter contradiction to the grim lines of his face. He starts to speak in his blunt manner and the essence of his words is one wondrous message:

The sea is about to rise and flood our island.

How did the Chief Warder learn of this? Not from any dubious weather forecasters who know nothing of our island, nor from any urgent call from the Central Prison authorities in the capital who scarcely remember our existence. The fact has come to the Chief Warder's knowledge solely through his own exhaustive studies, his poring day and night over the old diaries of our prison that stand volume by volume, massive and tall, in his locked bookcase. The jailers of old who died at their post (they could have known no other death) and whose bleached skeletons lie buried at the bottom of the sea took care to write a daily chronicle of all that occurred on the island. It is from these chronicles that the Chief Warder has learned about the flood tide, about the signs in nature portending it and about the destructive force of the water. Three times the prison house has been flooded, completely destroyed and built anew. Even I, the novice, knew this from my studies of the History of Prisons. Yet I had never imagined that it would be this tempest, this wild wind hurling itself against our walls, that would bring us the ancient flood tide once again.

Unthinking I take a few short steps nearer the desk, kindled by a new interest. Is it happiness, this glow inside me?

The Chief Warder lays his hand on the neck of one of his beloved dogs and starts stroking its fur voluptuously. In a low voice he tells me about the regulations that require the Chief Warder to escape from the island on the fateful day together with his men, to lock up the prisoners in their cells and to leave one or two jailers in charge, volunteers, worthy of the task. The little officer lowers his eyes. Who else should offer himself if not I, the young jailer who is so very eager to distinguish himself in the service?

Emotion grips me whenever the Regulations are spoken of in my presence, but on this occasion, when I hear that the Chief Warder has chosen me of all his men, I am stunned, I nearly fall at his feet. I bite my lip to contain a shout of exultation.

Do I wish another man to stay with me, inquires the Chief Warder, and his eyes show a glint of cunning. Serving in this jail, beside the two of us, there are a cook, a barber, an armorer and a locksmith. But I know what is in his mind.

"I want no one with me, sir," I reply softly.

No, I think, I want none of those functionaries, those trying to evade the pure naked function of jailer. And even as my eyes are watching his fondling hands and the pampered dogs at his feet, an idea flashes through my mind.

"Leave only your dogs with me, sir."

This time I have managed to take the little man by surprise. He cherishes those two dogs of his, is so attached to them as to arouse suspicion. He is a solitary man, childless, his wife away in the distant capital and none but the dogs left to him. They are dog and bitch, and he has bred and pampered them from puppies. Now I shall take them from him and turn them into proper prison dogs, fierce. How can he refuse me now that I am going to be left alone in this dark prison, left to face the rising sea? His hands tremble, he makes no reply. Softly he tells me of an ancient boat found on the island. It had been the jailers of old who had built it to save their own lives. It has recently been fitted out with a new engine brought over from the capital. This boat will avail me when the waters rise and flood the building – then I, too, shall escape. For thus say the wise Regulations: "When the waters shall prevail upon the earth, then shall the last jailer leave his prisoners and shall escape. Generations of prisoners come and go, but jailers are few and shall abide forever."

He hands me the key of the engine, tiny and bright. Tomorrow I shall be given all the heavy keys of the prison house.

Where will my master, the Chief Warder, flee to? To the mountains, the mountains of course. Even through the bars of the narrow prison windows you can see them, right to the dense growth bristling at their summits. There my master will flee with his men. Perhaps he will find a dry cottage. They say there is a hamlet there, low in a wadi between mountains. Who knows? His fate may yet be worse than mine. I, at any rate, have already raised my arm in parting salute. To my surprise he does not return it but rises from his chair, and a look of sorrow comes into his face. He leaves his dogs, sails around the desk, puts himself in front of me, rises on tiptoe and places both his small hairy paws on my shoulders in such a fatherly manner that a shiver runs through my body. His words, his obscure parting words, cut deep into the silence of my mind:

"Restrain your passions with the rising water, resist temptation and stand the test. Find it in yourself to escape, you and the dogs with you."

Good for you, Master.

At dawn, during a brief pause in the rain, the dogs thrust their heads through the two windows of the office where they have been locked up and howl at the little master who is deserting them. The fugitives with their luggage file in gloomy procession through the building; locking door after door, adding key after key to the heavy bunch jingling merrily in my hand. In the courtyard they show me the boat fastened with a rope to the building, and I give a careless nod. Barely patient, I accompany them to the gate, go outside with them, out to the plain, and lock the gate behind me. My eyes fly at once to the horizon, but I see nothing. The prison house is quite a distance from the sea, and it is only on golden days that one can make out a blue strip on the horizon. The fugitives climb into the barred prison van and crowd with their luggage on to the prisoners' seats. They measure me with their eyes. Are they glad to have escaped? Our parting is brief, unemotional: relationships are stiff within the framework of the Regulations. Presently the car drives off into the sandy plain surrounding us, accompanied by the dogs' wild barks of despair. The car is swallowed up by the heavy fog.

Now I am sole ruler in this house of stone. How wise to have built it on the plain, enabling me to see from afar all that may come and go, all that may attack or escape. I open the gate, enter the courtyard. Every time I open a door I lock it behind me at once. I am familiar with keys and fond of handling any of them, let alone the huge prison keys, their bare teeth frozen in an eternal gape. I have to pass many doors in order to reach the second storey, the cell-lined corridor. The prisoners have risen from their aimless sleep. They are already seated on their stools beside the doors, doors that are not made of solid sheets of iron but of grating, that the prisoners may always be visible through the bars and not be hatching plots. They resemble apes in cages, except that they are always silent and they do not move. Their crimes were committed long ago, even perhaps before I – their new young warder – saw the light of day. Now they are old, and their shaven skulls mask their baldness. The prison barber takes pains never to leave a single hair on their heads. He mows off everything with his shears, out of boredom. Most of them are heavy and fat. All these years they have been gorging on the state's food and drink, and they do nothing. There is no telling whether they are violent or wasted.

They watch me with tranquil eyes. They always sit facing the corridor, as though waiting. What are they waiting for now? Their breakfast, of course. The whining of the dogs imprisoned in the office is also changing tune from a whine of lament to one of hunger. I therefore hurry and unlock the kitchen, set myself at once to cook a meal according to the instructions pinned on the wall. Afterwards I load everything on a trolley and start rattling dishes through the dim windowless corridor. A small hatch opens between the bars of each door, and through it I am handed a bowl with the remnants of the previous meal congealed at the bottom and I hand back a fresh, full one. They are used to this back-and-forth exchange of bowls, and the whole routine is accomplished in utter silence. They must be aware that I am now their only guard. All that happens in this place is known to them even though, according to the Regulations, they are not allowed to talk among themselves, let alone talk to the jailers. What should we talk to them for? We are not interrogators, nor are we judges; only jailers guarding them lest they escape. The Law has been laid down, the sentence pronounced, and if they have not been brought to the gallows – that is their fate, and one does not discuss fate. I may have forgotten to mention that a loaded submachine gun hangs at all times suspended from a strap over my shoulder.

The food distribution is over. The dogs' howls are rending my ears. I unlock the office door and they burst out and leap at me, mad with joy, lick my face and hands. With great difficulty I manage to calm them down. From now on I am their master. I put their daily meat ration before them, the largest ration of all distributed in this place. They fall upon the meat, chew voraciously with their large molars, in rapture, their eyes rolling. I look on in silence at this gluttony, stand frozen on the spot till they have devoured everything. Then I prepare my own austere, frugal portion. Swiftly, indifferently, I gulp the tasteless food and go down to the courtyard to look at the storm.

Fog. I strain my eyes to make out water and see nothing. I prick up my ears to catch its murmur as one waiting for a beloved step, but the savage howling of the wind through the fog erases all sound. Impossible to learn anything about the progress of the sun. The world is gray from end to end. I return to the corridor. Silence; only the sound of the prisoners bent over their bowls, chewing on the last of their food.

My day is filled with activity. I wash the dishes, sweep the floor. From time to time I pick up the submachine gun suddenly, burst out of the kitchen and go wandering along the corridors. The inmates of the cages do not look at me. They are common people and the spiritual is beyond their ken. They have now opened their books and begun their daily reading. Ageing assassins with thrillers in their hands, tales of murder and obscenity out of the prison library, with their last pages torn (or ripped out maliciously), so that the readers never know about the capture of the criminal and linger to their satisfaction over the futility of the detectives in pursuit. Once a month we traverse the corridor with a trolley and collect the twenty-one books, shuffle them, and return with the trolley from the other end of the corridor. Some prisoners happen to get back their own book, some get a new-old one to read. It stands to reason that each of them knows all the books. Yet even now they sit there, their dim eyes straying over the tattered pages. Don't they know that their death is near? Don't they sense the rising tide? If they were to hoist themselves up a little to the slit high in the wall of their cell, they would be able to see the horizon stretching to the sea, or lift their eyes to the mountain tops.

Noon. A few lost rays of sunlight wander suddenly through the two narrow windows over the kitchen sink. I am warming up the midday meal. The dogs crawl into a corner for their daily copulation. Deplorable habits they have acquired in this jail. I stand watching them and a great sorrow fills my heart. The hours of the afternoon are once more spent in drudgery. Again I wash dishes, sweep floors, polish the doors. I am a servant to the prisoners, not their master. But when evening comes and darkness fills the building, and I have finished my work then a sweet weariness spreads through my limbs and I realize again with wonder that I am sole master of this entire building, without intermediaries, without commands. I and the Law alone. With hands rough from the day's work I take up the bunch of keys that accompanies me always and go rambling among the silent stones of my castle. I feel my way through the dark, the dogs ahead of me sniffing every corner. When I pass through the corridor I see that the eyes of my prisoners are tired, as though washed by a somber sea. Yet they haven't lifted a finger all day. I light the dim corridor lamp. The prisoners are never left in darkness, always in twilight. My eyes stray to the yellow pages tacked to the front of each cell. A blurred list of its inmate's crimes. It is decreed by the Chief Warder that their felonies should be recorded for us to see and never pity them. Pity is dangerous on so remote an island.

The hours of the night come to me like giant birds – each blacker than the one before. The prisoners do not raise their eyes, are still poring over their books. Nearly all of them have grown short-sighted from years of reading in bad light, and they sit with their faces on top of the print, their lashes grazing the page. Who cares about them going blind in jail? I enter the office, fill in the day's forms and lock the door on the dogs crouching among the piles of old documents and chronicles. Then I go to my cubicle, lock my door and secrete the keys beneath my pillow. I light a candle and by its feeble rays start taking my weapon apart in order to clean it. Hail lashes against the building, but not a single drop leaks in. Three times they built this place anew, and every time they improved upon the last. Now they will build it a fourth time. Except for the wind howling, the silence is absolute. Could any man wish for a silence deeper than this? True happiness comes and floods my heart again. I am alone here, but my solitude does not frighten me. For it is not a personal solitude but one ordained by the Regulations, and the Regulations are from the King. With a final click I attach the butt to the body of the submachine gun and lay it shining and steely on my bed, between the sheets. Then I lie down in my clothes on the hard narrow mattress, a jailer's mattress precluding deep sleep. The taut sheets, the folded blankets, the gun lying like a cruel child by my side – everything bears the monarchical emblems imprinted upon it. I pick up the Regulations Manual. My master, the Chief Warder, no longer reads the Regulations Manual, only the diaries left by the jailers of antiquity. But I know that the diaries are but commentary and the Manual is the main thing. I read the Manual alone, therefore; read slowly, thoroughly. After an hour or two fatigue makes the lines start humming within me like a soft chant, a lament. At midnight I force myself to shut the Manual, lest I be tempted to read all night. I am a member of the Prison System and I know that the prison needs my sleep, so that my head is clear at all times. I blow out the candle and remain lying with my eyes open to the darkness. Everything is locked, no one will break through the heavy doors. And who would go wandering on this bleak plain?

In the morning the sheets are twisted. Everything is in wild confusion. The gun has dropped to the floor, the keys have crept deep into the pillow, and the monarchical emblems have slipped, limp and crumpled, from under my head down to my nakedness. What dreams came to me? I do not wish to remember, I must not remember. I hasten to smooth the gray sheets and fold the blankets, efface the night's memory, shamefaced, and rush to see if the waters have come.

The two days preceding the flood tide pass like a gray dream filled with soft happiness and work. Every free moment I fly to the windows to look at the wide open world. Amazedly I discover that the storm is abating. The wind has completely died down and only a thin soft rain is drizzling from gray skies. A hush lies over everything. Can the Chief Warder have been mistaken? Is all this really but a prelude to the flood that will come? The silence of the far sea tells me nothing. Slowly my eyes travel to the other side of the island, to the great mountains, their impervious summits. No doubt the fugitives have arrived there by now. I do not in the least regret being here, waiting here still.

Faithfully I perform my daily labors, change the prisoners' bowls and feed the dogs, the tall dogs in heat who follow me with their long-legged tread, meek and faithful like a couple of foolish aristocrats come down in the world. In the evening I fill in the forms and write a few words of my own about the gray universe. And at night, in my locked cubicle, I become engrossed in the Manual once more.

The second day is also amazingly, excitingly gray. The skies are calm now, not a drop of rain. The plain lies still, suffused by an expectant hush, the whole universe in attendance. The temperature has risen with a sudden leap. But the sun has not broken through the gray shroud, and the day has gone by without any change in the light. Late in the afternoon, when the light began fading from the sky at last, I collected the two dogs, locked door after door behind me, descended the staircase, opened and locked the large iron gate, crossed the square prison yard, opened the gate in the outer wall and left the precincts, locking the last gate behind me like a man locking up his home. The dogs raced about madly in the open space. I began walking over the monotonous plain where there is no road, no mark – nothing but a dry sandy waste. The evening drew across the sea to meet me, passed through me and on to the darkening island. No wind, not the slightest whiff. I walked, drawing further and further away from the locked prison, the keys on my belt jingling softly, like bells. The dogs romped about me. They would dash off far ahead into the distance, then suddenly come tearing back to me in a furious rage, lick my hands and go roaming again. Sometimes they would stop, puzzling over some anonymous sandstone, sticking their damp muzzles into it, searching for the traces of some mysterious smell known to them alone. They had spent all their life in prison and were delighted with this unexpected outing. I, too, was gratified. I was going to see whether the sea was coming, and the prison house was transformed in my sight – by darkness or by distance – into a blurred shadow. Some may think that I could have gone, taken myself and the two dogs away and beyond the plain, and left the old prisoners locked in the silence behind me. The slight advantages we have in being at liberty to move about the corridors and wander of an evening into the plain around the prison may cause some people to believe that we jailers are free. But we are not. We, too, are imprisoned, but of our own accord. As yet we are innocent.

Perhaps that will explain why I stopped at last in my slow peaceful journey across the endless plain. No, I had not found the sea yet, but I had found everything dry and waiting for it. Darkness descends. The prison is an insignificant speck on the plain, but I know it is part of me.

The soft hazy air fills my eyes with longing. The dogs have stopped their ferreting about and come to stand by me, their ears cocked, listening too. I turn and start walking back. The dogs wonder why, without having achieved any purpose, reached any point, I suddenly stop midway and turn in my tracks. They defy me, continue in the direction of the sea till they vanish in the dusk; but in the end they come running in a wide arc back to me, and then once more they scamper merrily before me as though nothing had happened. Now the sun is setting. I can tell by the crimson streaks erupting over the mountains. By the time I reach the prison, darkness has covered everything. Flushed with happiness I open the gate in the wall. I am at peace. I find my prisoners seated in their cells, in complete darkness, their books trailing in their hands, patiently waiting for the dim light which I now turn on in their corridor. Everything is as it was. They are incapable of even thinking about flight. Only now do I realize how attached I have grown to this place. I shall not speak of the passion with which I fill in the day's forms.

At the break of dawn, in my dream, I hear the distant thrust. The first of the water is come. The invisible sea has hurled itself at the land and started its headlong advance. The dogs are restless. They have wakened and together with me they look out of the high windows and bark for no reason. The water appears to frighten them, somehow. For the time being the flood tide is nothing but a faint bluish line, as though the horizon itself were coming here, that same horizon that would never be visible except on the clearest of days. These are only playful waters as yet, casually they conquer the unresisting plain, as though surprised at themselves. These are only explorers, advancing in a crooked line and ready to yield to the first stone in their path, adapt themselves to the land for the sake of its conquest. So that when they reach the prison wall they halt respectfully before it. They mean no harm, they have only come to lick at the island, just lick it the way one of the dogs is licking my arm now in a dumb request for food.

I fling him away with a blow of my fist. Instead of savage, blood-thirsty animals, these two have been bred here into sentimental lap dogs with sad soulful eyes. I doubt if they are capable of attacking a man. Anything but a little grunting and growling is beyond them, and even these shows of menace will soon turn into sniveling.

A rhythmic banging of bowls against bars sounds from the corridor. The prisoners are demanding their food. The water has been distracting my attention and breakfast is long overdue. The prisoners have heard the water as well, but the limp bodies by the cell doors have not tensed; not a spark of excitement in their vacant eyes. I respect their silence and perhaps they, too, respect mine. I have heard it said that there were times when they would never stop talking and shouting among themselves, but over the years they had grown weary of each other and had limited themselves to strict necessities; before long they had found out that the only necessity was silence.

They have no contact with each other now, except through me.

As soon as I can spare a minute from my work I rush to the windows, stand staring at the waters, spellbound. Irresistibly the sea is urging its horizon on. Those first surprised explorers have already passed the prison house and are moving leisurely ahead, toying with every stone and conquering the entire plain in their offhand manner. Thus they will roll on till they reach the mountains, and there surprise will turn to adulation and their easygoing, playful domination will turn into a helpless fawning. But around the prison house the water is already swirling, endlessly flowing. Not a thin line any longer but a torrent, a close surging body of water turning the plain into a deep lake. Now it is reaching the top of the wall, towering, surmounting it, and in numerous sparkling cascades it drops into the courtyard, floods the tiles and rapidly approaches the prison house itself, licks the gray stones of its wall, plotting its evil and sure of victory. Caressed by the water, the boat rocks a little on its mooring.

The hours of the day go swiftly by. I look and look at the water and marvel. The prisoners do not raise their eyes from their books and sit wallowing in their stories. But in my brain the waters bore with a thin persistent wail. I do not think that the sound of the water can reach the distant mountains. I serve supper to my prisoners, amazed and hurt. Why will they not raise their heads? I collect the dirty bowls, wash the dishes. This is the third day that I have not eaten, just tasted my food. I am startled by the fast pace at which the tide is rising. Alone and deserted I wander about the corridors and suddenly my heart pines for all the people of the distant kingdom who are taking their pleasures and know nothing. Self-pity fills me, floods me. Joy and sorrow mingle and I crawl into a dark corner and cry a little. But soon my eyes dry, and once again I am a cruel guard bullying the frightened dogs. When I cross the corridor once more, and when I see my prisoners bent over their books, rage mounts in me and I cock my gun as in a dream and fire a long volley, piercing the twilit wall. Dust, smoke and a smell of sulphur. The prisoners are rigid in their cells. My Sovereign Liege, I am here, in this dark and distant corridor, lead me not into temptation. Again tears well up in my eyes: when shall I, too, go out into the mountains?

It is but a slight flutter. I pull myself together at once and return to work, clean the blackened gun. Afterwards I pass along the cells, collect the prisoners' buckets and empty their excrement into the sea.

Deep gray night, and the swirling of the water does not cease. A deadly silent world. This flood tide is nothing but the sea coming home. The sea will always come back and retake what it conquered once before. Let no one bear it malice for returning to trace its ancient crime. I look through the high windows. Softly the water has risen, has reached the windows of the ground floor. A black object sways near the wall – it is my escape boat slowly mounting towards me with the rising sea.

Are the prisoners growing alarmed? They must hear the howling of the water, they can see the rising water between the bars of their windows as well as I. Yet perhaps they are too old scramble up the walls of their cells. A mere glance at my face would tell them everything. I lock up the dogs, who have been following me – sad, their tails between their legs – wherever I go. For a moment I stand listening to the water, then I enter my cubicle, lock the door and light the candle. Tomorrow is the last day, no question about that. I shall escape with the keys. The building will crumble in the water, and I shall have the keys – that is the way it happens in the old legends. It is the perfect escape, the right one. Afterwards they will build a new prison here. Indeed, it would be a waste to relinquish this deserted plain where the sea comes from time to time and drowns the aging prisoners. But I shall escape with my life. With doorless keys I shall walk in front of the King's palace – a faithful servant, who may yet be honored in the capital.

I lie down in my clothes; always in my clothes. I take up the Regulations Manual and settle down to read, but I am too agitated still. The small cracked mirror by the closet reveals my pale face, the black rings under my eyes, the bloodless lips. When I declare that I sleep at night, it is only lest it be said of me that I violate the sleeping rules prescribed for jailers to promote vigilance by day. Actually, however, I lie wide-eyed hour after hour during most of the night. I lie clutching the thick square Manual, looking at its close print. It is divided into chapters and verses: instructions, laws, commandments. Yet there are times when I fancy that the Lawgiver is toying with me and has written nothing but obscure poetry. There is no explicit mention of the flood tide, but perhaps it is conveyed between the words. Fatigue envelops me. The figure of the teacher who used to instruct us in the Regulations Manual looms before my eyes. He was a strict, profound man, ever dressed in black. It was he that kindled my passion for the dry words. I lie lost in reverie, brooding over his figure till the flame dies out. I cannot sleep. The ceaseless gurgling of the water. Whenever I doze off the water rises in my dreams. In the middle of the night I start up, awake with sudden terror. I open the doors and see that the water has invaded the ground floor and is flooding the rooms. When I drag myself back through the corridor, I see the prisoners slouching on their stools, some reading by the faint light, some nodding over their books. One of them is always awake, to warn the others. Sometimes I have a desire to enter one of the cells and sit on a stool, like them, peacefully bent over my book.

Morning of my day of escape. The water is climbing sluggishly up the staircase. My head feels heavy. I trail along the corridors, draw near the two windows and look out. A gray sea stretching under gray skies. Wisps of fog floating. We are in the middle of the sea. Far, far into the distance the restless waters have swept, flooding the whole plain on their way to the mountains. Overnight the boat has risen an entire storey and is now floating up and down under the office windows. All I have to do is break through a window and jump into it.

There is a smell to the water, and the smell intoxicates me. Between the walls of the house the water is coming at me, a strange, alien mass. I descend to the last dry step of the staircase and the dogs follow me down with cautious tread, hesitating, slipping on the steps, their ears drooping; they lap a little at the water. Their lascivious passions have faded.

I spend all morning cleaning the house and making my preparations for escape. I intend to take nothing with me except the dogs, my weapon and, of course, the Regulations Manual; it is the copy presented to me upon my graduation from the course, and is inscribed with a splendid dedication from the Kingdom. The dogs sense that I am about to escape and do not let me out of their sight. The water is rising very slowly now. The flood tide has spent its impetus; now the sea is only finding its level on the plain, and it is due to flood the building in the process. I see a small puddle even now (and there is no knowing where it came from), collecting against the corridor threshold. At noon I divide all the food that is left in the house among the prisoners. Better that they die by drowning.

Afterwards I shut myself up in the office with the day's forms. I cannot recall what it was I wrote there, but I do know that I stayed a long time by the desk and that a strong emotion gripped me when I found the right words. Now I am scrubbing every corner of the house and arranging everything in its proper position. Actually, a strict order reigns in this place always, yet even this order may appear deceptive set against the severe demands of the Regulations. A swift glance at the windows covered with a thin haze tells me that dusk is hovering over the sea. I do not hurry myself on that account, not at all; it suits me well, departure in the black of night.

Out of the closet in my cubicle I take my black costume with the monarchical emblems imprinted on its lining. It is the formal attire for grand occasions, executions and such. The costume is creased here and there, but is still new. I have not worn it since the graduation ceremony of the course. I slip out of the dirty service overall, stride naked through the corridor, in full sight of the prisoners. I am not ashamed. I wash my limbs in the cold familiar water of the faucet, return to my cubicle and put on my clean clothing, smooth out the creases, pull on the high boots; I am ready for a journey into night. I shall light my flashlight and ford the darkness.

The water has flooded the top stair, arrives at the second landing like a guest sure of himself and his welcome. A single rivulet gushes forward suddenly, drawing a blind, timid line along the corridor, meandering over the crack between the tiles till it comes up against the wall. Soon the water will grip my hand in a cold wet salute. How strange to see it here, the flood of the distant sea here in this dim corridor. The moment has come to escape. The dogs wriggle joyously at my feet, their tails thumping hard against the floor; they, too, are excited at the thought of meeting their little master again. I don my coat, lash the dogs to my belt with short, tough straps, attach the keys to my buckle, hitch the gun on to my shoulder and take the Regulations Manual in my hand. I cannot deny that I am sorry to leave this dark prison house sinking in the sea. For three days I was sole ruler here, and I have grown attached to the long corridors.

Slowly I move along the cells and softly the keys jingle. One last inspection of my prisoners. They do not raise their heads from their books, some are dozing. Is that how they will part from me? They stay motionless, rooted to their stools with the placidity of very old, jail-hardened men, their striped prison garb emphasizing the drab ordinariness remaining here, in contrast to my festive clothes. The dogs are jerking at the straps attached to my belt, dragging me on. One of the prisoners is gnashing his teeth. Which one? I scan the cells with angry eyes and he falls silent. Are they really placid, or is the calm feigned? I am deserting them now. In my imagination I see my little boat steering swiftly for the mountains, and this deserted building with its prisoners caught between bars and battering sea. All that I leave here will remain outside the Law. I look at the small volume in my hand with surprise. Softly the Regulations have come, have flocked unnoticed from all corners where they belong and folded themselves back into the Manual; and with me, inevitably, they will go away from here.

Anarchy – I suddenly think of it, and I tremble.

I stop, pull back the panting dogs bent on escape. The Chief Warder has fled and has entrusted this place to me. Now I am about to escape. Whom shall I entrust the prison to? For a moment I consider leaving the beloved Manual here, in the middle of this dim corridor, at the heart of the flooded building, but I know that the water will sweep it away like a lifeless object. Suddenly the walls seem naked. I look at my prisoners, their bowed heads, and imagine them breaking into howls, tearing up the doors, breaking through secret tunnels, wrecking the whole crumbling prison in their rage and shattering the silence, this hard-won silence.

I could rip out the pages of my little book and paste up the Regulations on these walls, fuse them with the iron of the bars, knead them into the prisoners' food – but it will all be in vain, I think in despair. The prisoners see that I have stopped. Their eyes narrow as though in wonder: You still here? Our glances cross. Is there one among them worthy to receive the Regulations from my hand?

In a flash I make up my mind, boldly, as befits the personal (personal! – I could weep with joy) representative of the King in this jail. And then I have taken the keys from my belt, raised the gun to my waist and cocked it, and I turn on my heels and start opening the cells, one by one. The locks creak in amazement. Even the dogs appear shocked at the unthinkable deed. All the doors are unlocked. Twenty-one heavy iron doors. I command the whole length of the corridor with my short barrel. In a strong voice I order them out. The doors shriek, they open. The prisoners emerge, nearly all of them tall, their shaven heads bent; the dogs growl, terrified. A shiver of hatred passes through their bodies at the sight of the prisoners. The smell of ancient crimes is in their clothes still. With difficulty I manage to hold them back by their straps lest they break loose and attack them. The long line of prisoners passes before me in single file, splashing barefoot through the puddles. They climb the three steps to the office. They have not forgotten to take their books along, just in case I should bore them, the scoundrels.

Next I am seated like the Chief Warder in the chair behind the desk. The two dogs chained to my belt stand like haughty beasts of prey, one at each side of me. The gun is on the desk, its muzzle facing the prisoners. Instead of a young jailer all of a flutter I have twenty-one heavy, burnt-out prisoners before me. The smell of their sweat reaches my nostrils. An unbearable stench. I swing the oil lamp up over my head and the walls fill with long-faced shadows. I open the Regulations Manual. Where ought I to start? Can I teach it all to them? Every sentence in the Manual has some bearing upon another, no Regulation stands on its own. I therefore begin at the beginning. In a clear, eager voice I read out the first fairly simple Regulations. I make no attempt to explain, trusting to the power of the written word. It is brief, the time I can afford to linger here without endangering my life. I sense that they, lined up before my desk, are listening with startled attention. My voice is rapt with exaltation. All I want is to make them understand the Law that is abandoning them to their lot. Page after page turns under my fingers as I read, enunciating clearly, giving myself up to the words. Time passes. Their attention flags. They are feeling behind them for walls to lean against. A few even make bold to lower their eyes to their books and continue reading. I ignore them and accelerate my pace. I dare not raise my head from the book and see the utter incomprehension surrounding me. I know that the speed I am reading at makes it impossible for them to take in anything, but I would rather go over as many Regulations as possible. Indeed, even if I were to read slowly they would grasp nothing. The eagerness is there in my voice still. A whole hour passes. My hand holding the oil lamp is sagging with fatigue, my voice growing hoarse. The dogs have lain down on the floor. I skip whole pages, seek out only my favorite Regulations now. But the text is growing involved. I am coming to Regulations that are unfamiliar even to me. My speech is growing careless and confused. The flame is fading in the lamp. Still my prisoners stand before me, a dark mute mass. A few are asleep on their feet and I hear their soft snores. The letters are dissolving into the darkness and I fill in the missing words with the aid of my imagination, rapidly creating new regulations. They won't notice the difference. When my voice breaks at last, and the flame dies, I raise my eyes.

They show no reaction. I jump up to examine their faces. Now I see that some of them are standing there with their mouths sagging, lips trembling. I feel a momentary surge of pity; such old men. But in an instant I collect myself, move swiftly to the door and whisper a command. They file past me, close, so close. In a long shuffling line they descend the three steps to the corridor and slip quietly into their cells. They are disciplined to the core, obedient to the muzzle pointing at their backs. I follow them down the steps, halt at the mouth of the flooded corridor and listen to them dragging their stools back into place, settling down. Now I shall go and lock their cells, and flee to save my life. But what have I done? Have I tarried too long? I lower my hand to my belt to take the keys, and I do not find them. Madly I search through the pockets of my coat, turn my clothes inside out, go down on the floor, but the heavy bunch has vanished. I glance along the corridor. A deep hush. The water is caressing my boots.

My keys are stolen.

Sick with panic, in torment, I rush back up the three steps to the office. The dogs are dragged behind me on their straps. In vain I search the floor, the spot where I have been standing, hunt over the desk, snatch up the Manual that has remained there to look underneath. No doubt about it: the keys have been stolen from me.

I turn back to the corridor at once, tear down the three steps with the gun raised in my hand. If I find that they have come out of their open cells I shall mow them down to the last man. But when I reach the threshold of the corridor and pull myself up I find dead silence. Not one of them has left his cell. As yet they are lurking within, plotting their evil, unseen by me, not seeing me. I cannot advance into the corridor to search for the keys lest they attack me from behind. I have no choice but to stand here on the threshold, tense, my gun ready. They stay mute. Impossible to tell which of them is holding my keys. How skillfully they manage to communicate among themselves without speech, with invisible signs. An hour goes by, then two, I lean a little sideways against the wall. The dogs are lying at my feet. No, I am not miserable. On the contrary, this new and unforeseen trial rouses an intense excitement in me. I am still too determined to be miserable. Only a few times in my life have I been tested, and each new trial enriches my spirit. I have forgotten the boat rocking under the windows, forgotten the mountains. Open-eyed I stand, listening. The dogs too prick up their ears, absorb my excitement. I could roar commands into the dark void, but who would obey me now. I do not want to make a fool of myself at this difficult hour.

The current has slowed down, the water is almost, marvellously, still. I slacken the dogs' straps a little and they crawl up the three steps to find themselves a dry spot. Their eyes are sad now. They never really loved me, but this time I have plainly disappointed them. My apprehension grows from moment to moment. I am afraid to leave my place lest the prisoners break out and overrun the whole building, I am afraid to draw deeper into the corridor lest they attack me from behind.

The evening hours go quickly by. I feel hungry when my prisoners munch the food I have given them. By midnight my legs give way and I stumble against the steps. At last the water is touching my flesh. I sit on the floor and my new costume is stained by the black water. The muzzle of my gun is still pointing zealously at the cell openings, but I have to admit that, strained beyond bearing, my limbs are overcome by fatigue. For a moment I consider rising, going from cell to cell and shooting the inmates. Yet I am unable to call up a single Regulation that would in any way justify such an act. I am a jailer, and I may be called upon to die for the Regulations Manual.

My eyelids are as rocks upon my eyes. I who could master my sleep so well am crumbling with exhaustion. The dogs, too, are nodding by my side. They have crowded me against the wall and spread themselves over the entire floor space. Their tension has relaxed and they are sprawling in an ugly pose, their tongues lolling wet on the floor, their legs stuck out, giving off a repulsive smell. But I am awake, my Liege. I am awake here in this remote house of yours

that the sea is flooding. Are your prisoners awake as well? Certainly
they are, for they do as I do – subject to my behavior and awaiting my
collapse. Softly I repeat passages from the Manual to myself to ward
off sleep. My tired brain can only recall the first Regulations, the most
simple, most basic ones. For an instant the idea to rise and run, run
away from here with the last of my strength, crosses my mind. But I
still have the power to banish such weak thoughts.

The dogs' slumber is infecting me too. Who would have thought
that these dogs would betray me so in an hour of need? I try shouting,
beating them, but I cannot bring out a sound. I have lost my hold over
them. I am failing, sinking. Remember that I am in the middle of the
sea, and the sweetness of the water is enveloping my heart. I seem to
see shadows gliding through the corridor. Everything grows confused
before my defeated eyes. Am I asleep already? My finger remains on
the trigger. This much I know. I might even put a bullet through my
brain, but what good would that be? Is that what is demanded of me?
Will that stop them from fleeing to the mountains?

The gun is slipping. It is pointing at the floor now and I haven't the
strength to raise it. I lift my hand from my lap to look at the time, but
even if I could discern the dials I would not take in anything. It is
obvious now. I am asleep. I dream. It is my soul that is stretching like
a long dim corridor before me, it is from me that the shadows are
breaking forth.

Dawn, first light. The doors are open. The water is turning gray
again. Slow, so slow is the flood tide now. Imperceptible. Clearly a
kind of lull has set in, a moment of grace, of peace. I doze awhile and
wake, doze and wake. What is the trial I am failing? Only a trial of
wakefulness, of resisting sleep.

Dim light, shadows. The sound of water and the sound of steps.

All is lost.

They attack me in my dream before they attack me in the flesh.
Their hands are shaking with the exhaustion of a sleepless night and
with the long years of waiting. Many many hands, gnarled and cool.
They numb my head with fists that are not strong, that hurt but little.
They are frail. With little effort they slip the gun out of my hand, haul

me sleepy and lost along the corridor, lift me up and cast me into one of the cells. Me, and the two dazed animals pulled behind me. Through the feeding hatch they mockingly fling the Regulations Manual in after me, then lock the door with the stolen keys.

I maintain my calm, the superiority of my position. Take no heed of the tears in my eyes. They are not tears of sorrow but of joy. The blows hurt no longer. Imprisonment does not frighten me. I am not in despair. Here, perhaps, I shall gain insight into the real significance of the laws, here better than anywhere else. Here I shall understand the importance of imprisonment to the morality of the state. I am young still and need to perfect my personal knowledge of the Regulations Manual. Dank cell and bleak cold of dawn – have I made myself clear?

The fugitives stampede about the building. They do not speak but snarl at each other. They break through the windows, search for the boat. I hear their shouts as they fight for a place in the crowded boat. In no time some of them are being pushed overboard and rend the air with their drowning screams. Eternal prisoners, and even if they knew how to swim in youth they have forgotten over the long years. I hear the boat cutting its moorings. None of them knows how to start the engine and they throw it overboard and use the oars. They move off. A tiny, overloaded boat.

I dismiss them from my mind.

Yes, I fall asleep; and when I wake the sun is high in the sky and true silence enfolds the empty building. The water is rising no longer. Birds fill my window with gay twitter. I am happy once more. The tide has abated. The flood, surprisingly, has not turned out to be long-lasting. The birds know it is safe to come back, but not so the humans. They think I sailed my boat to the mountains long ago.

I fling myself down on the soiled mattress. The food left in this cell will last me for a time. Presently I shall sit on the stool and read the Regulations Manual. Now I realize the greatness of the Lawgiver who composed it as a book of verse, to be read psalm by psalm and grow truly serene, grow close to all that is far and beyond. But the dogs in my cell, the dogs are unquiet. They pace round and round the cell, hugging its walls with their heads down, hunting for a hole to escape through. They pay no attention to each other, only to the search for an outlet. Their passions have all condensed into the single passion for liberty. What shall I do with them? I cannot get them out of here.

I thought I had found peace but there is no peace. They race madly around me, the little cell is full of their long bodies. Even if I sit hunched in my corner they still bump into me on their restless circuits. From time to time they go straight for me, throw themselves hopelessly upon me with the full length of their bodies, lay their paws on my shoulders, lick my face with their long rough tongues, sometimes even biting a little. Their eyes are sad, tearful. I shut my book, stroke their heads. All the warmth that is left in me I lavish on them.

But they do not calm down. From time to time they hurl themselves at the bars of the door and break into a long wail for their real master. Their wolflike cry sends a shiver of pain through my heart. Who will carry my wail to my master?

They start circling me again. Caged, hungry, two disciplined dogs reverting to wild beasts. Will they rise against me? I place food before them – husks and salt herring. It is all I have. They sniff at it, nibble a piece and spit it out in disgust. It is not this food that they claim. Once more they pounce upon me, their temporary master, their hated master now. Lightly they bite me, lick my blood, intoxicated. A new passion is roused in them, a grim passion throbbing in their jaws. I try tying them up but they manage to slip their heads out of the straps. I try to soothe them, suffer them with infinite patience. My heart goes out to them. Tears are blinding my eyes.

The world is radiant with light. The glory of it. Still and smooth lies the water, joyously the sunbeams splinter. It is from this narrow window alone that one can see how vast it all is, how wide open. Nothing, no one from end to end. Over in the mountains they all must think that the sea has flooded the whole prison by now. No one will imagine that the last guard is imprisoned here in one of these cells, and is still alive. The dogs are hurting me, but the pain is sweet as yet. This, apparently, is my last trial. As yet, it is not much.

Nurit Zarchi

The Plague

Translated by Yael Lotan

In the time of the great plague in Jerusalem which killed a quarter of its inhabitants, the monks who lived on the mountain, at a distance of an hour and a half from the city, did not remain secluded in their cloister but entered the plague-stricken city to tend the sick and the dying.

The abbot, Alexander Monteiro, in his time a famous figure in Jerusalem, sent out his delegates according to a curious system: every morning a monk would set out for the beleaguered city, returning at night to sleep in the isolated hut in the monastery garden, so as not to infect his brethren. At dawn, when the brother on duty woke up, he had to ring a bell to let the others know that he was alive and ready to depart for the city. When the day broke and the bell was not heard, the monks lying awake in their cells knew that they had to choose a new delegate to leave that very day for the contaminated city.

One by one they would enter the chapel and draw lots before the image of the Virgin, and the one whose name came up would pack his belongings, carry his bedding down to the garden hut, and depart that morning.

It happened in the third month of the plague. The community was gathered in the chapel, and Abbot Monteiro studied the monks' pale, drawn faces. The previous week twenty-three brethren had taken part in the lottery, and this morning only twenty were left.

The Abbot watched them as they filed out through the door, all somewhat bowed and thin. But despite the great danger, not one of the monks sought to shirk his duty.

It was a hot day and Abbot Monteiro tried to open his window, pushing it against the branches of the cherry tree, which stretched as far as the pane. Under the tree lay cherry pits like minute skulls. Every year the monks and the birds raced to harvest the fruit. This year the birds had won and consumed all the red flesh. But now the fruit's rosiness reminded the Abbot of inflamed flesh, rather than of the tender cheek of an infant.

Beyond the garden stretched a poppy-strewn field, reddening the mountain's flank, and on its slopes, amid the protruding boulders, could be discerned the cyclamens with their slender throats, as airy and intangible a layer as the morning mist.

Feeling oppressed, Monteiro opened a hidden drawer in his desk, took out a bottle of choice Lebanon wine the color of amber, wiped the dust off it with a fold of his cassock, held the wineglass up against the light and poured in the translucent liquid. He sipped slowly, wondering about the mysterious ways of Providence that had chosen him to conduct this game which sentenced people to live or die.

Alexander Monteiro smiled bitterly to himself. Years had passed since the heads of his order barred his way up the Church hierarchy and left him to serve here, in Jerusalem, in a remote and wretched monastery. Had fortune favored him, he might have risen to become a senior figure in the Church Council in Rome, an appropriate position for one who aroused respect and fear alike. Abbot Monteiro, who had come up from the poor alleys as a youth, feared neither the lowly nor the great, but his thirst for power was as intense as his spiritual hunger. As the years passed, he looked back and tried to determine whether his fight had been driven by the principles of the faith or by the desire for power, but found no answer.

When the scandal had died down, or rather, after it had been hushed, he found himself in this monastery on a hillside near Jerusalem, in charge of a community of monks, mostly from Spain, a few from his own country, and some who had ended up here and he never found out whence they had come.

In his first years at the monastery, Abbot Monteiro was sunk in profound gloom, and month after month sent letters over the sea to his superiors in Rome, explaining, pleading and urging them to lighten his sentence and release him from this place to which he had been consigned.

The monastery put into his charge was indeed run-down and disheartening: the water cistern, the gardens, the stone walls – neglect was everywhere, and the monks themselves were ignorant and crude. They sat in the refectory in front of Abbot Monteiro, grabbing the food from the communal bowl with greasy fingers, which they would then wipe on their cassocks. When he warned them by striking the water jug with his fork, or pounding on the table with his fist, they would raise their faces from their plates and look at him with their little eyes set beneath narrow brows, their heads generally shaved, the better to withstand the summer heat in Jerusalem, and it was hard to tell if there was more hatred or ignorance in their gaze.

In his early years in Jerusalem, Abbot Monteiro used to spend his nights reading the books he had brought with him from home. He kept them in a chamber on top of the tower, and would go up there in the evening, light the lamp, finger the leather bindings and smell their scent, and be solaced.

For some time he continued to correspond with his metropolitan friends. Even when he realized that he would never be absolved, that his fate was sealed, he kept bestirring his soul to debate the higher issues.

Abbot Monteiro could not let go of the problem which had caused his downfall. He seemed to the people around him to be still possessed. And indeed, he too despaired when he realized that time was passing while he went on brooding about the question. As the years passed, weariness and guilt caused his letters to Rome to grow infrequent, until he stopped sending them altogether. And he began to believe, albeit dispassionately, that there was a hidden purpose in his having been sent hither, and that the life where you happen to be *is* your life. Moved by this cheerless but provocative idea, he began to restore the monastery, the stone wall, the grove, the vegetable garden and the water channels.

To his surprise, the monks who had hitherto regarded him with hostility, grew friendly when they saw that he had turned his mind to the place where he was.

Ten years passed, and then one day a letter arrived from the Ecumenical Council urging him to return. To his own surprise, he rejected the offer out of hand, either because he feared that the monastery in which he had invested most of his active years would start to decline and would soon be as bad as he had found it, or from a touch of residual vengefulness: "When I wanted to, you did not, and now it is I who refuses." Or maybe he feared that he no longer had the fiery passion which animated him in the past, and that the people who invited him to return would be disappointed in him as he had been disappointed in the heads of the Order, who nowadays seemed to him to be primarily cold authoritarians. So he stayed where he was and continued to direct the monastery, and might have lived out his life believing that nothing further would happen, and without knowing if the higher instruction had indeed achieved its purpose, the purpose of his passionate spirit, and whether it was weariness or modesty which affected him – but for something that occurred soon after the arrival of that letter.

Abbot Monteiro put the glass and the bottle of Lebanon wine back in the desk drawer, but the wine had not worked its expected effect and his heart remained as heavy as before.

This is what happened: one morning, some time after Abbot Monteiro had turned down his superiors' invitation and resolved to remain in Jerusalem, he took a walk in the monastery courtyard. The dew which had not yet evaporated from the grass soaked into the hem of his cassock, and the song of the birds, renewed each morning, sounded in the milky air. He gazed at the purplish mountains of Jerusalem, which contained their ancient thoughts as if they brought into the precincts of the monastery an even older gospel, but the landscape which had played such a major part in the history of Christianity did not move him.

He felt a touch on his shoulder. It was Brother Stefano, his devoted verger, who had risen even earlier and was walking in the garden some distance from the abbot, watching the latter, who seemed to be profoundly gloomy.

There was a strange expression on Brother Stefano's face, as though he had seen an impossible sight. Acting out of character, he took the abbot's sleeve and led him under the canopy of the cherry tree, which was then in full bloom like an entire pink cloud descended from heaven. Under the tree lay a baby bundled in a blanket, its open eyes laughing into the faces of Brother Stefano and the abbot as they stooped to look at it. It had evidently been placed there a short while before, but though they searched its little garments, they found no clue or hint as to who had left it there.

Abbot Monteiro and Brother Stefano were equally unfamiliar with the appearance of babies, but they both thought that the child they had found under the cherry tree was a perfect creature, with his clear features and his tiny sturdy limbs. The riddle of his origins was from the start bound up with the mystery of his beauty.

All that day the monks crept secretly, one by one, up the stairs to the abbot's cell to peep at the baby.

The following day the abbot gathered the community before the image of the Virgin and her Child, who now struck him as quite lacking in charm compared with his own baby. And, needless to say, they decided to keep the baby with them in the monastery, to take care of him and bring him up.

"Aaron" was the name with which Abbot Monteiro baptized the foundling, and he gave him his own surname, Monteiro.

Little Aaron grew into a handsome and good-natured boy, and although the brothers tended to pamper him, it did not do him any harm. Brother Stefano soon taught him to read and write, and the monks taught him the other skills, languages and crafts; he even mastered the arts of organ-playing and leather-stamping, which the monastery had specialized in for generations.

All the brothers unburdened themselves of knowledge which they had hitherto kept strictly secret so as to share it with him, and moreover instructed him in the lores of medicinal herbs, of wine-making and the blending of colors. They all regarded him without a doubt as the torch-bearer, the heir apparent.

In the evenings Abbot Monteiro would sit and talk to him at length about the proof of the existence of God, and other difficult matters suitable for a boy who was destined to join the order. Yet a delicacy of mind held the abbot back from discussing the matter of the virgin birth. He felt that it was inappropriate to raise such a sensitive issue with a boy who did not know his own origin.

Late one night, when Aaron was no longer a cherubic infant but a handsome lad whose looks recalled Donatello's David, Abbot Monteiro remained seated in his armchair for a long time after the lesson, sunk deep in thought. His weariness was tinged with unease. Aaron was indeed a clever boy and could answer his questions smartly, and yet...

Abbot Monteiro propped his heavy head on his forearms. What was the matter? He was conscious of the boy's superiority. Did the feeling stem from his admiration for youth and beauty, or a sense of inferiority before this boy who was not his son – or was it spiritual humility in the face of the foundling's reserve? Whatever it was, something was nagging at Abbot Monteiro and did not let up.

Occupied as the abbot was in the directorship of his monastery, he had nevertheless undertaken to teach the boys of the nearby village once a week, and it was when he observed on the face of one of those simple lads that expression of curiosity mingled with despair which reflects the constant impulse to overcome the darkness within or without, as the Netherlands sea seeks to overcome the shore, that he grasped the puzzle of his own boy: Aaron was entirely lacking in hunger. Perhaps the fact that he had never questioned the secret of his origin had extinguished all other hunger in him.

Aaron, thought Abbot Monteiro, moved like a somnambulist who, in his sleep, feels his own strength. Abbot Monteiro sighed. Yet it was this very quality, he thought, which created the strange and mysterious appeal of his eyes, his face, his curiously perfect limbs, as of one who had landed in a lesser world, whose presence was giving the world more than it could ever repay, one who always held the superior position of the beloved.

Abbot Monteiro sighed. He felt driven. The plague had imposed on him a burden of responsibility greater than he could bear.

There was a knock at the door. It was Brother Stefano. With his amiable, soothing face, the abbot's verger was one of those rare individuals in whom affection or regard for another person causes no resentment. But at this moment Abbot Monteiro could not interpret Brother Stefano's strange expression, until the verger handed him the letter.

Since the outbreak of the plague the consular mail had ceased to arrive, and the abbot could not imagine who could have written to him. Moreover, the monastery was taking stringent precautions to avoid exposure to anything that came from the city, for fear of infection. But Brother Stefano, his smile implying that he did not wish to know any more than he already did, and his gesture suggesting that now everything would fall into its proper place, laid the letter in the abbot's hand, went out and closed the door softly.

Abbot Monteiro looked at the letter. The sight of the writing aroused a sense of odd familiarity, which became clear as soon as he realized the identity of the writer.

Until a few years before, when he had ceased to maintain any inessential contacts with the land whence he had come, Abbot Monteiro had kept up one connection. He used to correspond, though with diminishing frequency, with a childhood friend, Lazarus, the son of a Jewish family who never, even when they were children, made any attempt to hide that fact.

The abbot would sometimes smile to himself, wondering what his superiors would think of him if they knew that the only person with whom he continued to discuss matters of the spirit was a Jew.

The two friends never referred in their letters to the scandal which had led to Monteiro's banishment, his raising of the question whether the virgin birth was actual or spiritual. Abbot Monteiro, being inordinately sensitive on the issue, interpreted Lazarus' silence on the subject to mean that he supported him, though in his most clear-headed moments he sensed that his friend Lazarus was laughing inwardly at him and at his questions.

And yet, the abbot felt, either by sheer intuition or from a vestige of their childish understanding, that Lazarus was on his side. There was nothing explicit about this. For instance, who but Lazarus would have thought of sending him that slip of a cherry tree, which under Brother Stefano's careful tending grew to be the finest cherry tree in the district of Jerusalem. Pilgrims to the Holy Land mentioned it in their letters as the cherry tree of the hillside monastery, the only one of its kind in the region. Though this year, Abbot Monteiro said to himself, looking out of the window at the cherry-stones strewn around the tree, the stench of death was everywhere. He opened the letter.

"My dear Monteiro," Lazarus wrote, "as you may have guessed, I am writing this letter in Jerusalem, having arrived here a little while ago with my daughter, after a long and wearisome journey via Genoa, Istanbul and Sidon. I have come here to die, in keeping with the custom of the Jews, who in their old age wish to be buried in the Holy Land. A bad sickness came over me, and I realized that my time was approaching. So, whether to take my old man's mind off matters, or because there is in me more faith than I had thought" – Abbot Monteiro smiled – "whatever the reason, here I am with my daughter in the plague-stricken city. And I find that although I have come here to die, I do not care to let death make a plaything of me. I certainly do not wish to entrust my daughter Tamah to him. Therefore I ask of you, my old friend and companion, to find me a place that is free of death whither I can hastily retire, before the plague has seized my daughter or me. In the name of our boyhood, which people are wont to call a wondrous time, I remain, your friend Lazarus."

Abbot Monteiro took up his quill. It was not difficult to accede to his old friend's request. There was in the village of Silwan – the ancient Siloam – a tile factory where in normal times, which now seemed immeasurably remote, some of the monks used to work. Here they produced the terrazzo squares which were known throughout the world as "Jerusalem floor tiles." Since the outbreak of the plague no one had gone there, and Abbot Monteiro had given it no thought until this moment.

But something stopped him from finishing his letter, which he intended to send to the city in the morning with the monk on duty.

For a moment he felt like an actor who finds himself on the stage, unable to remember his lines and at a loss to recover them. He laid the letter on his desk and left his office to attend to his usual occupations. But all day long his mind kept harking back to the matter, as though it offered an opening through which he might escape the imminent end, which was drawing nearer like dark ocean waves on a full-moon night.

Later Brother Stefano came to call the abbot to supervise the drawing of lots. The brothers were seated and ready, he said, and indeed Abbot Monteiro found them seated in the refectory before the great crucifix. Though it was already dark, the wicks in the oil lamps had not been turned up, and the faces of the brothers looked pale and gaunt in the dim yellowish light. Shadows moved on the walls as Abbot Monteiro looked around slowly, observing each man in turn, until he reached Aaron. His heart swelled even before his eyes rested on his pupil's white brow, his handsome, perfect face. Then he knew. And when the lots were drawn and the lad's name came up, Monteiro understood that it was God's will that his friend Lazarus' letter had come when it did.

That night Abbot Monteiro was unable to fall sleep, haunted by the thought that he might have sent the boy to the stricken city, and allowed fate to condemn him to death. No man believes in his own death, he thought, it is beyond comprehension. And yet, his own incomprehension might have caused the boy to lose his life before he had even tasted it.

A sudden disquiet seized him – could this be the voice of the Evil One? But he imagined the lad tossing on his cot on this night before his departure for the city, and resisted the impulse to conduct a scholastic debate with himself. He rang for Brother Stefano, who slept nearby, and ordered him to fetch the unfinished letter and to summon Aaron from his cell.

His appearance surprised the abbot. Once more his imagination had carried him too far: the boy looked calm and at ease. He was fully resolved to carry out his duty, and stood before his mentor as though he had nothing to lose, his green-gray eyes gazing at him with his usual attentive, matter-of-fact expression, clearly wondering why he had been summoned.

The abbot was deeply perturbed. Was it piety that he had inculcated in his disciple, or had his teaching grossly misdirected the soul of the infant whom fate had laid on his doorstep? For a moment it seemed to him that the plague itself was sent to force him to confront this question.

Aaron waited while Abbot Monteiro finished and sealed the letter, then called Brother Stefano to give it to a special messenger to take to the city. He gave Aaron another letter, bearing the address of the tile factory, and ordered him to give it to someone there who would be waiting for it. He told Stefano to give the boy adequate provisions, and instructed Aaron not to enter the city, but circle its walls to reach the village of Silwan.

"Surely not," the lad exclaimed, looking at the abbot uncomprehendingly. "Surely, Father, I must go into the city."

But Abbot Monteiro repeated his instructions in a firm voice, and made Aaron swear to obey him.

Monteiro accompanied his disciple to the door and then watched him through the window. For a moment the flaring torch revealed the boy's form in the night, then the glow shrank to a moving point of light in the darkness, which soon swallowed it up.

He sank into his chair, feeling so weighed down that he could hardly move a finger, but gradually his face cleared and he began to feel lighter and lighter. By the time the dawn broke through the high windows, he thought that if he were not too tired to rise, he might almost fly away like the cool white morning mist, animated by that sense of weightlessness we experience when it seems that we can lead fate on a string. When Brother Stefano knocked on his door and brought him his morning coffee and a slice of toasted bread, he found the abbot dressed and ready for the journey.

No one must find out that he had gone instead of Aaron, he said, and ordered Stefano to tell the community that the abbot had gone into retreat for a week.

Every morning for seven days Abbot Monteiro rode into the city on his donkey, moving among the dead and the dying as lightly as though he were bodiless. At first he took care to avoid drinking the water or tasting the food, but exhaustion and the horrors that met his eyes made him feel ashamed of his fear. Seeing small children whose livid and swollen faces suggested that they might not survive the day, his feelings were the reverse of Job's: Who am I, he asked himself, compared to these nestlings, whom love should have clutched to earthly life with its fierce talons, but who are struggling and soon, soon will fall into death's net.

Up in the monastery on the hillside the proximity of the divine order was plain and beyond question, but here in the city of Jerusalem, it dissolved in the face of death. If some supreme decree did in fact exist, Abbot Monteiro no longer knew if humility and courage were the means to attain it, or some dark impetus beyond all reason, beyond all custom and order, drawing him to that light which glowed from the city by night, bright as daylight, rising from the quarter where the plague victims were burned. It could be seen from afar, and by night Jerusalem looked like the lurid visions of St John.

In his heart of hearts Abbot Monteiro knew that he was negotiating with God when he offered himself as a substitute for his disciple, and he did not know whether or not he still wanted to believe in the divine order.

On the seventh evening, when Abbot Monteiro returned from the city to the monastery, his face was flushed and his whole body felt unwell. Too exhausted to wash himself, he lay down and wrapped himself in a blanket, which failed to stop his shivering. He heard footsteps approaching. Someone opened the door of his retreat. Someone made a fire, someone made a hot drink and brought it to his dry lips, spoonful after spoonful.

It is Brother Stefano, the feverish abbot thought to himself. He did not know how long he lay there before he was able to open his eyes. The shivering had stopped. Abruptly, he sat up on his cot. Aaron stood before him, his face pale and his eyes dark like those of a wild creature caught in the field.

"You!" he cried fiercely, waving a letter in his hand. "You! Why did you send me there, huh? Was it so I'd know what I was missing if I stayed out there, instead of being buried behind these damnable walls? Or so I would know how hard it is to give up that world, that life, and would not die without experiencing the pain of giving it up?"

Abbot Monteiro tried to hold his breath and let the wave pass, but Aaron went on furiously:

"Who gave you the right to keep me here, locked up in the worship of God? If it *is* God you worship, tell me, in whose name did you choose me to follow him – tell me, in whose name?"

Seeing foam on the boy's lips, Abbot Monteiro prayed it was only rage that produced it.

"You, you, you!..." Aaron shouted, waving his arms. "Who are you to take my place among the dead, and send me to the act of love? Are you God?!"

Abbot Monteiro gazed at him, pierced with sorrow.

"You will not decide for me whether I shall lie in a man's bed or a woman's," the young man said. His face looked chalk white in the firelight.

Even through the curtain of pain Abbot Monteiro could not but hear what was being said. He recalled the white visage of Brother Casparo, one of the Spanish monks, and his look when Aaron's name came up in the lottery. He had imagined that he knew all that went on in the monastery, yet evidently there were things he knew nothing of, things that his imagination had not compassed, and all the while he believed that his Aaron was safe and secure in his care.

"You! You!" – Suddenly a dam burst in the abbot's mind, and he recalled with painful vividness how he had felt when he resolved to join the monastic order. It was not a free choice, but a dark impulse;

he did not know whither he was fleeing, nor why or from what.

"Here is the letter your friend sent you," Aaron sneered. "But you two will not toy with me as though I were a child and you were fate. You will never read this letter!" And he threw it into the fire.

They both watched in silence as the tongues of flame licked the edge of the paper, flared up and consumed it, then subsided. Abbot Monteiro rose from his cot and walked slowly towards his pupil. But Aaron seized him by the collar before he could embrace him and dragged him outside.

"You!" he hissed, his face filled with loathing. "I alone will decide whether to go to the city tomorrow and do my duty, or disappear from this place and never be heard from again. And you – you shall only hear the echo, and perhaps not even that."

Abbot Monteiro could no more say if it was the right thing to do than if he had been bewitched, but he felt he had no other choice than to respect Aaron's wish. Somehow he made his way to his own room in the monastery and there he sat in his chair for the rest of the night, waiting for the sound of the bell. Did he doze off finally, in this, the longest night of his life? Or, if he was fully awake, how did he fail to hear the bell?

Abbot Monteiro was too shattered by grief to interpret the signs, and then at last morning came, silently and without the veils of mist that formerly filled the valley and hid the sunrise.

He rose with difficulty, aided by Brother Stefano, who pleaded with him desperately not to return to the sick city. But duty was the last thread that anchored his mind to sanity.

The columns of thick smoke were gone, only some embers still glowed here and there. He had to beware of the packs of hungry dogs that roamed through the city streets, but there was no mistaking the glimmer of hope in people's eyes. That night no one was struck down by the disease, and no one died of it thereafter. It was the end of the plague.

Nine months later Abbot Monteiro went out to the monastery garden before dawn. Nature seemed to be clothing herself luxuriously, as though to make people forget how fragile and tenuous life is, and how near oblivion. Everything that could flower did so extravagantly, and the bees buzzed feverishly over the spring display.

Abbot Monteiro stopped and looked around him. Since the plague he had had trouble sleeping. He would leave his room earlier than ever and go out into the garden at first light. Bluish mists rose from the gulleys, and if his gaze were not so sharp and deliberate, he might have forgotten where he was. Indeed, he thought, what matters the place where you are; it is all one. There was a touch of the illusion of eternity in that moment, and Abbot Monteiro knew it to be the greatest illusion of all. Everything stood still: the wind, the clouds hanging over the valley, even the sheep in the field stood motionless like pieces of an unfinished game of chess. A moment later, the world moved on, and the air whistled in its passage.

The birds sang aloud, as though their hearts were overflowing with beauty and sorrow. The sun rose, as yet gentle, without the violence that would blaze in later days, and gilded the cherry tree whose blossoming canopy spread wider than ever.

Abbot Monteiro went up to the tree, wishing that he could lay his soul under it. There was a small bundle lying at the foot of the trunk. The abbot stopped, then moved closer. It was a baby. Its eyes looked up at him, wide-open, unblinking, as the pagan gods were said to look. In these eyes the abbot seemed to see all the knowledge that a man might know and then forget, the knowledge which must forever remain ineffable. He stood and stared at the baby.

A thousand possibilities spun around in his mind like a kaleidoscope. Was there a governing principle at work here, or something that pretended to be one? What past events had led up to this moment? All these thoughts flashed through his mind simultaneously, as they are said to do in the minds of condemned men. The abbot drove away the possibilities that occurred to him. Despite his intense desire to grasp the symbol, he forced himself to see only a coincidence, a single fragile event in the current of events that the wind may at any moment disperse like foam on the water.

He looked around and saw no one. Deeply moved as though he had received absolution, yet too clear-headed to believe that he was being given a second chance, he bent down to the baby as Biblical Hagar bent over her son, and took him in his arms.

The End of the Millennium

Gafi Amir

By the Time You're Twenty-One, You'll Reach the Moon

Translated by Rachel Jacoby

A pal of mine from high school, Doron, is turning thirty. All day long he's been reading the Visa gift catalogue out of depression. I wanted to take him out somewhere to celebrate, but I got held up at work until six. The electricity went out and all the computers crashed. "Don't ask what's going on here," I apologize. Doron sounds pretty drunk when I call later that evening to let him know that I'm only just leaving. "That's fine," he says cheerfully, "just get over here and we'll watch the yuppies from the balcony." I cautiously ask what he's doing. "I'm reading the Visa catalogue," he says. "Come over. I want to show you something." "Okay," I say, "it'll take me ten minutes." In the end it takes a lot longer. We hug and then I give him his present: a big stuffed fur frog, with spots. "It's so great you came," he says. "This is terrific, it's like bringing someone a cockroach." But I show him how it croaks when you squeeze its stomach. "Listen, listen," I urge, "it sounds like a real croak." "Right on," says Doron. "I'll put it on top of the television. Come here, I want to show you something."

I follow him onto the balcony, telling him how I spent forty-five minutes looking for a parking space. I had a rough day, but that doesn't matter now. I'm finally here. "Right," Doron answers, "I've got to show you what I found." He picks up the catalogue and flips through the pages. "An electric Japanese foot-massager, isn't that awesome? And look," he says enthusiastically, "a pocketknife with twenty blades! I need something like that! Let's buy a rabbit! I've been reading this brochure since four and I can't get over it. Look at the possibilities!"

"Doron," I say patiently, "you don't need a rabbit. You're thirty years old. This rabbit is for up to age six."

"Yeah, yeah, I'm so ancient," he answers, annoyed. He rests the glass on the floor beside him. "I have more CDs and twice the magazines I had at twenty, and that's all there is to it. I thought that by thirty I'd already have a duplex in Ramat Aviv Gimmel and a wife who's a real babe and puts out every night. Listen," he says decisively, "I want a baby, Nurit."

So I think to myself, yeah, a baby. Sure. It jangles my nerves when I think about all my dreams that landed right in the junk heap. How I was going to be a supermodel. Crossing Sheinkin Street on a Friday afternoon, hanging on John Travolta's arm, while everyone's eyes just pop. How I would lose five kilos, win the Nobel Prize, and walk on stage in a tight black minidress with a plunging neckline. How I would become rich. And how someone would write a song about me. I don't want my friends to tell me out of the blue that they want a baby. Even if it is their birthday. "Fine," I say to him, "have a baby. Better for you to read the Visa catalogue." But he's not put off. He's totally wild about his fantastic idea. "Tell me," he asks excitedly, "what about you, don't you feel like having yourself a baby?" So I look at him in shock and go: "Doron!" "What," he says defensively, "it's amazing when you have a baby. You know what it's like? A friend of mine just had a baby. He comes home from work, takes a shower, stretches out on the couch, and puts the baby on his stomach!" And I think: God, don't be so descriptive. If we talk about this for one more millisecond, I'm going to get really blue. What do I need this for? So I say, annoyed: "Good, fine, okay," and he's surprised at me and disappointed, but doesn't say anything else.

We relax on the "King Plastic" chair on the balcony of the rented apartment on Melchett Street. We're surrounded by the enormous summer night melting patiently around us. We drink frozen vodka with frozen lemonade concentrate.

"It's great that summer's started," Doron says and stretches.

"Spring," I say to him. "Do you realize it's almost Passover? My father wants me to come to Jerusalem."

"Will you go?"

"He goes: 'Come on, let's be Jews once a year.' I told him I have to work, let him be a Jew once a year."

"Absolutely," Doron says. "Ditto."

Spring. Spring. Spring is like three Scud missiles for me because of all the bad things a spring night does to my serotonin. I get up in the morning and I see all that sun and I feel so satisfied. Like, sun! There it is, the sun! But when night falls, it hits me, wow: I get into this crazy hope mood. I start thinking about the last man I loved. He's living in Germany now and soon he'll come back to Israel. I start imagining how he'll come to my house, he'll knock on the door and all that. I get an attack of optimism as if life is really beautiful. Like he really meant it when he told me to wait for him. You know, spring is like a blast of lust and longing. More than the heart can stand. "Maybe this summer something really good will happen to us," I say to Doron, feeling the alcohol gently starting to get me high. So he takes my hand and promises warmly: "Nurit, by the time you're twenty-one you'll reach the moon." And we laugh. With relief. Light as flies. "One day," I tell him, "you'll make an important scientific discovery."[1] "Seriously," he says, "seriously, what do you most want to happen to you?" So I keep quiet. "Concentrate!" he says. "Tell me the one thing you most want to happen in your life." And I say, as if it's a question: "For Uri to come back to me? For him to come back from Germany tomorrow morning and say to me: 'Nurit, I missed you, you can't imagine how much, there's no way I can live without you?'" Then Doron drops my hand and goes: "Oy, Nurit." And I beg: "No, don't say it. I know myself." Just not tonight, with all of this blossoming all around. "But it's for your sake, you've got to..." Doron starts to say. "Look - yuppies," I say to him and point. From the balcony we can see rich Sheinkin types sallying out of their duplexes to make the rounds of the cafés, arms around each other as they go to stuff their

---

1. Both phrases are common fortunes on Hebrew Bazooka bubble-gum wrappers.

faces with pasta Alfredo and Italian ices. The name of the next snack food is probably already simmering away in their brains. Their creative ideas flutter around and crash into each other, making an awful racket in the neighborhood. Which is good, because if there was one instant of quiet here, just one instant of quiet, I would certainly hear myself wailing: "Come back to me, please, please, come back to me." Doron goes into the kitchen and comes back with a nearly empty bottle of Smirnoff. "You know what's really strange?" He stretches. "I woke up this morning completely sure I was twenty-nine. It was only after I brushed my teeth and made coffee that I suddenly realized it was impossible."

"You won't believe who I ran into on Friday," I say. "Out of the blue I saw Uzi at a party. What a laugh. Uzi, the guy who was Tali's boyfriend for ten years."

"Uzi?" Doron asks, falling back into his chair. "Uzi Dohar? Didn't he go to the States?"

"Now you'll die when you hear this, he's got this think tank in Houston. He explained it to me for an hour. I didn't understand a word. You should see him, he's turned into such a yuppie. Came to visit his parents, you know, with his American wife Susan."

"His American wife Susan," Doron repeats, amazed.

"One of those blondes," I say and close my eyes.

I remember how we were at twenty, when we got here from the settlement. Wrung out by this city and all its promises. It took a long time before we got our heads straight. After twenty the only way to make new friends was to fall in love with them, hate them, and then become platonic friends. We started a sandwich business, wandering all day between Asia House and the IBM office building with our straw baskets, selling health-food sandwiches, egg salad with alfalfa sprouts on whole-wheat bread, fucking all night on the Yarkon River bank, imagining that the crooked eucalyptuses were really the lap of nature. Yes, that was really the life. We could have stayed home and done it happily on our mattress, across from the TV set that only picked up Jordan TV from Amman, but we chose instead to throw on our harem pants and Birkenstocks and pedal slowly down Bnei Dan

Street on our bicycles, just so we could fall on our backs and feel the grass crackling underneath our brains. Looking for Alf and E.T. and all the stars of our childhood sailing through the sky. That was the first time I felt as if I really belonged to some generation.

"We were as fresh as quick-frozen broccoli," says Doron admiringly when I remind him of all this. "And how horny I was. All day long I thought about who I could fuck. Remember how often I used to make you pop?"

"Stop," I beg. "People aren't cans of fizzy drinks."

"I'm not a lech anymore," he answers mournfully. "I realized that a month ago, you know? That I'm not a lech anymore. When was it? I went to a party at the Perversity Club. A thousand girls, and not one of them did a thing for me. I said to myself, why do it, why should I start with the "you wanna dance?" routine. How about a dance? Want a drink? Want to come with me? Where did you go to school? What do you do for a living? Women pass on the street and I don't see them. There was a time when if I saw a blonde – I'd feel like I was on top of the world."

The best response I could think of was what my therapist always tells me when I spill my guts. Once a week I tell her how depressed I am and how I want to die and how I'm falling to pieces. She watches me attentively and says: "Aha." So I stare at him now, helplessly, and go: "Aha."

"Yesterday," he says, "I was someplace and I met someone, a girl. And I mean a girl, I'm telling you, Nurit. At most twenty. A guitar player. Just some chick. To cut a long story short, two in the morning she wakes me up, shakes me for half an hour. She goes: 'Wake up, Doron. C'mon, wake up. Please, wake up.' In the end I wake up, make like I'm half-asleep, and say to her: 'What?' She goes: 'Tell me, do I, like, interest you at all?'"

"I don't believe it."

"Believe it, Nurit, believe it."

"So what did you tell her?"

"I go: 'You bet you interest me,' and then I turn my back and go to sleep. But in my heart I'm thinking: 'Take a good look at these sheets

because you won't be setting eyes on them again.' My hormones
aren't what they used to be. I want love. I'm telling you, Nurit. Love."

I can't argue with him about that. I sip my lemonade slowly, let it
burn my throat. I think about all the time I had true love in my hand
and couldn't do a thing with it. I fill up with eight hundred spring
evening yearnings, like a disease. I read to him from the Visa
catalogue. Inflatable pillows. Preserves that never go bad. Run-proof
tights. The electric foot-massager. But he doesn't cheer up. I
remember all the sweet birthdays we used to have, with a clown and a
magician and surprise packages and chips and jelly beans and devil's
food cake. OK, those things don't really appeal to him, not now. "I'm
thirty," he says, "give me a break, Nurit." I try to cheer him up. I say
to him: "Hey, thirty isn't that much. Thirty is really pretty young." He
says to me: "Quit kidding me." And he's right. I can't say a thing. A
girlfriend of mine got married not long ago at the Ronit Ranch. I wore
my sheer tights. All night long I was shivering from the cold. A week
ago we went to see the anemones and irises on Mount Gilboa. Spring
messes with my mind. I think about Uri again. Hey, what are you
doing now? Who're you holding tight? I put the cup on the railing out
of easy reach and say hopefully: "Soon Uri's coming back from
Germany." "Quit that," he advises. "You have to get him out of your
head." "Sure," I say to him, "absolutely." "Seriously," says Doron.
"Seriously, Nurit, you're twenty-nine years old. It isn't right that at
twenty-nine every little thing gets you bent out of shape. It won't
work, do you understand?" I don't answer. He puts his hand on mine
on the arm of the chair. "You need to be tougher," he preaches at me
gently. "Really. For your own sake. You can't get like this every
time." But this wasn't just another fling. This wasn't just another one
of those shitty flings that help pass the time so well but don't do
anything for you. I really thought that, like, really, this was for real.
Somewhere in the sky Ursa Major and Ursa Minor are rising, and
Venus and Mars. A night full of stars like candy. Who else is lifting
his eyes to the sky on this dark night? Is he thinking about his life and
about love and all the things that were supposed to happen? Can he
feel his heart exploding with hope? I'm pretty drunk by the time I get

up, wavering a little on my legs. "Well, I've got to be on my way," I say to Doron. "I swear I have no idea how I'm going to drive home, and I can't even remember where I put the car. What a laugh." "Yeah," he agrees, "what a laugh. How're you going to find it?" "Wait a second," I say to him. "Don't laugh at me, please." But I'm laughing myself as I lie back down and open my eyes wide to look at the sky and broadcast telepathic messages: Come to me, come to me, come to me.

"You want to tell me exactly what you think you're doing there?" asks Doron and lies down beside me. And suddenly I know: he'll never come back home.

Yossi Avni

The Last Crusades

Translated by Dalya Bilu

When I started packing, they were showing a nature film on television; a mother turtle was digging in the sand on the seashore and laying her eggs, and after a while tiny, soft turtles broke out of the shells and rushed into the wet lap of the waves. Many dangers await them there, in the sea, said the narrator dramatically.

I smiled.

Every year soft, little babies with sad eyes come into the world. They grow up in ordinary apartments blocks in Ramat Gan or Holon, or in some country town surrounded by fields at the foot of the mountains. They cry like all babies, and nobody knows yet that they are little queers. They don't climb trees to find birds' nests, they don't tear their trousers at the knees. Quietly in the kitchen, they help their mother wash the dishes and bury their loving noses in her skirt. At school they don't play football, salty sweat doesn't run down their backs, and the girls don't peep at them and blush. In the afternoons, they learn to play the piano or the accordion, and sometimes they shut themselves in their rooms and write timid, ambiguous poems. They make sure to lock the bathroom door, and standing under the running shower they think about Nir's, or Alon's, or Oren's beautiful body, and at night they toss and turn in torment and detest themselves. In military service they don't volunteer for the elite units, salty sweat does not stream down their muscular thighs on strenuous marches, and when they are discharged, they harden their hearts to their mothers' despairing cries, pack a few clothes and a lot of dreams and drift one by one into the seductive embrace of the big city. What lies in store for them there, what dangers await them, our TV narrator should ask in a voice full of concern.

"What are you smiling about, look how much is left to do," said Shukie, and began to take down pictures and hanging plants. Shukie and I shared the three-room apartment on 46 Mazeh Street, near the water tower. According to the lease, we had less than a week in which to vacate it.

It was an enormous apartment and very old, its windows were painted bright blue and the gutters were Arab style, hollowed stone. I found it when I passed an estate agent's in Ben Yehuda Street and saw a note on the door: "Bargain: apartment with sea view." The agent climbed up to the third floor (it was a blazing hot day, his shirt stuck to his back), and furtively stripped away some cobwebs festooning the doorway. In spite of the squalor, or perhaps because of it, I liked the apartment.

"But where's the sea view?" I asked the agent.

He pushed open a crumbling wooden shutter and revealed a view of roofs patched with tar.

"You see the five solar heaters standing in a row?" he pointed to a remote roof.

"Yes."

"Look hard, you see the blurred patch between them?"

"Well?"

"That's the sea," he shrugged his shoulders and lit a cigarette.

I'd known Shukie for about two years; he was bald with an egg-shaped head, a bold, bony nose, and mainly a pair of enormous eyes, brimming with an immense, infinite thirst to seek a boyfriend. I say to seek, because sometimes it seemed he was keener on the search than on the actual find. Tall guys, short guys, young, middle-aged, accountants (accountants!) – he fell madly in love with all of them. Every two-three days, he would come home, his eyes moist with happiness, gasping for breath, as if drowning in intense emotion.

"Listen," he would lean weakly against the door jamb, "today I met a fabulous guy at the number 12 bus stop. Fabulous! I've never met such an amazing guy. His name's – um – Amit, twenty-seven, a captain in Intelligence. We sat and talked the whole night. What depth! What a sweetheart! (Huge eyes, shining with yearning.) We sat till dawn and talked, and then we cried together. We couldn't stop crying." He would sigh, sway with emotion and disappear into his room.

The next night I'd meet him in the kitchen.

"How's Amit?" I would ask with interest.

"Who?!" He would open his eyes wide in astonishment, as if I'd said – "Muammar Gadafi."

"Amit, the captain in Intelligence."

"Oh... him," he would stare at the sink with a look of contempt. "Who remembers him."

"I... I'm sorry," I'd mumble.

"*C'est la vie, mon chéri,*" he would open his hands and turn his bald head to the ceiling. "But listen..." his face would suddenly light up with a little secret. "This afternoon I went to the supermarket, and I saw this guy standing next to the cornflakes. We sat for hours next to the dairy products and talked. Just couldn't get up and say goodbye."

At this stage, I began to catch on.

"And afterwards you cried together and couldn't stop, right?" I asked carefully.

"How did you know?" He glanced at me with a misty, faraway look.

"Just did."

That was Shukie. For the last two weeks, ever since we received a clear-cut notice to quit the apartment, he had been busy spying on a soldier who lived across the street.

One night, the soldier left the window to his room open and in the 100-watt light fucked his girlfriend ferociously: first standing up, then on a chair (his uniform was hanging on its back), and lastly from behind. He had something to boast about, that soldier. Shukie groaned in agony, and from then on stayed stuck to the window. He was sure he had found the love of his life. At half past four he would come home from work and immediately cling to the window, in case the naked soldier showed up. More than once I found him training binoculars on the window and fingering his fly.

As for me, in those days I preferred a different, very clean method of getting my modest kicks: letters.

I rented a box at the post office near the Esther Cinema, and every day I went there and with trembling fingers opened the envelopes which arrived from all over the hungry city. Whole worlds were hidden between the lines; hundreds of handsome, sensitive young men, lonely and thirsty for a profound relationship. Some even included measurements and centimeters, to show how profound. Only rarely did I meet the letter writers; the disappointment of those dismal meetings taught me that one vague, healthy fantasy on paper was worth two pathetic meetings between the sheets. In my room, next to my bed, I would punch holes in the letters and add them to a thick file, and at night I would leaf through this file ("The Big Book of Lies," I wrote on it in red letters), until I fell asleep with a relaxed and unhopeful smile on my lips.

But one letter, which had reached the post office box a few days before, had revived an old curiosity in me. The anonymous young man wrote that he was twenty-six years old, that he wrote poetry and renovated old houses, and mainly: that he lacked experience with men. After some hesitation I got in touch with him, and arranged to meet him on the steps of the square, next to the ticket booths of the cinema.

"What are you smiling about," Shukie asked again and looked in astonishment at the little turtles rushing about the screen. His head was so shiny and egg-like that I had to restrain myself with difficulty from smashing a china plate on his skull. He began to pack his clothes into an enormous canvas case which was so old and shabby that it looked as if it was a survivor of the illegal immigrants camp in Cyprus.

"I'm going out, I have a date with someone in a few minutes," I said in a hurry and pulled on my blind-date shirt, the one that emphasizes my shoulders.

"Hang on a minute, I have to tell you about the soldier," Shukie began running after me, "he walks round in his underpants all day and smiles at me, I swear to you," but I was already outside in the street.

It was exactly seven o'clock.

Next to the ticket booths someone was leaning against the wall, and when he saw me he detached himself and a broad smile spread over his face. He was about forty, short, and he was trying so hard to pull in his stomach that it looked as if there was a cat inside there scratching him. I was furious about the cheap, contemptible trick he had played on me, but at the same time I felt very sorry for the lonely man standing opposite me in pointed shoes, smiling a repulsive smile.

"Joshua Jungman," he held out his hand.

"Pleased to meet you, Yaron Zehavi," I introduced myself.

"What a lovely name," he gushed, "why don't we go and sit down?"

We sat down on plastic chairs in a café that smelled strongly of urine.

"Remind me what you said about yourself in your letter," I said sweetly. I can be a real bastard sometimes.

"I'll be twenty nine soon," he looked at me with narrowed eyes and brushed his thinning hair back. (Twenty nine! Three whole years had passed since he sent that letter!) "And I'm inexperienced," he added in a voice full of mystery.

"What will you have to drink," asked the waiter and wiped a glass on his filthy apron.

"Two coffees," my companion made haste to order for both of us. "I'm paying," he announced chivalrously.

He looked at the concrete plaza and the fountain spitting fire and suddenly jumped up in astonishment.

"What is this?" he spluttered. "Where's the round square with the flowers? There was a square here once, wasn't there?"

I couldn't stand it any more. I put a couple of coins on the table and left at a run.

I loathed these people, stretching their legs in plastic chairs and spitting yellow phlegm on the pavement, I loathed the squalid cafés and the ugly square, I loathed the boiling asphalt and the sweat and the lies and the rot rising from the sewer outlets; I ran across Reines Street and the corner of Frischmann, and I didn't calm down until I reached the thicket of shady inner streets with the little gardens and bushy hedges planted all along them to protect their inhabitants from the heat.

There, at the entrance to one of the buildings in Spinoza Street, stood a youth in a crash helmet holding a thick envelope in his hand.

I walked past him; he was wearing dark trousers and the gap between the helmet and the gray shirt exposed a sturdy nape.

I went on walking.

"Excuse me," I heard a young voice behind me. I turned round.

The youth looked at the envelope and the numbers of the buildings alternately, and seemed completely at a loss.

"Do you happen to know where there's a vet living here? I have to deliver this envelope to number 18, but there's no vet here."

He removed his helmet and exposed a sweating brow. His beauty stopped my breath.

I looked at the envelope.

"It says here 18 Yisraelis Street, not Spinoza," I smiled at him. A hunk and a fool, just the way I like them.

"Hoy," the shamed youth hit his thigh with a giant hand.

"You haven't had enough to drink on such a hot day," I scolded him. "You really must come home with me and have something cold to drink."

He laughed in embarrassment, there were little drops of sweat hanging from his ears. What a bastard I am.

"46 Mazeh Street, third floor," I smiled at him and walked away.

At the corner I turned my head for a second; he was still standing there, looking after me.

When I got home Shukie was training his binoculars on the semi-darkness of his soldier's room in the opposite building, trying to squeeze a few bits of male nudity out of the lens to star in his nocturnal fantasies. From time to time he waved at the soldier with his hand.

The evening gathered, darkness climbed to the head of the water tower and was about to swoop down on the low trees and ficus bushes in the yard. The room was in a total mess; clothes hung on the chairs and piles of books were stacked on the floor. On the round wooden table next to the television stood the golden bronze horse I had once bought for a song on a bridge in Budapest from an old gypsy woman with blazing eyes; a strange burnished figurine of a knight mounted on a horse rearing up on its hind legs, holding a long cross studded with faded gemstones in his hand. A covetous antique dealer had once offered me several thousand shekels for it, but I preferred to stand it on the round table and see the dull gleam of the gemstones in the television screen.

At close to ten o'clock there was a knock on the door. Shukie tore himself from his observation point opposite the soldier's window and went to open the door. A squeaky sigh escaped his lips and he leaned unsteadily against the doorjamb, as if he had just seen the Buddha himself.

In the doorway stood the handsome youth in the helmet, his curls falling onto his forehead.

"I came for something cold to drink," he smiled.

"Come in, come in," I stood up weakly to welcome him and waved surreptitiously to Shukie to remove himself from the scene. He looked as if he wanted to slit my throat.

The youth came in and surveyed the room with interest. He put his helmet down on the bed, and then dropped his rucksack onto the floor, sank into the deep armchair, and stretched his legs out in front of him. Two gorgeous arms emerged from the gray T-shirt tightly fitting his strong body, and his knees moved against each other. I would have done anything to sit on his thighs and bury my face in his neck. As a first step I offered him a drink.

"Put in a lot of ice," he looked into my eyes.

"Whatever you say," I stammered and went to the kitchen.

Shukie stood next to the refrigerator and demanded an explanation. The soldier in the window was forgotten. I thrust him aside and returned to the room.

The youth drank two glasses of Pepsi (the ice cubes clinked in the glass like transparent diamonds) and sighed with pleasure. He looked at me in suspense.

"What's your name?" he asked quietly.

"Yossi. And yours?"

"Ehud."

I was silent. I didn't know what to say. I wanted him to stay there forever, in my armchair, and look at me with those soft doe eyes.

"I'm going to the army next week. They're sending me to tryouts for the Paratroops Corps," he said suddenly.

I saw him suffering on a back-breaking night march in the heart of the desert, rivers of sweat pouring down his young back, while I waited for him at the finishing line with a chocolate cake I'd baked with my own hands and wiped tears of emotion from my eyes at the sight of the red beret being pinned to his shoulder. The vision was so vivid that I blushed and sighed.

"I'm hot," complained Ehud. "I'm taking off my shirt."

I needed an ambulance. Intensive care.

He raised his hands to his nape, grabbed hold of the T-shirt, and pulled it over his head.

Shukie suddenly let out a kind of piercing wail. He was watching from somewhere, the sonofabitch.

I closed the door.

Ehud threw his head back until his hair fanned out and hung over the back of the chair. His neck and chest muscles were taut and proud. Tiny beads of sweat broke out of his navel and disappeared under the coarse material of his trousers. I found it increasingly difficult to breathe.

I stood up unthinking and sat down on the edge of the bed. He raised his head.

"Are you all right?" he asked.

"Uhuh."

He rose from the chair and came and sat next to me on the bed.

"I'm tired," he complained in a self-indulgent voice.

"Rest your head," I whispered.

He laid his head on my shoulder.

How can I describe that moment; the soft fall and flutter of his curls on my neck, the hard, precise fit of the bones of his head in the hollow of my shoulder, the sweetness of it, the dense, delicious sweetness percolating from my shoulder, seeping into the most secret tissues of my body and dripping into the invisible recess at the bottom of my back, close to my tailbone, and collecting there until it erupted in ever widening rings.

We sat like that for a few minutes. I was afraid to move, in case his head dropped off me and the spell was broken. I wanted to raise my hand and touch the tangle of his hair, but he opened his eyes and stretched slightly, as if he had returned from a distant journey.

"I have to go," he glanced at his watch.

"A little longer," I begged humbly.

He looked at me intently. His arms were holding the side of the bed so that a fine net of muscles stood out clearly. His knees played one against the other. A little flame danced behind the question in his eyes.

"Tomorrow," he said carefully, "I finish work at ten. I can come then, if you like."

"Sure," I swallowed my saliva.

He stood up and straightened out the bulge in his trousers. Then he hoisted his rucksack onto his shoulder.

I wrote my phone number on a slip of paper and pushed it into his hand. He stood there a moment longer, smiled at me strangely and left.

As soon as the door slammed Shukie's egghead popped out from behind the closet in the hall. He leaned weakly against the door and panted in an agony of desire.

"What's his name, where did you find him," he ran round me in circles and wouldn't let me be, "and what did he say about me, he must have said something about me, he was looking at me all the time."

But I didn't answer him. I was floating deep inside a cloud of cotton that Ehud had left behind him. Like a scene from a movie screened over and over again, I saw him smile and slam the door and smile again and slam the door, until the sweet heaviness overcame me and I shut my eyes and sat down in the kitchen and buried my face in my hands and said Ehud, Ehud.

Shukie turned up his nose in offended dignity and returned to his packing. He came and went between the rooms, opening and shutting suitcases with a bang and cursing in a low but distinct voice. From time to time he whispered, "Fabulous, fab-u-lous." After some time I went and stretched out in the armchair in my room, switched on the television and put my feet on the footstool. I was full of a great serenity.

On one of the channels they were showing pictures of the Andes, low clouds and wrinkled Indians wrapped in thick woolen coats. I thought about Ehud. Something in the screen looked strange to me, and I didn't know what it was. I switched to another channel; a group of women were sitting and talking about some George who hadn't come home, and there too I couldn't shake off the feeling that there was something missing. I looked hard: the little red lights! I couldn't see the gleam of the stones in the bronze figurine reflected on the screen!

I jumped up in alarm and looked around. The figurine of the knight riding the horse was nowhere to be seen. A bitter smile froze on my lips; now everything was clear. Ehud, that beautiful boy (if that was really his name), had only come here to make a buck at the end of the day's work. I remembered the strange way he had looked at me then too, on the pavement of Spinoza Street. I thought of all the stories about men who had been ripped off by beautiful, greedy rent boys – no doubt about it, he had immediately picked up with his avaricious senses the cry of loneliness engraved on the forehead of the man standing opposite him in the street, and hatched his schemes in his nasty little mind. And when I went out to the kitchen to get him something cold to drink and fantasize about his naked body, he simply stretched out his hand and buried the antique Hungarian knight in his rucksack, which he had thrown down next to the bed on purpose. Fool, fool, I couldn't stop hating myself, pathetic, foolish queer that I was.

All next day I went about in a black mood. I didn't know what hurt more: the burning insult, the old recognition – which had now received additional confirmation – that there was no more hope of finding love, or the loss of the precious figurine.

Shukie danced attendance on me with his shining bald dome, but I refused to talk to anyone. I didn't go to the post office either, to read the letters that had no doubt accumulated in my box like a pile of wormy muck.

Just before half past nine the phone rang. When it didn't stop ringing I picked up the receiver apathetically.

A young voice was on the line.

"It's me, Ehud," said the voice and trembled.

The sweetness drove me out of my mind. I couldn't afford to lose my cool.

"If you're Ehud, I'm Cleopatra," I said sarcastically.

"What?" the little shit tried to say something.

"If you don't return what you stole from me I'll go to the police!" I barked at him with the hatred that had been building up in me all day.

"Listen..." he croaked and fell silent. I saw his curls burning and writhing like snakes on his bare back.

"Murderer!" I yelled into the receiver at the top of my voice.

I myself was surprised by the voice that came out of my mouth. I'd only heard a voice like it once before, many years ago, when our Rumanian neighbor Fritzi found out that that her husband was cheating on her with her younger sister.

He breathed hard, as if he was waiting for the words to come, and then he hung up.

I felt a small measure of relief. I filled the tub with hot water and bubble bath and lay down in it, trying to banish the remnants of his dreamy figure from my mind. I remembered the mother turtle who laid her eggs every year in the warm sand, and the waves came and swept crowds of tiny turtles into the vast expanses of the sea. Maybe one day the sea would cast up a little surprise for me too.

There were two days left before we had to leave the apartment, and the dreary work of packing was proceeding at a leisurely pace.

At noon the agent climbed up to the third floor (his shirt was sticking to his back with the heat). He lit a cigarette and dropped the ash on the floor. Two bespectacled girls trailed behind him.

"But where's the view of the sea?" one of them asked.

Shukie and I collected the suitcases and parcels in a shapeless heap on the porch, a pile of clothes and books and broken dreams, and then we sat on the porch and drank cold juice.

"I put all kinds of important things in here," said Shukie, pulling a heavy-duty plastic bag out of the pile, "so they wouldn't get lost."

"What do you mean," I frowned.

"Here, look," he opened the bag calmly, pulling the sides apart, "the china vase from the kitchen, the pen collection, that little statue you had next to the television." Among the objects the proud head of the knight poked out and the dull tip of the cross, studded with old, reddish stones.

Shukie poured us each another glass of juice, and smiled faintly at the toes of his shoes. His bald head shone brilliantly in the sun.

Orly Castel-Bloom

Heathcliff

Translated by Dalya Bilu

It was war time. The soldiers of the regular army and the reserves weren't lying on a bed of roses. Once in a while, far from frequently, the fighting forces were given one or two days' leave. The leaves were short. Too short. The period of which we are speaking was a little after the middle of the war. Even though it was still going on, the public mood was one of weariness and saturation, as if it were already over. Loud voices began to be raised against it, and on the opposite side – dozens of reasons in favor of it. There were also people who weren't in the least bit interested in the war, to such an extent that they didn't really know who was winning and who was losing. Their hearts were set on different things entirely.

When Smadar came out of the movie theater it was still light. The flush on her face mingled with the red rays of the sun which were about to vanish at any minute behind an ugly office block. In her mind one word rampaged: Heathcliff. She was fourteen years old – so it was no wonder and even rather self-evident.

Her hands were wet with the tears she had quickly wiped away as she climbed the stairs to the exit, and they wet her ticket. She threw it away, damp and disintegrating, wiped away another tear, and crossed the road.

The spacious square was deserted. She sat down on the steps in front of the building, and lit a cigarette, which was hidden in the depths of her cloth purse.

Three motorcyclists a year older than she was rode past her. One of them noticed the girl smoking and whistled to his friends to stop. Smadar saw him and managed to wipe away another agitated tear.

He got off the bike.

"Want to come for a spin?" he asked.

The girl didn't answer.

"Want to come for a spin?" he asked again, and was not answered.

"Don't you understand Hebrew?" He was chewing gum.

Smadar went on inhaling in silence.

"Look, she's trembling," he crowed.

The second motorcylist kicked the gas pedal and rode around in the square in big circles.

The third smiled and also got off his bike.

"What's your story, Shula?" he said. "You don't want to come for a spin, so say so. You're not the first and you won't be the last."

"I don't want to," she said and stood up. From a distance she didn't look fourteen. She could easily have been eighteen.

The gum-chewer was annoyed. He approached her, removed the cigarette from her mouth and took a puff. The smile of the smiler froze. Smadar stretched her neck and looked at the two boys with contempt. She moved away and disappeared behind the concrete pillars.

"What have you done, Avner?" the smiler asked his friend angrily.

"I can't stand types like that. Not even pretty and they think they're Lady Di."

The smiler started his bike and joined their friend who was already deep in conversation with another young girl who had crossed his path. Avner raced after him, in order to prove to himself for the hundredth time that his horsepower was equal to that of his friend.

Smadar trailed along Ibn Gvirol Street. The taste of the cigarette was bitter. She looked around to make sure that nobody could see her and spat a big gob onto the pavement. When she raised her eyes, she turned red. Two eyes were watching her. They were Heathcliff's eyes. Green, slightly slanting and focused on her. She examined his look and consoled herself with the thought that spitting, after all, was a natural function, and Heathcliff's wild nature would not reject her because of it.

The penetrating look he had given her at first changed to a kind of smile. The green velvet coat he was wearing suited him. She undid the knot in her hair and let it fall loose. She was light, and Heathcliff, if he had wanted to, could have picked her up in one hand and galloped silently down the street with her.

A bus full of Arab workers stopped at the traffic lights near to her. Heathcliff and his horse disappeared in the direction of the top of the peak. There Heathcliff would go on shouting, and only the echoes of his shout would reach her straining ears. The Arab workers were exhausted and dozing. They had just finished an exhausting day's work and were on their way to a town in the south. Smadar didn't take the trouble to look into their faces. An Arab sitting in the middle of the bus whipped out a pistol, but she ignored him. Even when he aimed it at her and was about to shoot her, she didn't walk any faster. For ages she had wanted to be the victim of a terrorist attack. The traffic light changed and the bus drove off.

Smadar was left exposed, standing and looking upwards. The sky was full of stars, but the light was gray daylight. She shifted her gaze down a little and looked at the edges of the green hills, ignoring the antennas and electricity poles on the way. She couldn't see Heathcliff. His shout too was swallowed up in the noise of the traffic. The Arab workers were to blame for his flight. He seemed more noble to her. She went on walking, at a snail's pace, for a few more steps and stopped next to a big, thick tree.

In the evening there are no birds awake. They're all sleeping in the trees, camouflaged from human eyes, like guerilla fighters. Smadar peered into the depths of the tree. It was all black, and she could hardly make out the leaves. She tried to shake it to watch how the birds fly out, but the tree was hard and strong and its trunk was thicker than she was.

There should have been another cigarette in her purse. On her unpleasant journey through it she encountered lumps of sticky candies, and crumbs of antibiotic pills from her last bout of flu. From time to time she removed her hand from the purse and rubbed it against her trousers, or perhaps her long gray skirt.

For the third and last time, she promised herself, she dug her hand into the purse, and encountered a crumpled cigarette stuck to one of the candies. Gradually she drew the cigarette and the candy stuck to it up from the bottom of the purse. The purse was long and narrow and she had to move with great caution in order to prevent the many useless objects in it, among them a three-day-old cheese and olive sandwich, chewed-up pencils, a sharpener, and a lipstick cover, from tearing the delicate cigarette paper.

When she succeeded in removing the two objects from the purse, she began gently trying to separate them. This work demanded nimble fingers, but even the trembling hands of a junkie would have succeeded better than her two left hands. The cigarette split open, and the candy stuck to her hand. Smadar tried to remove it by shaking her hand, but it refused to drop off. In the end she got rid of it by rubbing her hand against a nearby notice board, and sat down despairingly on a yellow bench beside it. The feeling of hunger which had begun during the movie grew more acute, and she bit into the cheese sandwich. Her teeth encountered the olive pits which had been carelessly incorporated in the sandwich, and she spat them out into her palm.

Heathcliff dismounted his horse and sat down beside her. He stroked her face, and she dropped the olive pits. She rested her head against his chest and he stroked her tousled hair. Then she was afraid he would kiss her, because she had never kissed a man before. But Heathcliff only kissed her on her burning cheek and pushed her fringe out of the way so that he could see her eyes.

He didn't say a word, and Smadar longed to say to him in English: I love you, but she didn't want her foreign accent to betray her. It would be better too, she thought, if Heathcliff didn't know everything about her. She didn't know that Heathcliff knew and saw everything, and was nourished by her love for him like the earth is nourished by the rain falling on it.

The smell of rain-drenched earth rose in her nostrils. Perhaps it came from Heathcliff. He was sunk in thought, gazing at the horizon. Smadar dared to pass her fingers over his sharp profile, and he didn't move. Her nose stuck out too much, and she hoped he wouldn't touch it. Heathcliff turned his face to her and said nothing. There was a bond beyond words between them. and she didn't even dare to smile at him. He stood up and disappeared behind the green hills.

A little over a hundred meters separated Smadar from her parents' home, but she preferred to go on walking until she reached the green hills on the other bank of the river, which formed the northern border of the town.

She wanted it to be daylight so she could run and roll on the beautiful green grass. But the place was dark and frightening, and at any minute, if they felt like it, devils, witches and escaped murderers could emerge from the trees. The water of the river was black, and even the stars didn't dare to be reflected in it.

A stray dog slunk up and sniffed at her. How could she tell if the soul of this dog wasn't an imprisoned soul whose one desire was to get out and take its revenge?

The dog went on sniffing her. She threw a stick as far as she could and the dog ran after it and brought it back clenched between its teeth. It lay down next to her and yawned. Its breath was foul. It fell asleep.

The wind moved the branches of the trees. Smadar did not yield to her fear. She lay down on the damp lawn and rolled to and fro on it. The dog woke up. Smadar laid her head on her purse and encountered its painful corners.

She stood up and walked towards the only tree on the green bank.

At half past eight by her watch she called the place: Yorkshire.

She said to herself: "I don't owe anyone a thing. Not even the stupid bird that changes its position in the middle of the night. Nor the wolves that could come out of the ground and eat me up. I'm free. I belong to Heathcliff."

She lay on the grass and closed her eyes. She didn't want to open them, but the touch of a man's hand on her throat forced her to do so.

It was Heathcliff's hand. She murmured his name and he didn't reply. She wanted to ask him where he had been for the past hour, but he lay down on top of her and opened the buttons of her shirt. After a long kiss, Heathcliff calmed down and fell asleep. His breathing grew slower and slower. Her breathing was heavy. She lay on the lawns of Yorkshire naked as the day she was born, burning with shame. She didn't dare to move or ask him to move, even though his weight oppressed her. She looked for his horse, but she couldn't find it, and she assumed that it had gone to gallop alone in the open spaces. The dog looked at her yearningly, wanting to be petted. Heathcliff s body weighed heavily on her. There was pressure on her lungs. She shook him slightly, and he woke up. While he gently wiped away the bits of grass that were stuck to her brow, Smadar noticed that his coat was green, but not velvet as she had thought at first.

Heathcliff said to her: "I have to go," and Smadar knew that she would not see him for a long time. She had no idea how to stop him and make him stay. He stooped as he walked and buttoned his trousers. The dog followed him with its tail between its legs. She asked herself if she was pregnant or not. A melancholy expression spread over her young face.

Gail Hareven

Man in a Hat

Translated by Chaya Galai

This morning I killed a man. Or perhaps it wasn't a man, perhaps it was something else. He was wearing a suit. He had an Austrian hat with a feather. He wasn't tall. But for weeks he endangered my son's life.

Again and again, almost every time we spoke on the phone, I told my husband about it. Artzi won't deny it. But he said I should stop being funny. He said that if this man was harassing me, I should open my mouth and tell him so. Or perhaps it would be altogether better if I took Uri to kindergarten by a different route, why did we have to go along the boulevard? How can I? – I asked my husband – How can I take another route with the stroller, when there are cars parked on all the sidewalks, and every few minutes I have to step off the curb with Uri? My husband said that he trusted me to find a solution. I was young when we were married, and Artzi would like to feel that I'm growing up and becoming independent. Go to the police. Talk to the man. If the worst comes to the worst, you can murder him. That's what he said.

Artzi is tall, a good man. Once, for two months, I was the supply clerk in his brigade. Now there's another clerk there.

I killed a man this morning. And this evening I bathed Uri, put him in our bed, and lay down beside him till he fell asleep. Only then did I switch on the TV set, so that I missed the first half of the newscast, and later on not a word was said about it. I think that lots of people die without our being told anything at all. Sometimes they die in groups, and then it's really hard to mention all of them, and sometimes it's hard to know when exactly some of them died, because some people take a long time to die. The man in a hat – it seems to me – died quickly. Maybe he wasn't important enough to be mentioned. Anyway, while I was picking up the toys in the living room, they only talked about other people, and I'm quite sure of that, because I didn't leave the room till the newscast was over, even though I'd finished collecting the toys.

Artzi is a clever man. He's used to examining problems from several sides, but I think he hadn't really thought it through when he advised me to tell the man in a hat to stop endangering our son's life. Artzi loves Uri the way a father is supposed to. That's why I'll never ever remind him of what he asked me to do about the pregnancy, and I myself try to forget it, because nothing good can come of memories like that, and if you let them race about inside your head they could infect the child. Even if you don't say a word about them, they could be dangerous for him, because it's just that kind of thin memories, without words, that transmit easily, and that's the kind you have to be very careful of.

As far as my husband's feelings are concerned, I have absolutely no doubts, but even a man who's used to seeing things from above, over a wide range, can't always see everything. Artzi didn't see the stick that man had in his hand, and seeing isn't like hearing. Seeing is another thing. However many times I repeated: an Austrian hat, waving a stick about very, very dangerously, my husband, who's preoccupied by a great many things, didn't grasp it, and what's more, the telephone made it hard for me to deliver the message: every morning, on our way to kindergarten, this man in a hat comes towards us. Always at the same place along the boulevard. He has an old man's walking stick, and he sketches rapid circles with it so that it whistles through the air, and he marches along as if to the sound of an orchestra. Sometimes he throws it right up, and stretches his arm up high to catch it. Catches it and laughs. He does it over Uri's head, and the heads of other babies and children, because at that time of day there are lots of little children on the boulevard.

"Man in a hat" is a bad man. If he weren't so bad, the mothers might talk to him and ask him to stop, but the fact is that not one of them has the courage, and we just try to keep to one side, but still that stick whistles over our children. Some mothers, out of sheer fear, make an effort to smile into his laughter because maybe the smile will make him look them in the eye, and perhaps the look will prevent. Or it could be simply that they're hoping that because they're smiling, the children won't understand.

Children understand a lot. Uri is three, and I never switch on the news before he falls asleep, and even when he's sleeping, I keep the volume down low, in case he hears it in his sleep.

The man in the Austrian hat had a red face and a ruddy, fleshy nose like a drinker's, but I didn't smell any alcohol. A drunk might have been less dangerous. When I realized that my fear was only growing from day to day, I knew I had to act before it took me over completely. And then, last night, I heard the great doors again, and my body was flooded with such panic, and my heart pounded so hard, that I had to put my hand under Uri's cheek so that he wouldn't hear what was going on above and beneath him. In his sleep, Uri moved the hand away, mumbled something, and put his head back on my breast. The great doors are up there. All kinds of doors. Wooden gates. Hinged iron gratings. Sliding doors, as vast as a continent. An ear which is used to listening can distinguish between them. At special times you can hear the opening and closing, like the sound of icebergs cracking. The people who are being brought in are walking there. You can't see them. Just hear. Walking, walking, walking. Sometimes it's boots, sometimes the rustle of naked feet, a great rustling. And the worst of all is when all the kinds of marching mingle together.

This time it didn't last long, the way it does sometimes when more and more and more of them are moving, and it wasn't fast either, but when the doors closed, I knew that in the morning I was going to act.

Life and death always come suddenly. My mother was forty-six when I was born, and with everything that had happened to her, who would have thought that she was capable of giving birth. Uri also came as a surprise, and I also didn't think I could give birth, not yet, I

wasn't nineteen yet, my periods weren't even regular. Now Artzi
wants another child, if that's the way it is let's be a regular family, but
I haven't agreed yet. My husband sees our son only once a week,
when he breezes in from up north, and he doesn't understand how
much Uri depends on me. Artzi has a brother and sister. His mother,
brother and sister sometimes come visiting, to inspect me and to play
with Uri, but Uri just clings to me, and doesn't want to play. Artzi's
mother and sister suggest all kinds of plans: I should start studying, go
out to work, but how can I when kindergarten is only till twelve thirty
and then I have to come home and put him down to sleep, and apart
from me nobody can put Uri to sleep? "Let her be," my brother-in-law
says to his sister, "so what if she's not a career woman. Can't you see
that she herself is still a child?" and he places a hand on my shoulder.
They would never believe that I'm capable of going after the man with
the stick.

Things happen suddenly. If something happens to me in the night, if
Uri wakes up and I can't answer him... the door is locked, and he
couldn't open it on his own, the kindergarten teacher wouldn't
telephone for a few days, Artzi can't call me every morning, even
though I asked him to, it just isn't possible for him and that's a fact,
and you have to live with facts. Uri already knows how to take a cup
of water, and that's a change from the way it used to be, because a
baby could dehydrate in a few hours. He always asks me to pour it,
but in a crisis even little children can be wonderfully resourceful. The
refrigerator is closed tight, so he can't open it yet, but to drag a chair
to the sink and turn on the faucet, that he can do already. I leave his
cup on the kitchen counter every evening. I know the neighbors won't
hear him, that is, even if they hear a child crying and screaming, they
won't realize that they ought to break down the door instantly. They'll
think it's a baby crying and not a small child. They'll think it's regular
crying, not a catastrophe. People aren't sensitive about things like that,
not at all sensitive, and there's nobody to explain and teach. But all
the same, now that Uri's older, I have this kind of confidence that in
the end people will come and carry him out, there are always pictures

like that on the news, carrying them out, because often they do get them out in the end. In any case, there's no reason to worry, and it's not a good idea to worry. Suddenly-at-home-at-night, that's something that almost never happens to young women, and it's well known that it has nothing to do with palpitations, that there are different reasons altogether for those. And the sound of the great doors shouldn't terrify me. Many people are taken there, but many doesn't necessary mean us.

From a wider point of view, you understand that worries change, and then you don't stray back to old worries, you focus on what's important. On being properly prepared. That's what they ought to teach the mothers at the mother and baby clinic, I think. For example, when they explained how to start the babies on solid food and we were all happy, because there'll always be something to eat, I thought that I could chew it for him without swallowing it, that is, I wanted to believe I could and I concentrated hard on that. But then the book shelf in our house fell down, and Artzi had to come home, because I just couldn't stop crying, and it was only because I wasn't prepared and I wasn't concentrating on the right thing. My mother-in-law was whispering to my husband in the corner, and I knew what she was saying. Even though at the beginning she was on my side and Uri's, now, because of my mother, she's always afraid that there's something about our family. An illness, I mean. My mother's not sick the way she thinks, and what happened to her a woman like my mother-in-law could never understand, and even my husband can't understand, because I'm the only one who understands it, and that's something rare and very precious that it's almost impossible to explain. When I was born, my mother was so happy about me that she immediately became younger, and it was only because she was so sad because her baby didn't have a young mother. And a miracle happened to her, and it wasn't just a miracle for the short term, it was continuous, and because of that miracle, the more I grew, the younger she became. For my sake she gave up the years she already had and all the years of memories, at first it was a great effort, but afterwards, when she'd acquired the skill, she did it without even trying, and without taking notice of the way people laughed. When you love, nothing else matters. You even wear a short dress, braid your hair, wear buckled patent leather shoes, and block your ears so as not to hear what's going on up there... that's how it was till I got to be eight years old and so did she, and there, when we finally met, she stopped.

It's a tragedy that old people who are children, when they start getting younger and younger, don't have the strength to climb back up the way real children do, and they can't grow any more. So my mother, just because she loved me, stayed eight years old, while I went on growing till I became like a mother. And at my wedding, even under the canopy, I held her hand. Her head reached up to my shoulder, and she was wearing a white dress just like mine, except that in my case you could see my belly, and I couldn't taste the layered cake because I was nauseous. One day my mother will die, no question about it. And she'll be eight years old then.

Real children can run fast. Uri can run already, and he can march for miles. I read in the paper once that a child of his age does about twenty kilometers a day by running around. When I close my fingers around the calf of his leg, I can feel the muscles. He laughs and pushes me, and I gather him close to me and rub my cheek against the softest cheek in the world, and guard him fiercely but just a little, till he wriggles and slips out of my arms, and then I let him go, because you have to. If necessary, even now, I could still carry him in my arms. He weighs thirteen kilos. Artzi's troops carry much more weight on their marches, without dropping it. You can always rip up one of your garments to make a sling. But it's almost impossible to carry two by yourself.

"Man in a hat" didn't run, he just went on walking-walking fast, an unnatural kind of walk, a clownish walk not like a human being. I prepared everything the night before. I wrapped the hammer in my yellow sweater and put it in the bag with the diapers and the change of clothes. On second thoughts I realized that because of the weight, the bag might tear when it was hanging from the stroller handle, and to make quite sure, I put the white supermarket bag inside a thick nylon shoe bag.

At twenty-five to eight, Uri was dressed and ready, and at five to eight we were already waiting for Yaira at the kindergarten gate. It wasn't raining, and that was convenient for me, because I thought that an umbrella would only make things more difficult for me, and if I left it at the kindergarten, Yaira might run after me to hand it over.

We didn't meet the man in a hat, of course. His time is eight twenty.

And now, my husband is going to want to know why I couldn't get there that early every day, and avoid meeting the bad man. I have several answers to that. First of all, Uri falls asleep late and so he wakes up late, and I don't think it's right to wake him. At his age he needs his hours of sleep in order to grow and not be a midget. As it is, in the middle of the night I sometimes see him opening his eyes. Then why, Artzi will ask, why don't you go to kindergarten later? Well, Artzi, that's because all the children arrive by eight thirty at the latest, and if someone arrives later, Yaira makes a comment to the mother, and that's not pleasant for the child either. But even without Yaira's comments, Artzi, isn't it important for Uri to be like everyone else?

I remember it all precisely. By five past eight I was sitting in the *borekas* café. I bought hot chocolate from the machine and paid on the spot, so that I could sit down and get up without delay. At eight twenty I threw the styrofoam cup into the trash, and with long steps I started to follow the man. They say that some criminals are brilliant, I don't know about that, but anyway this criminal wasn't brilliant at all.

He didn't turn round even once to look at me, and no intuition told him he was being followed. He wasn't tall, not a bit tall. He was wearing a gray suit, his body was crammed into it like a pile of rags, and the stick was whistling all over the place.

A grandmother who was pushing a buggy tried to say something to him, but he moved away fast so she was left grumbling to herself above the baby, and his arm, suspended in the air as if the fingers had been amputated, his arm was already behind her. The grandmother was wearing a lot of lipstick, her hair was tinted an attractive shade of gray, and she had an attractive gray raincoat. She looked like an experienced woman, who wouldn't easily lose her head. I almost lingered to tell her not to be scared. If not for the baby, I might even have suggested that she join me. Some other morning I may approach her, and she'll explain that she left a pot simmering on the stove, and invite me to come home with her. Seated at the formica-topped table in the kitchen, we can consult one another about the kindergarten, because she may have an older grandchild who's already in kindergarten. And towards lunchtime we'll open a window and I'll help her with the frying, because I'm always ready to eat meatballs whenever they're offered to me, and I don't care what kind. There are all sorts of meatballs: fried with lots of breadcrumbs, cooked in spicy tomato sauce, tiny little soup meatballs... each woman's meatballs are a little different, even if they use the same recipe. I love the taste of other people's meatballs. Even in the army, where they added a mass of breadcrumbs, I loved them. In my husband's family, which is also mine, they never fry them. Except for Chinese, and they don't call that fried, just stir-fry.

"Man in a hat" walked along the boulevard till he came to the sea end, and then he turned right, into a street whose name I don't know and didn't have time to read on the street sign. It wasn't difficult to follow him. It was simple. And as I followed him, with the bag in my hand, I suddenly understood Artzi's quietness, where it comes from. When you're taking action, your heart is quiet. And as for me, for too long I waited and waited without taking action. And it's such a relief to get up and act. I never knew what a relief it was. I had the clarity of a woman who, for the first time, goes to the supermarket with a shopping list, which makes everything clear, and she can't understand how she could ever have done her shopping without it.

"Man in a hat" turned into an apartment house, a quite ordinary one, looking like any other building. Luckily for me, there were no buzzers there, so that there was no problem about following him. There was no difficulty. Almost.

Only when I followed him up the stairs did he turn and look at me. I saw a face like a revolting pink sponge. Eyes like marbles, a walking stick and a hat, and the feather made me as nauseous as if it had been shoved down my throat. For only a second he looked at me, but he said nothing. My hand was already inside the bag, and I didn't even hate him any more. It was just something that needed to be done, and not everything that has to be done is pleasant.

Afterwards there was the thwack of the hammer. I waited till he took out his key and stuck it in the lock. I'd fitted the pace of climbing the stairs to that. And I don't know if he screamed or if I did. I only remember the thwack of the hammer, the cracking sound sinking through the hat and a disgusting soft stuff. Like treading on a cockroach.

Then came the hard moment, because when he was right down there beneath me, I thought that I ought to lift up the tool again, and I couldn't do it. The lifting, that I could do, but not that cracking again, and the feel of the hat even through the tool.

He fell anyway. The hat stayed on his head and covered his face.

Why wasn't there an item about it on the news? Maybe he wasn't from here. Maybe after I went, the bodily parts fizzed and evaporated, and it's a good thing I didn't hear the tsssssssss... because I would surely have vomited. Perhaps all they found was an empty rag of skin, and nobody understood what it was, and a hat with a feather lying upside down. Cats dragged what was left behind the garbage cans. Better not to think.

And perhaps he really was a man. So fragile.

I hug my Uri, put my hand on his head and remember the feel of the open skull of a baby. The head only closes up after a year. And his heartbeats are still rapid and his chest is still soft.

I can't hear the doors tonight. Doors moving from their place very slowly, like icebergs floating over the continent. Sometimes they float for years over one continent so that another one is spared.

Mothers will always prefer their own child over anyone else. Even if they put a knife in my hand and said: this man, or else the child will scream, no mother would drop the knife on the concrete floor.

Bad man was fragile. Now I know it, and there's no reason to be afraid. I never asked Artzi if he'd killed a man close up. You can learn a great deal close up. If I'd been forced to look into his eyes, if it wasn't for the hat, maybe I wouldn't have summoned up the courage. And maybe I would. Mothers find the courage. And perhaps Artzi, who is an officer, looks them in the eye.

When he calls, I'll ask him, and I'll probably try to tell him all about it.

It's just that suddenly I think Artzi may not believe me, and then I'll be sad.

Judith Katzir

Schlafstunde[1]

Translated by Barbara Harshav

Once, when summer vacation stretched over the whole summer and tasted of sand and smelled of grapes and a redhead sun daubed freckles on your face and, after Sukkot, the wind whistled into a gang of clouds and we galloped home through the ravine in a thunderstorm and the rain stabbed your tongue with mint and pine and the neighborhood dogs set up a racket, barking like uncles coughing at intermission in a winter concert, and suddenly spring attacked with cats shrieking and the lemon trees blossoming and again came a *khamsin* and the air stood still in the bus but we got up only for Mrs. Bella Blum from the post office, a dangerous-child-snatcher who comes to us in bed at night with the wild gray hair of a dangerous-child-snatcher and narrow glasses on the tip of the sharp-as-a-red-pencil nose of a dangerous-child-snatcher and who smiles with the cunning flattery of a dangerous-child-snatcher and pokes dry-ice fingers into our faces, and only if we gave her all the triangular stamps could we somehow be saved or if we prayed to God, who disguised himself as a clown in the Hungarian circus and rocked, balancing himself on the tightrope under the blue canvas of the tent, in high-heeled shoes and wide red-and-white checked pants and then disguised himself as an elephant, turned his wrinkled behind to us and went off to eat supper.

Once, when the world was all golden through the sparkling Carrera

---

1. German: literally, an hour of rest; siesta

vase in the living room on the credenza, which maybe vanished with all the other furniture as soon as we left the room and we peeked through the keyhole to see if it was still there but maybe it saw us peeking and rushed back and a horrible gang of thieves was hiding out in the garage under the supermarket and only Emil and you could solve the mystery because obviously you were going to be an important detective they'd write books about and I'd be your assistant and we experimented with invisible ink made of onion skins and we heated the note in the candle so the writing would emerge and then we trained ourselves to swallow it so it wouldn't fall into enemy hands and we did other training exercises, in self-defense and in not-revealing-secrets even if they torture you and tie you to a bed and put burning matches under your toenails, and we mixed up poison from dirt and leaves and crushed shells and we kept it in yogurt jars and we drew a skull and crossbones on them and hid them with all our other treasures.

When the summer vacation stretched over the whole summer and the world was all gold and everything was possible and everything was about to happen, and Uncle Alfred was still alive and came for afternoon tea and Grandfather and Grandmother went to rest between two and four and left us endless time, we snuck up the creaky wooden steps behind the house to our little room in the attic which was headquarters, and we stood at the window where you could view the whole sea beyond the cemetery and you touched my face with your fingertips and said you loved me.

Now we're gathered here, like sad family members at a departure in an airport, around the departures board at the entrance, where somebody's written in white chalk, two zero zero, Aaron Green, funeral, and I look at the woman sitting on the stone bench next to you, a round straw hat shading her eyes and ripening her mouth to a grape and the sun polishes two knives of light along her tanned shins and then I go up to the two of you, take off my sunglasses and say quietly, Hello, and you stand up hastily, Let me introduce you, this is my wife. My cousin. I discern the sparkle of the ring and the white teeth among the shadows and touch her soft hand with long long fingers and say again, Hello. And the undertakers, busy at work like angels in their white shirtsleeves, bearded faces, sweaty, carrying on a stretcher the shriveled body under the dark dusty cloth, the head almost touching the fat black behind of the gravedigger, the legs dangling in front of the open fly of the second one, and a frosty wind blowing inside me, as then, and I seek the memory in your eyes but you lower them to her, take hold of her arm and help her up and my spy's eyes freeze on her rounded belly in the flowered dress and see inside her all your children you buried behind the house, in the grove, in the summer vacation between seventh and eighth grade, when on the first morning, as every year, Grandfather came to pick me up from home in his old black car, with Misha, the office chauffeur, who dressed himself up in my honor in a white visor cap and a huge smile with a gold tooth. Misha put my red suitcase in the trunk and opened the back door for me with a bow and a wink and we went to pick you up from the railroad station near the port. On the way, I stuck my head between him and Grandfather and asked him to tell me again how he played for the king of Yugoslavia and Misha sighed and said, That was a long time ago, but I remember it as if it was yesterday. I was a child then, maybe nine, maybe ten, and I played the trumpet better than anybody in the whole school and one day they brought me a blue suit with gold buttons and a tie and stockings up to my knees and a cap with a visor and said, Get dressed, and they put me next to a flag and said, Play, and I played so beautiful and strong and King Pavel came in and the flag rose to the top of the pole and the trumpet sparkled like that in the sun and so did the gold buttons, who would have believed a little Jewish boy like that playing trumpet for the king and he came to me and stroked my head and asked, What's your name, and I told him, Misha, and Mama was standing there and crying so they had to hold her up and Papa said to her, Now I'm happy we have him, because at first he didn't want me at all, they went to Austria just for a vacation and when they came back Mama said, I'm pregnant, and Papa told her, Five is enough, get an abortion, but Mama was very stubborn, like Albert Einstein's mother, his father didn't want him either, and then he was terrible in school and the teachers called the father and the father said to him, Albert, you're seventeen years old now, not a child, what will become of you, but when he was twenty-six he met Lenin and Churchill and showed them the theory of relativity and there were a lot of discussions, and he became famous all over the world, so when I hear about abortions I say, Who knows what can come out of that child, why kill a human being. Misha sighed again and lit a cigarette. In the distance you could already see the big clock over the railroad station. At five to nine we arrived. Grandfather and I went down to the platform and Misha waited in the car. Two porters in gray caps were leaning on their rusty carts, looking at one another from time to time with half-closed eyes and smoking stinky cigarettes from yellow packs with a picture of black horses. I was so excited I had to pee and I hopped around from one foot to the other. At nine o'clock on the dot we heard a long happy whistle of the locomotive pulling five rumbling cars. The porters woke up, stomped on their cigarettes with huge shoes and started running back and forth along the platform shouting, Suitcases, suitcases. Terrified, I looked for your face among the hundreds of faces, crushed and scared, against the glass of the windows. Then the doors opened with a hiss and you came down, the very first one, wearing the short jeans all the kids had and a green shirt with emblems on the pockets that only a few had and a checked detective hat they had brought you from England and no other kid had, and you stood there like that next to your father's black suitcase, and looked around with eyes scrunched up like two green slits under your disheveled fair curls, and once again I felt the pain between my throat and my stomach that clutched my breath every time I saw you and even when I thought about you, and I shouted, Here Uli, here Uli, and I ran to you, and then you saw me and smiled and we embraced, and Grandfather came too, and tapped you on the shoulder and said, How you've grown, Saul, and he didn't take your suitcase because you were already thirteen and a half and stronger than he, and you put it in the trunk, next to my red one. And Misha took us to Grandfather's office on Herzl Street, whose walls were covered with big shiny pictures with lots of blue, pictures of beautiful places in Israel, the Sea of Galilee and the Dead Sea and Rosh Ha-Nikra and Eilat, where there were rest homes, and the government paid him to send Holocaust survivors there, and I always imagined how they arrived there by train, wearing funny coats and hats with sad yellow faces underneath them as in the pictures they showed us in school on Holocaust-and-Heroism Day, and they line up there in a long row with all their suitcases tied with rope, and everybody enters in a line and takes off his coat and hat and gets a bright-colored swimsuit and an orange cap, and they sit in loungers in the sun and swim in the sea and eat a lot and convalesce and after a week grow fat and tanned and smiling like the people in the advertisements and then they're sent home because new survivors came on the train and are already waiting in line. Until once, on Saturday, we went with Grandfather and Grandmother and Misha to visit one of those rest homes, called Rosh Ha-Nikra Recreation Village, and there was no line of survivors at the entrance, and there was no way to know who was a Holocaust survivor and who was just a normal person because they all had fat, droopy potbellies and nobody looked especially sad, they were all swimming in the pool and gobbling sandwiches and guzzling juice and talking loud and playing bingo. So we made up a system to check who was a real survivor, but I didn't have the courage, I just watched from a distance as you passed among the loungers on the lawn next to the pool and whispered into everybody's ear, Hitler, and I saw that most of the people didn't do anything, just opened their eyes wide in a strange kind of look, as if they were waking up from some dream and hadn't had time yet to remember where they were and they closed their eyes right away and went on sleeping and only one man, big and fat with a lot of black hair on his chest and on his back like a huge gorilla, got up and chased you all over the lawn huffing and puffing, his eyes red and huge, and finally he caught you and slapped you and shook your shoulders hard and barked, *Paskutstve holerye, paskutstve holerye*, and you came back to me with red ears, and you didn't cry and you said it didn't really hurt, but from then on, every time they mentioned Hitler, in school or on television, I would think of the gorilla from the rest home instead of the real Hitler with the little mustache and dangling forelock.

In the afternoon we went down, as always on the first day of vacation, to eat in the Balfour Cellar, and the tall thin waiter, who looked like a professor – Grandfather told us that many years ago he really had been a professor in Berlin, wearing glasses in a silver frame and a beard the same color and a black bowtie – gave a little bow because he knew us, and especially Grandfather, who was a regular customer, and pulled out the chairs for us to sit down, and quickly put menus in front of us and said, What will you have, Herr Green, even though Grandfather always ordered the same thing, roast with puree of potatoes and sauerkraut, and a bunch of purple grapes for dessert, and the regular customers around the tables knew us and smiled and waved at us with white napkins, and as I ate I gazed at the two plywood cooks hanging on the wall in their high chef's hats and long aprons and black mustaches curving upward like two more smiles on their mouths, and they looked back at me, leaning on half a wooden barrel sticking out of the wall, which was full, I was sure, of very very good sauerkraut. And once you told me that the restaurant had a secret cellar right underneath us and that was why it was called the Balfour Cellar, and in the cellar there were lots more barrels like those and all of them were full of sauerkraut that could last a long time in case of another Holocaust, and then the limping newspaper seller came in wearing a dirty gray undershirt soaked with sweat and yelled, Paper get your paper, until the whole restaurant was filled with his sour breath, and Grandfather beckoned to him, and he came to our table and gave him the paper with a black hand, and Grandfather paid him twenty *grush* even though right next door to the restaurant there was a clean kiosk that had papers and soda and ice-cream-on-a-stick. Then we went back home on the steep road that went past the gold dome and you could see the whole bay from there, and on the way we fooled around on the back seat and played pinch-me-punch-me and boxed and yelled and called each other names, and Grandfather suddenly turned around and said quietly and earnestly, Don't fight, children, human beings have to love and pity one another, for in the end we all die. And we didn't understand what he meant but we stopped, and Misha winked at us in the mirror, and told us about Louis Armstrong, who was the greatest trumpet player and had the deepest lungs, and when Betty Grable who had the prettiest legs in Hollywood got cancer he came with his whole orchestra to play for her on the hospital lawn under her window. Then we got to the house, and Grandmother opened the door, her tight hairdo rolled in a braid around her scalp, and pecked each of us on the cheek and said, Now *Schlafstunde*, which always sounded to me like the name of a cake like Schwartzwalder Kirschtorte or Sachertorte or Apfelstrudel, which she would bake because they reminded her of her home overseas, and the steamy fragrant café when outside it was cold and snowing, but Dr. Schmidt didn't allow her to eat them because she had high blood sugar which is very dangerous for the heart. So she only served it to us and Uncle Alfred and Grandfather, who always said politely, No thank you, and refused to taste a single bite even though he was very healthy. But sometimes, when he went to walk Uncle Alfred to the gate, Grandmother would cut herself a small slice and eat it with quick bites, bent over her plate, and Grandfather would come back, stand in the door and observe her back with a tender look, and wait until she was finished, and only then would he come into the living room and sit down with the newspaper, pretending he hadn't seen. They went to their room, and we went out to the grove behind the house and stretched a strong rope between two pine trees and tried to balance on it like that clown we once saw when we were little and Grandfather took us to the Hungarian circus in Paris Square, where there were purebred horses and panthers with yellow eyes and trained elephants and a beautiful acrobat with long blond hair and the face of an angel who danced on the tightrope with a golden parasol in her hand, and we decided we'd run away and join that circus after we were trained, but now we only managed to creep along on the rope, and you explained to me that it's important to know in case you have to cross over water. Then we climbed up to our espionage headquarters under the roof, which sometimes was Anne Frank's hiding place, where we'd huddle together trembling under the table and munch on potato peels and call each other Anne and Peter and hear the voices of German soldiers outside and drop onto the green velvet sofa which Grandmother brought with her when she came to Israel on the ship, and when one of the two wooden headrests collapsed they bought a new sofa for the living room and brought this one here, because it's a shame to throw out a good piece of furniture, and suddenly you said in a pensive voice, Interesting what you feel after you die, and I said, After you die you don't feel anything, and we tried to close our eyes tight and block our ears and hold our breath to feel dead, but it didn't work because even with our eyes closed we could see colors and you said, Maybe by the time we get old they'll invent some medicine against death, and I said, Maybe you'll be a scientist and invent it yourself and you'll be famous like Albert Einstein. Then we played writing words with our finger on each other's back and whispering them. First we wrote the names of flowers, narcissus and anemone and cyclamen, and names of animals, panther and hippopotamus, and names of people we knew, but after a while you said that was boring, and it was hard to guess because of our shirts, so I took off my shirt and lay down on the sofa, my face in the smell of dust and perfume and cigarette smoke that lingered in the upholstery from days gone by, and I felt how your nice finger slowly wrote words we never dared to say, first a-s-s and then t-i-t and finally w-h-o-r-e, and while I whispered the words in a soft voice between the cushions of the sofa I felt my face burning and my nipples which had just started to sprout hardening against the velvet.

In the afternoon Grandfather and Grandmother came out of the bedroom with pink cheeks, twenty years younger, and at five o'clock on the dot Uncle Alfred came and we never understood exactly how he was related to us, maybe he was one of Grandmother's distant cousins, and her mouth grew thin as a thread whenever his name was mentioned and Grandfather would roar with rage, Bastard, and we didn't know why they didn't like him, whether it was because he was poor or because he once tried to be an opera singer in Paris or some other reason we couldn't guess, and why they entertained him so nicely in spite of it, and Grandmother served him tea and cake, which he would drink and eat and smack his thick red lips and tell again, his eyes melting with regret, about how he was a student in the Paris Conservatoire and lived in a teeny-tiny attic without a shower and without a toilet in the Place de la République, and ate half a baguette-with-butter a day, but at seven in the evening he would put on his only good suit and a bowtie and sprinkle eau-de-cologne on his cheeks and go to the opera, where he would stand under a decorated lighted arch and steal the occasional notes that slipped out through the lattices and caress the statues of the muses and the cornices of the angels, and in the intermission he would mingle with the audience and go inside, because then they didn't check tickets, and find himself an empty seat in one of the balconies, and so with sobbing heart and damp as a clutched handkerchief he saw the last acts of the most famous operas in the world. And here he would usually stand up, sway like a jack-in-the-box, clasp the back of the armchair with his plump fingers, and burst into an aria from *Rigoletto* or *La Traviata* or *The Marriage of Figaro*, and his voice was frail and fragrant and sweet like the tea he had just drunk, and only at the end did it squeak and break like glass, and Grandmother's thin hands smacked one another in dry applause and Grandfather lowered his eyes to the squares of the carpet and muttered, Bravo, bravo, and we didn't know why Uncle Alfred was thrown out of the Conservatoire one day and didn't become a great singer in the Paris opera, and Grandmother wouldn't tell us, she only clenched her mouth even tighter, as if a huge frog would leap out if she opened it. And Uncle Alfred would sit down and sigh and wipe his reddish nose like a strawberry with a wrinkled handkerchief he pulled out of the left pocket of his jacket, and he would hold out his arms to invite us to ride on both sides of the chair, and hug our waists and tell about the cafés of Montparnasse and Montmartre, which was a meeting place for writers and artists and students, and from his mouth strange names flowed with a wonderful sound I'd never heard before anywhere, like Sartre and Simone de Beauvoir and Cocteau and Satie and Picasso, and then he'd caress your hair and say, You'll be an artist too someday, and stroke your back and say, Or a writer, and press his little white hand on your leg with the short jeans and say, Or a musician, and go on strumming with his fingers on your smooth bare thigh as if he were playing a piano, and he didn't say anything to me. He couldn't know that someday, on a steamy shuddering mid-summer afternoon, we'd be standing in the old cemetery at Carmel Beach, our shamed backs to his tombstone, on which were the words, in gold letters he'd requested, of the Chinese poet from Mahler's *Lied von der Erde*:

> *When sorrow draws near,*
> *The gardens of the soul lie wasted,*
> *Joy and song wither and die,*
> *Dark is life and so is death.*
> *Now it is time, companions!*
> *Drain your golden goblets to the dregs.*

Our backs to his tombstone and our faces to Grandfather wrapped in a sheet, he hurrying to slip into an eternal *Schlaffstunde* next to Grandmother, who had died one winter many years before, but they didn't take us to the funeral because they didn't want us to catch cold and miss school, and our faces to the cantor, whose closed eyes were turned to the sky as he trilled his *"El maleh rakhamim shokhen bamromim,"* and to your father who had turned completely gray, muttering *"Yitgadal v'yitkadash sh'me raba"* and to my mother hiding her face in her hands, ripping her shirt, and to the old people responding Amen, their familiar faces mocking me under their wrinkled masks, waving at me sometimes and smiling around the tables in the Balfour Cellar which isn't there anymore, and sometimes dozing off on the loungers of the rest home which was closed years ago, and here's Misha, who is almost no older but without the visor hat and the smile with the gold tooth, and he's wearing a black skullcap and noisily wiping his nose, and my gaze is drawn to the shriveled sharp face of a stooped little old woman which is stamped on my memory as if it had accompanied me throughout my childhood, though I can't remember where, and I turn to you and seek in your eyes which don't look straight at me, in your faded face and in the white threads in your hair, desire a sharp wild pain in me like the whistle of the train now galloping along the shore on its way to the new station at Bat-Galim, but only tatters of memories are pulled from me, connecting to one another with their tails like the colored handkerchiefs from the box of the magician in the Hungarian circus, and about a week after vacation started you didn't want to join the circus or practice balancing on the tightrope between the pines and you didn't want to play Anne Frank or Emil and the Detectives, you didn't want to play anything with me, you just sat under the big pine tree all day long and read little books with crinkled bindings and you looked worried and sad and full of secret thoughts under your checked cap. At first I tried not to disturb you even though I was insulted, but by the third day I had had enough. I waited until afternoon and when Grandfather and Grandmother went for their *Schlafstunde*, I crept up behind you, grabbed the book named *The Confession of the Commander's Lover* with a picture on the cover of a soldier in a brown uniform with black boots up to his knees aiming a huge pistol at a blonde sprawling in the snow between his legs and wearing only panties and a bra. I hid the book, and said I wouldn't give it back until you told me what was going on. You looked at me strangely through your long light lashes and said, Swear on the black grave of Hitler that you won't tell anyone in the world ever. I swear, I whispered solemnly, and to myself I imagined a deep black hole where the big hairy Hitler of the rest home was standing. Then you told me that recently, ever since you started reading those books, it swelled up in your pants and became so hard you had to rub it with your hand until a kind of white liquid sprayed out of it and that was the most wonderful feeling you ever had in your life, like the explosion of a shooting star, but afterward you were worried because in school they explained to you that women get pregnant from it, and when you wash your hands it goes into the pipes of the sewer along with the water and flows into the sea and a lot of women swim in the sea and it could get into them under their bathing suits, and not all of it would go into the sink either because among millions of little seeds some twenty or thirty were bound to be left on your hand, and sometimes you had to go on the bus afterward or to basketball or scouts, and it could get on the money you paid the driver, and from the driver's hands to the tickets he gives the girls and women of all ages, and then they go back home and go to the bathroom and tear toilet paper and wipe themselves and it gets inside them and they don't even know, and now thousands of women are walking around the streets with babies from you in their swollen bellies, and not only here in Israel, because the sperm can be washed away in the water and even go as far as Europe. An abashed spark of pride glimmered in your eyes for a moment and died out. I sat silently awhile and thought, chewing on dry pine needles. That was a really serious problem. Meantime you were tossing pine cones, trying to hit the tree trunk opposite, thunk, thunk, thunk. Suddenly I had an idea. I stood up and ran to the kitchen, opened the drawer next to the sink which had all kinds of things you need in a house, matches and bandaids and rubber bands, and took out a few plastic sandwich bags Grandmother used to pack food for the road when we went on a Saturday visit to one of the rest homes, and I ran back and gave it to you and said, Here, do it in this and bury it in the ground. From that day on, the worry and the pride disappeared from your face and we were friends again and played all the old games, and only sometimes did you suddenly stop and give me long pensive looks, and at night I'd creep into the kitchen and count the bags to know how many were missing, and I'd go out barefoot to the fragrant dark grove with gloomy treetops and the sound of rustling and chirping and howling and mysterious hissing, and I'd find the places where dry pine needles were piled up and the earth was loose, and I'd dig with feverish curious hands and panic and bring up the plastic bags from their graves and look at the wonderful liquid in the moonlight for a long time. One day you added the crinkled little books to our treasure and said, I don't need this garbage anymore, I can invent better stories myself, and I said, You'll surely be a writer someday, and I remembered that Uncle Alfred had said it before me. So we tore the pages out of the books and sat down to cut out the words, especially the coarsest ones, and pasted them into scary anonymous threatening letters to the gang of criminals under the supermarket and to Mrs. Bella Blum of the post office, and we gorged ourselves on the chocolate we had stolen earlier from Grandmother's kitchen, where she kept it for baking her cakes, and it tasted a little like almond paste, and suddenly you touched my face with your fingertips, as if to wipe off a chocolate mustache, and you went behind me and wrote slowly on my back, word after word, I-love-you, and hugged me tight. You lay on the sofa, and I lay down on top of you, my face in the soft shadow between your shoulder and your neck, a smell of paste and starch from your green shirt, and your damp fingers stroked the back of my neck for a long time, trembled, hovered over my hair. Stuck together without moving, almost without breathing, only our hearts galloping like horses in a mad race, and I slowly stroked your face, as if I were sculpting it anew, your fair curls and your smooth brow and your eyelids with a whole world underneath them and your little nose that a finger could slide down like a ski to your lips, where a hot draft breathed on my frozen finger, and you pull up my shirt, your cool hand on my back down and up, then up and down to that nice place where if we were cats our tails would start, and I put my mouth on your mouth, taste the stolen chocolate, our tongues meet, circle, and push each other like two panicky wrestlers, and I tug the shirt up off your smooth chest and my shirt up off my breasts, to press my nipples hard from the cold against the warm soft skin of your panting belly, and I feel a sweetness between my legs as if honey had spilled and a little of it drops on my panties, and that makes me open them and move back and forth on your thigh, and you hug me tight and suck my lips like lemon drops and you put my hand on the hard bulge in your shorts and your face becomes serious and fragile so in it I can see what no one before me has ever seen, and I breathe fast-fast like a little animal without memories, my melted belly stuck to yours the sweetness in my panties more and more until it hurts until I can't and suddenly those spasms inside me the first time so strong and sharp and long and then shorter and faster like flutterings but I don't shout so they won't wake up and I want it never to end but finally it does end and I fall on you breathless as if I had run the sixty-meter-dash, and I see that you too are half fainting, struggling to swallow air, your face burning, and I get off you and lie beside you and discover a big spot on your pants and, excited, I inhale the sharp smell rising from the two of us, a smell not like any other.

Then you looked at me with flashing green eyes and you smiled and kissed me on my cheek, and you wildly pushed aside the hair stuck to your brow and sat up and took off your shirt in one movement and said, Take off yours too. And I took off mine, and you laid your head on my stomach, and we rested like that awhile, my hand stirring your damp hair, and fingers of sun pierced the chinks in the shutter and spread golden fans on the walls. Then I stroked your back and said your skin was soft as velvet, and you said mine was soft as water, and you kissed my stomach and drew strange forms on it with your lips, and you said, When you lie on your back your breasts are as flat as mine, and you licked my nipples, and your tongue was a little rough like a cat's, and you licked and licked until they got hard as cherry pits, and again I felt sweet and smooth between my legs and I wanted it to go on as before, but Grandmother's voice rose from downstairs, sharp and probing, like the periscope of a submarine, Children, where are you, five o'clock tea and cake. We put on our shirts fast and came down and you went to change your pants, while I looked in the gilded mirror in the vestibule. My eyes sparkled like cups of sky, and the whole world, the furniture in the living room and Grandfather and Grandmother and Uncle Albert looked far away and unreal but sharp and clear, as on a stage.

That night I couldn't sleep because I missed you too much, you were sleeping quietly in the room at the end of the hall and maybe your body was dreaming of me. I wanted so much to come to you in the dark and hug you and hear you breathing, but Grandmother was always strict about you sleeping in your father's old room and me in my mother's room, next to their room, so I controlled myself and thought about tomorrow, about the ceremony we planned down to the smallest detail after dinner, when Uncle Alfred had gone and Grandfather and Grandmother sat down in the living room to watch the Friday night news on television, and we whispered back and forth in the kitchen, and we could hear Menachem Begin the new Prime Minister giving a speech about Auschwitz and the Six Million, and then he announced he was willing to meet in Jerusalem with President Sadat, and Grandfather said, At last that idiot came out with something good, and Grandmother called us, You should see this, important news, but we knew that tomorrow's ceremony was much more important, and especially what would come afterward, and there was no way I could stop the film that kept repeating over and over on the dark screen, the film we starred in. And suddenly, from their room, I heard Grandmother scream in a whisper, Aaron, Aaron, and Grandfather woke up and said gently, Yes, Minna, and Grandmother said she couldn't fall asleep, and she told him quietly, but I could hear every word, that in the morning, as she was walking around in the supermarket with the cart to buy food for the Sabbath, she suddenly felt that her mother was standing next to her, in a black fur coat, the one she wore years ago when they said goodbye at the railroad station, and her face was as pale and terrified as it was then, and she told her something, but Grandmother didn't pay attention because she said to herself, It's summer now, why is Mother wearing a fur coat, and before she could understand, her mother wasn't there anymore. I've not been calm ever since, Grandmother went on in a harsh whisper, I'm sure it's something very bad. From her face I know something awful is going to happen. Grandfather didn't say anything, he just sang her something very quiet, a tune of yearning without words, and repeated it over and over until it filled me completely, until I fell asleep.

The next day was the Sabbath. Grandfather and Grandmother woke us early to go with them to visit the rest home in Tiberias, and were surprised when we muttered from under the covers that we were tired and wanted to stay home, but they gave in. I remembered what I had heard at night from their room, and I thought to myself, How can ghosts wander around in our supermarket, and why didn't Grandfather comfort her and tell her it was all her imagination and nothing bad would happen, and suddenly I thought, Maybe that whole conversation didn't happen and I only dreamed it, and I decided not to tell anybody, not even you. Grandmother made hard-boiled egg sandwiches for our lunch, and prepared food to take on the road, and my heart began to pound when I heard the drawer next to the sink open and Grandmother whisper to herself, Funny, I remember there was a whole package here. Finally she wrapped it in waxpaper because Misha was already honking for them outside, and pecked each of us on the cheek and said, We'll be back by seven thirty tonight, behave yourselves, and they left. As soon as the hum of the motor disappeared around the corner, we leaped out of bed and met in the hall, and we started to do everything exactly according to the plan we had concocted last night down to the last detail. First each of us took a long and thorough bath, shampooing our hair and cleaning our ears. Then we wrapped ourselves in our sheets, which we tied at the shoulder like Greek togas, and I put on perfume from all the bottles I found on Grandmother's dressing table, and I smeared my lips and cheeks with a lot of red, and my eyes with blue. Then we cut off the tops of the pink flowers Grandmother had bought for the Sabbath, in the golden vase on the credenza, and we plaited two wreaths for our heads. Then we went into the kitchen but didn't eat breakfast because we couldn't swallow a thing, but from Grandmother's hiding place for candles, next to the hiding place for chocolate, we stole six *yahrzeit*[2] candles, she always kept it full of them because there was always a *yahrzeit* for somebody in her family who had remained over there, and from the sewing box covered with flowered cloth we took a pair of scissors, and from Grandfather's linen drawer we took a white handkerchief, and from the pantry a glass of wine, and from the library a small Bible your father got as a bar-mitzvah present from his school, and barefoot we went up to our room in the attic with all those things. Then we closed the shutter on the day and on the cemetery and we made it absolutely dark, and we lit the *yahrzeit* candles and set them about the room, which was filled with the shadows of scary demons dancing on the ceiling and the walls, and we left one candle on the table, and we put the Bible next to it, and you asked, You ready, and I whispered, Yes, and my heart was pounding, and we stood facing each other, and we put one hand on the Bible and we raised the other with thumb and pinkie together as

---

2. Yiddish: Anniversary of a relative's death, according to the Hebrew calendar.

in the scouts' oath, and I looked straight into your eyes where the flames of the candles were burning and repeated after you slowly, solemnly:

> *I swear by God and by the black grave of Hitler,*
> *I swear by God and by the black grave of Hitler,*
> *I will never marry another woman,*
> *I will never marry another man,*
> *And I will love only you forever,*
> *And I will love only you forever.*

Then we hugged each other and almost couldn't breathe because we knew that that oath was strong as death and to make it even stronger we cut the words out of the Bible and pasted them on a sheet of paper by the light of the candle. The two Gods we found right away in the creation, and woman in the story of Adam and Eve, and grave in the part about the Tomb of the Patriarchs. Then we found man and swear and I and of and you and another and love and the and black and will and never. The rest of the words, Hitler and marry and forever, we couldn't find, so we pasted them together from separate letters. When it was all ready, you wrapped the glass in the handkerchief, put it on the floor and stamped on it hard with your bare foot. The glass broke and a big spot of blood spread over the cloth. You dipped your finger in it and signed your name under the oath. Now you, you said. I took a deep breath, picked up a piece of glass, and scratched my big toe hard, from the bottom, so nobody would see the cut, squeezed a drop of blood onto my finger and signed a shaky signature next to your name. Then we wrote the date, the regular date and the Hebrew date, and the exact address, Presidents' Boulevard, Mount Carmel, Haifa, Israel, Middle East, Continent of Asia, Earth, Solar System, Galaxy, Cosmos. Now we'll tear the oath in two and each of us will keep the half with the other's signature, I said what we had planned to do, and you were silent for a moment and suddenly you said, No, let's wrap it up and bury it under the big pine tree, someplace where we can always find it. I thought to myself that we mustn't change the plan, but I didn't say anything. We folded the paper in the aluminum foil of yesterday's chocolate and put it in an empty matchbox, which we wrapped in more paper and in a plastic bag you had left over from the ones you stole from the drawer, and we went downstairs. We dug a deep pit with our hands next to the trunk and hid our package, more important than anything in the world, but when we covered it with earth and tamped it down with our feet and piled pine needles on it, I became very sad all of a sudden, and I didn't know why.

When we got back to the room, the *yahrzeit* candles were still burning and the demons kept jumping wildly on the walls. I knew what was about to happen but I wasn't scared. I thought about Anne Frank and how the Germans caught her before she really had a chance to love her Peter, when she was exactly my age, and I said to myself, I will have a chance. We took off the wreaths and the Greek togas and we spread one sheet on the sofa underneath us, and we lay down, and covered ourselves with the other one, and I caressed your whole body which was warm and breathing fast, and I walked my tongue among hills of light and soft shadows and paths of soap and sweat under the sheet, and suddenly you were over me on all fours and looking at me with sparkling yellow eyes and a savage smile, and I wanted that to happen, and I whispered, Come, and you asked, Does it hurt, and I said, No, and I could hear your heart drumming on my breasts rhythmically I-love-you-1-love-you, and I was filled with tremendous pride.

Then heavy steps grated on the stairs and I whispered, The Germans, and I started trembling, and we held each other tight and pressed against the wall, and the door opened, and in the opening in a halo of light stood Uncle Alfred. They apparently forgot to tell him they were going away and that he shouldn't come today for tea. He looked at our sweaty bodies and the handkerchief spotted with blood and the pink flowers scattered over the floor and the *yahrzeit* candles, and he rubbed his strawberry-nose in embarrassment, and his eyes were fixed on some point on your stomach, maybe your belly button, as he stammered, What's this, children, it's forbidden, at your age, you shouldn't, if Grandmother finds out. We covered ourselves with the sheet and looked at him cautiously and silently like cats. He lowered his eyes to the shiny tips of his shoes and went on, Of course I'll have to tell her, who would have thought, children, cousins, and God forbid there'll be a baby with six fingers on each hand, or two heads, or a little tail like a pig, this is very dangerous, who would have thought. And he wagged his head from the right shoe-tip to the left shoe-tip, as if he were setting up a shiny-shoe contest. Then he looked at you again, and said with no stammering now that he was willing not to tell anybody on condition that you agreed to meet him here tomorrow afternoon, so he could talk to you and explain what a serious thing it was we had done. Why only him, I burst out to defend you, and Uncle Alfred said he regarded you as responsible and that with your sense and talent he hadn't expected anything like this from you. I agree, you said quietly, and he left. As soon as the door closed behind him we jumped off the couch, stood at the window again, with one hand on the Bible and the other in the air, with thumb and pinkie together, and I repeated after you an oath we composed on the spot:

> *And even if we have a baby*
> *With six fingers on each hand*
> *Or two heads*
> *Or a little tail like a pig*
> *We will love it as if it was a completely normal baby*
> *With five fingers and one head*
> *And no tail at all.*

Then we dressed and cleaned up everything fast before Grandfather and Grandmother got back home. Except the dark red spot, blossoming on the green velvet, that we left as a souvenir. Before I fell asleep, I could hear Grandmother whispering into the golden vase on the sideboard, Funny, I remember buying flowers for the Sabbath, and Grandfather comforting her gently, Well, my memory's not what it used to be either, how could I forget to tell Alfred not to come today for tea.

In the middle of the night I felt horribly nauseous, ran to the bathroom and stuck my finger down my throat and suddenly I felt I was throwing up sand, enormous amounts of wet sand, it filled my mouth and gritted between my teeth, and I spat and threw up, threw up and spat, and then something else was vomited up from me with the sand, and I looked into the toilet. A tiny black dog floating stiffly on his side, his legs spread out, his gums exposed in a creepy smile, watching me with a gaping dead eye. In horror I slammed down the lid. Outside it was beginning to turn light.

I wandered around among the trees with my hands in my pockets, kicking pine cones. You'd been up there for more than half an hour, closed in the room. What did he have to tell you that took so much time. I couldn't control myself anymore. I went up very quietly, opened the door a little, and peered in. The two of you were sitting on the sofa. With big opera gestures Uncle Alfred was explaining something to you that I couldn't hear and from time to time he put his cotton hand on your leg. Then he wrapped his arm around your shoulders and put his face which was always flushed, almost purple, close to your face which was ashen. Suddenly he looked up and saw me. A shadow passed over his eyes. I fled downstairs. I lay under the big pine tree, right over the oath we buried yesterday, and I looked at the green sparkling needles that stabbed the clouds which today were in the shape of a huge white hand. I waited. Time passed, more time, a lot of time passed, and you didn't come down. I remembered the dream I had last night, and I shivered with cold. At last the door opened and Uncle Alfred came out breathing deeply as he went unsteadily down the steps. He buttoned his jacket and rang the front door bell. Grandmother opened the door, said, Hello Alfred, and he went into the house. Then you came running out, you lay down beside me, hid your head against my belly, and muffled your howls of anguish. Your whole body shook. I held you. What happened, what did he tell you, I whispered. We have to kill him, you cried. Your hot tears were absorbed by my shirt. I had never seen you cry like that. But what happened, what did he do, I asked again. We have to kill him we have to kill him, you wailed, your feet kicking the ground. But what did he do, hit you, tell me what he did, I pleaded. You lifted your burning wet face where the tears and the snot were running but you didn't care, and you said quietly, Today I'm going to kill him. I looked into your red eyes, with two black pits in them, and I knew that today Uncle Alfred would die.

Within minutes we had a fatal solution of poison made of shells ground up with two ants, a mashed piece of pine cone, and yellow dog-doo. We mixed it all up with pine tar so the ingredients would stick together. My job was to ask Grandmother if I could make the tea today, and to pour the poison into Uncle Alfred's cup. I chose the big black cup for him so I wouldn't confuse it with another and also because I thought the poison would work better in a black cup. I added five spoons of sugar and stirred it well, trying to hear what they were saying in the living room to make sure he wasn't telling on us in spite of everything. They were talking very quietly and only separate words reached me, Dr. Schmidt, chest X-ray, diagnosis, and Dr. Schmidt again. They were talking about diseases. I calmed down. On the tea cart I also put the special double-layer *Schwartzwaldertorte* that Grandmother had baked and I didn't understand what it was in honor of, maybe it was his birthday today. As soon as I entered with the tray, they shut up. Uncle Alfred said, Thank you, and a sad smile clouded his face. You came in too, your eyes dry now, and we huddled together in the chair, waiting with awful tension to see him drink and die on the spot. First he greedily polished off three pieces of cake. Then he sipped noisily, smacked his lips, faced us, and declared, Now I will sing you the first *Lied* from Mahler's *Lied von der Erde*. He cleared his throat twice, clasped his hands on his stomach, and started singing in German which we couldn't understand. His voice burst out of his chest as a solemn trumpet blast, rose to a great height both bold and trembling like a tightrope walker, and suddenly it fell and plunged into a dark abyss, where it struggled with fate, pleaded, prayed, shouted like a hollow echo, whimpered, abased itself, his face that of a drowning man, tears flowed from his eyes and from Grandmother's eyes too, she understood the words, and even Grandfather blew his nose a few times, and we looked at each other and knew the poison we had mixed was also a magic potion, and we held our breath to see him sink into the carpet in the middle of the song, but Uncle Alfred finished it with a long endless shout and his arms waved to the sides and hit the credenza, and the gold vase teetered a moment in surprise and then slid off and smashed on the floor into sparkling slivers. Uncle Alfred sat down, panting heavily, and whispered, Sorry, and Grandmother said, It's nothing, and she came and kissed him on the cheek and Grandfather didn't look at the squares of the carpet and didn't murmur, Bravo, but shook his hand and looked into his eyes and said, Wonderful, wonderful, and Uncle Alfred took another sip of the poisoned tea, and stood up to go, and said to us, Goodbye, and caressed you with his gaze, but we didn't answer, we only looked at him with hatred, and they accompanied him to the door, and wished him good luck, and Grandfather patted him on the shoulder and said, Be strong, Alfred, and Uncle Alfred said hesitantly, Yes, and the door closed behind him and Grandfather and Grandmother looked at each other a moment, and Grandmother nodded her head and brought a broom and dustpan and swept up the slivers.

At night I woke up to the sound of coughing and an awful screeching laughter and I heard Grandmother telling Grandfather in the kitchen, Now I know what she said, now I know what she wanted to tell me then. And the awful laugh was heard again, as if it weren't Grandmother laughing but some demon inside her. I got up to peer from behind the door, and I saw her sitting at the table, her long hair disheveled and in her nightgown and her mouth stained with cherry juice and chocolate, a knife clutched in her fist over the ruins of Alfred's double-layer cake, and Grandfather in pajamas grabbing her wrist and pleading, Enough, enough now, you've already eaten too much, and Grandmother struggled to free her hand and the screeching voice of the demon burst out of her, Just one more little piece, just one more little piece, and Grandfather held her and cried, Don't leave me alone, Minna, please don't leave me alone, I can't make it alone. I ran away from there to your room. Your breathing was heavy, uneven. I got in under your blanket and hugged you and put my head next to yours. The pillow was soaked.

The next day we went with Misha and Grandfather and

Grandmother who sat in front, her braid now pinned together, and Misha let them off at Rambam Hospital and took us to the beach at Bat-Galim, and we took off our clothes and had our bathing suits on underneath, and Misha looked like a lifeguard with his visor cap and broad chest, all he needed was a whistle. He sat down in a beach chair at the edge of the water, and you ran into the sea with a spray splashing colorfully and you plunged into the waves, and I ran in behind you and also plunged because I wanted to feel what you were feeling, and my eyes burned and I swallowed salt water, and when I came back to shore, you were already standing there and shaking your curls, and we sat down on the sand next to Misha, leaning against his sturdy legs, and we watched the sea and were silent because none of us had anything to say. Then I asked Misha to tell us again how he played for the king of Yugoslavia because I knew how much he liked to tell it, and I thought maybe that would save the situation. He was silent a moment, and suddenly he said quietly, It wasn't I who played for the king, it was another boy, he was also called Misha, and he played better than I did, so they chose him to wear the uniform with gold buttons, and the trumpet sparkled in the sun, and the flag went up to the top of the flagpole, it was so beautiful I'll never forget it, and King Pavel came and patted his head and his mother cried so they had to hold her up, and I stood there in the line with all the children and I cried too. He wiped his nose, and then he went on, as if to himself, But that Misha isn't here anymore, Hitler took him, all of them, all of them, my parents too, my brothers and sisters, I'm the only one alive, the sixth child, the one they didn't want, because Papa and Mama got married very young, they were cousins, but the family decided to marry them off at thirteen, that's how it was done in those days, and every year they had a baby, every year a baby, until Papa said, enough. But then they went for a vacation in Austria and when they came back Mama was pregnant again. Misha fell silent and lit a cigarette, and then he said out of the blue, Your grandfather is a fine man, there aren't many people like him. We quietly watched a young man who finally managed to walk on his hands and a man who threw a stick in the water and his big dog charged in barking and swam and brought the stick out in his mouth and the man patted his head. I took an ice-cream stick and drew a house and a tree and the sun on the wet sand, and the waves came and erased my picture. And the sea slowly turned yellow and we got chilly so we dressed and went to get Grandfather and Grandmother, who were waiting for us at the entrance to the hospital with gray faces and looking suddenly very old.

A few days later Grandmother told us that Uncle Alfred had died in the hospital. She wiped her tears and said, He had a disease in his lungs and the operation didn't succeed. But we knew the real reason, and we didn't dare look at each other as we walked with Grandmother, who was weeping for Alfred and for herself, and with Grandfather, who was weeping for Grandmother, and with our parents and the other three people we didn't know, behind the undertakers busy like angels in white shirtsleeves and sweaty faces, carrying the shriveled body on a stretcher under a dark dustcloth, the head almost touching the fat black behind of the first gravedigger, the legs dangling in front of the open fly of the second one, and I thought, It could be anyone under the cloth, maybe it's not him, but when we got to the open grave the cantor said his name and a desperate crying burst out of me because I knew you couldn't move time backward. And you stood silently on the other side of the black grave, and I knew that Uncle Alfred would always be between us, and after the funeral your father would take you home, long before the end of summer vacation because Grandmother already didn't feel well, and in a few months, in the winter, she would die too, and Grandfather would close the office on Herzl Street and move to an old people's home, and he would go on talking to her all those years as if she were still beside him, and we would never again be together in our little room under the roof, and only sometimes, before sleep came, you would crouch over me on all fours and look at me with yellow pupils and I would whisper to you, Come, and I would feel your heart drumming on my breasts, until the last flutter. I wipe my tears and go with all the old people to put a little stone on the grave, and now everyone is turning to go, but I stay another moment at Uncle Alfred's yellowed marble, I know you're standing here next to me. Up close you can see that I too have lines at the corner of my mouth and many gray hairs, and both of us are reciting in our hearts the lines from the first *Lied* of *Das Lied von der Erde*, whose words we didn't understand then, and I put a little stone under the words and you put a little stone and then you put your hand on my shoulder and say, Let's go. My mother and your father are walking in front of us, whispering about the city's plan to destroy the old house and dig up the grove to build an expensive apartment building on the site, and I see the ground, which can no longer contain all we buried there, trembling and splitting open it will split open and the highrise cracking and collapsing. Misha comes up behind us and sighs and says, If you could only go backward in life, even one minute, and I know exactly what minute he wants to go back to. And at the gate stands the stooped-over old woman whose shriveled face is so familiar, and she grabs my sleeve with a trembling hand and screeches, Maybe you don't remember me but I remember your grandfather very well, he was a regular customer of mine, in the old post office. You're Mrs. Bella Blum from the post office, I whisper and my heart turns pale, and for a split-second I see eyeglasses on the end of a sharp nose, gray hair, icy fingers reaching out for the necks of children and triangular stamps, and I remember the anonymous threatening letters, and I glance over at you, but you're looking at your shoes covered with dust and you say, I have to go, we have a meeting at the factory, and once again I touch her soft hand under the purplish straw hat. Suddenly a strong wind comes from the sea and snatches the hat off her head and rolls it down the path, and she runs after it among the tombstones in her fluttering flowery dress, with her rounded belly, with the locks of her chestnut hair, flinging out her full arms to catch it, but the hat mocks her, it flies into the sky like a purple butterfly, and just as it's about to alight on the sharp top of the cypress, it changes its mind, flips over twice and lands on the tombstone of Abba Hushi the famous mayor of Haifa, and you and Misha and all the other men volunteer to get it for her and you jump around among the graves, but the hat is already far away from there, crushed and ashamed between Hanoch ben Moshe Gavrieli born in the city of Lodz and Zilla Frumkin model wife and mother, who lie crowded next to each other, and all of you are flushed and sweating, but the hat pulls away again with a splendid somersault and soars, and you chase it, look up and wave your hands, like survivors on a desert island to an airplane, then the hat loses its balance and spins around itself like a dancer with a jumble of purple ribbons and lands with a bang outside the gate and lies on its side and laughs with its round mouth, and she runs to it, heavy and gasping and bends over and picks it up and waves it high in the air and brimming with joy she turns to you with sparkling eyes, I got it, I got it.

Etgar Keret

Shoes

Translated by Marganit Weinberger-Rotman

On Holocaust Memorial Day, our teacher Sara took us on a No. 57 bus to visit the Museum of Volhynia Jewry, and I felt very important. All the kids in the class except me, my cousin, and one other boy, Druckman, had families that came from Iraq. I was the only one with a grandfather who died in the Holocaust. Volhynia House was very beautiful and ritzy, all made of black marble, like millionaires' houses. It was full of sad black-and-white pictures and lists of people and countries and dead folks. We walked past the pictures in pairs and the teacher said, Don't touch! But I did touch one picture, made of cardboard, showing a thin pale man who was crying and holding a sandwich in his hand. The tears were streaming down his cheeks like the divider lines you see on the highway, and my partner, Orit Salem, said she'd tell the teacher that I touched it, and I said I didn't care, she could tell whoever she wanted, even the principal, I didn't give a damn. It's my Grandpa and I'll touch whatever I want.

After the pictures, they took us into a big hall and showed us a movie about little children who were shoved into a truck and then suffocated by gas. Then a skinny old man got up on the stage and told us what bastards and murderers the Nazis were and how he took revenge on them, he even strangled a soldier with his bare hands till he died. Djerby, who was sitting next to me, said the old man was lying; the way he looks, there was no way he could make a soldier bite the dust. But I looked the old man in the eye and believed him. He had so much anger in his eyes, that all the freaked-out hot-heads I've ever seen seemed like small change in comparison.

Finally, when he finished telling us what he'd done during the Holocaust, the old man said that what we'd just heard was relevant not only to the past but also to what goes on nowadays, because the Germans still exist and still have a country. He said he was never going to forgive them, and that he hoped we would never ever go visit their country either. Because when he went to Germany with his parents fifty years ago everything looked nice, but it ended in hell. People have short memories, he said, especially where bad things are concerned. People tend to forget, he said, but you won't forget. Every time you see a German, you'll remember what I told you. Every time you see German products, whether it's a television set (because most television sets here are made by German manufacturers) or anything else, you should always remember that underneath the fancy wrapping there are parts and tubes that they made out of the bones and skin and flesh of dead Jews.

On the way out Djerby said again that he'd bet anything the old man never strangled anybody in his life, and I thought to myself it was lucky that we had a made-in-Israel refrigerator at home. Why look for trouble?

Two weeks later my parents came back from a trip abroad and brought me a pair of sneakers. My older brother had secretly told my Mom that that was what I wanted, and she got me the best pair in the world. Mom smiled as she handed me the present. She was sure I had no idea what was inside. But I recognized the Adidas logo on the bag right away. I took out the shoebox and said thank you. The box was rectangular, like a coffin, and inside was a pair of white shoes with three blue stripes and the inscription *Adidas* on their side; I didn't have to open the box to know what they looked like. "Let's put them on," my mother said and took off the wrapping, "to make sure they fit." She was smiling the whole time, and had no idea what was going on. "They're from Germany, you know," I told her, squeezing her hand tightly. "Of course, I know," Mom smiled, "Adidas is the best brand in the world." "Grandpa was from Germany, too," I tried to give her a hint. "Grandpa was from Poland," Mom corrected me. For a moment she became sad, but she got over it in no time. She slipped one shoe on my foot and started to tie the laces. I kept quiet. I realized there was nothing doing. Mom didn't have a clue. She'd never been to Volhynia House. Nobody had ever explained it to her. For her, shoes were just shoes and Germany was Poland. I let her put the shoes on me and didn't say a thing. There was no point in telling her and making her even sadder.

I thanked her again and kissed her on the cheek and said I was going out to play ball. "You be careful, eh?" my Dad called, laughing, from his armchair in the front room, "Don't wear out the soles right away." I looked again at the pale leather covering my feet. I looked at them and remembered everything the old man who had strangled a soldier said we should remember. I touched the blue Adidas stripes and remembered my cardboard grandfather. "Are the shoes comfortable?" my mother asked. "Sure they're comfortable," my brother answered for me. "These aren't cheap Israeli sneakers. These are the same sneakers that the great Cruiff wears." I tiptoed slowly towards the door, trying to put as little weight as I could on the shoes. And so I made my way gingerly to the Monkey Park. Outside, the kids from the Borochov neighborhood had made up three teams: Holland, Argentina and Brazil. It so happened that Holland needed a player, so they agreed to let me join in, even though they never take anyone who's not from Borochov.

At the beginning of the game I still remembered not to kick with the tip of my shoe, so it wouldn't hurt Grandpa, but after a while I forgot, just like the old man at Volhynia House said people tend to do, and I even managed to kick a tie-breaking goal. But when the game was over I remembered, and looked at the shoes. All of a sudden they were really comfortable, much bouncier than when they were in the box. "Some goal, eh?" I reminded Grandpa on the way home, "that goalie didn't know what hit him." Grandpa didn't answer, but judging by the tread I could tell that he was pleased too.

Mira Magen

Will Somebody Please Shut the Gate

Translated by Sondra Silverston

A few months before Mother's madness was officially announced, though there were hints that something out of the ordinary was happening and our daily routine suffered small blows, life went on and the days were all pretty much alike.

She spread slices of pickled cucumber on the windowsill and said that once the sun dried them out pure cucumber would be left, that there was enough water in the tap anyway and it was just inflating the cucumber, but the sun shrivelled them into transparent greenish rags spotted with dried seeds which she ate and ate and her mouth reeked of rotten bay leaves and neglected teeth. Then there was the business about the windows that we weren't allowed to close because there wasn't enough air for five pairs of nostrils and if everyone exhaled their carbon dioxide into the closed apartment, the air would be poisoned. But when the strong autumn winds blew through the rooms and the windows swung wildly on their hinges, banging their frames and rattling the panes, it was clear that something new was happening.

Father oiled the wood of the windowsill because the vinegar from the pickles had erased the paint and eaten away the glaze. He didn't tell Mother to stop it, just as he didn't tell her that the cold coming in through the open windows was giving us goose bumps, just as he didn't tell her that there was nothing wrong with her stomach, but the more she folded her hands over her stomach and said she was wasting away, the more reasons he found to fix his Subaru. He tightened bolts, stretched belts, wiped the windows with damp cloths until they shone like mirrors and you could see the neighbors' houses reflected in them. He shook out the rubber mats and spread them on the asphalt driveway and he scrubbed the headlights with the green dish-washing liquid, and only when the darkness thickened so that he couldn't tell the pliers from the screwdriver did he close his toolbox, gather up the rags and go upstairs.

There were no signs that Mother was wasting away. After all, when someone is wasting away they get smaller and smaller, but not one centimeter of Mother's meter sixty-two was missing, her ring was still tight on her finger like a thin gold canal between two banks of thick flesh, her belt was buckled as always on the third hole and, as always, when she leaned against the doorjamb the top of her head reached the bottom nail of the mezuzah. I believed that she was wasting away from the inside, that her intestines were growing shorter, her blood draining away, her heart shrinking and only her outer skin remained inflated, covering the general desiccation taking place inside.

So many things changed all at once that, from fear, I began to count the things that were still the same and did not panic at sudden tears or shrieks that turned into laughter. One of those things was Talia's morning. She would stand in front of the mirror combing her hair to her heart's content, the black plastic comb rearranging the varying shades of brown and gold, and the steady rhythm of Talia's hand remained constant despite Mother's screaming, Enough with that mirror. The shouts grew louder, rattling the mirror, but Talia would continue to arrange each strand of hair slowly and painstakingly. When it became unbearable Father would try to imprison the noise and violated the latest decree by closing the kitchen window, but the insulation was less than perfect and the neighbors heard. The Baumans' curtains moved and half of Mrs. Bauman's face filled the slit between them, then the opening narrowed to the width of her ear and she had to decide whether to devote it to her eye or her ear.

I didn't understand how Talia was able to wrap herself in a kind of membrane and detach herself from the screaming, and how day by day she perfected this membranous ability of hers. I thought that if I tried hard enough I could be as good at it as she was. When I wrapped my sandwich in waxed paper and Mother screamed that I was getting on her nerves with that noisy paper and that was enough and get on with it, I couldn't go on like Talia and I didn't finish folding the paper over the sandwich and the mayonnaise dripped on my fingers and then she screamed, You think I didn't see you wiping your hands on your dress, and I didn't answer. The truth is that I didn't wipe them on my dress, and when I bit my nails in the first lesson the nail slivers I swallowed had enough mayonnaise on them to last me the whole lesson.

With Talia and me Mother's nerves were like a lizard's severed tail. Only Uli didn't irritate her, and when she ran her fingers through his soft hair they stayed straight and didn't curl on his forehead and didn't feel his hot scalp and all the fears accumulated inside his little skull. He sat on the living-room floor for hours lining up a long row of red Lego pieces, attaching one to the other, making sure that their sides fitted together without a crack. When there were no red pieces left he pulled out his shoelaces and tried to thread them through again, pushing the hard plastic tip of the lace into the holes until the plastic began to split and spread from so much pushing and wouldn't go through and Uli tried again and again and the tips of the laces broke altogether, and finally he went to kindergarten with his shoes untied and the teacher glued the split plastic, re-threaded the laces and tied two bows.

Those shoes of Uli's had a function, those two little brown things were part of the arrangements I made to maintain order amid all the changes taking place in the house. Every evening after he fell asleep I set them side by side between the legs of his bed and every once in a while I checked to see that the angle hadn't changed, that the soles were touching each other neatly with the little hollow in the middle. Those shoes that had taken the shape of Uli's feet were a kind of good-luck charm protecting me from the chameleons of that house.

More than once I woke up in the middle of the night and heard the bats that had swerved from their usual route and were flying through the yard upside down like a plane that has been hit, crashing into the window, their black bellies gleaming in the dark, and the moths began hovering backwards, their antennae gone. I threw off my blanket and ran to Uli's bed to check if the shoes were obeying the order I had imposed on them, to be sure beyond the shadow of a doubt that they were still in the same position, the heels a centimeter from the edge of the floor tile, and then I went into the kitchen to see if the faucet was still dripping at the same obedient rate. Talia said that the faucet got on her nerves and darn it when were they going to fix it, but I hoped they wouldn't fix it so that I would still be able to hear an old familiar sound amidst all the new sounds that cropped up every day in that house.

Official confirmation of madness arrived on the health clinic's white stationery, with the words Mental Health Clinic printed in blue on either side of the red emblem. Father ran around with it to the National Insurance Institute and the municipality to arrange for allowances and discounts, and from being opened and refolded by a lot of clerks it became smudged at the edges with brown fingerprints until the letter looked like paper that had been left to spin in the washing machine and came out wrinkled like an old cotton handkerchief.

You could say that that paper reorganized our lives and the days took on a new routine. Even Uli knew that Mother was in a special hospital and that if Bauman or other neighbors asked questions we were to say that she had stomach problems. Father stopped grooming our Subaru, and the back window was once again covered with dust and children drew the word *slob* and all sorts of other comments in the dust, and on damp nights water dripped onto the windshield from the roof, leaving muddy brown circles.

We only visited Mother once, and in honor of the occasion I picked an anemone from the flowerbed at school. Talia, in a tight-fitting denim skirt and a black blouse, her brown-gold hair combed back, resting on the back of her neck like a honey-colored scarf, rattled the house keys and hurried me, Come on now hurry so we can catch the three-o'clock bus. I put the anemone in an empty olive jar and we left.

The bouncing of the bus shook the water in the jar and a woman said, Little girl what's this, you shouldn't take water on a bus, and when we got off a little water spilled on my shoe and my sock got wet but the anemone stayed fresh and its petals became transparent in the sun, so that you could see the thin veins crisscrossing them.

Mother was wearing her green track suit and eating chicken and rice and some grains of rice fell on the suit and some hung from the corners of her mouth. She didn't say hello or sit down or anything. The man sitting next to her had the exact same food on his tray, he was chewing on a chicken bone and Mother smiled at him and put the remains of her rice on his plate saying, Take it, eat, and she tidied up his plate, separating the rice from the gnawed bones and he scraped the rice from Mother's mouth with a long yellow nicotine-stained finger. Talia twisted the strap of her handbag tightly around her thumb, her nail turned blue but she didn't stop and she stood there taut as an ironed sheet and when Mother said again, Eat, eat, she roared hello Mother in a voice I had never heard before, three patients stopped eating and stared at her with empty eyes and rice fell off their spoons suspended in the air on the way from their plates to their mouths, but Mother didn't hear and kept on with her Eat, eat, and her thigh inside the green sweat suit brushed against the blue pants he was wearing. Then he pushed his plate to the middle of the table, and when he took Mother's hand and placed it on his knee and began to move it very slowly up his thigh to the unmentionable place in his pants, Talia pulled me out of there and water spilled from my jar onto the bathrobe of one of the patients. Talia was silent all the way home and didn't wipe the tears that ran down her cheeks. Once the wind blew one of her tears onto my chin and I didn't wipe it off either, there was practically no water left in the jar and nobody scolded me on the bus, but two women stared at us and whispered to each other, I don't know if it was because of how beautiful Talia was or because she was crying. Talia remained silent and I noticed that the black eye of the anemone was watching the leaves the whole time but it couldn't prevent the widest leaf from starting to wither.

During that time there was no one around to ask for explanations when I was late home from school. And that's why I could take all the time I wanted between one step and the other on my way home. I stood for hours under the almond tree watching the wind blow the blossoms about, thousands of pieces of white blossom drifting down the sidewalk and I gathered them up into the empty sandwich bag and when I opened it at home, the delicate scent of the almond tree drifted out and overcame the smell of mayonnaise, and I crushed the petals and smeared the damp mess on my forehead and throat. There was a kind of relief about this blossoming of the almond tree, it was so completely certain that every year in February the branches would be covered with the white plumage that would then change to green, always always in the same order and at the same time. An almond tree is not one of those things you can surprise – what does it care if the wind bangs windows that can't be closed for fear of carbon dioxide, it doesn't count the loaves of bread which are more numerous from day to day because there is no hot food. I was so envious of the patience of trees and the exact order in which things happened to them that I lingered outside for hours to collect more proof of this. After the almond trees in February, anemones bloomed in the flowerbeds at school and then tulip bulbs thickened under their twisted green leaves, and during the Passover vacation the schoolyard was all yellow with wild mustard and chrysanthemums. Under my bed, fig leaves piled up and turned yellow still hanging on their stems, Talia said I should throw out all that junk but I knew that when the windows started banging and the noise hurt my ears, all I had to do was look at those leaves and calm down.

One evening Father came home from work, stuck his head in the kitchen sink and turned the faucet on full force and the water dripped from his tangled hair onto the floor and the counter and he dried himself with a worn kitchen towel and said, Children, Mother's coming back tomorrow. His face was red from being rubbed and his hair stood on end like a hedgehog's and once again I could hear that noise that hurt my ears because the kitchen window was banging like crazy. Uli stopped chewing his bread and ran to his Lego, and Talia wrapped herself in her membrane, detached from Father's words, her face closed up tight, her eyes staring at a color photo of a model in a magazine. I tried to learn from her whether this was good news or bad but I didn't succeed, I only saw how her jaw was sticking out, and I knew that she was clenching her teeth very hard. In the long silence it seemed to me that the walls were breathing, small squeaks could be heard, something cracking, I was sure they were groaning in distress and I couldn't stand it anymore, so I said, Too bad that she's coming back and my hand moved of its own accord to protect my cheek from the expected slap, but Father didn't slap me, he stood as unmoving as a troll doll, a big drop of water glistening on his earlobe like an earring.

Why now, I thought, maybe we can delay her, maybe somebody can run over there and close the heavy gates. Why right now when I've almost managed to silence the commotion in my head and I already have a few ways of calming myself down, and I've even got used to the glittering eyeballs of the neighbors peering out at us from the peepholes in their doors, they haven't bought the story about stomach problems for a long time now. I wanted the days to stay the same and there really was a kind of uniformity about them, and all of a sudden she's coming back.

When we heard the doors of the Subaru slam shut we stood in the hallway like an honor guard, Talia first, then me, and Uli behind me, very close together and because I was in the middle I could feel the heat coming from both of them and the trembling. I had some chinaberries in my pockets for security and I kept stroking them till they were warm and damp, they helped me to overcome the terrible ringing that sent sparks flying up into my brain and stopped up my ears.

I didn't give Mother my hand when she came in because it was in my pocket clutching those berries, and when she bent over Uli I saw that she had become thin, her bones were sticking out under her purple blouse. Father led her into the living room as if she were a glass stem, his big hand encircling her white one, and she let him lead her to the biggest and fanciest of our three armchairs. She sat down very slowly without moving her head as if it were fixed in a permanent position, just bent her body into a sitting position and said, I'm terribly thirsty, those pills dry me out completely. Talia rushed to the kitchen to make lemonade, Uli sat on the floor near the TV and stirred his Lego and I stood still with the chinaberries in my hand and had no idea what is done on such occasions. Father helped her unbuckle her shoes, there were red marks on her white feet from the straps and I decided that the best thing for me to do was to concentrate on the feet business and not think about anything else.

Why are you afraid of me, she asked and all the windows banged at once, don't be afraid, I take medicine and I'm fine I just need to get stronger, and I saw that her ring had slipped down to her knuckle and she was twisting it around and around on her finger. Get a hold of yourself, I said to myself, think about the patience of the old fig tree, go to your room and touch the leaves, but the space under my bed was empty and clean, Talia had thrown out everything.

They didn't suspect anything at the grocery when I took five jars of pickled cucumbers and said that Father would pay later. The jars were much heavier than I had expected and my right shoulder hurt. Everyone was still sitting in the living room when I spilled the contents on the windowsill in the kitchen, five rows, ten cucumbers in each row, dark green, close together, glittering in the sun, the strong wind outside ruffled the Baumans' curtains, now and then widening the gap between them. I had been careful to open all the windows earlier, even the small one in the bathroom that we never opened, and all the cabinets and all the drawers, everything was open to enlarge the space and lessen the danger of carbon dioxide, and now that everything was open and air was flowing freely through the house I could allow myself to stand quietly in the kitchen and look at what was happening outside. The Baumans' curtains fluttered like a giant butterfly, the thin fringes edging the pink gauze blew about in the wind like Talia's hair. I think Mrs. Bauman's eye was blue, or maybe it just seemed that way because the sky was reflected in her glasses.

Winds blew through the space between our building and theirs, the last fingers of light played on the walls. I waited for darkness when the flight of the bats begins, and they take off all at once from the south side of the building and the moon lights up their heavy bellies. Strange creatures, thick membranes connect their digits and they fly through the yard in total blindness, and maybe this whole flying business is not as complicated as I thought and I emptied the chinaberries out of my pockets to get rid of the weight and they bounced against the windows of the neighbors below us until they finally landed on the ground. I rolled up my sleeves and bared my elbows and started to move them up and down in a uniform, controlled motion and felt that if I could only get a little better at it I could detach myself from the ground and hover, and then my flight would be as transparent and delicate as a dragonfly's, and Mrs. Bauman's shrieks, Help! the girl is jumping, didn't distract me and from moment to moment the motion of my elbows became smoother, more delicate and precise, almost perfect.

Ronit Matalon

A Borrowed Convertible

Translated by Marsha Weinstein

They drove to Rosh Pina in a gleaming, gap-roofed convertible that Maurice borrowed from Shlomo, a buddy who owned a garage. Lily M. went, and Maurice went, and Margalit his daughter went, along with her collection of cardboard boxes which she stuffed into an old makeup case of Lily M.'s shaped like a suitcase and lined with red satin bunting. Toward evening they set out in a taxi for the garage on Hamasger Street, where they waited forever in a wood-paneled room with a large fan that swung left, swung right, and faced forward toward Maurice, tousling his hair and blowing his thick forelock up over his forehead like a weird crown.

Maurice, in his good suit, stretched out in a armchair and dozed off, his head resting on one of the small, filthy pillows that were strewn about the room.

Lily M. laughed. "You're a real sight, with your hair like that," she said, bending over to remove a wad of chewing gum from the heel of her shoe.

Maurice opened his eyes at once, in utter silence. He stared straight ahead as if there were no difference between sleeping and waking but for the hushed sense of doom that had just made him open his eyes; a still sense of doom that was insinuated by the wall opposite and by the window set in that wall, which looked out at tall buildings; a stifling sense of doom that was portended in the curtain shielding the window, which stirred with the fan's breeze, then hung inert; a canny, enigmatic sense of doom.

"What time is it?" he asked, rising and striding toward the door that divided the waiting room from the office. He rapped at the door, fixed his hair. "Just a couple more minutes, a couple minutes more," came a voice from inside. "There's no rush, Shlomo," Maurice said. "We've got time."

The girl lay on the floor at his feet, arranging wrapped boxes in a square the size of the floor tiles. He looked at her as he turned towards the adjacent bathroom, his gaze lingering on her socks, which sliced into the flesh of her pudgy legs. Suddenly overcome with rage, he said: "What are you getting all dirty for now?"

She was humming something softly, setting the boxes down carefully and running her finger along their sides to straighten them.

She had a strange face. A crooked, hawklike nose, especially the line of the nostrils, protruded distressingly far above the sliver-thin lips, which were always parted as if holding a bubble of saliva; her usual expression was one of perplexity. Pale, nearly invisible lashes guarded her dull-brown, beady eyes, where a cruel, cold spark sometimes flashed, devouring her pleasantly homely features and transforming them into something else, something harsh and terrible to look at.

At night she would stand by his bed in her long, white nightgown, arms clasped behind her back and knees touching the bed frame, her gaze piercing the darkness until he woke in alarm, pulling the sheet over his head and kicking the sleeping Lily M. : "Get her out of here," he'd say, trembling. "Take her away."

Once every two months he picked the child up from his mother's house, bringing slender tubes of perfumeries, and gifts: wicker baskets of mangoes on a bed of straw; beribboned, cellophane-wrapped packages of candied fruit or marzipan arranged in a heart; giant chocolate bunnies, their eyes and ears outlined with stiff white icing; strings of glass beads; little girls' pink purses decorated with charming, innocent drawings of blond girls in straw hats, or lambs or squirrels on dark-green lawns, bathed in a rain of yellow polka dots.

"Look, Margalit," he said, opening the purse for her, pointing out its attractions: a zippered pocket for coins; a removable, two-sided mirror; a secret compartment in the bottom. "Look, Margalit."

The child opened the purse cautiously, examining the various compartments in turn and then placing it back in its box, conscientiously resealing the long, sticky ribbon. "It's very nice, Maurice," she said. "I'll put it away and make sure it doesn't get lost."

"Why don't you put it in your suitcase," he suggested. "What have you got that suitcase for, anyway?' She thought a moment, raising her vulnerable, beady eyes with their light, translucent lashes. "I can't," she said at last. "I'll put it someplace else."

Maurice buttoned his jacket, missing a button; he unbuttoned it and began again. Her halting, graceless, clumsy speech, rushing and whistling like a large shell pressed to his ear, made him dizzy, drew him down to turbid depths.

"C'mon," he said. "Let's go."

They went to pick up Lily M. from the boutique. Afterwards, Maurice promised, they would go get ice cream at the beach.

He put on dark sunglasses and tucked a silk scarf into his shirt collar. "How do I look?" he asked.

"You look very nice, Maurice," the child replied.

"You didn't even look," he said angrily. "You answered me without looking."

"I looked at you before," she said panting, trying to catch up with him.

On the way they stopped at a kiosk that sold nuts and candies and bought anise lozenges for Lily M., and candy-coated peanuts. Maurice rationed the child to a handful of peanuts at a time. "Don't chew them," he explained. "It's better to suck on them, like candy. The coating melts. They taste better that way."

When they reached the corner near the boutique, Maurice said, "I'll wait here. You go get her."

He leaned against an electricity pole, crossing his legs and combing his hair with a small plastic comb he pulled from his pocket. Behind the dark glasses his shiny, narrow eyes ranged over the sidewalk, fixing on one thing or another, then letting it go, forgetting what they had been looking for.

He had taken to waiting for her on that corner since he had borrowed two thousand shekels from Etti, the boutique owner, and failed to pay her back. He'd tried various tactics: detouring down long side streets that circumvented the boutique, changing the tenor of his voice on the telephone. Recently, Etti had threatened to fire Lily M. after he'd passed a bad check from his mother's checkbook.

From his post across the street he made out a familiar figure. He tensed, relaxing only when the figure crossed the street in the other direction. Soon he was slack with relief, alternately perusing the headlines in a newspaper he had bought at the kiosk and observing the movements of the passersby, which seemed to encircle him in a pleasant way, gladdening in its commonplaceness, a positive and not unfamiliar routine that allayed his anxiety for a time and made him feel anchored in the world, surrounded by sensible things, by simple deeds and uncomplicated intentions.

"Gotcha!" Lily M. cried from behind, startling him. She was wearing a short, flowered dress and high-heeled, cheap shoes whose leather was peeling. Maurice looked at them derisively, still shaken by her capriciousness. "What's that supposed to be, those shoes?" he asked.

"They're just regular shoes," said Lily M.

They turned toward the beach in single file, Maurice leading, walking quickly, pulling up his lapels to shield his neck, Margalit following with her large, blue suitcase, and Lily M. alternatively falling behind and catching up, her heels tap-tapping, her arm reaching over Maurice's shoulder to grab a handful of peanuts. "Here," he said, stopping suddenly, handing her the bag. "You hold it."

When they arrived at the promenade that ran the length of the beach, Maurice began looking for a coffee shop right on the water, down on the sand. They walked until Lily M.'s feet hurt. "There's no such place," she shouted from behind, tottering on her high heels.

"Yes there is," Maurice said. "I tell you there is."

Where the beach meets Allenby Street they found a kiosk whose owner had set chairs and tables out on the sand. Lily M. took off her shoes and ran to the water to wash her feet. Maurice sat down, shaking sand out of his pants cuff, and lit a cigarette. "What's new in school?" he asked the girl, who sat staring at her feet digging in the sand.

"Nothing," she said.

Lily M. came back. "The water's great," she said. "I'm going right back in. You coming?" she asked Margalit. The child shook her head "no," gathering the edges of her skirt carefully under her. "C'mon," Lily M. said, grabbing her arm, "come on in." She dragged the chunky, hesitant child to the water's edge. "Take your shoes off and come in," Lily M. said.

"No," replied the child.

"Go on," Maurice cried from behind. "Enjoy yourself a little, now that we're here."

The child flopped down on the sand. "I'll push you in," Lily M. threatened good-naturedly. She dragged the girl to the water and pushed her from behind, until her chubby body was submerged to the waist. "Well?" Lily M. called. "How's the water?"

The girl shut her eyes and stood unmoving for a few minutes. Then she plunged her head into the water. "Going diving?" Lily M. chuckled, splashing water on herself.

Suddenly Lily M. grew alarmed. "What d'you think you're doing?" she cried. "Take your head out of the water!" The girl's dark, frizzy locks floated on the surface. "Come out, I said!" Lily M. shrieked, pulling at the child, huffing and puffing.

"Did you see that?" Lily M. asked Maurice as they neared the table, dripping, their legs muddied.

Maurice ordered lemonade and Danish for them all. "You want a popsicle?" he asked the child. "Yes, Maurice," she answered, pulling apart the Danish to remove the raisins.

Maurice shredded an empty cigarette pack. "So what do you say about this business?" he asked Lily M.

"What business?" she replied, gulping her lemonade and squeezing the water out of her hair. "I was so thirsty," she said.

"That aunt of yours in Rosh Pina," he said.

"You still thinking about that?" she asked.

"I need ten grand to pay Etti and close the deal with that guy for the office furniture. He's squeezing me," he said.

"She won't give you a cent. Forget it," Lily M. said.

"But she owes your parents," he said, dropping shreds of cigarette pack and sweeping sand over them with his foot.

"She owes my parents, not me," said Lily M.

"Why not give it a try?" he asked, leaning toward her and grabbing her wrist. "What d'you care? It's worth a try."

For more than six months, he'd been living in her two-room apartment on Allenby Street which stank of cat piss and ammonia. The stench clung to everything, to the piles of clothes before and after laundry that nightly migrated from the double bed to the floor and, in the morning, studded with strands of hair, dust and clumps of plaster that had fallen from the ceiling, migrated back to the bed; to the kitchen utensils and the sticky counter; to the napkins and the white and beige lace doilies hand-crocheted by Lily M.'s mother, that adorned every conceivable and inconceivable surface – armchair rests, tables, shelves.

He had moved in with her after he'd been forced to leave his own apartment, which had doubled as his office, in the middle of the night out of fear of his creditors. It had had two telephone lines, venetian blinds, an enormous poster of Paris at night, wall-to-wall carpeting, a cuckoo clock, and an umbrella stand by the door.

On sleepless nights, wrapped in a silk bathrobe embroidered with dragons that a friend had brought back from Hong Kong, he would stretch out in his executive chair – at the touch of a side lever it moved into a reclining position – staining papers with cigarette ash and chewed toothpicks.

He'd started, as he said, "at the bottom:" a third-rate magician who performed at birthdays and other parties. For several months he apprenticed himself to Caliostro, the real thing. He was with him morning, noon, and night. He ate with him, drove his children to after-school activities, did the shopping and cooked like crazy. Caliostro paid him an apprentice's wages and used him as a cover for his night-time absences from home. Money ended their professional relationship, and their friendship: Maurice got Caliostro a performance at a private party held by one of his friends. According to Caliostro, Maurice had pocketed a sizable finder's fee. Maurice denied it, packed his things, and left the same day with his pride intact.

He printed up business cards, bought the necessary props, and began to perform. For a while he tried to convince Margalit to join him as his personal assistant. Standing on a little stool in front of her, wearing a black magician's cape and waving his short arms like a large, crippled chicken, he talked and talked about acrobats and acrobat families – fathers and daughters, mothers and sons, sometimes whole families.

On one occasion she did give in to his entreaties. At his command, she hid under a table covered with a long tablecloth, and handed him props. When the performance was over, she stepped out from under the table but tripped over a mesh cage of white doves that predicted fortunes from cards. The doves spilled out and flew around the room, dropping feathers on to the refreshments and alighting on window ledges. She stood in the center of the room, chewing on her dress collar and covering her ears with the palms of her hands. Maurice was embarrassed. Indignant, he dragged her back to his mother's house and locked her in the bedroom as punishment, berating her for hours from the other side of the door.

In any case, his business as an independent magician didn't thrive. The low fees he charged to curry favor, the taxis, the clothes, the gifts he gave to guests of honor, all ruined him: his expenses far exceeded his income.

A Wild-West style wedding that he planned once for a neighbor couple, with cowboy costumes for the guests, can-can dancers and a tommy gun salute after the ceremony, led him to become an impresario.

He sold the rabbits and the doves, the capes, the boxes and ropes for a song, ran around for two months to find five guarantors so he could borrow twenty thousand shekels from the bank, and opened an office. He needed a secretary.

He interviewed Lily M. three times before he finally hired her. He wanted a "friendly atmosphere," he said.

Her real name was Lily Marmelstein. She was the daughter of elderly, middle-class parents who had a little shop in the south end of the city that sold sewing supplies. "Very simple people, very simple," Maurice determined with some discontent after they had shown reserve toward him, and polite aversion.

She soon changed her name to Lily M. He preferred short names, he said. She was glad. She began to dress with more care; she dyed her hair ash blond and gathered it in a chignon. She sipped white wine with dinner and affected a slight nasal twang. She made a habit of fingering her long strands of pearls.

Maurice, who wanted to branch out to receptions and catering in the homes of diplomats and the wealthy, taught her French. He obtained a book for beginners with the French alphabet and monosyllabic words with illustrations. She often bungled her pronunciation of the "e," and more often was distracted by the illustrations: the cat, she thought, looked like a dog, and the chair had only three legs.

Maurice despaired. He tore the illustrations out of the book, crumpled them and threw them in the wastebasket. At the sight of her protruding eyes staring at him – the eyes of a gullible, distressed lamb – he relented. "My baby," he said sitting her on his lap and burying his face in her neck. "You don't know a thing, do you?" he said, rocking her on his knees from side to side in consolation and appeasement: "You don't know a thing; not a thing."

They abandoned the French and moved on to cooking. Maurice inquired about importing escargots and shrimp, purchased whole sets of tablecloths and serving utensils, and compiled complicated menus.

It was a fraught time. Yesterday's goblets of champagne and leftovers of Cordon Bleu lay on large china platters among mountains of paper, newspaper clippings and full ashtrays. Crème Anglaise simmered on the stove in the narrow, stuffy kitchenette. People came and went, came and went, talking of deals, barter arrangements, tax laws. Telephones never ceased ringing in the midst of lengthy, multi-course meals that were held on the balcony, from whose right edge one could glimpse the sea.

Maurice served. Wearing a white chef's hat and swathed in an apron wound twice around his narrow waist, he never touched the food. He grew gaunt. At night, when the drunken guests, whose faces he barely recognized, had finally gone, he chewed on stumps of carrots and cucumbers, sitting beside the table still laden with dessert bowls, slices of half-eaten bread, and empty bottles of wine and beer.

He and Lily M. sat on the balcony until morning's first light, dissolute in their evening clothes beside the festive table. Lily M. fell asleep stretched across two chairs, her dress hiked slightly above her knees, revealing a long run in one stocking. Maurice drank his fourth cup of coffee and stared at the chilly, empty street. Tall, dense trees closed in on the balcony from the left, dropping withered leaves onto the railing and table and concealing the lighted appliance store whose broken alarm rent the street with an incessant wail, which seeped slowly into the ineffectual, viscous thoughts of numbers and calculations that had been preoccupying him for some time. Sometimes he would fixate on a single number, rolling it over and over in his mind before letting it go and pulling another from the serpentine chain of numbers. "Fifty grand," he thought. "Fifty thousand clear," he ruminated, and paused for a moment: the wail had stopped.

When she woke, blinking in the strong light, he was already leafing through the financial pages of the morning papers. She went to wash her face, on the way touching his shoulder, massaging it lightly. "Didn't you sleep?" she asked. "No, I didn't," he replied, leaning aside to evade her grasp, part of his shoulder staying warm even after she had gone into the bathroom, half asleep and stumbling over furniture, taking with her the warmth and innocence of those whose sleep is tranquil, he thought. Recoiling inside, he held her accountable for having slept like that so close to him, oblivious. "An earthquake wouldn't have roused her," he thought, immediately ashamed of himself of the grudge he bore her, of the envy he felt at her provocative, undisturbed sleep, the recollection of which became more vivid the moment he thought of the word "provocative," whose very sound seemed to bare sharp teeth, devouring the shame he had felt only moments before.

In the mornings she went shopping, equipped with the list of goods he had given her and orders regarding substitutes, if necessary – orders that confused her and intimidated her. She came back mostly with badly-sewn dresses and ugly knickknacks purchased in the southernmost streets of the city. Within two weeks he had dispensed with her presence in the office. She couldn't type, she made spelling errors, she forgot the mail and urgent messages, she drowsed at business meetings.

Sometimes, when they sat facing one another toward evening in the empty office, both preoccupied with their own affairs, he would suddenly notice her plucking her eyebrows or doing a crossword puzzle in a women's magazine, chomping on an apple and spraying droplets of juice onto the pages. Repulsed by her banality, by his own banality, he resolved to end the affair neatly that very day, to send her away with a nice gift and some flowers, and to find another, more worthy secretary.

His ribs ached. In an effort to determine the source of the pain he rubbed them, counting them as he went, then pressed them hard, first with his fingers and then with his fist, to eradicate the previous, mysterious ache. He bent over the desk, pretending to go through his papers, and in the darkness beneath it he dug his fists into his ribs, straining to see as the light waned, disassembling her figure in the armchair opposite him, first her head – "it all starts with the head," he thought – then watching all of her crumble except for the bright red spot that was her dress – "the little whore," he thought, amazed at his directness.

"Lily," he called. "Lily."

Shivering, he plunged his fists between his thighs. "I'm sick," he said.

She put him to bed, covering him with a blanket and turning on the light. "No, turn off the light," he pleaded. Then she lay down beside him, slowly pulling his hand out from under the blanket and bringing it to her lips. "My poor baby," she said. "You never stop working." Her bulging eyes with their fake eyelashes gleamed in the light that seeped in through the blinds, or maybe it was from the sadness they reflected, a heart-wrenching, grown-up sadness, as if she knew something, as if there was something she knew, one thing she understood that he never would. He clung to her, laying his head on her breast and listening to the drumming of her heart, sinking into her, pushing on until the noise stopped, all the noise except for that one, rhythmic sound.

"Say something, Lily," he said.

"Like what?" she asked.

"Something, anything, it doesn't matter," he said.

In the morning, wearing a pink, woolly robe, she brought him coffee and toast in bed and propped another pillow behind his back. Stubble had grown on his sunken cheeks, emphasizing the hidden pallor of a dark-skinned face. Coffee dripped from the cup to the saucer; he mopped up the little puddle with paper napkins, twisting his face in revulsion. He sipped in silence, staring into the cup, his eyes dim and harboring ill. "Take your things and go," he said.

She found a job as a saleswoman in a boutique and moved into her parents' old apartment. They didn't meet for two months, until one night he knocked at her door. When she opened it, she couldn't see anyone in the dark corridor. Clasping two plastic bags, Maurice leaned on the door jamb and turned aside. "I'm in trouble," he said. Lily M. served tea in the living room whose heavy wooden furniture was arranged in a row: a carved table, a buffet, another table, an armchair, a special cabinet for the record player. A thick, striped curtain covered the width of one wall. "But I don't have a thing," said Lily M. "Not a thing."

They lay down on her parents' high double bed. Maurice talked and talked, smoking cigarettes and playing with the ends of her hair. At five in the morning he awoke, thoroughly chilled. He searched the closet for something to wear and found a white chiffon nightshirt that buttoned down the front. He woke again at 9 a.m. Quietly he took off the nightshirt and put it back in its place, then he shaved, washed, dressed, and waited. By eleven they were at the bank. Lily M. mortgaged her apartment. Then they went for a swim, and had a picnic. Maurice made sandwiches of black bread, charcoal-broiled chicken, tomatoes, spicy Tunisian salad, and choice cheeses. They opened a bottle of wine. Dessert consisted of fresh fruit and chocolate. That night, before they went out, perfumed and heavy after a long afternoon nap, Maurice dressed her as he once had, in a little black dress with a slit up the side, black flat shoes, a string of pearls and matching earrings. He brushed her hair carefully and gathered it in a loose knot at her nape. Grabbing her shoulders, he stood her back from his body and looked her over, his gaze veiled.

It was night when they reached a broad house shrouded in darkness, with two flat wings facing one another, like two large palms.

For a long time they had wandered the streets of the village, leaning over to read the small signs set in doors and stone walls. "What kind of place is this?" Maurice asked standing still, surveying the area. "Trees and stones. It's like a cemetery."

Again he wandered from house to house, confused by the similar yards, retracing his steps, crisscrossing the streets and peering at signs, all the while shaking out his hands, which were red from holding the steering wheel for so long.

Lily M. trailed after him at some distance from the thick hedges. There was fluttering there, bugs, moths. She soon tired and sat down to rest on a large stone by the side of the road, munching on a hamburger they had bought at a gas station concession stand. "Forget it, Maurice," she said over and over, licking her ketchupy fingers.

An old man walked past her, leading a large dog on a leash. He stopped in front of her, pulling his slack pants up toward his waist, and stared. Lily M. held the remains of the bun out to the dog: "C'mere honey, have a bite," she cajoled.

Maurice came running from the end of the street, his tie flailing. "Fanny," he asked, panting, "where does Fanny live?" The man said nothing, passing his hand over the dog's wide head. Man and dog looked at him for a while. "Fanny?" he finally said in a thick, broken accent. He gave a lengthy explanation in vague, incomprehensible language, his hand pointed ahead of them toward a clump of lights at the top of a hill to the left.

Maurice favored going on foot; in any case they would have to stop every few minutes to check, and it was nice out.

They barely managed to wake the child who was sleeping in the back seat, and had to support her on either side as they lumbered up the steep road. For a while Maurice carried her in his arms, then gave up. "She's heavy," he complained, examining his wrinkled shirt with concern. "Come on, give me your hand," he said, offering her his arm. "Don't open your eyes, just move your legs and I'll lead you." That was what they did. Maurice led the child, whose eyes were shut; Lily M., alongside them, carried the blue suitcase and a large bouquet of flowers wrapped in cellophane, a gift for the aunt.

A green wooden fence interlaced with fuchsia bushes surrounded the house. In front was a cast-iron gate, wound twice around with barbed wire. Maurice worked on it for long minutes, breaking his thumbnail. "What's the old lady afraid of?" he muttered, binding a handkerchief around his thumb.

In the end they jumped over the gate. Maurice went first, then extended a hand to Lily M. as he cowered on a tile to the side of the path, out of range of the lawn sprinkler. Margalit's dress got caught in the short, spiked poles of the gate. Lily M. grabbed her legs and Maurice carefully extricated the material. "It's all right," he promised.

All at once festive colored lights went on in the yard above their heads, strung from the gate to the roof beams above the main door. A voice called out: "Who's there?" Maurice and Lily M. glanced at each other.

"Answer," Maurice whispered.

"Who's there?" the voice called again.

"It's me, auntie," said Lily M.

"Louder," Maurice instructed, "she can't hear you."

"It's me, Lily," Lily called to a lighted window on the ground floor. The door opened a crack and they walked toward it, then stood on the porch.

"Who's there with you?" the aunt asked.

"Nobody, auntie. It's just Maurice, my boyfriend, and his daughter and me," Lily M. called.

"I can hear you," she said, coming out toward them wrapped in a large shawl. "What are you shouting for? Come closer," she commanded. "Come closer. What have you done to your hair?' she said scrutinizing Lily M., reaching out and touching her hair. "It's like straw," she said.

Maurice joked, "You know, a different color every day."

The aunt turned to face him. "So you're the divorced magician?" she interrogated him.

He nodded, retreating till his way was blocked by a large clay pot.

"Very well," she said. "Come in."

They crowded onto one sofa in the long white living room, which was practically empty of furniture. "What a huge room!" Maurice whistled in awe, getting up and pacing the room, his hands stuck in his pants' pockets. "How much d'you think a place like this is worth?" he asked. Opening a window wide and looking out. Outside it was cold, impervious, secretive. The blank, silent houses with their fences and neglected wood and metal signs were embroidered into the thatch of trees and undergrowth, adhering to some principle, lying very very low in the good landscape that was generous to all, to rich and poor, sick and healthy, old and young. He leaned out, opening his mouth wide to gulp cool air, to burrow deep into the landscape, disappear into it and slough off the cares, the grime, the restlessness that had tormented him, consumed his soul. "Take everything!" he would say, merciful and pure. "Take everything," he would say walking away from it all, his head held high, taking only the shirt on his back and a few small mementos, wiping his face on his sleeve to hold back the tears and the pity.

A door slammed behind him. The aunt appeared carrying a tray full of juice glasses. Painstakingly, she wiped each glass with a kitchen towel before serving it. "It's fantastic here, really," Maurice said. Excited, he hoped to placate her with compliments. She placed her body in the wide armchair opposite them, resting her glass on its wooden arm, and stared at the girl. "Where are your people from?" she asked the child.

Maurice burst out laughing, spraying juice all about him. "We're of Egyptian stock, Nona. Egyptians," he said. "We Egyptians know how to eat. Baklawa, you ever heard of it?"

"Had some once," she said drily.

The child studied a large oil painting on the wall above the dining table. She went up to it, extending a hand to touch the globs of purple and green paint. "What's it a painting of?" she asked suddenly.

"It's a Galilean landscape," the aunt replied. "Don't touch it."

Maurice joined the child beside the painting. "Very interesting," he said, somewhat absentmindedly. Out of the corner of his eye he followed the conversation between Lily M. and her aunt.

"Your father said he'd send twelve plates, but he sent only six," the aunt's voice grew louder. "You tell him that, you tell him every word I said."

Lily M. mumbled something, playing nervously with her hands in her lap, pulling her silver ring on and off.

He went over to a pile of records and looked through it, chose one and placed it on the old record player in the corner of the room. "C'est une chanson," Yves Montand's voice crooned, deep and velvety in the large room, drowning out the aunt's complaints. Her cheeks puffing and reddening, she called out: "Really! Really!"

He grabbed her strong, freckled hand and brought it to his lips: "Come dance with me, Nona," he coaxed her. Gently he pulled her toward the center of the room, whispering "shhh" when she tried to evade his grasp. Throwing his head back and mouthing the words of the song, he waltzed her in grand, wide, easy sweeps the length of the room, to the French doors that opened onto the garden in the backyard. There, at the end of a winding white path, the girl stood with her blue suitcase, trying to find the crickets whose clicking was the only sound coming from the edge of the garden.

Lily M. went out to her. "Come on inside, it's dark out," she said, though she herself continued to stand there barefoot, smoothing her concave stomach and prominent hip bones under her tight dress. She picked a rose and plucked its petals, crushing them between her fingers until the palms of her hands were covered with a sticky, pink paste. "When are we leaving?" the girl asked.

"I don't know," answered Lily M., flopping down onto a bench cemented there. "When we're done with things here, I guess." She yawned, and scratched a pimple on her chin. "I'd love to be in bed right now," she said.

It took a while for them to notice that the large room had become very quiet. Lily M. straightened up: "What's going on in there?" she asked.

The needle of the record player slipped. No one was there. Beyond the living room wall, from the stairs that led up to the second floor, came the sound of loud voices and the tapping of footsteps. Then Maurice appeared. His dark narrow face shone. A flower was stuck in his lapel. "What's wrong?" Lily M. asked in alarm.

"Nothing," he said, lighting a cigarette, shielding the flame from the wind. "Everything's fine," he said

"Where's my aunt?" asked Lily M.

"She's making an omelet in the kitchen," he said. "Go talk to her."

She looked at him for a moment, then got up and walked off toward the kitchen. Before she had reached the door, she changed her mind and came back.

"Did you say anything to her?" she asked.

"Me?" asked Maurice in amazement.

She turned away, burying her face in her shoulder, behind the curtain of her hair. "You never tell the truth," she whimpered, starting to cry. "Never a word of truth."

He was overcome by a coughing fit and loosened the knot of his tie. "Lily," he coughed. "Lily, you're doing me an injustice here. Really, Lily, you're not being fair. Come on," he said, taking hold of her hands, then pressing her hunched shoulders to his chest. "Come on, let's go wash your face. Come with me."

When they came back she was leaning on his arm, dragging her left leg a little. He patted her hand and pushed her slowly toward the kitchen. He caressed the back of her neck before slowly closing the door.

The child had moved back inside. She was leaning on the suitcase, waving her arms in front of her, tracing shapes in the air. He went out to the garden, came back, made a circuit of the room, listened for a while behind the kitchen door, then sat down on the sofa. "What are you doing?" he asked the child.

"Nothing," she said. "Playing."

"What kind of game is that you're playing?" he wondered aloud.

"Nothing special. A game," she said.

He went back to pacing the room, stroking his chin and glancing at the clock. He stopped beside her, watching in wonderment as her fingers played in the air, bent, stretched, and pointed straight ahead at some invisible object. "Want me to teach you a magic trick in the meantime?" he asked.

Her arms, still extended in mid-air, stopped moving. "All right," she said with some hesitation, getting up to sit opposite him.

Maurice held a cigarette between the fingers of one hand and drew the fingers of the other over it, as if to estimate its length. "You take a cigarette," he began, "and light it. You grab it very tightly with your teeth – see? You move it from side to side in your mouth, up and down, up toward your nose. Then you open your mouth, all at once," he gulped, "so it jumps into your mouth. Then you blow out smoke from your nose and ears – see? Three, four times... and finally," he cheered, waving his arms before her eyes, "you pull the cigarette out of your sleeve – see?" He bowed deeply to her.

The child blinked, haltingly touched her lips. "From which sleeve?" she asked.

"What d'you mean, 'from which sleeve'?" he said, his knee jiggling nervously.

"From which sleeve do you pull out the cigarette?" she insisted.

"It doesn't matter," he said. "It doesn't matter what sleeve, the main thing is that you pull it out. Now," he announced, "it's your turn."

Lily M. came in, quietly closing the kitchen door behind her. "Well?" he asked, stuffing the pack of cigarettes into his pocket. She shook her head.

"She didn't agree?" he asked in astonishment.

"She won't give us a penny," said Lily M., taking her patent leather pocket book off the table. "Let's go."

He forcefully pulled the pocket book out of her hands, turned it inside out and looked at it in panic, not knowing what to do. The thought "I'm ruined" flashed through his mind like the neon sign of a sign company opposite an apartment he had lived in years ago, a one-and-a-half room place not far from the stadium in Yad Eliahu. Where exactly it had been he couldn't recall, though he panned the familiar streets in his mind's eye. He knew the name of the street had had something to do with a rabbi, it ended in "ra" – no, not "Ezra." The number "12a" echoed in his head, conjuring an image of the entry where kids had scrawled graffiti, and of the stairwell, which had always smelled of fatty chickens frying. Suddenly engulfed by a wave of nausea, he grabbed his head and, wobbling from side to side, ran out to the garden.

"Maurice!" Lily M. called, running out after him barefoot. "Maurice!"

The clink of silverware, the opening and shutting of doors and the nervous, regular rattle of a refrigerator crept into the silence of the white unfamiliar room, leaking under the kitchen door along with a narrow strip of light. The child walked in Lily M.'s high-heeled shoes toward the French doors, then the length of the room and back again toward the French doors, deliberately scrunching up her toes so as not to slip.

The ringing of a phone upstairs froze her to her spot, until the steady flow of silence and its rustlings began again.

She stepped out of the shoes and carried the suitcase to the carpet, opening it with care: first using the tiny key, then popping the right and the left latches in turn. Quietly she removed the wrapped boxes one by one, the humming of the crickets and the murmur of broken conversation wafting through the French doors. It was her habit once a day to empty the suitcase and brush the satin lining with a small brush she removed from the cloth pocket on the inside of the lid. She turned the suitcase upside down and rapped on its bottom to remove any lingering dust and then, tense, weak with the pleasure and suffering the tension brought her, carefully chose those parcels worthy of being the first to be put back, swallowed up, placed full of promise on the shiny cloth.

"You're sick, Maurice. You're sick, you're sick" a voice outside insisted, saying it over and over without cease. "You're sick, Maurice. You're sick, sick."

She placed a blue rectangular box in the corner, surveyed the colored boxes that were left, and waited.

The thing had to be done quietly, in solitude, with dedication and reverence.

At first, when Lily M. had given her the suitcase, it had been simple, almost mechanical; only the damaged objects, the ones that were torn or dirty, were weeded out. Some of them were laundered or repaired and others were discarded. But then things got complicated. An idea got stuck in her head. What that idea was she did not know, but she felt it the way one feels the presence, behind one's back, of someone in the doorway. A strange sensation grew inside her, a dissatisfaction concerning the suitcase, something in the suitcase, or in the desecration of the suitcase.

The objects and the suitcase – the suitcase and the objects – had to be in total symmetry, in perfect, ultimate harmony, unsullied by one iota of disorder or error.

She strove for a completely flat surface of objects in the bottom of the suitcase, without extrusions or indentations and with corners formed by straight angles. This dictated a completely different sort of selection, which soon also governed the colors of the objects and their coordination with the red lining of the suitcase. She was especially troubled by the objects that were flush against the sides of the suitcase: if they were the right size then they weren't the right color, and vice versa. She moved objects, and exchanged them for other objects whose main advantage was their suitability to the suitcase. She exchanged them again and again.

It was an exhausting game. For many weeks she was empty of everything, except for the suitcase. In the meantime, something developed inside her. The empty cardboard boxes that Maurice brought from his office, boxes whose wrapping was chosen with care, took the place of the objects she had lined up against the sides of the suitcase. Soon she had exchanged all of the objects, including those that had been in the center of the suitcase, for wrapped cardboard boxes with straight sides.

For an hour or more she was busy with the boxes. Her tongue poked out slightly over her lower lip, which she bit, and her face held the expression that she reserved for the suitcase and its organization. When she tired of this, she locked the suitcase with the key and placed the key in an empty candy box that she hid in her pocket.

She played with the long fringes of the carpet. She braided all the strands on one side and skipped between the braids. Then she went to the other side. Suddenly the aunt was standing in the doorway, her hand on the light switch. "It's a shame to waste electricity," she said, turning off the central light and switching on a standard lamp with a parchment shade bearing ancient Egyptian figures. She was wearing striped pajamas and her head was wrapped in a white rag that she had fastened above her forehead. "Where are they?" the aunt asked.

The girl was mesmerized by the flat, back-lit silhouettes of beautiful brown youths wielding spears and harpoons. She could barely tear her eyes away to look up in appreciation at the aunt and ask: "What?"

Maurice burst into the room at a run, his shirt open. "Come," he said. "We're going." By the time the girl had lumbered out of the house, Maurice was already past the lawn; she could just make him out at the end of the path, hurrying her along with a wave of his arm. When they reached the steeply-pitched asphalt road that led to the car, they could hear Lily M. from behind.

"Wait, Maurice," she called, panting, her high-heeled shoes in her hand.

Maurice kept running, pulling the child after him by the arm. "Go away," he shouted at Lily M. "Go away." For a few minutes she disappeared from sight, but then suddenly reappeared from behind some bushes, kicking up gravel with her feet.

"Wait, Maurice, wait," she cried, taking a shortcut through a small grove to their right, fleet-footed, catching up with them, now only a few feet away.

Maurice looked back, wiping his face on his shirt sleeve. Suddenly he bent forward, scooped up a fistful of gravel and hurled it at her. "Get away, leave me alone," he shouted, flinging stones over his shoulder aimlessly, opening his fist and letting them fall to the ground.

Hastily he slammed the car doors behind them, turned the radio on full blast, turned the key in the ignition and drove off.

The girl in the back seat extended her hand, fingers spread, into the wind outside. Bent, spike-topped trees raced by, one after the other, At an empty junction with a traffic light, he looked at her in the rearview mirror. "You cold, sweetie?" he asked. She nodded, curled up in one corner of the seat. Maurice pressed a button and the automatic, flexible top slowly rose above them, gradually blocking the sky. Abruptly it flopped back with a buzzing sound. "What's going on?" Maurice protested, pounding the button in annoyance and groping along the length of the lighted dashboard. "What the hell is this?" The top rose and fell, rose and fell, alternately revealing and concealing the sky all the way to the freeway junction at the edge of the big city.

Shoham Smith

Guadeloupe

Translated by Dalya Bilu

It happened in Guadeloupe, the island that lies in the Pacific Ocean. The volcano of Guadeloupe was conspiring to erupt at any moment.

Let the reader take shelter and wait, for what we are concerned with here isn't an ordinary volcano but a woman, a Guadeloupian, a secretary by profession and utterly nervous.

Her boss' success went to his head and sat there like a fat louse, as he ordered her to type, at once, in duplicate, to punch holes, to file; and bring some coffee, instant, two sugars, that's all, and not to make such a big deal out of it.

But Guadeloupe, well, she was fed up with being told all the time what to do, and her fuses blew, just like Bob Beamon in the thin air of Mexico City.

So that she and her nerves could spend a few moments in private, she shut the door to her room and went over to the corner, where a window, Swiss scenery and snow – in August – grew on a calendar. The plan rose to her head of its own accord, she didn't have to open a single drawer.

Beneath Switzerland stood the photocopying machine called Xerox. She lifted the lid, took a chair, climbed up and lay down on the glass. All kinds of limbs spilled over the sides. She collected them and tidied them up, so that everything would fit into the format. She closed the lid on herself gently, like you close the lid on a coffin or cover a baby.

Then she pressed "ON" and closed her eyes real tight, so as not to be dazzled.

From closing her eyes so hard she fell asleep. From sleeping so soundly she didn't hear the creaking birthpangs of the machine nor see herself being born. Her self born from the Xerox was very much like herself; same secretary, same smile, what's there to say? A carbon copy. Two hundred percent her.

Her eyes were already open, she was enveloped in the white reality around her – she was almost convinced that she was in paradise or at least in Switzerland, until she realized that the white was the top of the walls; the ceiling was so close, immediately she was swept by an urge to give it a hard kiss. Why not? Even an island sometimes longs to lose its boundaries.

Her waist level had risen by a meter. Her knee peeped through the key hole. Her broad pelvis, one of the many Achilles heels she nurtured, had also doubled in width. Luckily the Xerox magnifies everything in proportion and not the way it usually happens, that if something grows a little, right away its hang-ups develop in geometric progression, too. The most accurate word to describe the woman who emerged from the Xerox would be: *monument.*

All of this, everything that happened behind the closed door and must sound to you like a tedious lecture – didn't take longer than a few seconds. Time is an amazing schizophrenic, time is manic. Time flew, and the door opened to welcome it.

Ah, what a laugh it was, to observe the situation from above: her boss, terrified in his chair, as tiny as an out-of-control pilotless plane, dwarfish, even if he were to overcome his paralysis and stand up, he would hardly reach her ankle.

Anxiously, he watched those legs marching toward him. "Just don't lose your nerve," she repeated to herself, "Keep cool," walk slowly and softly, and quietly lest her pity be roused, lest the whole plan go down the drain.

When she reached him she picked him up by his white collar, which was already soaking wet with cold sweat. He cursed himself and wept in silence. Why did he have to be such a big spender and invest in sky and scenery, what was wrong with his last office, as if the sky only existed on floor forty-four. His feet drew little whirlpools in the air. He was positive that this was it.

But the secretary had other plans for him.

"Just you wait," she said, "it's not over yet." He felt her hand, the one holding his neck, bringing him closer to her face, looking at him eye to eye, like he used to do with his chihuahua when it was a puppy and left its poop on the carpet.

"Now," she said, making her way to the Xerox machine, "I'm going to make you **this small**."

And so she did. It was very simple. All the buttons were already set, all she had to do was change the percentages from enlargement to reduction, and to press. Before she closed the lid on him she still managed to hear all kinds of voices promising her bonus shares, exclusive monopolies, compound interest, and other paired words which think that if there are two of them, then they've got the world in their pocket. She tried to imagine to herself what it would feel like to have the world swelling in your pants pocket, like a prick. If I was a man, she said to herself, that's probably what I would think. She didn't know how to explain why she was suddenly very happy to be a woman and not a man.

She took a deep breath and pressed.

And she waited.

Until something emerged, something the size of a fountain pencil. Minuscule fingers and a Lilliputian snout, a shining bare pate. A sweet little dwarf, she almost duplicated a dozen. Luckily she stuck to the original plan. She turned away and sat down, overflowing the leather armchair, while he, a kinetic executive toy, was placed among the papers on the desk, and regiments of words stood on the ramp of her tongue ready to jump, like paratroopers, into the unknown. Terrified, the eyes of the boss watched the hand, beginning to move, writhing toward him like an anaconda. He knew it was the end, that his life was about to turn into puree. Now, he thought, I'll see it passing before my eyes.

And indeed this is what happened. His entire miserable life passed before him frame by frame and it was definitely no thriller, he had to admit, all in all his life had been quite dull and dreary. Apart from that there were all sorts of parts which did not find favor in his eyes or his ears. Whoever said that the movies were silent was either lying or dead. Because that's a fact: the boss heard the barking of the chihuahua very clearly. He remembered how it peed joyfully in his honor every evening when he came home from work. And how, instead of being happy in return, he would shove the chihuahua's gleaming nose into the puddle and say Pfui! And how the insulted chihuahua would nevertheless try to lick his cheek, and how he wouldn't let it, even though it felt nice, because it wasn't educational.

A warm wetness trickled down his cheek. He thought about his chihuahua, which would be left without him, who would look after it? He knew that he looked very unprofessional and even foolish crying, but it made no difference to him. By now he didn't care about anything any more. His head emptied out its entire contents (mainly figures and facts). If only a good fairy would show up here, he thought, one of those blonde ones with a wand and a wish, I would ask her to let me pet the chihuahua, one last time.

There was once a wise man who said "Everything is water," and then another, even wiser, came along and said "Everything flows." They were both right. The island of Guadeloupe was sunk up to the neck in the ocean, the boss streamed tears. And Guadeloupe the secretary? Something strange happened to her, too.

A sweet torrent of spit flooded her mouth. Spit is neither a joke nor words. All the nasty words she was about to pour onto the boss' head dissolved in an instant. What's happening here? She was alarmed. Was she losing control? Where were the fantasies painted by her demonic desire; how she would lay him on the desk and pull off his legs one after the other, and all his other limbs too, one by one, or – and this could be even more fun – force him to type her an apology by jumping from key to key. What had gone wrong, that suddenly all these ideas did not seem so splendid?

She sat in the armchair, an overgrown secretary, sister to Og of Ashtaroth, choked with emotion, and how could she have guessed that her heart too had doubled itself. Suddenly she felt like cupping the boss in her hand and stroking him.

The boss' closed eyes did not prevent him from looking into the cruel reality. He knew all too well that there are no good fairies. Neither in Guadaloupe nor at all. He dreamt that he was his own chihuahua, and that he was being stroked, and also that it was him stroking the chihuahua. Shivers of happiness shook him. Rivers of tenderness streamed through his body. Then he dreamt that he was gliding through the air, that he was being covered, and then there was a great, dazzling light, the kind that penetrates even closed eyes. Mommy, he thought in terror, this must be the light they talk about, the one you see at the end of the dark tunnel, before you... he didn't want to say the word.

"You can open your eyes," he heard a soft voice. He had no idea if he was in paradise, hell, or limbo. Oh my God, he thought, I knew it, God's a woman.

Gadi Taub

You Never Can Tell

Translated by Shira Atik

By the time I heard that this Naama woman (whom I barely know) had knocked down a girl, she had already completed her six months of community service. She had done community service instead of sitting in a prison cell for six months. She got off easy. At first they wanted to charge her with hit-and-run, because she kept on driving and didn't stop until she crashed into an electricity pole. But she wasn't running away. It's just that she was in shock and didn't know what she was doing. She didn't even try to get out of the car.

When the police came, she was still inside with the engine running. The air conditioner, too. People were standing around peering into the car, but the doors were locked, and when they knocked on her window she didn't respond. Itamar told me that when the cops found her, she was sitting there with her hands on the steering wheel, wearing her sunglasses. She had injured her forehead in the crash, and a thin line of blood was streaming down behind her glasses. He heard all these details in court. And he also told me that the girl's parents called Naama every few days. So she wouldn't forget what she had done to them, they said. Since then, she never answers the phone herself. If nobody else is around, she lets the machine pick it up. It happened near the house I live in now, on Balfour Street, not far from the Maccabi health clinic. She killed a twelve-year old girl.

We met in Eilat long before this happened. It was a few weeks before my release from the army. I was on leave, and I went to Eilat with a girl named Lena. She was a year older than me. At one time she had been my older sister's friend, and she used to visit us a lot, but then they had a falling-out. When I was in high school I was in love with her.

I was surprised that she agreed to go with me. I wasn't really serious when I asked her. I just said it, I hadn't even been planning to go myself. All this happened in my sister's apartment. I think it was Lena's first time there.

In Eilat, we rented an apartment for thirty-five dollars a night. One room, with a kitchen and a small shower room and toilet. But it had everything, even a television set. Not that we watched it, but it was there. It was a pleasant second-floor apartment in some complex. Although it didn't have an air conditioner, it did have a Desert Cooler. At that time of year, it was hot as hell outside. Really sweltering. The road surface was blinding. You could feel the hot air in your nostrils when you inhaled. In that kind of heat, it's nice to walk into a cool house. You feel your skin cool down the minute you get inside. In the beginning, it also seems dark, but then your eyes get used to it.

On the day we arrived, we spent the morning at the beach and the afternoon napping. We hung up our clothes and closed the blinds. Lena took the closet near the wall and I took the one next to it. The shelves inside were lined with paper. When we finished unpacking, the closet was still pretty much empty. It was big enough for an entire family's wardrobe. We put a sheet on the bed, and took out two more sheets to cover ourselves. Then we went to sleep. Lena was out in a matter of seconds. She was lying on her stomach, her face turned towards me. The blinds were almost completely closed, but there was still a little light. I looked at her face. I was glad that she was there, and that I was there, and that we had four days together. I didn't think I would be able to fall asleep. I wanted to kiss her. I moved closer to her, until I could feel her breath. I thought I could just get a tiny bit closer, and then I could kiss her. She was only an inch away from my face. She was breathing quietly, like a little girl. She's very pretty. There's something special about her face.

I rolled onto my back and thought about all the things we would do.

How we would go to the beach and lie there all day. I was afraid we wouldn't have anything to say to each other. But four days is a long time. A lot can happen in four days. I took a deep breath, stretched, and turned to face her. I don't know how long it took for me to fall asleep. A long time. I could have skipped the nap altogether, and just lain there looking at her, but in the end I did fall asleep. I fell asleep on my hand.

In the afternoon we got up and walked into town to do some shopping. We bought wine and hot dogs and frozen french fries, and we cooked dinner in the apartment. We drank an entire bottle of wine with the meal. I did most of the drinking. Later, when we went back into town to hang out in some pub, I realized that I was a little bit drunk. I was dizzy, but in a pleasant way. I felt a bit unstable. When my feet hit the sidewalk, it was like I was walking down a staircase in the dark, groping for the bottom step.

The pub was very noisy, and we hardly spoke. We laughed a little, but that was it. Lena smoked, too. She doesn't usually smoke, but it's different when you're in Eilat. We watched all the sex-crazed natives hitting on the tourists. They have no shame. And the fact is, they get what they want. They live here, and they know what they're doing. We spent the whole evening watching which ones were successful and which ones weren't, and while we watched, we drank. Time passed slowly; we weren't in any rush. When we finished our drinks, we'd order more. My skin was hot from being in the sun all morning, and the cold beer made me feel good. The music was good, too. A little dated, but OK.

We stayed there until two in the morning. Lena didn't want to go anywhere else. And it was driving me mad, this feeling that she was close enough for me to smell her hair and her moisturizer. I tried to catch her eye a few times, but she wouldn't meet my gaze. I should have realized that there was nothing there to pursue, but people don't understand what they don't want to understand. That's how it is. If I hadn't gotten drunk and vomited, I would have made a pass at her that same evening. But I was plastered. I barely made it home. I don't remember how we got home. I don't remember anything between the pub and the apartment, except that I threw up outside the pub and was still nauseated afterwards. When we got back, I wanted to throw up again. I went straight to the bathroom and sat down on the floor. Lena followed me in and turned on the light, but I asked her to turn it off. I rested my chin on the toilet seat and waited. I remember that the floor felt cold, and that everything seemed to be spinning. I didn't vomit in the end. I don't know how long I sat there in the dark. Lena finally got me up and helped me into bed. Then she put a mattress on the floor for herself. I lay there in the dark, on my back, in my underwear, and stared at the light bulb dangling from the ceiling. The room was hot. I kept my eyes open; if I closed them, my head would start to spin.

The next morning, I was the first one up. I awoke with a headache at 6 a.m. Outside it was quiet and still cool. I lay in bed for another hour or so; then I got up, showered, and made myself some black coffee.

When Lena got up a few hours later, we tidied up and went to the beach. We lay there all day, sleeping and sunbathing. Every so often, we'd put on suntan lotion. She would do my back and I would do hers, but I didn't exploit the situation. Slowly, I began to feel better. By late afternoon, I was even hungry. The sun had cured me of my nausea. That morning, I'd felt like everything was wrecked because of what had happened overnight. But as the day went on, the feeling lifted. We even shared a couple of laughs over what had happened. Everything was going well.

But that night, when we were out dancing at the disco, I did exactly what I should have known not to do. I was a little tipsy, and in the middle of one of the dances I grabbed her in my arms and embraced her. She tried to break away from me. She pushed my chest with both her hands, digging her thumbs into my ribcage. "No," she said. And she meant it, too. She was very serious. But even if I had managed to restrain myself at that particular moment, it was bound to happen later on. Maybe the next night, or maybe after we got back from Eilat, but sooner or later it would have happened. I was in love with her and it was inevitable.

She kept pushing me away. "That's enough," she said. I was still holding her, and there was a moment when I wanted to kiss her by force. There was a moment like that. But I didn't do it. I held her for another minute, then let go. After that, nothing was the same. And when we got back to the apartment, things got even worse. I shouldn't have begged. I could see that all she wanted was for me to stop, but I was in too deep. I tried to hold her hand. Finally, she went into the bedroom and left me standing there in the kitchen. She started packing her bags. After a few minutes, I followed her in and lay down on the bed. I watched her until she was done. I didn't say another word – there was nothing to say.

That night, after she left, I started smoking again. After fourteen months. I didn't have any cigarettes on me, but I went outside and mooched one off a stranger. Then I went into town. By then it was pretty empty. I found a cigarette machine in one of the pubs, bought a pack, then went down to the beach. I walked along the sand and the gravel towards the Jordanian border, and I looked at the lights of Aqaba. I was drunk, and the lights looked blurry, like they were floating in the air. I could feel my legs. I felt that if I sat down on the sand I would start to cry. I wanted to sit, but I held myself up.

I went back through the hotel area, towards the airport; then I turned left and walked past the new city center, through the neighborhoods where the local people live. Then I started back to the apartment. I wasn't sure exactly how to go. I wandered around until I found the right street. By the time I finally got to the apartment, it was almost daybreak. The lobby was still dark, though. I sat on the stairs. I suddenly felt like I couldn't go inside. I didn't want to see the kitchen, or the dishes we had eaten from, or the bed we had slept in. Already, I couldn't think about anything besides Lena and how I'd ruined everything. I smoked another cigarette, then went back towards the beach. I walked around the lagoon until I found a patch of sand where I could lie down. The sun was starting to rise, but it was still breezy. I was tired. I lay on my side, next to a boat that shielded me from the wind, and put my head down on my arms. Some cold air seeped in behind my collar, but I felt alright anyway. I felt like if I lay there without moving, and without thinking about anything, I would be OK.

When I got back to the apartment, I saw that she had left seventy shekels on the kitchen table. This covered her half of the rent. She must have caught the late-night bus, or maybe she left early in the morning. Perhaps she found somewhere else to sleep. I have no idea.

I stayed in Eilat for the three remaining days of my leave. I don't know how I passed the time. Most nights, I wandered around the beach or went to the pubs. One night I even went to a disco. Not to dance, though, just to look. I sat at a small black table that was bolted to the floor, and I drank. I came for the noise and for the people. It cheered me up a little bit. As a rule, the nights were easier. During the day, I mostly stayed inside. I dozed off, or watched educational TV, or just lay there doing nothing. I slept and ate very little. I had no appetite, even though I had a hole in the pit of my stomach. I felt it constantly. Whenever it gnawed at me, I drank some wine and smoked a cigarette. That always fills me up a little. Once or twice I went downstairs to get a pita sandwich, but I couldn't get it down. I would eat a little, then chuck the rest.

On my last day there, when I was supposed to go back to the army, I called in sick. They don't usually give you any trouble when you're about to get discharged. If they had given me a hard time I would have gone to the regional officer, but it didn't come to that. In fact, it actually worked out well for them. When the deputy battalion commander heard that I was in Eilat, he told me straight out not to go back to the base. At first, I didn't understand what he meant; I thought he was making fun of me. But then he explained himself. He told me they were sending down a crew to update their reference points, and that he was short one soldier. Then he instructed me to wait for him at noon the next day at the airport's military terminal.

The following day, they arrived: Itamar, my unit's operations officer, a sergeant I didn't know, and Naama, whom I also didn't know at the time. She was an intelligence officer in Southern Command. This was about a year and a half before she knocked down the girl.

Our assignment was to review two hundred reference points and check their addresses and diagrams against those listed. We had to update anything that had changed, and mark down new addresses if any had been erased. Itamar and the sergeant, whose name was Haimon, were in uniform; Naama was wearing an army shirt with jeans. The mission was supposed to take us two days, but they gave us three just in case. At any rate, we finished in a day and a half. We drove like maniacs. Itamar was the one who really tore up the road, though I must admit I didn't drive that cautiously myself.

On the first day, only Itamar drove. Naama sat next to him with the maps, and Haimon and I sat in the back. I didn't get out of the jeep all day, except to pee. I didn't even help them look for the reference points. I just sat there. It was good, that drive. I managed not to think about anything. I watched the scenery roll by, and the shoulders of the road. Itamar drove like a lunatic. Going downhill was terrifying. I felt it in my gut. Sometimes I even closed my eyes, which made it even scarier.

It was almost nightfall when we reached Eilat, and we went straight to my apartment. It was better than the accommodation that had been set up for us at the naval base, that's for sure. After we brought up our stuff, Naama went to take a shower. Itamar turned on the overhead light and closed the door. Meanwhile, I sat in a chair with my feet up on the windowsill. I unbuttoned my army shirt and lit a cigarette. The window was open. Ten minutes later, Naama came out of the shower and Itamar went in. And that was the first time I really paid any attention to Naama. She was wearing a cropped t-shirt and underpants. Her hair was wet. She had smooth, tan skin. I looked at her. Itamar looked, too, on his way into the shower. Only Haimon didn't seem to notice. He just lay on the bed and read the paper. When she was finished arranging her bag, she walked over to the window and looked outside. I tilted my chair back and stared at her legs. Her underpants were white. She had a nice body. That was the first time I started to think about her that way. And she could tell that I was staring.

"You see that building?" I asked. She looked where I was pointing. "There was a fire there yesterday. I saw it."

"There?" she said, pointing to the building opposite. By the light of the streetlamps, you could see the soot on the wall above the first-floor windows. The window frames were charred, and the blinds were completely distorted from the flames. There really had been a fire, but it had happened earlier, before I even got to Eilat.

"You should have seen the people leaving the building," I said. "I've never seen anything like it."

She kept looking out the window, but she was listening. "Was anyone hurt?"

I said no. "But after they all went out," I said, "they went back in to get their stuff. They kept running in and out, the husband and wife. The children stayed outside. They brought out pictures, chairs, kitchen appliances, a television, a stereo system. They even took out all kinds of food: frozen meat, bottles, you name it. I don't know why."

"How do you know nobody was hurt?"

"If somebody was hurt, they wouldn't have taken out all those other things, right?"

"I suppose," she said.

I lit another cigarette and threw the match out the window. "In the end, they even managed to take out the refrigerator," I said. Then I was quiet for a moment. Both of us were quiet. Naama stared at the burnt windows. It was pitch black inside the house.

"The upstairs neighbors also started carrying out their stuff," I said. "They were afraid the flames would reach their apartment, too. By the time the firefighters came, they couldn't even get into the downstairs apartment. It was in ashes. So they stood outside and watched the fire."

She thought for a minute. "And nothing happened to the other apartments?"

I leaned my chair further back. "Apparently not," I said. I gestured towards the building with my chin. There were lights on in the second-floor apartment. I looked outside, then at her. She had nice legs. And a nice ass. She came closer and put her hand on the windowsill. "When did they get here?" she asked.

"What?" I didn't know what she was talking about.

"The firefighters, when did they get here?"

"It took them twenty minutes," I said. "Maybe fifteen."

"That's a long time," she said.

I shrugged my shoulders. I don't know what's considered a long time in these kinds of situations.

"Once, my father's store burned down," she said. She went to get a cigarette from her bag. I thought she would bring over a chair and sit down next to me, but she didn't come back. While Itamar was in the shower, she walked around the room arranging her things. When Haimon went in to shower, Itamar dragged a chair over and sat next to me. He also put his feet up on the windowsill. He was barefoot. I looked outside and didn't say a word. I didn't have the energy for a conversation. But it wasn't just that. I couldn't stop thinking about Lena. And that took everything out of me.

After we'd been sitting there in silence for a while, he started asking me what I was planning to do after my discharge. I looked behind me. Naama was still busy sorting through her bag. Just then, I had this urge to get the hell out of there. Their things were scattered all over the room, and the floor was full of wet footprints. The overhead light was on. The mattress that Lena had slept on was leaning against the wall. I wanted to get out. Mostly, I didn't want to talk to Itamar. It was an effort just to move my mouth. I didn't know how I would make it through a whole night with them. If I could have, I would have simply stood up and left. But I stayed. When Itamar started talking to me, I thought about Lena. Ever since the night she left, I'd been tormented by thoughts about what would have happened if I hadn't tried to come on to her. Plus my stomach was empty.

Itamar started telling me about the work he was going to do when he got out of the army. He had a friend who was already doing it. He was working for a company that cleaned the exteriors of old houses. They had a special machine that sprayed a pressurized jet of water. Instead of responding, I just kept saying "uh-huh" over and over again to show that I was listening. Or I would nod my head. He described how they were suspended from the walls while they were working, like rappellers. With special masks and safety goggles. I kept on looking outside; then I threw my cigarette butt out the window. I felt like I could have started crying. I could have, too, very easily. But I stopped myself.

Haimon came out of the shower in a pair of shorts and sat down on the bed. He put his bag between his legs and took out a huge jar of moisturizer. He started spreading the lotion all over his face. He has dry skin. He noticed me staring at him, and he stared back for a moment; then he went back to what he was doing.

I got up and went to the kitchen. I was looking for the red wine. I had an open bottle in the refrigerator. Naama was standing there leaning back on the table, eating some pita with mayonnaise. She looked at me but didn't speak. I opened the fridge. Aside from another jar of mayonnaise, some jam, and a container of olives, it was empty. There were some yogurts in the door, but that's it. I took out the wine, threw the cork into the sink, and took a swig from the bottle.

"Have a drink," said Naama. She dipped her pita in the mayonnaise. There was some mayo on the rim of the jar, and she got a little on her fingers. I toasted her with the bottle and went back to my seat by the windowsill. Itamar sat there quietly, and I certainly wasn't about to initiate a new conversation. He stretched out his hand, and I passed him the bottle.

When Haimon was finished getting dressed, he packed up his bag and pushed it back under the bed. "I'm off," he said. Everyone turned to look at him, but he didn't elaborate. Itamar said goodbye. Naama just nodded at him. He stood there in the middle of the room for another minute; then he left.

"We're not going?" asked Naama.

Itamar stood up. "We are," he said. He looked at Naama, then at me. I stayed where I was. "You're not coming?" he asked.

I said no. I told them I was tired, and that I wanted to sleep. But that's not what I intended to do. I waited for them to leave; then I took off my shirt and turned off the light. I went back to my spot and sat there in the dark. I looked out the window. I wasn't tired. I thought about how she shouldn't have come to Eilat with me in the first place if she hadn't wanted to. I didn't force her to come with me; she chose to. But what difference did it make now? I finished the wine, and I smoked, and I continued to look out the window with my feet on the windowsill. I felt myself calming down, slowly. Little by little, I was able to think about other things. I tried not to think about how they were all coming back here to sleep, about their belongings strewn all over the floor. I hoped I could fall asleep before they came back and turned on the light and opened their bags and rummaged around for their toothbrushes. In the end, I did get into bed. I don't know what time it was. Late.

When they got back, I was lying in the dark under a sheet, smoking. I heard their footsteps on the stairs. I snuffed out my cigarette in the empty packet that I was using as an ashtray, and dropped the butt on the floor next to the bed. When they put the key into the lock, I was buried under the sheet, pretending to be asleep. I heard them come in, and even though my eyes were closed and my face was covered up, I could tell that they had turned on the light. Again, I was overcome by this feeling that I was about to burst into tears. I listened to their laughter, and to the sound of the water running in the bathroom sink. I couldn't wait for all of this to be over. And the whole time, I was conscious of the light. I heard Itamar say something, I couldn't tell what. Then Naama laughed. They were drunk. Itamar brushed his teeth and tried to talk at the same time. I closed my eyes and breathed deeply. All I wanted to do at that moment was to get up and smack them. That's what was going through my head. I saw myself standing up and pounding Itamar's face against the edge of the sink until blood flowed out of his mouth, blood mingled with the foam from his toothpaste. Then they came into the room and arranged their mattresses on the floor next to the bed. I stayed perfectly still until the lights were off and they were lying down. I heard them laughing a little more, then whispering, and then they began. I don't know why, but it made me feel better all of a sudden. There I was, lying in bed, and the two of them were fucking on the mattress next to me. Slowly, silently, I turned over and looked at them. It was dark, but I could still see them, more or less. At any rate, I could hear them just fine. I don't know why but it amused me, the whole idea that I was lying there awake, not giving a damn about the two of them fucking next to my bed. It made me feel better.

When they were done, they turned over and Naama lit up a cigarette. They talked about how the ATM had swallowed Itamar's bank card, and wondered how he would get by with whatever cash he had on him. They spoke quietly. Itamar said he had been waiting for it to happen, because his card was bent out of shape. He moved his hands in the dark to show what it had looked like. "It's been like that for two months," he said, "and I knew it was going to happen. But in Eilat?"

Naama mimicked him. "'In-Ei-Lat'?" she said. "Why shouldn't it happen in Eilat?"

"I don't know, I just thought it wouldn't," he said. "Oh, shit!"

Then suddenly I noticed that Haimon wasn't there. I thought about asking them where he was, and this thought did me in. I tried to stifle a giggle. I had to clamp my lips together to keep the giggle from escaping, because by then my stomach was already in spasms. But they had no idea. They kept on talking. I lay there in silence and tried to relax. But then it erupted. I didn't mean for it to happen, it just did. At first it was just a kind of "ppfff" sound, but when I thought about what would go through their minds when they heard me laughing, I started to crack up. For a moment, they were just stunned. Then Itamar started laughing, and then Naama. She got up on her knees and the sheet slipped off her body. She was naked. "You son of a bitch," she screamed, and she started hitting me with her pillow. She was laughing at the same time, and she could hardly talk. I lifted my hand to shield myself from the pillow. She was hitting Itamar, too. "It's not funny!" she yelled. But she couldn't stop laughing either.

After she composed herself, she lay back down and covered herself up. We had all calmed down. But when I thought about asking them my original question, I started laughing again. I laughed so hard I felt it in both my stomach and my temples. My forehead broke out in a cold sweat.

"You could have at least told us you were awake," said Naama. But she started laughing mid-sentence.

"I wanted to know," I began, and I tried to collect myself enough to finish the sentence, "what happened to Haimon."

Itamar, who had pulled himself together by now, went hysterical. He started laughing like a lunatic. An officer in the Israeli army. Naama was also convulsed with laughter. We laughed until our stomachs hurt. I don't know how long it had been since I laughed like that. And this time, it took us a long time to calm down. We were lying there in the dark, and every time we were finally quiet, someone would start up again.

Finally, we were over it. I could feel all the muscles in my face and my stomach. I could feel how my expression was turning serious again. I was no longer smiling. I knew I'd have trouble falling asleep, and once again, all I wanted to do was get away from there. Away from the apartment, and from these people, and from their things scattered all over the room.

The next day, nobody mentioned what had happened. Nobody even hinted at it. Except for when Haimon came in, and Naama and I looked at each other and smiled. This was at seven in the morning; we had just woken up and were starting to make breakfast. The kitchen blinds were open and it was cool. There was even a little breeze. Itamar was shaving, and Naama and I were alone. I wanted to talk to her. This was the first time that I felt O.K. Relaxed, anyway. She was slicing vegetables for a salad, and I was slicing olives for an omelet. Both of us were in shirts and underpants. We were barefoot. I even wanted to tell her about Lena. To get it off my chest. Not to go into too much detail, just to let her know it had happened. But in the end I didn't say anything. I didn't want Itamar to barge in while I was talking. I took out a glass bowl and put the olives in it. Then I cracked the eggs and beat them. Naama finished dicing the onion, and she put it into the salad. She held the cutting board at an angle and pushed the vegetables into the bowl with her knife.

"We only have soy oil," I said.

She turned around to look at me. "What?" she said. She flicked her hair back.

"We only have soy oil," I said. "For the salad."

"That's OK," she said. "It's better than what they have in the army." I took out the bottle of oil and handed it to her.

I put some butter in a pan and turned on the burner. Just as I was pouring in the eggs, Haimon walked in. It was at that moment that Naama and I smiled at each other.

He stood where he was, by the door. He had a toothbrush in his shirt pocket.

"Hello," he said.

We said hello back.

He looked around. "Where's Itamar?"

Itamar came out of the bathroom to see who was at the door, but he left the water running. He had shaving cream on his neck. "What's up?" he asked Haimon.

Haimon gestured with his head. "I want to go to Jerusalem," he said. "You can manage without me. I'll go back to the base on Thursday, by myself." He had one hand shoved in his pocket.

All of a sudden, Itamar remembered that he was the officer in charge here. He was half naked, dressed in shorts, with shaving cream all over his face. But he was still in charge. He thought it over for a minute. I didn't think he would consent to it. I thought that he would take this chance to show us that he wasn't a sucker. But he agreed. He didn't even make a face. Haimon dragged his bag out from underneath the bed, and sat down.

"Do you want something to eat?" Naama asked.

He said no. Then he opened his bag and took out the jar of moisturizer. Itamar went back to shaving, and Naama and I sat down to eat. Haimon stripped down to his underwear and started applying the lotion. He still hadn't finished when Itamar came out of the bathroom.

"You're hitchhiking?" asked Itamar, buttoning his army shirt.

"Yes."

"You don't want to see if there's any room on the transport plane to Sde Dov?"

Haimon reached into the jar for some more lotion. "No. There's no point in checking. You can't get on a transport anyway, not without connections."

Itamar reached behind his back to tuck in his shirt. He's a good-looking guy, Itamar. "If there's room, they'll take you," he said. "Even if you don't have connections. What do they care? They're flying anyway."

Haimon spread lotion on his legs. "That's not how it works," he said.

"Did you check, at least?"

Haimon shrugged his shoulders. Itamar stared at him for a minute, then went back to the bathroom.

Naama sat down at the table. She sliced a lemon and squeezed it onto her salad. I slid the omelet onto the plates and sat down across from her. Naama and I started eating. Haimon kept on moisturizing.

When Itamar came out, he sat with us. He cut himself some bread and started eating his omelet, a slice of bread in one hand and a fork in the other. "Can we make some coffee?"

Naama stopped chewing. She looked at me. "I think we can," she said. "I think the kettle is working." She pointed at the electric kettle. Itamar was looking at me, too.

"Yeah, it's working," I said. But I didn't get up.

Suddenly I thought of asking him if I could drive. I didn't say anything, but I was hoping that when we got to the jeep, he would suggest it himself. Naama filled up the kettle. Then we went on eating, and we hardly spoke. Itamar was daydreaming, staring at an invisible spot on the table. Maybe he was still half-asleep. At any rate, I wasn't about to disturb him. I wasn't in the mood for an early-morning chat.

When we were finished eating, it suddenly occurred to Itamar that he had to make sandwiches. He and Naama started preparing them, while I filled up the cooler with water. Then we went down to the jeep. Naama was carrying the file with the reference points and the maps.

When we were outside, I asked Itamar if he would let me drive.

"Once we're out of the city," he said. He put the cooler and the bag with the sandwiches on the floor near the back seat. Naama sat next to the driver's seat. Itamar climbed in and started the engine.

When we left the city, he really did pull over and switch seats with me. Naama stayed in the front, next to me. I was really wild that day. Sometimes I really shook them up. Naama, at least. But she didn't say anything.

We got back to the apartment at two thirty. We had finished all our work, and we still had almost two days left. I turned off the engine and hopped out. I was the only one who hadn't gotten out of the car all day, except for once or twice. Naama and Itamar marked down all the reference points. It felt strange, standing on the asphalt in the parking lot. You get used to the tremors of the motor and the bumps of the road; there's a particular feeling you get in your legs when you're going downhill.

It was hot. The sun was strong, and glared off the houses. It's the kind of heat that you can't get away from. Itamar took off his sunglasses and lifted up the back seat. He was looking for something in the box beneath it. Naama tried to help him. She went to the back of the jeep and put her foot on the step, but when she tried to hoist herself up, she burnt her knee on the edge of the exhaust. It was a pretty serious burn. She screamed, then grabbed her leg. Her whole face was twisted in pain. Itamar sat her down on the curb. He sent me upstairs for a bag of ice. I went, but there wasn't any ice.

By the time I came out of the lobby, he had already gotten her back into the jeep. I went over to them. "There isn't any," I said.

Itamar climbed into his seat. "There isn't any in the freezer?"

"No."

He put his hand on the stick shift. "I thought I saw some," he said.

I shrugged my shoulders. Naama wasn't crying, but she was grimacing. She was grasping her thigh with her hands, as though it took all her willpower not to touch the burn.

"I'm taking her to the army clinic," Itamar said. He started the engine. I watched the jeep until it turned off the road; then I went up to the apartment.

They didn't get back until evening. While they were gone, I managed to take a cold shower, sleep for a bit, and shower again. They came back half an hour after I woke up. My hair was still wet. I sat by the window, barefoot, in my underwear, my feet up on the sill.

It was quiet outside. The sun was setting and there was a breeze, but it was still hot. The room was tidy by then. Naama's belongings were in her bag, and Itamar's clothes were on the chair. His shirt was draped over the back of the chair, and his pants were on top of the seat, folded beneath his bag. It was a pleasant time of day. I was disappointed when I heard the jeep coming down the street. I heard Itamar turning off the engine, and I heard them climbing out of the jeep and going up the steps. Aside from that, it was quiet. I remember thinking then that it wasn't so bad. I still felt it all the time, but by now it wasn't so bad. And perhaps it was better here in Eilat than anywhere else.

Naama came in first, and Itamar followed. She tossed something onto the bed: a long orange box. Itamar closed the door.

"What's that?" I asked, pointing at the box.

"Nylon bags," said Naama. She had a large gauze pad on her leg, stuck on with band-aids and covered with white netting. The gauze was stained orange from the iodine. She put her leg up on the bed and touched the bandage with her fingertips. "So that I can shower."

I leaned my chair back. "What?"

Naama looked up. "What do you mean, what?"

"What's so that you can shower?"

"Oh, the bags," she said. Then she thought of something. "Are there any rubber bands around here?"

I shrugged my shoulders. Itamar went into the kitchen and started opening the drawers, but he couldn't find anything. He came out and stood in the middle of the room with his hands on his hips.

"Why do you need bags to take a shower?"

"I'm not allowed to get it wet," she said.

Itamar looked at her without speaking. Then he said, "You have a rubber band." He pointed towards Naama. He spoke as though he had unearthed something terribly important. We both stared at him. His finger remained poised in mid-air. "You have a rubber band," he repeated. I didn't know what he was talking about. Neither did Naama.

"You have a rubber band in your hair," he said.

Naama lifted her hand and touched her ponytail. It really was pulled back with a rubber band. She removed it and shook out her hair; then she sat on the bed to see if it would fit over her leg. It did.

"Itamar," she said, "you're a genius."

Itamar smiled and shook his head. He's no genius, Itamar. But he's alright.

Naama took out the roll of bags and pulled one off. She tore the bottom open, slid it over her leg, and stretched the rubber band over it. Then she went to take a shower. I put on a shirt and a pair of shorts and told Itamar I was going for a walk. I had no desire to be in the apartment with them. On my way out, I heard Naama turn on the water.

It was quiet outside. I turned off our street and started walking uphill, away from the beach. The streets were almost empty. The shops had just closed, and it was starting to get dark. I turned left onto one of the newer streets, not far from the supermarket. The asphalt was still pitch-black, and the houses were new, but even so, it was dirty. There was nothing in front of any of the houses. No gardens, no flowerpots, nothing. I stopped for a minute and leaned on a fence. You could see the mountains between the houses. It was really on the outskirts of the city. On the other side of these houses there was nothing but desert. I had this strange sense that if I really focused, I could think about something other than Lena. But if I got distracted, even for a minute, the thoughts would return. I craved a cigarette, but I hadn't brought my pack with me. Or my matches. I looked around in search of a smoker, but there was nobody on the street. Just some kids in a parking lot. I went back to the main street, towards the supermarket, to see if any of the kiosks were open. I wanted a cigarette so badly that I almost broke into a run, but I didn't. Then I remembered that I didn't have my wallet, and I slowed down.

By the time I got back, it was almost dark. Naama and Itamar were sitting in the kitchen drinking coffee. The fluorescent light was on. Naama was wearing a black miniskirt and a black tank top, with no bra. She has a nice chest, Naama. Itamar wasn't wearing a shirt.

I said hello, and they answered without looking up. At first I didn't understand what was happening. Naama was holding her cigarette above Itamar's coffee cup, and they were looking at each other. The ash was about to drop.

"Enough," said Itamar.

"It always has to be me?" asked Naama.

I shut the door behind me and walked up to them. "It's not my fault," said Itamar. There was an ember resting on the froth in Naama's cup. "Stop," he said. He was smiling, but he wasn't sure if this was a joke or if she was serious. She looked into his eyes. She had this wicked kind of smile.

"Enough, OK?" Itamar was laughing.

Naama leaned forward and rested both elbows on the table. Her cigarette was still poised above the cup, and she raised a finger as though she were about to flick off the ash. She ground her teeth from side to side. "That's it," said Itamar, "I'm moving the cup." He reached out, but Naama shook her head no, and he stopped. I went over to the sink and got myself a glass of water.

"I'm taking my cup," Itamar said.

But the moment he touched it, Naama flicked her ash into his coffee. Just like that. I don't think he'd even taken a sip yet.

"What a bitch," he said. Then he turned to me. "What a bitch," he said.

Naama smiled and raised her eyebrows. She took a drag from her cigarette. Itamar stood up. "I'm making myself a fresh cup," he said, "and I'm not making one for you."

"OK, darling," Naama answered. She raised her knee a bit and touched her bandage. From where I stood I could see her underwear. I stayed there until she put her leg back down; then I turned off the light and got into bed. There was still light shining from the kitchen. I lay on my stomach, just as I had done on the day that Lena and I arrived. I smoothed the sheet over the part of the bed where she had slept. I wished I had never started anything with her. If I hadn't tried anything, at least she would have stayed.

Itamar came in a minute later. "Did you turn off the light on purpose?" he asked.

I said yes, and he left me alone and went back to the kitchen. I was in a bad mood and I was hungry, but I couldn't bring myself to eat anything. I tried to imagine how things would be in, say, another six months. Would I forget about this whole business with Lena, or would it still be haunting me? I turned over onto my back and stared at the ceiling. I heard them talking in the kitchen.

After a few minutes, Itamar came back. He took out his shirt. "We're going out to get some food," he said. "Are you coming?"

I said no. I stood up to get a cigarette; then I went back to bed. I took a cup with me for an ashtray. But as they were about to leave, I suddenly remembered something. I raised my head and leaned on my elbow. "Itamar," I said. They both stopped. Naama turned on the light in the corridor. "You know this apartment costs money."

"It's OK," said Itamar. "Don't worry about it."

"OK," I said, and I lay back down. They waited by the door for another minute, as though they expected me to say something else. Then they said goodbye and left.

I had planned to spend that evening just as I had the previous one: alone. But after half an hour, I couldn't stay in the apartment anymore. I put on long pants and shoes, and I went out. I walked over to the resort area to look for them at the Yacht Club where some French band was performing Beatles music; then I went to the Flea in Your Ear. Only then did I realize that they were probably downtown. And they were. They were at a Middle Eastern restaurant, where all the tables were outside. I sat down at their table. They had already eaten, and their plates were covered with leftovers. Itamar had had chicken.

"You guys want to come dancing?" I asked.

Itamar looked at Naama. She looked at me, then pointed under the table. I looked down. She was pointing at her burn.

"But let's go out for a drink, anyway," she said. They had already had a beer. I told them that it was OK with me. Itamar was also up for it.

We went to one of the pubs in town. We thought we'd sit for a while, then walk around. But we stayed there all evening. What's

funny is that it was the same pub I had gone to with Lena the night I
got drunk. And I was making every effort to get drunk this time, too.

We ordered three pints of draft beer; when we were finished, we
ordered more. We drank and smoked and laughed. By the third round,
we were pretty wasted. We sat in a half-circle around the table, Itamar
and I on the sides and Naama in the middle. We were sitting close
together. When Naama leaned forward, I could see her breasts. Itamar
was looking, too. I saw him leaning back and staring, and I smiled at
him so he would know I'd caught him in the act. He laughed and
raised his glass. He was still smiling while he drank. Then we started
to play that game, the one with the napkin and the coin. You put a
paper napkin over the glass, and then you put a coin on top of the
napkin. Everyone has to burn a hole in the napkin with their cigarette.
Whoever makes the coin fall has to drink a shot of vodka. At first,
Naama kept losing. But when they brought out her second glass, she
had another idea. "Hang on," she said. She flattened both hands on the
table and straightened her elbows. She was totally plastered. "I can't
drink anymore," she said. She raised her fingertips off the table. "But
listen. Instead of drinking, give me another assignment." She cupped
the shotglass between her hands.

"What is this, Truth or Dare?" asked Itamar.

Naama shot him a look. Then she slipped her hand between his
legs. She rubbed his cock through his pants. Maybe she thought I
wasn't looking. "No, sweetie," she said, "it's not Truth or Dare." She
paused. "Well?"

Itamar and I looked at each other. He reached over to the next table
to grab a few more napkins. Naama turned to me. "Well?"

My shoulder was touching her shoulder, and my face was right near
her face. We looked at each other. There was a moment of silence.
"Take off your underpants," I said.

She looked at me for another minute; then she did it. She stood up
partway and, without lifting her skirt, pulled her underpants down to
her knees. Itamar looked under the table. So did I. Then she drew her
knees together, and the underpants slid down onto the floor. She lifted

them up with her foot, grabbed them with her hand, and placed them on the table. Right in the center. I looked around. Nobody was watching us. She leaned back and folded her arms.

"Perfect," said Itamar. He took her underpants off the table and put them on her lap. I stood up to start a new round. I fished the coin out of the glass and placed it over a fresh napkin. Suddenly I felt her hand. She was pushing her underpants into my pocket.

We sat there for another hour or two. At first the assignments were just French kisses, but then it got much more raunchy. Itamar had to take off his underpants, too, but he did it in the bathroom. Both of us had another beer. Plus we split Naama's vodka. We poured it into our beers.

At about two thirty, we headed back to the apartment. The three of us were hugging and kissing the whole way home. Naama's underpants were still in my pocket. When we got there, we didn't even bother to turn on the light. We just collapsed on the mattresses, and Itamar and I took off Naama's clothes, and in the process, our own clothes as well. Naama kept things from really degenerating. All three of us were there, but we took turns fucking her. I don't know how long it went on. I only remember that when I was fucking her, she held my head between her hands and said my name. She said it over and over again. Quietly, like she was talking to herself. I remember feeling like I wasn't really there. My hands were on the mattress, on either side of her head. I lifted myself on top of her by straightening my elbows. I stared at her, as though I weren't taking part in any of this. Every now and then she would raise herself up and we'd kiss, but mostly she kept stroking my face and murmuring my name.

Once we got back from Eilat, I didn't see her anymore. And after I got out of the army, I didn't see Itamar either. The first news I heard of her was three years later, when I bumped into Itamar at a building supplies store in B'nei Brak. He was working there as a salesman. We talked a little. I sat on a chair between the tools and the cans of plaster, and Itamar sat behind the counter. He told me what had happened. This was already after she had finished her six months of community service, her alternative to prison time. He told me how she had knocked down the girl, and how she had stayed in the car until the police arrived. Afterwards, I thought about her for a long time. About how she sat there with her sunglasses on, in the car that was impaled on the electricity pole, with the motor still running. And about the people who gathered around and gawked at her. I don't know how you feel after something like that happens to you. Killing a young girl is the kind of thing that you can't forget, ever. We talked about this, and Itamar said she was doing OK. She's thick-skinned. But with something like that, you never can tell.

Uzi Weill

You'll Be Dead

Translated by Chaya Galai

It's funny now to remember the snow of '72, my first snow. I've been living in Oslo for five years now, and the amount of snow that falls here every winter would be enough to create an ocean in the middle of the Negev desert. The woman I've been living with for the past five years grew up in the Norwegian snow and she loves to see how the sight thrills me each time afresh, when winter comes. To tell you the truth, after two years I stopped being so thrilled, but she gets such a kick out of seeing me go outside after the first night of snow, and going wild in the garden like a Jerusalemite seeing the sea for the first time, that I've gone on doing it ever since, keeping up my show of enthusiasm. I do it in order to see her standing at the door of the little house, rubbing her hands together in the cold air, all smiles and shining eyes, delighted to have succeeded in giving me something I never had back home, something that's all hers, and when I go back in she hugs me and says, You're crazy, that's what you are, and she feels like the Norwegian ambassador to the United Nations, bestowing her love on me on behalf of the entire nation. And so, for five years in succession, I've gone on pretending that it's the snow that makes me happy.

But this story is about the first snow of my life, in the winter of '72, on top of Mount Meron. I hadn't thought about it for years, not until three days ago, here in Oslo, when I ran into my first girlfriend. We were together for two and a half years. We met in high school, she was my first woman, and for a time we even lived together, before we were drafted. When we were both in the army, we met less and less frequently and drifted apart. We kept it up for eight months and then it was over. She was the one who decided. Of course. I didn't know it at the time, but I'll never be capable of being the one who decides to leave. I'm faithful by nature, and even when all the love has been exhausted, the fidelity remains. I'm not capable of sending away a woman who's allowed me to love her. I'll always be the one standing on the railroad platform waving a handkerchief, never turning and going, always standing and watching till the train disappears into the distance. That encounter with her, on the outskirts of snowy Oslo, after so many years, was like finding the rubber ball you lost when you were a child, and suddenly there it is in the storage closet, and your heart is filled with the sweet, sharp fragrance of memory, much sharper than the time itself, which was quite wretched and intense and certainly far from sweet. People touch, stamp themselves on one another and then vanish, but the imprint endures forever, changing the image of the person whose heart has been imprinted, for better or worse. The winter when we parted, things could have ended very badly.

I was in the army. My battery was stationed at the top of Mount Meron, and winter was late that year. I was one of three recruits who were sent on a long, rigorous course held in a godforsaken base in the Negev. The conditions were arduous, the nights were bitterly cold, we lived in little field tents, two to a tent, and ate out of mess tins, and our officers were tough and strict. I didn't like the whole setup and I kept hoping some miracle would happen and they'd kick me out straight back to the battery. The miracle didn't happen, but I managed to pick quarrels with everyone, particularly my direct commander. One evening I was alone in the tent. I was lying in the dark on my sleeping bag on the hard ground, thinking how shitty life was. Apart from my commander and two guards on duty at the other side of the camp, who were out of sight, I was all alone. Everyone else had gone off to see a movie at the nearby airforce base, and I'd chosen to stay behind. I was thinking about Anat, my girlfriend, and how things hadn't been going well for quite some time, and how we were drifting apart. Suddenly I heard a noise outside.

"Edri, out!" It was my commander. I took a deep breath and crawled out.

"What's your weapon doing outside while you're in there?"

"It isn't, it's here inside," I said. He didn't believe me, so I took my rifle out of the tent to show him.

"So who's is that?" he asked and pointed to a rifle that was lying about two meters behind the tent, in the dark. I shrugged and went over to check. It was just a stick. I showed it to him.

"OK," he said. "Tell me, Edri, who's Anat Levinson?"

My heart pounded. That was her name. Nothing could have been more weird and offensive than hearing him utter her name.

"Why?" I asked, wary.

He took out a letter. "This came for you, from your unit at Meron."

I stretched out a hand.

"No," he said. "First let's have thirty pushups."

"What!?"

"Thirty. Get down, move!"

He had the letter in his hand, with her handwriting on the envelope. After almost a year in the army, Anat was the only thing in my life that remained as pure and as sweet as I had once wanted life to be, the only thing it was worth getting up in the morning for and making it through another day. Her letter in his hand was the nearest thing to sacrilege that a secular individual like me could feel.

"Give it here," I said, my voice trembling.

"No, Edri, not so fast. You know what? Make it twenty five. Down, move it, *yalla*."

To this day I don't know if he really meant it or was just bluffing, and was planning to pat me on the shoulder a minute later. He grinned, and his grin looked to me like mockery of the weakness he'd uncovered in me: love for a woman.

"*Yalla*, Edri. I'm not going to wait all night."

I cocked the rifle and pointed it at him. The smile was wiped off his face with the same speed it takes a train to run someone down.

"Edri, what's wrong with you, drop it immediately."

I couldn't speak.

"Edri, what's wrong with you?!"

"Let go of that letter."

"Edri, drop that gun!"

"I'll shoot you," I said, clutching the rifle. He froze.

"I'll shoot you," I repeated. "Throw me the letter."

"Edri, you'll be getting yourself into deep shit."

"And you'll be dead." My voice shook. I yelled: "Throw me that letter!"

And he threw it.

"Now turn around and get out of here," I said.

"This is really going to cost you."

"It is?" I said. "There's nobody here. It's my word against yours. And I can be such a good little boy that nobody's going to believe you."

He remained rooted to the spot. His hands were trembling. Then he turned and went. I put down the rifle and picked up the letter. I stood there like that for a few minutes, the letter in my hand. Only then did I grasp what I'd done. I took a deep breath and crawled into the tent holding the rifle and the letter. I lay down on the sleeping bag, removed a bothersome stone from under my head, took the flashlight out of my kit-bag and opened the letter. It wasn't long, only one page. I switched on the flashlight and started reading:

"Yoav,

This letter is very hard for me, but I've decided to sit down and write it. I'm going to try to say it as simply as I can.

I'm having a hard time. I can't go on like this. For the past few months we haven't been good for one another. You know what I'm talking about. I think that the truth is we're quite bored with one another, and we go on this way because it's convenient. Because we're used to each other. But we're not really enjoying it, are we? Yoavi, I'm not saying "we" to hide the fact that it's only me, I think the truth is that you're also a little bored. Perhaps it's more difficult for you, because you're a long way off and all by yourself, but when you're with me, you're not as happy as you used to be.

I'm not blaming you or myself, or anyone. Two and a half years is a long time. It's no fun any more, Yoavi. I'm still very attached to you and I love you, but it's not the real thing, we're bored with one another. I don't want you to be hurt. I'm thinking about myself but I'm really thinking about you a little, as well. You don't love me either the way you once did. And I don't either. So maybe it's over. Maybe. Maybe we just need to take a little break from each other, to see other people for a while. OK, I know it probably sounds terrible. Here I am in Tel Aviv and I can see anyone I want, and you're stranded there on a mountain with thirty other males. But I'm not going to erase what I've written because that's what I feel, at least where I'm concerned. I want a little freedom, so let's take a break, OK? When you come to town we'll talk about it.

Don't be mad at me. You're still part of me, part of my life, being without you seems to me a bit like living someone else's life. But we're not having fun together any more, and perhaps that means it's over.

Don't be mad, this is hard for me as it is.

Au revoir,

Me."

I read the letter over and over again, and then I folded it and put it back in the envelope. I put it down beside me, and lay there with my eyes open. Several hours passed, everyone came back from the movie, there was a racket going on around me, my tentmate came in and went out again, the racket died down, in the end everyone went to sleep and I was still lying there. In the end I went outside, lit a cigarette and went over to the gun emplacement to smoke it. I was chockful of dry, painful sorrow, but I couldn't even cry. I was dog-tired, dirty, heavy, with the bitter taste of too many cigarettes in my mouth. I was sorry I had no alcohol with me. I went back to the tent, slid into the sleeping bag and tried to sleep. For hours I lay awake, and fell asleep only towards morning.

We were roused at five thirty in the morning. I crawled out of the tent and began to fold my sleeping bag. In the distance I saw the commander approaching, with a movement order in his hand.

"Take it," he said. "You're being posted back to your base. You're finished with this course."

I took the order from him.

"And don't look so pleased with yourself. You'll find a little surprise waiting for you there."

I watched him walk away. Then I packed all my gear. I put on my dress uniform and said goodbye to the other guys. They must have heard something, because they all had very grave expressions. It took time for them to realize that I wasn't in the know, and the cook was the one who volunteered the information.

"Edri, I don't know what you've done, but you're in deep shit with him," he said. "Your CO at Meron is that jerk's uncle."

So that's the way it is, I thought, that's it. He doesn't need witnesses, he doesn't even need to lodge a complaint. The CO will come over to the battery, and put me up on a charge about something or other, a button out of place, a grain of dirt in the rifle barrel, if you look hard enough you can always find something. He'll court martial me himself, and I'll get a stiff sentence in the stockade.

"The CO is retiring from the service in five days' time," I said.

"Well, keep hoping that he has more important things to do in the next five days," said the cook.

I nodded goodbye, and went. The base was a long way from the nearest town, and by the time I reached my parents' apartment in Tel Aviv it was evening. I called Anat but there was no reply. Exhausted, I lay down on my bed, reread the letter and thought, Wow, what a great week it's been, she's leaving me and I'm going to jail. Fantastic! I was so tired that I fell asleep with the letter in my hand.

When I woke up it was already 9 a.m. I got up and packed. Without great hopes, I called Anat again and this time she answered.

"Anat," I said.

"Yoav," she said, surprised. "You're here?"

"Yes. Are you free?"

"Yes," she said and fell silent.

Eventually I said: "I got your letter."

We were silent for another half a minute. Then we arranged to meet. She turned up in her father's big, new car.

I climbed in and we drove away and it was all over. There was nothing more to say. It's hard to describe that feeling, sitting beside someone who's suddenly decided that she's not yours any more. To look at, she was the same person, but I wasn't allowed to touch the Anat who drove me that morning. I couldn't speak, knowing that every word I said was only taking her further away from me and sealing her heart. She'd already made her decision. That's the true betrayal. It's not, like people think, when the woman you love leaves you for somebody else, but when she doesn't allow you to love her any more.

That's not to say that I didn't speak all the same. It's easy to be clever when it's all over, when you're alone in bed. But while it's happening, you keep on trying with all the strength you have left. It was like stroking her with nettles. You try to stroke her, but all you're doing is hurting her more and more, till she shrinks into herself. In the end she drove me to the bus stop. I watched her hands on the wheel and changing gears, I knew what those skilled hands had been able to do to me, and I thought to myself, take a good look, that's the last time you'll ever see her touching something that way. We parted.

At the bus terminal I bought a bottle of vodka and when I reached Mount Meron, five hours later, I'd already finished half of it. I got off the bus and sat down to wait for transportation to my unit. By the time I reached the gate of my base, up on the peak, another hour had gone by. My head spinning from the liquor, I swayed my way in. The guard at the gate yelled at me: "Yoav, Yoav, how's it going, you're in real shit, bro, huh?"

I grinned at him and went towards my room. The entire base was no bigger than an average parking lot, but under the influence of that half bottle, which I still remember kindly, I doubted I could get there without collapsing. I braced myself and made it. When I walked in, my two roommates were sprawled on their beds.

"Edri, Edri," they shouted as I entered. I grinned at them. Within seconds, more than ten people were crowded into the room, patting me on the shoulder and offering me free legal advice. They all knew that I was in the hot seat. The battery commander came in.

"OK," he said. "Everyone who doesn't belong in here, out on the double!!" They left slowly and very noisily.

"Do you want to talk in my office?" he asked and looked at my roommates.

"No, that's OK."

"Right," he said. "I've been hearing some unpleasant stories about you. From the CO. I heard that you threatened your commander with a weapon."

I shrugged. "That's not exactly what happened," I lied.

He gazed at me. "The CO will be here tomorrow morning," he said. "There's no reason for him to come, he's retiring from the service in four days' time. If he's coming, it's because of you."

I was silent. He paced the room, sighed and said: "Edri, Edri, tell me, why did you have to get yourself into this mess. If he's coming up from the valley especially for you four days before he's due to retire, then you're in deep shit. He's coming to screw you. He'll find some fuck-up, and I'll have to put you up on a charge and then he'll try you. Straight to the stockade."

I continued to gaze at him.

He breathed deeply and nodded: "OK, there's nothing to be done. Get settled here, go and eat something. Today you're excused from guard duty."

"Thanks," I said. He nodded again as if he couldn't believe it and went out. My roommates pounced on me, demanding all the details, but I didn't supply them. I sat on my bed and felt nausea welling up. After a few minutes, the world started spinning around me. I went out and staggered towards the latrines, where I stood for a long time, vomiting my guts out. The world came to a halt. I stood with my head under the cold water faucet, and then I dried myself and went back to my room. People were coming in steadily, in the hope of hearing more about my exploits. I drank a great deal of tea and refused to talk about it. In fact, I scarcely said a word.

Then it was evening, and after the meal, during which I was forced to listen to all possible types of advice on "how to avoid a court martial without really trying," I went into my room and closed the door. The stove was lit and the room was warm. My two roommates put on their greatcoats, balaclavas and padded boots and went out on guard duty. I lay in bed and couldn't fall asleep. I switched on the radio, and the songs sounded harsh and remote. Slowly, as the hours passed, they began to soften. I closed my eyes and fell asleep for a while. I awoke when one of my roommates came back and got into bed. He was asleep within a few seconds. The radio was playing an unfamiliar tune, and outside I could hear the guards talking, like another distant radio, tuned to a different station. I listened quietly. Suddenly I thought of Anat and began to cry. For a long time I lay there in the dark, the tears welling out of my eyes, till they came to an end. I gaped into the darkness, and couldn't fall asleep. At three in the morning it started to snow, at first softly, and after about an hour in increasing quantities. The guards woke everyone up and shouted: "Snow, snow," and they all ran out and started playing, hurling snowballs and building snowmen. The snow went on falling without letting up for a moment. In the morning it was still snowing, the water pipes froze and all the roads to the base were blocked. They radioed us that access to our mountain was also blocked. The snow went on falling in quantities unprecedented for decades, and food and fuel were flown in to us by helicopter. Nobody had anticipated such a severe winter, and the snow fell and fell for five consecutive days. All the roads were closed and the CO never turned up to avenge his nephew, and by the time the snow let up and the roads were cleared, I already had a new CO, who knew nothing about the whole affair, and the snow went on falling. In all my life I've never seen such beautiful snow.

Biographical Notes

Ruth Almog

Ruth Almog (b. 1936, Petah Tikva, Israel) comes from a German-Jewish Orthodox family. She studied literature and philosophy, trained as a teacher and has taught at elementary school and university level. Since 1967 she has been on the editorial staff of the literary section of *Haaretz*. Her novel *Roots of Light* won the 1989 Brenner Prize; in 2001 she was awarded the Agnon Prize, and in 2004 the Newman Prize. She has also been awarded two prizes for children's literature.

Nissim Aloni

Nissim Aloni (1926–1998) was born in Tel Aviv and fought in the 1948 War of Independence. His first play, *Most Cruel the King*, was staged by the Habimah Theater in 1953. After studying modern European drama in Paris, he wrote and directed *The King's New Clothes*, a turning point in Israeli theater. His plays have been translated into French and English. He has also published a collection of short stories, *The Owl*. Aloni was awarded the Israel Prize for Theater.

Gafi Amir

Gafi Amir (b. 1966, Givatayim, Israel) began her journalistic career while still serving in the IDF. She has worked as a radio writer and presenter, television researcher and newspaper columnist. Amir published her first novel at age 21 and has since published two more novels and two collections of short stories. She has also written television scripts and co-authored a play.

Aharon Appelfeld

Aharon Appelfeld (b. 1932, Czernowitz, Rumania) spent his childhood in a concentration camp and wandering alone in Nazi-occupied Ukraine, finally making his way pre-state Israel in 1946. A Hebrew University graduate, he is now Professor Emeritus of Literature at Ben Gurion University of the Negev. His novels, short stories and essays, most of them on Holocaust themes, have been translated into many languages. He has been awarded the Brenner Prize, the Bialik Prize, the Israel Prize (1983), the National Jewish Book Award (USA, 1989), the Prix Médicis Etranger (France, 2004) and the Nelly Sachs Prize (Germany, 2005).

Yossi Avni

Yossi Avni (a pseudonym; b. 1962, Israel) spent several years as an officer in the IDF. He then went on to study law and Middle Eastern history at the Hebrew University of Jerusalem. Avni began publishing fiction in 1987. He has published two collections of short stories and novellas, and one novel.

Hanoch Bartov

Hanoch Bartov (b. 1926, Petah Tikva, Israel), novelist, playwright and journalist, served in the British Army's Jewish Brigade in World War II and fought in Israel's War of Independence. His first novel was published in 1953. Among other awards, Hanoch Bartov has received the 1965 Shlonsky Prize for his novel *The Brigade*, the 1985 Bialik Prize for *In the Middle of it All* and the 1998 President's Award for Literature.

Yitzhak Bar-Yosef

Yitzhak Bar-Yosef (b. 1949, Tel Aviv), son of writer Yehoshua Bar-Yosef, graduated from the Hebrew University of Jerusalem with a BA in Jewish history and theater studies and an MA in comparative literature. He has published three novels and four short-story collections and works as a journalist for a daily newspaper.

Ehud Ben-Ezer

Ehud Ben-Ezer (b. 1936) belongs to one of the founding families of Petah Tikva. He studied philosophy and kabbala at the Hebrew University of Jerusalem. Ben-Ezer writes children's books as well as fiction and nonfiction for adults, and is a literary critic. His first novel, *The Quarry*, was made into a movie in 1990. He received the Ze'ev Prize in 1994.

Yitzhak Ben-Ner

Yitzhak Ben-Ner (b. 1937, Kfar Yehoshua, Israel) writes screenplays and plays; he is also a film critic and a journalist. He has published a number of novels and collections of stories for adults and children. Several of his works have been adapted for the screen, television and theater. He has received the Agnon-Jerusalem Prize (1981), the Bernstein Prize and the Ramat Gan Municipal Literary Prize.

Yossl Birstein

Yossl Birstein (1920-2003, b. Poland) left home at the age of seventeen for Australia. He served in the Australian army during World War II and in 1950 immigrated to Israel. For several years he was a shepherd at Kibbutz Gvat. He later worked in professions ranging from banker to radio storyteller. Birstein wrote novels and stories in both Yiddish and Hebrew.

Orly Castel-Bloom

Orly Castel-Bloom (b. 1960, Tel Aviv) studied film at Tel Aviv University, and began publishing in 1987. She has published 11 books for adults and one children's book. Her novel, *Dolly City*, has been included in UNESCO's Collection of Representative Works, and in 1999 she was named one of the 50 most influential women in Israel. Castel-Bloom has received the Tel Aviv Prize (1990), the Alterman Prize (1993), the Prime Minister's Prize twice (1994, 2001) and the Newman Prize (2003).

Shulamit Gilboa

Shulamit Gilboa (b. 1943, Tel Aviv) has published two collections of short stories and three novels. She has a BA in Hebrew Literature and an MA in Philosophy from Tel Aviv University. Since 2005 she has been the literary editor of the daily *Yedioth Ahronoth*. She has received the Tel Aviv Literature and Art Fund Award, and a writing stipend from Oxford (1999). Her bestseller, *Four Men and a Woman* was awarded the Publishers Association's Golden and Platinum Book Prizes.

David Grossman

David Grossman (b. 1954, Jerusalem) studied philosophy and drama at the Hebrew University of Jerusalem and later worked as a radio editor and broadcaster. He has written six novels, a play, a number of short stories and novellas, and children's books, as well as three books of nonfiction, including interviews with Palestinians and Israeli Arabs. He is one of the most read and translated Israeli authors. Among Grossman's many awards: the Premio Grinzane (Italy, 1996), the Chevalier de l'Ordre des Arts et des Lettres (France, 1998), the Valumbrosa Prize (Italy), the Prix Eliette von Karayan (Austria), the Buxtehude Bulle (Germany, 2001), the Sapir Prize (2001), and the Bialik Prize (2004).

Gail Hareven

Gail Hareven (b. 1959, Jerusalem) is the daughter of writer Shulamit Hareven. She writes on politics and feminist issues, reviews books for the daily *Maariv* and other publications, and teaches writing and feminist theory. She has written books for adults and children as well as plays, five of which have been staged. In 2002 she received the Sapir Prize for her novel, *My True Love*.

Shulamith Hareven

Shulamith Hareven (1930-2003, b. Warsaw, Poland) immigrated to pre-state Israel in 1940. She served in the Haganah underground and as a medic in the 1948 War of Independence. One of the founders of Israel's Army Radio and later an IDF officer, she was a war correspondent in the 1970s. She published poetry, novels, short stories, essays and children's books, and worked as a newspaper columnist on social, cultural and political issues.

Yehudit Hendel

Yehudit Hendel (b. 1926, Poland) was born into a rabbinic family and immigrated to pre-state Israel in 1930 as a small child. Her first book was published in 1950. She is the author of several novels and short-story collections; many of her works have been adapted for stage, screen, television and radio. She has received several literary prizes, including the Jerusalem Prize, the Bialik Prize, and the Israel Prize (2003).

Yoel Hoffmann

Yoel Hoffmann (b. 1937, Hungary) immigrated to pre-state Israel as an infant. His mother's early death and a childhood spent boarding with relatives as well as in children's homes before his father's remarriage figure prominently in his prose. He is a professor at Haifa University, where he teaches Japanese poetry, Buddhism and philosophy; he has also translated Japanese poetry into Hebrew. Hoffmann has written novels, short stories and a book for children. He received the Bialik Prize in 2002.

Amalia Kahana-Carmon

Amalia Kahana-Carmon (b. 1926, Kibbutz Ein Harod) served as a wireless operator in the 1948 War of Independence, and studied philology and library sciences at the Hebrew University of Jerusalem.

She has written novels, novellas, short stories and essays and has been Writer-in-Residence at Tel Aviv University and the Oxford Center for Hebrew Postgraduate Studies. She has receved the Brenner Prize (1985), the Newman Prize (1990), the Bialik Prize (1994), the ACUM Prize (1995), the President's Prize (1997) and the Israel Prize for Literature (2000).

Yoram Kaniuk

Yoram Kaniuk (b. 1930, Tel Aviv) fought and was wounded in the 1948 War of Independence. A painter and journalist, he lived in New York for ten years, returning to Israel in 1961. His novels have been translated into 20 languages. Kaniuk has received the Prix des Droits de l'Homme (France, 1997), the President's Prize (1998), the Bialik Prize (1999), the Prix Méditerranée Etranger for his work *Exodus: The Odyssey of a Commander* (France, 2000), the Book Publishers Association's Gold Book Prize (2005) and the Newman Prize (2006). *Adam Resurrected* will be made into a feature film in 2006, directed by Paul Shrader.

Judith Katzir

Judith Katzir (b. 1963, Haifa, Israel) studied literature and film at Tel Aviv University. She is currently an editor for Hakibbutz Hameuchad/ Siman Kriah publishing house and teaches creative writing. She began publishing short stories in the Israeli press in the 1980s. In addition to literary prizes for individual stories, Katzir has received the Book Publishers Association's Gold and Platinum Book Prizes, the Prime Minister's Prize (1996), and the French WIZO Prize.

Amos Kenan

Amos Kenan (b. 1927, Tel Aviv) was a member of the pre-state anti-British military underground movement. He became known as a political dove soon after Israel was established and in the 1970s co-founded the Israeli-Palestinian Council. A leading columnist, he has written for the daily *Yedioth Ahronoth*, and is also a painter, sculptor, playwright and novelist. He has written a number of books: short-story collections, novels and nonfiction. Amos Kenan was awarded the Brenner Prize (1999).

Yehoshua Kenaz

Yehoshua Kenaz (b. 1937, Petah Tikva, Israel), studied philosophy and Romance languages at the Hebrew University of Jerusalem, and French literature at the Sorbonne. A translator of French classics into Hebrew, he has worked on the editorial staff of the daily paper *Haaretz*. He has published five novels and two books of novellas and stories. Kenaz has received the Alterman Prize (1991), the Newman Prize (1992), the ACUM Prize (1994) and the Bialik Prize (1995).

Etgar Keret

Etgar Keret (b. 1967, Tel Aviv) is the most popular writer among Israeli youth today. Since 1992, he has published four books of stories, a novella and three graphic novels. Bestsellers at home, his books have also received international acclaim. *Missing Kissinger* has been listed among the 50 most important Israeli books of all time. "The Nimrod Flip-Out" was published in Francis Ford Coppola's magazine, *Zoetrope* (2004). Keret has received the Book Publishers Association's Platinum Prize several times, and the Ministry of Culture's Cinema Prize. His movie, *Skin Deep*, won 1st Prize at several international film festivals, and was awarded the Israeli Oscar. Keret lectures in the television and film department at Tel Aviv University.

Yeshayahu Koren

Yeshayahu Koren (b. 1940, Kfar Saba, Israel) studied philosophy and Hebrew literature at the Hebrew University of Jerusalem. He has published a novel and several collections of short stories. His work has been translated into a number of languages.

Yitzhak Laor

Yitzhak Laor (b. 1948, Pardes Hanna, Israel) is a poet, playwright and novelist. A graduate in theater and literature from Tel Aviv University, he is a literary critic and op-ed writer for daily *Haaretz*. He has published collections of poems, plays, three novels, a collection of stories and two collections of essays.

Shulamit Lapid

Shulamit Lapid (b. 1934, Tel Aviv) majored in Oriental studies at the Hebrew University of Jerusalem. A former chair of the Hebrew Writers' Association, she is the author of four collections of short stories, nine novels, and several plays and books for children. Lapid has received the Prime Minister's Prize, the International Theater Institute Award (1988), and the Newman Prize.

Savyon Liebrecht

Savyon Liebrecht (b. 1948, Munich, Germany) was born to Holocaust survivor parents who immigrated to Israel soon after her birth. She studied philosophy and literature at Tel Aviv University and began publishing in 1986. She has published two novels, six collections of stories and novellas, television scripts and plays. She has received the Alterman Award (1987), the Amelia Rosselli Prize (Italy, 2002), and the Maior-Amalfi Award (Italy, 2005). In 2005, she was nominated Playwright of the Year in Israel.

Mira Magen

Mira Magen (b. Kfar Saba, Israel) was born to an Orthodox family. She studied psychology and sociology before turning to nursing, and has worked as a nurse at Hadassah University Medical Center in Jerusalem. She has published four bestselling novels and one collection of stories. Magen was awarded the Prime Minister's Prize in 2005.

Ronit Matalon

Ronit Matalon (b. 1959, Israel) is of Jewish-Egyptian origin and was born in an outlying town. She studied literature and philosophy at Tel Aviv University. Matalon has been a journalist (covering the first Intifada) as well as a critic and book reviewer for the daily *Haaretz*; she teaches at the Camera Obscura Academy for the Arts in Tel Aviv. She has published two novels, one collection of short stories, one collection of essays, and a children's book which was made into a film.

Aharon Megged

Aharon Megged (b. 1920, Wroclawek, Poland), came to Tel Aviv as a child. After twelve years on a kibbutz, he left and became a literary editor, journalist and novelist. Megged has been Writer-in-Residence at Haifa and Oxford Universities. From 1980 to 1987, he was the president of the Israeli branch of P.E.N. Megged has published over 40 books and has received many literary awards, most recently the ACUM Prize (1990), the Newman Prize (1991), the Agnon Prize (1996), the President's Prize (2001) and the Israel Prize for Literature (2004).

Reuven Miran

Reuven Miran (b. 1944, Israel), was raised in the Jezreel Valley and now lives in Benyamina. He holds an MA in philosophy from the Sorbonne, and is a publisher and translator from French to Hebrew. Miran has published novels, short stories, books for children and film scripts. He is the recipient of the BBC World Service Prize, the Ashman Prize for Literary Achievement (1995), and the French Ministry of Culture Award.

Igal Mossinsohn

Igal Mossinsohn (1917–1994) was born in Petah Tikva, Israel, and was a prolific author, playwright and inventor. He was active in the pre-state underground and fought in the Palmach during the 1948 War of Independence. A number of his plays have been staged in Israel, and his 40-volume *Hasamba* adventure stories for children were widely popular. He was the recipient of the Ussishkin Prize and the Cleveland Prize.

Shlomo Nitzan

Shlomo Nitzan (1921-2006, b. Liepaja, Latvia) came to pre-state Israel in 1935. As a young man, he worked as a carpenter, waiter and gardener. He began publishing stories in the 1940s. During the 1948 War of Independence he was a military correspondent and edited a series of pocket books for soldiers. An editor, short story writer and novelist for both children and adults, he received several awards, including the Brenner Prize.

Yitzhak Orpaz

Yitzhak Orpaz (b. 1923, Zinkov, Russia) immigrated to pre-state Israel in 1938. During World War II, he fought in the Jewish Brigade. Orpaz studied philosophy and literature at Tel Aviv University. He lived for some years on a kibbutz and has pursued a number of professions, including construction, diamond cutting, editing and teaching. He has published short stories, novels and poetry, and has for Life Achievement (2005). received several prizes, including the Bialik Prize (1986), the Prime Minister's Prize (2004) and the Israel Prize for Life Achievement (2005).

Amos Oz

Amos Oz (b. 1939, Jerusalem), novelist, short-story writer and essayist, lived on a kibbutz from the age of fifteen. He studied philosophy and literature at the Hebrew University. Since 1986 he has lived in the southern town of Arad and teaches literature at Ben Gurion University of the Negev. Oz has published eleven novels, three books of short stories and seven books of essays and books for children. He has written widely on the Israel-Arab dispute and is a leading figure in the Peace Now movement. Among Oz's many prizes: the French Prix Fémina Etranger (1988), the Frankfurt Peace Prize (1992), the French Légion d'Honneur (1997), the Israel Prize (1998) and the Goethe Prize (2005). Oz is one of Israel's most renowned writers; his work has been published in some thirty languages.

Dorit Peleg

Dorit Peleg (b. 1953, Haifa) lives in Tel Aviv, and holds workshops in creative writing. The author of two novels and four short story collections and novellas, she received the Prime Minister's Prize for her novel *Miss Fanny's Voice.*

Yotam Reuveny

Yotam Reuveny (b. 1949, Lasi, Rumania) immigrated to Israel in 1964. After his army service and several years on a kibbutz, he joined the editorial staff of the daily *Haaretz* in 1972 and has also worked for the daily *Yedioth Ahronoth.* He has published short stories, novels and poetry, and translates French and English literature into Hebrew. Reuveny has participated in the International Writing Program at Iowa University.

David Schütz

David Schütz (b. 1941, Berlin) came to Israel with his brother at the age of seven. After his army service, he studied history and philosophy at the Hebrew University of Jerusalem. He is a film producer and scriptwriter. Schütz has published five novels, two collections of short stories and novellas, and a children's book.

Dan Benaya Seri

Dan Benaya Seri (b. 1935, Jerusalem) has lived in Jerusalem all his life. He spent many years as a civil servant in the Ministry of Agriculture. He has written two novels and several short stories and novellas about the world of Sephardi Jews in Jerusalem. His novella, *The Thousand Wives of Naftali Siman-Tov*, was adapted for the screen.

Yaakov Shabtai

Yaakov Shabtai (1934–1981) was born in Tel Aviv and spent ten years on a kibbutz before returning to the city. He published two novels, a number of plays, one collection of short stories and a children's book. His novel, *Past Continuous*, is considered one of the high points of contemporary Hebrew prose: it was awarded the 1986 Kenneth B. Smilen Literary Award. Shabtai died prematurely of a heart attack and was awarded the Agnon Prize posthumously. In 1999, the City of Tel Aviv named a street after him.

Nathan Shaham

Nathan Shaham (b. 1925, Tel Aviv), served with the elite Palmach unit in Israel's 1948 War of Independence, and is a member of Kibbutz Beit Alpha. He has been publishing novels, short stories and plays since 1944. He served as Israel's cultural attaché in New York (1977–1980), and was editor-in-chief of Sifriat Poalim Publishing House. Shaham has published almost 40 books. He has received the American National Jewish Book Award (1992), the Newman Prize (1993), the Bialik Prize (1998) and the Italian ADEI-WIZO Prize (2005).

David Shahar

David Shahar (1926–1997) was a fifth-generation Jerusalemite. He was the author of several novels, children's book, collections of short stories, and seven volumes of a historical saga based in

Jerusalem. His work has been widely translated. A former chair of the Hebrew Writers' Association, he was awarded the French Prix Médicis Etranger, the Bialik Prize, and the Agnon Prize. He was also appointed Commandant de L'Ordre des Arts et des Lettres by the French government.

Moshe Shamir

Moshe Shamir (1921–2004) was born in Safed, Israel, and spent most of his life in Tel Aviv. He was a novelist, journalist, playwright, children's author, literary critic and political figure. In 1948 he founded and was the first editor of the Israeli army weekly, *Bamachane*. He was a member of the Knesset from 1977 to 1981. Shamir was a recipient of the Israel Prize for Literature (1988) and the ACUM Prize for Life Achievement (2002).

Shoham Smith

Shoham Smith (b. 1966, Jerusalem) currently lives in Tel Aviv. Smith studied industrial design at the Bezalel Art Academy, and has an MA in literature. She writes book reviews and has published two collections of short stories as well as four children's books.

Benjamin Tammuz

Benjamin Tammuz (1919–1989) immigrated to Tel Aviv from Russia at the age of five. He studied law and economics at Tel Aviv University and art history at the Sorbonne. For many years he was the literary editor of the newspaper *Haaretz*, and was also Israel's cultural attaché in London. A prolific author of both children's and adult literature, he received several literary prizes, including the Ze'ev Prize (1972). His novel, *Minotaur*, was selected Book of the Year in England in 1981.

Gadi Taub

Gadi Taub (b. 1965, Jerusalem) studied at Tel Aviv University and received his Ph.D at Rutgers University. He teaches communications at the Hebrew University of Jerusalem. Taub has hosted many television shows for children as well as a weekly talk show on Israel's Army Radio, and has written scripts for children's television. He has been a columnist for the daily *Maariv* and is co-editor of the journal *Mikarov*. Taub has published a book of short stories, a collection of essays and five books for children. He was awarded the Ze'ev Prize in 2000.

Uzi Weill

Uzi Weill (b. 1964, Israel) was raised in Tel Aviv where he still lives. He is a writer, journalist, translator and television scriptwriter. Weill has published one novel and two collections of stories. Two films have been based on his short stories.

A.B. Yehoshua

A.B. Yehoshua (b. 1936, Jerusalem) studied Hebrew literature and philosophy at the Hebrew University of Jerusalem and is currently professor of literature at Haifa University. He has published numerous novels, short stories, plays and essays and is one of the most internationally known Israeli authors. Yehoshua has received several awards in Israel and abroad, among them the Brenner Prize, the Alterman Prize, the Bialik Prize, the Israel Prize for Literature and, most recently, the Giovanni Boccaccio Prize (Italy, 2005) and the Viareggio Prize (Italy, 2005).

S. Yizhar

S. Yizhar (Yizhar Smilansky, 1916-2006, b. Rehovot, Israel) fought in the 1948 War of Independence and held a Knesset seat for seventeen years as a member of the political parties headed by David Ben Gurion.

He received his Ph.D from the Hebrew University of Jerusalem, and was a Professor Emeritus of Tel Aviv University. Yizhar is considered Israel's most illustrious writer. He wrote novels, novellas and short stories for adults and children. He was awarded the Brenner Prize, the Bialik Prize, the Israel Prize for Literature, and the Emet Prize for Art, Science and Culture.

Nurit Zarchi

Nurit Zarchi (b. 1941, Jerusalem) is the daughter of writer Israel Zarchi. After her father's early death, she was raised in Kibbutz Geva, and later studied at the Hebrew University of Jerusalem. She has worked as a journalist, and has taught creative writing to adults and children. Zarchi has published over eighty books for children as well as short stories, novels, essays, and poetry. She has received every major Israeli award for children's literature and has twice received an IBBY Honor Citation. She has also been awarded the Bialik Prize.

Acknowledgements

Copyright of the original Hebrew works © ACUM and/or the authors.

For the English translations published here, the editor and publishers are grateful for permission to include the following copyright material:

Ruth Almog, first published in *Moment Magazine/Forthcoming*, No. 5, New York, 1984. Copyright © The Institute for the Translation of Hebrew Literature.

Nissim Aloni, first published in *Hebrew Short Stories*, Tel Aviv, The Institute for the Translation of Hebrew Literature & Meggido, 1965. Copyright © The Institute for the Translation of Hebrew Literature.

Gafi Amir, first published in *Israel: A Traveller's Literary Companion*, Berkeley, CA., Whereabouts Press, 1996. Copyright © 1996 Rachel Jacoby. Reprinted by permission of Whereabouts Press.

Aharon Appelfeld, first published in *In the Wilderness*, Jerusalem, Ah'shav, 1965. Copyright © Ah'shav.

Yossi Avni, first published in *Cherries in the Icebox*, London, Loki Books, 2002. Copyright © The Institute for the Translation of Hebrew Literature.

Hanoch Bartov, first published in *P.E.N.* Israel, 1995. Copyright © Riva Rubin.

Ehud Ben-Ezer, first published in *Ariel* No. 81, Jerusalem, 1990. Copyright © Chaya Amir.

Yitzhak Ben-Ner, first published in *Ariel* No. 53, Jerusalem, 1983. Copyright © Yitzhak Ben-Ner.

Birstein, Yossl, "What Did I Do in those First Days in Australia," first published in *P.E.N.*, Israel, 1997. Copyright © Karen Alkalay-Gut.

David Grossman, first published in *The Oxford Book of Hebrew Short Stories*, Oxford, Oxford University Press, 1996. Copyright © The Institute for the Translation of Hebrew Literature.

Yehudit Hendel, first published in *New Women's Writing from Israel*, Ilford, Vallentine Mitchell, 1996. Copyright © The Institute for the Translation of Hebrew Literature.

Yoel Hoffman, first published in *Katschen & The Book of Joseph*, New York, New Directions, 1998. Copyright © Yoel Hoffman. Reprinted by permission of New Directions Publishing.

Amalia Kahana-Carmon, first published in *P.E.N.* Israel, 1991. Copyright © Amalia Kahana-Carmon.

Yoram Kaniuk, first published in *Midstream*, Vol. 19, No. 8, New York, 1973. Copyright © *Midstream*. Reprinted by permission of *Midstream*.

Judith Katzir, first published in *Closing The Sea*, New York, Harcourt Brace Jovanovich, 1992. Copyright © Judith Katzir.

Yehoshua Kenaz, first published in *Musical Moment and Other Stories*, Vermont, Steerforth Press, 1995. Copyright © The Institute for the Translation of Hebrew Literature.

Etgar Keret, first published in *Modern Hebrew Literature*, Nos. 20/21, Tel Aviv, 1998. Copyright © The Institute for the Translation of Hebrew Literature.

Yeshayahu Koren, first published in *Modern Hebrew Literature,* No. 4, 1990. Copyright © The Institute for the Translation of Hebrew Literature.

Yitzhak Laor, first published in *Israel: A Traveller's Literary Companion*, Berkeley, CA., Whereabouts Press, 1996. Copyright © Sheila Jellen. Reprinted by permission of Whereabouts Press.

Shulamit Lapid, first published in *P.E.N.,* Israel, 1993. Copyright © Shulamit Lapid.

Savyon Liebrecht, first published in *Jewish Spectator*, Vol. 53, No. 3, Santa Monica, 1988. Copyright © The Institute for the Translation of Hebrew Literature.

Mira Magen, first published in *New Women's Writing From Israel*, Ilford, Vallentine Mitchell, 1996. Copyright © The Institute for the Translation of Hebrew Literature.

Aharon Megged, first published in *The Oxford Book of Hebrew Short Stories*, Oxford, Oxford University Press, 1996. Copyright © The Institute for the Translation of Hebrew Literature.

Reuven Miran, first published in *Formations*, Vol. 1, No. 3, Madison, Wisc., 1985. Copyright © The Institute for the Translation of Hebrew Literature.

Yitzhak Orpaz, first published in *The Oxford Book of Hebrew Short Stories*, Oxford, Oxford University Press, 1996. Copyright © The Institute for the Translation of Hebrew Literature.

Amos Oz, first published in *Where the Jackals Howl and Other Stories*. New York, Harcourt Brace Jovanovich, 1981. Copyright © Harcourt, Inc. Reprinted by permission of Harcourt, Inc.

Yaakov Shabtai, first published in *Not Just Milk and Honey*, New Delhi, National Book Trust, 1998. Copyright © The Institute for the Translation of Hebrew Literature.

Nathan Shaham, first published in *The Oxford Book of Hebrew Short Stories*, Oxford, Oxford University Press, 1996. Copyright © The Institute for the Translation of Hebrew Literature.

David Shahar, first published in *News from Jerusalem*, Boston, Houghton Mifflin, 1974. Copyright © David Shahar.

Moshe Shamir, first published in *P.E.N.*, Israel, 1995. Copyright © Moshe Shamir.

Shoham Smith, first published in *Modern Hebrew Literature*, No. 19, Tel Aviv, 1997. Copyright © The Institute for the Translation of Hebrew Literature.

Benjamin Tammuz, first published in *A Rare Cure*, Tel Aviv, Hakibbutz Hameuchad, 1981. Copyright © The Institute for the Translation of Hebrew Literature.

A.B.Yehoshua, first published in *Three Days and a Child*, New York, Bantam Doubleday, 1970. Copyright © The Institute for the Translation of Hebrew Literature.

S.Yizhar, first published in *Modern Hebrew Literature*, No. 18, Tel Aviv, 1997. Copyright © The Institute for the Translation of Hebrew Literature.